LAURELL K. HAMILTON
ANITA BLAKE™
VAMPIRE HUNTER
Guilty Pleasures

ANITA BLAKE
VAMPIRE HUNTER
Guilty Pleasures

Anita Blake is the Executioner.
She raises the dead and kills vampires.
So you would think that vampires would avoid her like the proverbial
plague. But there's something out there they fear even more, a killer
targeting the most powerful vampires in the city. The Master Vampire
of St. Louis makes her an offer she can't refuse: if she wants to save
the life of her best friend, the Executioner will join forces with
the very creatures she would rather kill.

WRITER **LAURELL K. HAMILTON**
ADAPTATION **STACIE RITCHIE** (ISSUES 1-5) & **JESS RUFFNER-BOOTH** (ISSUE 6)
ARTWORK **BRETT BOOTH**   COLORS **IMAGINARY FRIENDS STUDIOS** (WITH MATT MOYLAN)
LETTERS & DESIGN **BILL TORTOLINI** (WITH SIMON BOWLAND)   EDITORS **MIKE RAICHT & SEAN JORDAN**
SPECIAL THANKS TO **MELISSA MCALISTER, ANN TREDWAY, JONATHON GREEN,
MERRILEE HEIFETZ, JASON & DARLA COOK**

Cory Levine *Collection Editor* John Denning *Assistant Editor* Jennifer Grünwald & Mark D. Beazley *Editors, Special Projects*
Jeff Youngquist *Senior Editor, Special Projects* Ruwan Jayatilleke *Senior Vice President of Development*
David Gabriel *Senior Vice President of Sales* Tom Marvelli *Vice President of Creative*
Joe Quesada *Editor in Chief* Dan Buckley *Publisher*

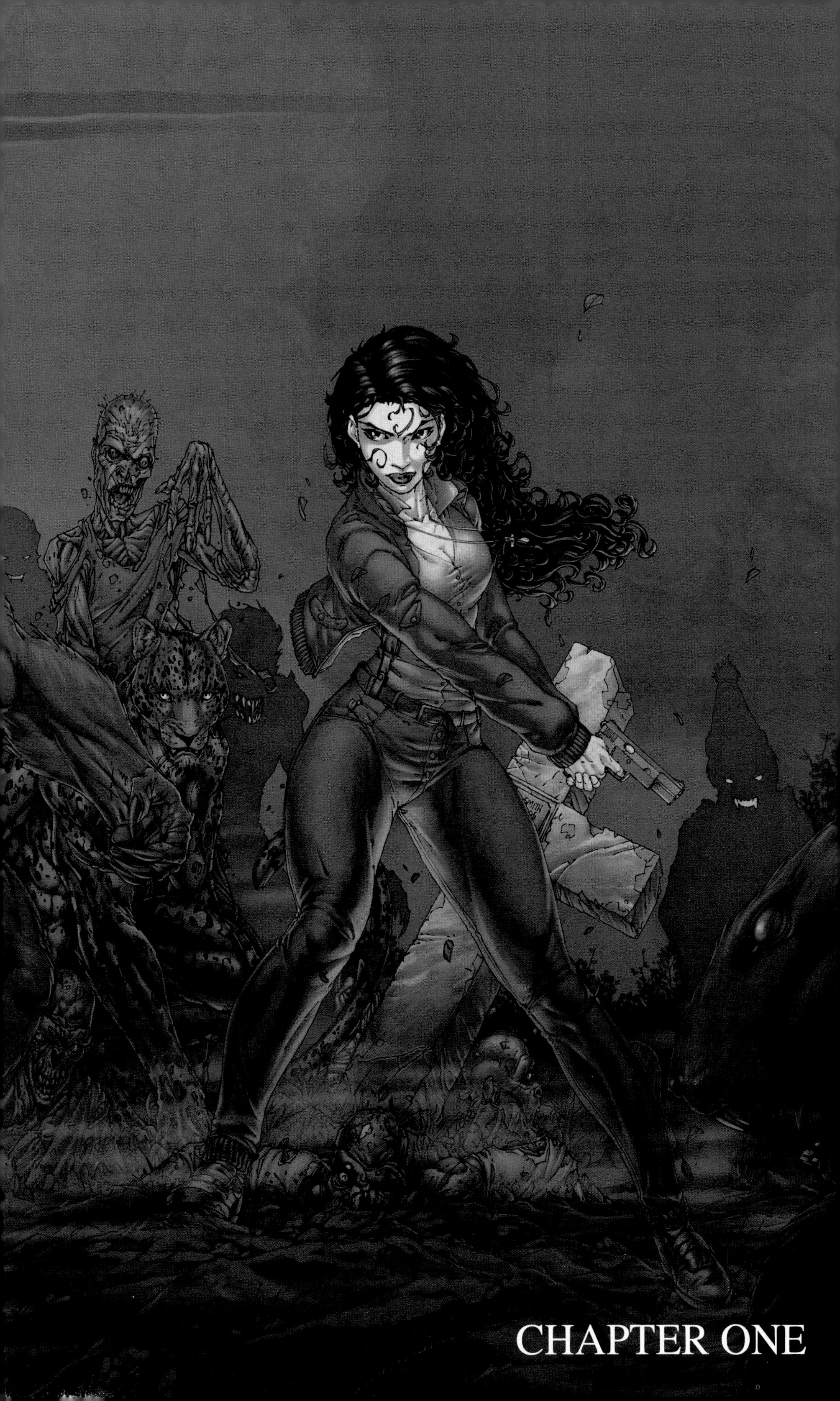

CHAPTER ONE

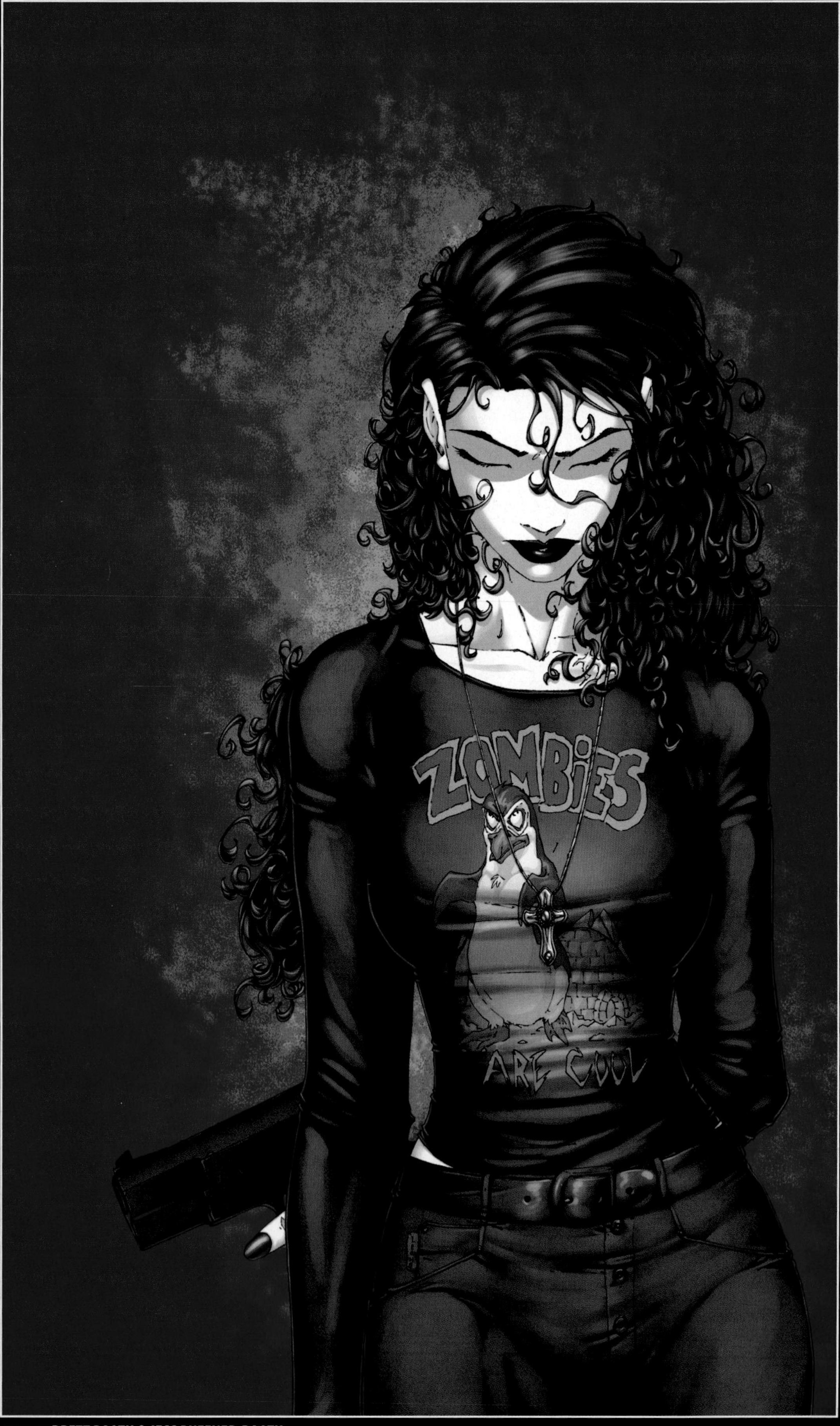
ZOMBIES
ARE COOL

COVER BY: **BRETT BOOTH & JESS RUFFNER-BOOTH**

LLIE McCOY HAD BEEN JERK BEFORE HE DIED.

HIS BEING DEAD DIDN'T CHANGE THAT.

MIND IF I SMOKE?

YES, I DO.

DAMN, YOU AREN'T GOING TO MAKE THIS EASY FOR ME, ARE YOU?

NO.

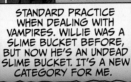

GEEZ, I LOVE IT. YOU'RE AFRAID OF ME.

NOT AFRAID, JUST CAUTIOUS.

I NEED TO REMEMBER NOT TO LOOK HIM IN THE EYE, NOW THAT HE'S DEAD.

STANDARD PRACTICE WHEN DEALING WITH VAMPIRES. WILLIE WAS A SLIME BUCKET BEFORE, BUT NOW HE'S AN UNDEAD SLIME BUCKET. IT'S A NEW CATEGORY FOR ME.

YOU DON'T HAVE TO ADMIT IT. I CAN SMELL THE FEAR ON YOU, ALMOST LIKE SOMETHIN' TOUCHING MY FACE, MY BRAIN.

YOU'RE AFRAID OF ME, 'CAUSE I'M A VAMPIRE.

WHAT CAN I SAY? HOW DO YOU LIE TO SOMEONE WHO CAN SMELL YOUR FEAR?

I WANT TO ASK HIM HOW IT FEELS TO BE DEAD.

I'VE KNOWN OTHER VAMPIRES, BUT WILLIE IS THE FIRST I'VE KNOWN BEFORE AND AFTER DEATH.

IT'S A PECULIAR FEELING.

WHY ARE YOU HERE, WILLIE?

WHAT DO YOU WANT?

HEY, I'M HERE TO GIVE YOU MONEY.

TO BECOME A CLIENT.

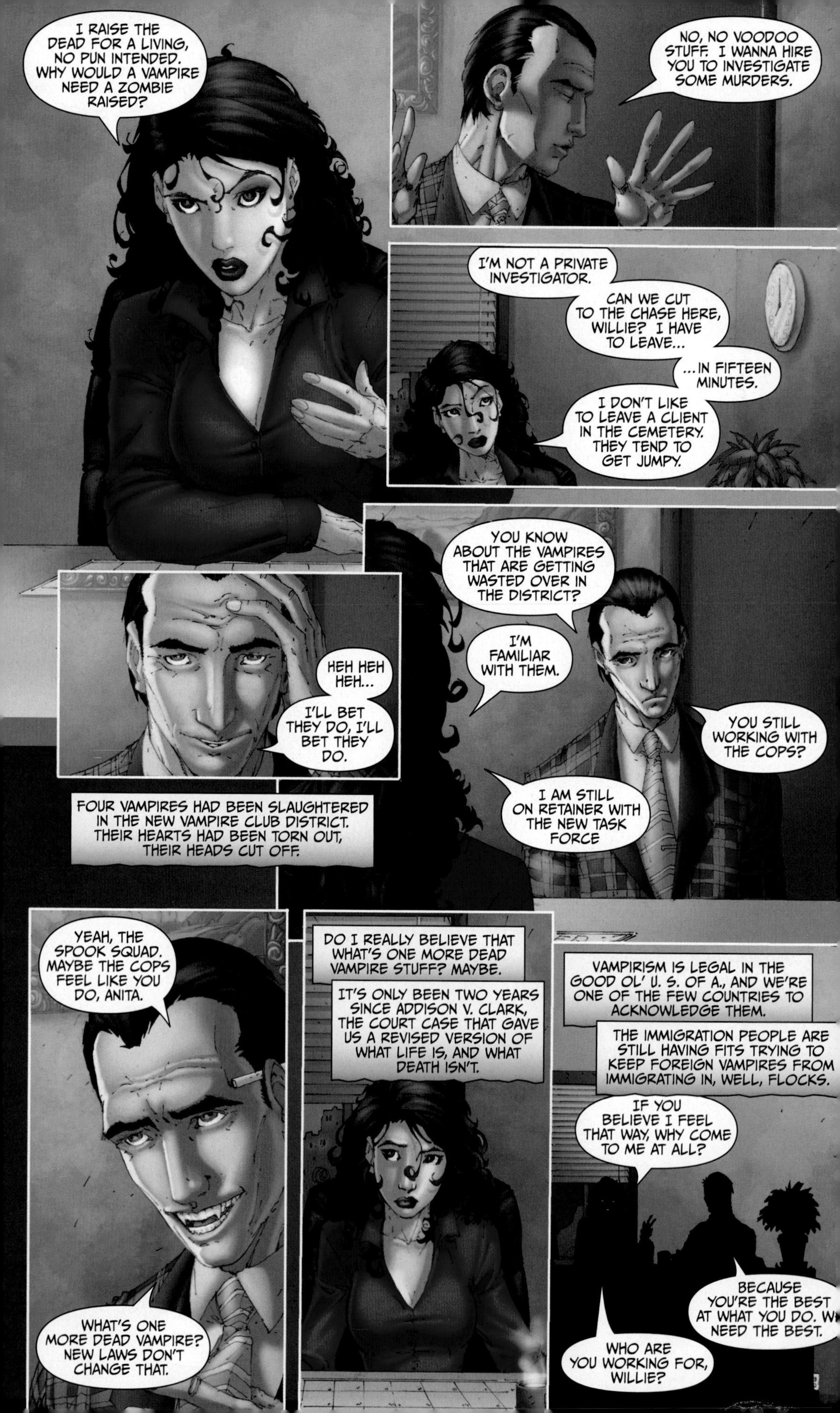
I RAISE THE DEAD FOR A LIVING, NO PUN INTENDED. WHY WOULD A VAMPIRE NEED A ZOMBIE RAISED?
NO, NO VOODOO STUFF. I WANNA HIRE YOU TO INVESTIGATE SOME MURDERS.
I'M NOT A PRIVATE INVESTIGATOR.
CAN WE CUT TO THE CHASE HERE, WILLIE? I HAVE TO LEAVE...
...IN FIFTEEN MINUTES.
I DON'T LIKE TO LEAVE A CLIENT IN THE CEMETERY. THEY TEND TO GET JUMPY.
YOU KNOW ABOUT THE VAMPIRES THAT ARE GETTING WASTED OVER IN THE DISTRICT?
I'M FAMILIAR WITH THEM.
HEH HEH HEH...
I'LL BET THEY DO, I'LL BET THEY DO.
YOU STILL WORKING WITH THE COPS?
I AM STILL ON RETAINER WITH THE NEW TASK FORCE
FOUR VAMPIRES HAD BEEN SLAUGHTERED IN THE NEW VAMPIRE CLUB DISTRICT. THEIR HEARTS HAD BEEN TORN OUT, THEIR HEADS CUT OFF.
YEAH, THE SPOOK SQUAD. MAYBE THE COPS FEEL LIKE YOU DO, ANITA.
WHAT'S ONE MORE DEAD VAMPIRE? NEW LAWS DON'T CHANGE THAT.
DO I REALLY BELIEVE THAT WHAT'S ONE MORE DEAD VAMPIRE STUFF? MAYBE.
IT'S ONLY BEEN TWO YEARS SINCE ADDISON V. CLARK, THE COURT CASE THAT GAVE US A REVISED VERSION OF WHAT LIFE IS, AND WHAT DEATH ISN'T.
VAMPIRISM IS LEGAL IN THE GOOD OL' U. S. OF A., AND WE'RE ONE OF THE FEW COUNTRIES TO ACKNOWLEDGE THEM.
THE IMMIGRATION PEOPLE ARE STILL HAVING FITS TRYING TO KEEP FOREIGN VAMPIRES FROM IMMIGRATING IN, WELL, FLOCKS.
IF YOU BELIEVE I FEEL THAT WAY, WHY COME TO ME AT ALL?
BECAUSE YOU'RE THE BEST AT WHAT YOU DO. W NEED THE BEST.
WHO ARE YOU WORKING FOR, WILLIE?

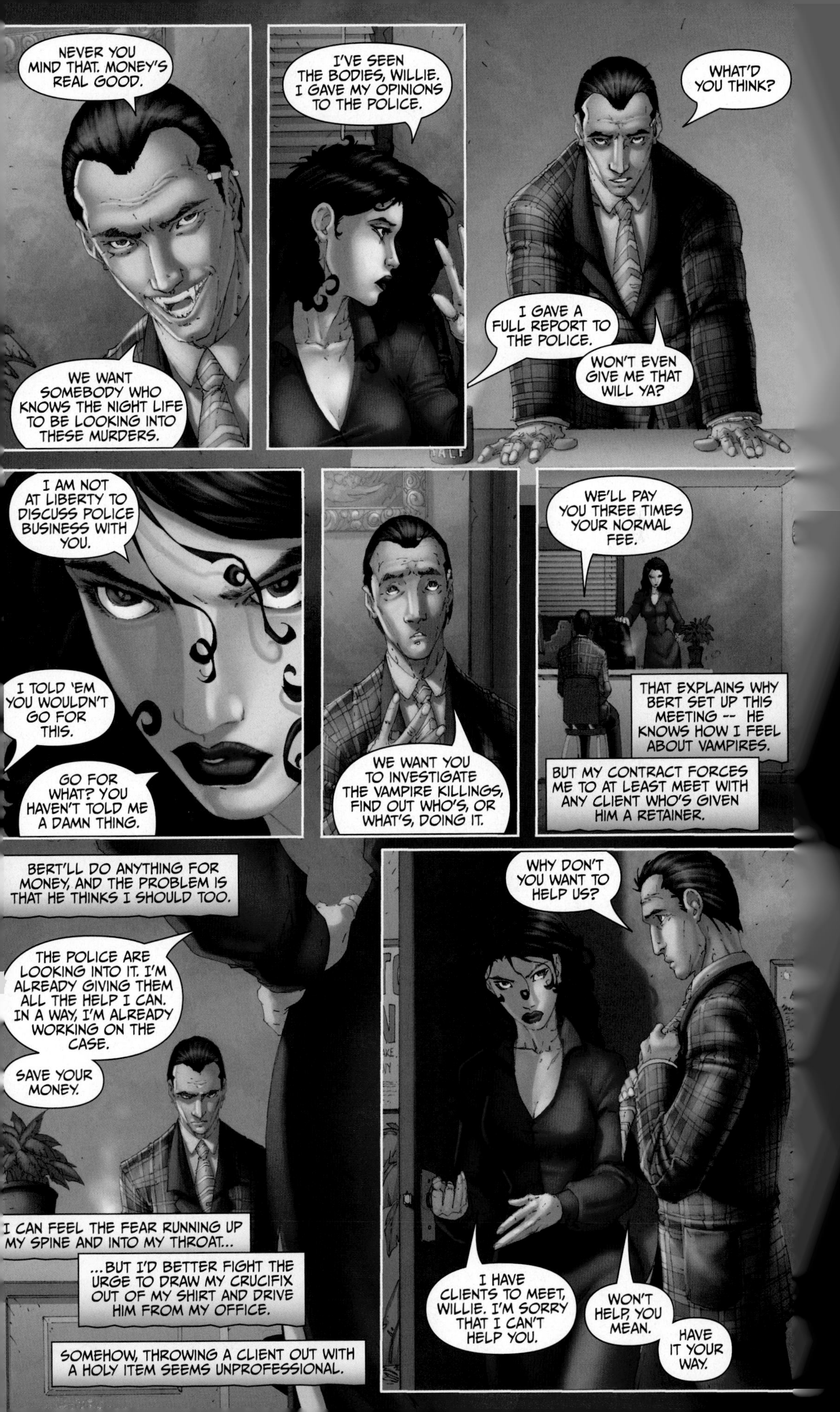
NEVER YOU MIND THAT. MONEY'S REAL GOOD.
WE WANT SOMEBODY WHO KNOWS THE NIGHT LIFE TO BE LOOKING INTO THESE MURDERS.
I'VE SEEN THE BODIES, WILLIE. I GAVE MY OPINIONS TO THE POLICE.
WHAT'D YOU THINK?
I GAVE A FULL REPORT TO THE POLICE.
WON'T EVEN GIVE ME THAT WILL YA?
I AM NOT AT LIBERTY TO DISCUSS POLICE BUSINESS WITH YOU.
I TOLD 'EM YOU WOULDN'T GO FOR THIS.
GO FOR WHAT? YOU HAVEN'T TOLD ME A DAMN THING.
WE WANT YOU TO INVESTIGATE THE VAMPIRE KILLINGS, FIND OUT WHO'S, OR WHAT'S, DOING IT.
WE'LL PAY YOU THREE TIMES YOUR NORMAL FEE.
THAT EXPLAINS WHY BERT SET UP THIS MEETING -- HE KNOWS HOW I FEEL ABOUT VAMPIRES.
BUT MY CONTRACT FORCES ME TO AT LEAST MEET WITH ANY CLIENT WHO'S GIVEN HIM A RETAINER.
BERT'LL DO ANYTHING FOR MONEY, AND THE PROBLEM IS THAT HE THINKS I SHOULD TOO.
THE POLICE ARE LOOKING INTO IT. I'M ALREADY GIVING THEM ALL THE HELP I CAN. IN A WAY, I'M ALREADY WORKING ON THE CASE.
SAVE YOUR MONEY.
I CAN FEEL THE FEAR RUNNING UP MY SPINE AND INTO MY THROAT...
...BUT I'D BETTER FIGHT THE URGE TO DRAW MY CRUCIFIX OUT OF MY SHIRT AND DRIVE HIM FROM MY OFFICE.
SOMEHOW, THROWING A CLIENT OUT WITH A HOLY ITEM SEEMS UNPROFESSIONAL.
WHY DON'T YOU WANT TO HELP US?
I HAVE CLIENTS TO MEET, WILLIE. I'M SORRY THAT I CAN'T HELP YOU.
WON'T HELP, YOU MEAN.
HAVE IT YOUR WAY.

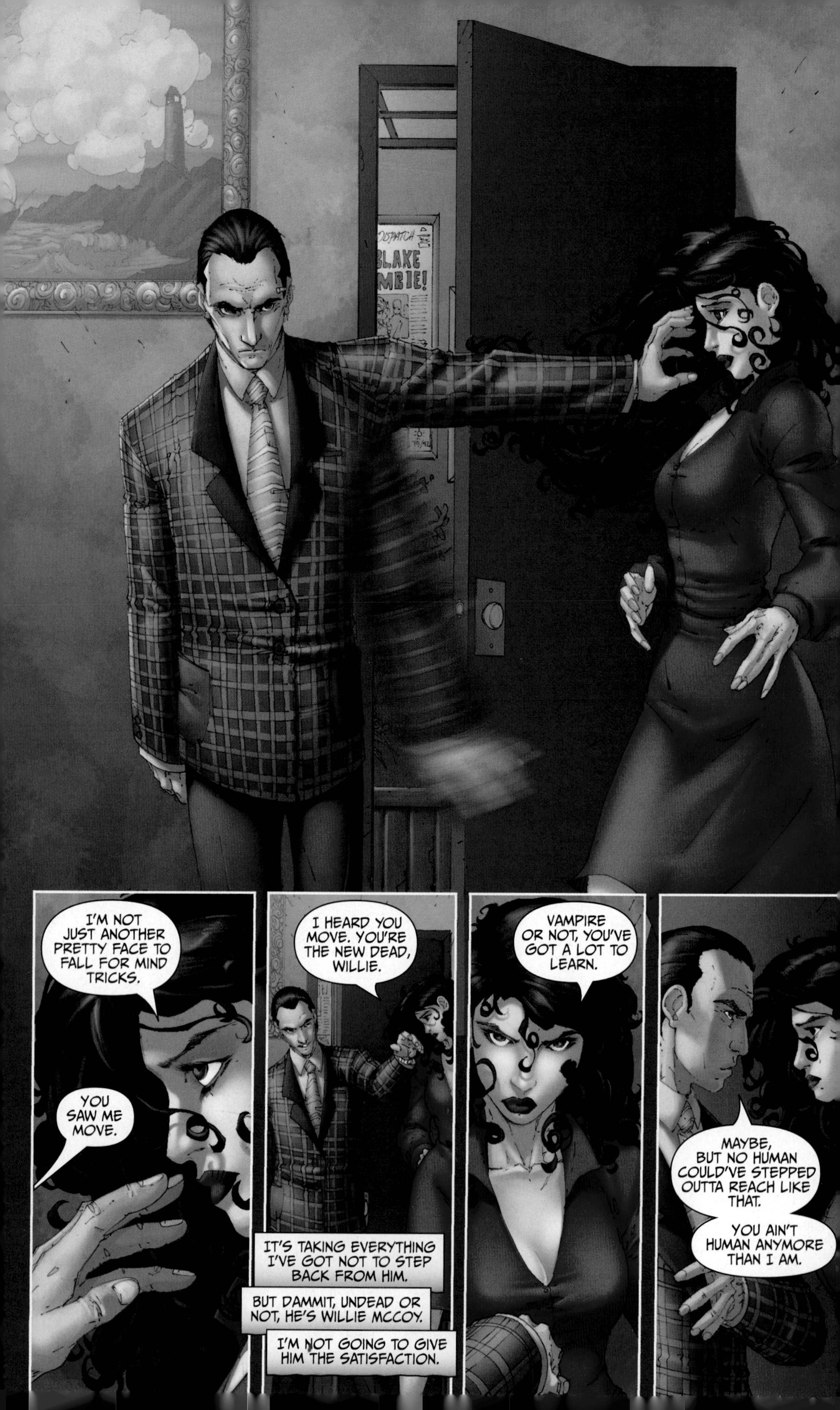

DISPATCH
BLAKE
ZOMBIE!
I'M NOT JUST ANOTHER PRETTY FACE TO FALL FOR MIND TRICKS.
YOU SAW ME MOVE.
I HEARD YOU MOVE. YOU'RE THE NEW DEAD, WILLIE.
IT'S TAKING EVERYTHING I'VE GOT NOT TO STEP BACK FROM HIM.
BUT DAMMIT, UNDEAD OR NOT, HE'S WILLIE MCCOY.
I'M NOT GOING TO GIVE HIM THE SATISFACTION.
VAMPIRE OR NOT, YOU'VE GOT A LOT TO LEARN.
MAYBE, BUT NO HUMAN COULD'VE STEPPED OUTTA REACH LIKE THAT.
YOU AIN'T HUMAN ANYMORE THAN I AM.

I REALLY HAVE TO BE GOING NOW. THANK YOU FOR THINKING OF ANIMATORS, INC.

WHY WON'T YOU WORK FOR US? I GOTTA TELL 'EM SOMETHING WHEN I GO BACK.

TELL THEM, WHOEVER THEY ARE, THAT I DON'T WORK FOR VAMPIRES.

A FIRM RULE?

CONCRETE.

I WISH YOU HADN'T SAID THAT, ANITA. THESE PEOPLE DON'T LIKE ANYBODY TELLING 'EM NO.

I THINK YOU'VE OVERSTAYED YOUR WELCOME. I DON'T LIKE TO BE THREATENED.

IT AIN'T A THREAT, ANITA. IT'S THE TRUTH.

MY KNEES FEEL WEAK. BUT THERE ISN'T TIME FOR ME TO SIT HERE AND SHAKE.

I KEEP A 9MM BROWNING HIGH-POWER IN MY DESK. THE GUN WEIGHED A LITTLE OVER TWO POUNDS, SILVER-PLATED BULLETS AND ALL. SILVER WON'T KILL A VAMPIRE OUTRIGHT, BUT IT MAKES THEM HEAL THE WOUND HUMAN-SLOW.

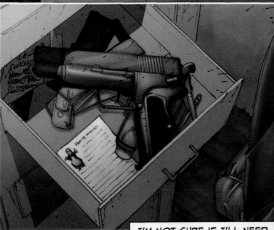

I'M NOT SURE IF I'LL NEED IT TODAY, BUT IT NEVER

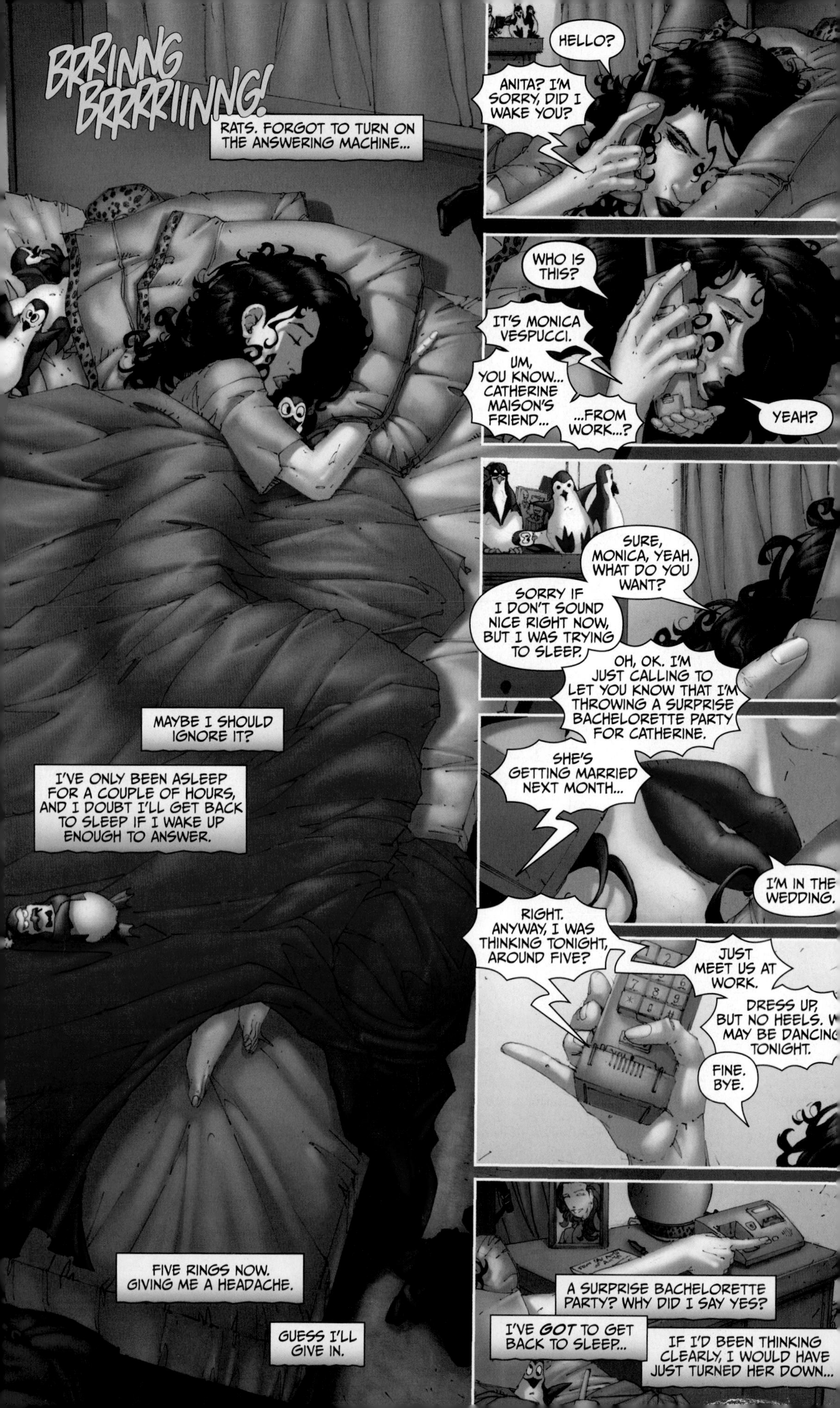
BRRINNG BRRRRIINNG!
RATS. FORGOT TO TURN ON THE ANSWERING MACHINE...
MAYBE I SHOULD IGNORE IT?
I'VE ONLY BEEN ASLEEP FOR A COUPLE OF HOURS, AND I DOUBT I'LL GET BACK TO SLEEP IF I WAKE UP ENOUGH TO ANSWER.
FIVE RINGS NOW. GIVING ME A HEADACHE.
GUESS I'LL GIVE IN.
HELLO?
ANITA? I'M SORRY, DID I WAKE YOU?
WHO IS THIS?
IT'S MONICA VESPUCCI.
UM, YOU KNOW... CATHERINE MAISON'S FRIEND...
...FROM WORK...?
YEAH?
SURE, MONICA, YEAH. WHAT DO YOU WANT?
SORRY IF I DON'T SOUND NICE RIGHT NOW, BUT I WAS TRYING TO SLEEP.
OH, OK. I'M JUST CALLING TO LET YOU KNOW THAT I'M THROWING A SURPRISE BACHELORETTE PARTY FOR CATHERINE.
SHE'S GETTING MARRIED NEXT MONTH...
I'M IN THE WEDDING.
RIGHT. ANYWAY, I WAS THINKING TONIGHT, AROUND FIVE?
JUST MEET US AT WORK.
DRESS UP, BUT NO HEELS.
MAY BE DANCING TONIGHT.
FINE. BYE.
A SURPRISE BACHELORETTE PARTY? WHY DID I SAY YES?
I'VE GOT TO GET BACK TO SLEEP...
IF I'D BEEN THINKING CLEARLY, I WOULD HAVE JUST TURNED HER DOWN...

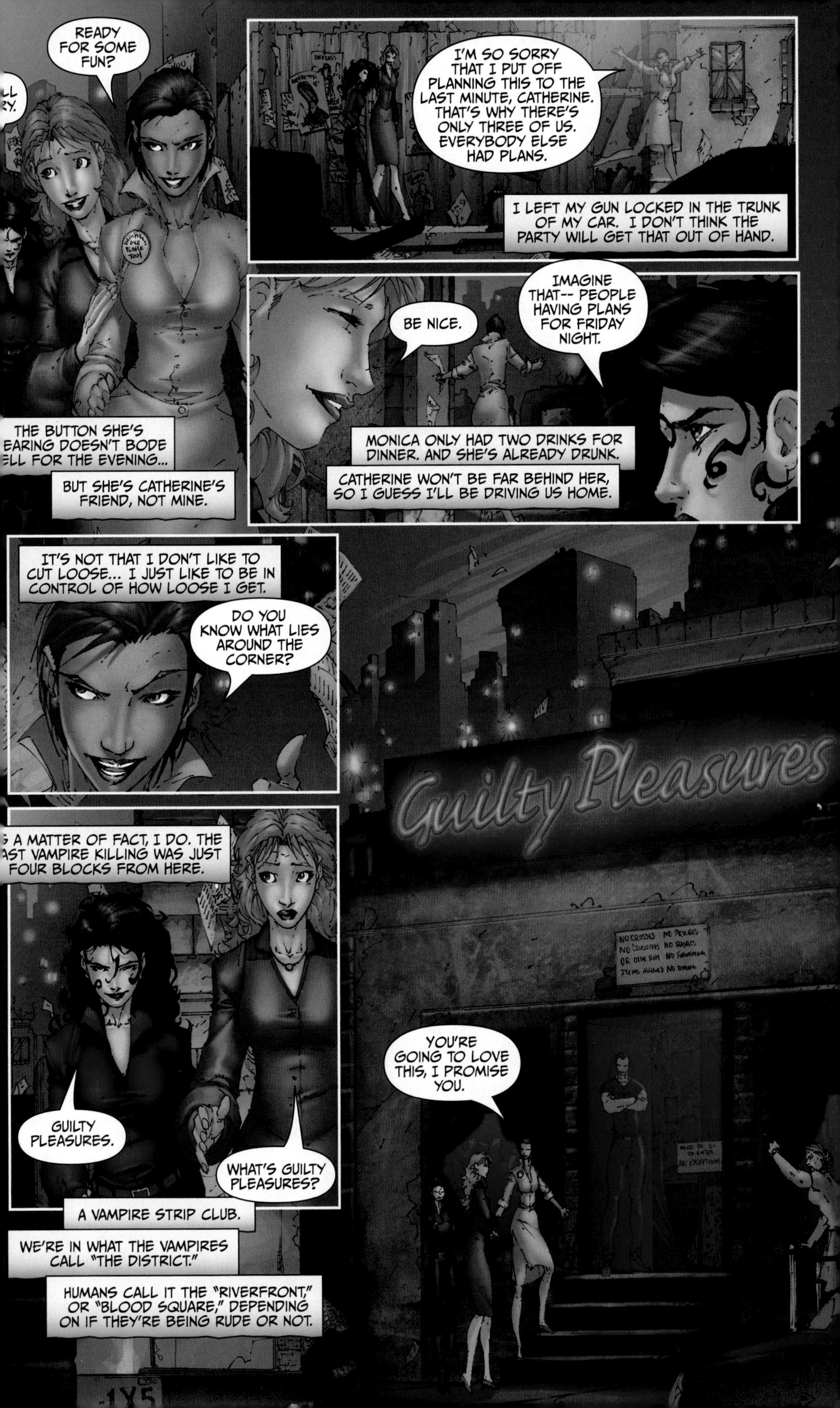

READY FOR SOME FUN?
I'M SO SORRY THAT I PUT OFF PLANNING THIS TO THE LAST MINUTE, CATHERINE. THAT'S WHY THERE'S ONLY THREE OF US. EVERYBODY ELSE HAD PLANS.
I LEFT MY GUN LOCKED IN THE TRUNK OF MY CAR. I DON'T THINK THE PARTY WILL GET THAT OUT OF HAND.
THE BUTTON SHE'S EARING DOESN'T BODE ELL FOR THE EVENING...
BUT SHE'S CATHERINE'S FRIEND, NOT MINE.
IMAGINE THAT-- PEOPLE HAVING PLANS FOR FRIDAY NIGHT.
BE NICE.
MONICA ONLY HAD TWO DRINKS FOR DINNER. AND SHE'S ALREADY DRUNK.
CATHERINE WON'T BE FAR BEHIND HER, SO I GUESS I'LL BE DRIVING US HOME.
IT'S NOT THAT I DON'T LIKE TO CUT LOOSE... I JUST LIKE TO BE IN CONTROL OF HOW LOOSE I GET.
DO YOU KNOW WHAT LIES AROUND THE CORNER?
A MATTER OF FACT, I DO. THE AST VAMPIRE KILLING WAS JUST FOUR BLOCKS FROM HERE.
GUILTY PLEASURES.
WHAT'S GUILTY PLEASURES?
A VAMPIRE STRIP CLUB.
WE'RE IN WHAT THE VAMPIRES CALL "THE DISTRICT."
HUMANS CALL IT THE "RIVERFRONT," OR "BLOOD SQUARE," DEPENDING ON IF THEY'RE BEING RUDE OR NOT.
Guilty Pleasures
YOU'RE GOING TO LOVE THIS, I PROMISE YOU.

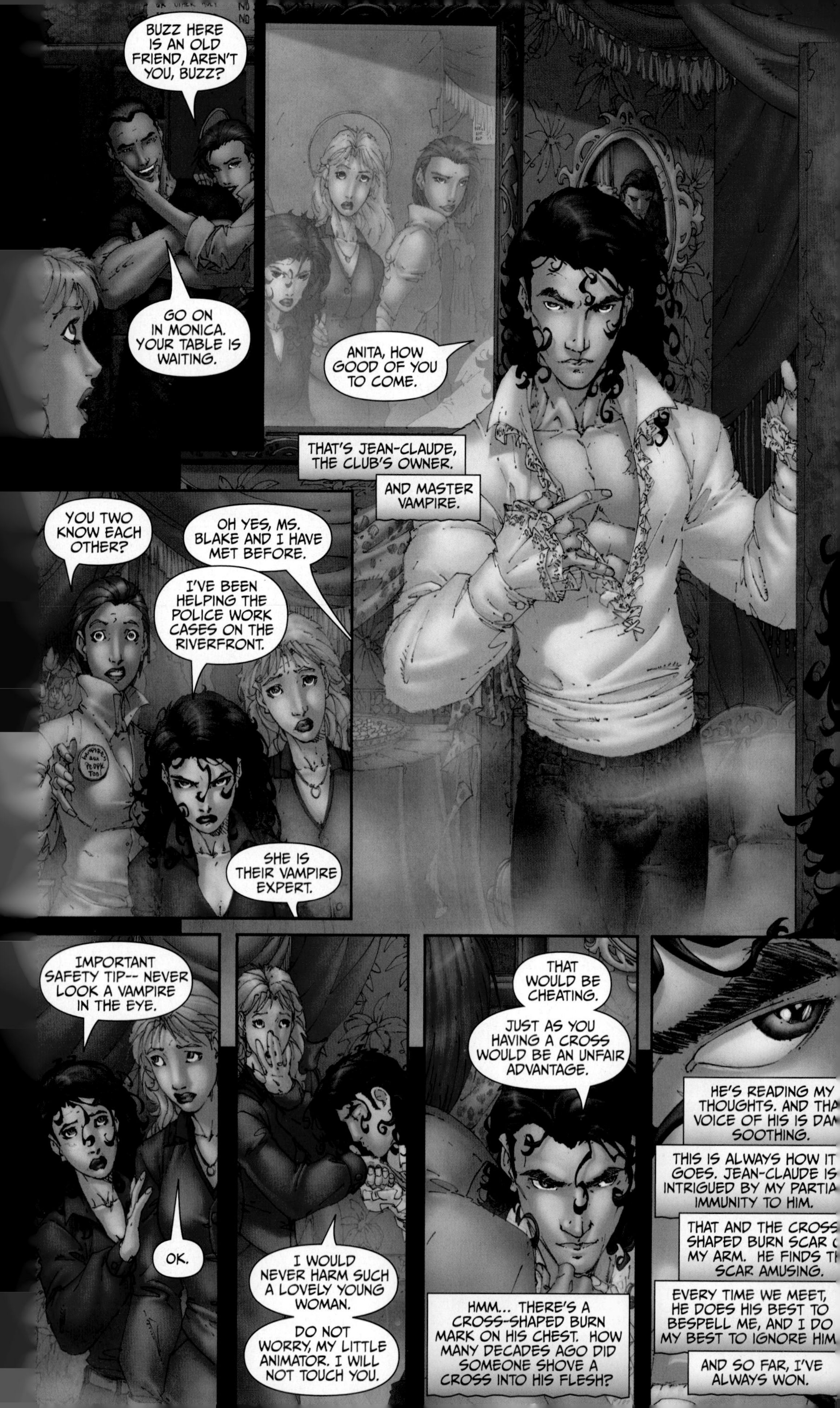

BUZZ HERE IS AN OLD FRIEND, AREN'T YOU, BUZZ?
GO ON IN MONICA. YOUR TABLE IS WAITING.
ANITA, HOW GOOD OF YOU TO COME.
THAT'S JEAN-CLAUDE, THE CLUB'S OWNER.
AND MASTER VAMPIRE.
YOU TWO KNOW EACH OTHER?
OH YES, MS. BLAKE AND I HAVE MET BEFORE.
I'VE BEEN HELPING THE POLICE WORK CASES ON THE RIVERFRONT.
SHE IS THEIR VAMPIRE EXPERT.
IMPORTANT SAFETY TIP-- NEVER LOOK A VAMPIRE IN THE EYE.
OK.
I WOULD NEVER HARM SUCH A LOVELY YOUNG WOMAN.
DO NOT WORRY, MY LITTLE ANIMATOR. I WILL NOT TOUCH YOU.
THAT WOULD BE CHEATING.
JUST AS YOU HAVING A CROSS WOULD BE AN UNFAIR ADVANTAGE.
HMM... THERE'S A CROSS-SHAPED BURN MARK ON HIS CHEST. HOW MANY DECADES AGO DID SOMEONE SHOVE A CROSS INTO HIS FLESH?
HE'S READING MY THOUGHTS. AND THA VOICE OF HIS IS DAM SOOTHING.
THIS IS ALWAYS HOW IT GOES. JEAN-CLAUDE IS INTRIGUED BY MY PARTIA IMMUNITY TO HIM.
THAT AND THE CROSS SHAPED BURN SCAR MY ARM. HE FINDS T SCAR AMUSING.
EVERY TIME WE MEET, HE DOES HIS BEST TO BESPELL ME, AND I DO MY BEST TO IGNORE HIM.
AND SO FAR, I'VE ALWAYS WON.

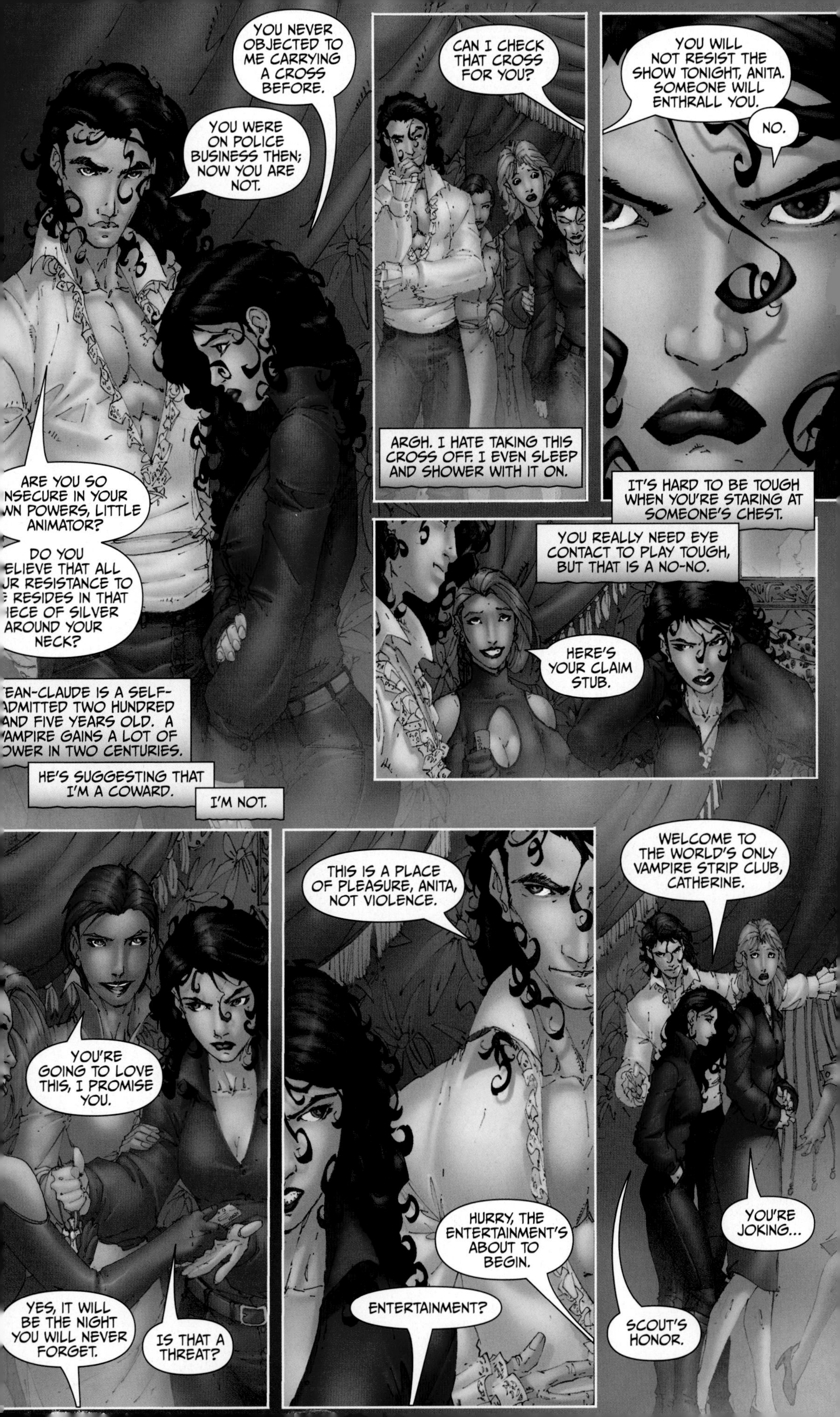
YOU NEVER OBJECTED TO ME CARRYING A CROSS BEFORE.
YOU WERE ON POLICE BUSINESS THEN; NOW YOU ARE NOT.
ARE YOU SO NSECURE IN YOUR WN POWERS, LITTLE ANIMATOR?
DO YOU ELIEVE THAT ALL UR RESISTANCE TO E RESIDES IN THAT IECE OF SILVER AROUND YOUR NECK?
EAN-CLAUDE IS A SELF-ADMITTED TWO HUNDRED AND FIVE YEARS OLD. A VAMPIRE GAINS A LOT OF OWER IN TWO CENTURIES.
HE'S SUGGESTING THAT I'M A COWARD.
I'M NOT.
CAN I CHECK THAT CROSS FOR YOU?
ARGH. I HATE TAKING THIS CROSS OFF. I EVEN SLEEP AND SHOWER WITH IT ON.
YOU WILL NOT RESIST THE SHOW TONIGHT, ANITA. SOMEONE WILL ENTHRALL YOU.
NO.
IT'S HARD TO BE TOUGH WHEN YOU'RE STARING AT SOMEONE'S CHEST.
YOU REALLY NEED EYE CONTACT TO PLAY TOUGH, BUT THAT IS A NO-NO.
HERE'S YOUR CLAIM STUB.
YOU'RE GOING TO LOVE THIS, I PROMISE YOU.
YES, IT WILL BE THE NIGHT YOU WILL NEVER FORGET.
IS THAT A THREAT?
THIS IS A PLACE OF PLEASURE, ANITA, NOT VIOLENCE.
HURRY, THE ENTERTAINMENT'S ABOUT TO BEGIN.
ENTERTAINMENT?
WELCOME TO THE WORLD'S ONLY VAMPIRE STRIP CLUB, CATHERINE.
YOU'RE JOKING...
SCOUT'S HONOR.

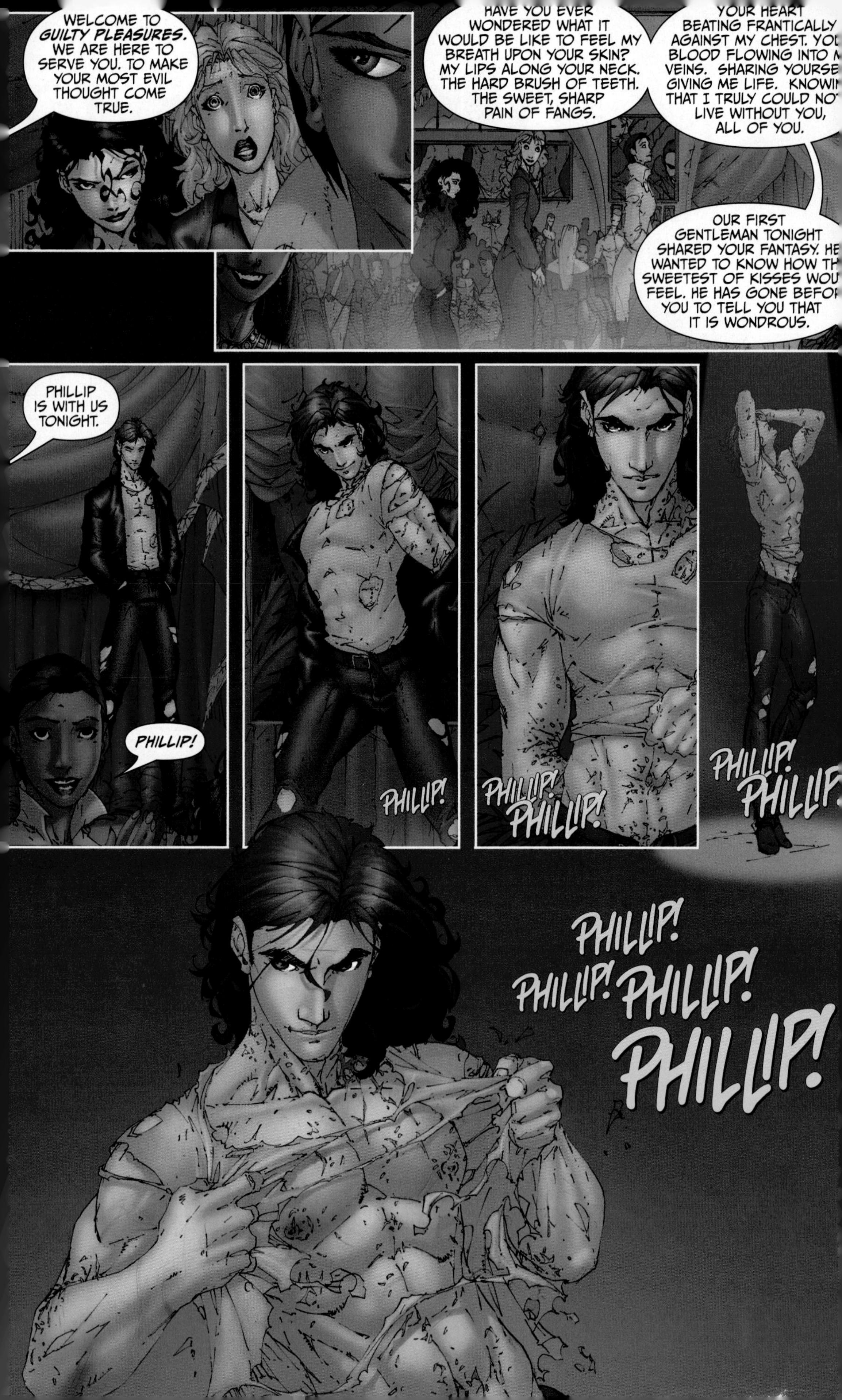
WELCOME TO *GUILTY PLEASURES.* WE ARE HERE TO SERVE YOU. TO MAKE YOUR MOST EVIL THOUGHT COME TRUE.
HAVE YOU EVER WONDERED WHAT IT WOULD BE LIKE TO FEEL MY BREATH UPON YOUR SKIN? MY LIPS ALONG YOUR NECK. THE HARD BRUSH OF TEETH. THE SWEET, SHARP PAIN OF FANGS.
YOUR HEART BEATING FRANTICALLY AGAINST MY CHEST. YOU BLOOD FLOWING INTO M VEINS. SHARING YOURSE GIVING ME LIFE. KNOWIN THAT I TRULY COULD NOT LIVE WITHOUT YOU, ALL OF YOU.
OUR FIRST GENTLEMAN TONIGHT SHARED YOUR FANTASY. HE WANTED TO KNOW HOW TH SWEETEST OF KISSES WOU FEEL. HE HAS GONE BEFOR YOU TO TELL YOU THAT IT IS WONDROUS.
PHILLIP IS WITH US TONIGHT.
PHILLIP!
PHILLIP!
PHILLIP! PHILLIP!
PHILLIP! PHILLIP!
PHILLIP! PHILLIP! PHILLIP! PHILLIP!

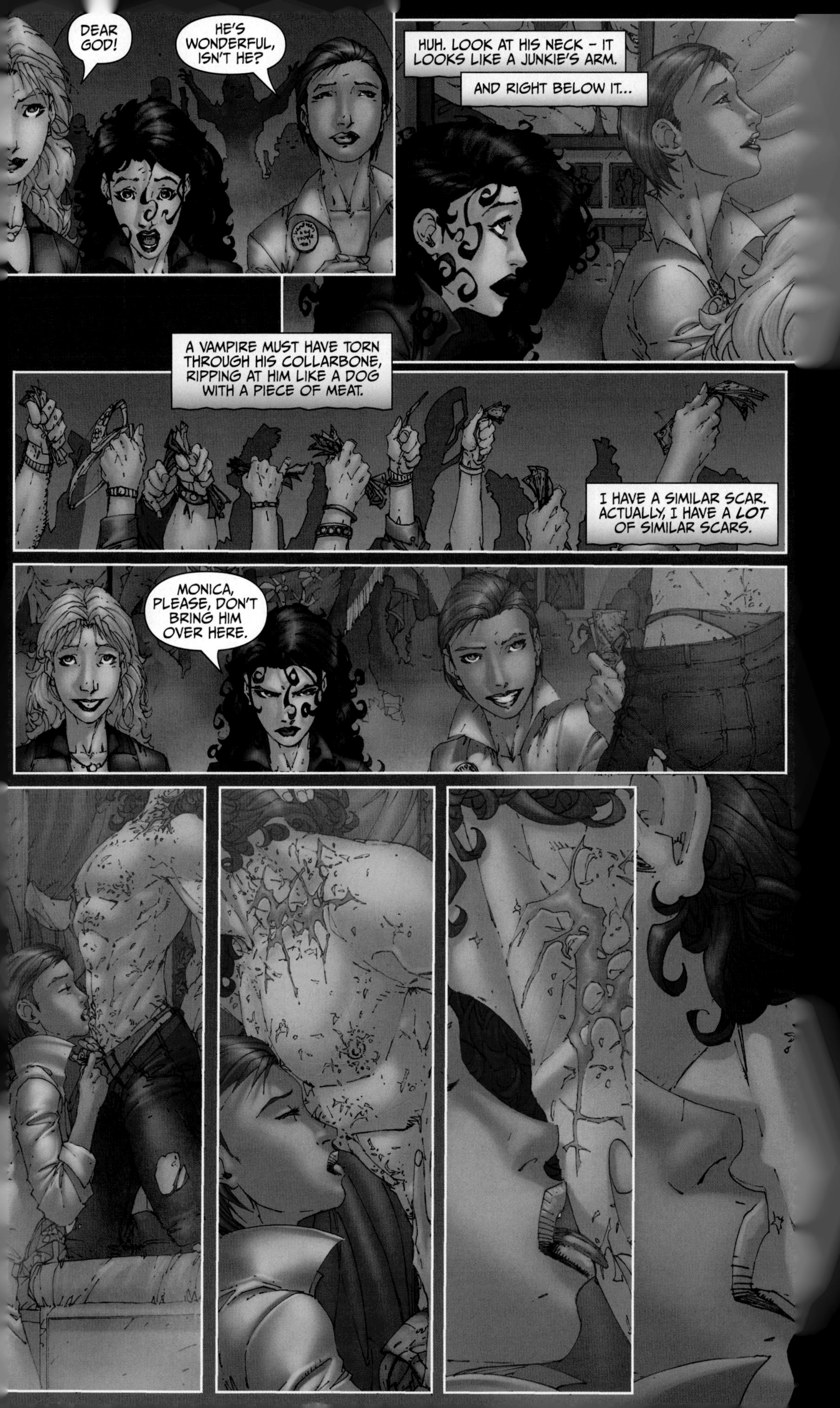
DEAR GOD!
HE'S WONDERFUL, ISN'T HE?
HUH. LOOK AT HIS NECK – IT LOOKS LIKE A JUNKIE'S ARM.
AND RIGHT BELOW IT...
A VAMPIRE MUST HAVE TORN THROUGH HIS COLLARBONE, RIPPING AT HIM LIKE A DOG WITH A PIECE OF MEAT.
I HAVE A SIMILAR SCAR. ACTUALLY, I HAVE A *LOT* OF SIMILAR SCARS.
MONICA, PLEASE, DON'T BRING HIM OVER HERE.

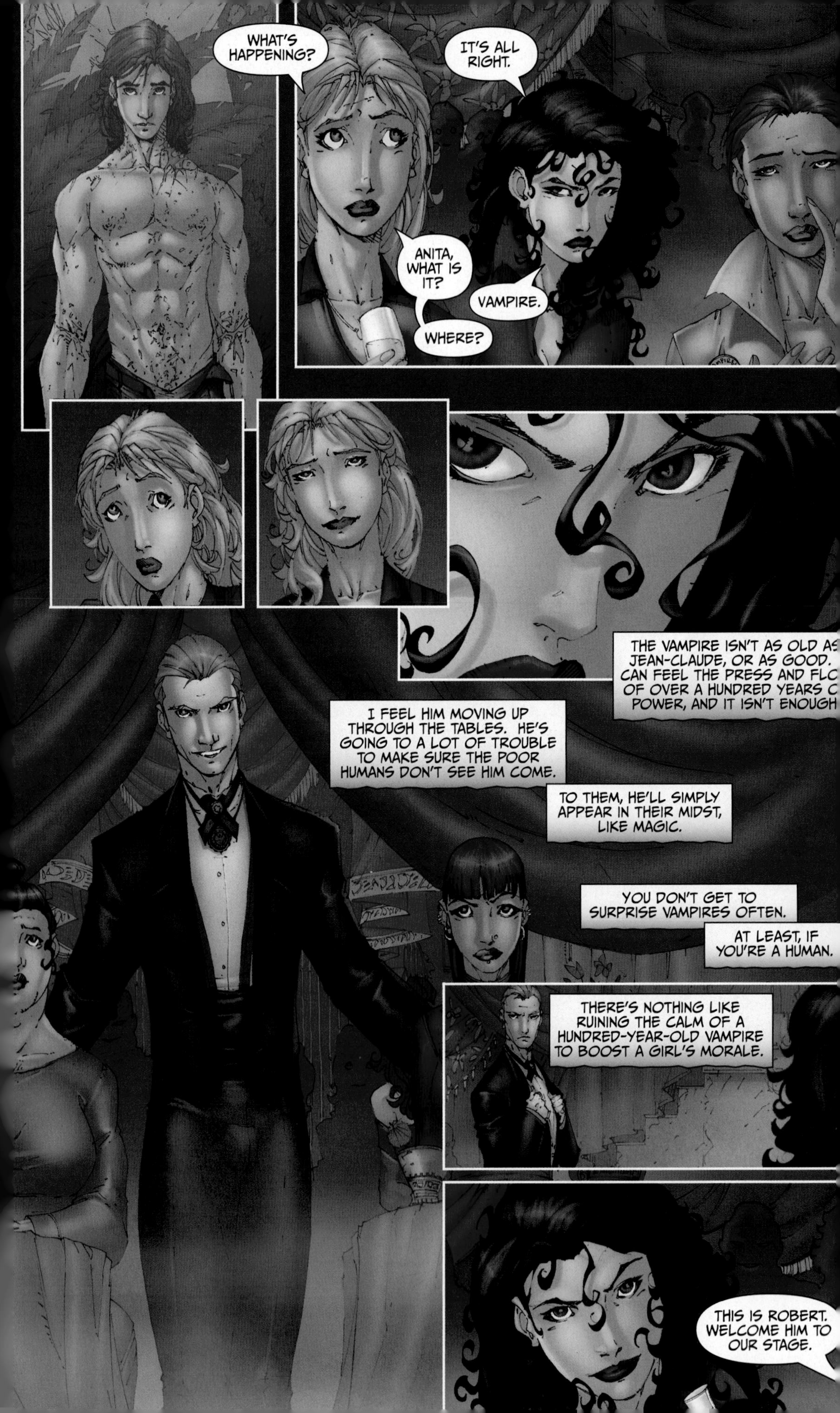
WHAT'S HAPPENING?
IT'S ALL RIGHT.
ANITA, WHAT IS IT?
VAMPIRE.
WHERE?
THE VAMPIRE ISN'T AS OLD AS JEAN-CLAUDE, OR AS GOOD. CAN FEEL THE PRESS AND FLO OF OVER A HUNDRED YEARS O POWER, AND IT ISN'T ENOUGH
I FEEL HIM MOVING UP THROUGH THE TABLES. HE'S GOING TO A LOT OF TROUBLE TO MAKE SURE THE POOR HUMANS DON'T SEE HIM COME.
TO THEM, HE'LL SIMPLY APPEAR IN THEIR MIDST, LIKE MAGIC.
YOU DON'T GET TO SURPRISE VAMPIRES OFTEN.
AT LEAST, IF YOU'RE A HUMAN.
THERE'S NOTHING LIKE RUINING THE CALM OF A HUNDRED-YEAR-OLD VAMPIRE TO BOOST A GIRL'S MORALE.
THIS IS ROBERT. WELCOME HIM TO OUR STAGE.

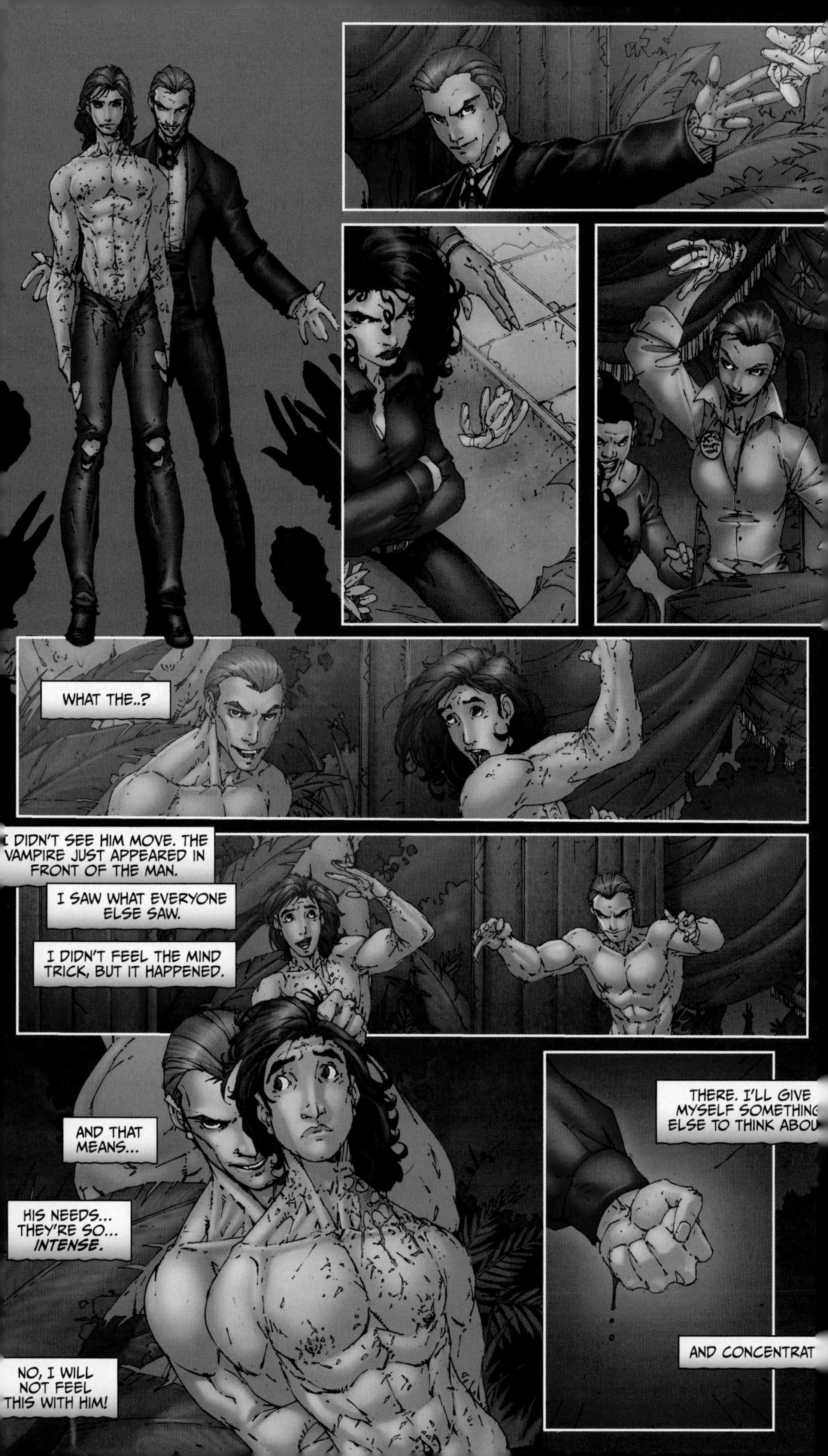

WHAT THE..?
I DIDN'T SEE HIM MOVE. THE VAMPIRE JUST APPEARED IN FRONT OF THE MAN.
I SAW WHAT EVERYONE ELSE SAW.
I DIDN'T FEEL THE MIND TRICK, BUT IT HAPPENED.
AND THAT MEANS...
HIS NEEDS... THEY'RE SO... *INTENSE.*
NO, I WILL NOT FEEL THIS WITH HIM!
THERE. I'LL GIVE MYSELF SOMETHING ELSE TO THINK ABOU
AND CONCENTRAT

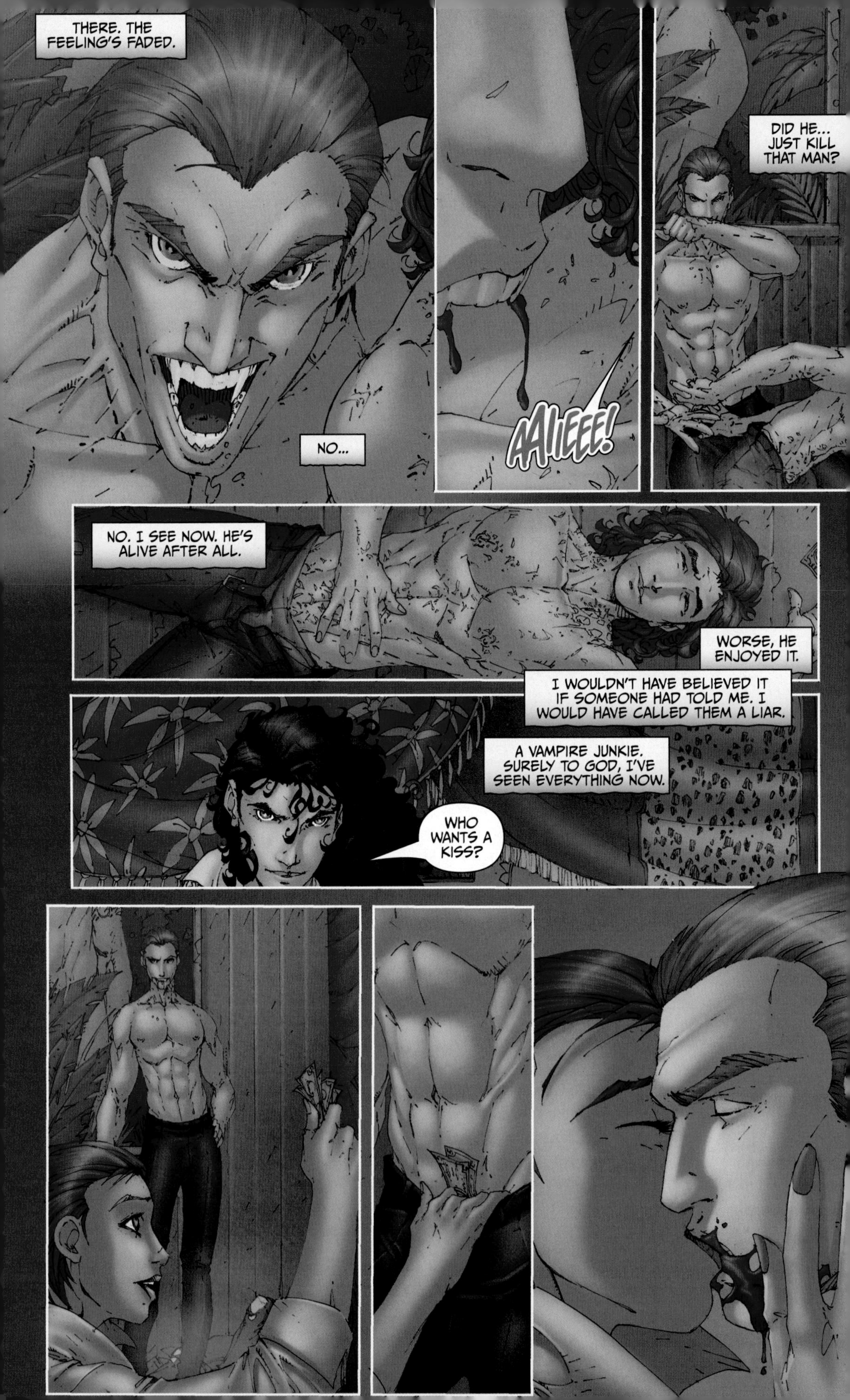
THERE. THE FEELING'S FADED.
NO...
AAIIEEE!
DID HE... JUST KILL THAT MAN?
NO. I SEE NOW. HE'S ALIVE AFTER ALL.
WORSE, HE ENJOYED IT.
I WOULDN'T HAVE BELIEVED IT IF SOMEONE HAD TOLD ME. I WOULD HAVE CALLED THEM A LIAR.
A VAMPIRE JUNKIE. SURELY TO GOD, I'VE SEEN EVERYTHING NOW.
WHO WANTS A KISS?

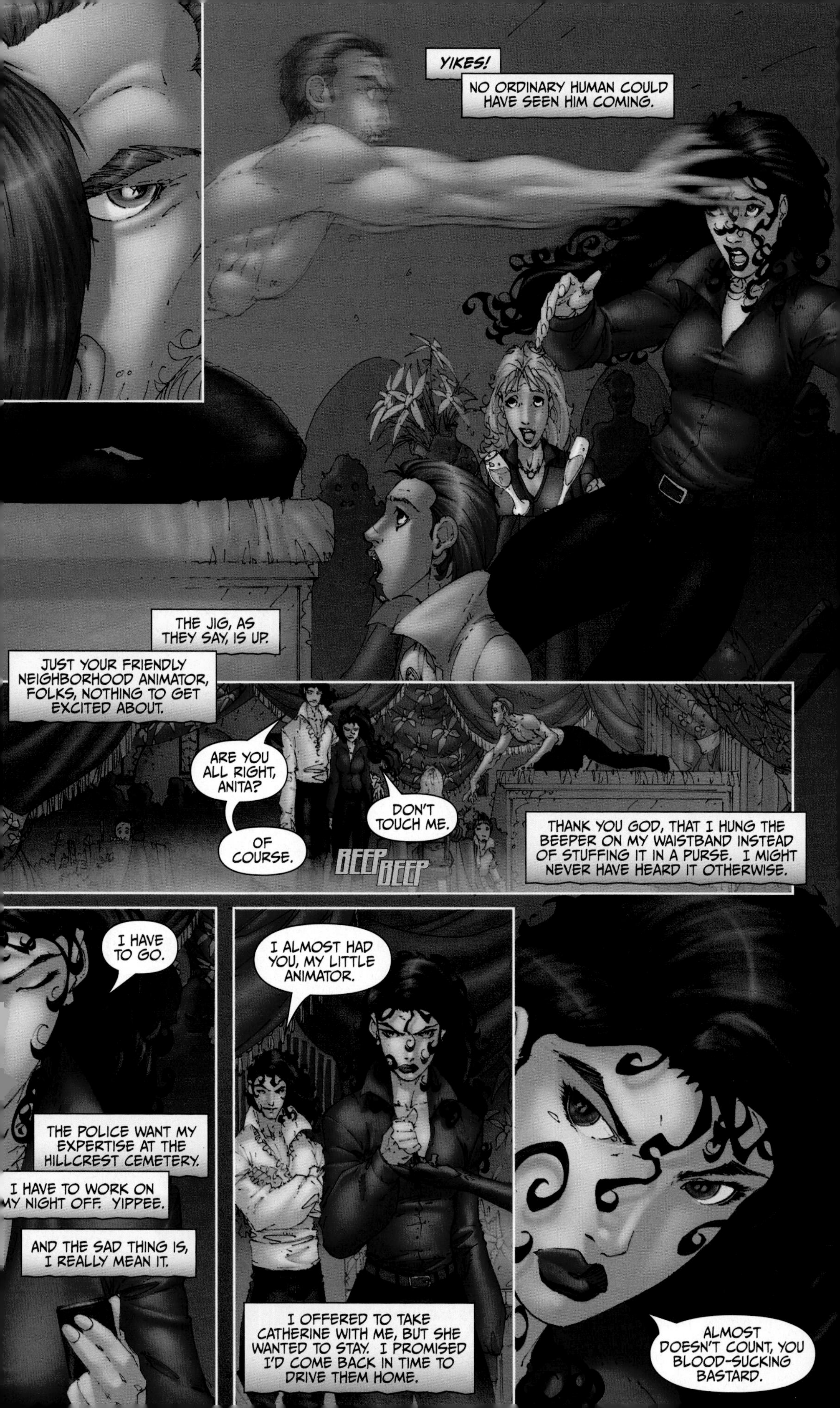

YIKES!
NO ORDINARY HUMAN COULD HAVE SEEN HIM COMING.
THE JIG, AS THEY SAY, IS UP.
JUST YOUR FRIENDLY NEIGHBORHOOD ANIMATOR, FOLKS, NOTHING TO GET EXCITED ABOUT.
ARE YOU ALL RIGHT, ANITA?
OF COURSE.
DON'T TOUCH ME.
BEEP BEEP
THANK YOU GOD, THAT I HUNG THE BEEPER ON MY WAISTBAND INSTEAD OF STUFFING IT IN A PURSE. I MIGHT NEVER HAVE HEARD IT OTHERWISE.
I HAVE TO GO.
THE POLICE WANT MY EXPERTISE AT THE HILLCREST CEMETERY.
I HAVE TO WORK ON MY NIGHT OFF. YIPPEE.
AND THE SAD THING IS, I REALLY MEAN IT.
I ALMOST HAD YOU, MY LITTLE ANIMATOR.
I OFFERED TO TAKE CATHERINE WITH ME, BUT SHE WANTED TO STAY. I PROMISED I'D COME BACK IN TIME TO DRIVE THEM HOME.
ALMOST DOESN'T COUNT, YOU BLOOD-SUCKING BASTARD.

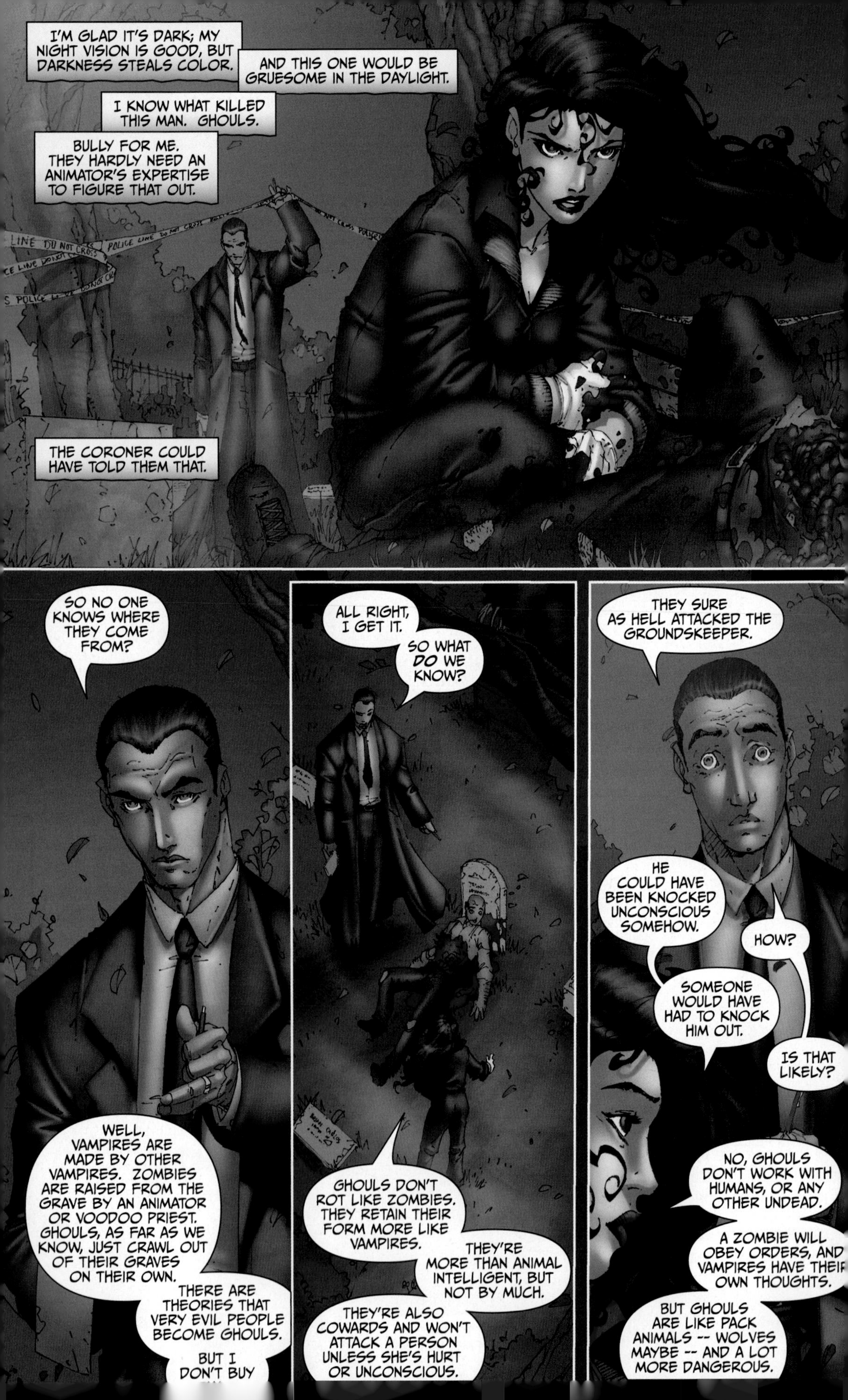

I'M GLAD IT'S DARK; MY NIGHT VISION IS GOOD, BUT DARKNESS STEALS COLOR.
AND THIS ONE WOULD BE GRUESOME IN THE DAYLIGHT.
I KNOW WHAT KILLED THIS MAN. GHOULS.
BULLY FOR ME. THEY HARDLY NEED AN ANIMATOR'S EXPERTISE TO FIGURE THAT OUT.
THE CORONER COULD HAVE TOLD THEM THAT.
SO NO ONE KNOWS WHERE THEY COME FROM?
WELL, VAMPIRES ARE MADE BY OTHER VAMPIRES. ZOMBIES ARE RAISED FROM THE GRAVE BY AN ANIMATOR OR VOODOO PRIEST. GHOULS, AS FAR AS WE KNOW, JUST CRAWL OUT OF THEIR GRAVES ON THEIR OWN.
THERE ARE THEORIES THAT VERY EVIL PEOPLE BECOME GHOULS.
BUT I DON'T BUY
ALL RIGHT, I GET IT.
SO WHAT DO WE KNOW?
GHOULS DON'T ROT LIKE ZOMBIES. THEY RETAIN THEIR FORM MORE LIKE VAMPIRES.
THEY'RE MORE THAN ANIMAL INTELLIGENT, BUT NOT BY MUCH.
THEY'RE ALSO COWARDS AND WON'T ATTACK A PERSON UNLESS SHE'S HURT OR UNCONSCIOUS.
THEY SURE AS HELL ATTACKED THE GROUNDSKEEPER.
HE COULD HAVE BEEN KNOCKED UNCONSCIOUS SOMEHOW.
HOW?
SOMEONE WOULD HAVE HAD TO KNOCK HIM OUT.
IS THAT LIKELY?
NO, GHOULS DON'T WORK WITH HUMANS, OR ANY OTHER UNDEAD.
A ZOMBIE WILL OBEY ORDERS, AND VAMPIRES HAVE THEIR OWN THOUGHTS.
BUT GHOULS ARE LIKE PACK ANIMALS -- WOLVES MAYBE -- AND A LOT MORE DANGEROUS.

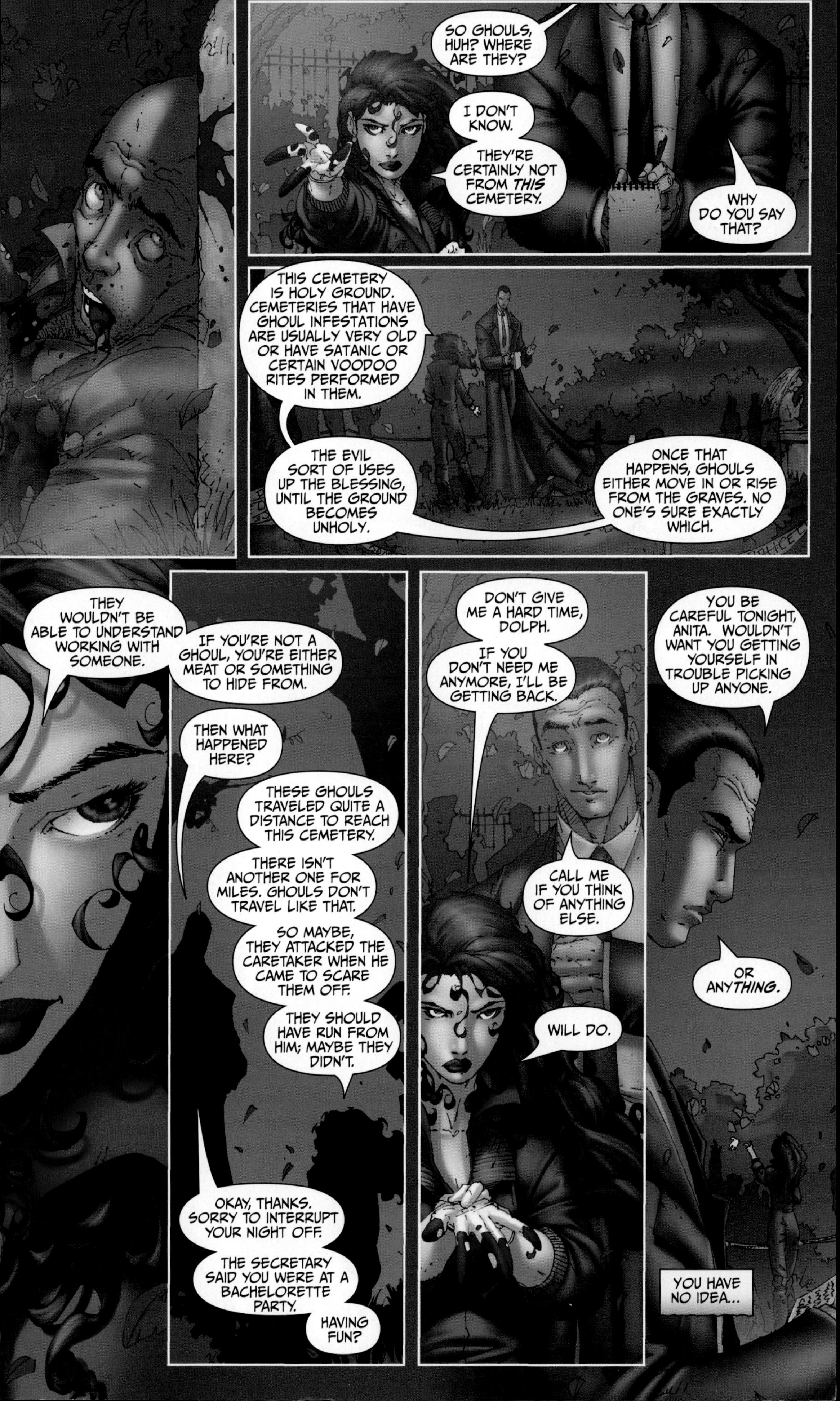
SO GHOULS, HUH? WHERE ARE THEY?
I DON'T KNOW.
THEY'RE CERTAINLY NOT FROM THIS CEMETERY.
WHY DO YOU SAY THAT?
THIS CEMETERY IS HOLY GROUND. CEMETERIES THAT HAVE GHOUL INFESTATIONS ARE USUALLY VERY OLD OR HAVE SATANIC OR CERTAIN VOODOO RITES PERFORMED IN THEM.
THE EVIL SORT OF USES UP THE BLESSING, UNTIL THE GROUND BECOMES UNHOLY.
ONCE THAT HAPPENS, GHOULS EITHER MOVE IN OR RISE FROM THE GRAVES. NO ONE'S SURE EXACTLY WHICH.
THEY WOULDN'T BE ABLE TO UNDERSTAND WORKING WITH SOMEONE.
IF YOU'RE NOT A GHOUL, YOU'RE EITHER MEAT OR SOMETHING TO HIDE FROM.
THEN WHAT HAPPENED HERE?
THESE GHOULS TRAVELED QUITE A DISTANCE TO REACH THIS CEMETERY.
THERE ISN'T ANOTHER ONE FOR MILES. GHOULS DON'T TRAVEL LIKE THAT.
SO MAYBE, THEY ATTACKED THE CARETAKER WHEN HE CAME TO SCARE THEM OFF.
THEY SHOULD HAVE RUN FROM HIM; MAYBE THEY DIDN'T.
OKAY, THANKS. SORRY TO INTERRUPT YOUR NIGHT OFF.
THE SECRETARY SAID YOU WERE AT A BACHELORETTE PARTY.
HAVING FUN?
DON'T GIVE ME A HARD TIME, DOLPH.
IF YOU DON'T NEED ME ANYMORE, I'LL BE GETTING BACK.
CALL ME IF YOU THINK OF ANYTHING ELSE.
WILL DO.
YOU BE CAREFUL TONIGHT, ANITA. WOULDN'T WANT YOU GETTING YOURSELF IN TROUBLE PICKING UP ANYONE.
OR ANYTHING.
YOU HAVE NO IDEA...

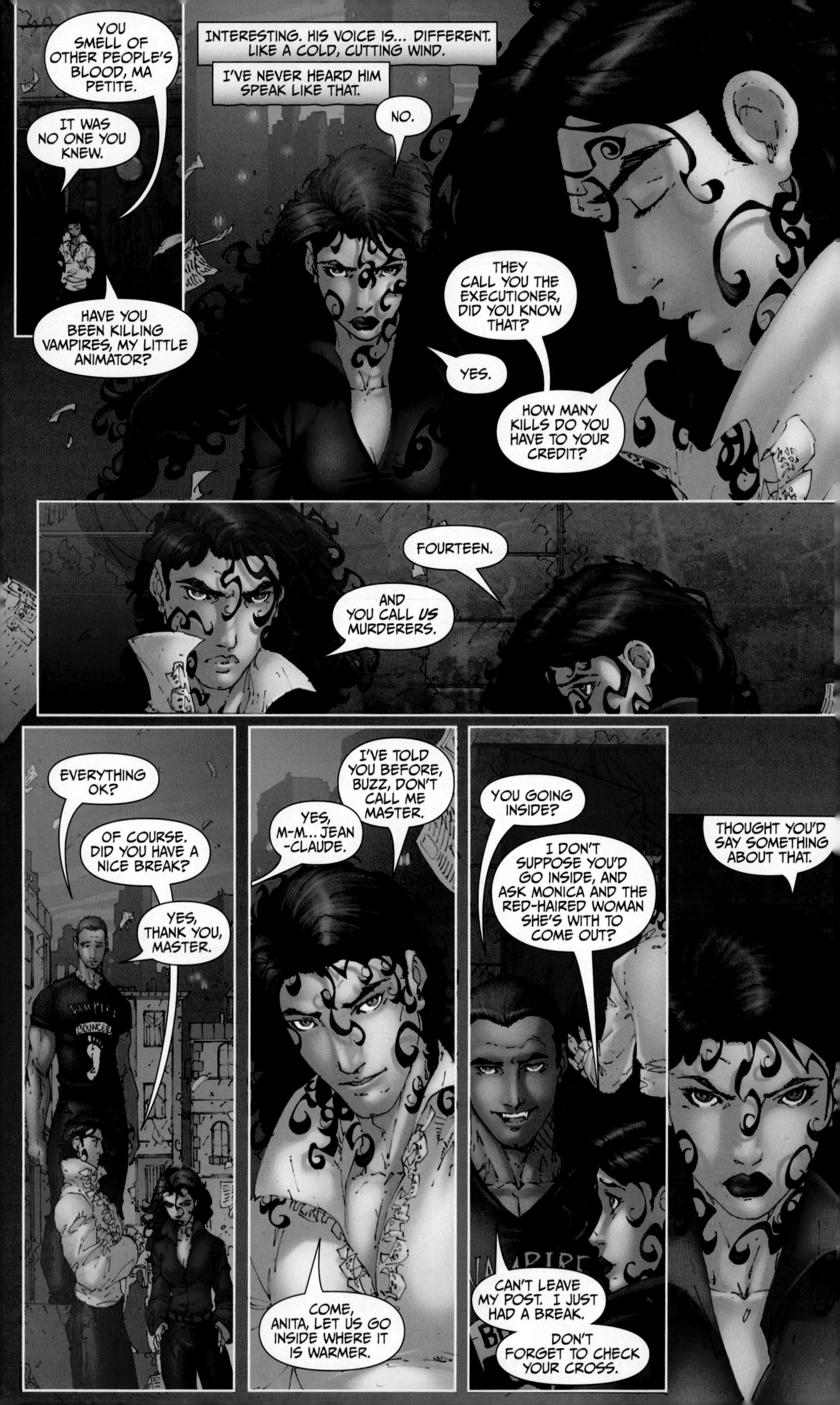
YOU SMELL OF OTHER PEOPLE'S BLOOD, MA PETITE.
IT WAS NO ONE YOU KNEW.
HAVE YOU BEEN KILLING VAMPIRES, MY LITTLE ANIMATOR?
INTERESTING. HIS VOICE IS... DIFFERENT. LIKE A COLD, CUTTING WIND.
I'VE NEVER HEARD HIM SPEAK LIKE THAT.
NO.
THEY CALL YOU THE EXECUTIONER, DID YOU KNOW THAT?
YES.
HOW MANY KILLS DO YOU HAVE TO YOUR CREDIT?
FOURTEEN.
AND YOU CALL US MURDERERS.
EVERYTHING OK?
OF COURSE. DID YOU HAVE A NICE BREAK?
YES, THANK YOU, MASTER.
I'VE TOLD YOU BEFORE, BUZZ, DON'T CALL ME MASTER.
YES, M-M... JEAN-CLAUDE.
COME, ANITA, LET US GO INSIDE WHERE IT IS WARMER.
YOU GOING INSIDE?
I DON'T SUPPOSE YOU'D GO INSIDE, AND ASK MONICA AND THE RED-HAIRED WOMAN SHE'S WITH TO COME OUT?
CAN'T LEAVE MY POST. I JUST HAD A BREAK.
DON'T FORGET TO CHECK YOUR CROSS.
THOUGHT YOU'D SAY SOMETHING ABOUT THAT.

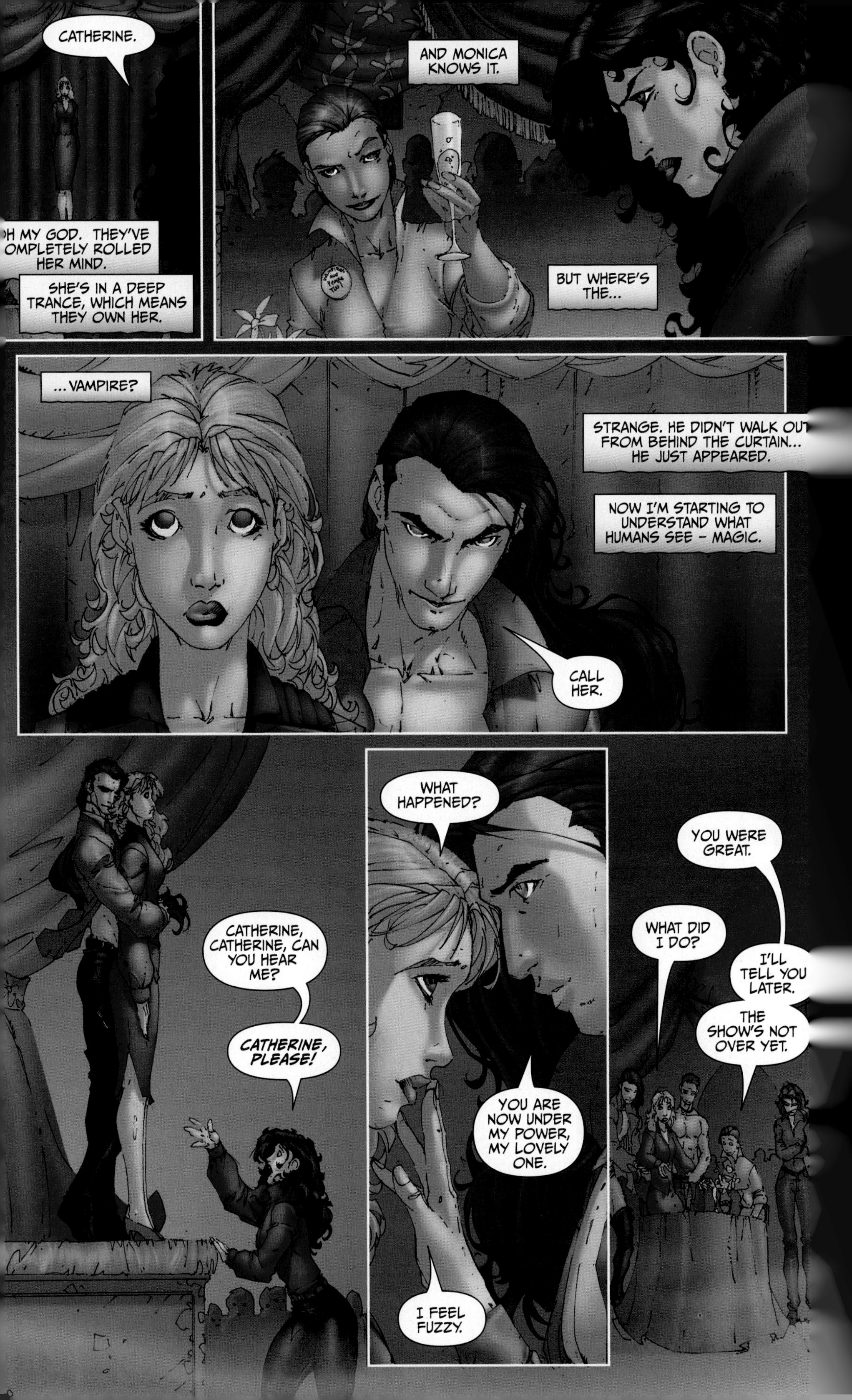
CATHERINE.
H MY GOD. THEY'VE OMPLETELY ROLLED HER MIND.
SHE'S IN A DEEP TRANCE, WHICH MEANS THEY OWN HER.
AND MONICA KNOWS IT.
BUT WHERE'S THE...
...VAMPIRE?
STRANGE. HE DIDN'T WALK OUT FROM BEHIND THE CURTAIN... HE JUST APPEARED.
NOW I'M STARTING TO UNDERSTAND WHAT HUMANS SEE – MAGIC.
CALL HER.
CATHERINE, CATHERINE, CAN YOU HEAR ME?
CATHERINE, PLEASE!
WHAT HAPPENED?
YOU ARE NOW UNDER MY POWER, MY LOVELY ONE.
I FEEL FUZZY.
YOU WERE GREAT.
WHAT DID I DO?
I'LL TELL YOU LATER.
THE SHOW'S NOT OVER YET.

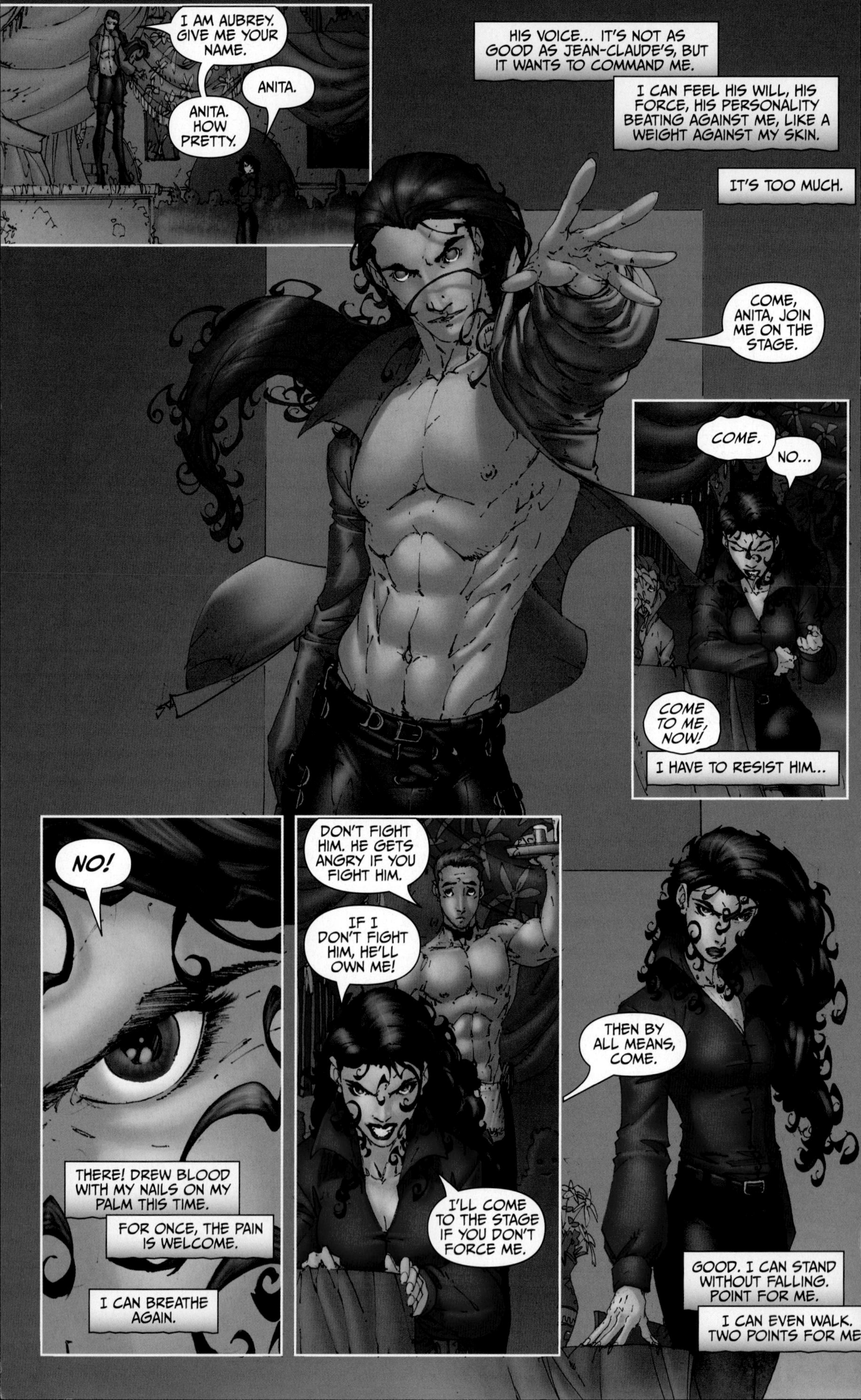
I AM AUBREY. GIVE ME YOUR NAME.
ANITA.
ANITA. HOW PRETTY.
HIS VOICE... IT'S NOT AS GOOD AS JEAN-CLAUDE'S, BUT IT WANTS TO COMMAND ME.
I CAN FEEL HIS WILL, HIS FORCE, HIS PERSONALITY BEATING AGAINST ME, LIKE A WEIGHT AGAINST MY SKIN.
IT'S TOO MUCH.
COME, ANITA, JOIN ME ON THE STAGE.
COME.
NO...
COME TO ME, NOW!
I HAVE TO RESIST HIM...
NO!
THERE! DREW BLOOD WITH MY NAILS ON MY PALM THIS TIME.
FOR ONCE, THE PAIN IS WELCOME.
I CAN BREATHE AGAIN.
DON'T FIGHT HIM. HE GETS ANGRY IF YOU FIGHT HIM.
IF I DON'T FIGHT HIM, HE'LL OWN ME!
I'LL COME TO THE STAGE IF YOU DON'T FORCE ME.
THEN BY ALL MEANS, COME.
GOOD. I CAN STAND WITHOUT FALLING. POINT FOR ME.
I CAN EVEN WALK. TWO POINTS FOR ME

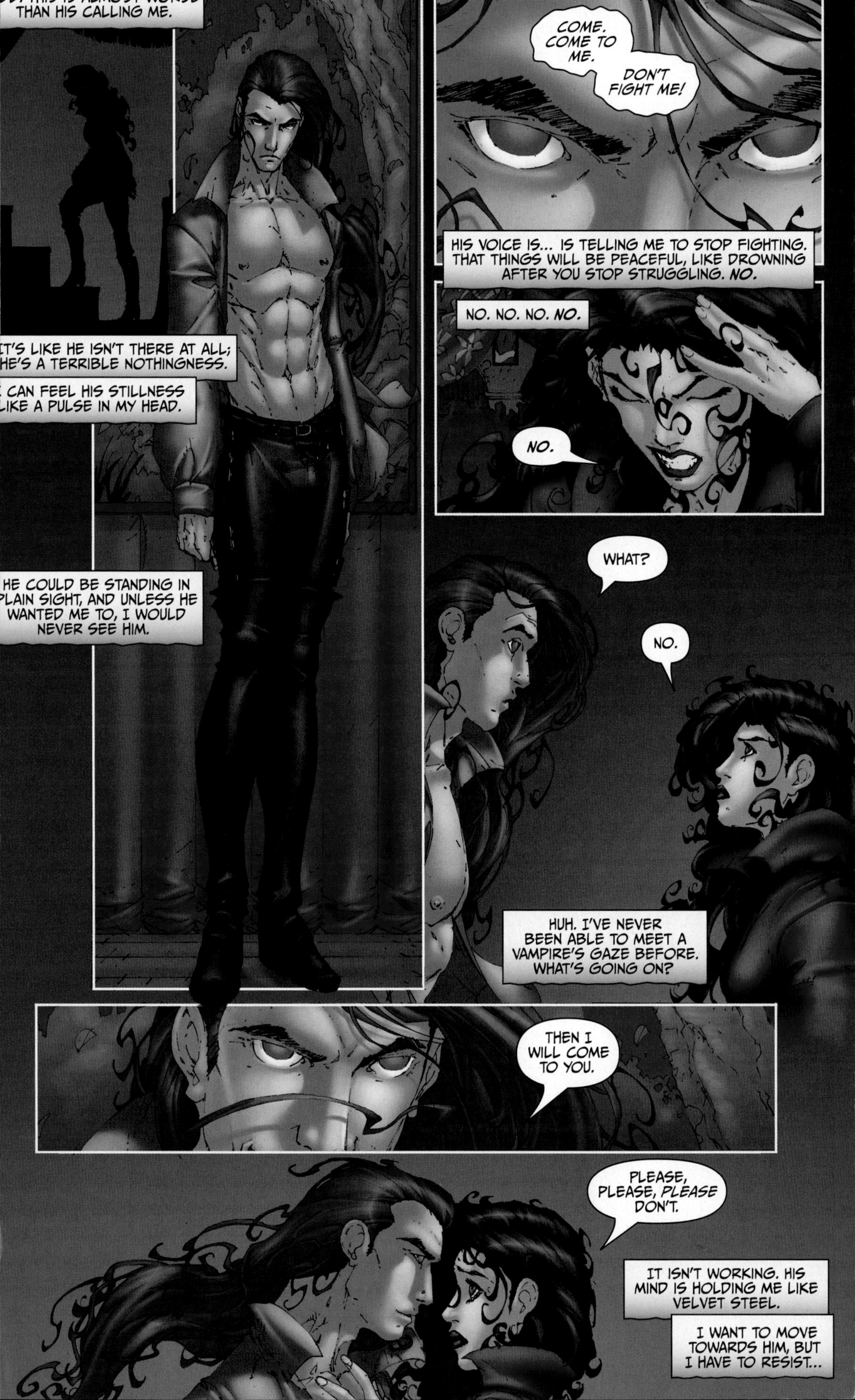

THAN HIS CALLING ME.
IT'S LIKE HE ISN'T THERE AT ALL; HE'S A TERRIBLE NOTHINGNESS.
I CAN FEEL HIS STILLNESS LIKE A PULSE IN MY HEAD.
HE COULD BE STANDING IN PLAIN SIGHT, AND UNLESS HE WANTED ME TO, I WOULD NEVER SEE HIM.
COME. COME TO ME.
DON'T FIGHT ME!
HIS VOICE IS... IS TELLING ME TO STOP FIGHTING. THAT THINGS WILL BE PEACEFUL, LIKE DROWNING AFTER YOU STOP STRUGGLING. *NO.*
NO. NO. NO. *NO.*
NO.
WHAT?
NO.
HUH. I'VE NEVER BEEN ABLE TO MEET A VAMPIRE'S GAZE BEFORE. WHAT'S GOING ON?
THEN I WILL COME TO YOU.
PLEASE, PLEASE, *PLEASE* DON'T.
IT ISN'T WORKING. HIS MIND IS HOLDING ME LIKE VELVET STEEL.
I WANT TO MOVE TOWARDS HIM, BUT I HAVE TO RESIST...

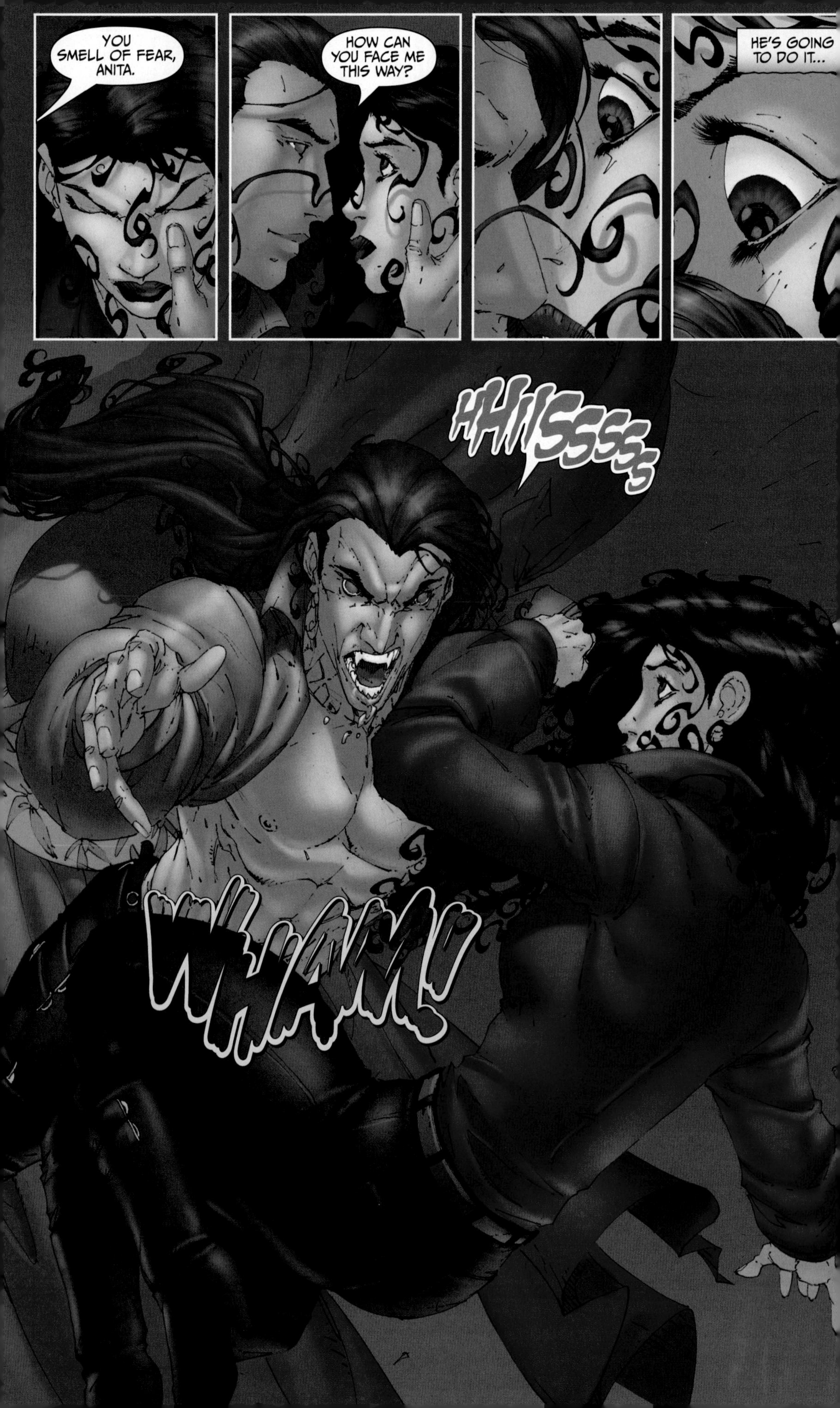
YOU SMELL OF FEAR, ANITA.
HOW CAN YOU FACE ME THIS WAY?
HE'S GOING TO DO IT...
HHIISSSSS
WHAM!

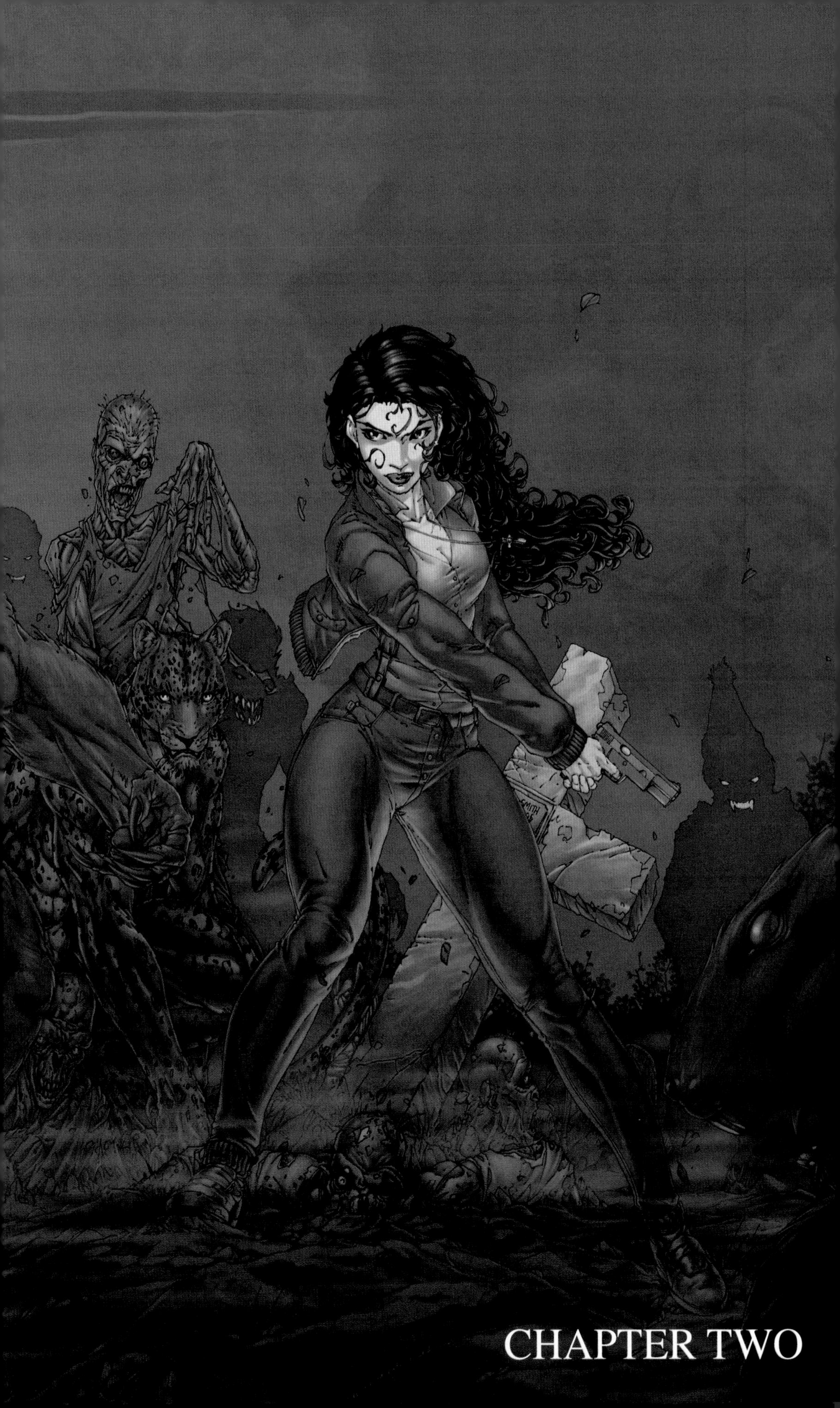

CHAPTER TWO

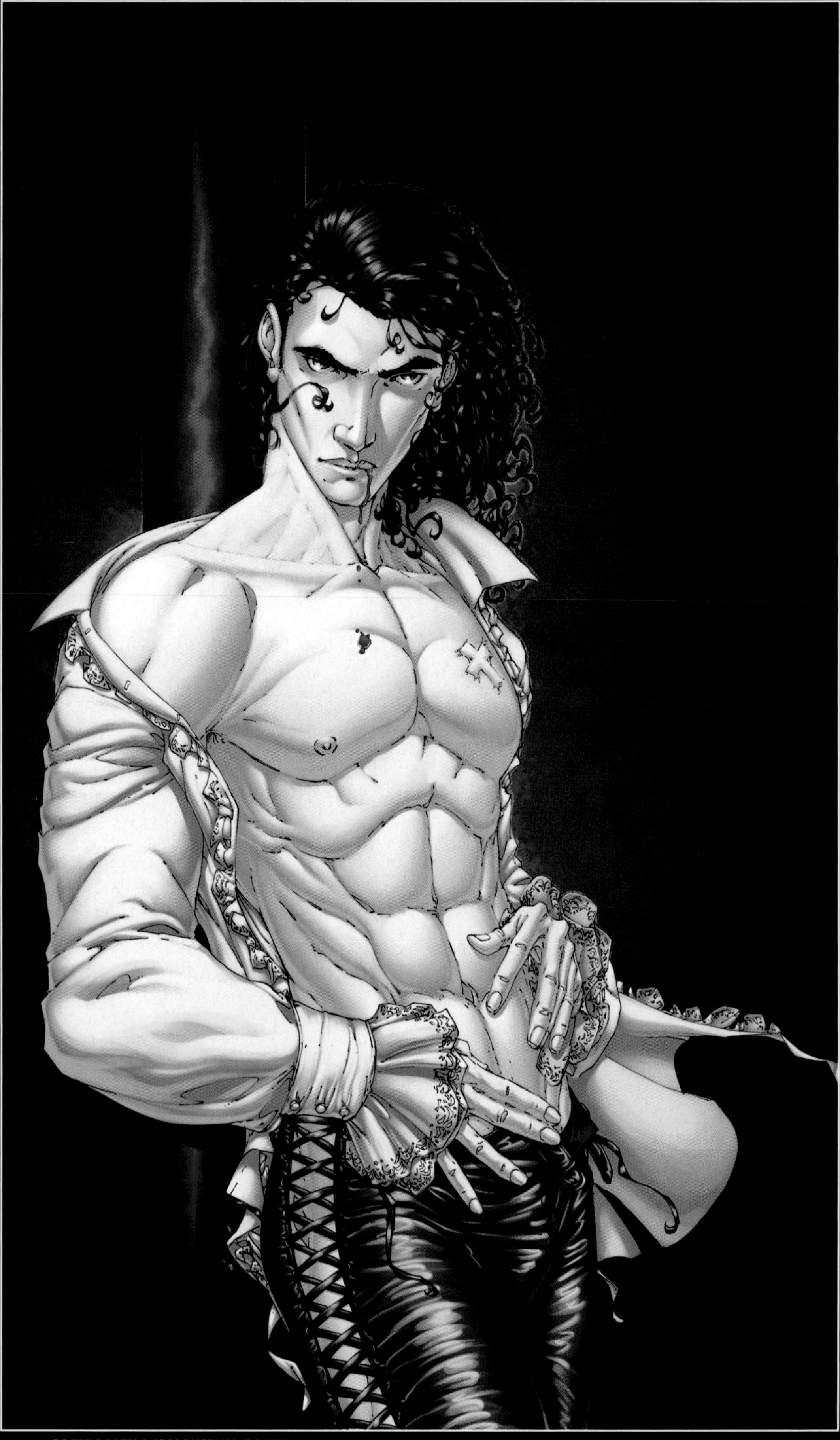

COVER BY: BRETT BOOTH & JESS RUFFNER-BOOTH

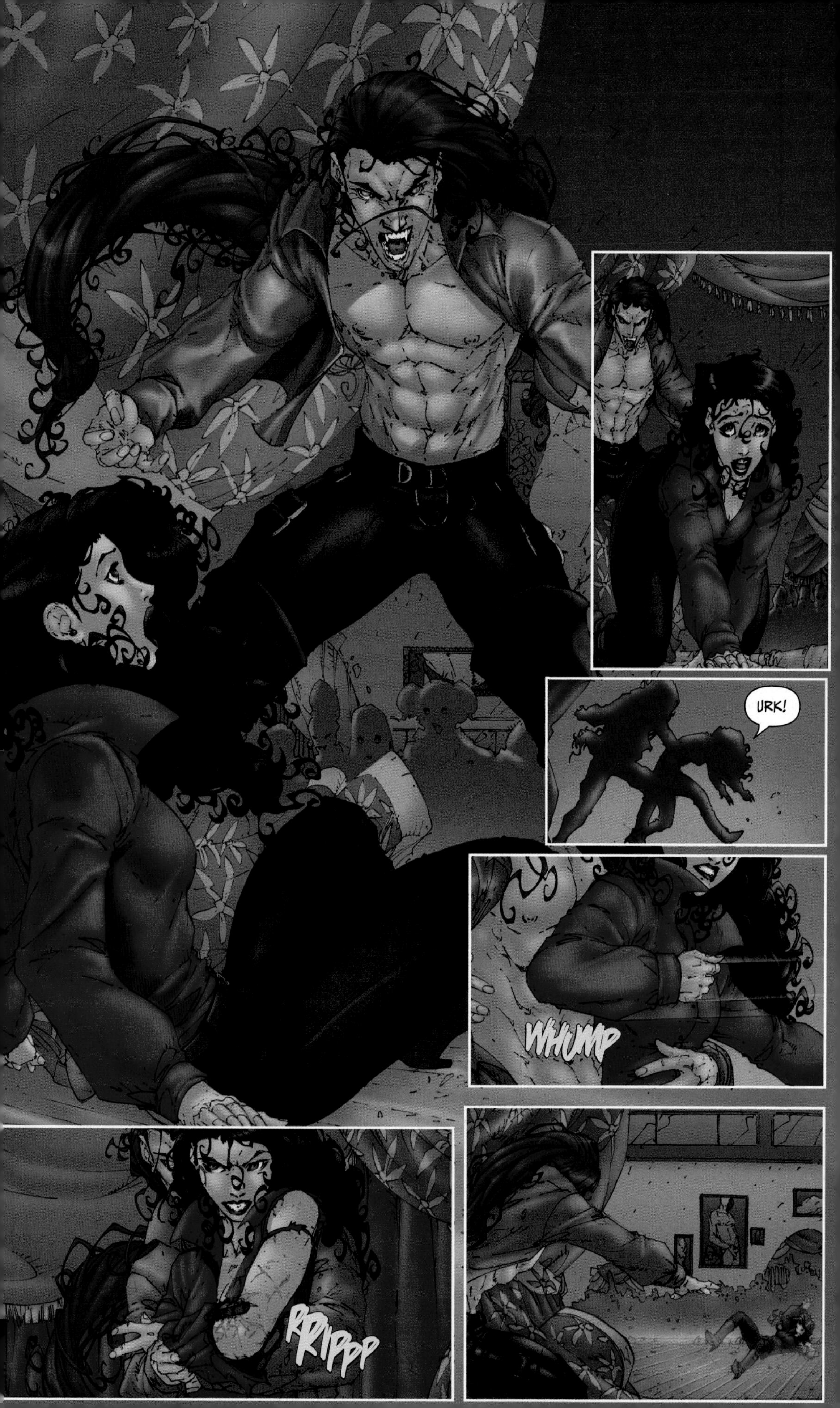
URK!
WHUMP
RRIPPP

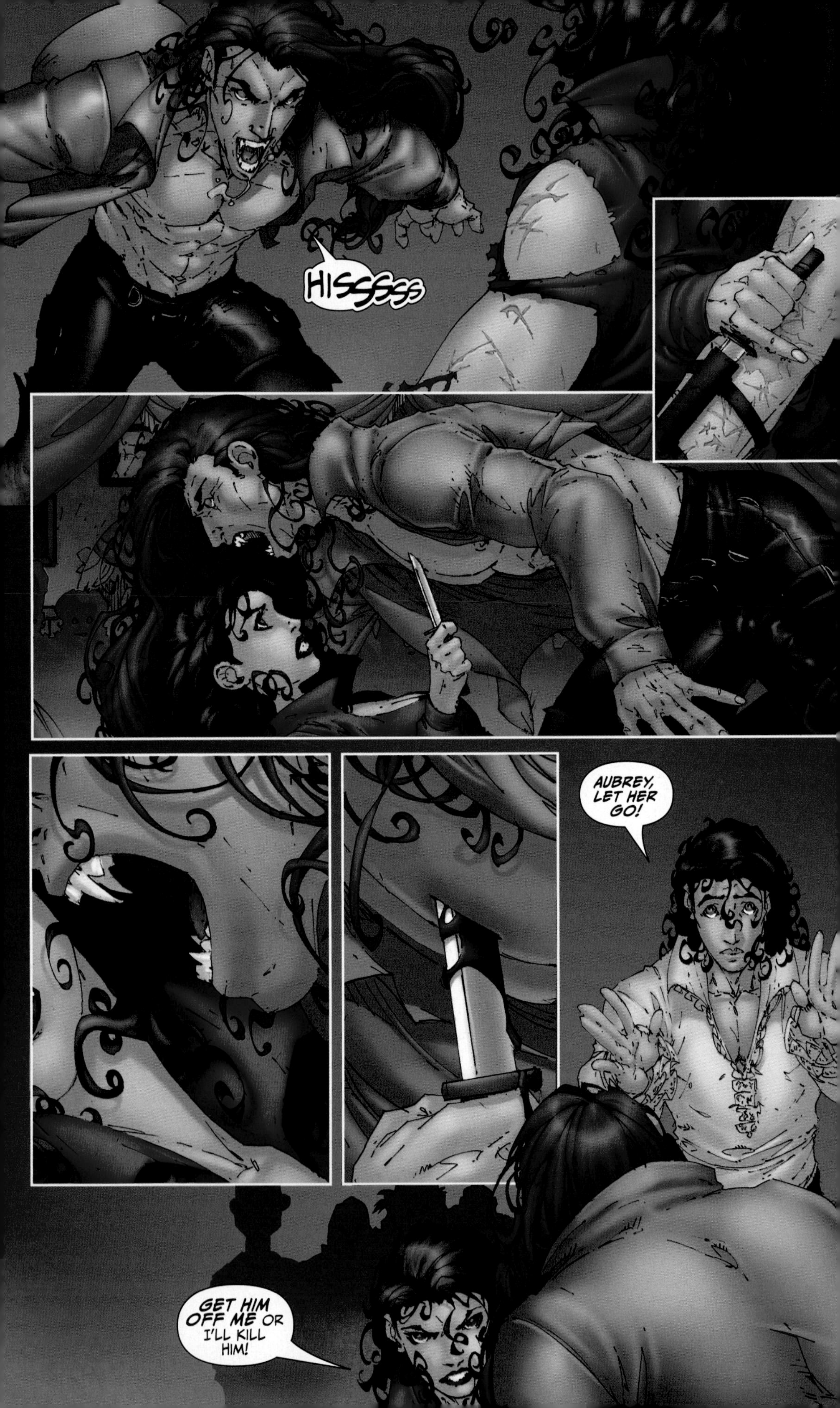
HISSSSSS
AUBREY, LET HER GO!
GET HIM OFF ME OR I'LL KILL HIM!

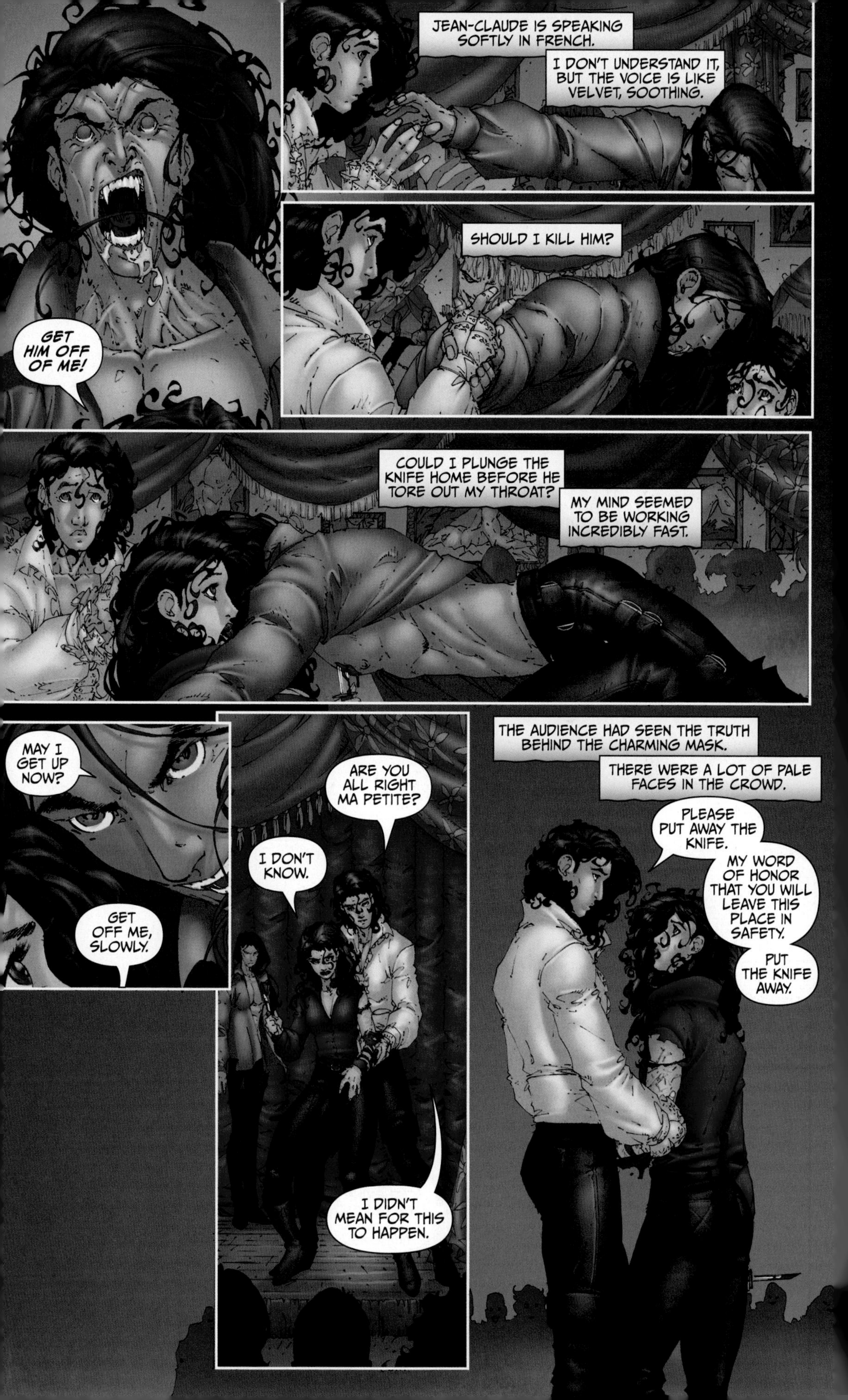
JEAN-CLAUDE IS SPEAKING SOFTLY IN FRENCH.
I DON'T UNDERSTAND IT, BUT THE VOICE IS LIKE VELVET, SOOTHING.
GET HIM OFF OF ME!
SHOULD I KILL HIM?
COULD I PLUNGE THE KNIFE HOME BEFORE HE TORE OUT MY THROAT?
MY MIND SEEMED TO BE WORKING INCREDIBLY FAST.
MAY I GET UP NOW?
GET OFF ME, SLOWLY.
ARE YOU ALL RIGHT MA PETITE?
I DON'T KNOW.
I DIDN'T MEAN FOR THIS TO HAPPEN.
THE AUDIENCE HAD SEEN THE TRUTH BEHIND THE CHARMING MASK.
THERE WERE A LOT OF PALE FACES IN THE CROWD.
PLEASE PUT AWAY THE KNIFE.
MY WORD OF HONOR THAT YOU WILL LEAVE THIS PLACE IN SAFETY.
PUT THE KNIFE AWAY.

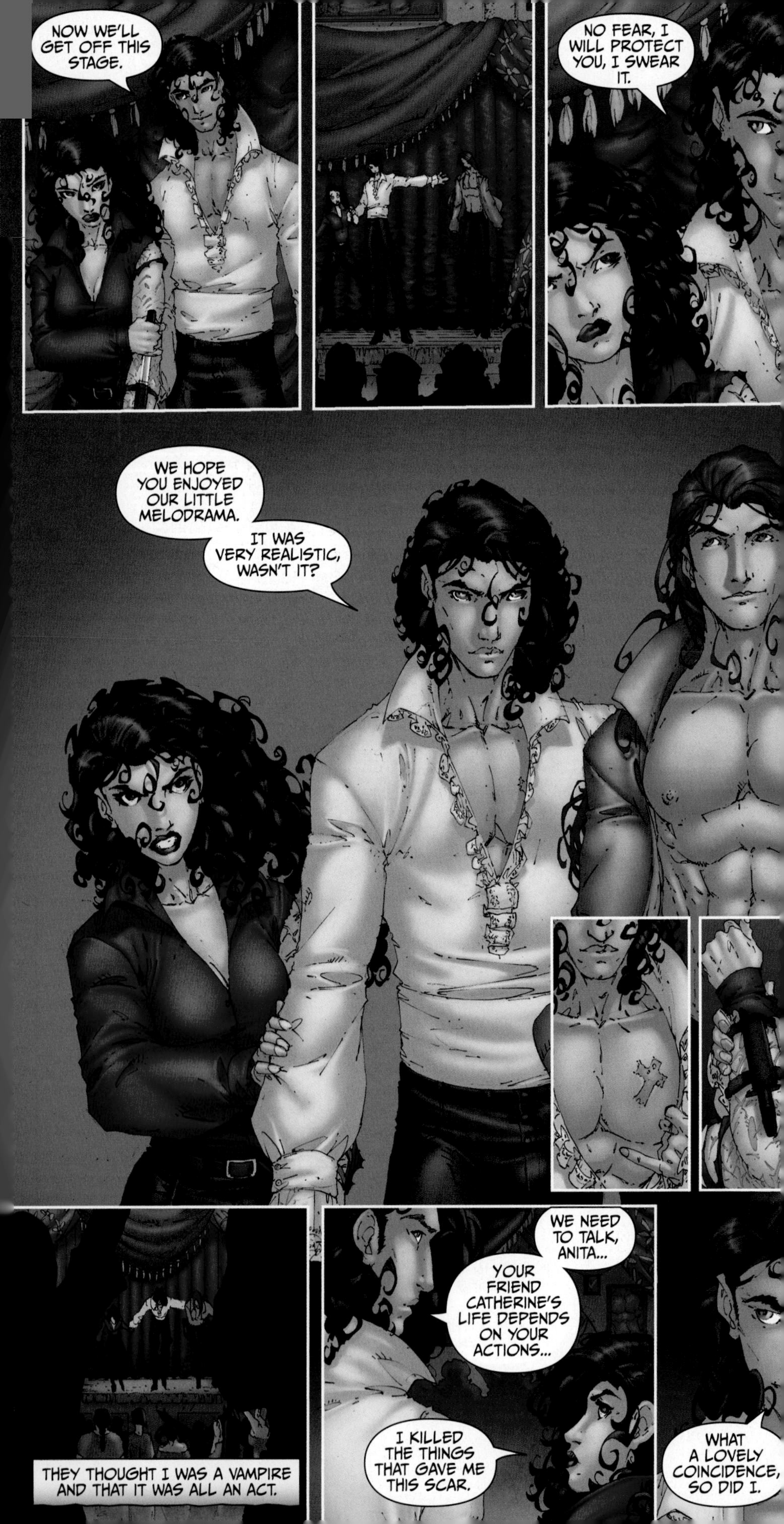
NOW WE'LL GET OFF THIS STAGE.
NO FEAR, I WILL PROTECT YOU, I SWEAR IT.
WE HOPE YOU ENJOYED OUR LITTLE MELODRAMA.
IT WAS VERY REALISTIC, WASN'T IT?
THEY THOUGHT I WAS A VAMPIRE AND THAT IT WAS ALL AN ACT.
WE NEED TO TALK, ANITA...
YOUR FRIEND CATHERINE'S LIFE DEPENDS ON YOUR ACTIONS...
I KILLED THE THINGS THAT GAVE ME THIS SCAR.
WHAT A LOVELY COINCIDENCE, SO DID I.

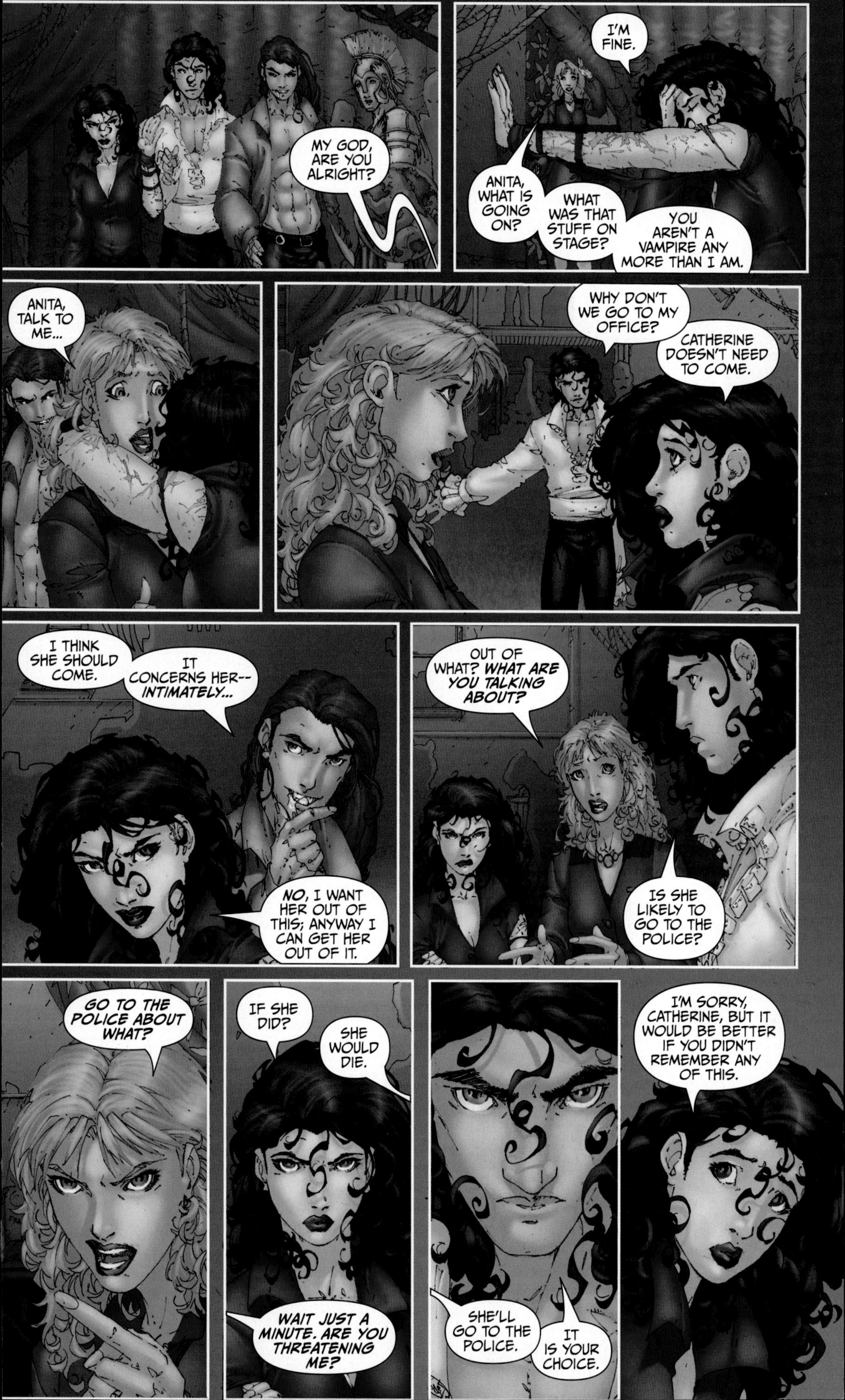
MY GOD, ARE YOU ALRIGHT?
I'M FINE.
ANITA, WHAT IS GOING ON?
WHAT WAS THAT STUFF ON STAGE?
YOU AREN'T A VAMPIRE ANY MORE THAN I AM.
ANITA, TALK TO ME...
WHY DON'T WE GO TO MY OFFICE?
CATHERINE DOESN'T NEED TO COME.
I THINK SHE SHOULD COME.
IT CONCERNS HER-- *INTIMATELY...*
NO, I WANT HER OUT OF THIS; ANYWAY I CAN GET HER OUT OF IT.
OUT OF WHAT? *WHAT ARE YOU TALKING ABOUT?*
IS SHE LIKELY TO GO TO THE POLICE?
GO TO THE POLICE ABOUT WHAT?
IF SHE DID?
SHE WOULD DIE.
WAIT JUST A MINUTE. ARE YOU THREATENING ME?
SHE'LL GO TO THE POLICE.
IT IS YOUR CHOICE.
I'M SORRY, CATHERINE, BUT IT WOULD BE BETTER IF YOU DIDN'T REMEMBER ANY OF THIS.

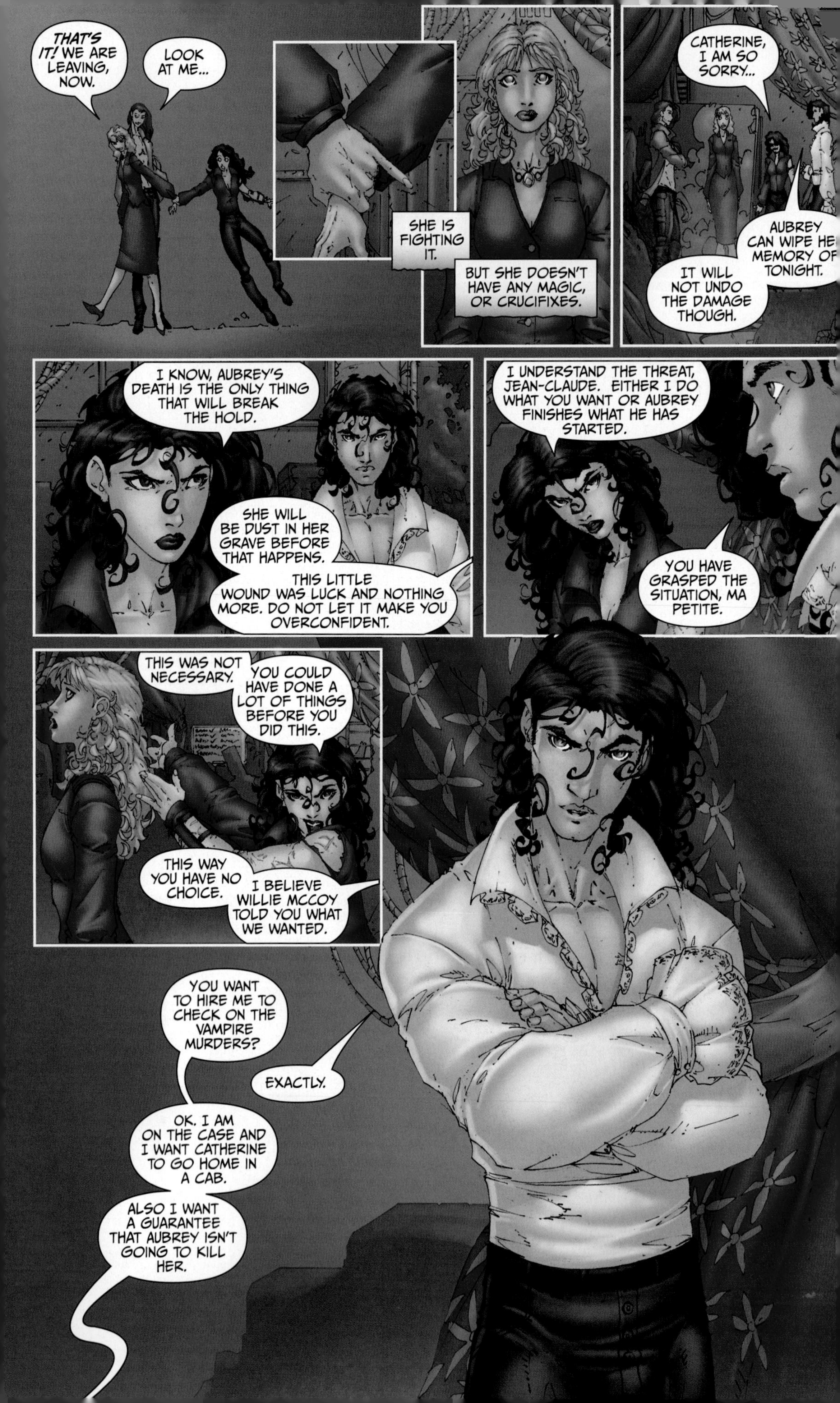
THAT'S IT! WE ARE LEAVING, NOW.
LOOK AT ME...
SHE IS FIGHTING IT.
BUT SHE DOESN'T HAVE ANY MAGIC, OR CRUCIFIXES.
CATHERINE, I AM SO SORRY...
AUBREY CAN WIPE HE MEMORY OF TONIGHT.
IT WILL NOT UNDO THE DAMAGE THOUGH.
I KNOW, AUBREY'S DEATH IS THE ONLY THING THAT WILL BREAK THE HOLD.
SHE WILL BE DUST IN HER GRAVE BEFORE THAT HAPPENS.
THIS LITTLE WOUND WAS LUCK AND NOTHING MORE. DO NOT LET IT MAKE YOU OVERCONFIDENT.
I UNDERSTAND THE THREAT, JEAN-CLAUDE. EITHER I DO WHAT YOU WANT OR AUBREY FINISHES WHAT HE HAS STARTED.
YOU HAVE GRASPED THE SITUATION, MA PETITE.
THIS WAS NOT NECESSARY.
YOU COULD HAVE DONE A LOT OF THINGS BEFORE YOU DID THIS.
THIS WAY YOU HAVE NO CHOICE.
I BELIEVE WILLIE MCCOY TOLD YOU WHAT WE WANTED.
YOU WANT TO HIRE ME TO CHECK ON THE VAMPIRE MURDERS?
EXACTLY.
OK. I AM ON THE CASE AND I WANT CATHERINE TO GO HOME IN A CAB.
ALSO I WANT A GUARANTEE THAT AUBREY ISN'T GOING TO KILL HER.

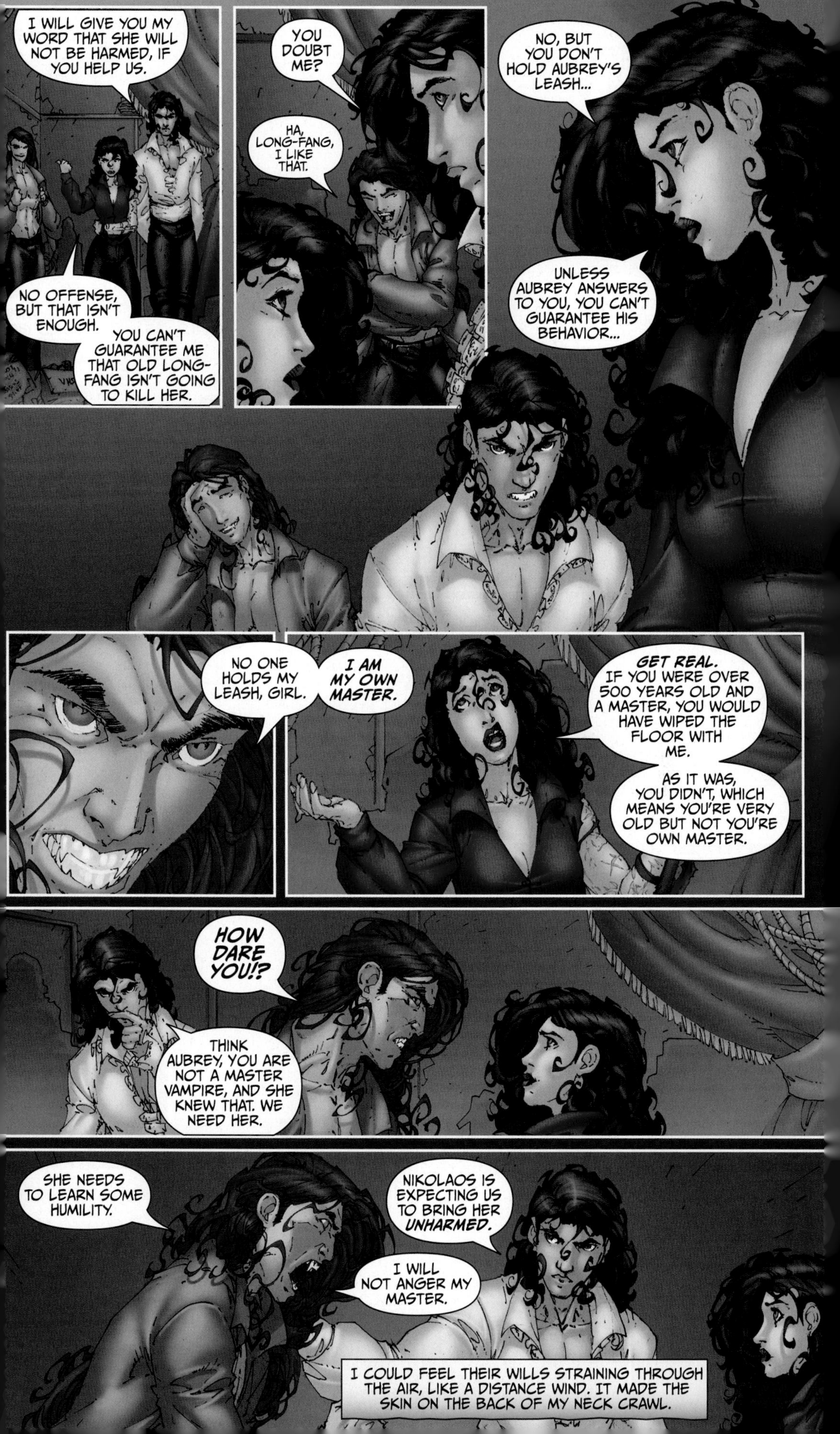
I WILL GIVE YOU MY WORD THAT SHE WILL NOT BE HARMED, IF YOU HELP US.
NO OFFENSE, BUT THAT ISN'T ENOUGH.
YOU CAN'T GUARANTEE ME THAT OLD LONG-FANG ISN'T GOING TO KILL HER.
YOU DOUBT ME?
HA, LONG-FANG, I LIKE THAT.
NO, BUT YOU DON'T HOLD AUBREY'S LEASH...
UNLESS AUBREY ANSWERS TO YOU, YOU CAN'T GUARANTEE HIS BEHAVIOR...
NO ONE HOLDS MY LEASH, GIRL.
I AM MY OWN MASTER.
GET REAL. IF YOU WERE OVER 500 YEARS OLD AND A MASTER, YOU WOULD HAVE WIPED THE FLOOR WITH ME.
AS IT WAS, YOU DIDN'T, WHICH MEANS YOU'RE VERY OLD BUT NOT YOU'RE OWN MASTER.
HOW DARE YOU!?
THINK AUBREY, YOU ARE NOT A MASTER VAMPIRE, AND SHE KNEW THAT. WE NEED HER.
SHE NEEDS TO LEARN SOME HUMILITY.
NIKOLAOS IS EXPECTING US TO BRING HER UNHARMED.
I WILL NOT ANGER MY MASTER.
I COULD FEEL THEIR WILLS STRAINING THROUGH THE AIR, LIKE A DISTANCE WIND. IT MADE THE SKIN ON THE BACK OF MY NECK CRAWL.

I WILL NOT ANGER *MY* MASTER.

IF THEY WANTED ME SCARED, THEY WERE DOING A HELL OF A JOB.

WHO IS NIKOLAOS?

THAT QUESTION IS NOT OURS TO ANSWER.

WHAT THE HELL IS THAT SUPPOSED TO MEAN?

WHAT ABOUT MONICA?

ARE YOU WORRIED FOR HER SAFETY?

IT HIT ME THEN. THE WHOLE THING WAS A SETUP.

SHE WAS THE LURE TO GET CATHERINE AND ME DOWN HERE.

YES.

I WANTED TO GO BACK OUT AND SMASH MONICA'S FACE IN.

LET US PUT YOUR FRIEND IN A CAB, OUT OF HARM'S WAY.

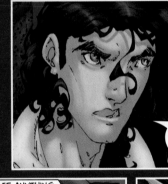

THE MORE I THOUGHT ABOUT IT, THE BETTER IT SOUNDED. AND THEN, AS IF BY MAGIC...

EVERYTHING GOING ACCORDING TO PLAN?

DO NOT HARM HER, ANITA. SHE IS UNDER OUR PROTECTION.

I SWEAR TO YOU THAT I WILL NOT LAY A FINGER ON HER TONIGHT. I JUST WANT TO TELL HER SOMETHING.

IF ANYTHING HAPPENS TO CATHERINE, I WILL SEE YOU *DEAD*.

THEY WILL BRING ME BACK AS ONE OF THEM.

I WILL *CUT OUT* YOUR HEART.

THEN I WILL *BURN IT* AND *SCATTER* THE ASHES IN THE RIVER.

DO YOU UNDERSTAND ME?

I THINK SHE BELIEVED I'D DO IT. PEACHY KEEN.

I HATE TO WASTE A REALLY GOOD THREAT.

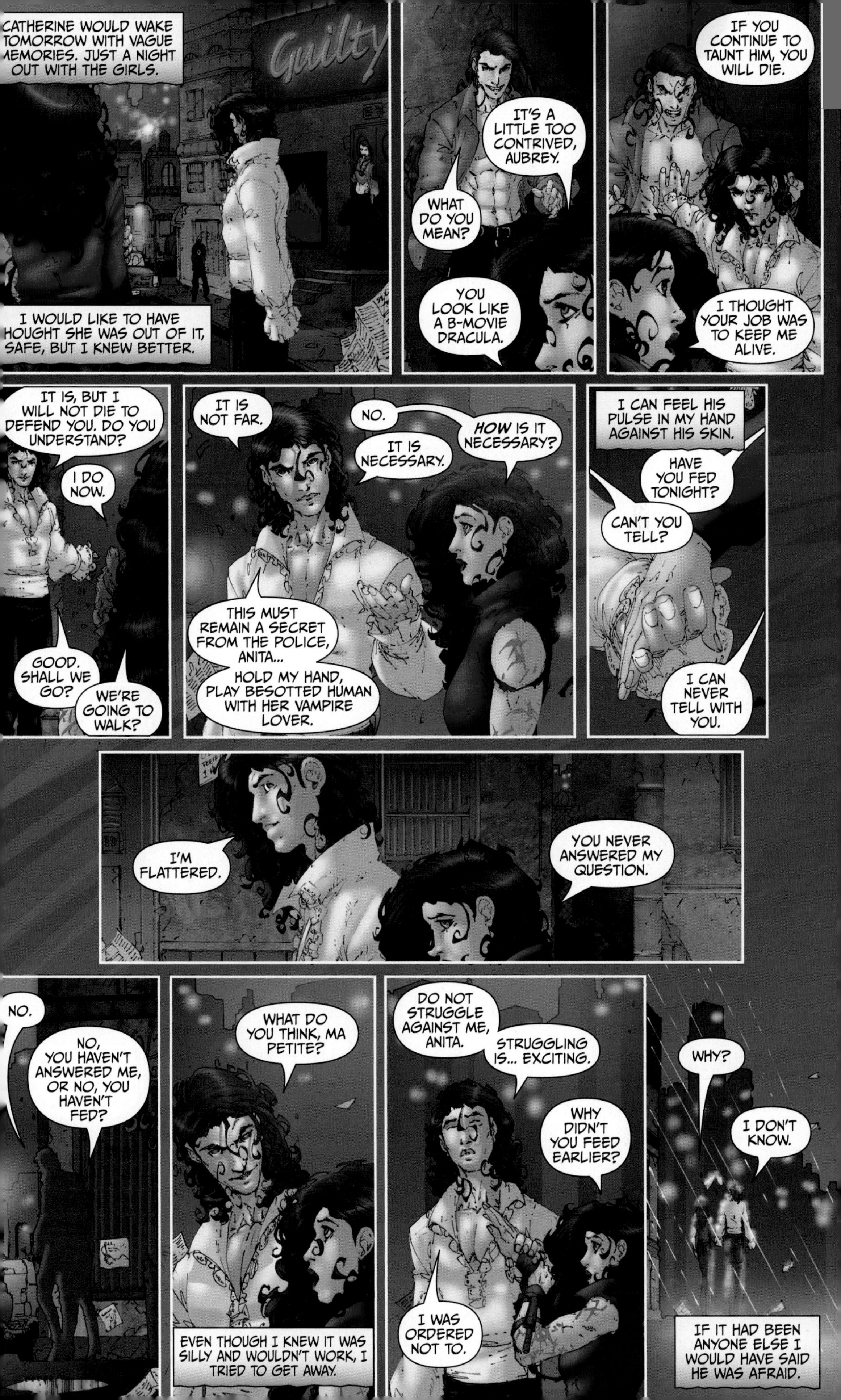
CATHERINE WOULD WAKE TOMORROW WITH VAGUE MEMORIES. JUST A NIGHT OUT WITH THE GIRLS.
Guilty
I WOULD LIKE TO HAVE THOUGHT SHE WAS OUT OF IT, SAFE, BUT I KNEW BETTER.
IT'S A LITTLE TOO CONTRIVED, AUBREY.
WHAT DO YOU MEAN?
YOU LOOK LIKE A B-MOVIE DRACULA.
IF YOU CONTINUE TO TAUNT HIM, YOU WILL DIE.
I THOUGHT YOUR JOB WAS TO KEEP ME ALIVE.
IT IS, BUT I WILL NOT DIE TO DEFEND YOU. DO YOU UNDERSTAND?
I DO NOW.
GOOD. SHALL WE GO?
WE'RE GOING TO WALK?
IT IS NOT FAR.
NO.
IT IS NECESSARY.
HOW IS IT NECESSARY?
THIS MUST REMAIN A SECRET FROM THE POLICE, ANITA...
HOLD MY HAND, PLAY BESOTTED HUMAN WITH HER VAMPIRE LOVER.
I CAN FEEL HIS PULSE IN MY HAND AGAINST HIS SKIN.
HAVE YOU FED TONIGHT?
CAN'T YOU TELL?
I CAN NEVER TELL WITH YOU.
I'M FLATTERED.
YOU NEVER ANSWERED MY QUESTION.
NO.
NO, YOU HAVEN'T ANSWERED ME, OR NO, YOU HAVEN'T FED?
WHAT DO YOU THINK, MA PETITE?
EVEN THOUGH I KNEW IT WAS SILLY AND WOULDN'T WORK, I TRIED TO GET AWAY.
DO NOT STRUGGLE AGAINST ME, ANITA.
STRUGGLING IS... EXCITING.
WHY DIDN'T YOU FEED EARLIER?
I WAS ORDERED NOT TO.
WHY?
I DON'T KNOW.
IF IT HAD BEEN ANYONE ELSE I WOULD HAVE SAID HE WAS AFRAID.

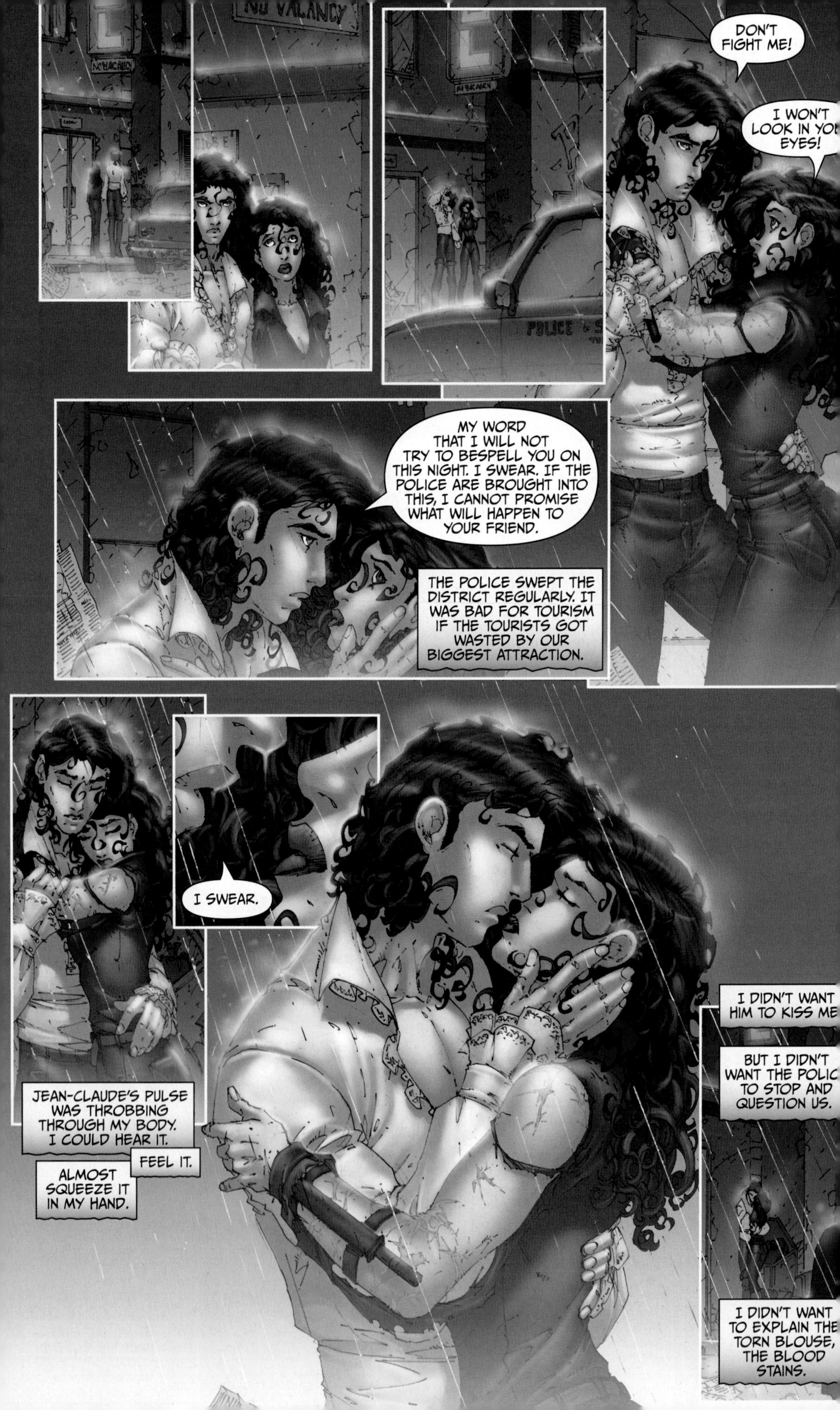

NO VACANCY
DON'T FIGHT ME!
I WON'T LOOK IN YO EYES!
MY WORD THAT I WILL NOT TRY TO BESPELL YOU ON THIS NIGHT. I SWEAR. IF THE POLICE ARE BROUGHT INTO THIS, I CANNOT PROMISE WHAT WILL HAPPEN TO YOUR FRIEND.
THE POLICE SWEPT THE DISTRICT REGULARLY. IT WAS BAD FOR TOURISM IF THE TOURISTS GOT WASTED BY OUR BIGGEST ATTRACTION.
I SWEAR.
JEAN-CLAUDE'S PULSE WAS THROBBING THROUGH MY BODY. I COULD HEAR IT.
FEEL IT.
ALMOST SQUEEZE IT IN MY HAND.
I DIDN'T WANT HIM TO KISS ME
BUT I DIDN'T WANT THE POLIC TO STOP AND QUESTION US.
I DIDN'T WANT TO EXPLAIN THE TORN BLOUSE, THE BLOOD STAINS.

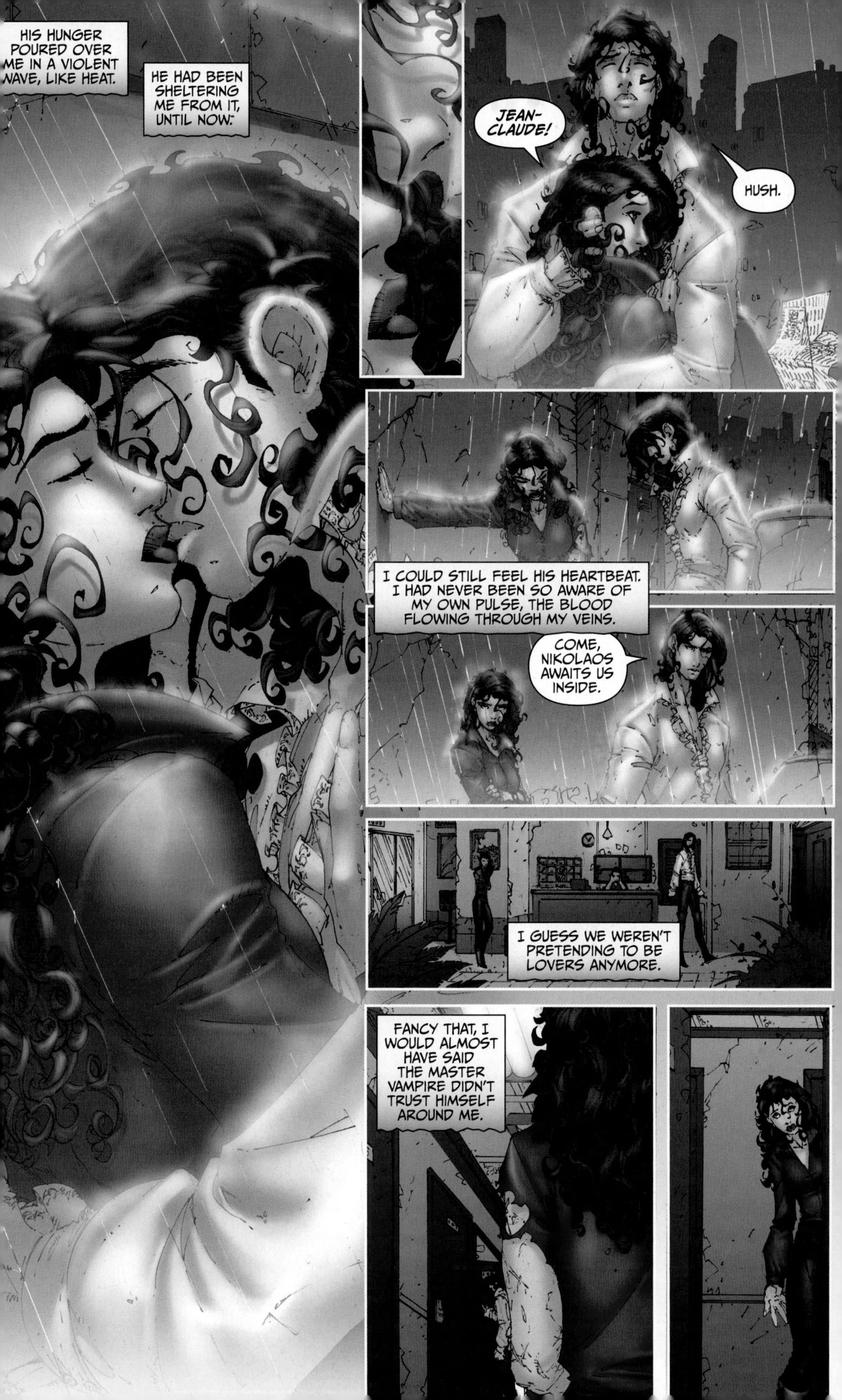
HIS HUNGER POURED OVER ME IN A VIOLENT WAVE, LIKE HEAT.
HE HAD BEEN SHELTERING ME FROM IT, UNTIL NOW.
JEAN-CLAUDE!
HUSH.
I COULD STILL FEEL HIS HEARTBEAT. I HAD NEVER BEEN SO AWARE OF MY OWN PULSE, THE BLOOD FLOWING THROUGH MY VEINS.
COME, NIKOLAOS AWAITS US INSIDE.
I GUESS WE WEREN'T PRETENDING TO BE LOVERS ANYMORE.
FANCY THAT, I WOULD ALMOST HAVE SAID THE MASTER VAMPIRE DIDN'T TRUST HIMSELF AROUND ME.

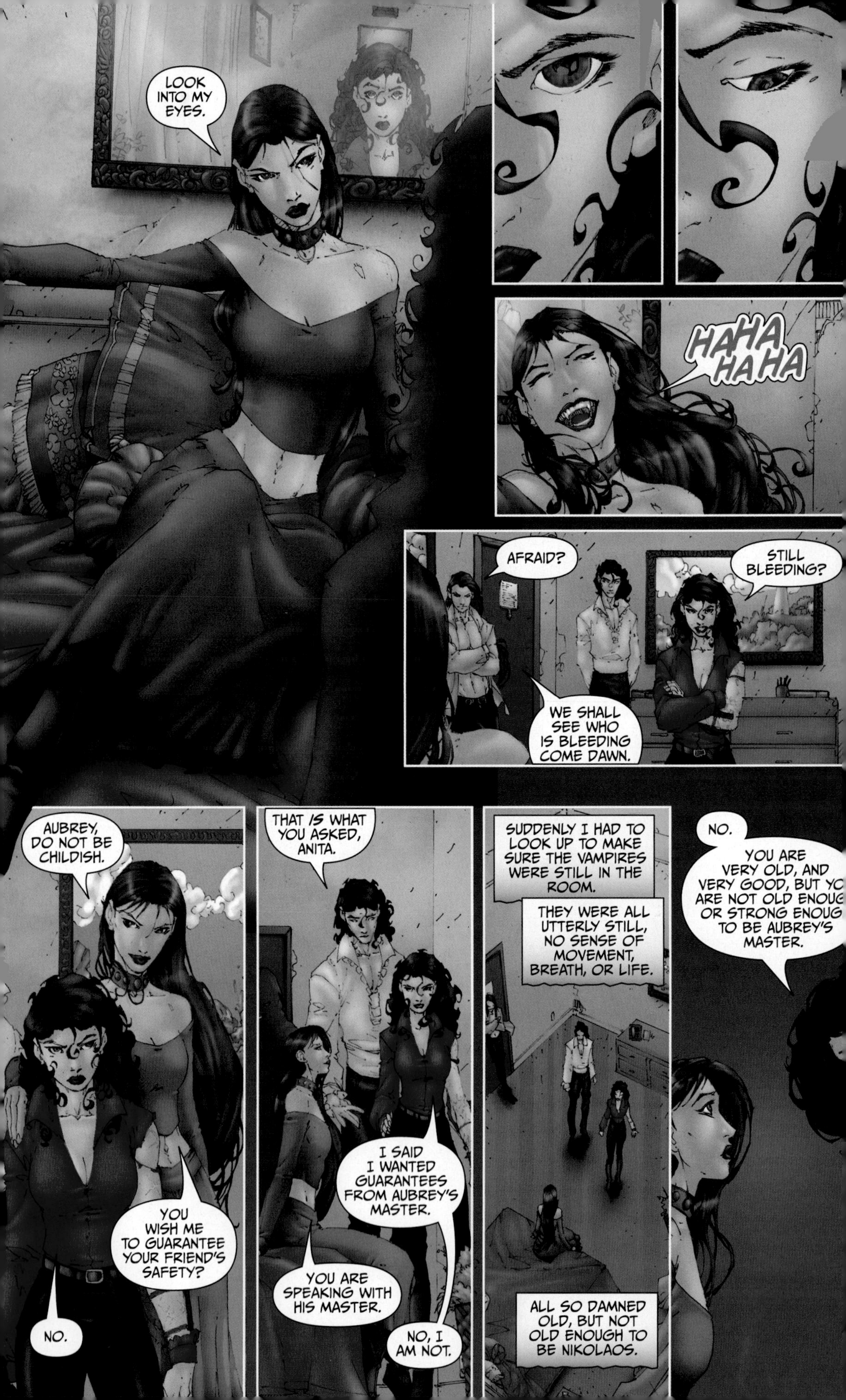
LOOK INTO MY EYES.
HAHA HAHA
AFRAID?
STILL BLEEDING?
WE SHALL SEE WHO IS BLEEDING COME DAWN.
AUBREY, DO NOT BE CHILDISH.
YOU WISH ME TO GUARANTEE YOUR FRIEND'S SAFETY?
NO.
THAT IS WHAT YOU ASKED, ANITA.
I SAID I WANTED GUARANTEES FROM AUBREY'S MASTER.
YOU ARE SPEAKING WITH HIS MASTER.
NO, I AM NOT.
SUDDENLY I HAD TO LOOK UP TO MAKE SURE THE VAMPIRES WERE STILL IN THE ROOM.
THEY WERE ALL UTTERLY STILL, NO SENSE OF MOVEMENT, BREATH, OR LIFE.
ALL SO DAMNED OLD, BUT NOT OLD ENOUGH TO BE NIKOLAOS.
NO.

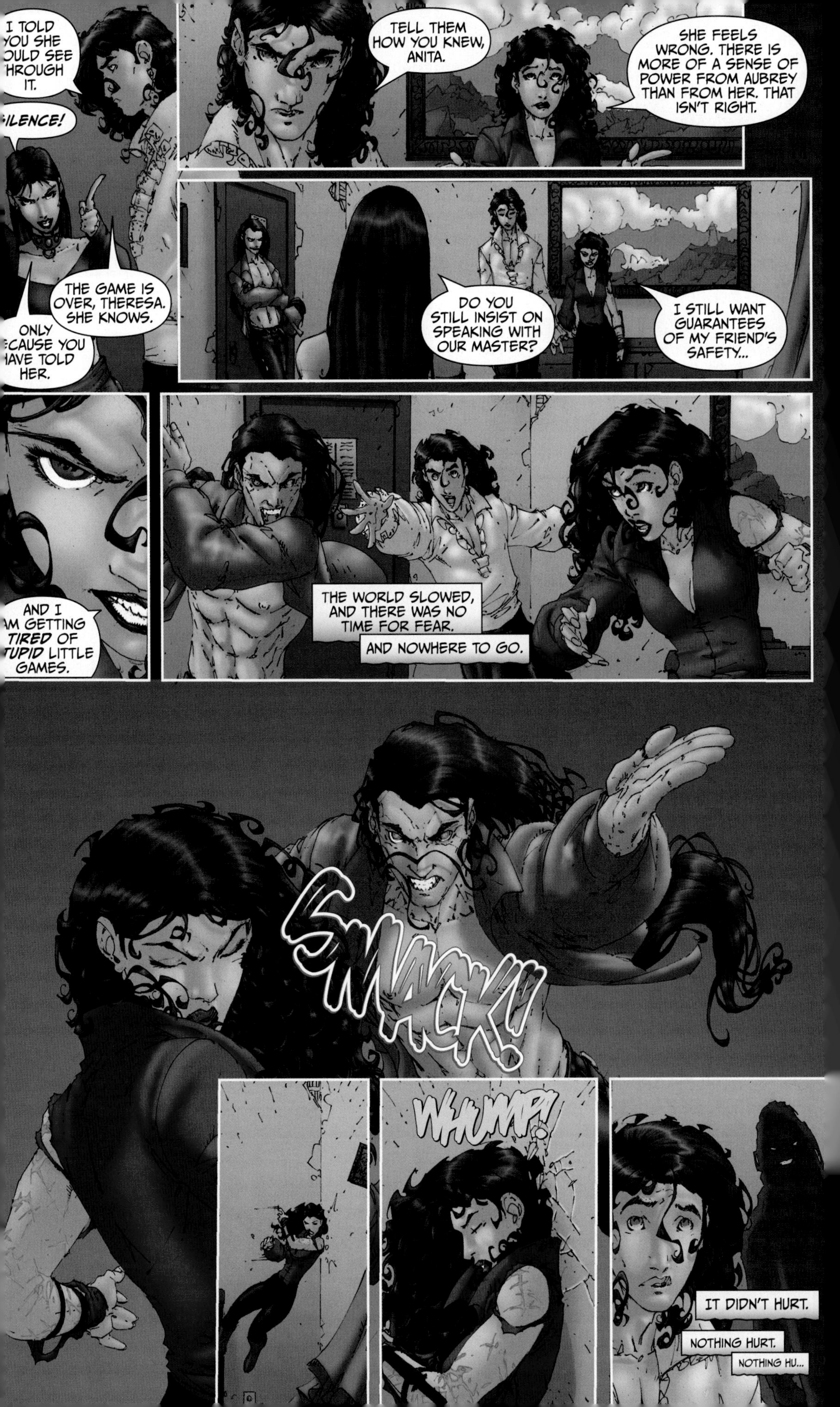
I TOLD YOU SHE OULD SEE HROUGH IT.
ILENCE!
THE GAME IS OVER, THERESA. SHE KNOWS.
ONLY ECAUSE YOU AVE TOLD HER.
TELL THEM HOW YOU KNEW, ANITA.
SHE FEELS WRONG. THERE IS MORE OF A SENSE OF POWER FROM AUBREY THAN FROM HER. THAT ISN'T RIGHT.
DO YOU STILL INSIST ON SPEAKING WITH OUR MASTER?
I STILL WANT GUARANTEES OF MY FRIEND'S SAFETY...
AND I AM GETTING TIRED OF TUPID LITTLE GAMES.
THE WORLD SLOWED, AND THERE WAS NO TIME FOR FEAR.
AND NOWHERE TO GO.
SMACK!!
WHUMP!
IT DIDN'T HURT.
NOTHING HURT.
NOTHING HU...

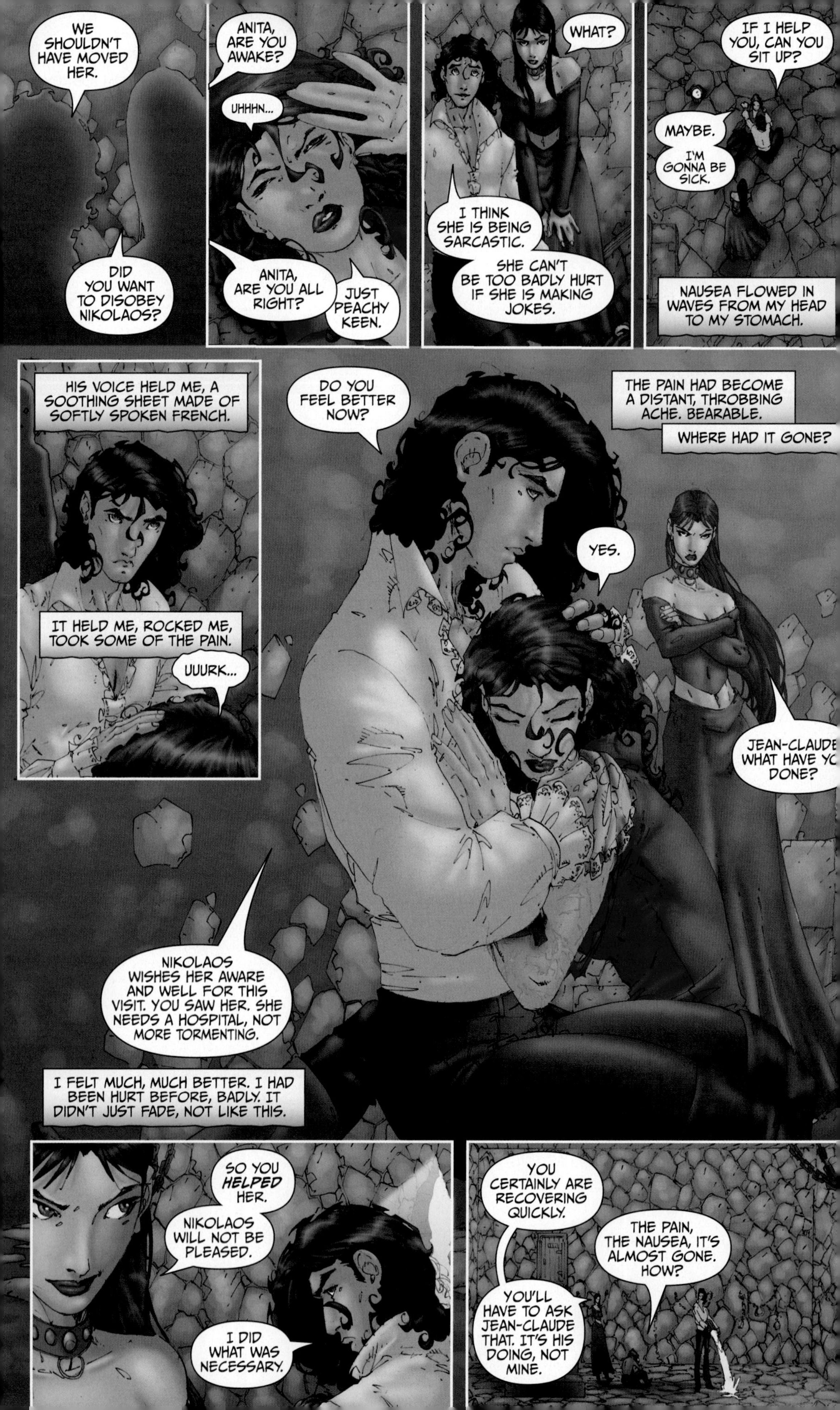

WE SHOULDN'T HAVE MOVED HER.
DID YOU WANT TO DISOBEY NIKOLAOS?
ANITA, ARE YOU AWAKE?
UHHHN...
ANITA, ARE YOU ALL RIGHT?
JUST PEACHY KEEN.
WHAT?
I THINK SHE IS BEING SARCASTIC.
SHE CAN'T BE TOO BADLY HURT IF SHE IS MAKING JOKES.
IF I HELP YOU, CAN YOU SIT UP?
MAYBE.
I'M GONNA BE SICK.
NAUSEA FLOWED IN WAVES FROM MY HEAD TO MY STOMACH.
HIS VOICE HELD ME, A SOOTHING SHEET MADE OF SOFTLY SPOKEN FRENCH.
IT HELD ME, ROCKED ME, TOOK SOME OF THE PAIN.
UUURK...
DO YOU FEEL BETTER NOW?
THE PAIN HAD BECOME A DISTANT, THROBBING ACHE. BEARABLE.
WHERE HAD IT GONE?
YES.
JEAN-CLAUDE WHAT HAVE YO DONE?
NIKOLAOS WISHES HER AWARE AND WELL FOR THIS VISIT. YOU SAW HER. SHE NEEDS A HOSPITAL, NOT MORE TORMENTING.
I FELT MUCH, MUCH BETTER. I HAD BEEN HURT BEFORE, BADLY. IT DIDN'T JUST FADE, NOT LIKE THIS.
SO YOU **HELPED** HER.
NIKOLAOS WILL NOT BE PLEASED.
I DID WHAT WAS NECESSARY.
YOU CERTAINLY ARE RECOVERING QUICKLY.
THE PAIN, THE NAUSEA, IT'S ALMOST GONE. HOW?
YOU'LL HAVE TO ASK JEAN-CLAUDE THAT. IT'S HIS DOING, NOT MINE.

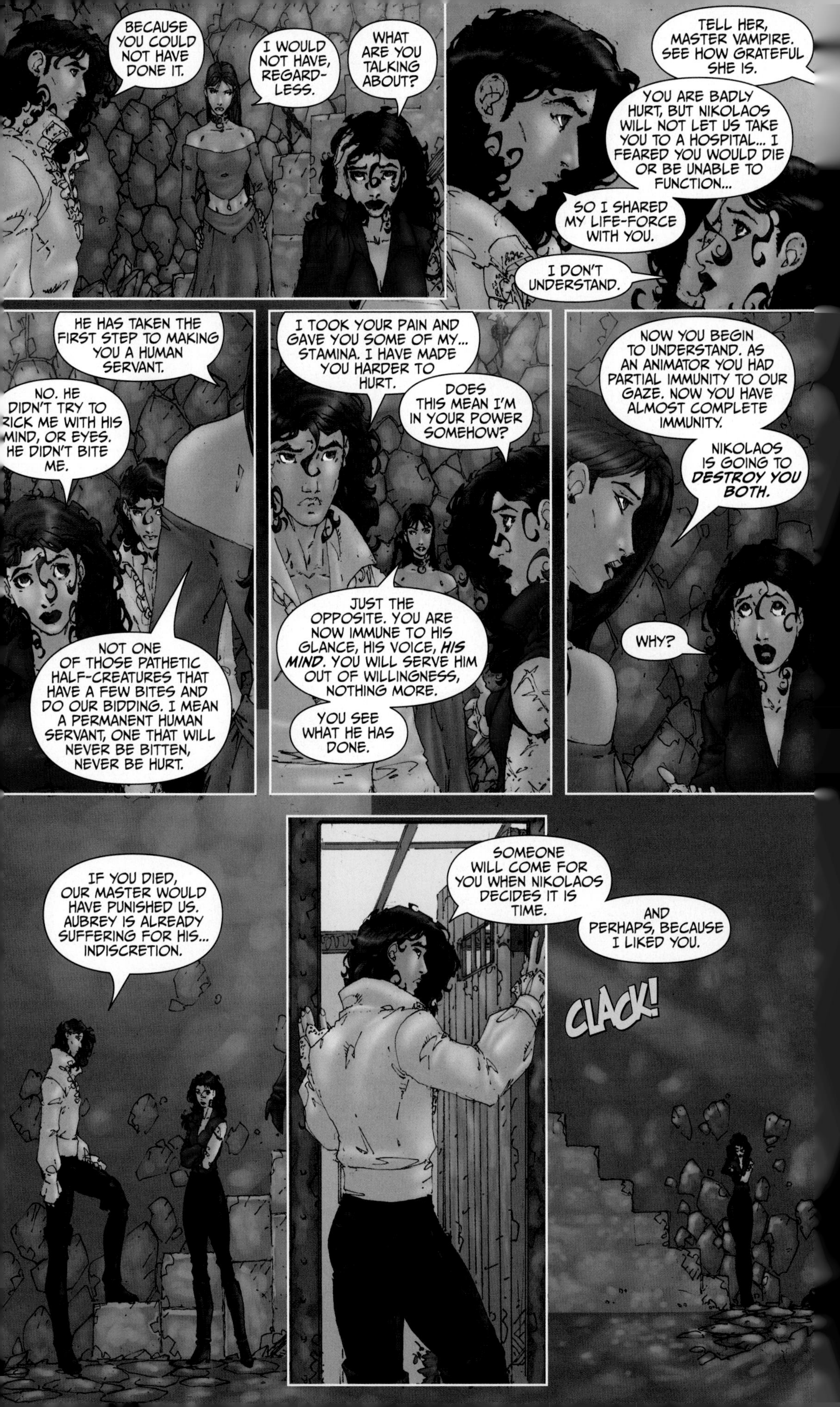

BECAUSE YOU COULD NOT HAVE DONE IT.
I WOULD NOT HAVE, REGARD-LESS.
WHAT ARE YOU TALKING ABOUT?
TELL HER, MASTER VAMPIRE. SEE HOW GRATEFUL SHE IS.
YOU ARE BADLY HURT, BUT NIKOLAOS WILL NOT LET US TAKE YOU TO A HOSPITAL... I FEARED YOU WOULD DIE OR BE UNABLE TO FUNCTION...
SO I SHARED MY LIFE-FORCE WITH YOU.
I DON'T UNDERSTAND.
HE HAS TAKEN THE FIRST STEP TO MAKING YOU A HUMAN SERVANT.
NO. HE DIDN'T TRY TO TRICK ME WITH HIS MIND, OR EYES. HE DIDN'T BITE ME.
NOT ONE OF THOSE PATHETIC HALF-CREATURES THAT HAVE A FEW BITES AND DO OUR BIDDING. I MEAN A PERMANENT HUMAN SERVANT, ONE THAT WILL NEVER BE BITTEN, NEVER BE HURT.
I TOOK YOUR PAIN AND GAVE YOU SOME OF MY... STAMINA. I HAVE MADE YOU HARDER TO HURT.
DOES THIS MEAN I'M IN YOUR POWER SOMEHOW?
JUST THE OPPOSITE. YOU ARE NOW IMMUNE TO HIS GLANCE, HIS VOICE, HIS MIND. YOU WILL SERVE HIM OUT OF WILLINGNESS, NOTHING MORE.
YOU SEE WHAT HE HAS DONE.
NOW YOU BEGIN TO UNDERSTAND. AS AN ANIMATOR YOU HAD PARTIAL IMMUNITY TO OUR GAZE. NOW YOU HAVE ALMOST COMPLETE IMMUNITY.
NIKOLAOS IS GOING TO DESTROY YOU BOTH.
WHY?
IF YOU DIED, OUR MASTER WOULD HAVE PUNISHED US. AUBREY IS ALREADY SUFFERING FOR HIS... INDISCRETION.
SOMEONE WILL COME FOR YOU WHEN NIKOLAOS DECIDES IT IS TIME.
AND PERHAPS, BECAUSE I LIKED YOU.
CLACK!

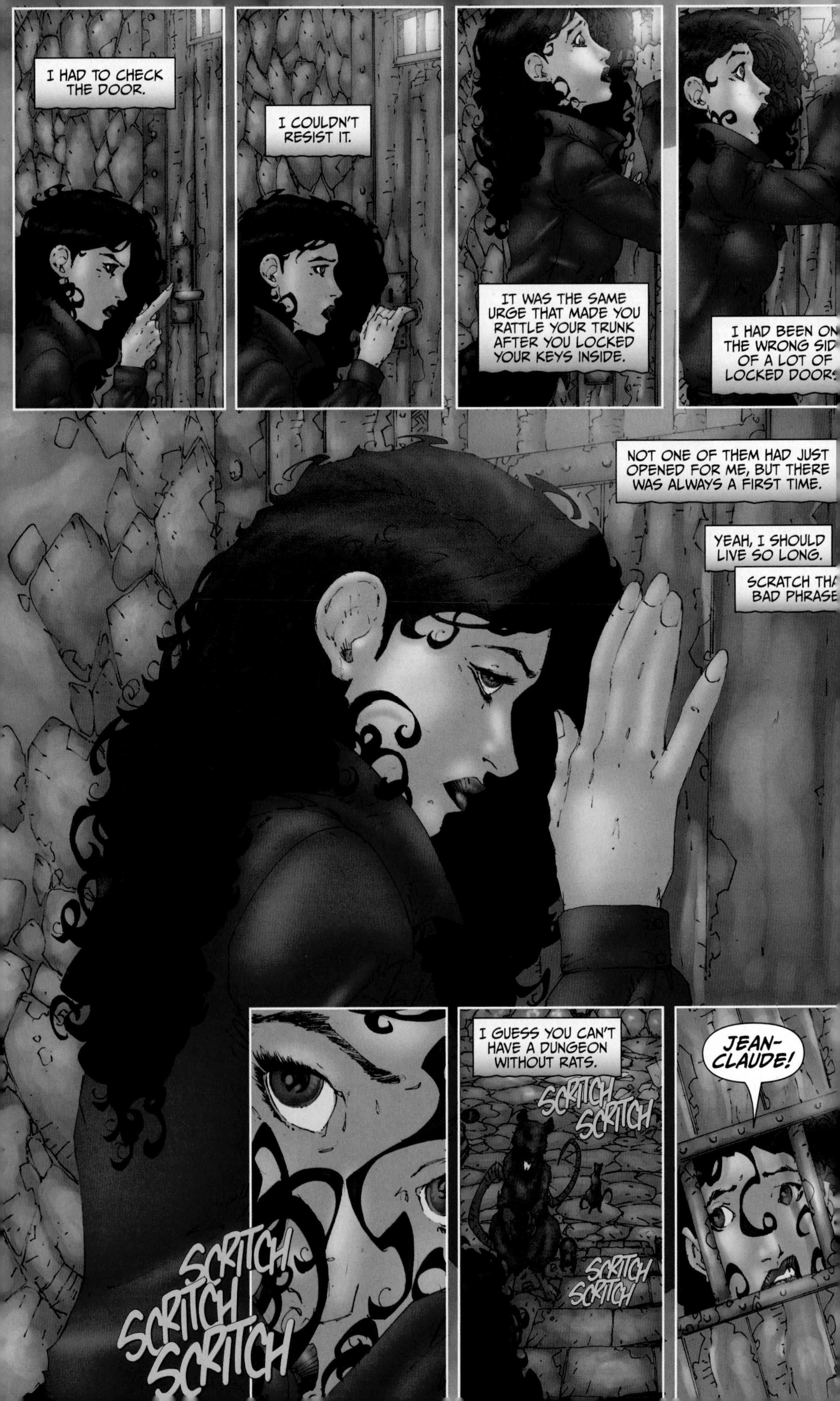

I HAD TO CHECK THE DOOR.
I COULDN'T RESIST IT.
IT WAS THE SAME URGE THAT MADE YOU RATTLE YOUR TRUNK AFTER YOU LOCKED YOUR KEYS INSIDE.
I HAD BEEN ON THE WRONG SID OF A LOT OF LOCKED DOORS
NOT ONE OF THEM HAD JUST OPENED FOR ME, BUT THERE WAS ALWAYS A FIRST TIME.
YEAH, I SHOULD LIVE SO LONG.
SCRATCH THA BAD PHRASE
SCRITCH! SCRITCH SCRITCH
I GUESS YOU CAN'T HAVE A DUNGEON WITHOUT RATS.
SCRITCH SCRITCH
SCRITCH SCRITCH
JEAN-CLAUDE!

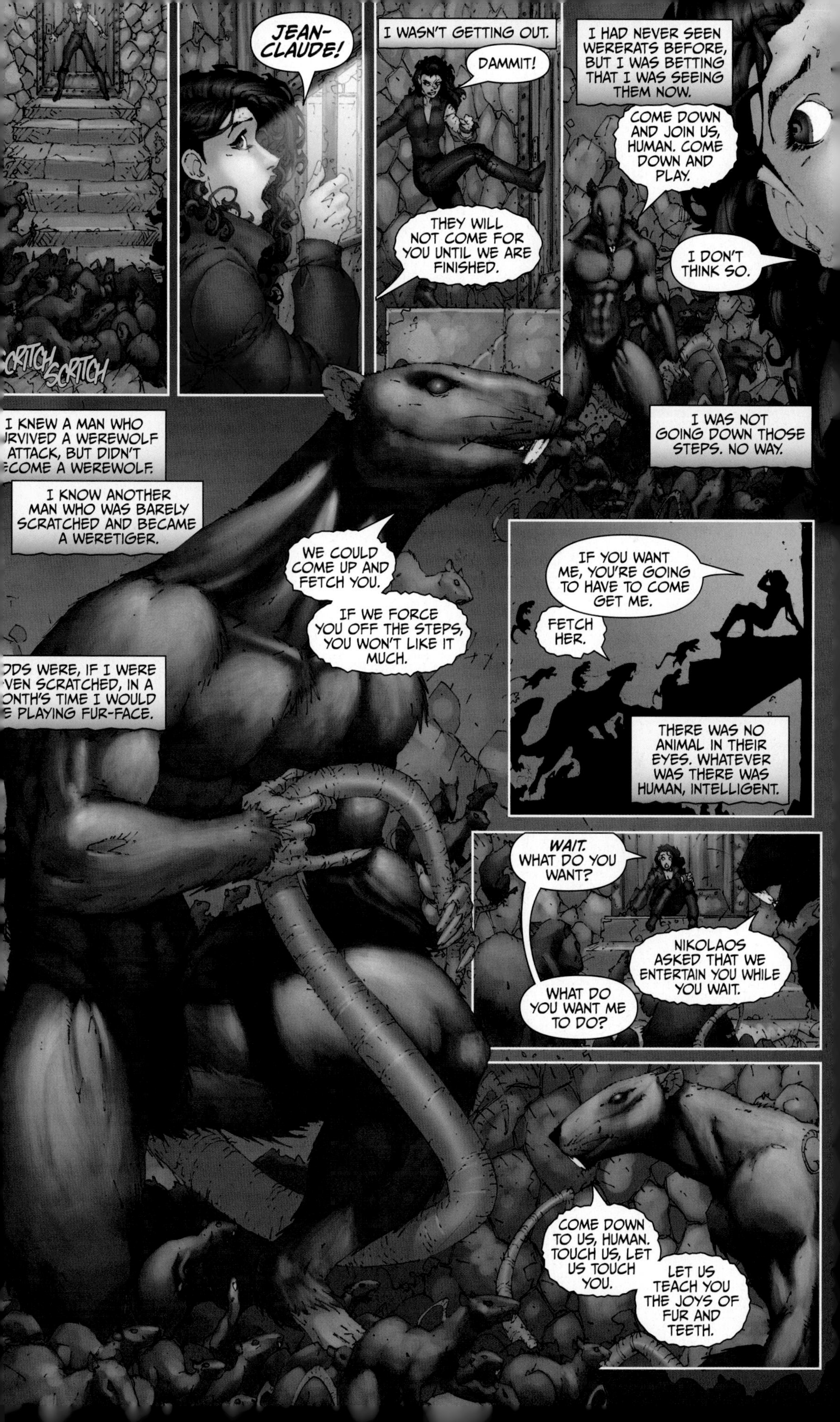
JEAN-CLAUDE!
SCRITCH SCRITCH
I WASN'T GETTING OUT.
DAMMIT!
THEY WILL NOT COME FOR YOU UNTIL WE ARE FINISHED.
I HAD NEVER SEEN WERERATS BEFORE, BUT I WAS BETTING THAT I WAS SEEING THEM NOW.
COME DOWN AND JOIN US, HUMAN. COME DOWN AND PLAY.
I DON'T THINK SO.
I WAS NOT GOING DOWN THOSE STEPS. NO WAY.
I KNEW A MAN WHO URVIVED A WEREWOLF ATTACK, BUT DIDN'T ECOME A WEREWOLF.
I KNOW ANOTHER MAN WHO WAS BARELY SCRATCHED AND BECAME A WERETIGER.
WE COULD COME UP AND FETCH YOU.
IF WE FORCE YOU OFF THE STEPS, YOU WON'T LIKE IT MUCH.
DDS WERE, IF I WERE VEN SCRATCHED, IN A ONTH'S TIME I WOULD E PLAYING FUR-FACE.
IF YOU WANT ME, YOU'RE GOING TO HAVE TO COME GET ME.
FETCH HER.
THERE WAS NO ANIMAL IN THEIR EYES. WHATEVER WAS THERE WAS HUMAN, INTELLIGENT.
WAIT. WHAT DO YOU WANT?
NIKOLAOS ASKED THAT WE ENTERTAIN YOU WHILE YOU WAIT.
WHAT DO YOU WANT ME TO DO?
COME DOWN TO US, HUMAN. TOUCH US, LET US TOUCH YOU.
LET US TEACH YOU THE JOYS OF FUR AND TEETH.

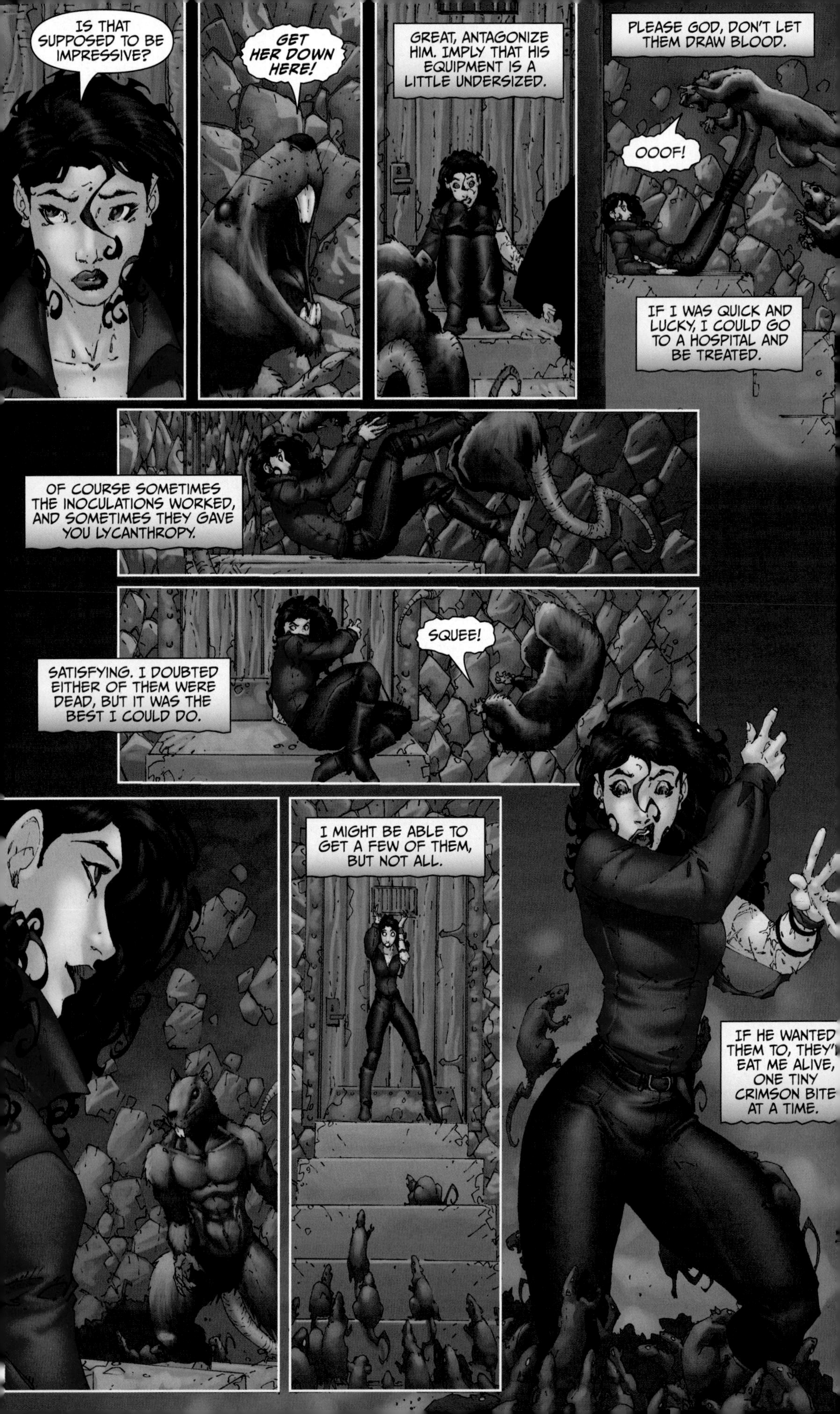

IS THAT SUPPOSED TO BE IMPRESSIVE?
GET HER DOWN HERE!
GREAT, ANTAGONIZE HIM. IMPLY THAT HIS EQUIPMENT IS A LITTLE UNDERSIZED.
PLEASE GOD, DON'T LET THEM DRAW BLOOD.
OOOF!
IF I WAS QUICK AND LUCKY, I COULD GO TO A HOSPITAL AND BE TREATED.
OF COURSE SOMETIMES THE INOCULATIONS WORKED, AND SOMETIMES THEY GAVE YOU LYCANTHROPY.
SATISFYING. I DOUBTED EITHER OF THEM WERE DEAD, BUT IT WAS THE BEST I COULD DO.
SQUEE!
I MIGHT BE ABLE TO GET A FEW OF THEM, BUT NOT ALL.
IF HE WANTED THEM TO, THEY'D EAT ME ALIVE, ONE TINY CRIMSON BITE AT A TIME.

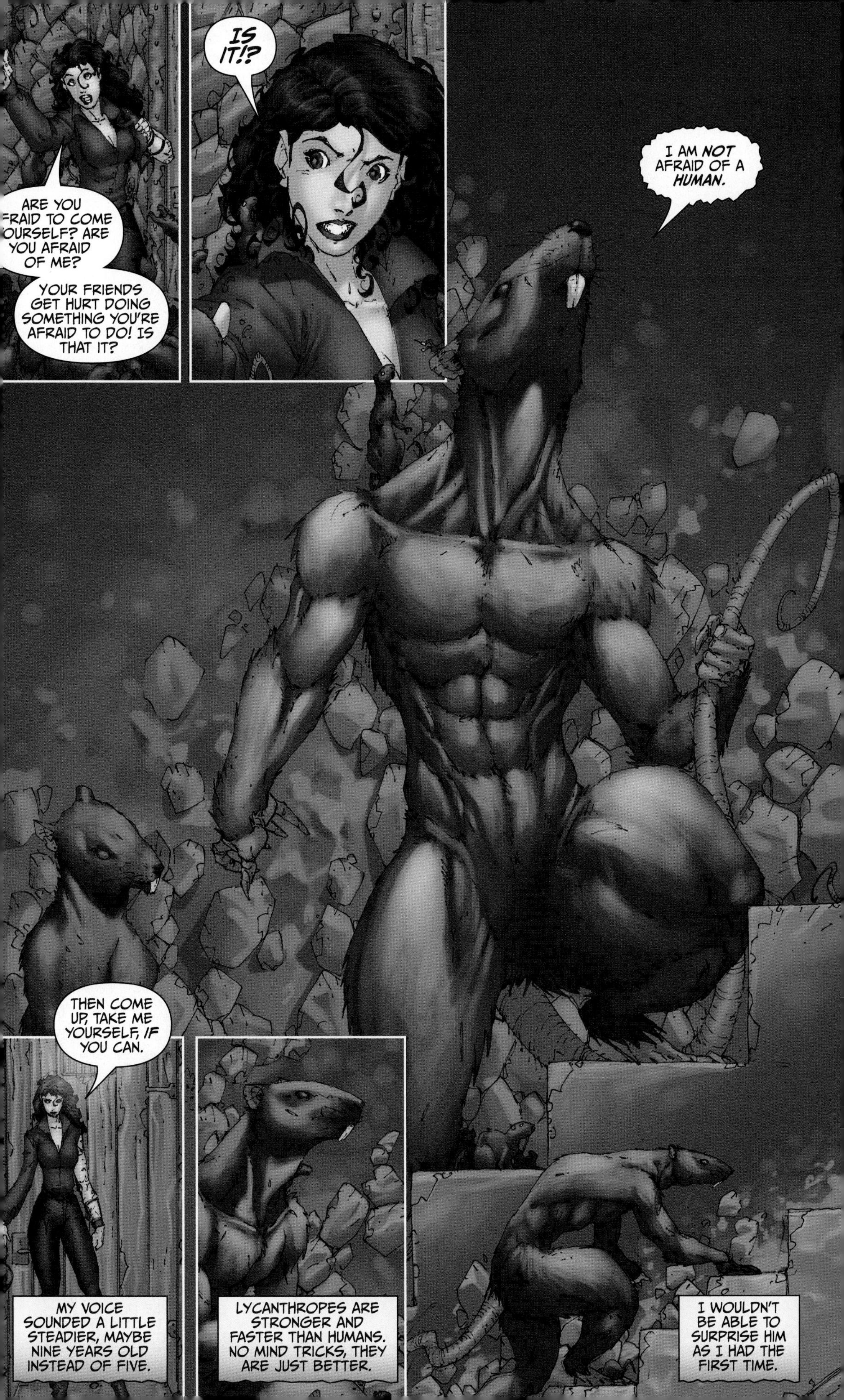
ARE YOU AFRAID TO COME YOURSELF? ARE YOU AFRAID OF ME?
YOUR FRIENDS GET HURT DOING SOMETHING YOU'RE AFRAID TO DO! IS THAT IT?
IS IT!?
I AM NOT AFRAID OF A HUMAN.
THEN COME UP, TAKE ME YOURSELF, IF YOU CAN.
MY VOICE SOUNDED A LITTLE STEADIER, MAYBE NINE YEARS OLD INSTEAD OF FIVE.
LYCANTHROPES ARE STRONGER AND FASTER THAN HUMANS. NO MIND TRICKS, THEY ARE JUST BETTER.
I WOULDN'T BE ABLE TO SURPRISE HIM AS I HAD THE FIRST TIME.

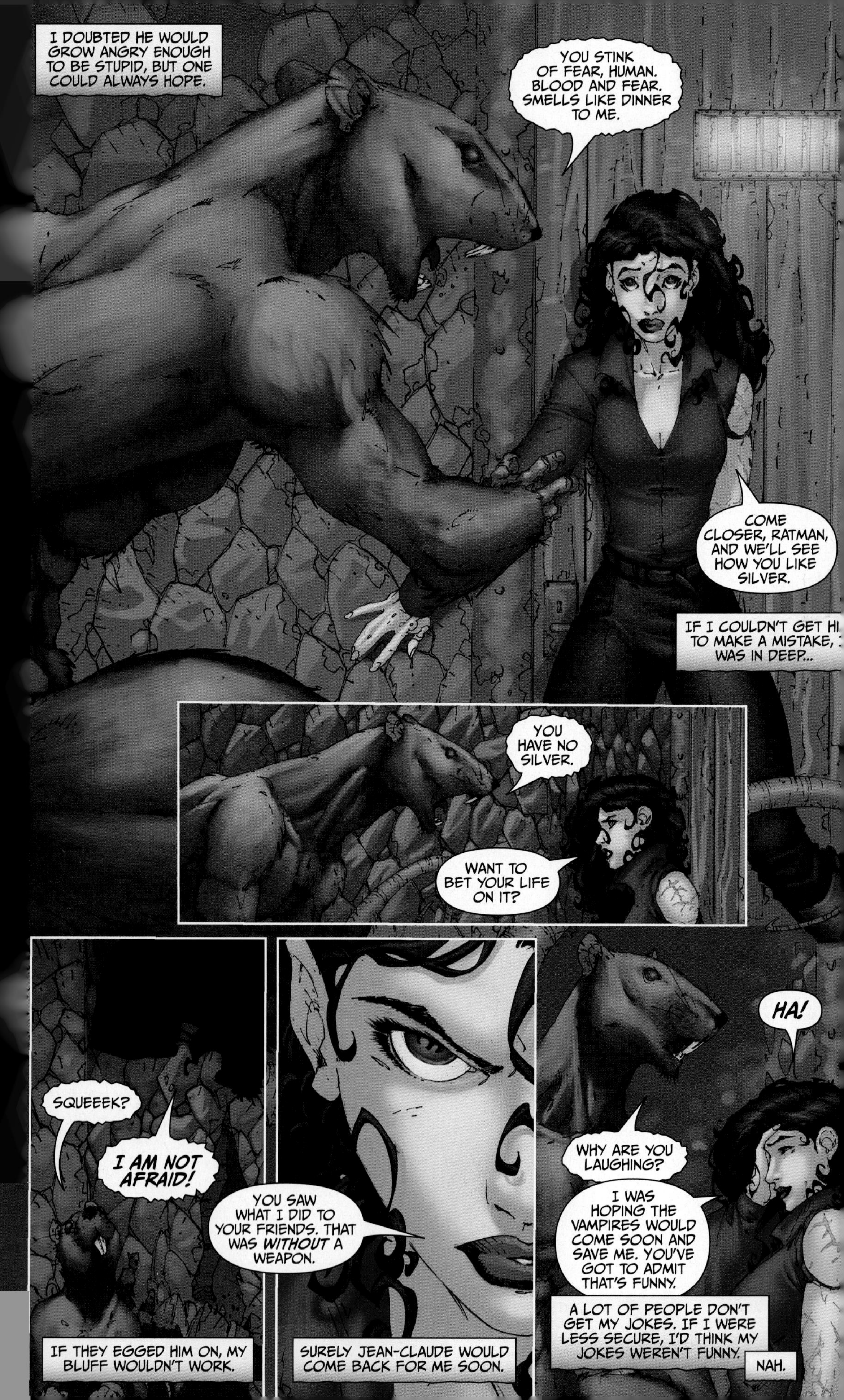
I DOUBTED HE WOULD GROW ANGRY ENOUGH TO BE STUPID, BUT ONE COULD ALWAYS HOPE.
YOU STINK OF FEAR, HUMAN. BLOOD AND FEAR. SMELLS LIKE DINNER TO ME.
COME CLOSER, RATMAN, AND WE'LL SEE HOW YOU LIKE SILVER.
IF I COULDN'T GET HI TO MAKE A MISTAKE, WAS IN DEEP...
YOU HAVE NO SILVER.
WANT TO BET YOUR LIFE ON IT?
SQUEEEK?
I AM NOT AFRAID!
IF THEY EGGED HIM ON, MY BLUFF WOULDN'T WORK.
YOU SAW WHAT I DID TO YOUR FRIENDS. THAT WAS *WITHOUT* A WEAPON.
SURELY JEAN-CLAUDE WOULD COME BACK FOR ME SOON.
HA!
WHY ARE YOU LAUGHING?
I WAS HOPING THE VAMPIRES WOULD COME SOON AND SAVE ME. YOU'VE GOT TO ADMIT THAT'S FUNNY.
A LOT OF PEOPLE DON'T GET MY JOKES. IF I WERE LESS SECURE, I'D THINK MY JOKES WEREN'T FUNNY.
NAH.

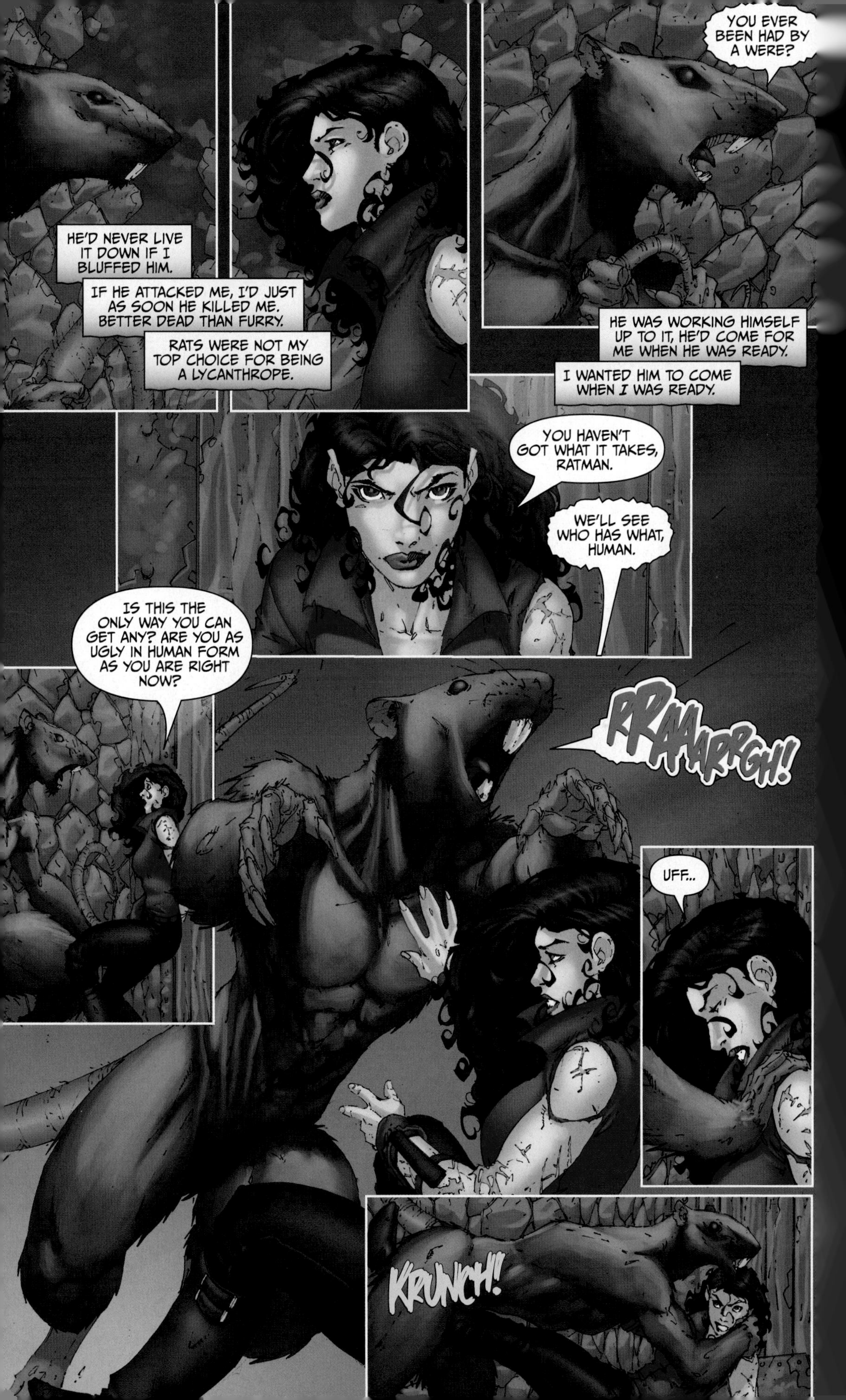
YOU EVER BEEN HAD BY A WERE?
HE'D NEVER LIVE IT DOWN IF I BLUFFED HIM.
IF HE ATTACKED ME, I'D JUST AS SOON HE KILLED ME. BETTER DEAD THAN FURRY.
RATS WERE NOT MY TOP CHOICE FOR BEING A LYCANTHROPE.
HE WAS WORKING HIMSELF UP TO IT, HE'D COME FOR ME WHEN HE WAS READY.
I WANTED HIM TO COME WHEN I WAS READY.
YOU HAVEN'T GOT WHAT IT TAKES, RATMAN.
WE'LL SEE WHO HAS WHAT, HUMAN.
IS THIS THE ONLY WAY YOU CAN GET ANY? ARE YOU AS UGLY IN HUMAN FORM AS YOU ARE RIGHT NOW?
RRAAAARRGH!
UFF...
KRUNCH!

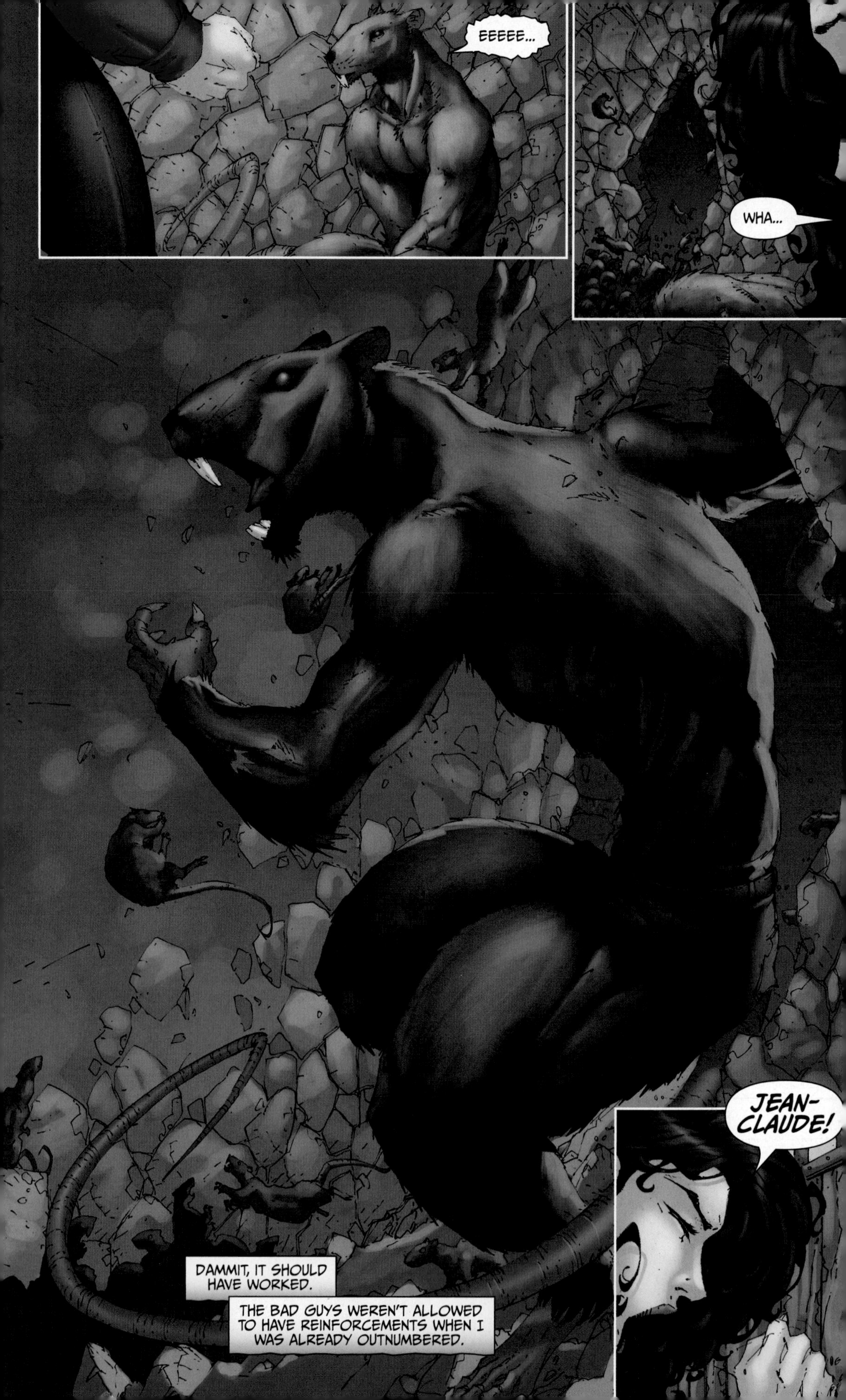
EEEEE...
WHA...
JEAN-CLAUDE!
DAMMIT, IT SHOULD HAVE WORKED.
THE BAD GUYS WEREN'T ALLOWED TO HAVE REINFORCEMENTS WHEN I WAS ALREADY OUTNUMBERED.

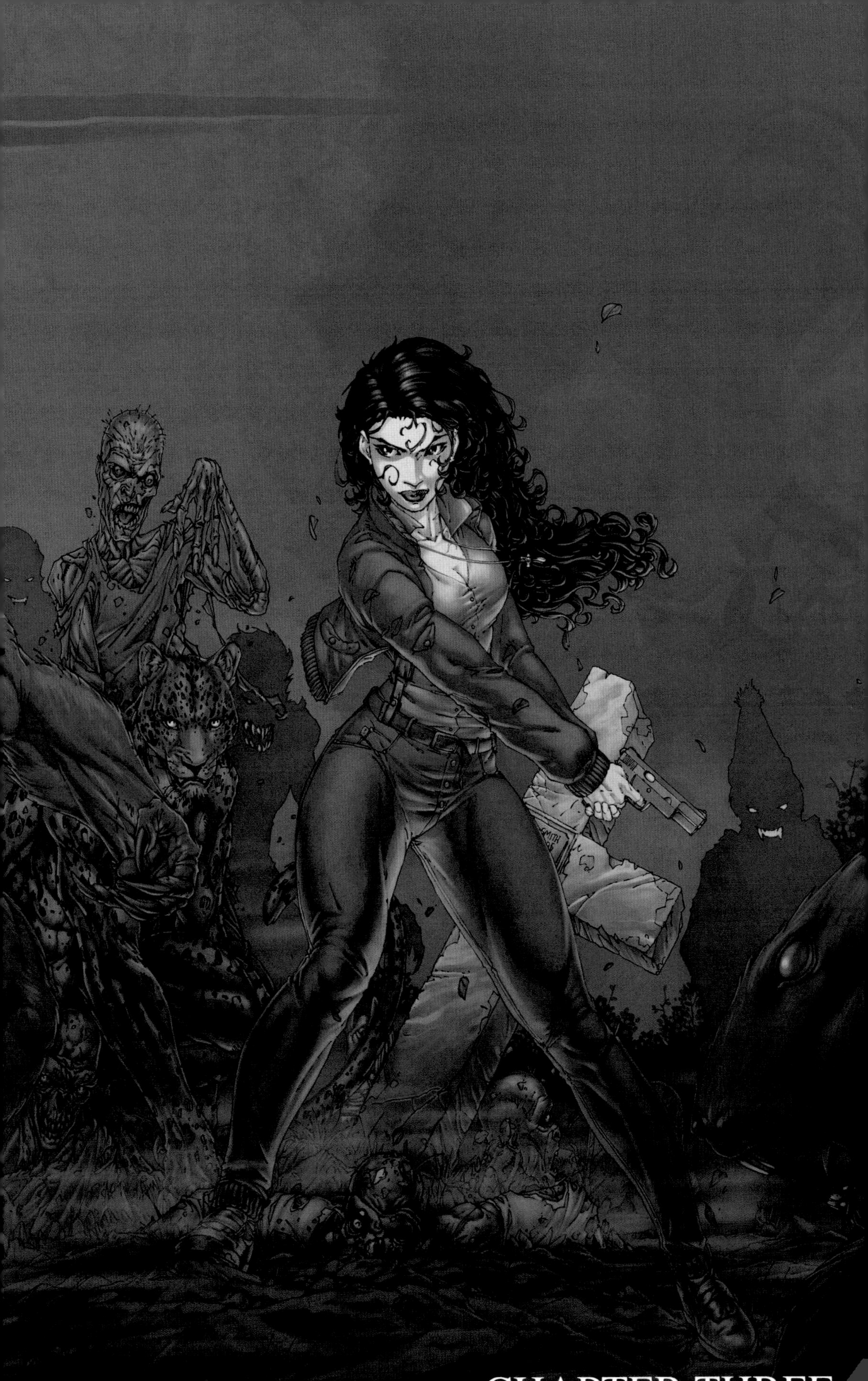

CHAPTER THREE

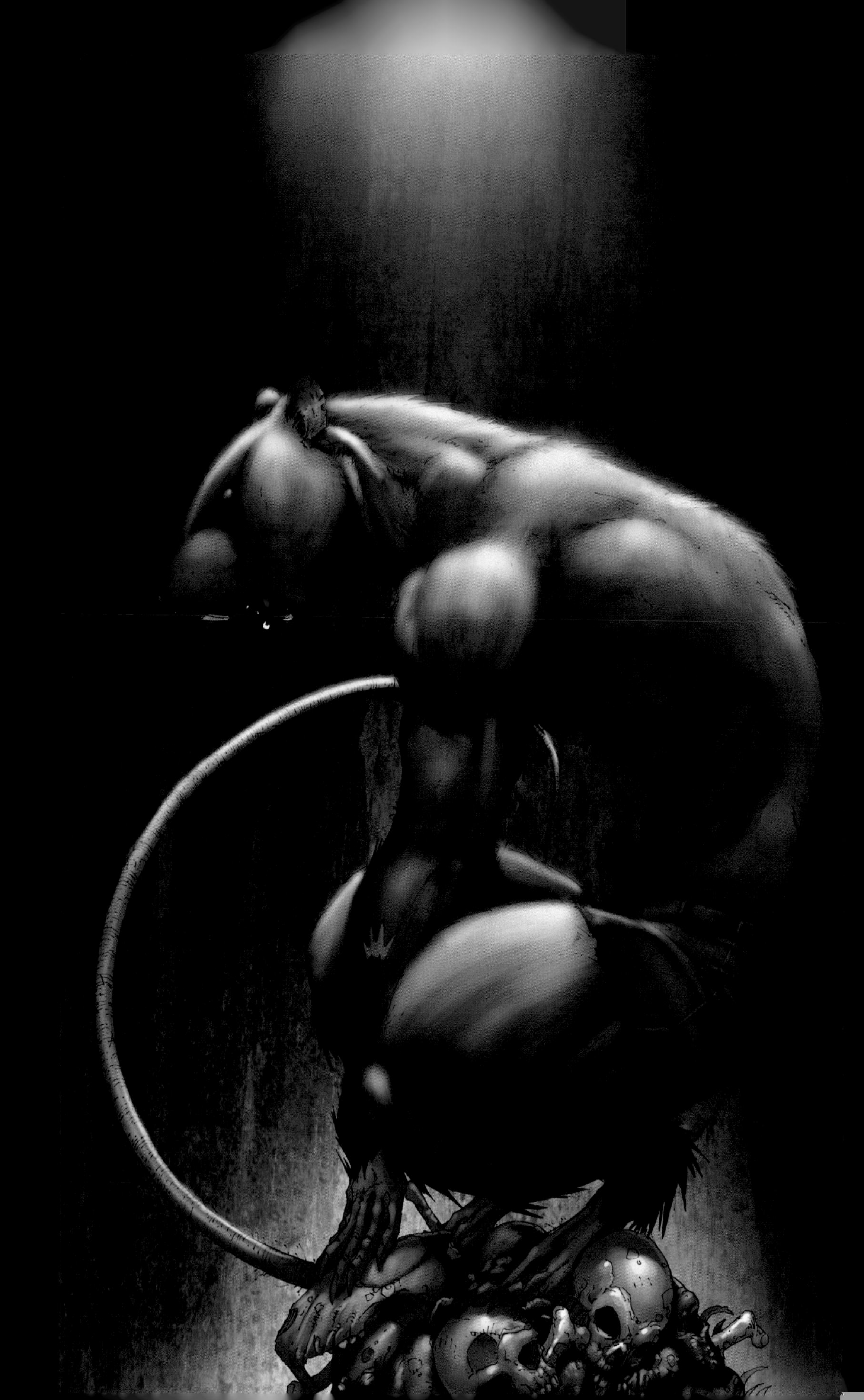

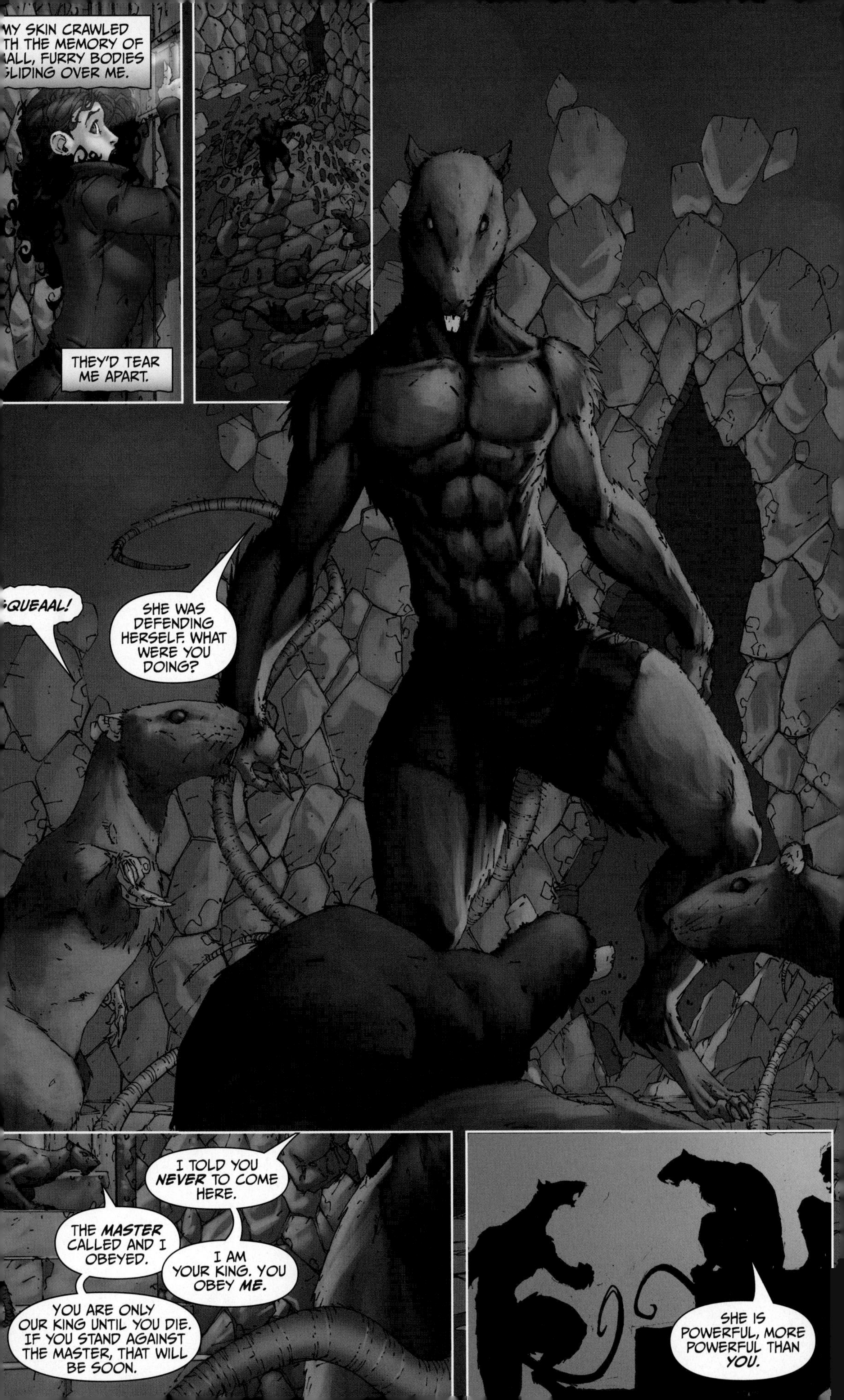
MY SKIN CRAWLED
TH THE MEMORY OF
ALL, FURRY BODIES
GLIDING OVER ME.
THEY'D TEAR ME APART.
SQUEAAL!
SHE WAS DEFENDING HERSELF. WHAT WERE YOU DOING?
I TOLD YOU NEVER TO COME HERE.
THE MASTER CALLED AND I OBEYED.
I AM YOUR KING. YOU OBEY ME.
YOU ARE ONLY OUR KING UNTIL YOU DIE. IF YOU STAND AGAINST THE MASTER, THAT WILL BE SOON.
SHE IS POWERFUL, MORE POWERFUL THAN YOU.

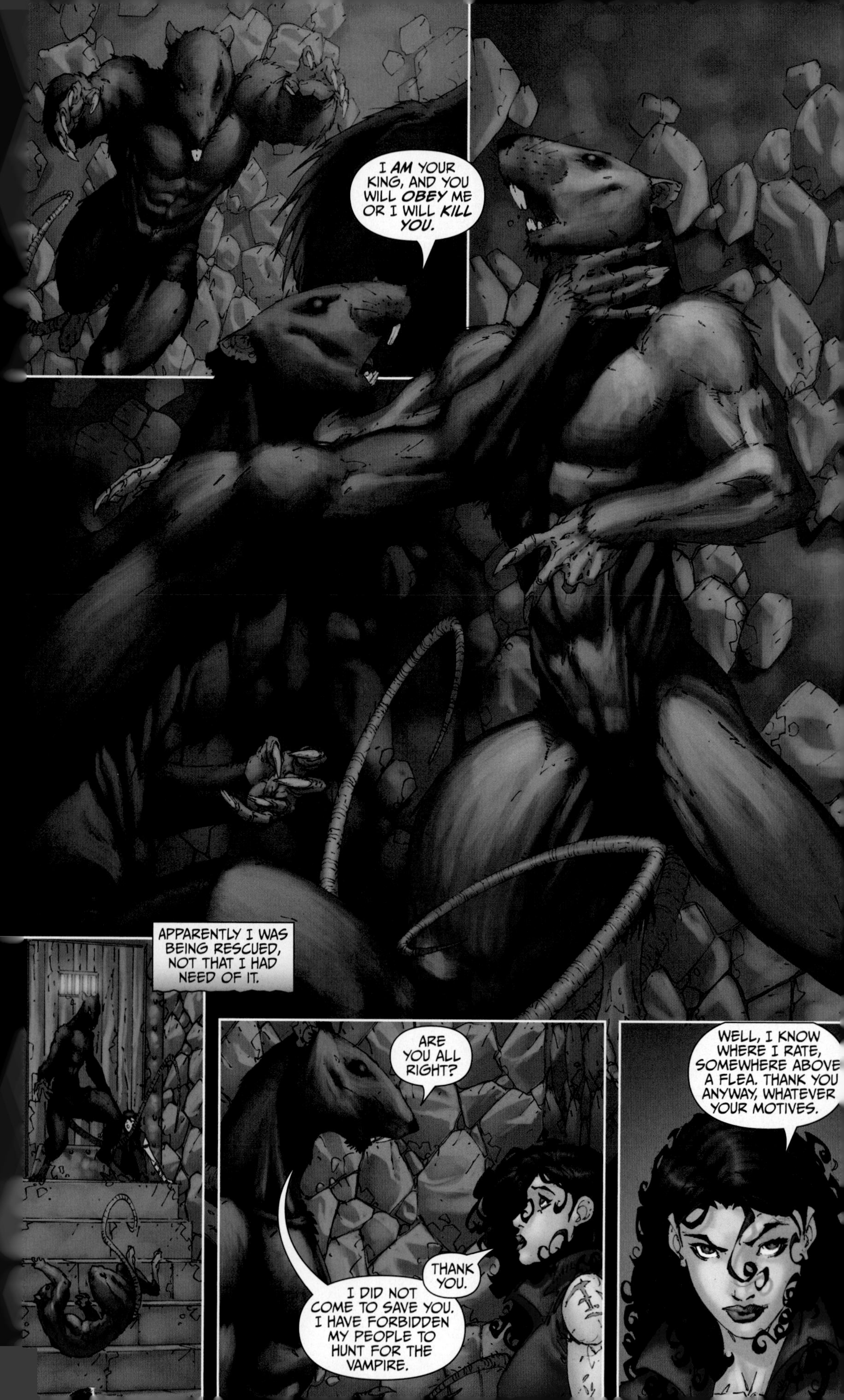
I AM YOUR KING, AND YOU WILL OBEY ME OR I WILL KILL YOU.
APPARENTLY I WAS BEING RESCUED, NOT THAT I HAD NEED OF IT.
ARE YOU ALL RIGHT?
THANK YOU.
I DID NOT COME TO SAVE YOU. I HAVE FORBIDDEN MY PEOPLE TO HUNT FOR THE VAMPIRE.
WELL, I KNOW WHERE I RATE, SOMEWHERE ABOVE A FLEA. THANK YOU ANYWAY, WHATEVER YOUR MOTIVES.

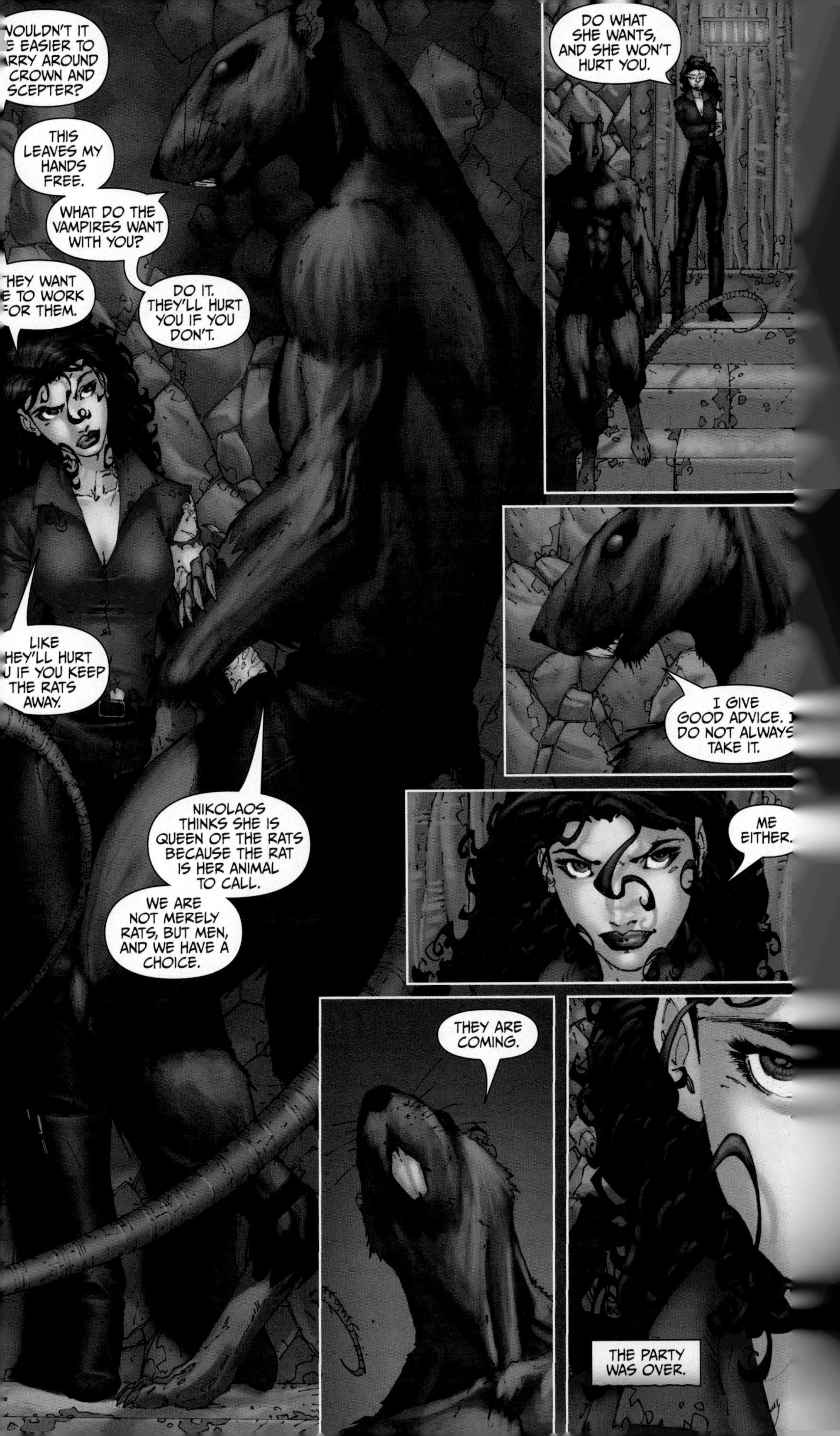
VOULDN'T IT E EASIER TO ARRY AROUND CROWN AND SCEPTER?
THIS LEAVES MY HANDS FREE.
WHAT DO THE VAMPIRES WANT WITH YOU?
HEY WANT E TO WORK FOR THEM.
DO IT. THEY'LL HURT YOU IF YOU DON'T.
DO WHAT SHE WANTS, AND SHE WON'T HURT YOU.
LIKE HEY'LL HURT U IF YOU KEEP THE RATS AWAY.
NIKOLAOS THINKS SHE IS QUEEN OF THE RATS BECAUSE THE RAT IS HER ANIMAL TO CALL.
WE ARE NOT MERELY RATS, BUT MEN, AND WE HAVE A CHOICE.
I GIVE GOOD ADVICE. DO NOT ALWAYS TAKE IT.
ME EITHER.
THEY ARE COMING.
THE PARTY WAS OVER.

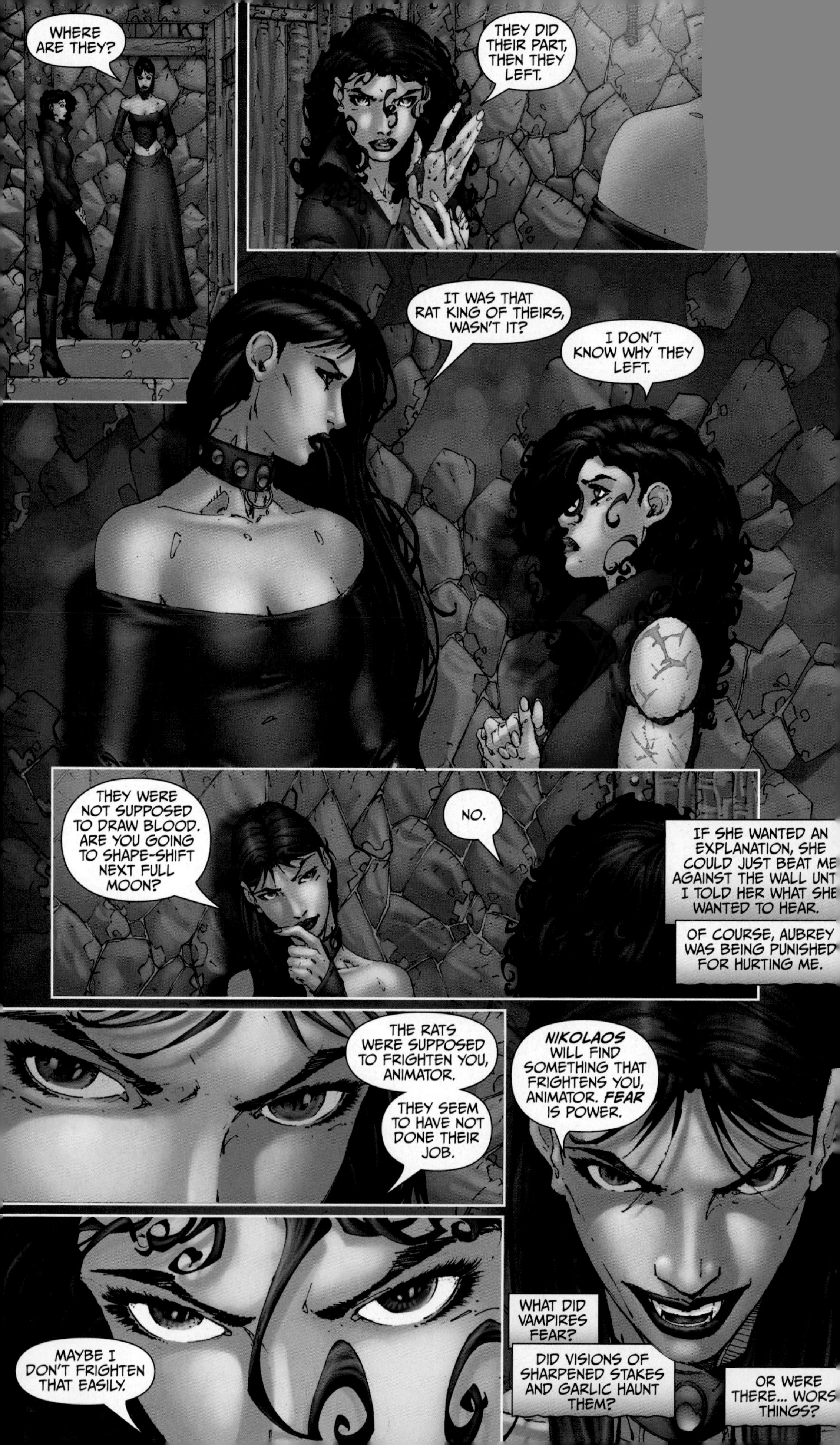
WHERE ARE THEY?
THEY DID THEIR PART, THEN THEY LEFT.
IT WAS THAT RAT KING OF THEIRS, WASN'T IT?
I DON'T KNOW WHY THEY LEFT.
THEY WERE NOT SUPPOSED TO DRAW BLOOD. ARE YOU GOING TO SHAPE-SHIFT NEXT FULL MOON?
NO.
IF SHE WANTED AN EXPLANATION, SHE COULD JUST BEAT ME AGAINST THE WALL UNT I TOLD HER WHAT SHE WANTED TO HEAR.
OF COURSE, AUBREY WAS BEING PUNISHED FOR HURTING ME.
THE RATS WERE SUPPOSED TO FRIGHTEN YOU, ANIMATOR.
THEY SEEM TO HAVE NOT DONE THEIR JOB.
NIKOLAOS WILL FIND SOMETHING THAT FRIGHTENS YOU, ANIMATOR. *FEAR* IS POWER.
MAYBE I DON'T FRIGHTEN THAT EASILY.
WHAT DID VAMPIRES FEAR?
DID VISIONS OF SHARPENED STAKES AND GARLIC HAUNT THEM?
OR WERE THERE... WORS THINGS?

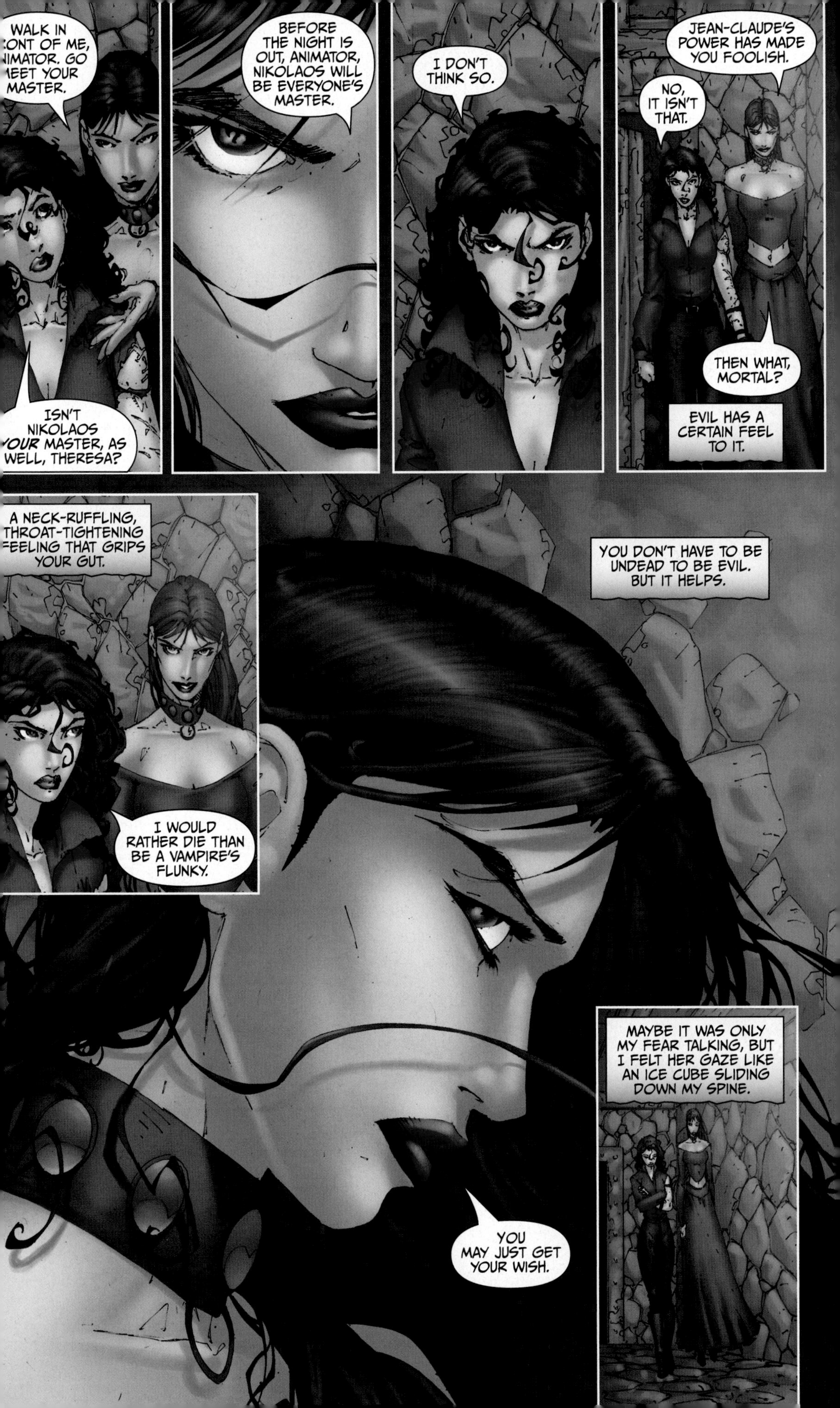

WALK IN RONT OF ME, NIMATOR. GO MEET YOUR MASTER.
ISN'T NIKOLAOS YOUR MASTER, AS WELL, THERESA?
BEFORE THE NIGHT IS OUT, ANIMATOR, NIKOLAOS WILL BE EVERYONE'S MASTER.
I DON'T THINK SO.
JEAN-CLAUDE'S POWER HAS MADE YOU FOOLISH.
NO, IT ISN'T THAT.
THEN WHAT, MORTAL?
EVIL HAS A CERTAIN FEEL TO IT.
A NECK-RUFFLING, THROAT-TIGHTENING FEELING THAT GRIPS YOUR GUT.
I WOULD RATHER DIE THAN BE A VAMPIRE'S FLUNKY.
YOU DON'T HAVE TO BE UNDEAD TO BE EVIL. BUT IT HELPS.
MAYBE IT WAS ONLY MY FEAR TALKING, BUT I FELT HER GAZE LIKE AN ICE CUBE SLIDING DOWN MY SPINE.
YOU MAY JUST GET YOUR WISH.

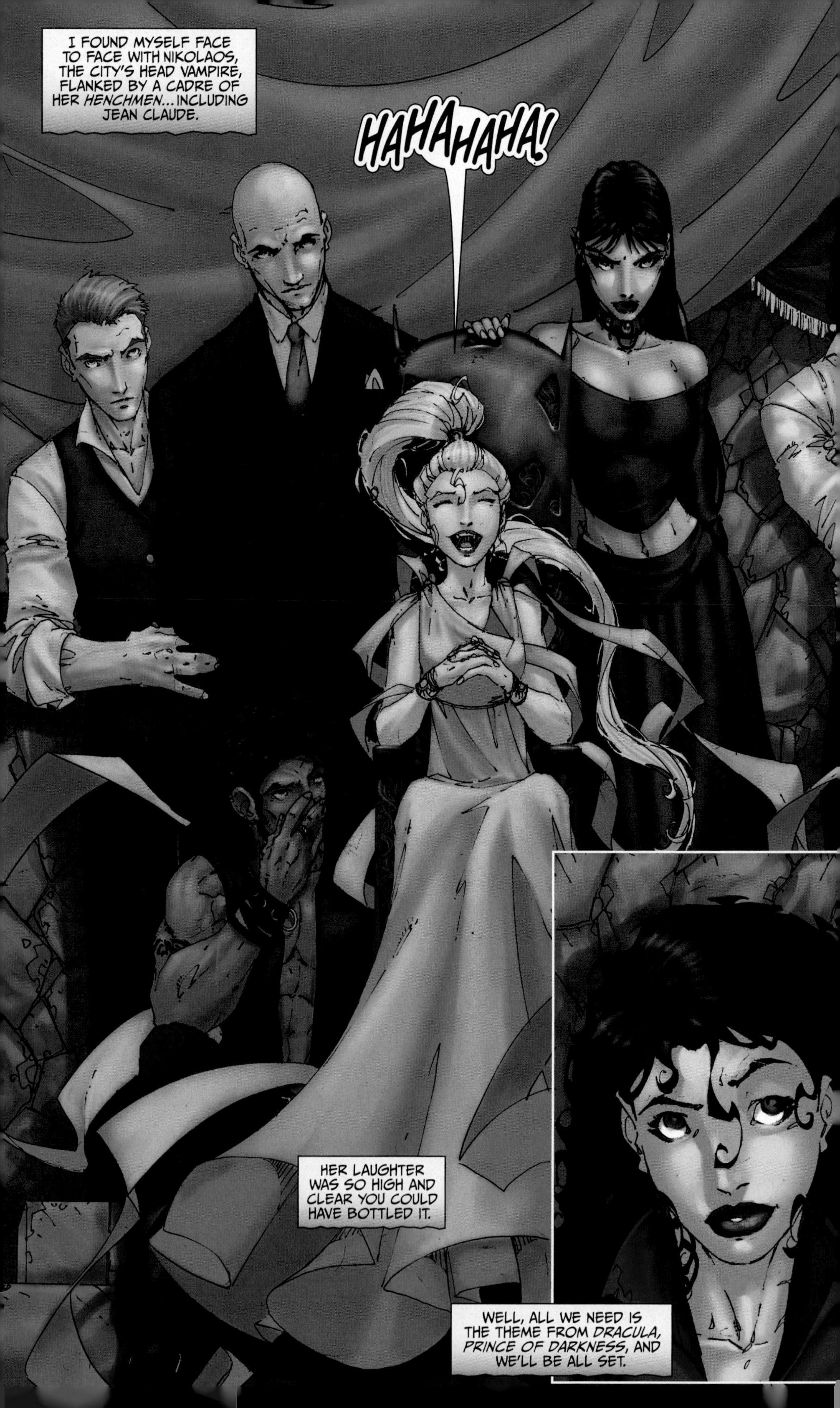
I FOUND MYSELF FACE TO FACE WITH NIKOLAOS, THE CITY'S HEAD VAMPIRE, FLANKED BY A CADRE OF HER *HENCHMEN*... INCLUDING JEAN CLAUDE.
HAHAHAHAHA!
HER LAUGHTER WAS SO HIGH AND CLEAR YOU COULD HAVE BOTTLED IT.
WELL, ALL WE NEED IS THE THEME FROM *DRACULA, PRINCE OF DARKNESS*, AND WE'LL BE ALL SET.

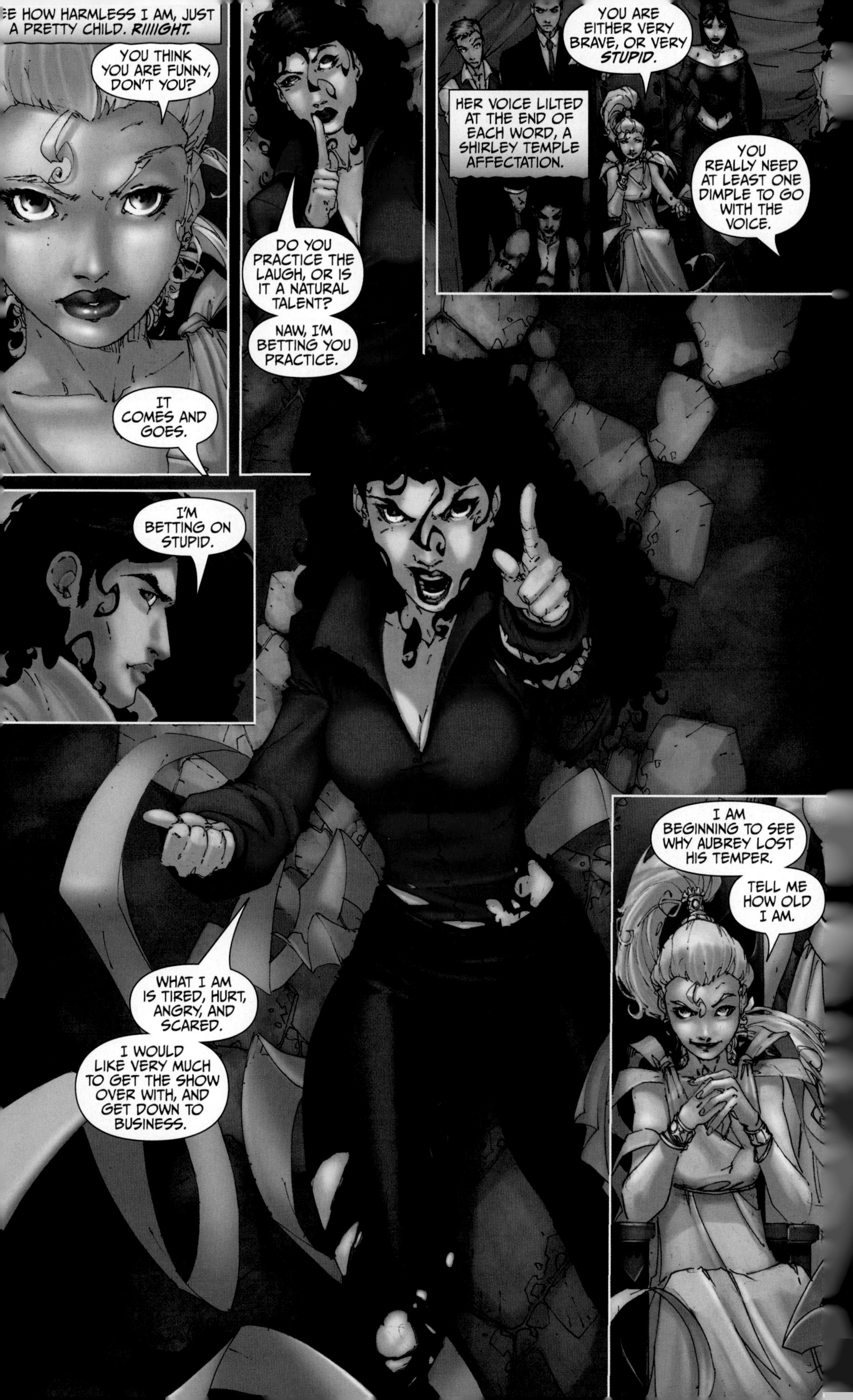

...E HOW HARMLESS I AM, JUST A PRETTY CHILD. RIIIIGHT.
YOU THINK YOU ARE FUNNY, DON'T YOU?
IT COMES AND GOES.
DO YOU PRACTICE THE LAUGH, OR IS IT A NATURAL TALENT?
NAW, I'M BETTING YOU PRACTICE.
YOU ARE EITHER VERY BRAVE, OR VERY STUPID.
HER VOICE LILTED AT THE END OF EACH WORD, A SHIRLEY TEMPLE AFFECTATION.
YOU REALLY NEED AT LEAST ONE DIMPLE TO GO WITH THE VOICE.
I'M BETTING ON STUPID.
I AM BEGINNING TO SEE WHY AUBREY LOST HIS TEMPER.
TELL ME HOW OLD I AM.
WHAT I AM IS TIRED, HURT, ANGRY, AND SCARED.
I WOULD LIKE VERY MUCH TO GET THE SHOW OVER WITH, AND GET DOWN TO BUSINESS.

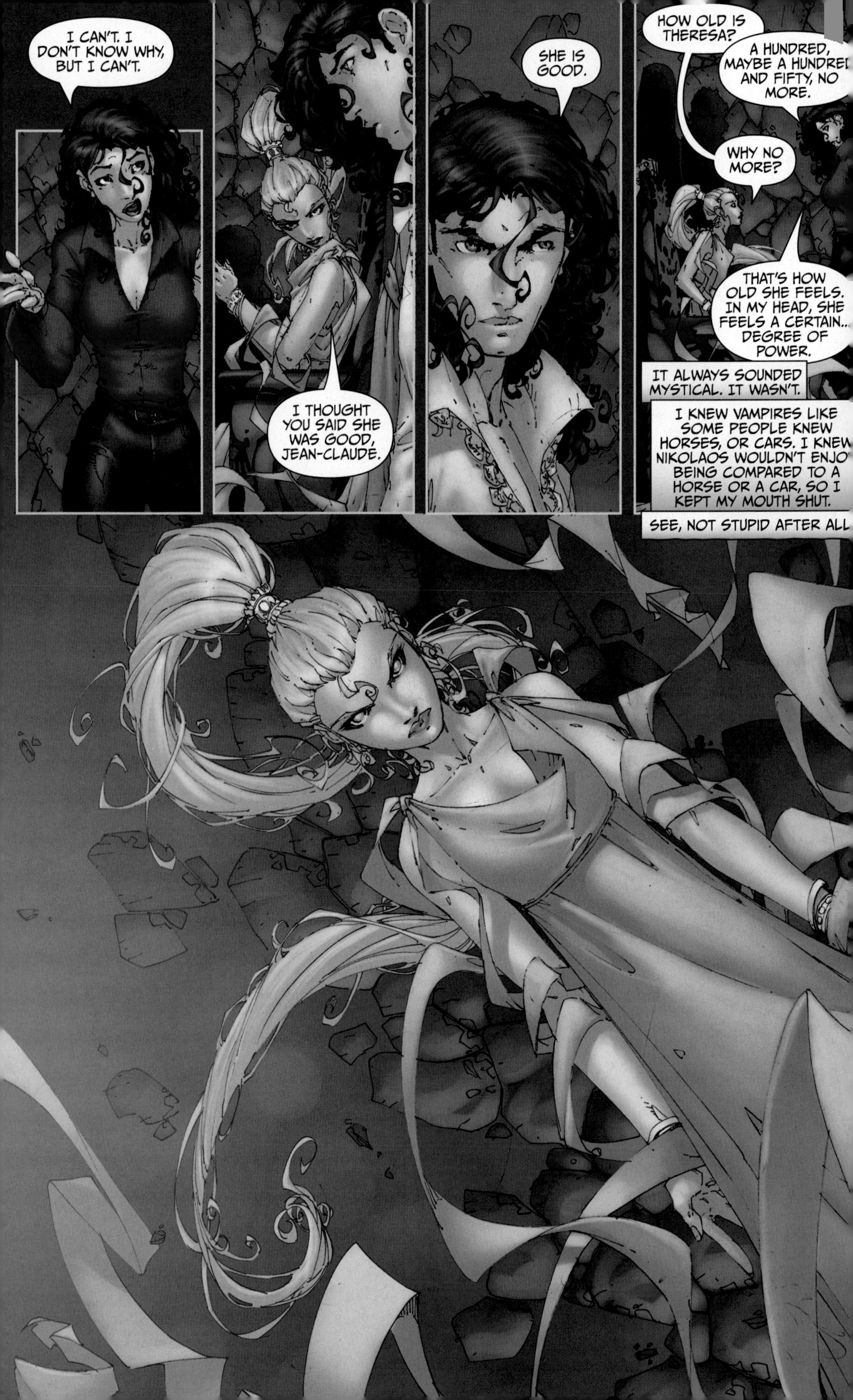
I CAN'T. I DON'T KNOW WHY, BUT I CAN'T.
I THOUGHT YOU SAID SHE WAS GOOD, JEAN-CLAUDE.
SHE IS GOOD.
HOW OLD IS THERESA?
A HUNDRED, MAYBE A HUNDRE AND FIFTY, NO MORE.
WHY NO MORE?
THAT'S HOW OLD SHE FEELS. IN MY HEAD, SHE FEELS A CERTAIN... DEGREE OF POWER.
IT ALWAYS SOUNDED MYSTICAL. IT WASN'T.
I KNEW VAMPIRES LIKE SOME PEOPLE KNEW HORSES, OR CARS. I KNEW NIKOLAOS WOULDN'T ENJO BEING COMPARED TO A HORSE OR A CAR, SO I KEPT MY MOUTH SHUT.
SEE, NOT STUPID AFTER ALL

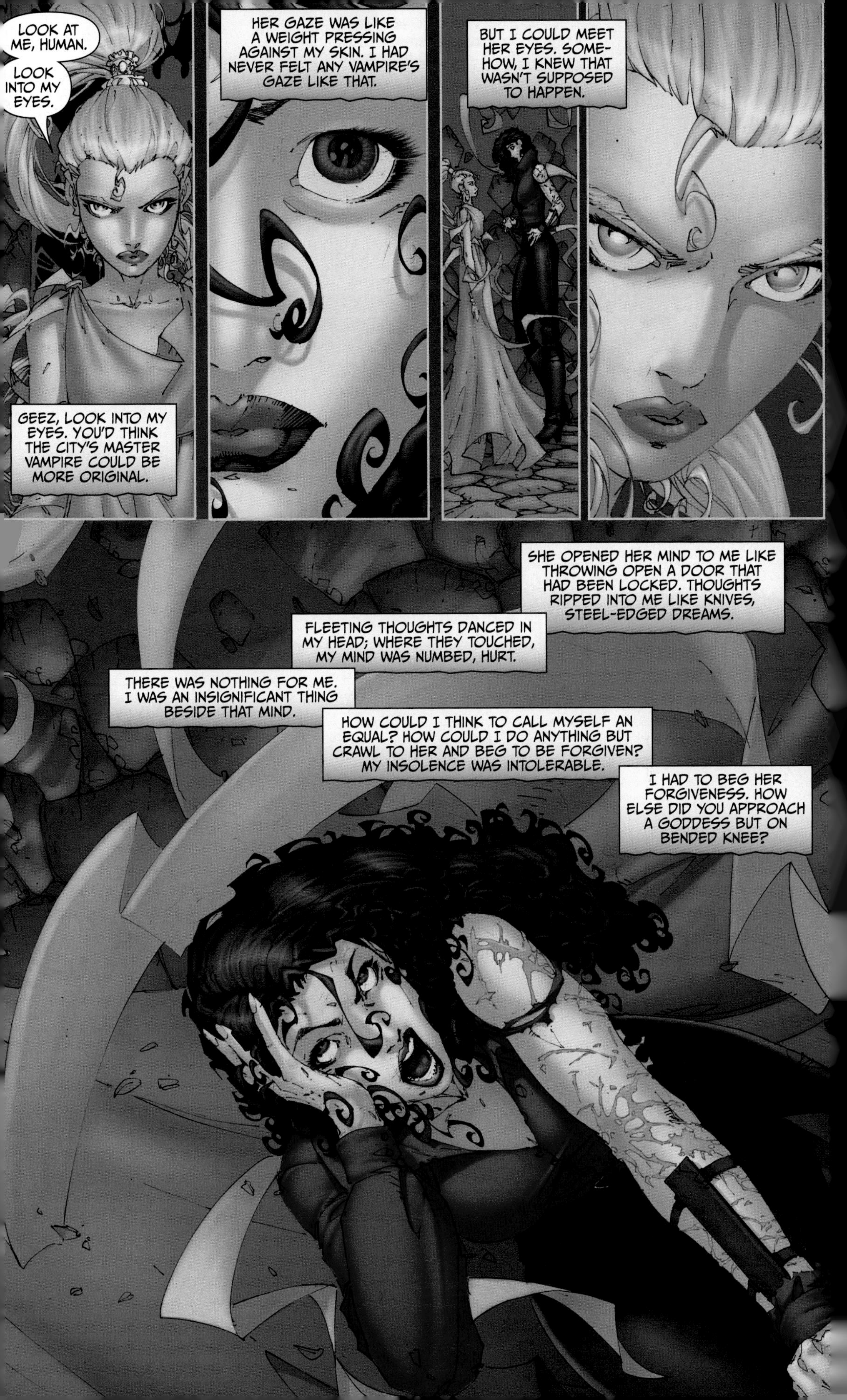
LOOK AT ME, HUMAN.
LOOK INTO MY EYES.
GEEZ, LOOK INTO MY EYES. YOU'D THINK THE CITY'S MASTER VAMPIRE COULD BE MORE ORIGINAL.
HER GAZE WAS LIKE A WEIGHT PRESSING AGAINST MY SKIN. I HAD NEVER FELT ANY VAMPIRE'S GAZE LIKE THAT.
BUT I COULD MEET HER EYES. SOME-HOW, I KNEW THAT WASN'T SUPPOSED TO HAPPEN.
SHE OPENED HER MIND TO ME LIKE THROWING OPEN A DOOR THAT HAD BEEN LOCKED. THOUGHTS RIPPED INTO ME LIKE KNIVES, STEEL-EDGED DREAMS.
FLEETING THOUGHTS DANCED IN MY HEAD; WHERE THEY TOUCHED, MY MIND WAS NUMBED, HURT.
THERE WAS NOTHING FOR ME. I WAS AN INSIGNIFICANT THING BESIDE THAT MIND.
HOW COULD I THINK TO CALL MYSELF AN EQUAL? HOW COULD I DO ANYTHING BUT CRAWL TO HER AND BEG TO BE FORGIVEN? MY INSOLENCE WAS INTOLERABLE.
I HAD TO BEG HER FORGIVENESS. HOW ELSE DID YOU APPROACH A GODDESS BUT ON BENDED KNEE?

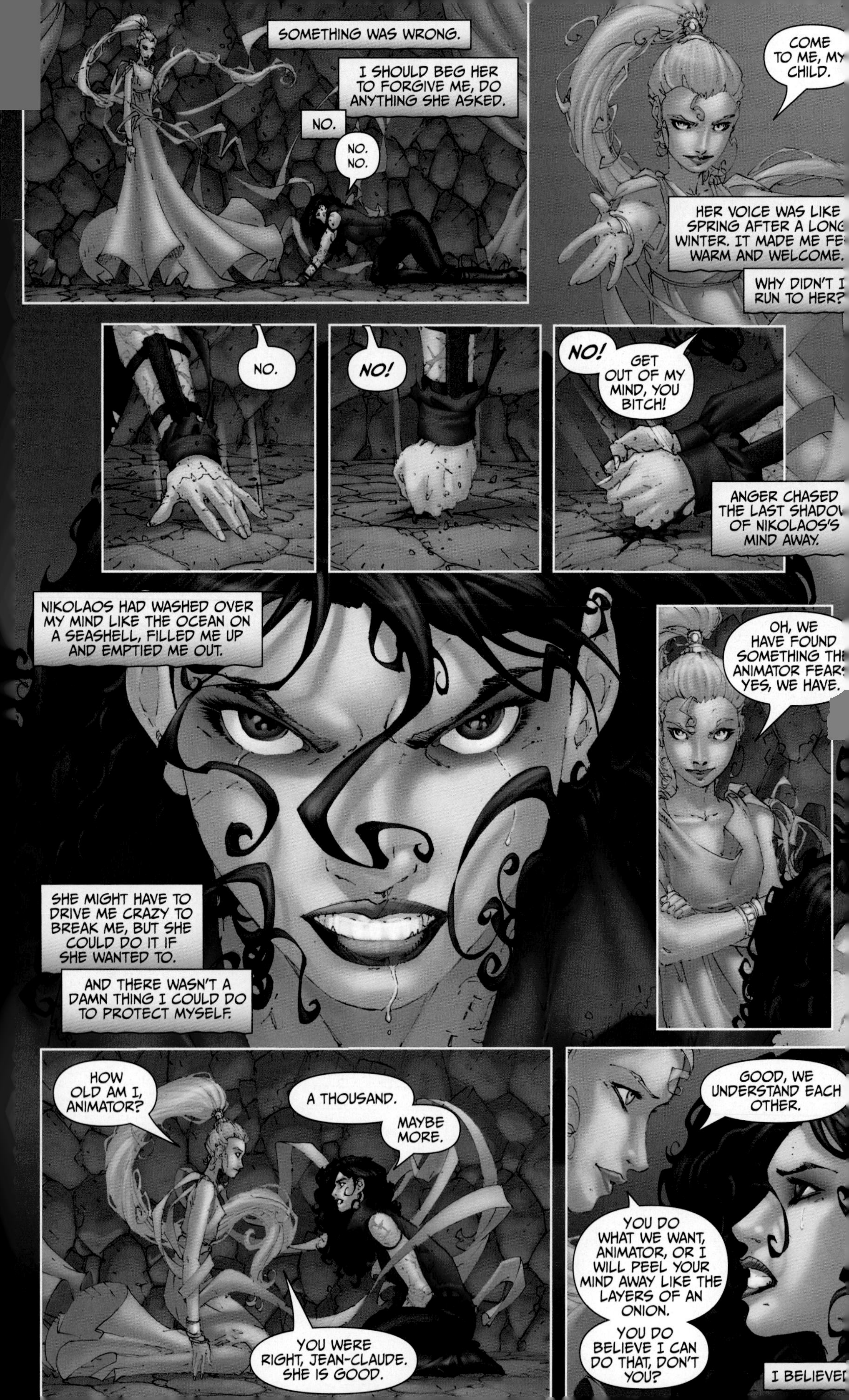
SOMETHING WAS WRONG.
I SHOULD BEG HER TO FORGIVE ME, DO ANYTHING SHE ASKED.
NO.
NO. NO.
COME TO ME, MY CHILD.
HER VOICE WAS LIKE SPRING AFTER A LONG WINTER. IT MADE ME FE WARM AND WELCOME.
WHY DIDN'T I RUN TO HER?
NO.
NO!
NO! GET OUT OF MY MIND, YOU BITCH!
ANGER CHASED THE LAST SHADOW OF NIKOLAOS'S MIND AWAY.
NIKOLAOS HAD WASHED OVER MY MIND LIKE THE OCEAN ON A SEASHELL, FILLED ME UP AND EMPTIED ME OUT.
OH, WE HAVE FOUND SOMETHING TH ANIMATOR FEAR YES, WE HAVE.
SHE MIGHT HAVE TO DRIVE ME CRAZY TO BREAK ME, BUT SHE COULD DO IT IF SHE WANTED TO.
AND THERE WASN'T A DAMN THING I COULD DO TO PROTECT MYSELF.
HOW OLD AM I, ANIMATOR?
A THOUSAND.
MAYBE MORE.
YOU WERE RIGHT, JEAN-CLAUDE. SHE IS GOOD.
GOOD, WE UNDERSTAND EACH OTHER.
YOU DO WHAT WE WANT, ANIMATOR, OR I WILL PEEL YOUR MIND AWAY LIKE THE LAYERS OF AN ONION.
YOU DO BELIEVE I CAN DO THAT, DON'T YOU?
I BELIEVED

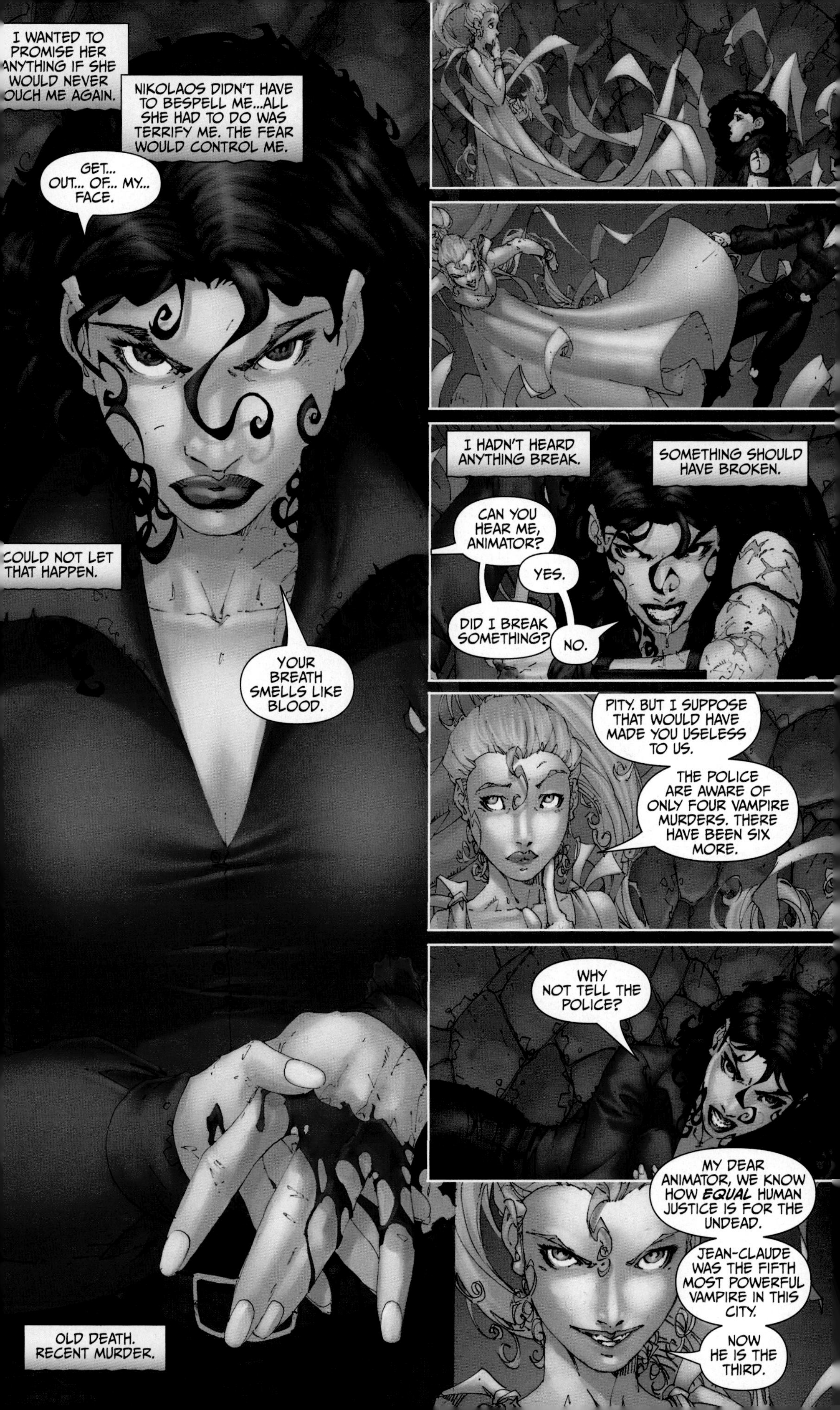

I WANTED TO PROMISE HER ANYTHING IF SHE WOULD NEVER TOUCH ME AGAIN.
NIKOLAOS DIDN'T HAVE TO BESPELL ME...ALL SHE HAD TO DO WAS TERRIFY ME. THE FEAR WOULD CONTROL ME.
GET... OUT... OF... MY... FACE.
COULD NOT LET THAT HAPPEN.
YOUR BREATH SMELLS LIKE BLOOD.
OLD DEATH. RECENT MURDER.
I HADN'T HEARD ANYTHING BREAK.
SOMETHING SHOULD HAVE BROKEN.
CAN YOU HEAR ME, ANIMATOR?
YES.
DID I BREAK SOMETHING?
NO.
PITY. BUT I SUPPOSE THAT WOULD HAVE MADE YOU USELESS TO US.
THE POLICE ARE AWARE OF ONLY FOUR VAMPIRE MURDERS. THERE HAVE BEEN SIX MORE.
WHY NOT TELL THE POLICE?
MY DEAR ANIMATOR, WE KNOW HOW EQUAL HUMAN JUSTICE IS FOR THE UNDEAD.
JEAN-CLAUDE WAS THE FIFTH MOST POWERFUL VAMPIRE IN THIS CITY.
NOW HE IS THE THIRD.

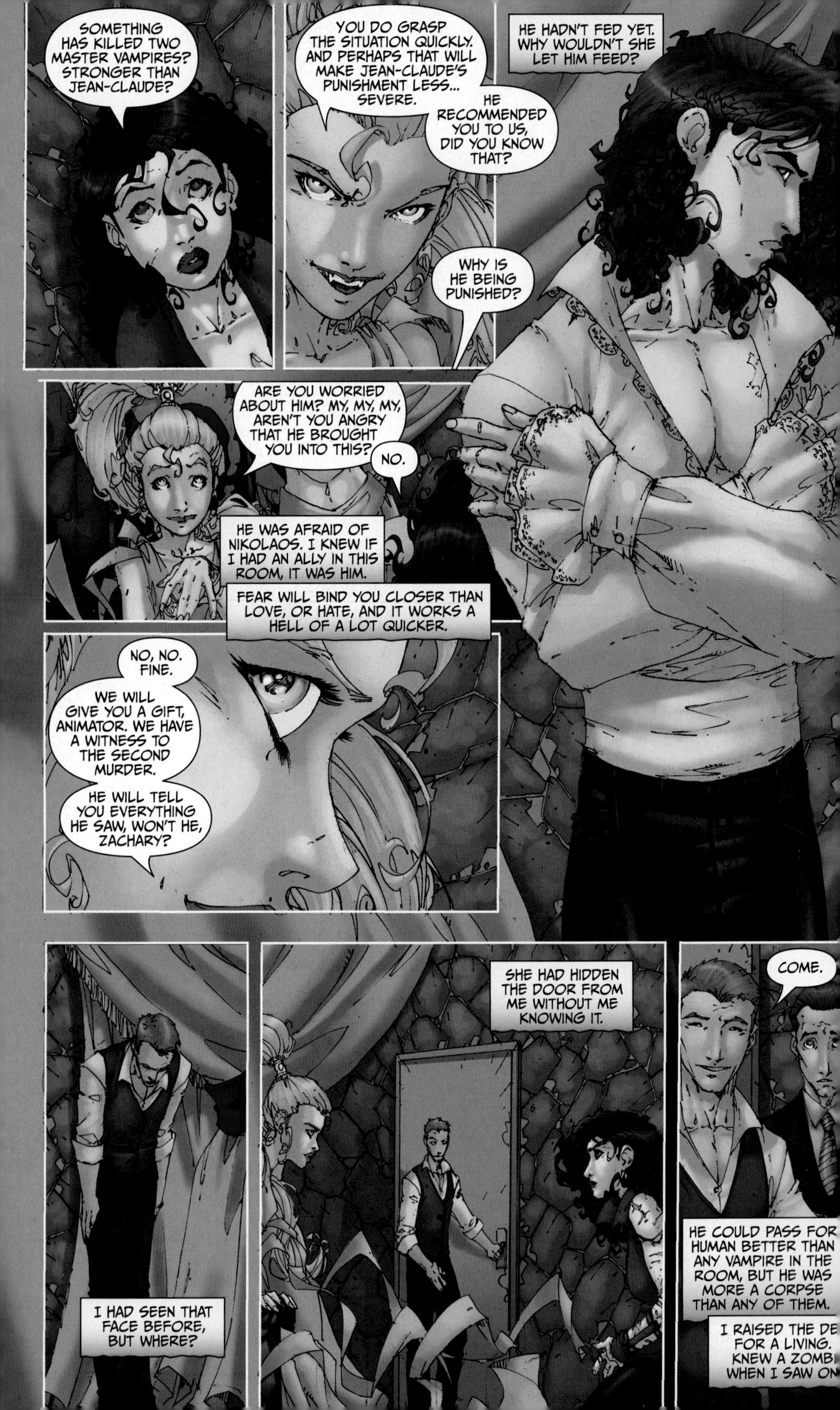
SOMETHING HAS KILLED TWO MASTER VAMPIRES? STRONGER THAN JEAN-CLAUDE?
YOU DO GRASP THE SITUATION QUICKLY. AND PERHAPS THAT WILL MAKE JEAN-CLAUDE'S PUNISHMENT LESS... SEVERE.
HE RECOMMENDED YOU TO US, DID YOU KNOW THAT?
WHY IS HE BEING PUNISHED?
HE HADN'T FED YET. WHY WOULDN'T SHE LET HIM FEED?
ARE YOU WORRIED ABOUT HIM? MY, MY, MY, AREN'T YOU ANGRY THAT HE BROUGHT YOU INTO THIS?
NO.
HE WAS AFRAID OF NIKOLAOS. I KNEW IF I HAD AN ALLY IN THIS ROOM, IT WAS HIM.
FEAR WILL BIND YOU CLOSER THAN LOVE, OR HATE, AND IT WORKS A HELL OF A LOT QUICKER.
NO, NO. FINE.
WE WILL GIVE YOU A GIFT, ANIMATOR. WE HAVE A WITNESS TO THE SECOND MURDER.
HE WILL TELL YOU EVERYTHING HE SAW, WON'T HE, ZACHARY?
I HAD SEEN THAT FACE BEFORE, BUT WHERE?
SHE HAD HIDDEN THE DOOR FROM ME WITHOUT ME KNOWING IT.
COME.
HE COULD PASS FOR HUMAN BETTER THAN ANY VAMPIRE IN THE ROOM, BUT HE WAS MORE A CORPSE THAN ANY OF THEM.
I RAISED THE DE
FOR A LIVING.
KNEW A ZOMB
WHEN I SAW ON

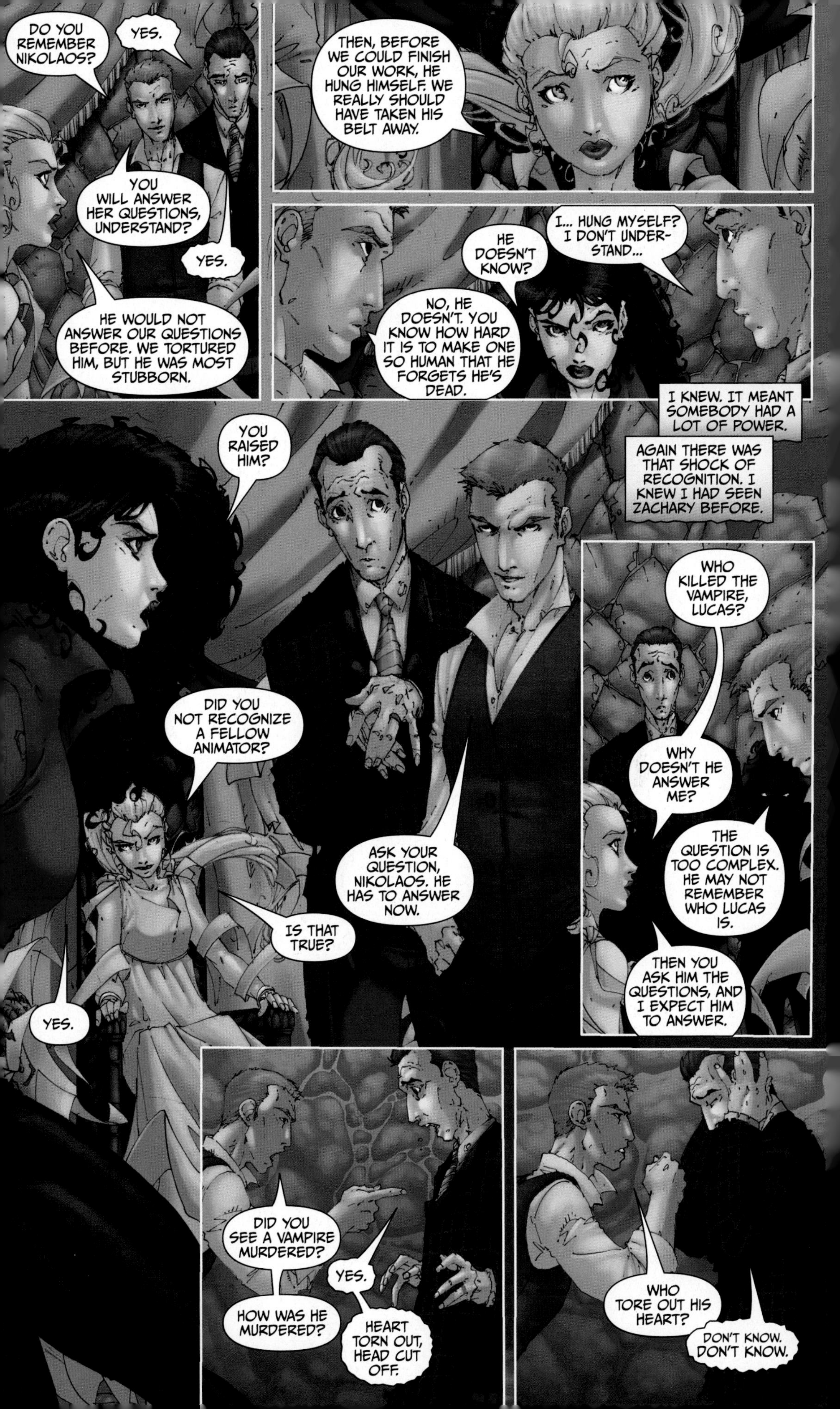
DO YOU REMEMBER NIKOLAOS?
YES.
YOU WILL ANSWER HER QUESTIONS, UNDERSTAND?
YES.
HE WOULD NOT ANSWER OUR QUESTIONS BEFORE. WE TORTURED HIM, BUT HE WAS MOST STUBBORN.
THEN, BEFORE WE COULD FINISH OUR WORK, HE HUNG HIMSELF. WE REALLY SHOULD HAVE TAKEN HIS BELT AWAY.
I... HUNG MYSELF? I DON'T UNDER-STAND...
HE DOESN'T KNOW?
NO, HE DOESN'T. YOU KNOW HOW HARD IT IS TO MAKE ONE SO HUMAN THAT HE FORGETS HE'S DEAD.
I KNEW. IT MEANT SOMEBODY HAD A LOT OF POWER.
AGAIN THERE WAS THAT SHOCK OF RECOGNITION. I KNEW I HAD SEEN ZACHARY BEFORE.
YOU RAISED HIM?
DID YOU NOT RECOGNIZE A FELLOW ANIMATOR?
ASK YOUR QUESTION, NIKOLAOS. HE HAS TO ANSWER NOW.
IS THAT TRUE?
YES.
WHO KILLED THE VAMPIRE, LUCAS?
WHY DOESN'T HE ANSWER ME?
THE QUESTION IS TOO COMPLEX. HE MAY NOT REMEMBER WHO LUCAS IS.
THEN YOU ASK HIM THE QUESTIONS, AND I EXPECT HIM TO ANSWER.
DID YOU SEE A VAMPIRE MURDERED?
YES.
HOW WAS HE MURDERED?
HEART TORN OUT, HEAD CUT OFF.
WHO TORE OUT HIS HEART?
DON'T KNOW. DON'T KNOW.

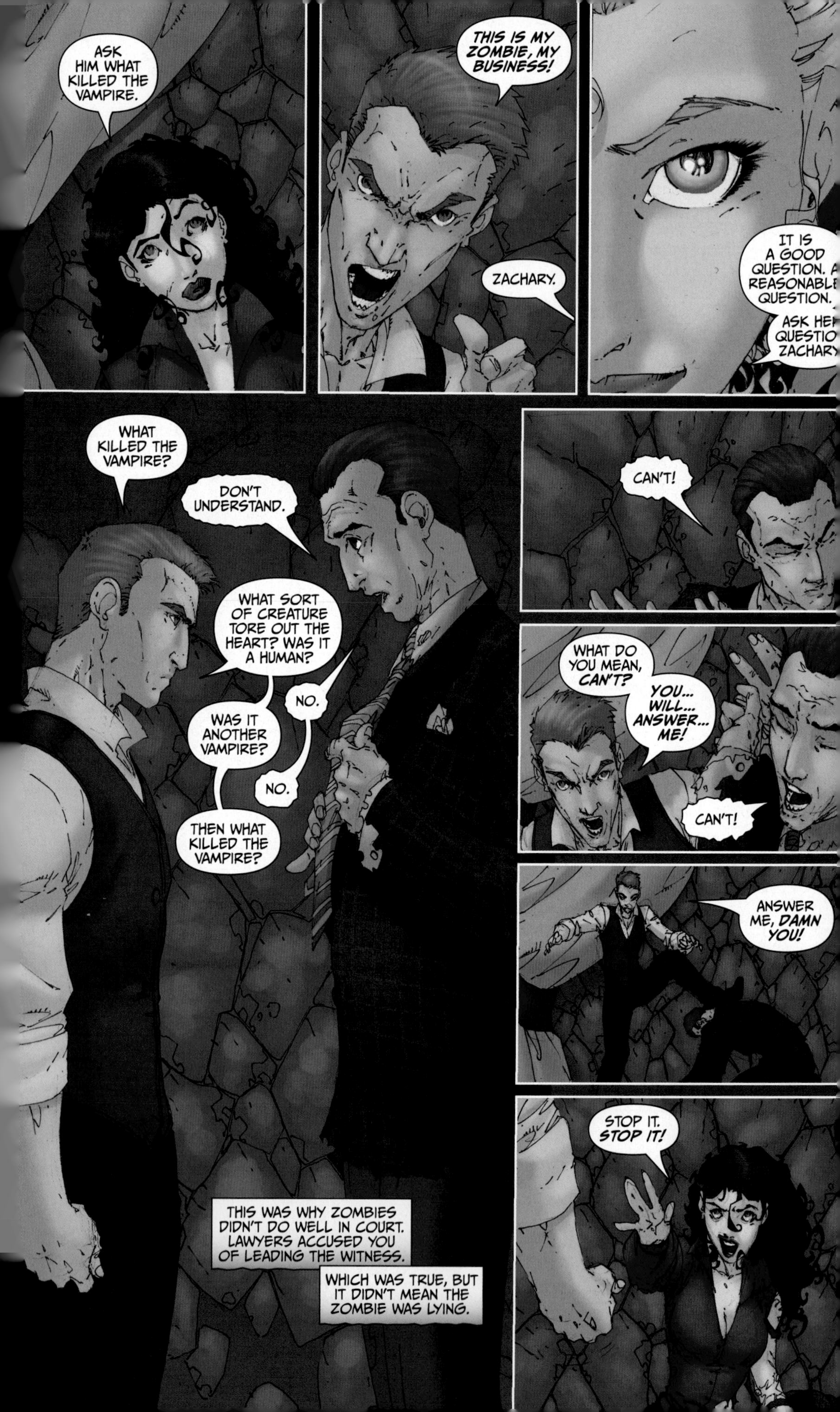
ASK HIM WHAT KILLED THE VAMPIRE.
THIS IS MY ZOMBIE, MY BUSINESS!
ZACHARY.
IT IS A GOOD QUESTION. A REASONABLE QUESTION.
ASK HER QUESTION, ZACHARY.
WHAT KILLED THE VAMPIRE?
DON'T UNDERSTAND.
WHAT SORT OF CREATURE TORE OUT THE HEART? WAS IT A HUMAN?
NO.
WAS IT ANOTHER VAMPIRE?
NO.
THEN WHAT KILLED THE VAMPIRE?
THIS WAS WHY ZOMBIES DIDN'T DO WELL IN COURT. LAWYERS ACCUSED YOU OF LEADING THE WITNESS.
WHICH WAS TRUE, BUT IT DIDN'T MEAN THE ZOMBIE WAS LYING.
CAN'T!
WHAT DO YOU MEAN, CAN'T?
YOU... WILL... ANSWER... ME!
CAN'T!
ANSWER ME, DAMN YOU!
STOP IT. STOP IT!

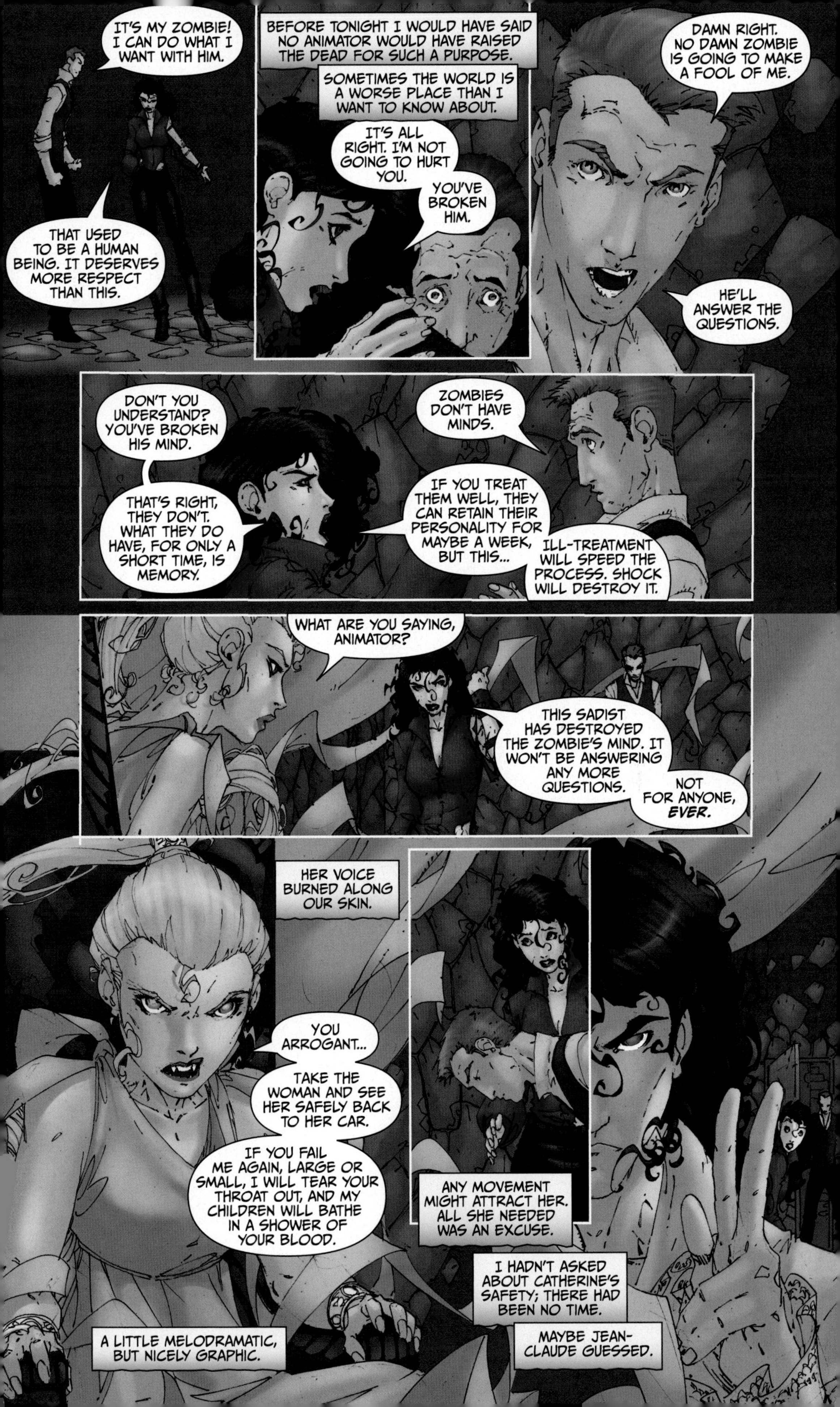

IT'S MY ZOMBIE! I CAN DO WHAT I WANT WITH HIM.
THAT USED TO BE A HUMAN BEING. IT DESERVES MORE RESPECT THAN THIS.
BEFORE TONIGHT I WOULD HAVE SAID NO ANIMATOR WOULD HAVE RAISED THE DEAD FOR SUCH A PURPOSE.
SOMETIMES THE WORLD IS A WORSE PLACE THAN I WANT TO KNOW ABOUT.
IT'S ALL RIGHT. I'M NOT GOING TO HURT YOU.
YOU'VE BROKEN HIM.
DAMN RIGHT. NO DAMN ZOMBIE IS GOING TO MAKE A FOOL OF ME.
HE'LL ANSWER THE QUESTIONS.
DON'T YOU UNDERSTAND? YOU'VE BROKEN HIS MIND.
ZOMBIES DON'T HAVE MINDS.
THAT'S RIGHT, THEY DON'T. WHAT THEY DO HAVE, FOR ONLY A SHORT TIME, IS MEMORY.
IF YOU TREAT THEM WELL, THEY CAN RETAIN THEIR PERSONALITY FOR MAYBE A WEEK, BUT THIS...
ILL-TREATMENT WILL SPEED THE PROCESS. SHOCK WILL DESTROY IT.
WHAT ARE YOU SAYING, ANIMATOR?
THIS SADIST HAS DESTROYED THE ZOMBIE'S MIND. IT WON'T BE ANSWERING ANY MORE QUESTIONS.
NOT FOR ANYONE, *EVER.*
HER VOICE BURNED ALONG OUR SKIN.
YOU ARROGANT...
TAKE THE WOMAN AND SEE HER SAFELY BACK TO HER CAR.
IF YOU FAIL ME AGAIN, LARGE OR SMALL, I WILL TEAR YOUR THROAT OUT, AND MY CHILDREN WILL BATHE IN A SHOWER OF YOUR BLOOD.
A LITTLE MELODRAMATIC, BUT NICELY GRAPHIC.
ANY MOVEMENT MIGHT ATTRACT HER. ALL SHE NEEDED WAS AN EXCUSE.
I HADN'T ASKED ABOUT CATHERINE'S SAFETY; THERE HAD BEEN NO TIME.
MAYBE JEAN-CLAUDE GUESSED.

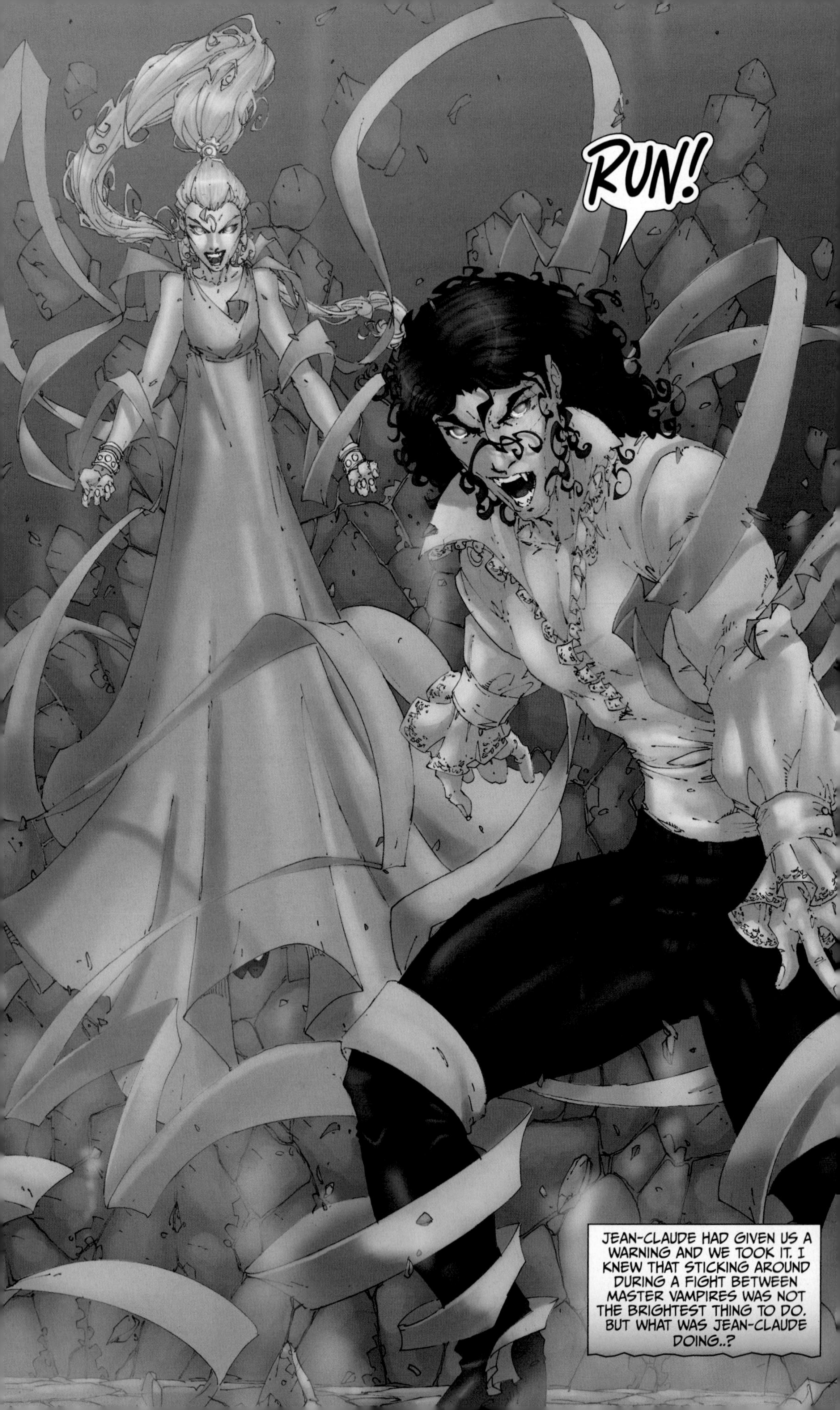
RUN!
JEAN-CLAUDE HAD GIVEN US A WARNING AND WE TOOK IT. I KNEW THAT STICKING AROUND DURING A FIGHT BETWEEN MASTER VAMPIRES WAS NOT THE BRIGHTEST THING TO DO. BUT WHAT WAS JEAN-CLAUDE DOING..?

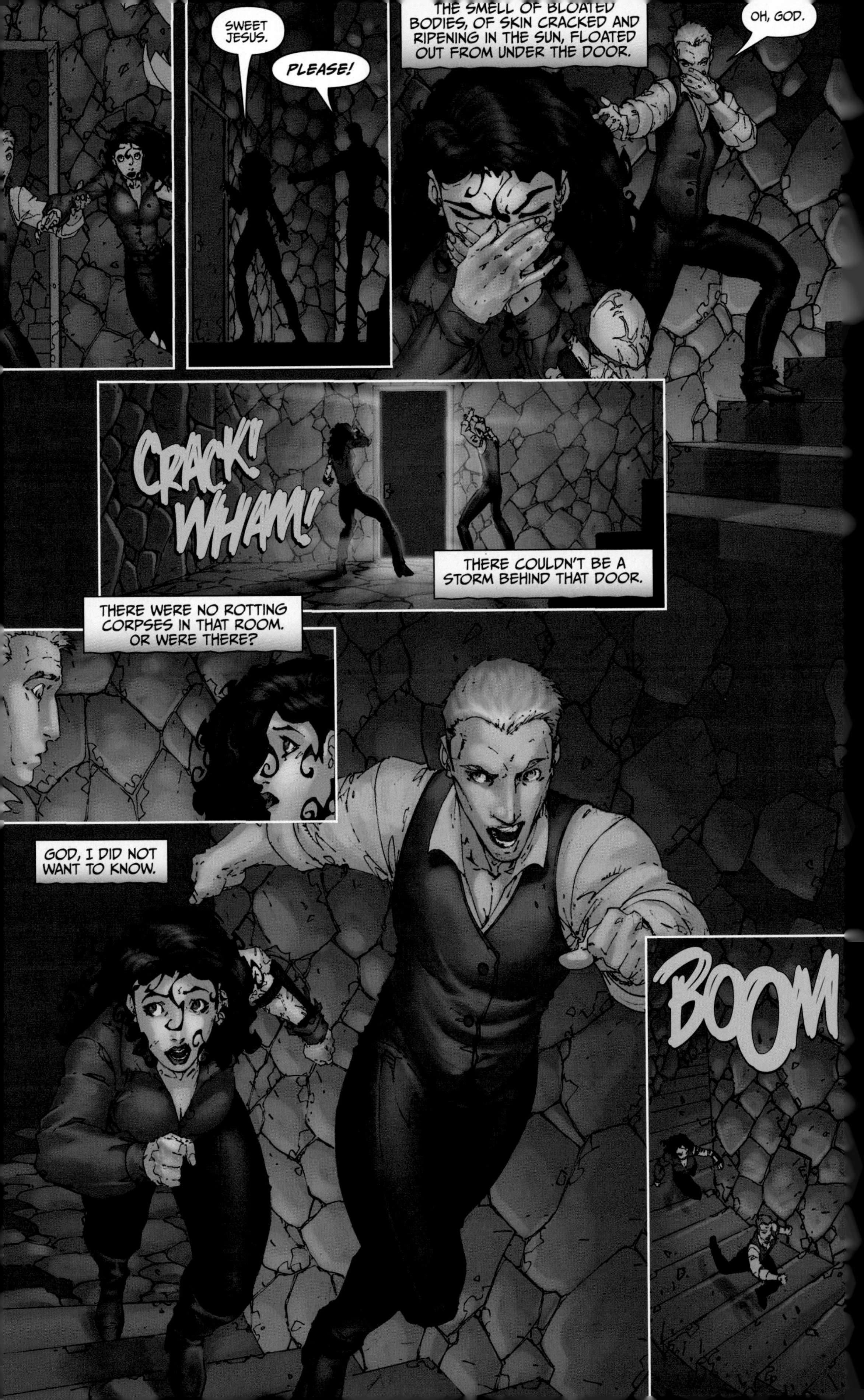
SWEET JESUS.
PLEASE!
THE SMELL OF BLOATED BODIES, OF SKIN CRACKED AND RIPENING IN THE SUN, FLOATED OUT FROM UNDER THE DOOR.
OH, GOD.
CRACK! WHAM!
THERE COULDN'T BE A STORM BEHIND THAT DOOR.
THERE WERE NO ROTTING CORPSES IN THAT ROOM. OR WERE THERE?
GOD, I DID NOT WANT TO KNOW.
BOOM

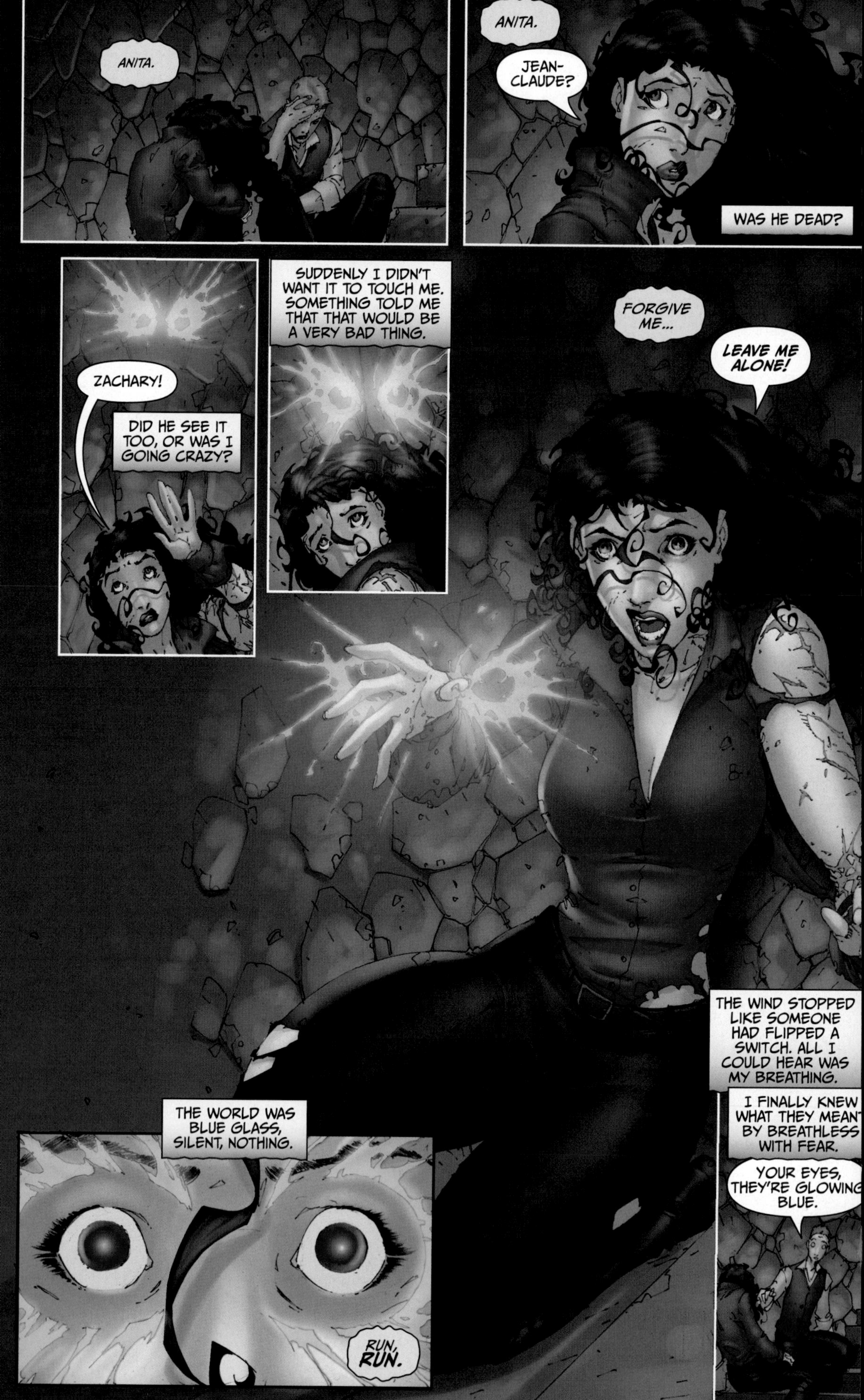
ANITA.
ANITA.
JEAN-CLAUDE?
WAS HE DEAD?
ZACHARY!
DID HE SEE IT TOO, OR WAS I GOING CRAZY?
SUDDENLY I DIDN'T WANT IT TO TOUCH ME. SOMETHING TOLD ME THAT THAT WOULD BE A VERY BAD THING.
FORGIVE ME...
LEAVE ME ALONE!
THE WIND STOPPED LIKE SOMEONE HAD FLIPPED A SWITCH. ALL I COULD HEAR WAS MY BREATHING.
I FINALLY KNEW WHAT THEY MEANT BY BREATHLESS WITH FEAR.
YOUR EYES, THEY'RE GLOWING BLUE.
THE WORLD WAS BLUE GLASS, SILENT, NOTHING.
RUN, RUN.

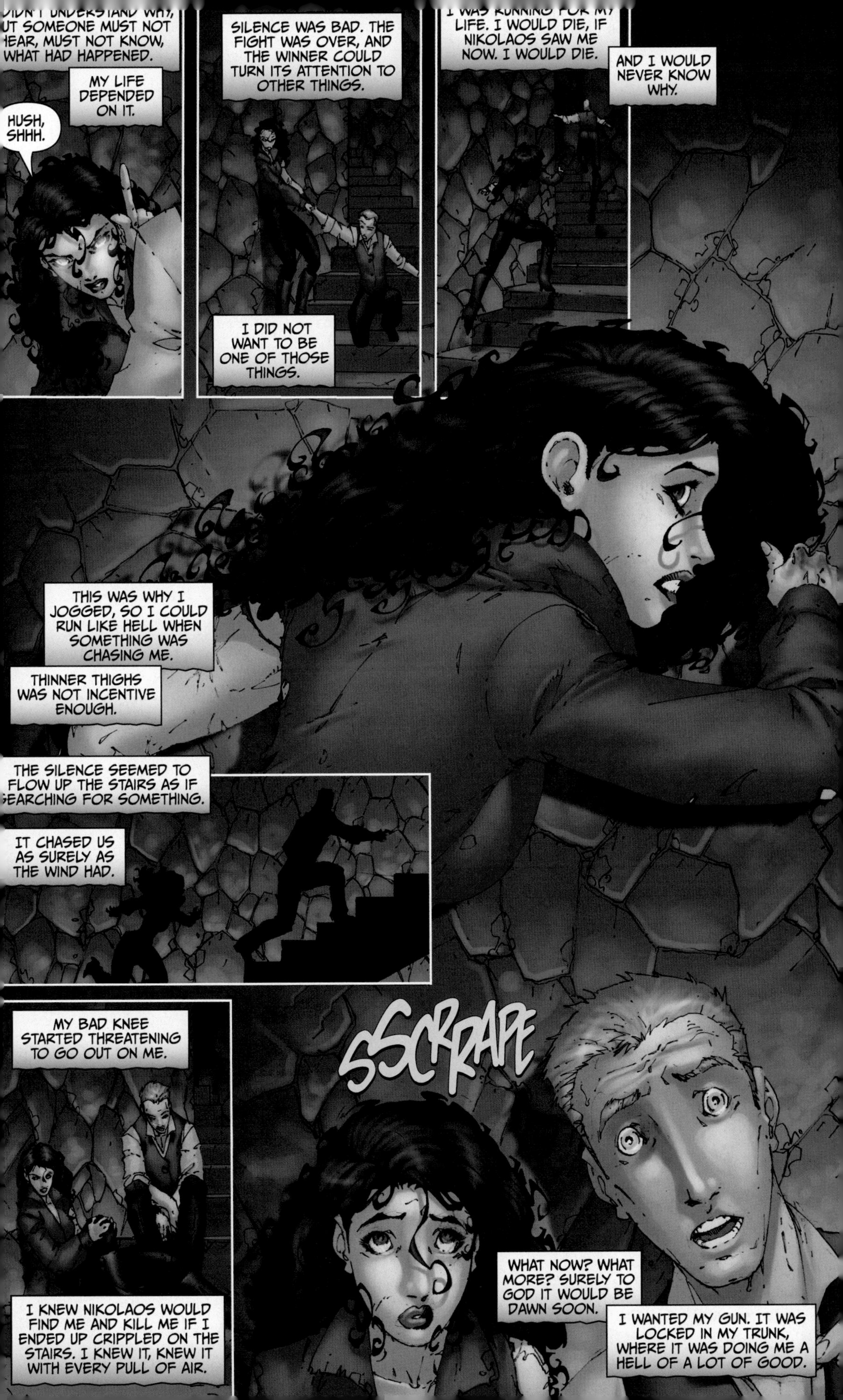

IDN'T UNDERSTAND WHY, UT SOMEONE MUST NOT HEAR, MUST NOT KNOW, WHAT HAD HAPPENED.
MY LIFE DEPENDED ON IT.
HUSH, SHHH.
SILENCE WAS BAD. THE FIGHT WAS OVER, AND THE WINNER COULD TURN ITS ATTENTION TO OTHER THINGS.
I DID NOT WANT TO BE ONE OF THOSE THINGS.
I WAS RUNNING FOR MY LIFE. I WOULD DIE, IF NIKOLAOS SAW ME NOW. I WOULD DIE.
AND I WOULD NEVER KNOW WHY.
THIS WAS WHY I JOGGED, SO I COULD RUN LIKE HELL WHEN SOMETHING WAS CHASING ME.
THINNER THIGHS WAS NOT INCENTIVE ENOUGH.
THE SILENCE SEEMED TO FLOW UP THE STAIRS AS IF SEARCHING FOR SOMETHING.
IT CHASED US AS SURELY AS THE WIND HAD.
MY BAD KNEE STARTED THREATENING TO GO OUT ON ME.
I KNEW NIKOLAOS WOULD FIND ME AND KILL ME IF I ENDED UP CRIPPLED ON THE STAIRS. I KNEW IT, KNEW IT WITH EVERY PULL OF AIR.
SSCRAPE
WHAT NOW? WHAT MORE? SURELY TO GOD IT WOULD BE DAWN SOON.
I WANTED MY GUN. IT WAS LOCKED IN MY TRUNK, WHERE IT WAS DOING ME A HELL OF A LOT OF GOOD.

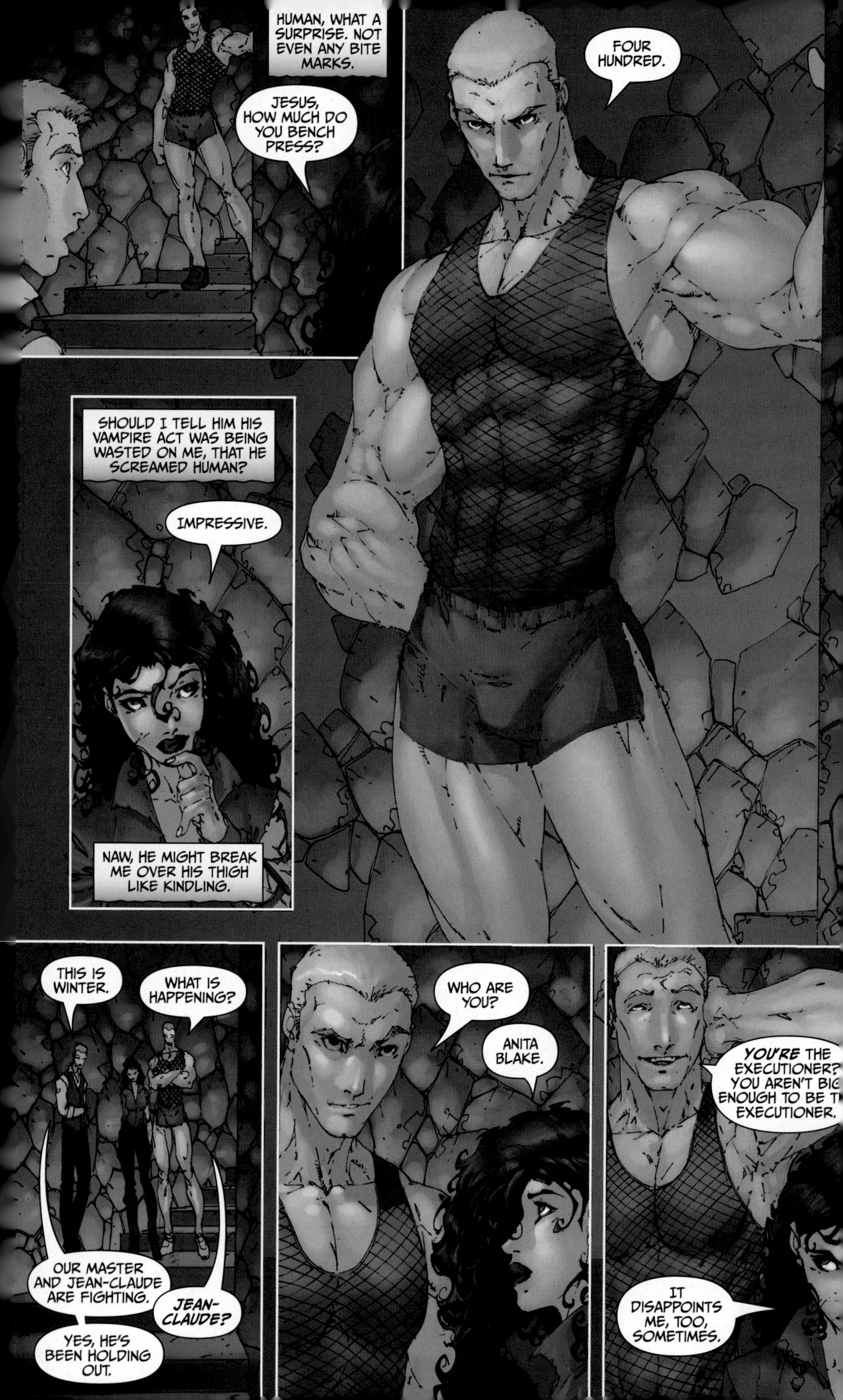
HUMAN, WHAT A SURPRISE. NOT EVEN ANY BITE MARKS.
JESUS, HOW MUCH DO YOU BENCH PRESS?
FOUR HUNDRED.
SHOULD I TELL HIM HIS VAMPIRE ACT WAS BEING WASTED ON ME, THAT HE SCREAMED HUMAN?
IMPRESSIVE.
NAW, HE MIGHT BREAK ME OVER HIS THIGH LIKE KINDLING.
THIS IS WINTER.
WHAT IS HAPPENING?
OUR MASTER AND JEAN-CLAUDE ARE FIGHTING.
JEAN-CLAUDE?
YES, HE'S BEEN HOLDING OUT.
WHO ARE YOU?
ANITA BLAKE.
YOU'RE THE EXECUTIONER? YOU AREN'T BIG ENOUGH TO BE THE EXECUTIONER.
IT DISAPPOINTS ME, TOO, SOMETIMES.

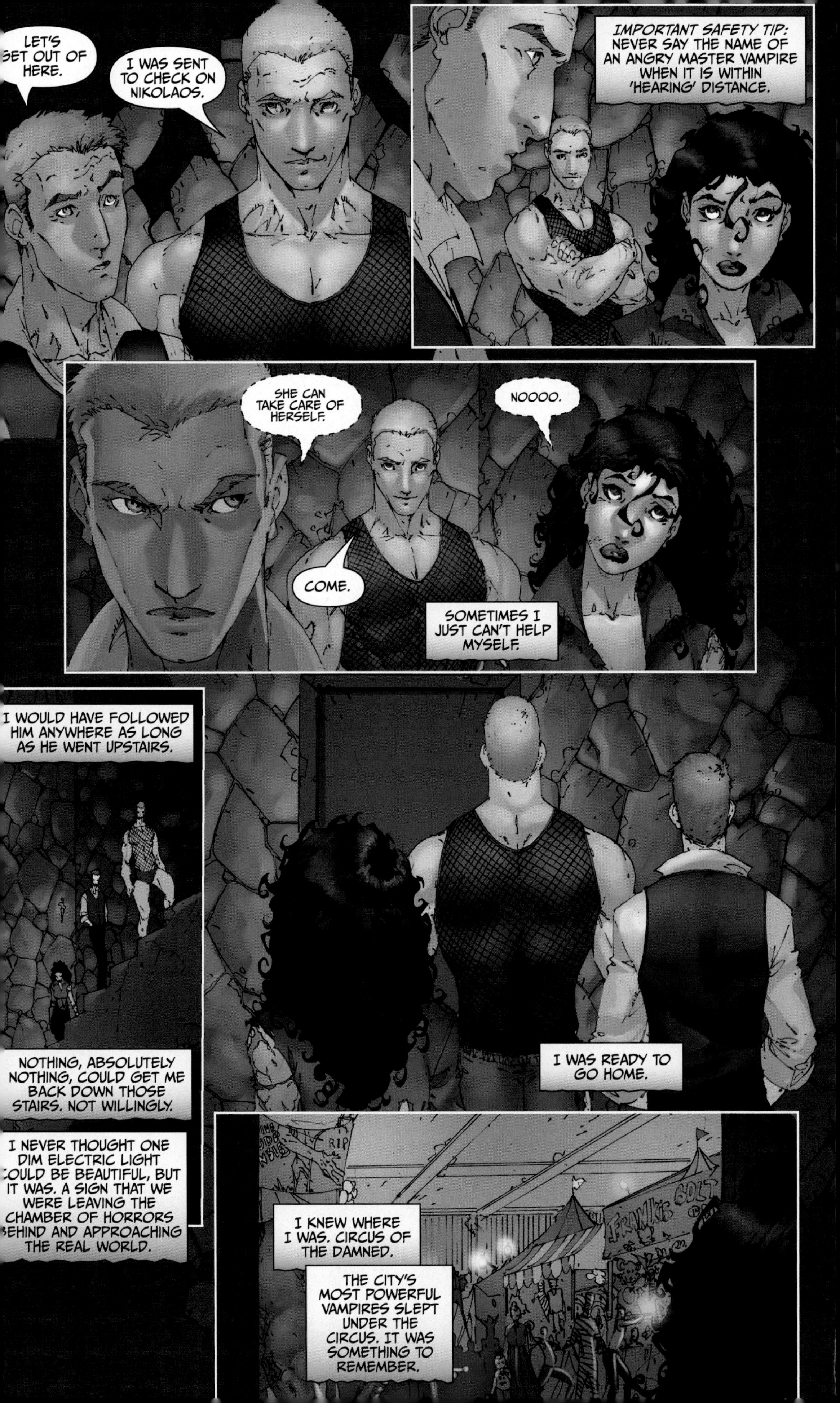
LET'S GET OUT OF HERE.
I WAS SENT TO CHECK ON NIKOLAOS.
IMPORTANT SAFETY TIP: NEVER SAY THE NAME OF AN ANGRY MASTER VAMPIRE WHEN IT IS WITHIN 'HEARING' DISTANCE.
SHE CAN TAKE CARE OF HERSELF.
NOOOO.
COME.
SOMETIMES I JUST CAN'T HELP MYSELF.
I WOULD HAVE FOLLOWED HIM ANYWHERE AS LONG AS HE WENT UPSTAIRS.
NOTHING, ABSOLUTELY NOTHING, COULD GET ME BACK DOWN THOSE STAIRS. NOT WILLINGLY.
I NEVER THOUGHT ONE DIM ELECTRIC LIGHT COULD BE BEAUTIFUL, BUT IT WAS. A SIGN THAT WE WERE LEAVING THE CHAMBER OF HORRORS BEHIND AND APPROACHING THE REAL WORLD.
I WAS READY TO GO HOME.
I KNEW WHERE I WAS. CIRCUS OF THE DAMNED.
THE CITY'S MOST POWERFUL VAMPIRES SLEPT UNDER THE CIRCUS. IT WAS SOMETHING TO REMEMBER.

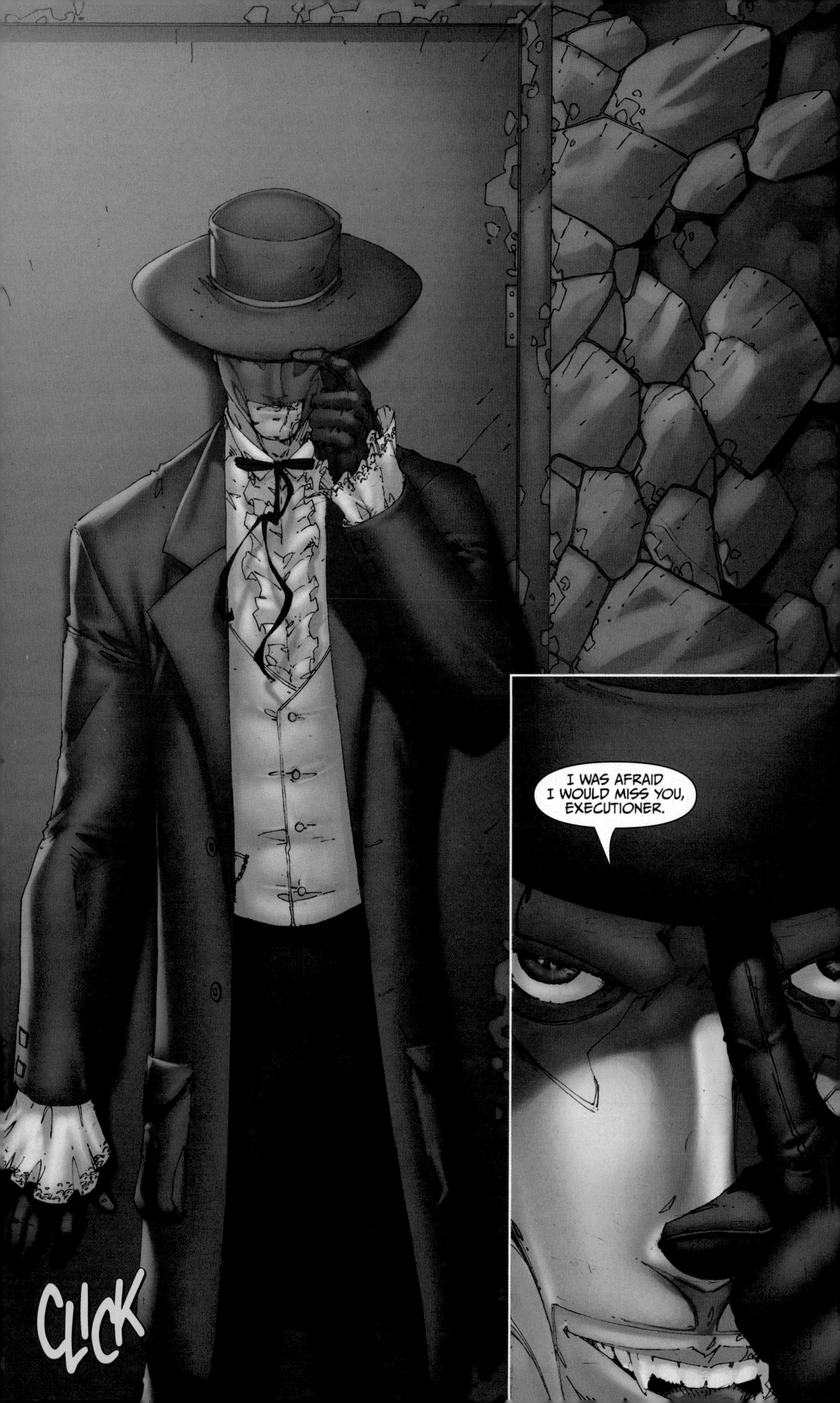
I WAS AFRAID
I WOULD MISS YOU,
EXECUTIONER.
CLICK

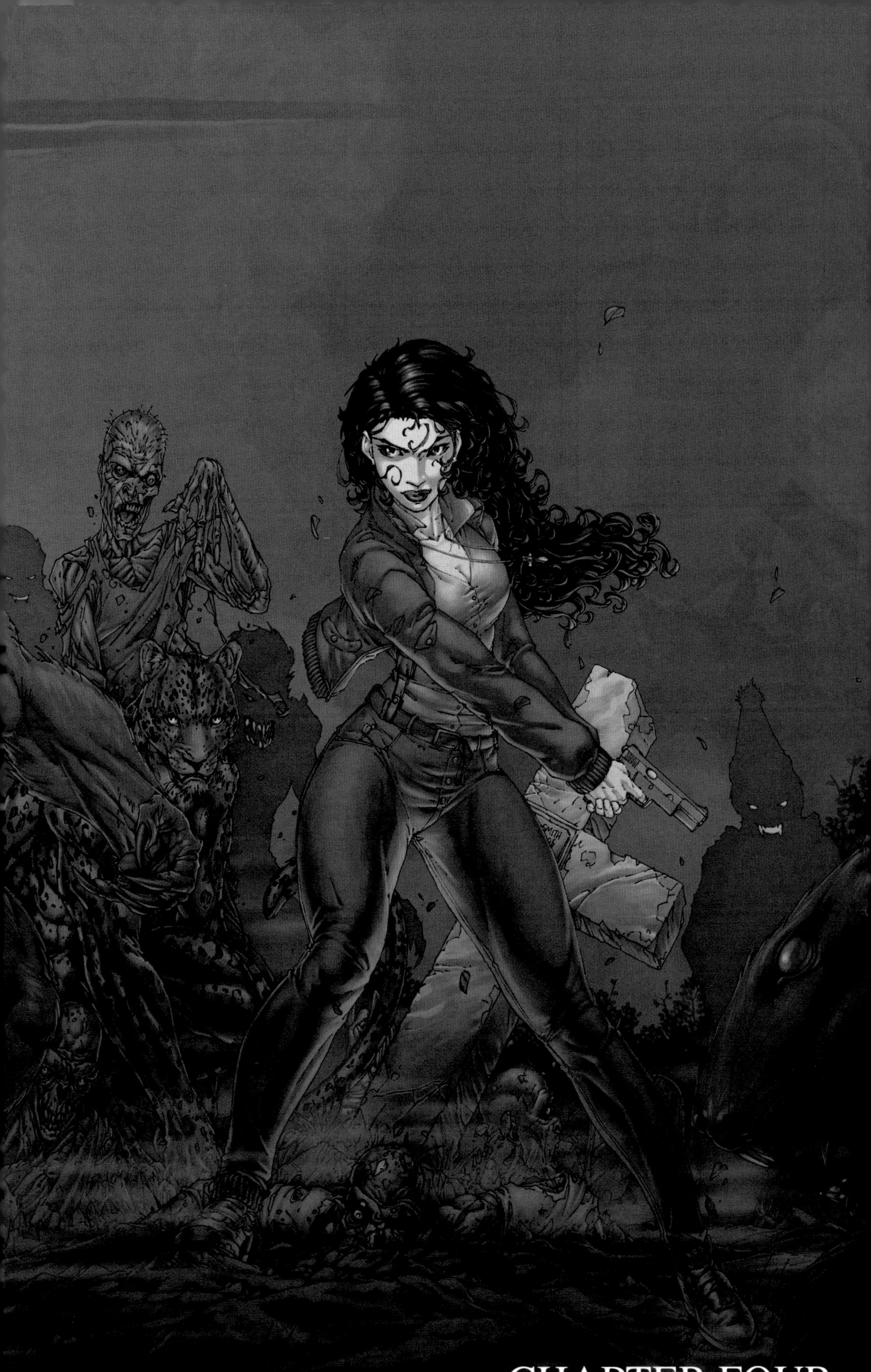

CHAPTER FOUR

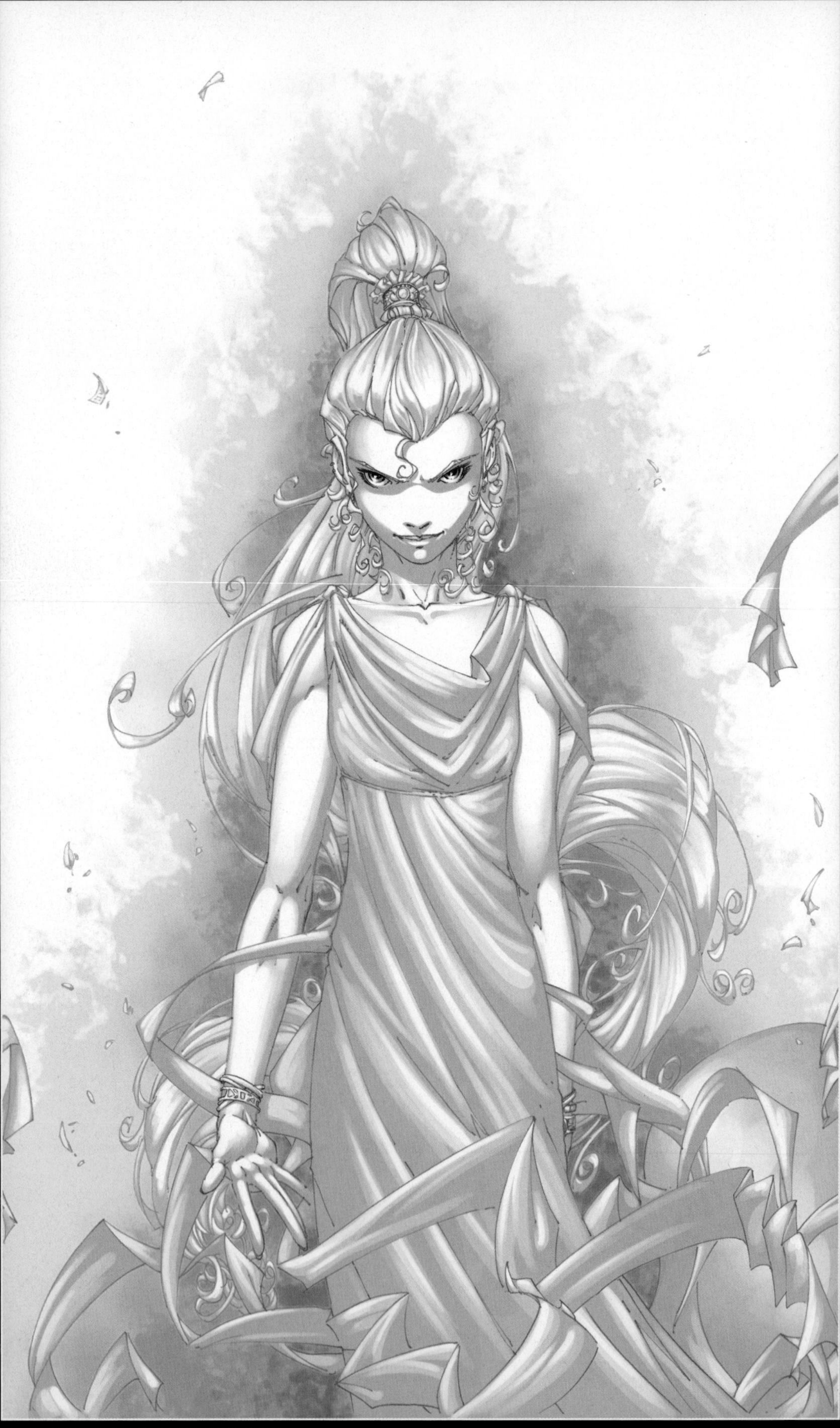

COVER BY: BRETT BOOTH & JESS RUFFNER-BOOTH

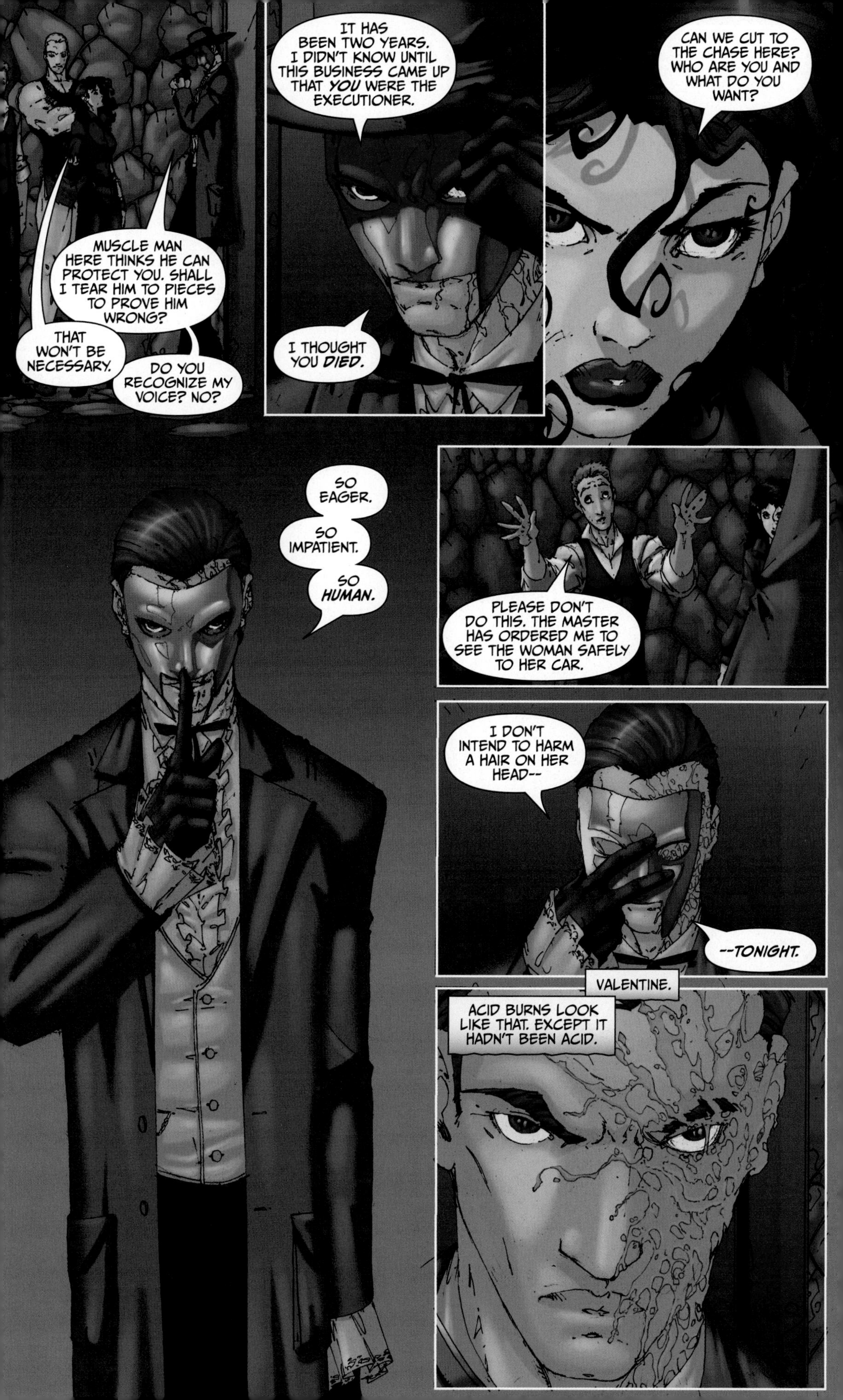
MUSCLE MAN HERE THINKS HE CAN PROTECT YOU. SHALL I TEAR HIM TO PIECES TO PROVE HIM WRONG?
THAT WON'T BE NECESSARY.
DO YOU RECOGNIZE MY VOICE? NO?
IT HAS BEEN TWO YEARS. I DIDN'T KNOW UNTIL THIS BUSINESS CAME UP THAT *YOU* WERE THE EXECUTIONER.
I THOUGHT YOU *DIED.*
CAN WE CUT TO THE CHASE HERE? WHO ARE YOU AND WHAT DO YOU WANT?
SO EAGER.
SO IMPATIENT.
SO *HUMAN.*
PLEASE DON'T DO THIS. THE MASTER HAS ORDERED ME TO SEE THE WOMAN SAFELY TO HER CAR.
I DON'T INTEND TO HARM A HAIR ON HER HEAD--
--TONIGHT.
VALENTINE.
ACID BURNS LOOK LIKE THAT. EXCEPT IT HADN'T BEEN ACID.

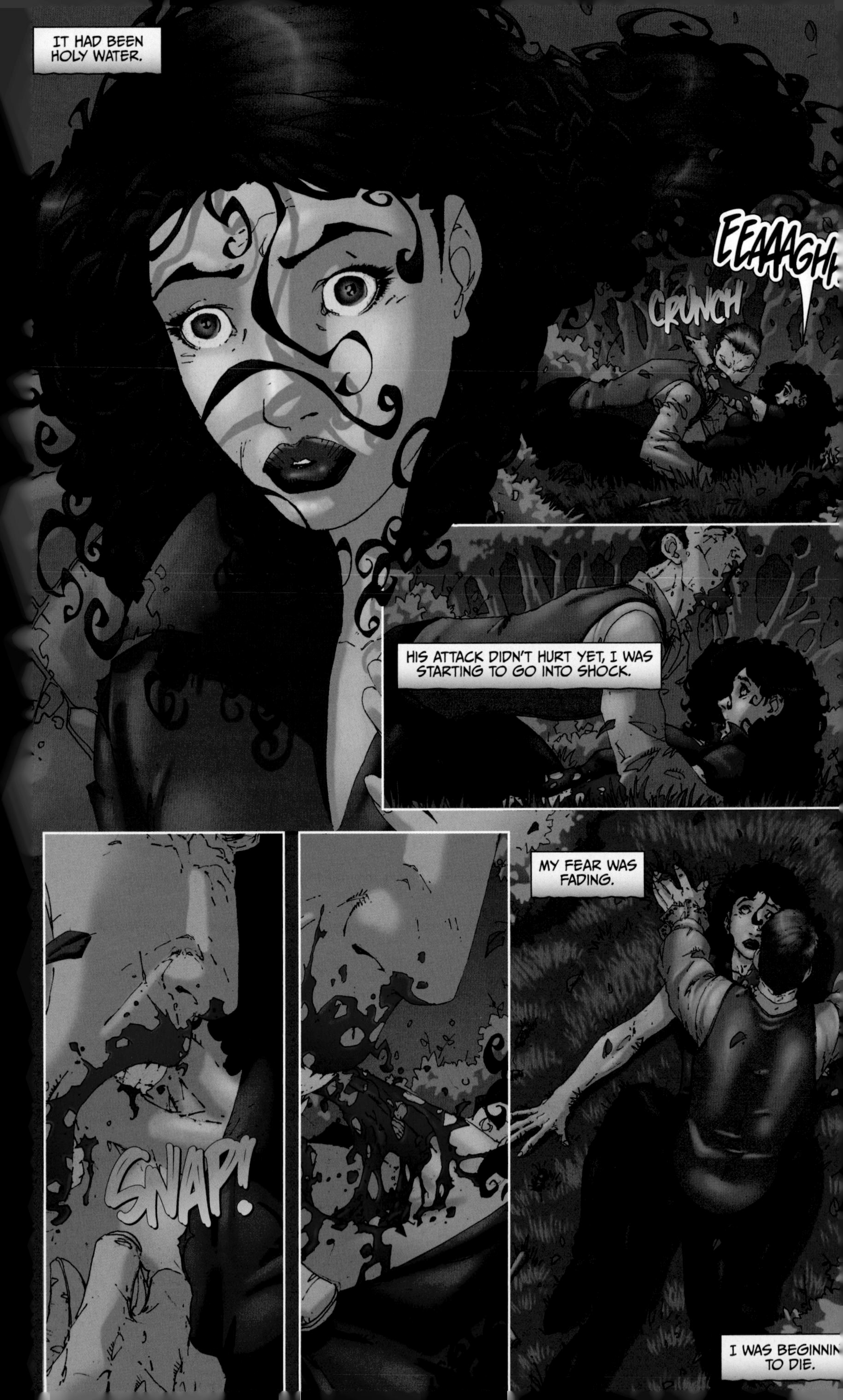
IT HAD BEEN HOLY WATER.
EEAAAGH!
CRUNCH
HIS ATTACK DIDN'T HURT YET, I WAS STARTING TO GO INTO SHOCK.
SNAP!
MY FEAR WAS FADING.
I WAS BEGINNIN TO DIE.

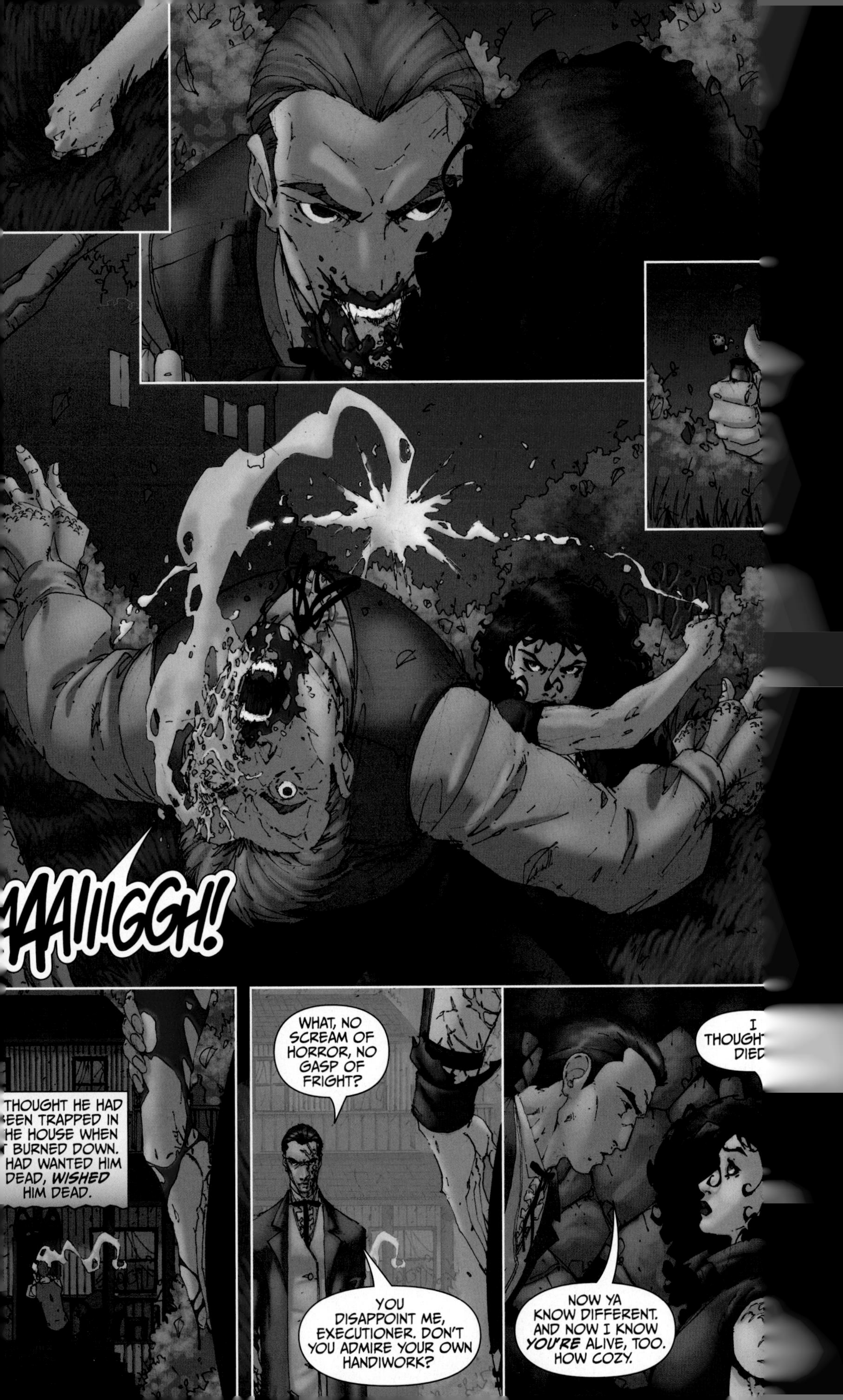

AAIIIGGH!
THOUGHT HE HAD
EEN TRAPPED IN
HE HOUSE WHEN
T BURNED DOWN.
HAD WANTED HIM
DEAD, WISHED
HIM DEAD.
WHAT, NO SCREAM OF HORROR, NO GASP OF FRIGHT?
YOU DISAPPOINT ME, EXECUTIONER. DON'T YOU ADMIRE YOUR OWN HANDIWORK?
I THOUGHT DIED
NOW YA KNOW DIFFERENT. AND NOW I KNOW YOU'RE ALIVE, TOO. HOW COZY.

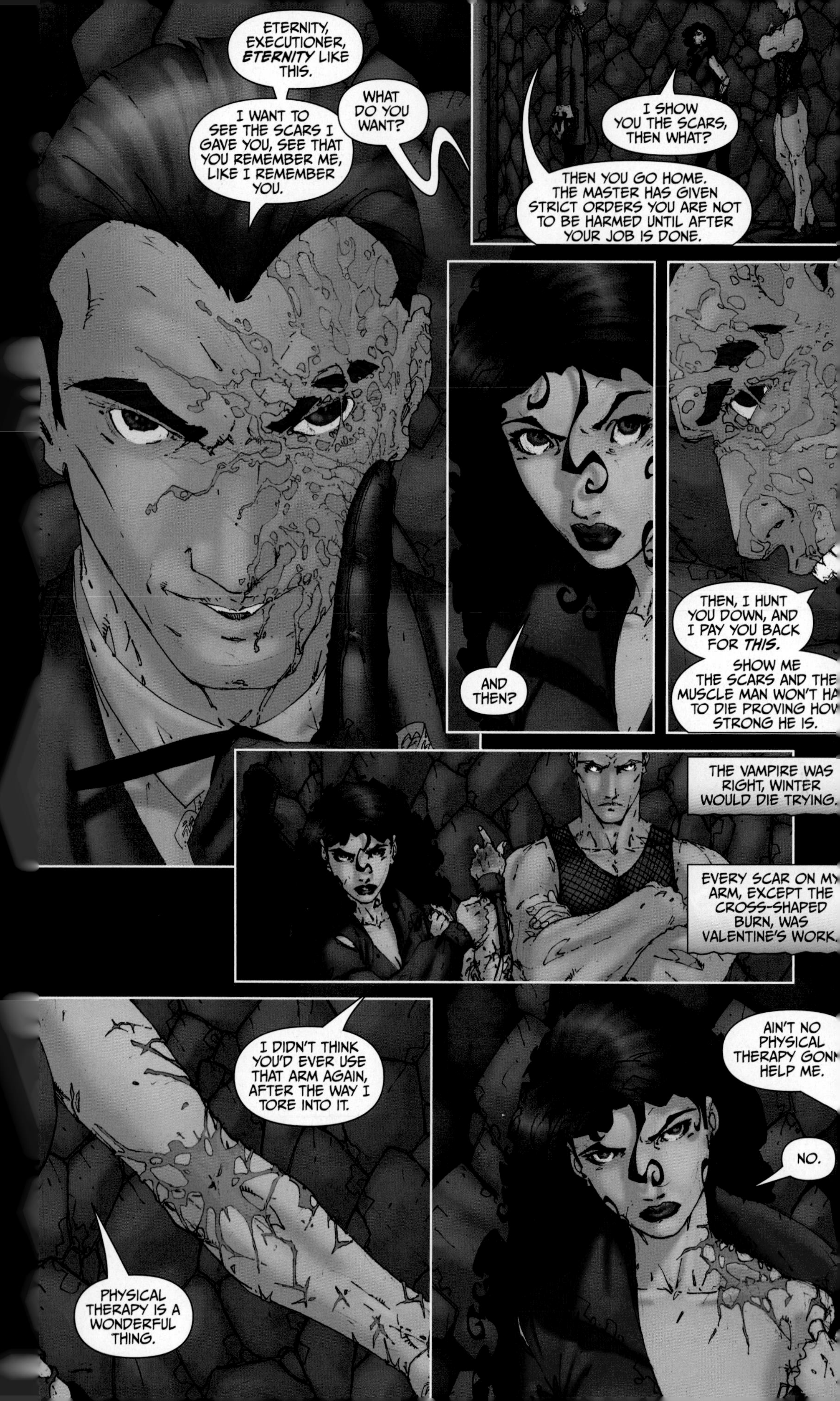
ETERNITY, EXECUTIONER, *ETERNITY* LIKE THIS.
I WANT TO SEE THE SCARS I GAVE YOU, SEE THAT YOU REMEMBER ME, LIKE I REMEMBER YOU.
WHAT DO YOU WANT?
I SHOW YOU THE SCARS, THEN WHAT?
THEN YOU GO HOME. THE MASTER HAS GIVEN STRICT ORDERS YOU ARE NOT TO BE HARMED UNTIL AFTER YOUR JOB IS DONE.
AND THEN?
THEN, I HUNT YOU DOWN, AND I PAY YOU BACK FOR *THIS.*
SHOW ME THE SCARS AND THE MUSCLE MAN WON'T HA TO DIE PROVING HOW STRONG HE IS.
THE VAMPIRE WAS RIGHT, WINTER WOULD DIE TRYING.
EVERY SCAR ON MY ARM, EXCEPT THE CROSS-SHAPED BURN, WAS VALENTINE'S WORK.
I DIDN'T THINK YOU'D EVER USE THAT ARM AGAIN, AFTER THE WAY I TORE INTO IT.
PHYSICAL THERAPY IS A WONDERFUL THING.
AIN'T NO PHYSICAL THERAPY GONN HELP ME.
NO.

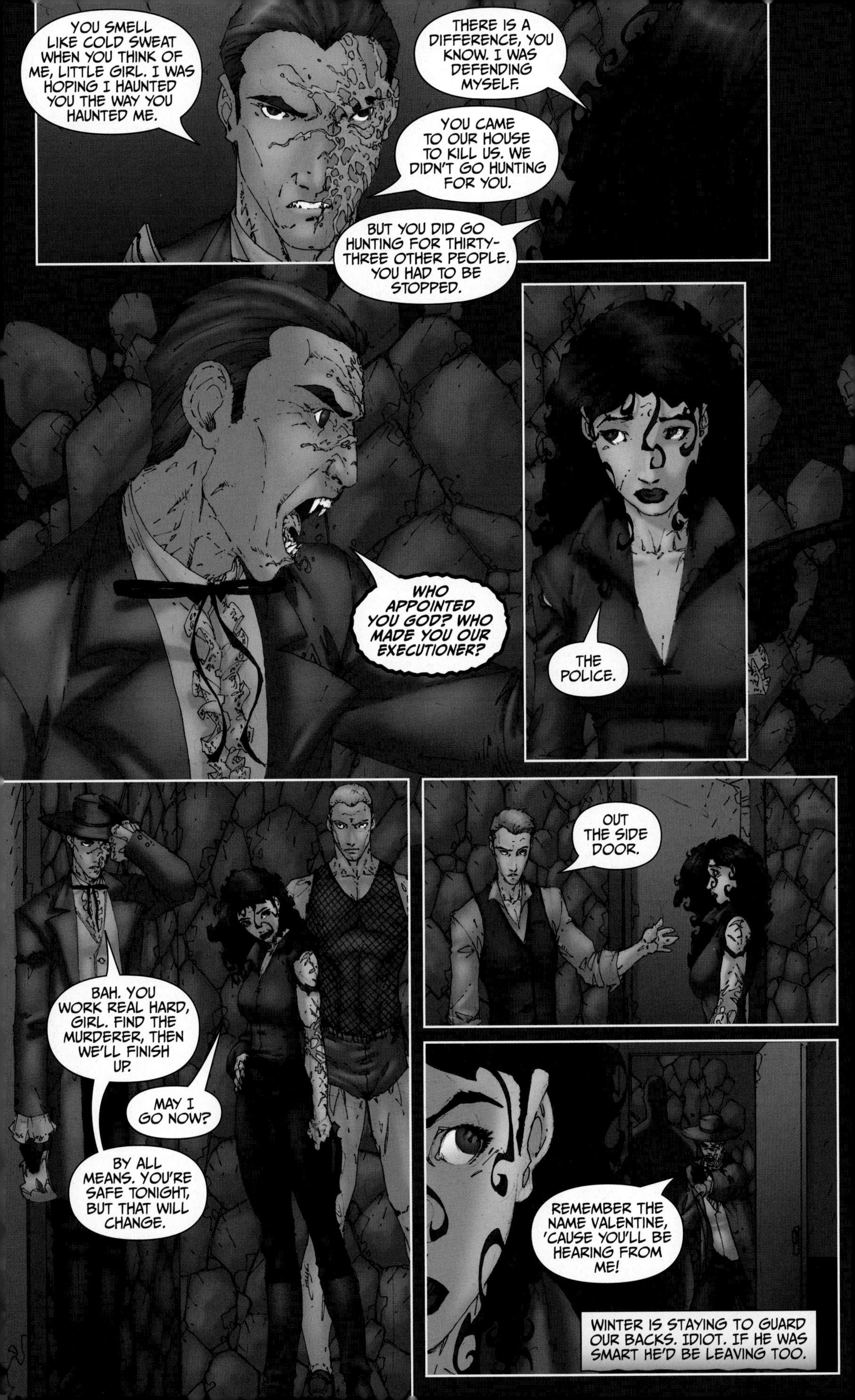

YOU SMELL LIKE COLD SWEAT WHEN YOU THINK OF ME, LITTLE GIRL. I WAS HOPING I HAUNTED YOU THE WAY YOU HAUNTED ME.
THERE IS A DIFFERENCE, YOU KNOW. I WAS DEFENDING MYSELF.
YOU CAME TO OUR HOUSE TO KILL US. WE DIDN'T GO HUNTING FOR YOU.
BUT YOU DID GO HUNTING FOR THIRTY-THREE OTHER PEOPLE. YOU HAD TO BE STOPPED.
WHO APPOINTED YOU GOD? WHO MADE YOU OUR EXECUTIONER?
THE POLICE.
BAH. YOU WORK REAL HARD, GIRL. FIND THE MURDERER, THEN WE'LL FINISH UP.
MAY I GO NOW?
BY ALL MEANS. YOU'RE SAFE TONIGHT, BUT THAT WILL CHANGE.
OUT THE SIDE DOOR.
REMEMBER THE NAME VALENTINE, 'CAUSE YOU'LL BE HEARING FROM ME!
WINTER IS STAYING TO GUARD OUR BACKS. IDIOT. IF HE WAS SMART HE'D BE LEAVING TOO.

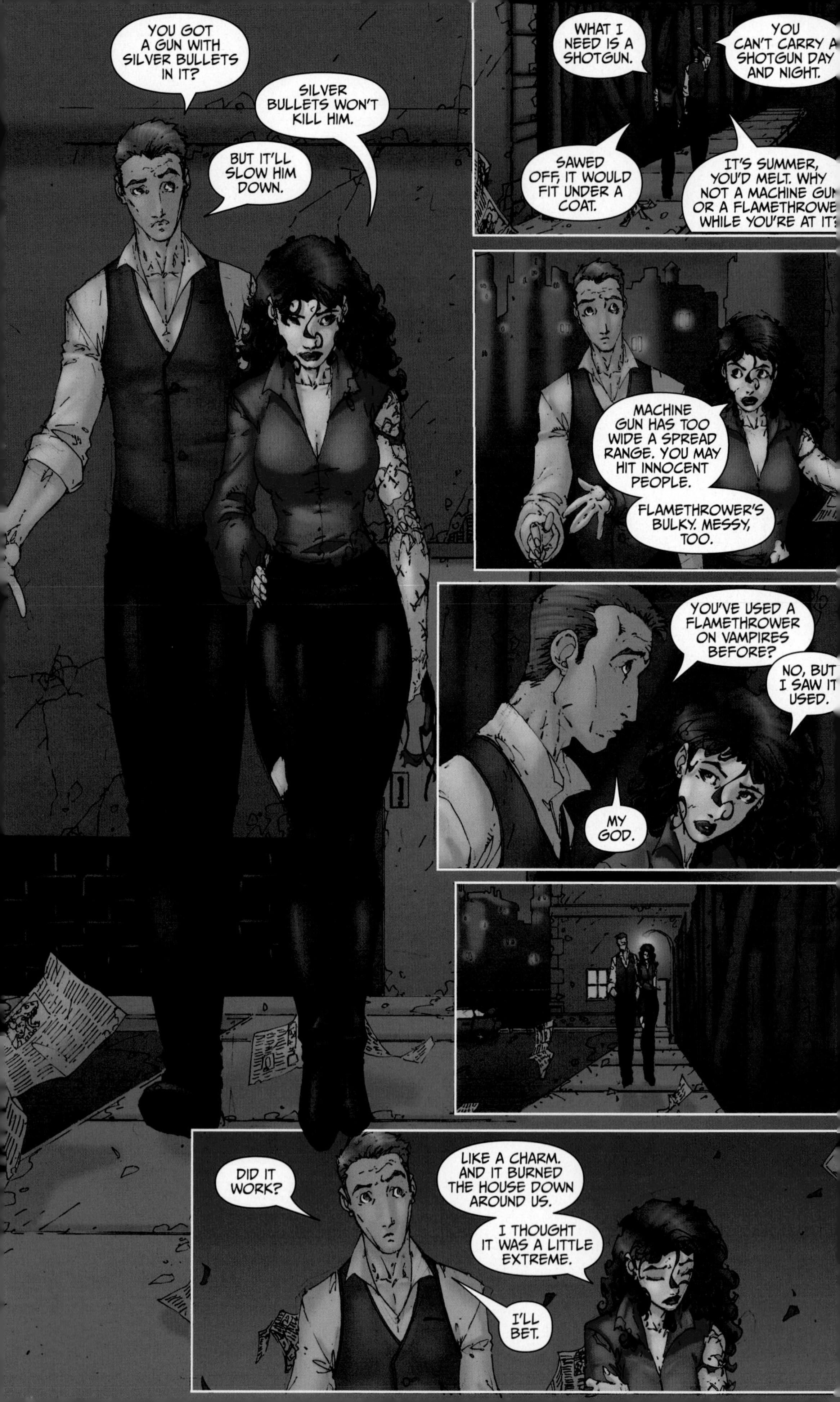

YOU GOT A GUN WITH SILVER BULLETS IN IT?
SILVER BULLETS WON'T KILL HIM.
BUT IT'LL SLOW HIM DOWN.
WHAT I NEED IS A SHOTGUN.
YOU CAN'T CARRY A SHOTGUN DAY AND NIGHT.
SAWED OFF, IT WOULD FIT UNDER A COAT.
IT'S SUMMER, YOU'D MELT. WHY NOT A MACHINE GUN OR A FLAMETHROWER WHILE YOU'RE AT IT?
MACHINE GUN HAS TOO WIDE A SPREAD RANGE. YOU MAY HIT INNOCENT PEOPLE.
FLAMETHROWER'S BULKY. MESSY, TOO.
YOU'VE USED A FLAMETHROWER ON VAMPIRES BEFORE?
NO, BUT I SAW IT USED.
MY GOD.
DID IT WORK?
LIKE A CHARM. AND IT BURNED THE HOUSE DOWN AROUND US.
I THOUGHT IT WAS A LITTLE EXTREME.
I'LL BET.

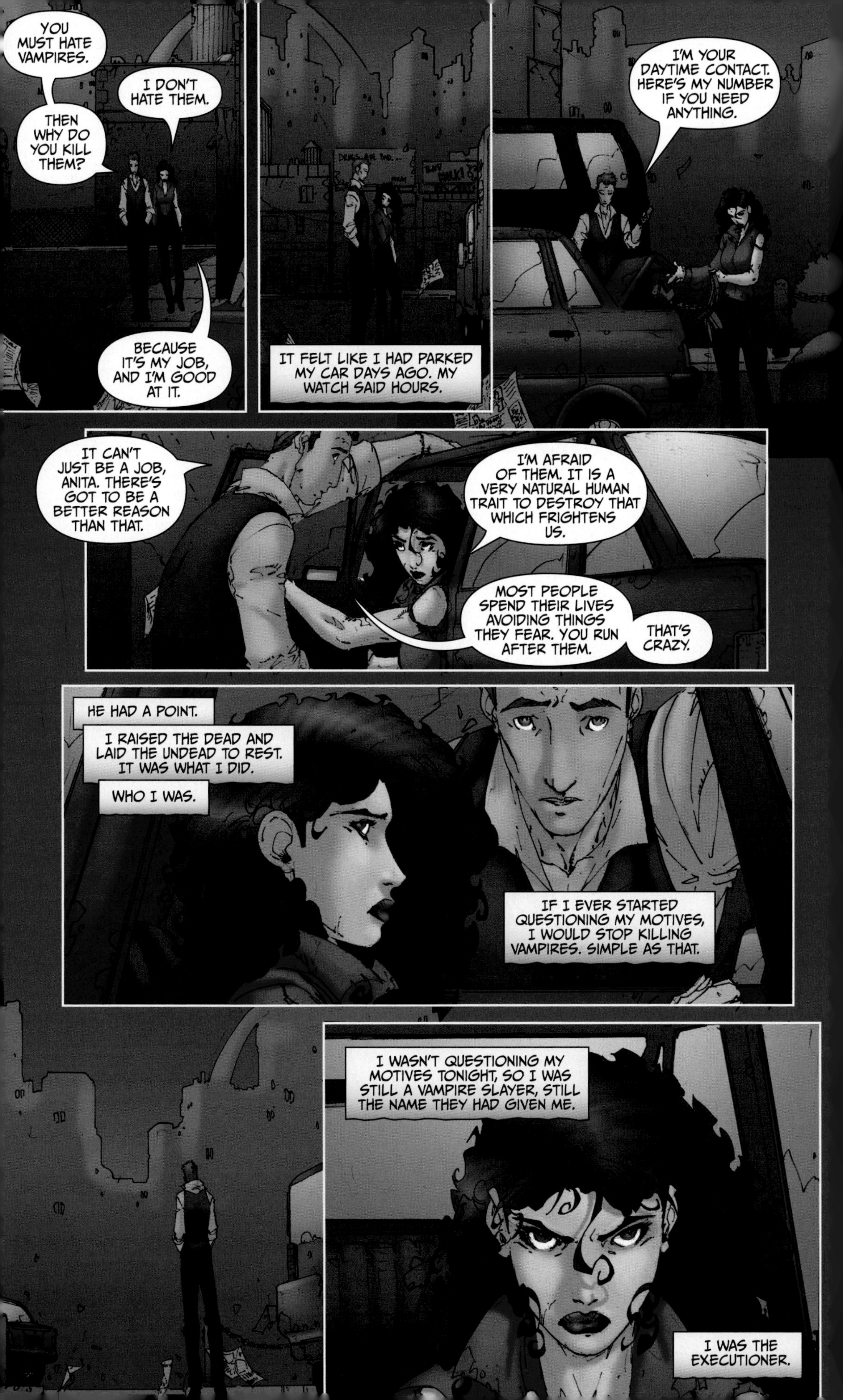
YOU MUST HATE VAMPIRES.
I DON'T HATE THEM.
THEN WHY DO YOU KILL THEM?
BECAUSE IT'S MY JOB, AND I'M GOOD AT IT.
IT FELT LIKE I HAD PARKED MY CAR DAYS AGO. MY WATCH SAID HOURS.
I'M YOUR DAYTIME CONTACT. HERE'S MY NUMBER IF YOU NEED ANYTHING.
IT CAN'T JUST BE A JOB, ANITA. THERE'S GOT TO BE A BETTER REASON THAN THAT.
I'M AFRAID OF THEM. IT IS A VERY NATURAL HUMAN TRAIT TO DESTROY THAT WHICH FRIGHTENS US.
MOST PEOPLE SPEND THEIR LIVES AVOIDING THINGS THEY FEAR. YOU RUN AFTER THEM.
THAT'S CRAZY.
HE HAD A POINT.
I RAISED THE DEAD AND LAID THE UNDEAD TO REST. IT WAS WHAT I DID.
WHO I WAS.
IF I EVER STARTED QUESTIONING MY MOTIVES, I WOULD STOP KILLING VAMPIRES. SIMPLE AS THAT.
I WASN'T QUESTIONING MY MOTIVES TONIGHT, SO I WAS STILL A VAMPIRE SLAYER, STILL THE NAME THEY HAD GIVEN ME.
I WAS THE EXECUTIONER.

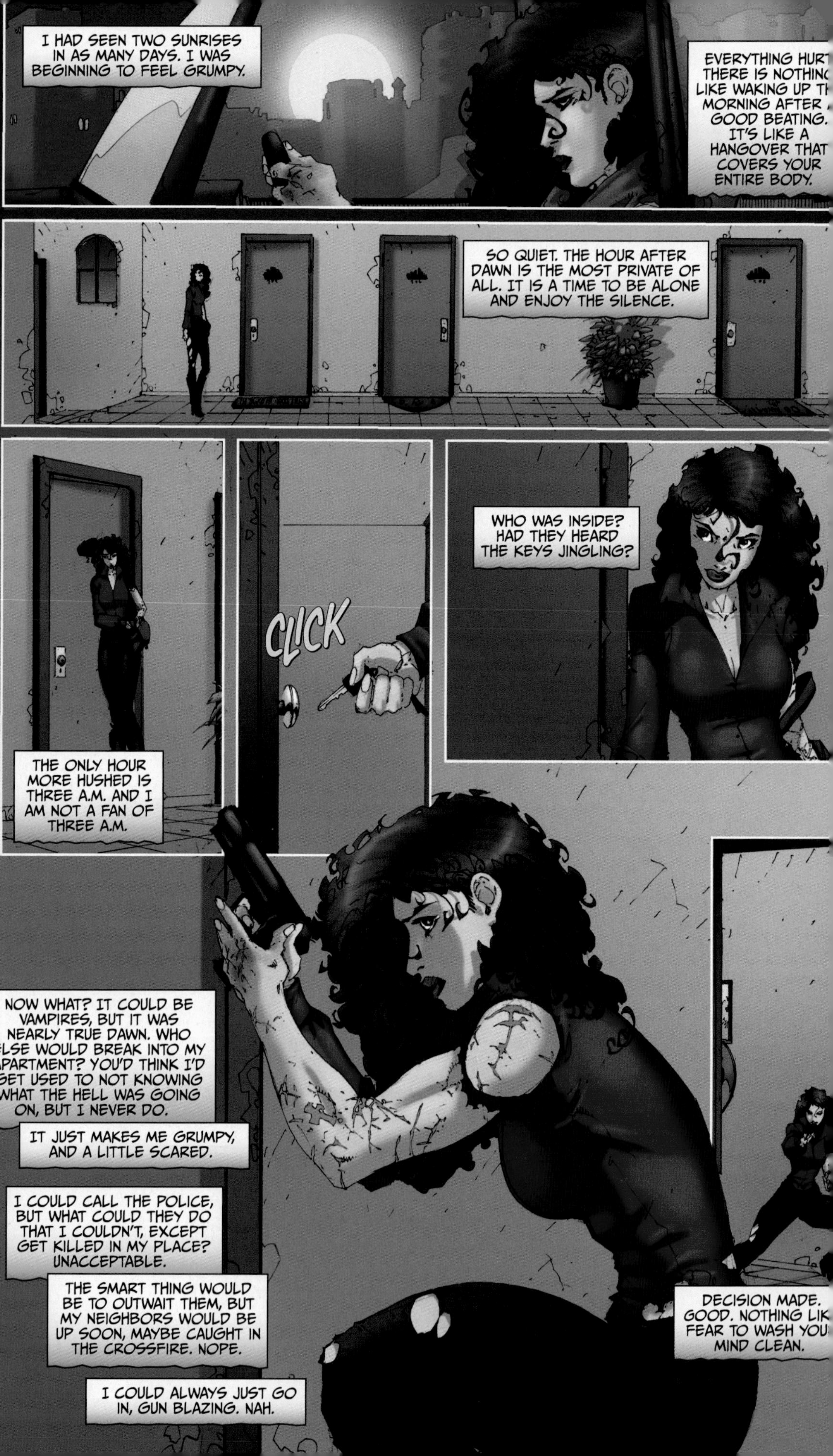
I HAD SEEN TWO SUNRISES IN AS MANY DAYS. I WAS BEGINNING TO FEEL GRUMPY.
EVERYTHING HURT. THERE IS NOTHING LIKE WAKING UP TH MORNING AFTER A GOOD BEATING. IT'S LIKE A HANGOVER THAT COVERS YOUR ENTIRE BODY.
SO QUIET. THE HOUR AFTER DAWN IS THE MOST PRIVATE OF ALL. IT IS A TIME TO BE ALONE AND ENJOY THE SILENCE.
THE ONLY HOUR MORE HUSHED IS THREE A.M. AND I AM NOT A FAN OF THREE A.M.
CLICK
WHO WAS INSIDE? HAD THEY HEARD THE KEYS JINGLING?
NOW WHAT? IT COULD BE VAMPIRES, BUT IT WAS NEARLY TRUE DAWN. WHO ELSE WOULD BREAK INTO MY APARTMENT? YOU'D THINK I'D GET USED TO NOT KNOWING WHAT THE HELL WAS GOING ON, BUT I NEVER DO.
IT JUST MAKES ME GRUMPY, AND A LITTLE SCARED.
I COULD CALL THE POLICE, BUT WHAT COULD THEY DO THAT I COULDN'T, EXCEPT GET KILLED IN MY PLACE? UNACCEPTABLE.
THE SMART THING WOULD BE TO OUTWAIT THEM, BUT MY NEIGHBORS WOULD BE UP SOON, MAYBE CAUGHT IN THE CROSSFIRE. NOPE.
I COULD ALWAYS JUST GO IN, GUN BLAZING. NAH.
DECISION MADE. GOOD. NOTHING LIK FEAR TO WASH YOU MIND CLEAN.

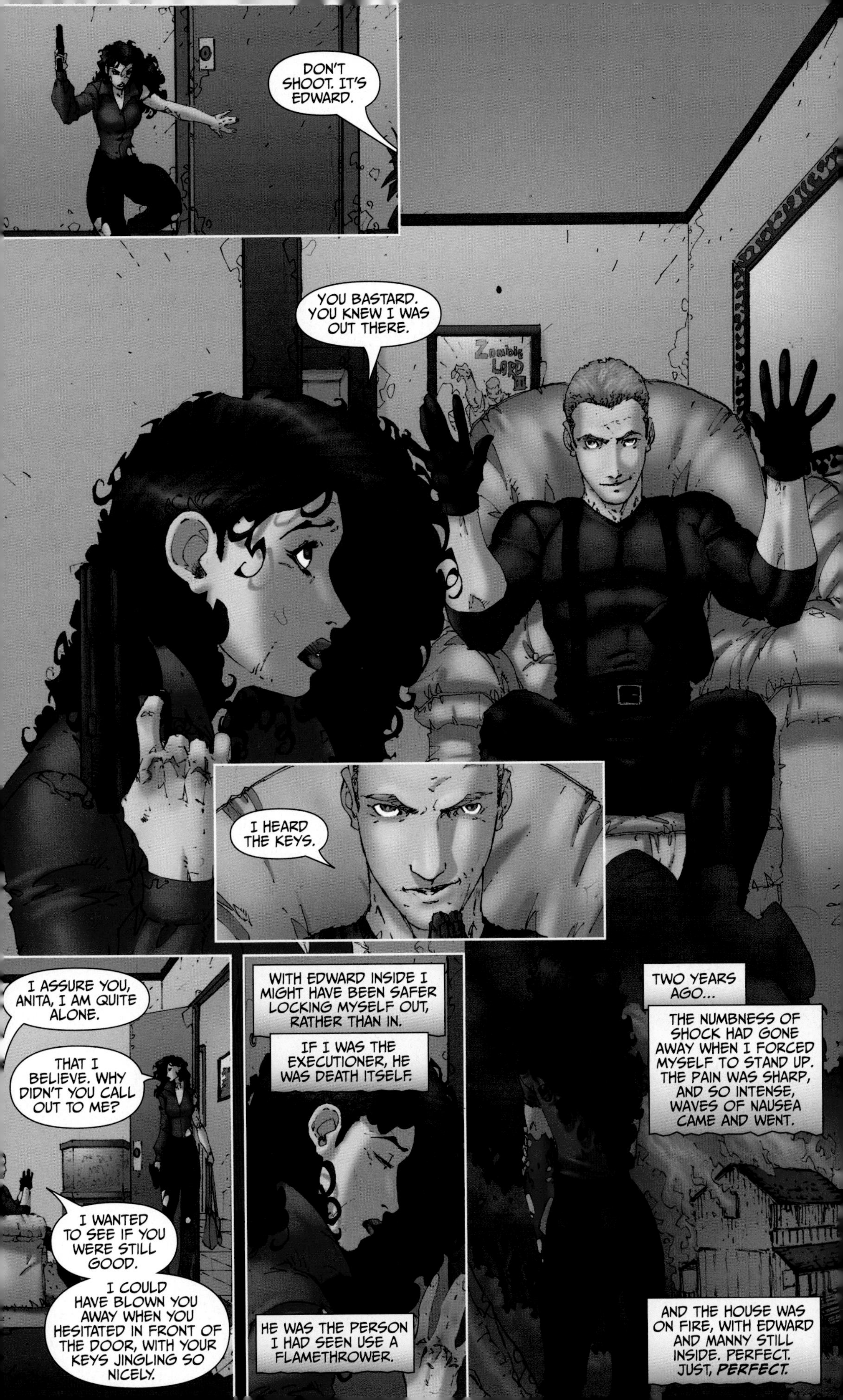
DON'T SHOOT. IT'S EDWARD.
YOU BASTARD. YOU KNEW I WAS OUT THERE.
ZOMBIE LORD III
I HEARD THE KEYS.
I ASSURE YOU, ANITA, I AM QUITE ALONE.
THAT I BELIEVE. WHY DIDN'T YOU CALL OUT TO ME?
I WANTED TO SEE IF YOU WERE STILL GOOD.
I COULD HAVE BLOWN YOU AWAY WHEN YOU HESITATED IN FRONT OF THE DOOR, WITH YOUR KEYS JINGLING SO NICELY.
WITH EDWARD INSIDE I MIGHT HAVE BEEN SAFER LOCKING MYSELF OUT, RATHER THAN IN.
IF I WAS THE EXECUTIONER, HE WAS DEATH ITSELF.
HE WAS THE PERSON I HAD SEEN USE A FLAMETHROWER.
TWO YEARS AGO...
THE NUMBNESS OF SHOCK HAD GONE AWAY WHEN I FORCED MYSELF TO STAND UP. THE PAIN WAS SHARP, AND SO INTENSE, WAVES OF NAUSEA CAME AND WENT.
AND THE HOUSE WAS ON FIRE, WITH EDWARD AND MANNY STILL INSIDE. PERFECT. JUST, PERFECT.

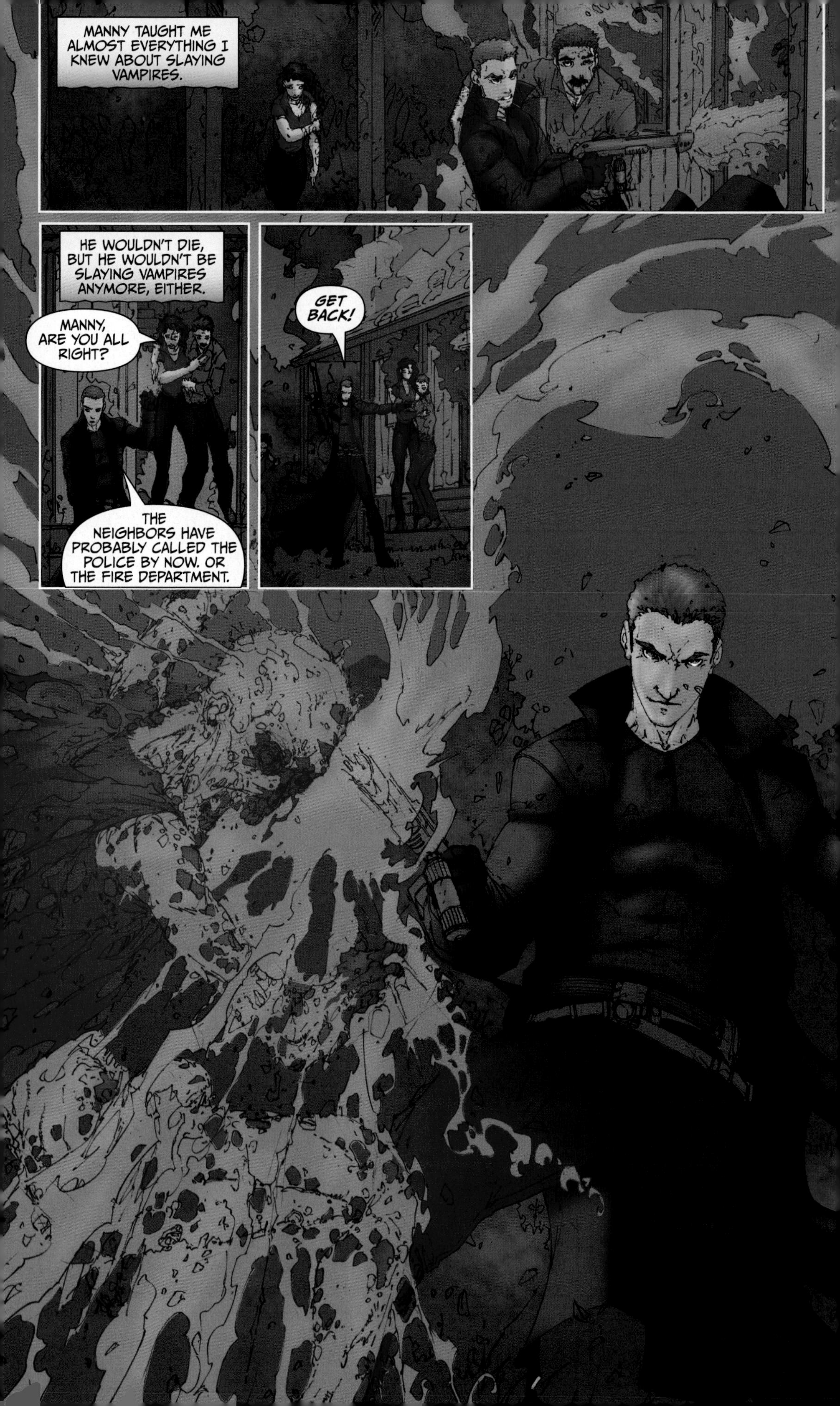
MANNY TAUGHT ME ALMOST EVERYTHING I KNEW ABOUT SLAYING VAMPIRES.
HE WOULDN'T DIE, BUT HE WOULDN'T BE SLAYING VAMPIRES ANYMORE, EITHER.
MANNY, ARE YOU ALL RIGHT?
THE NEIGHBORS HAVE PROBABLY CALLED THE POLICE BY NOW. OR THE FIRE DEPARTMENT.
GET BACK!

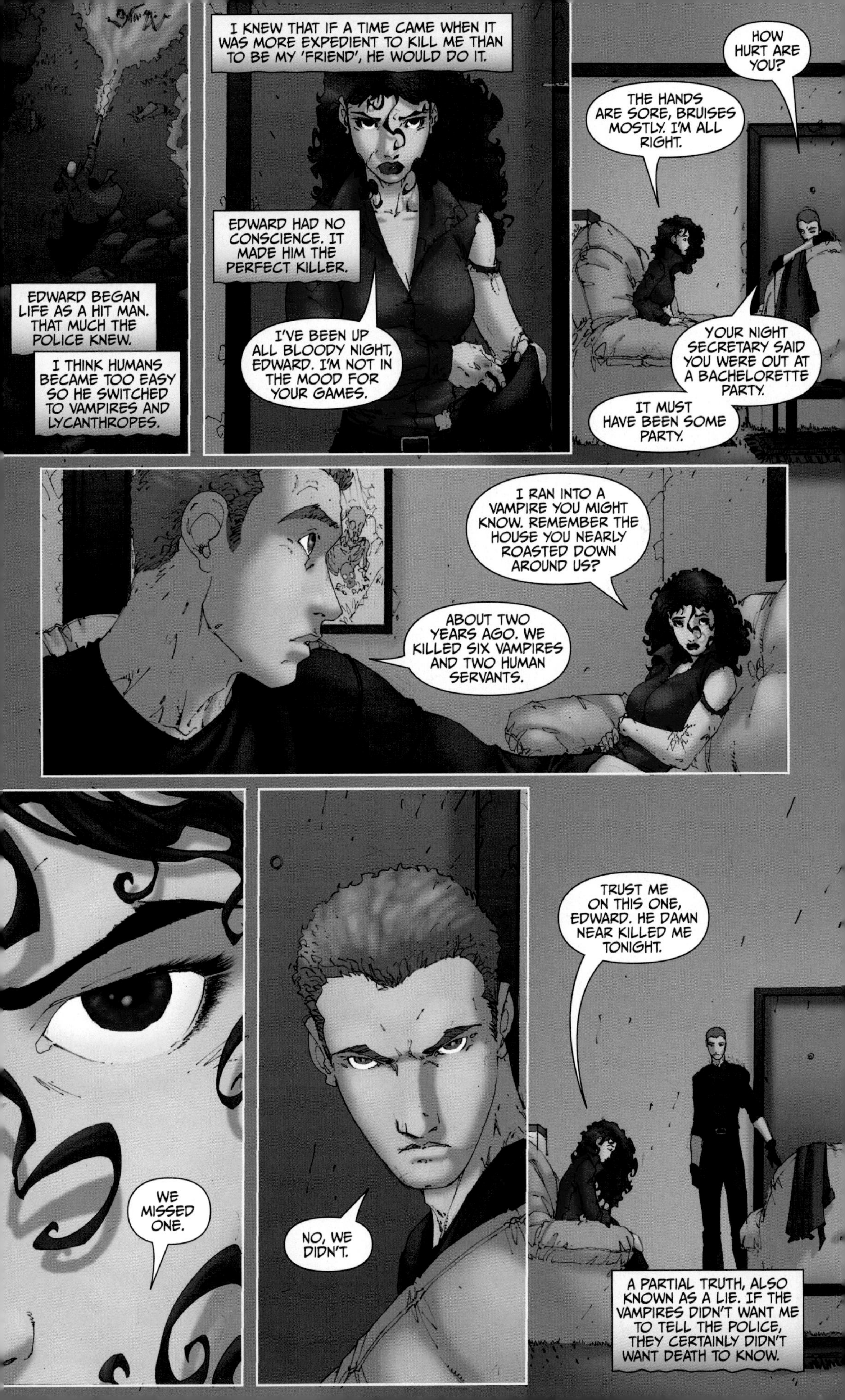
EDWARD BEGAN LIFE AS A HIT MAN. THAT MUCH THE POLICE KNEW.
I THINK HUMANS BECAME TOO EASY SO HE SWITCHED TO VAMPIRES AND LYCANTHROPES.
I KNEW THAT IF A TIME CAME WHEN IT WAS MORE EXPEDIENT TO KILL ME THAN TO BE MY 'FRIEND', HE WOULD DO IT.
EDWARD HAD NO CONSCIENCE. IT MADE HIM THE PERFECT KILLER.
I'VE BEEN UP ALL BLOODY NIGHT, EDWARD. I'M NOT IN THE MOOD FOR YOUR GAMES.
HOW HURT ARE YOU?
THE HANDS ARE SORE, BRUISES MOSTLY. I'M ALL RIGHT.
YOUR NIGHT SECRETARY SAID YOU WERE OUT AT A BACHELORETTE PARTY.
IT MUST HAVE BEEN SOME PARTY.
I RAN INTO A VAMPIRE YOU MIGHT KNOW. REMEMBER THE HOUSE YOU NEARLY ROASTED DOWN AROUND US?
ABOUT TWO YEARS AGO. WE KILLED SIX VAMPIRES AND TWO HUMAN SERVANTS.
WE MISSED ONE.
NO, WE DIDN'T.
TRUST ME ON THIS ONE, EDWARD. HE DAMN NEAR KILLED ME TONIGHT.
A PARTIAL TRUTH, ALSO KNOWN AS A LIE. IF THE VAMPIRES DIDN'T WANT ME TO TELL THE POLICE, THEY CERTAINLY DIDN'T WANT DEATH TO KNOW.

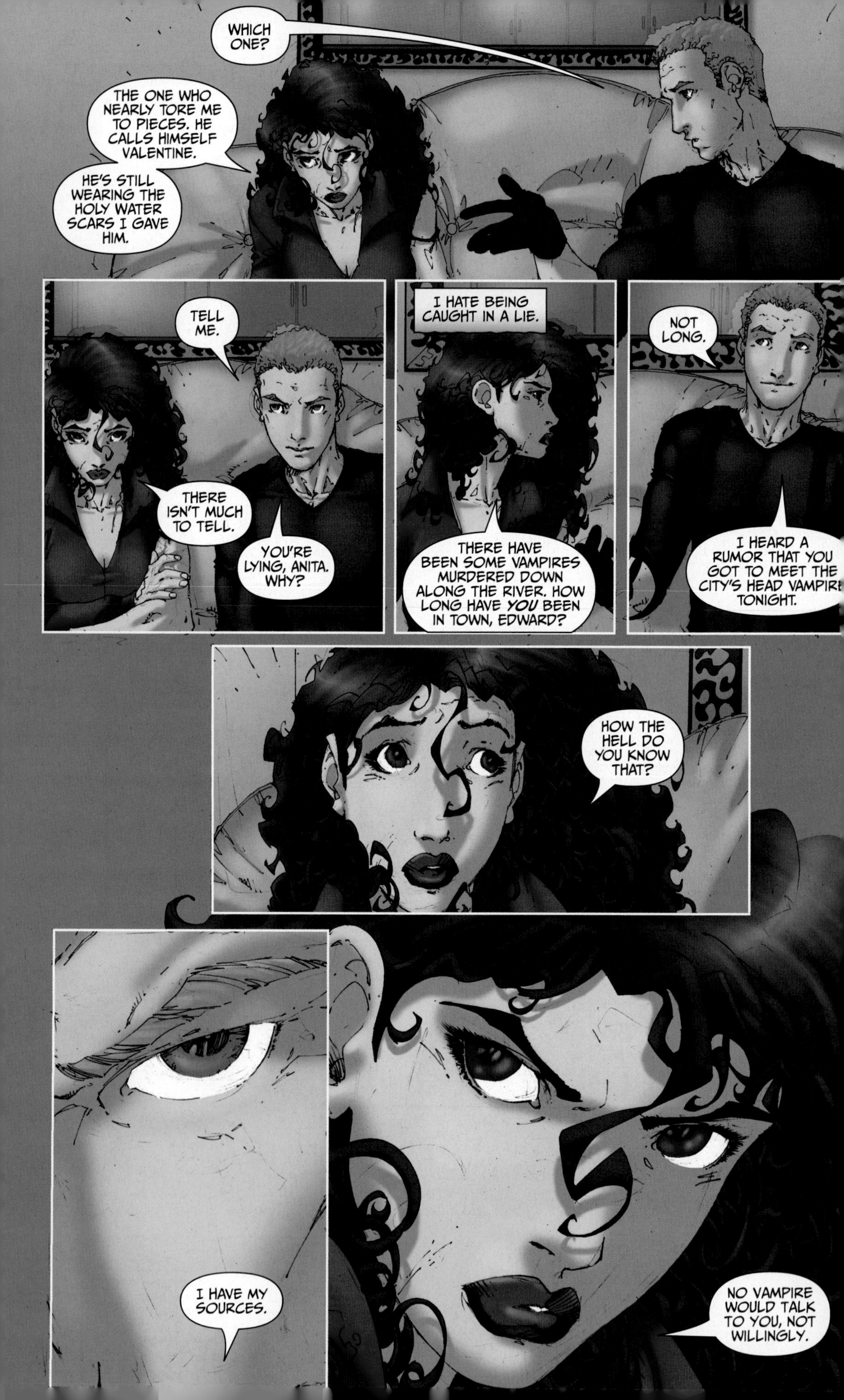
WHICH ONE?
THE ONE WHO NEARLY TORE ME TO PIECES. HE CALLS HIMSELF VALENTINE.
HE'S STILL WEARING THE HOLY WATER SCARS I GAVE HIM.
TELL ME.
THERE ISN'T MUCH TO TELL.
YOU'RE LYING, ANITA. WHY?
I HATE BEING CAUGHT IN A LIE.
THERE HAVE BEEN SOME VAMPIRES MURDERED DOWN ALONG THE RIVER. HOW LONG HAVE *YOU* BEEN IN TOWN, EDWARD?
NOT LONG.
I HEARD A RUMOR THAT YOU GOT TO MEET THE CITY'S HEAD VAMPIRE TONIGHT.
HOW THE HELL DO YOU KNOW THAT?
I HAVE MY SOURCES.
NO VAMPIRE WOULD TALK TO YOU, NOT WILLINGLY.

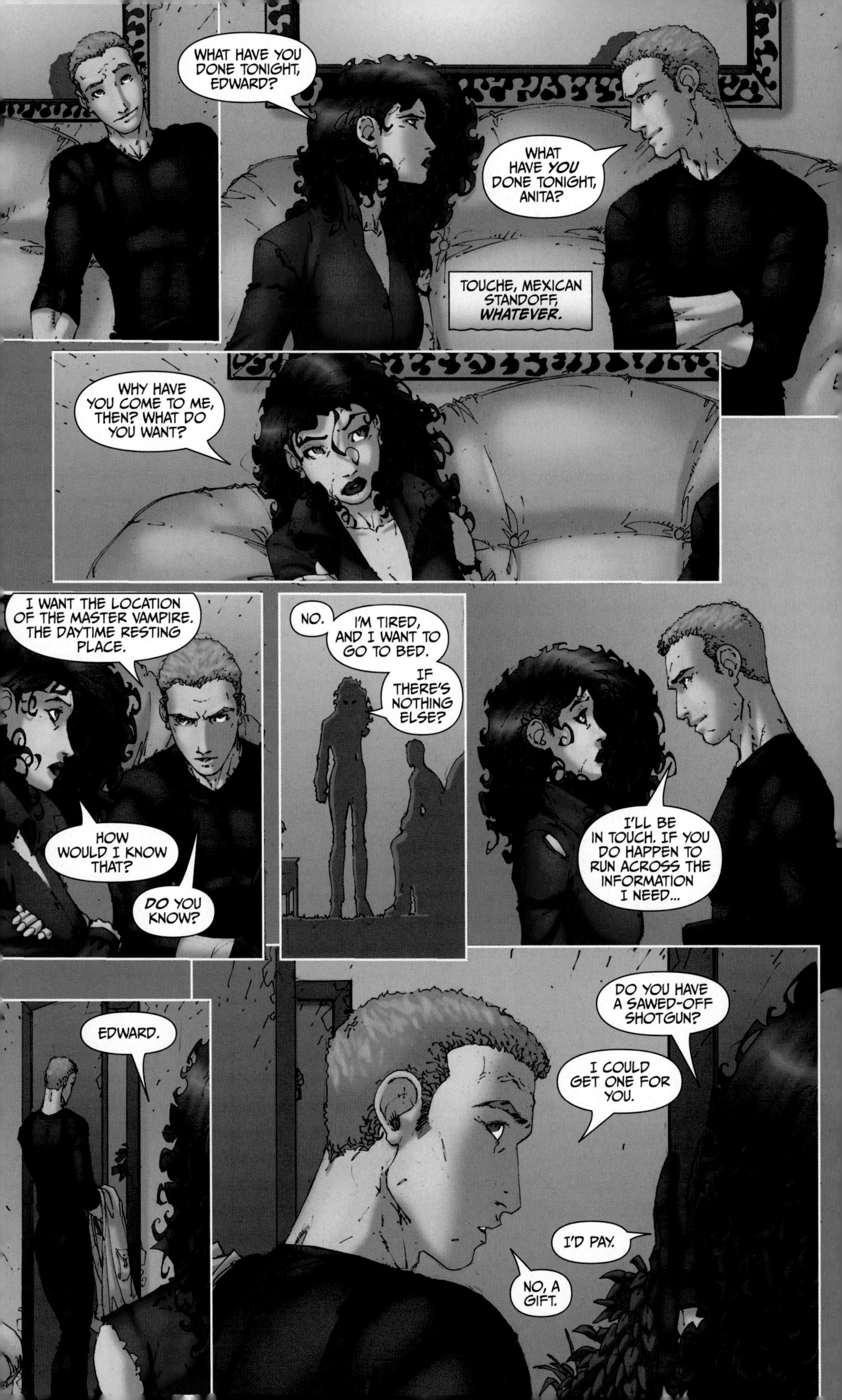

WHAT HAVE YOU DONE TONIGHT, EDWARD?
WHAT HAVE YOU DONE TONIGHT, ANITA?
TOUCHE, MEXICAN STANDOFF, WHATEVER.
WHY HAVE YOU COME TO ME, THEN? WHAT DO YOU WANT?
I WANT THE LOCATION OF THE MASTER VAMPIRE. THE DAYTIME RESTING PLACE.
HOW WOULD I KNOW THAT?
DO YOU KNOW?
NO.
I'M TIRED, AND I WANT TO GO TO BED.
IF THERE'S NOTHING ELSE?
I'LL BE IN TOUCH. IF YOU DO HAPPEN TO RUN ACROSS THE INFORMATION I NEED...
EDWARD.
DO YOU HAVE A SAWED-OFF SHOTGUN?
I COULD GET ONE FOR YOU.
I'D PAY.
NO, A GIFT.

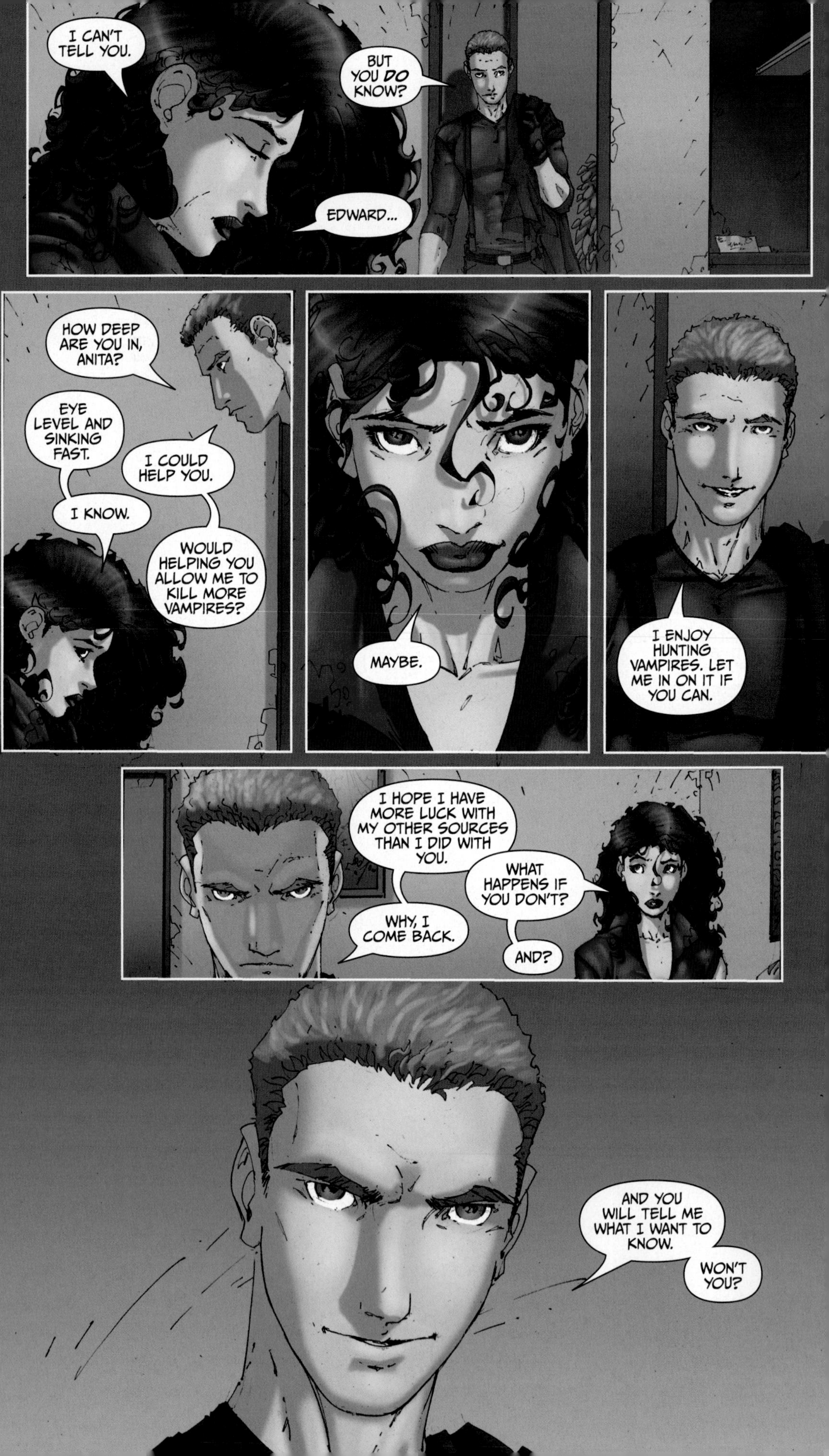
I CAN'T TELL YOU.
BUT YOU DO KNOW?
EDWARD...
HOW DEEP ARE YOU IN, ANITA?
EYE LEVEL AND SINKING FAST.
I COULD HELP YOU.
I KNOW.
WOULD HELPING YOU ALLOW ME TO KILL MORE VAMPIRES?
MAYBE.
I ENJOY HUNTING VAMPIRES. LET ME IN ON IT IF YOU CAN.
I HOPE I HAVE MORE LUCK WITH MY OTHER SOURCES THAN I DID WITH YOU.
WHAT HAPPENS IF YOU DON'T?
WHY, I COME BACK.
AND?
AND YOU WILL TELL ME WHAT I WANT TO KNOW.
WON'T YOU?

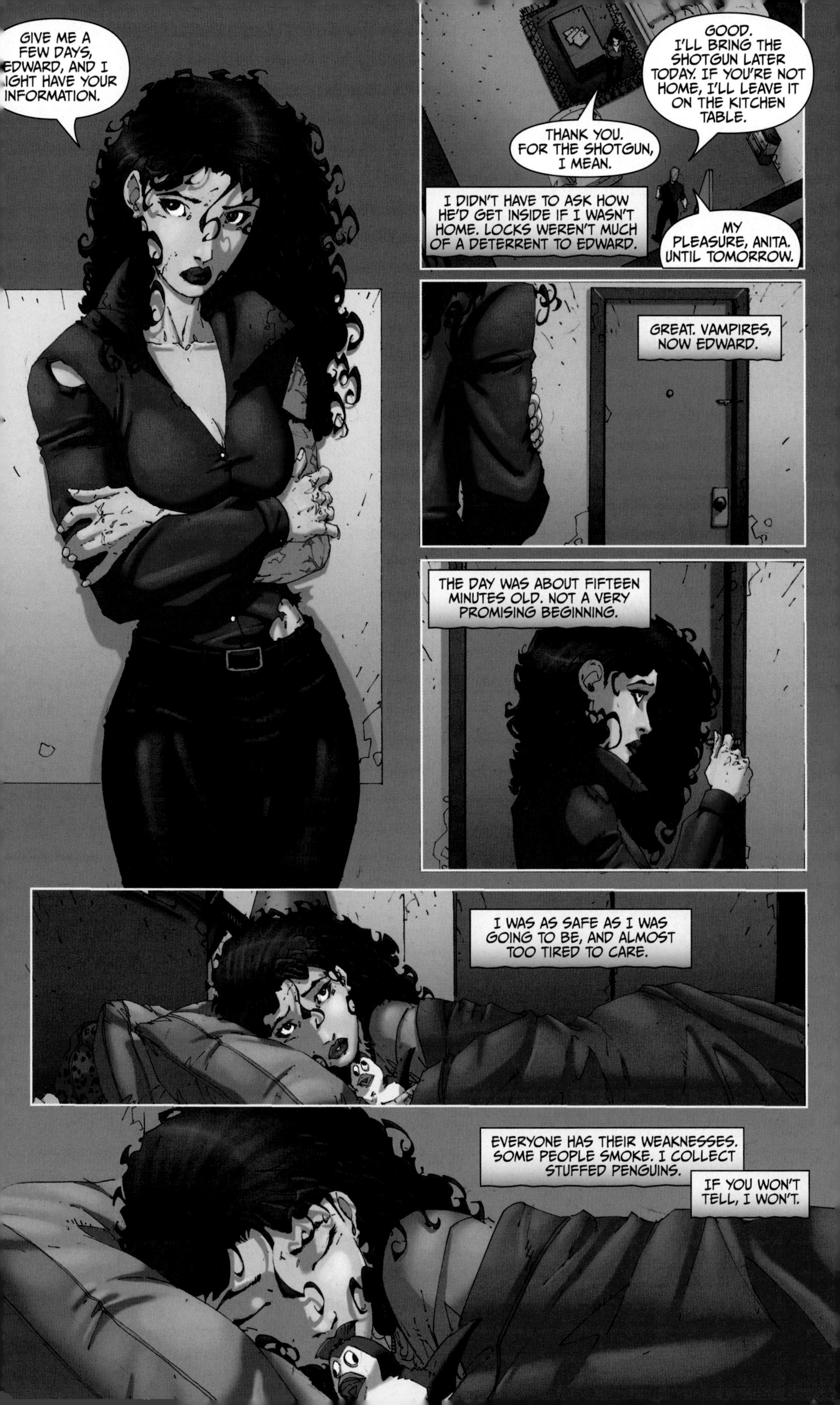
GIVE ME A FEW DAYS, EDWARD, AND I MIGHT HAVE YOUR INFORMATION.
THANK YOU. FOR THE SHOTGUN, I MEAN.
GOOD. I'LL BRING THE SHOTGUN LATER TODAY. IF YOU'RE NOT HOME, I'LL LEAVE IT ON THE KITCHEN TABLE.
I DIDN'T HAVE TO ASK HOW HE'D GET INSIDE IF I WASN'T HOME. LOCKS WEREN'T MUCH OF A DETERRENT TO EDWARD.
MY PLEASURE, ANITA. UNTIL TOMORROW.
GREAT. VAMPIRES, NOW EDWARD.
THE DAY WAS ABOUT FIFTEEN MINUTES OLD. NOT A VERY PROMISING BEGINNING.
I WAS AS SAFE AS I WAS GOING TO BE, AND ALMOST TOO TIRED TO CARE.
EVERYONE HAS THEIR WEAKNESSES. SOME PEOPLE SMOKE. I COLLECT STUFFED PENGUINS.
IF YOU WON'T TELL, I WON'T.

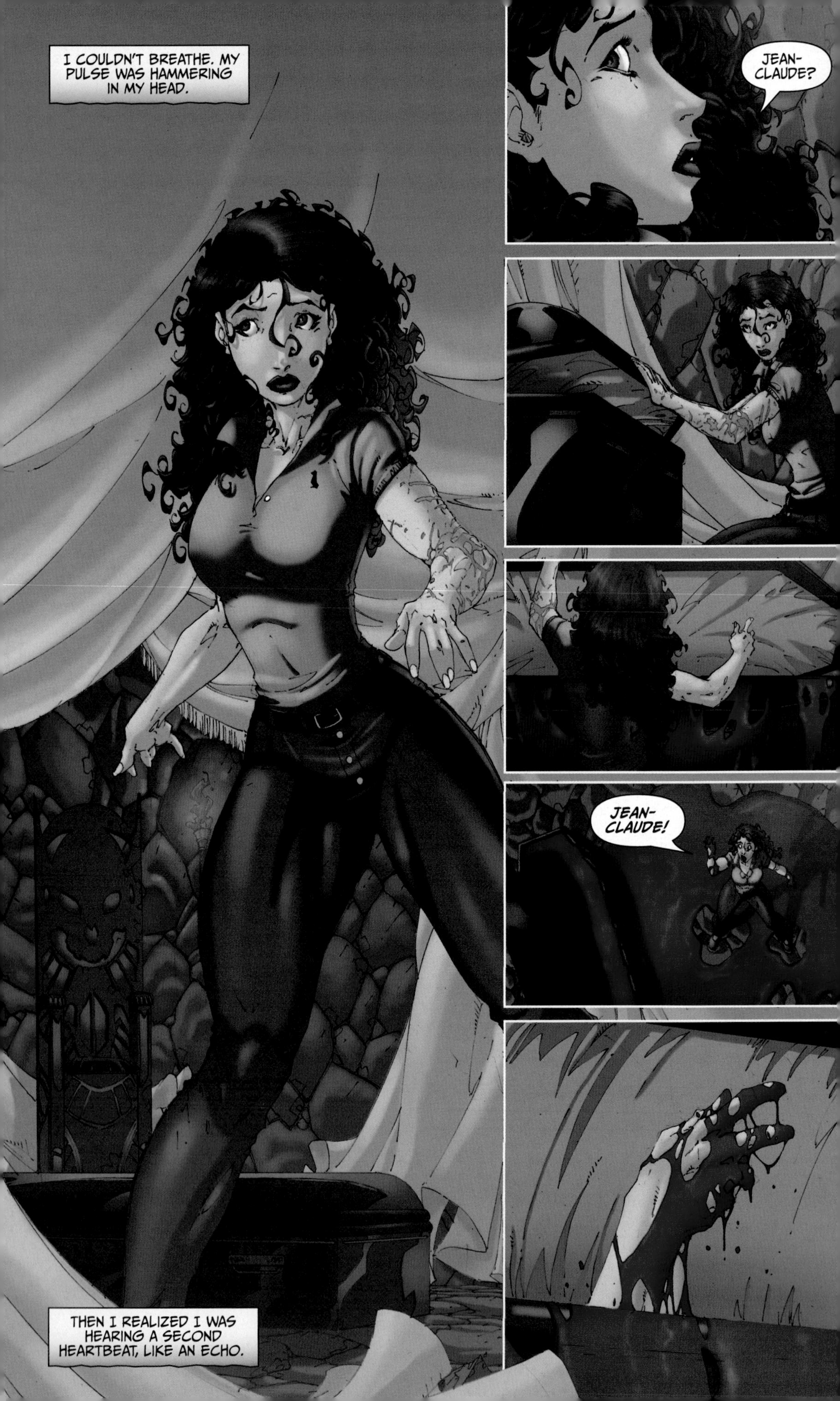
I COULDN'T BREATHE. MY PULSE WAS HAMMERING IN MY HEAD.
THEN I REALIZED I WAS HEARING A SECOND HEARTBEAT, LIKE AN ECHO.
JEAN-CLAUDE?
JEAN-CLAUDE!

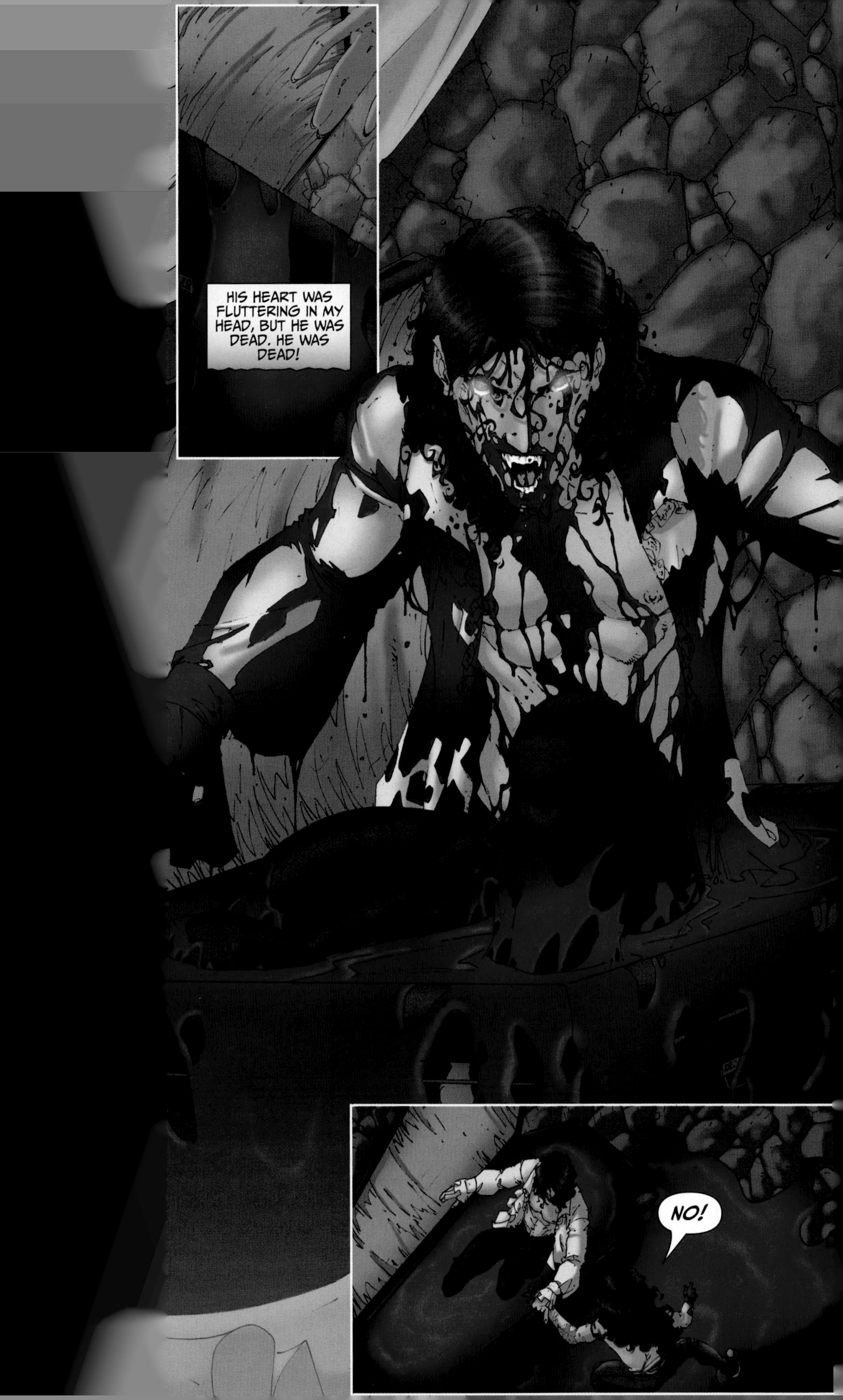
HIS HEART WAS FLUTTERING IN MY HEAD, BUT HE WAS DEAD. HE WAS DEAD!
NO!

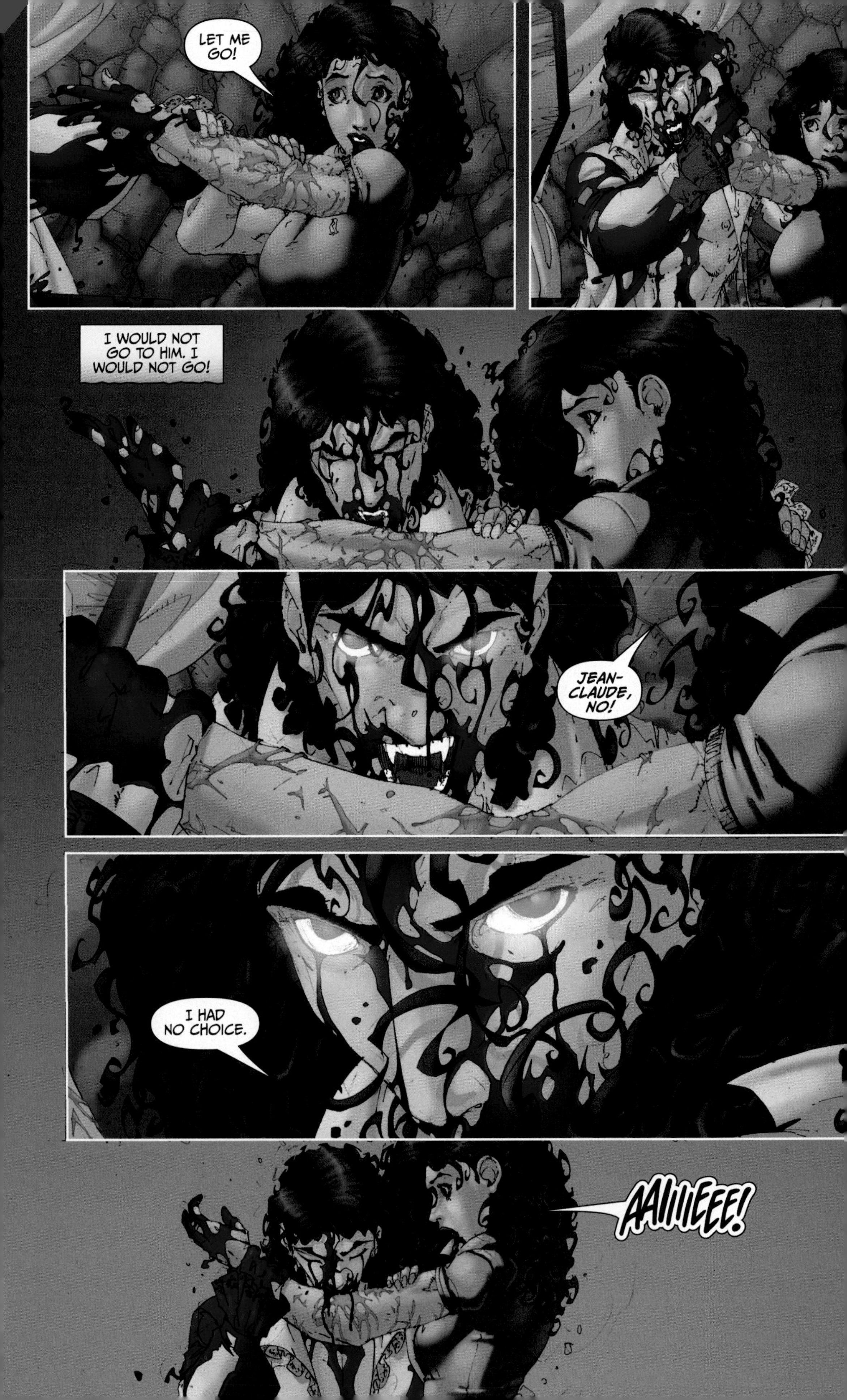
LET ME GO!
I WOULD NOT GO TO HIM. I WOULD NOT GO!
JEAN-CLAUDE, NO!
I HAD NO CHOICE.
AAIIIIEEE!

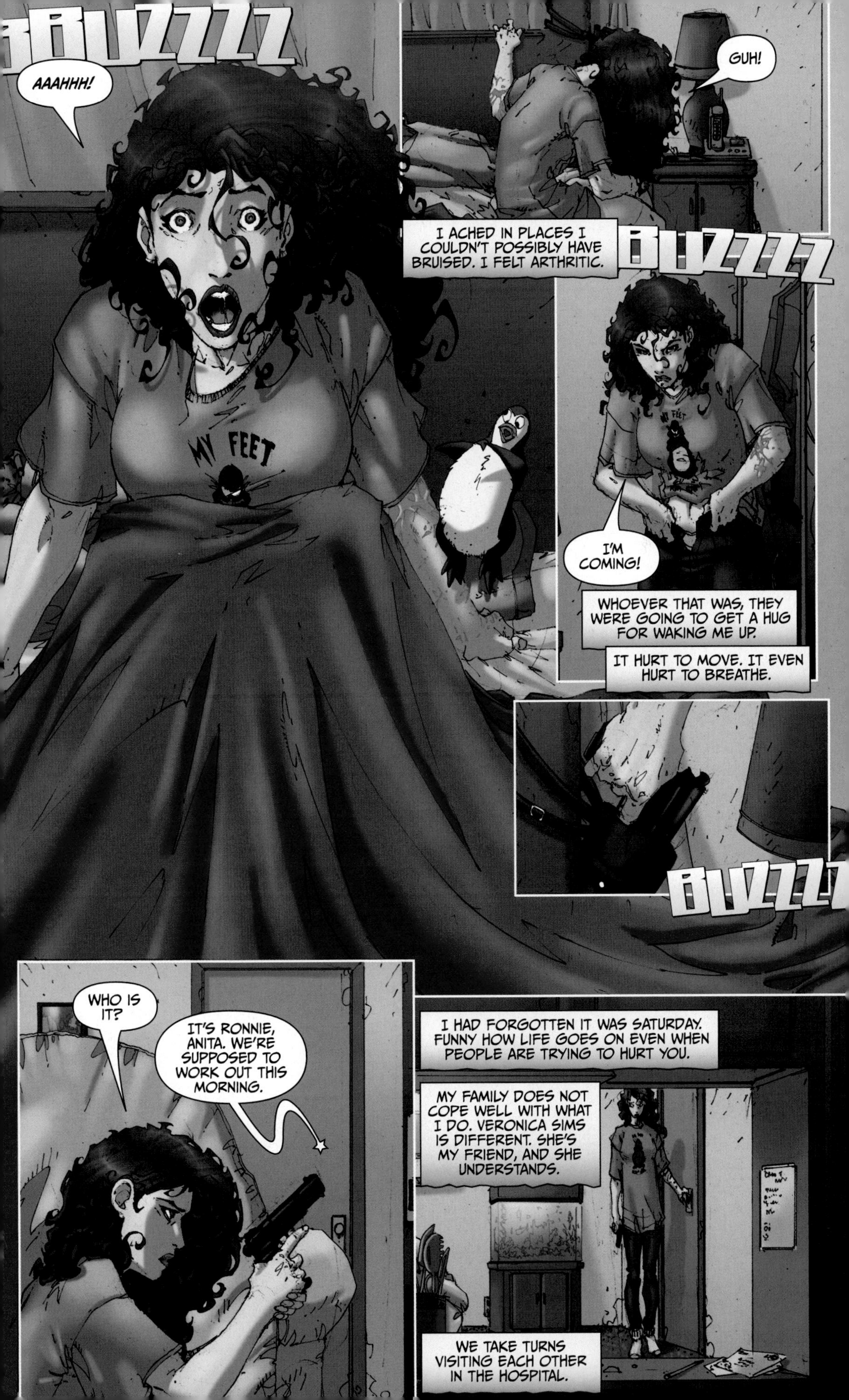
BUZZZZ
AAAHHH!
MY FEET
GUH!
I ACHED IN PLACES I COULDN'T POSSIBLY HAVE BRUISED. I FELT ARTHRITIC.
BUZZZZ
I'M COMING!
WHOEVER THAT WAS, THEY WERE GOING TO GET A HUG FOR WAKING ME UP.
IT HURT TO MOVE. IT EVEN HURT TO BREATHE.
BUZZZZ
WHO IS IT?
IT'S RONNIE, ANITA. WE'RE SUPPOSED TO WORK OUT THIS MORNING.
I HAD FORGOTTEN IT WAS SATURDAY. FUNNY HOW LIFE GOES ON EVEN WHEN PEOPLE ARE TRYING TO HURT YOU.
MY FAMILY DOES NOT COPE WELL WITH WHAT I DO. VERONICA SIMS IS DIFFERENT. SHE'S MY FRIEND, AND SHE UNDERSTANDS.
WE TAKE TURNS VISITING EACH OTHER IN THE HOSPITAL.

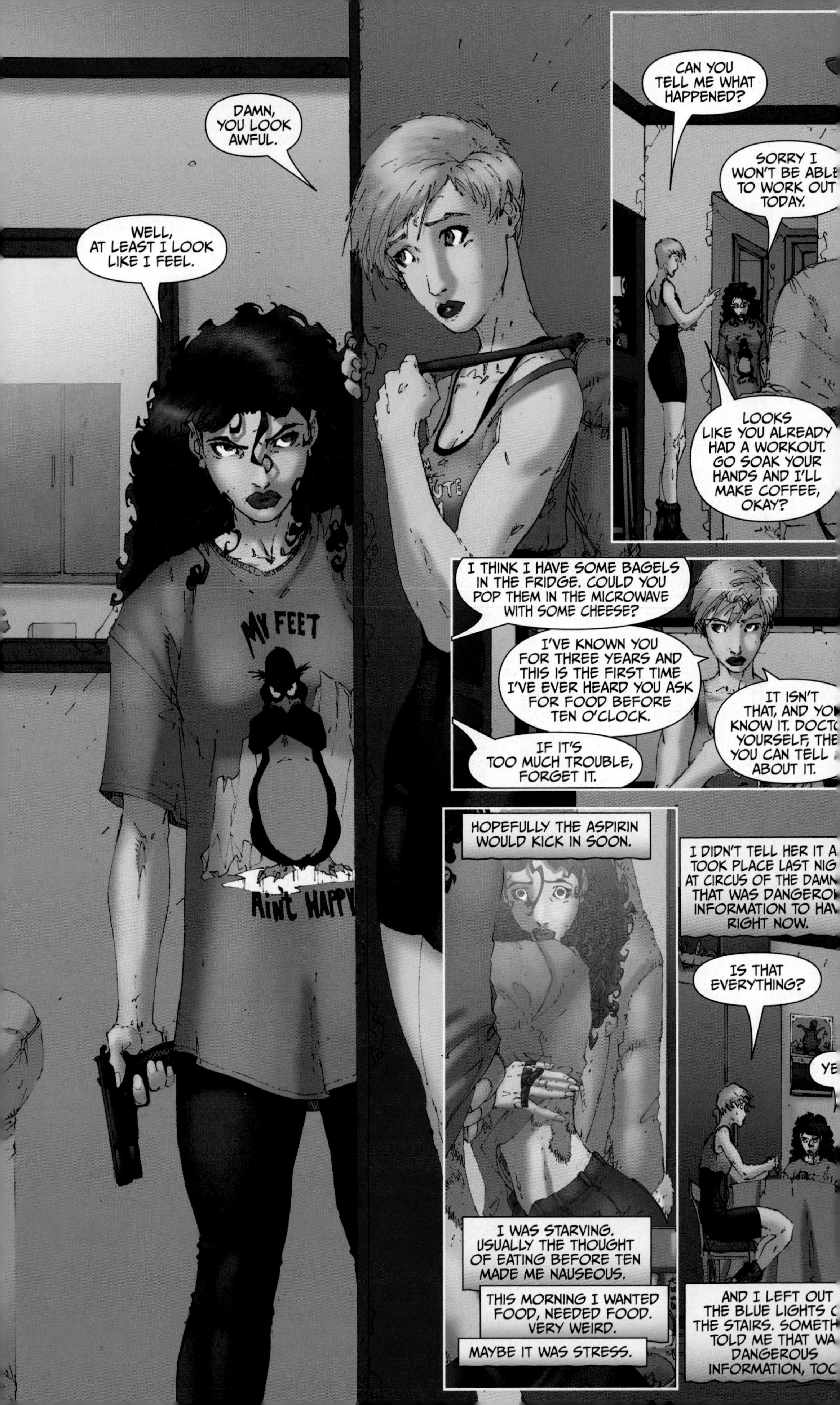

DAMN, YOU LOOK AWFUL.
WELL, AT LEAST I LOOK LIKE I FEEL.
MY FEET AIN'T HAPPY
CAN YOU TELL ME WHAT HAPPENED?
SORRY I WON'T BE ABLE TO WORK OUT TODAY.
LOOKS LIKE YOU ALREADY HAD A WORKOUT. GO SOAK YOUR HANDS AND I'LL MAKE COFFEE, OKAY?
I THINK I HAVE SOME BAGELS IN THE FRIDGE. COULD YOU POP THEM IN THE MICROWAVE WITH SOME CHEESE?
I'VE KNOWN YOU FOR THREE YEARS AND THIS IS THE FIRST TIME I'VE EVER HEARD YOU ASK FOR FOOD BEFORE TEN O'CLOCK.
IF IT'S TOO MUCH TROUBLE, FORGET IT.
IT ISN'T THAT, AND YO KNOW IT. DOCTO YOURSELF, THE YOU CAN TELL ABOUT IT.
HOPEFULLY THE ASPIRIN WOULD KICK IN SOON.
I WAS STARVING. USUALLY THE THOUGHT OF EATING BEFORE TEN MADE ME NAUSEOUS.
THIS MORNING I WANTED FOOD, NEEDED FOOD. VERY WEIRD.
MAYBE IT WAS STRESS.
I DIDN'T TELL HER IT A TOOK PLACE LAST NIG AT CIRCUS OF THE DAMN THAT WAS DANGERO INFORMATION TO HAV RIGHT NOW.
IS THAT EVERYTHING?
YE
AND I LEFT OUT THE BLUE LIGHTS THE STAIRS. SOMETH TOLD ME THAT WA DANGEROUS INFORMATION, TOO

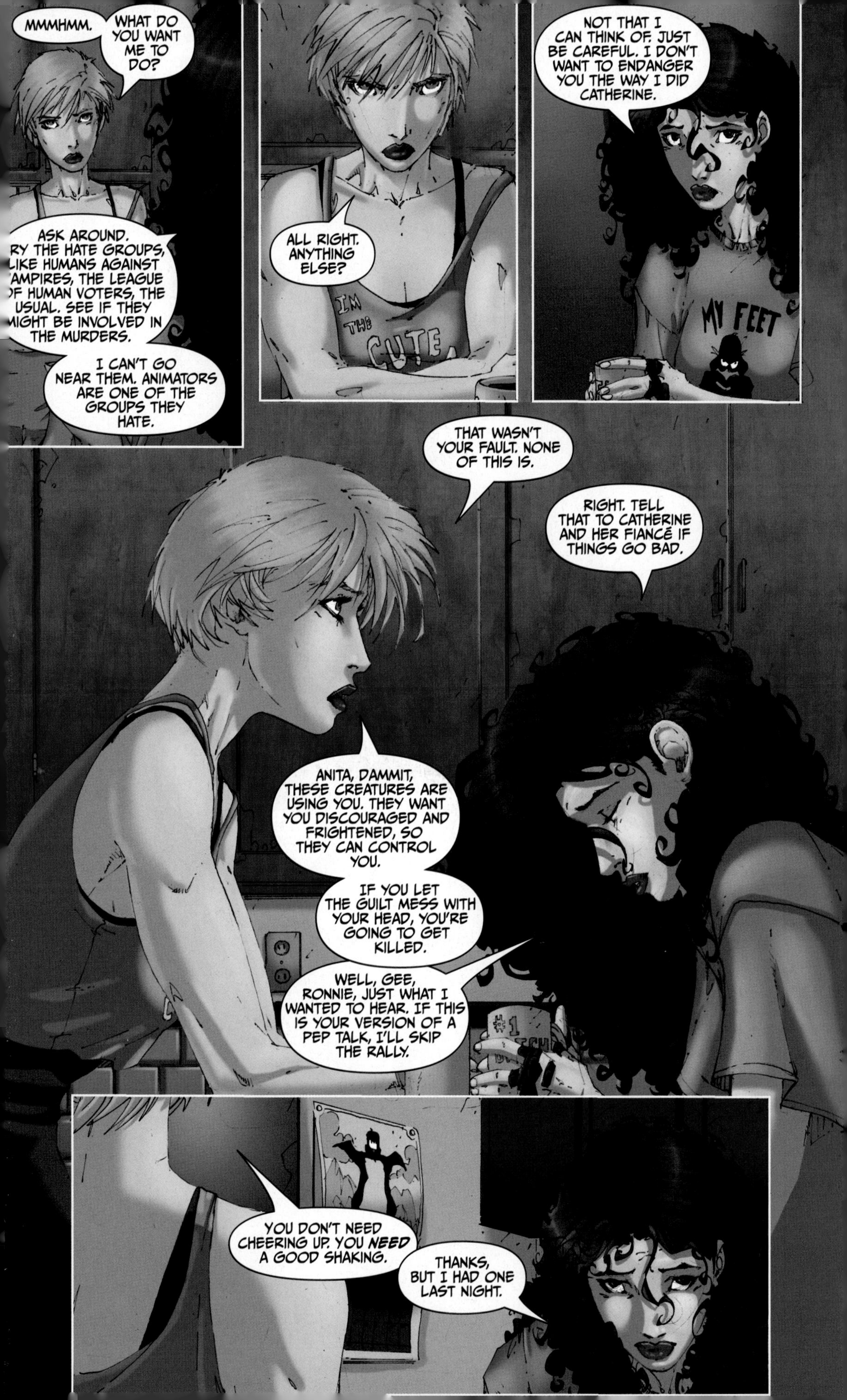

MMMHMM.
WHAT DO YOU WANT ME TO DO?
ASK AROUND. RY THE HATE GROUPS, LIKE HUMANS AGAINST AMPIRES, THE LEAGUE OF HUMAN VOTERS, THE USUAL. SEE IF THEY MIGHT BE INVOLVED IN THE MURDERS.
I CAN'T GO NEAR THEM. ANIMATORS ARE ONE OF THE GROUPS THEY HATE.
ALL RIGHT. ANYTHING ELSE?
NOT THAT I CAN THINK OF. JUST BE CAREFUL. I DON'T WANT TO ENDANGER YOU THE WAY I DID CATHERINE.
THAT WASN'T YOUR FAULT. NONE OF THIS IS.
RIGHT. TELL THAT TO CATHERINE AND HER FIANCÉ IF THINGS GO BAD.
ANITA, DAMMIT, THESE CREATURES ARE USING YOU. THEY WANT YOU DISCOURAGED AND FRIGHTENED, SO THEY CAN CONTROL YOU.
IF YOU LET THE GUILT MESS WITH YOUR HEAD, YOU'RE GOING TO GET KILLED.
WELL, GEE, RONNIE, JUST WHAT I WANTED TO HEAR. IF THIS IS YOUR VERSION OF A PEP TALK, I'LL SKIP THE RALLY.
YOU DON'T NEED CHEERING UP. YOU ***NEED*** A GOOD SHAKING.
THANKS, BUT I HAD ONE LAST NIGHT.

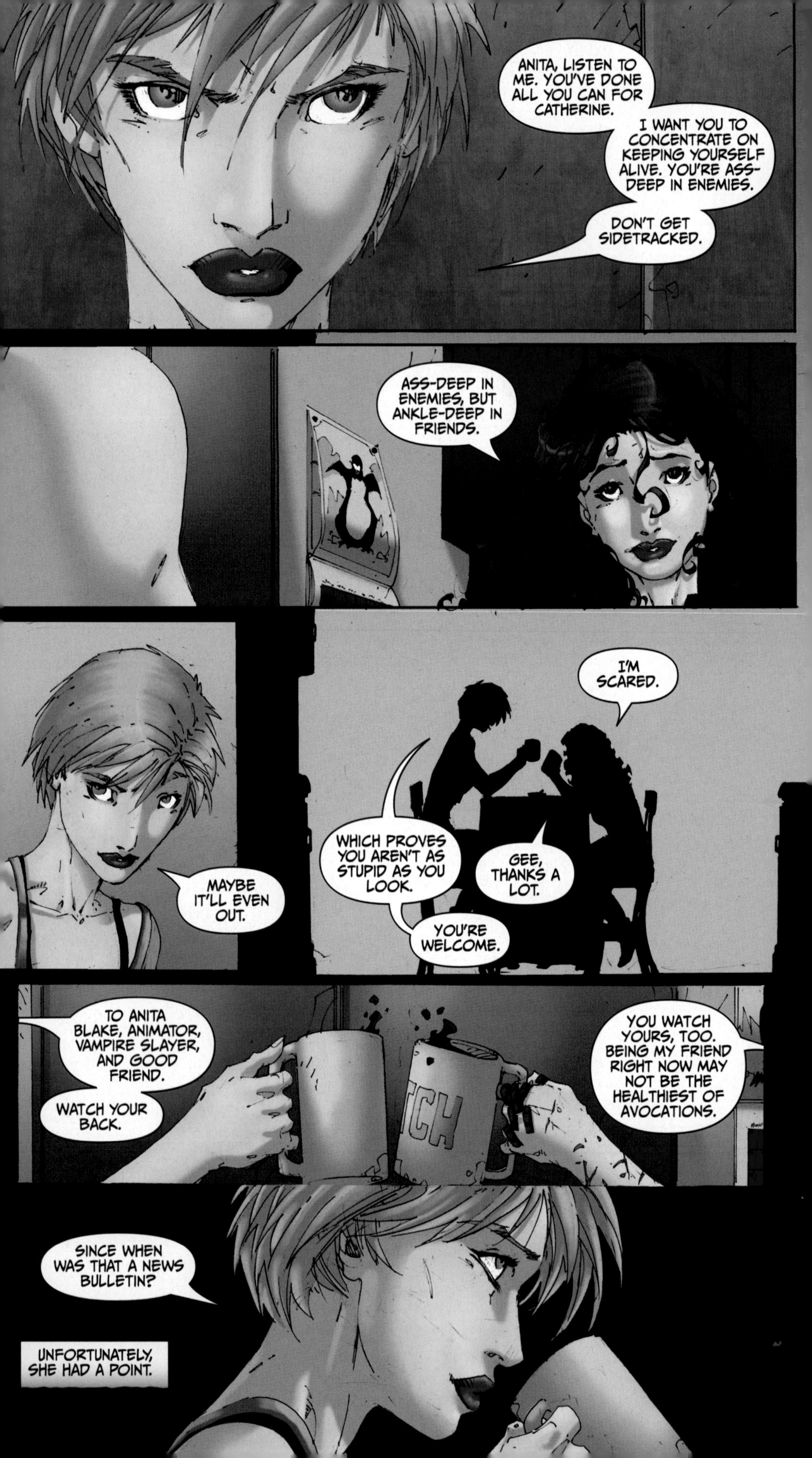

ANITA, LISTEN TO ME. YOU'VE DONE ALL YOU CAN FOR CATHERINE.
I WANT YOU TO CONCENTRATE ON KEEPING YOURSELF ALIVE. YOU'RE ASS-DEEP IN ENEMIES.
DON'T GET SIDETRACKED.
ASS-DEEP IN ENEMIES, BUT ANKLE-DEEP IN FRIENDS.
MAYBE IT'LL EVEN OUT.
I'M SCARED.
WHICH PROVES YOU AREN'T AS STUPID AS YOU LOOK.
GEE, THANKS A LOT.
YOU'RE WELCOME.
TO ANITA BLAKE, ANIMATOR, VAMPIRE SLAYER, AND GOOD FRIEND.
WATCH YOUR BACK.
YOU WATCH YOURS, TOO. BEING MY FRIEND RIGHT NOW MAY NOT BE THE HEALTHIEST OF AVOCATIONS.
SINCE WHEN WAS THAT A NEWS BULLETIN?
UNFORTUNATELY, SHE HAD A POINT.

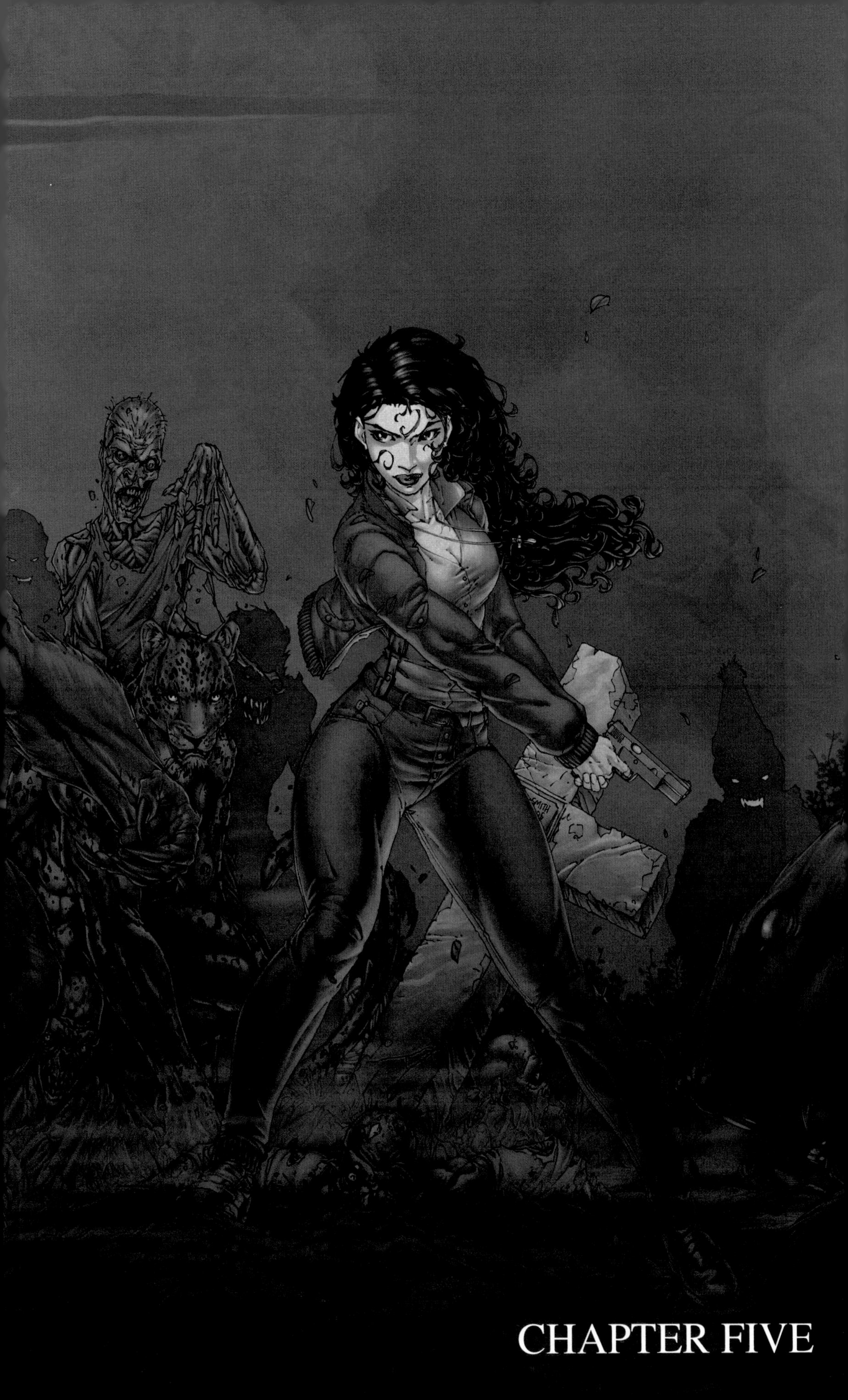

CHAPTER FIVE

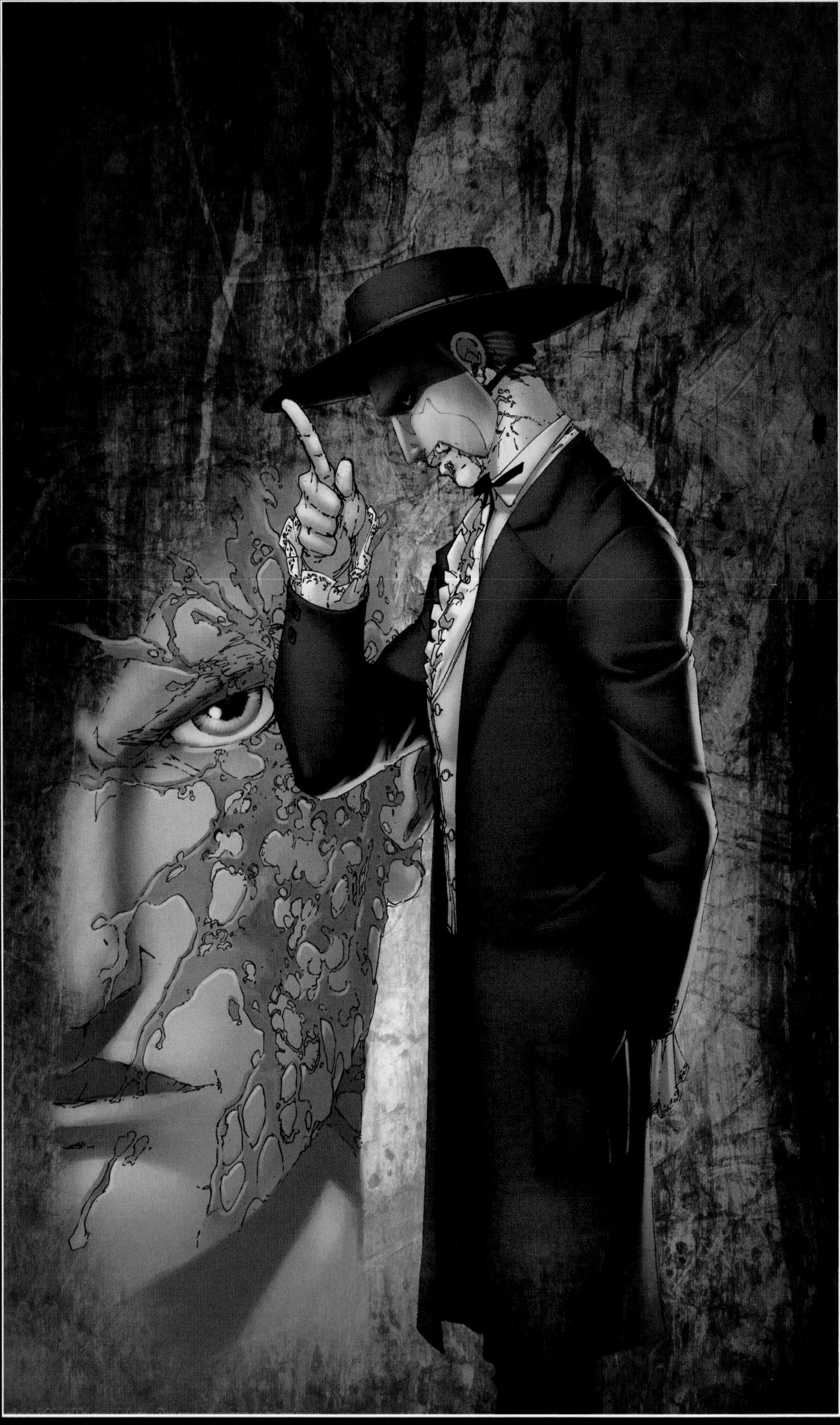

COVER BY: BRETT BOOTH & IMAGINARY FRIENDS STUDIO

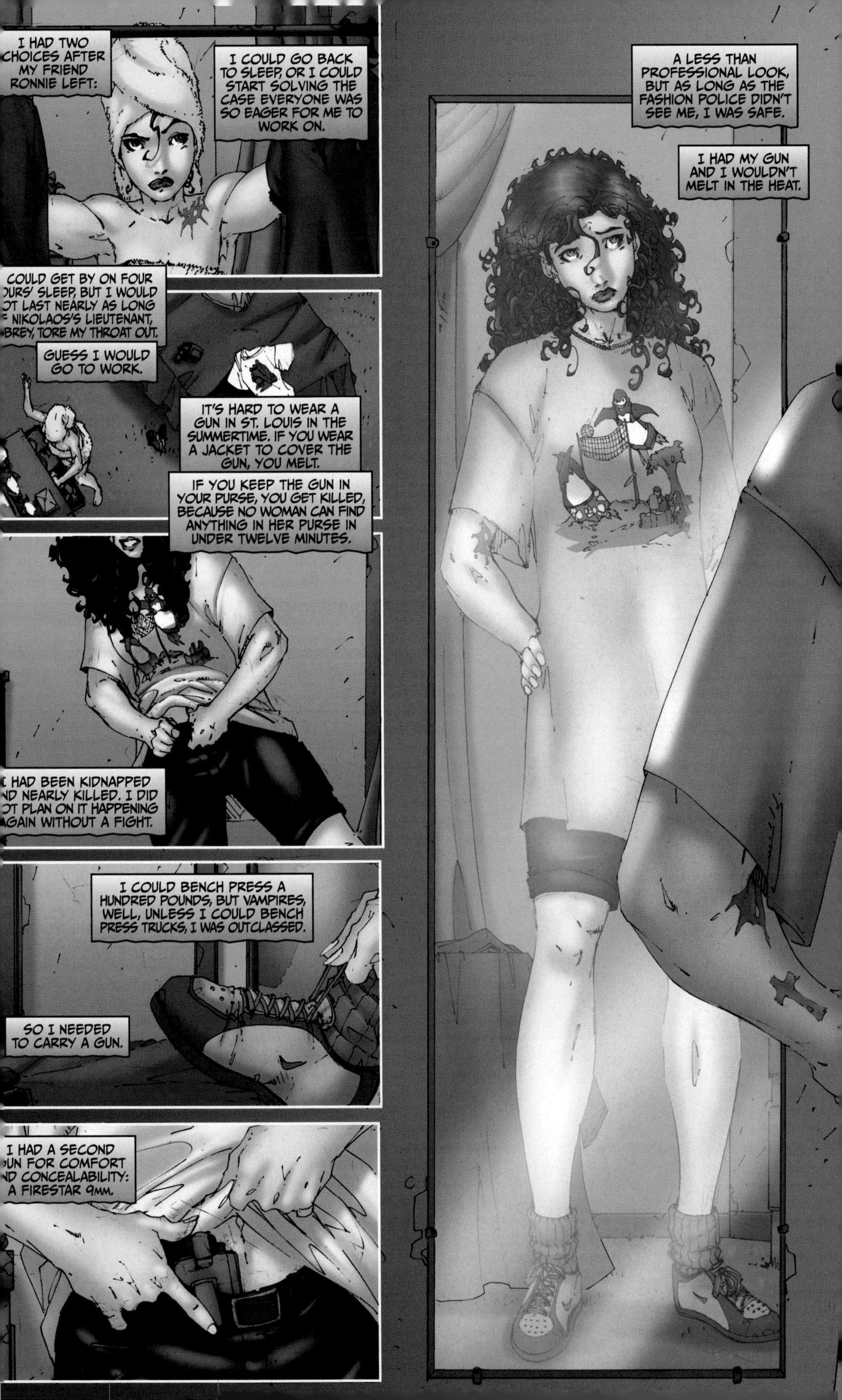
I HAD TWO CHOICES AFTER MY FRIEND RONNIE LEFT:
I COULD GO BACK TO SLEEP, OR I COULD START SOLVING THE CASE EVERYONE WAS SO EAGER FOR ME TO WORK ON.
COULD GET BY ON FOUR OURS' SLEEP, BUT I WOULD OT LAST NEARLY AS LONG F NIKOLAOS'S LIEUTENANT, BREY, TORE MY THROAT OUT.
GUESS I WOULD GO TO WORK.
IT'S HARD TO WEAR A GUN IN ST. LOUIS IN THE SUMMERTIME. IF YOU WEAR A JACKET TO COVER THE GUN, YOU MELT.
IF YOU KEEP THE GUN IN YOUR PURSE, YOU GET KILLED, BECAUSE NO WOMAN CAN FIND ANYTHING IN HER PURSE IN UNDER TWELVE MINUTES.
I HAD BEEN KIDNAPPED ND NEARLY KILLED. I DID OT PLAN ON IT HAPPENING AGAIN WITHOUT A FIGHT.
I COULD BENCH PRESS A HUNDRED POUNDS, BUT VAMPIRES, WELL, UNLESS I COULD BENCH PRESS TRUCKS, I WAS OUTCLASSED.
SO I NEEDED TO CARRY A GUN.
I HAD A SECOND GUN FOR COMFORT ND CONCEALABILITY: A FIRESTAR 9MM.
A LESS THAN PROFESSIONAL LOOK, BUT AS LONG AS THE FASHION POLICE DIDN'T SEE ME, I WAS SAFE.
I HAD MY GUN AND I WOULDN'T MELT IN THE HEAT.

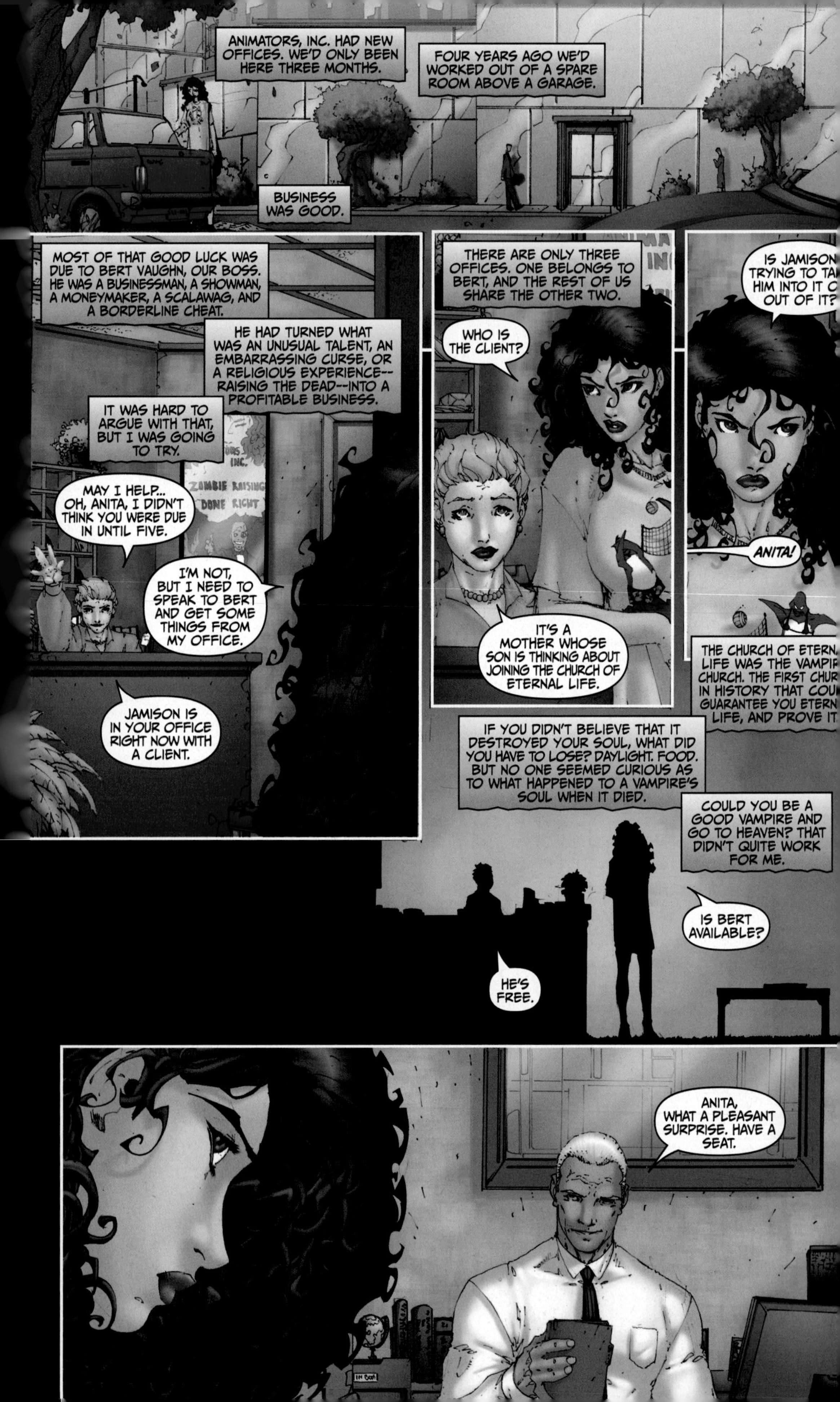

ANIMATORS, INC. HAD NEW OFFICES. WE'D ONLY BEEN HERE THREE MONTHS.
FOUR YEARS AGO WE'D WORKED OUT OF A SPARE ROOM ABOVE A GARAGE.
BUSINESS WAS GOOD.
MOST OF THAT GOOD LUCK WAS DUE TO BERT VAUGHN, OUR BOSS. HE WAS A BUSINESSMAN, A SHOWMAN, A MONEYMAKER, A SCALAWAG, AND A BORDERLINE CHEAT.
HE HAD TURNED WHAT WAS AN UNUSUAL TALENT, AN EMBARRASSING CURSE, OR A RELIGIOUS EXPERIENCE--RAISING THE DEAD--INTO A PROFITABLE BUSINESS.
IT WAS HARD TO ARGUE WITH THAT, BUT I WAS GOING TO TRY.
ZOMBIE RAISING DONE RIGHT
MAY I HELP... OH, ANITA, I DIDN'T THINK YOU WERE DUE IN UNTIL FIVE.
I'M NOT, BUT I NEED TO SPEAK TO BERT AND GET SOME THINGS FROM MY OFFICE.
JAMISON IS IN YOUR OFFICE RIGHT NOW WITH A CLIENT.
THERE ARE ONLY THREE OFFICES. ONE BELONGS TO BERT, AND THE REST OF US SHARE THE OTHER TWO.
WHO IS THE CLIENT?
IT'S A MOTHER WHOSE SON IS THINKING ABOUT JOINING THE CHURCH OF ETERNAL LIFE.
IS JAMISON TRYING TO TA
HIM INTO IT O
OUT OF IT?
ANITA!
THE CHURCH OF ETERN
LIFE WAS THE VAMPIR
CHURCH. THE FIRST CHUR
IN HISTORY THAT COU
GUARANTEE YOU ETERN
LIFE, AND PROVE IT
IF YOU DIDN'T BELIEVE THAT IT DESTROYED YOUR SOUL, WHAT DID YOU HAVE TO LOSE? DAYLIGHT. FOOD. BUT NO ONE SEEMED CURIOUS AS TO WHAT HAPPENED TO A VAMPIRE'S SOUL WHEN IT DIED.
COULD YOU BE A GOOD VAMPIRE AND GO TO HEAVEN? THAT DIDN'T QUITE WORK FOR ME.
IS BERT AVAILABLE?
HE'S FREE.
ANITA, WHAT A PLEASANT SURPRISE. HAVE A SEAT.
IN BOX

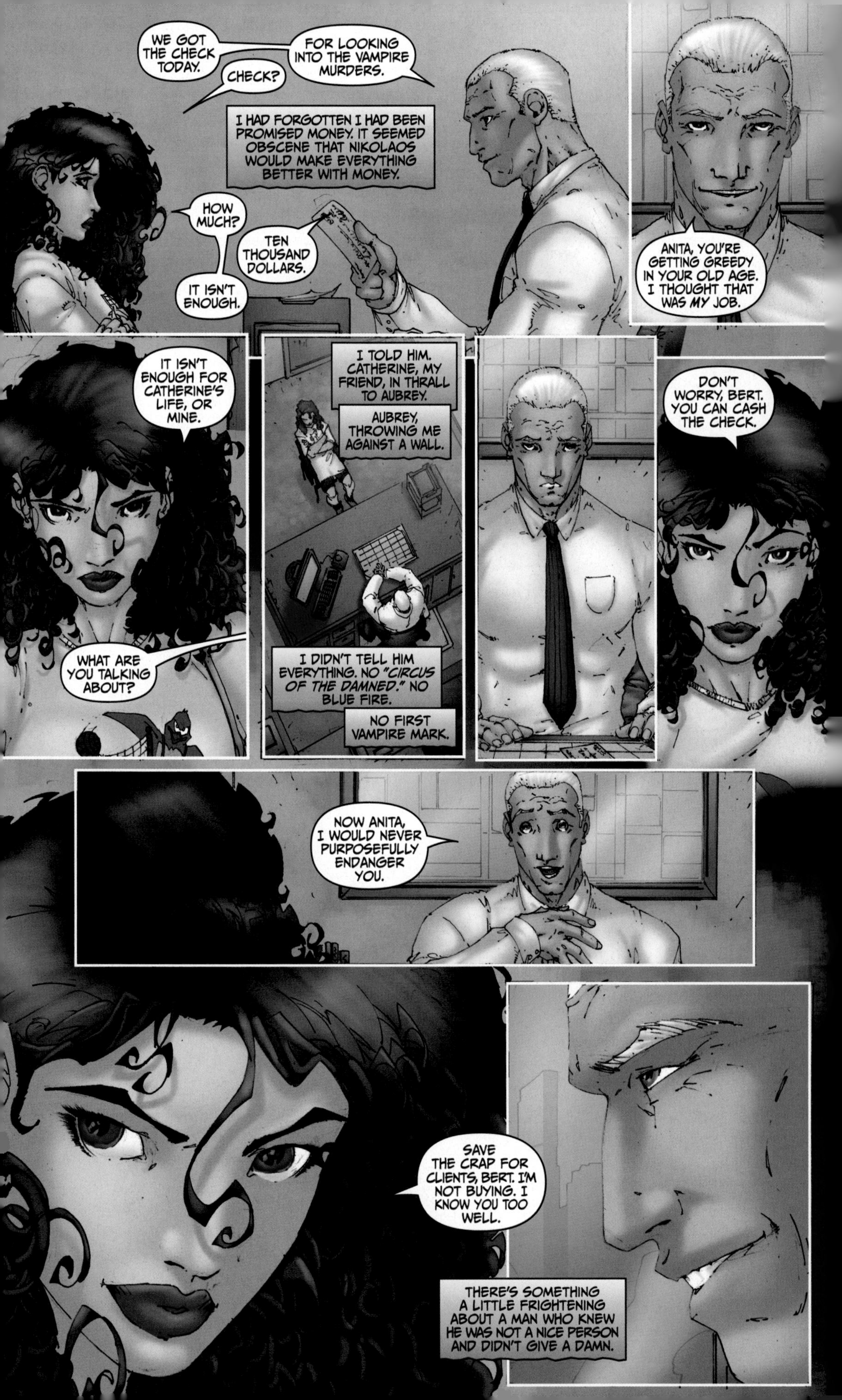
WE GOT THE CHECK TODAY.
CHECK?
FOR LOOKING INTO THE VAMPIRE MURDERS.
I HAD FORGOTTEN I HAD BEEN PROMISED MONEY. IT SEEMED OBSCENE THAT NIKOLAOS WOULD MAKE EVERYTHING BETTER WITH MONEY.
HOW MUCH?
TEN THOUSAND DOLLARS.
IT ISN'T ENOUGH.
ANITA, YOU'RE GETTING GREEDY IN YOUR OLD AGE. I THOUGHT THAT WAS MY JOB.
IT ISN'T ENOUGH FOR CATHERINE'S LIFE, OR MINE.
WHAT ARE YOU TALKING ABOUT?
I TOLD HIM. CATHERINE, MY FRIEND, IN THRALL TO AUBREY.
AUBREY, THROWING ME AGAINST A WALL.
I DIDN'T TELL HIM EVERYTHING. NO "CIRCUS OF THE DAMNED." NO BLUE FIRE.
NO FIRST VAMPIRE MARK.
DON'T WORRY, BERT. YOU CAN CASH THE CHECK.
NOW ANITA, I WOULD NEVER PURPOSEFULLY ENDANGER YOU.
SAVE THE CRAP FOR CLIENTS, BERT. I'M NOT BUYING. I KNOW YOU TOO WELL.
THERE'S SOMETHING A LITTLE FRIGHTENING ABOUT A MAN WHO KNEW HE WAS NOT A NICE PERSON AND DIDN'T GIVE A DAMN.

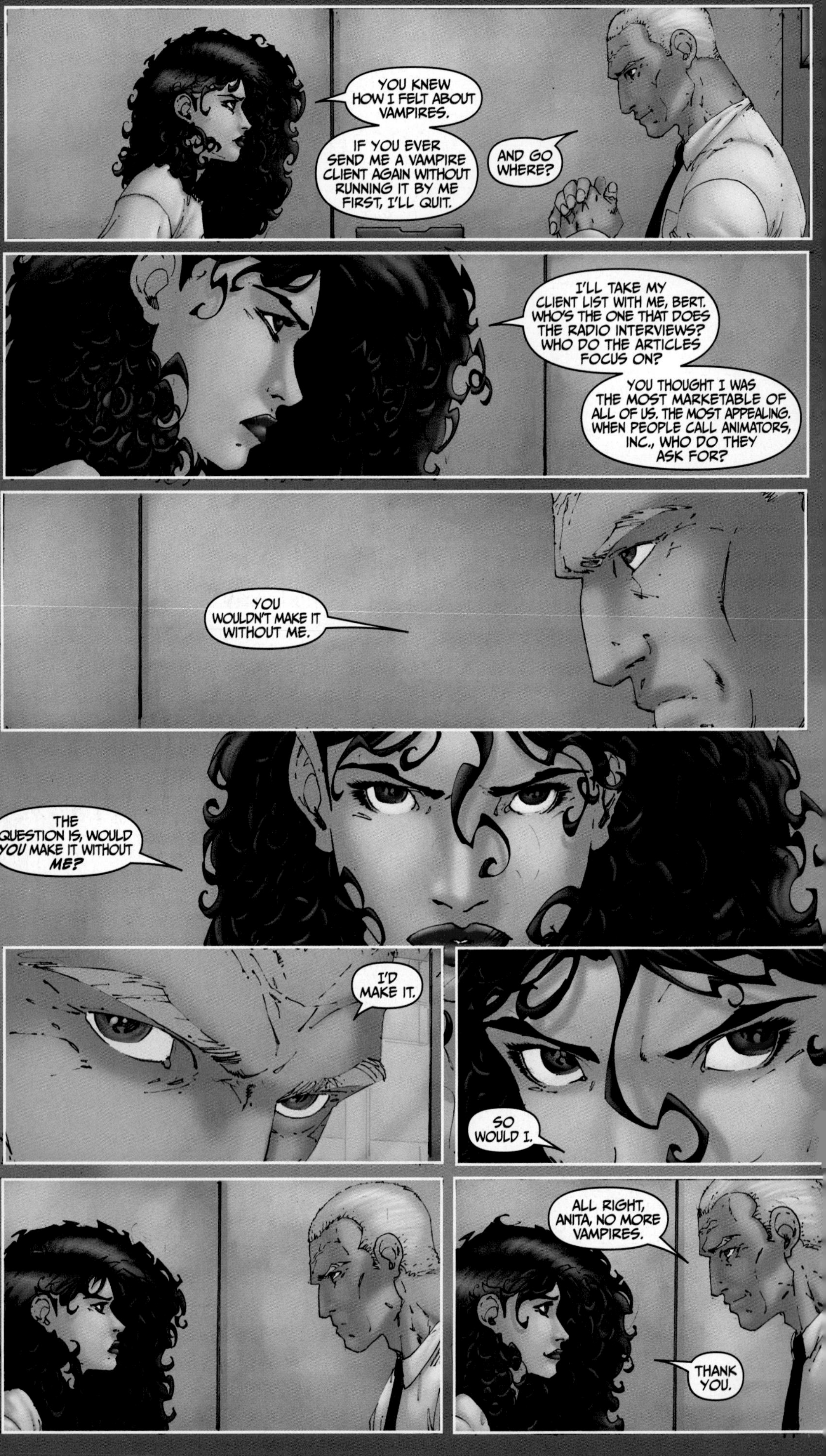
YOU KNEW HOW I FELT ABOUT VAMPIRES.
IF YOU EVER SEND ME A VAMPIRE CLIENT AGAIN WITHOUT RUNNING IT BY ME FIRST, I'LL QUIT.
AND GO WHERE?
I'LL TAKE MY CLIENT LIST WITH ME, BERT. WHO'S THE ONE THAT DOES THE RADIO INTERVIEWS? WHO DO THE ARTICLES FOCUS ON?
YOU THOUGHT I WAS THE MOST MARKETABLE OF ALL OF US. THE MOST APPEALING. WHEN PEOPLE CALL ANIMATORS, INC., WHO DO THEY ASK FOR?
YOU WOULDN'T MAKE IT WITHOUT ME.
THE QUESTION IS, WOULD *YOU* MAKE IT WITHOUT ***ME?***
I'D MAKE IT.
SO WOULD I.
ALL RIGHT, ANITA, NO MORE VAMPIRES.
THANK YOU.

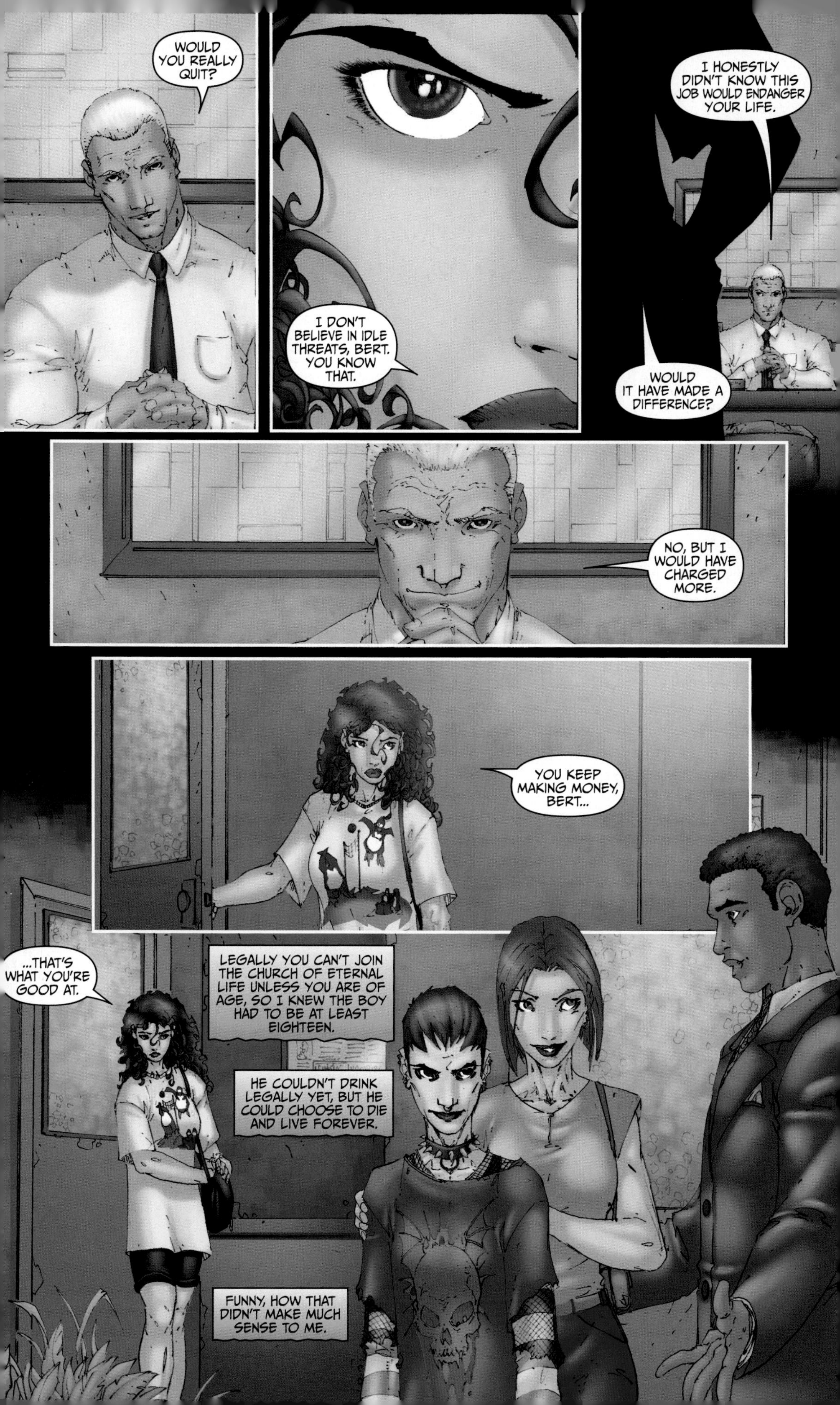

WOULD YOU REALLY QUIT?
I DON'T BELIEVE IN IDLE THREATS, BERT. YOU KNOW THAT.
I HONESTLY DIDN'T KNOW THIS JOB WOULD ENDANGER YOUR LIFE.
WOULD IT HAVE MADE A DIFFERENCE?
NO, BUT I WOULD HAVE CHARGED MORE.
YOU KEEP MAKING MONEY, BERT...
...THAT'S WHAT YOU'RE GOOD AT.
LEGALLY YOU CAN'T JOIN THE CHURCH OF ETERNAL LIFE UNLESS YOU ARE OF AGE, SO I KNEW THE BOY HAD TO BE AT LEAST EIGHTEEN.
HE COULDN'T DRINK LEGALLY YET, BUT HE COULD CHOOSE TO DIE AND LIVE FOREVER.
FUNNY, HOW THAT DIDN'T MAKE MUCH SENSE TO ME.

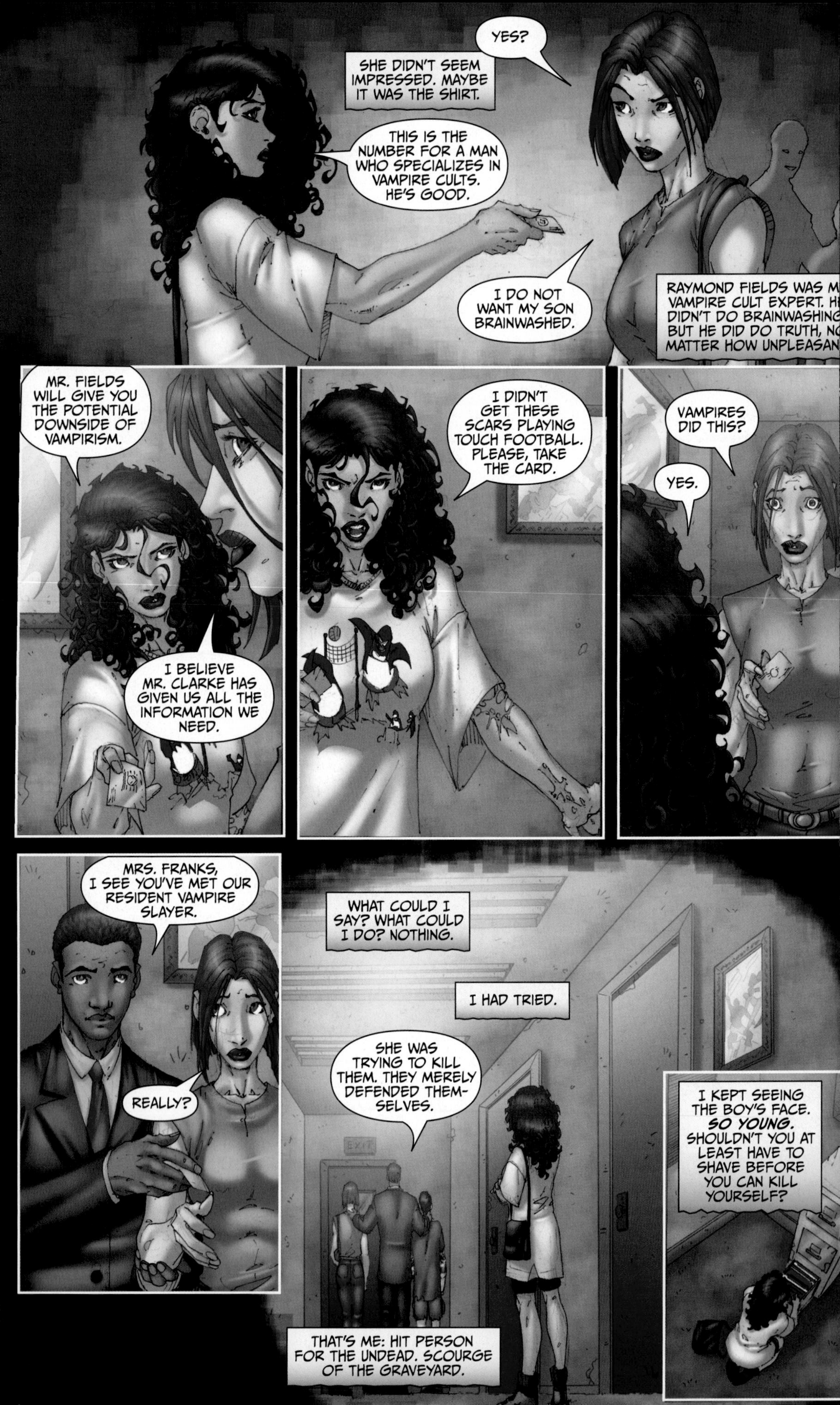
SHE DIDN'T SEEM IMPRESSED. MAYBE IT WAS THE SHIRT.
YES?
THIS IS THE NUMBER FOR A MAN WHO SPECIALIZES IN VAMPIRE CULTS. HE'S GOOD.
I DO NOT WANT MY SON BRAINWASHED.
RAYMOND FIELDS WAS MY VAMPIRE CULT EXPERT. HE DIDN'T DO BRAINWASHING, BUT HE DID DO TRUTH, NO MATTER HOW UNPLEASANT.
MR. FIELDS WILL GIVE YOU THE POTENTIAL DOWNSIDE OF VAMPIRISM.
I BELIEVE MR. CLARKE HAS GIVEN US ALL THE INFORMATION WE NEED.
I DIDN'T GET THESE SCARS PLAYING TOUCH FOOTBALL. PLEASE, TAKE THE CARD.
VAMPIRES DID THIS?
YES.
MRS. FRANKS, I SEE YOU'VE MET OUR RESIDENT VAMPIRE SLAYER.
REALLY?
WHAT COULD I SAY? WHAT COULD I DO? NOTHING.
I HAD TRIED.
SHE WAS TRYING TO KILL THEM. THEY MERELY DEFENDED THEMSELVES.
EXIT
THAT'S ME: HIT PERSON FOR THE UNDEAD. SCOURGE OF THE GRAVEYARD.
I KEPT SEEING THE BOY'S FACE. SO YOUNG. SHOULDN'T YOU AT LEAST HAVE TO SHAVE BEFORE YOU CAN KILL YOURSELF?

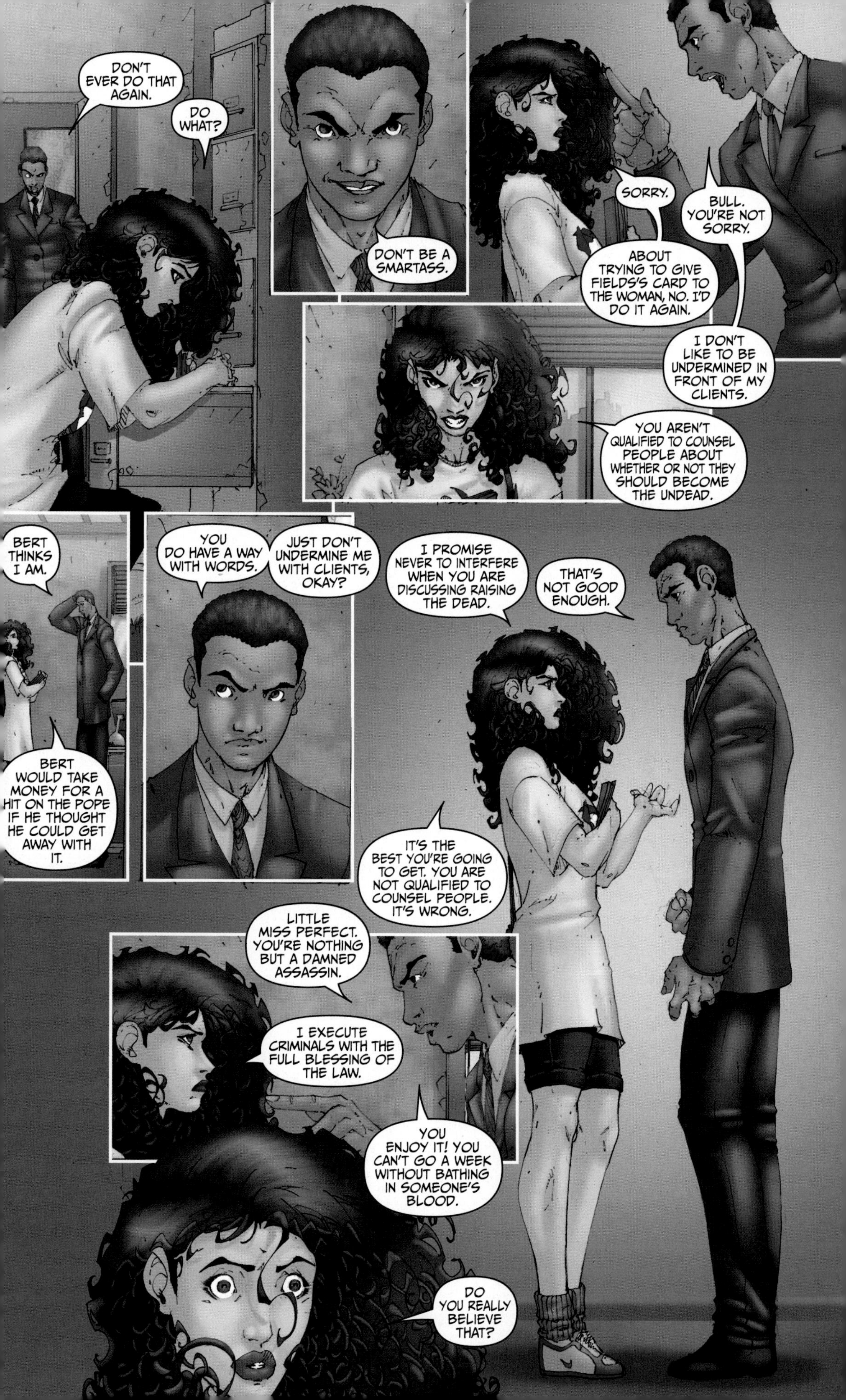

DON'T EVER DO THAT AGAIN.
DO WHAT?
DON'T BE A SMARTASS.
SORRY.
BULL. YOU'RE NOT SORRY.
ABOUT TRYING TO GIVE FIELDS'S CARD TO THE WOMAN, NO. I'D DO IT AGAIN.
I DON'T LIKE TO BE UNDERMINED IN FRONT OF MY CLIENTS.
YOU AREN'T QUALIFIED TO COUNSEL PEOPLE ABOUT WHETHER OR NOT THEY SHOULD BECOME THE UNDEAD.
BERT THINKS I AM.
BERT WOULD TAKE MONEY FOR A HIT ON THE POPE IF HE THOUGHT HE COULD GET AWAY WITH IT.
YOU DO HAVE A WAY WITH WORDS.
JUST DON'T UNDERMINE ME WITH CLIENTS, OKAY?
I PROMISE NEVER TO INTERFERE WHEN YOU ARE DISCUSSING RAISING THE DEAD.
THAT'S NOT GOOD ENOUGH.
IT'S THE BEST YOU'RE GOING TO GET. YOU ARE NOT QUALIFIED TO COUNSEL PEOPLE. IT'S WRONG.
LITTLE MISS PERFECT. YOU'RE NOTHING BUT A DAMNED ASSASSIN.
I EXECUTE CRIMINALS WITH THE FULL BLESSING OF THE LAW.
YOU ENJOY IT! YOU CAN'T GO A WEEK WITHOUT BATHING IN SOMEONE'S BLOOD.
DO YOU REALLY BELIEVE THAT?

I DON'T KNOW.

POOR MISUNDERSTOOD LITTLE VAMPIRES. THE HUMAN SERVANTS WHO BRANDED M ARM BELONGED TO A VAMPI THAT SLAUGHTERED TWENT THREE PEOPLE BEFORE TH COURTS WOULD GIVE ME THE GO-AHEAD.

THIS VAMPIRE KILLED TEN PEOPLE, PERSONALLY. HE SPECIALIZED IN LITTLE BOYS, SAID THEIR MEAT WAS MOST TENDER.

HE'S NOT DEAD, JAMISON. HE GOT AWAY. BUT HE FOUND ME LAST NIGHT AND THREATENDED MY LIFE.

YOU DON'T UNDERSTAND THEM.

NO! *YOU* DON'T UNDERSTAND THEM.

TOUCHING HIM WAS AGAINST THE RULES. NEVER TOUCH ANYONE IN A FIGHT UNLESS YOU WANT VIOLENCE.

I'M SORRY, JAMISON.

I DON'T KNOW IF HE UNDERSTOOD WHAT I WAS APOLOGIZING FOR.

WHAT ARE THE FILES FOR?

THE VAMPIRE MURDERS.

YOU TOOK THE MONEY?

YOU KNEW ABOUT IT?

I TOLD BERT YOU WOULDN'T WORK FOR VAMPIRES.

MONEY TALKS, JAMISON, EVEN TO ME.

YOU DIDN'T DO IT FO MONEY. WHA WAS IT?

JAMISON THOUGHT VAMPIRES WERE FANG PEOPLE. THEY WERE VE CAREFUL TO KEEP HIM THE NICE, CLEAN FRING

HE COULD AFFORD TO PRETEND, OR IGNORE, OR EVEN LIE TO HIMSELF.

ANYTHING THAT CAN KILL VAMPIRES COULD MAKE MEAT PIES OUT OF HUMAN BEINGS. I NEED TO CATCH THAT MANIAC BEFORE HE, SHE, OR IT, DOES JUST THAT.

IT WASN'T A BAD LIE, AS LIES GO. IT WAS EVEN PLAUSIBLE.

YOU THINK YOU CAN CATCH SOMETHING THE MASTER VAMPIRES CAN'T?

THEY SEEM TO THINK SO.

ANITA, ARE YOU READY TO GO?

IT WAS PHILLIP. I HADN'T RECOGNIZED HIM WITH HIS CLOTHES ON.

WE NEED TO TALK.

PHILLIP, I DIDN'T EXPECT TO SEE YOU SO SOON.

JAMISON CLARKE, THIS IS PHILLIP... A FRIEND.

SO, YOU'RE ANITA'S... FRIEND.

GOOD GRIEF. "FRIEND" IS WHAT PEOPLE CALL THEIR LOVERS. JAMISON WOULD TELL EVERYONE, THE SMIRKING LITTLE CREEP.

WELL, WE HAVE TO GO NOW. COME ALONG, PHILLIP.

NICE TO MEET YOU PHILLIP. I'M SURE THE REST OF THE GUYS WHO WORK HERE WOULD LOVE TO MEET YOU SOMETIME.

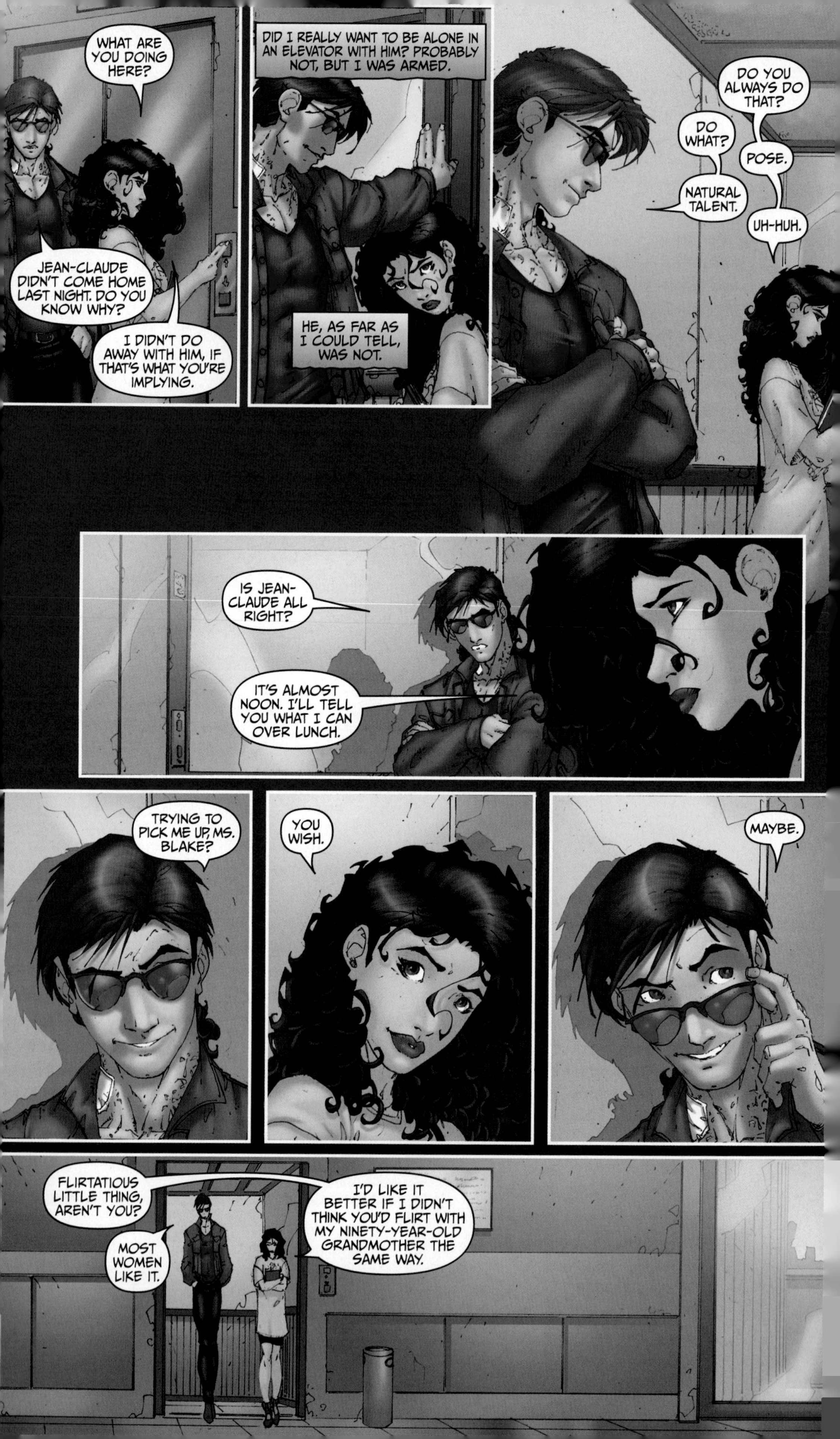
WHAT ARE YOU DOING HERE?
JEAN-CLAUDE DIDN'T COME HOME LAST NIGHT. DO YOU KNOW WHY?
I DIDN'T DO AWAY WITH HIM, IF THAT'S WHAT YOU'RE IMPLYING.
DID I REALLY WANT TO BE ALONE IN AN ELEVATOR WITH HIM? PROBABLY NOT, BUT I WAS ARMED.
HE, AS FAR AS I COULD TELL, WAS NOT.
DO YOU ALWAYS DO THAT?
DO WHAT?
POSE.
NATURAL TALENT.
UH-HUH.
IS JEAN-CLAUDE ALL RIGHT?
IT'S ALMOST NOON. I'LL TELL YOU WHAT I CAN OVER LUNCH.
TRYING TO PICK ME UP, MS. BLAKE?
YOU WISH.
MAYBE.
FLIRTATIOUS LITTLE THING, AREN'T YOU?
MOST WOMEN LIKE IT.
I'D LIKE IT BETTER IF I DIDN'T THINK YOU'D FLIRT WITH MY NINETY-YEAR-OLD GRANDMOTHER THE SAME WAY.

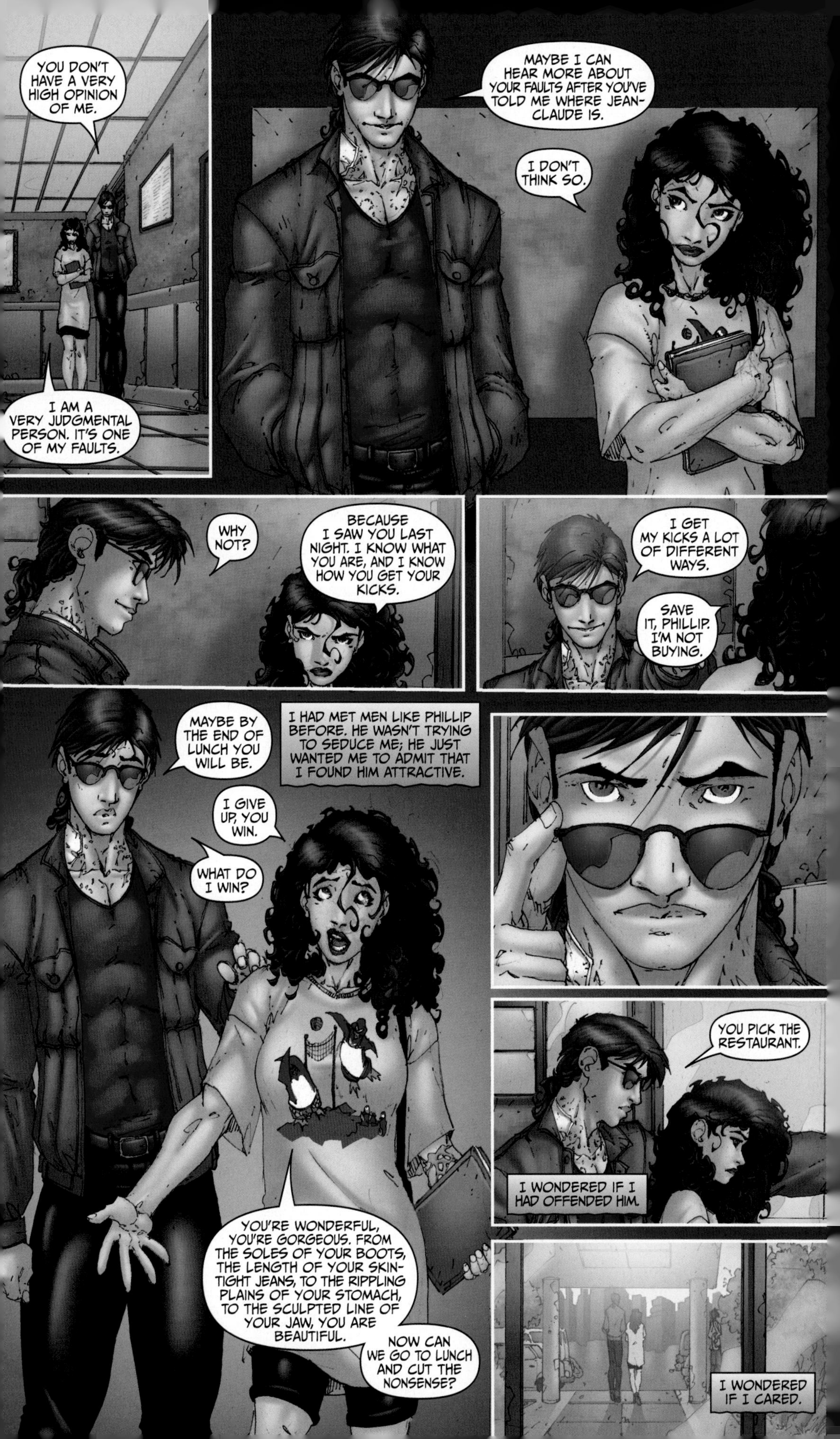
YOU DON'T HAVE A VERY HIGH OPINION OF ME.
I AM A VERY JUDGMENTAL PERSON. IT'S ONE OF MY FAULTS.
MAYBE I CAN HEAR MORE ABOUT YOUR FAULTS AFTER YOU'VE TOLD ME WHERE JEAN-CLAUDE IS.
I DON'T THINK SO.
WHY NOT?
BECAUSE I SAW YOU LAST NIGHT. I KNOW WHAT YOU ARE, AND I KNOW HOW YOU GET YOUR KICKS.
I GET MY KICKS A LOT OF DIFFERENT WAYS.
SAVE IT, PHILLIP. I'M NOT BUYING.
MAYBE BY THE END OF LUNCH YOU WILL BE.
I HAD MET MEN LIKE PHILLIP BEFORE. HE WASN'T TRYING TO SEDUCE ME; HE JUST WANTED ME TO ADMIT THAT I FOUND HIM ATTRACTIVE.
I GIVE UP, YOU WIN.
WHAT DO I WIN?
YOU'RE WONDERFUL, YOU'RE GORGEOUS. FROM THE SOLES OF YOUR BOOTS, THE LENGTH OF YOUR SKIN-TIGHT JEANS, TO THE RIPPLING PLAINS OF YOUR STOMACH, TO THE SCULPTED LINE OF YOUR JAW, YOU ARE BEAUTIFUL.
NOW CAN WE GO TO LUNCH AND CUT THE NONSENSE?
YOU PICK THE RESTAURANT.
I WONDERED IF I HAD OFFENDED HIM.
I WONDERED IF I CARED.

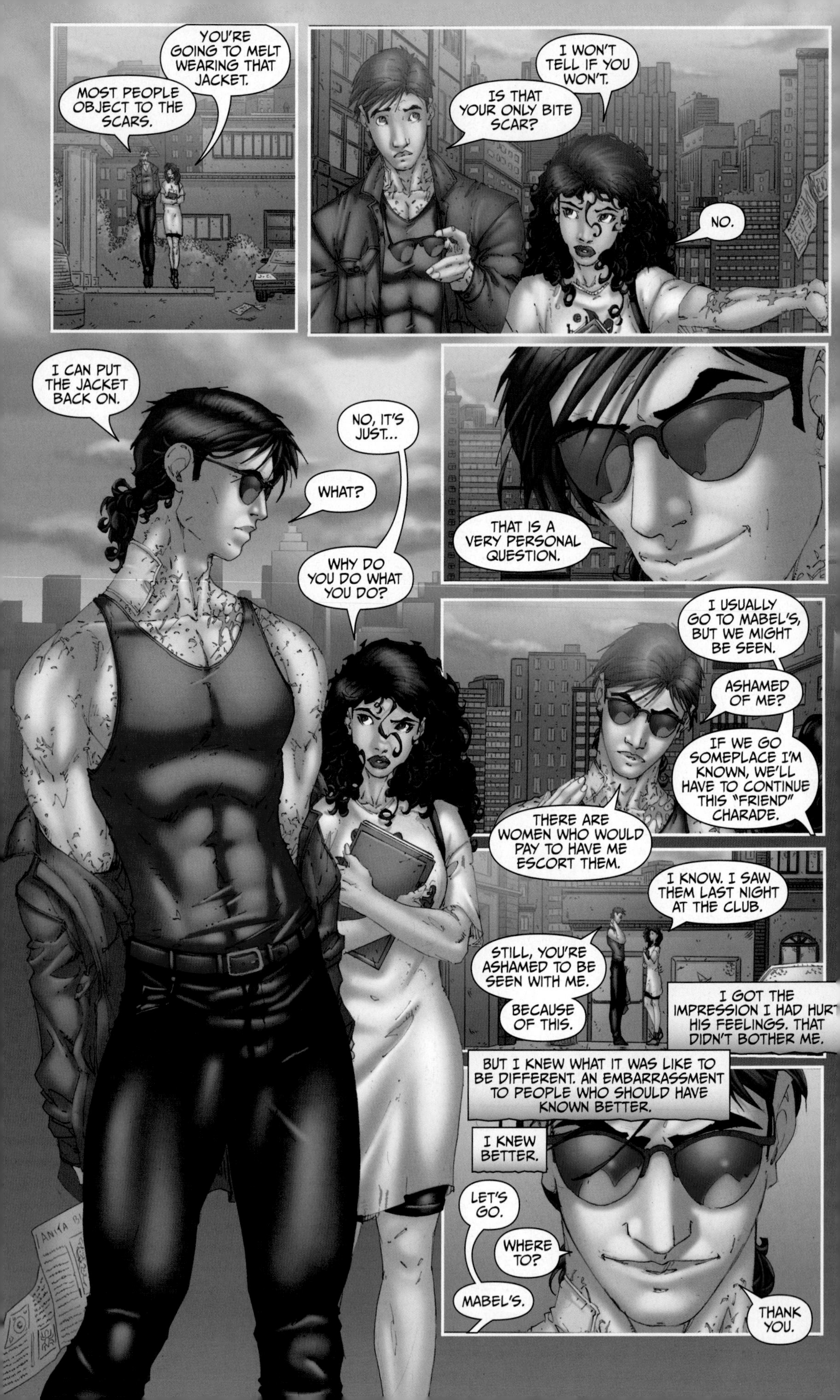

MOST PEOPLE OBJECT TO THE SCARS.
YOU'RE GOING TO MELT WEARING THAT JACKET.
I WON'T TELL IF YOU WON'T.
IS THAT YOUR ONLY BITE SCAR?
NO.
I CAN PUT THE JACKET BACK ON.
NO, IT'S JUST...
WHAT?
WHY DO YOU DO WHAT YOU DO?
THAT IS A VERY PERSONAL QUESTION.
I USUALLY GO TO MABEL'S, BUT WE MIGHT BE SEEN.
ASHAMED OF ME?
IF WE GO SOMEPLACE I'M KNOWN, WE'LL HAVE TO CONTINUE THIS "FRIEND" CHARADE.
THERE ARE WOMEN WHO WOULD PAY TO HAVE ME ESCORT THEM.
I KNOW. I SAW THEM LAST NIGHT AT THE CLUB.
STILL, YOU'RE ASHAMED TO BE SEEN WITH ME.
BECAUSE OF THIS.
I GOT THE IMPRESSION I HAD HURT HIS FEELINGS. THAT DIDN'T BOTHER ME.
BUT I KNEW WHAT IT WAS LIKE TO BE DIFFERENT. AN EMBARRASSMENT TO PEOPLE WHO SHOULD HAVE KNOWN BETTER.
I KNEW BETTER.
LET'S GO.
WHERE TO?
MABEL'S.
THANK YOU.

ABEL'S IS A [CA]FETERIA, BUT [T]HE FOOD IS [W]ONDERFUL.

HI, BEATRICE. THIS IS PHILLIP.

HI, PHILLIP.

ON SATURDAYS IT WAS NEARLY DESERTED.

DID SHE NOTICE THE SCARS? DID IT MATTER TO HER?

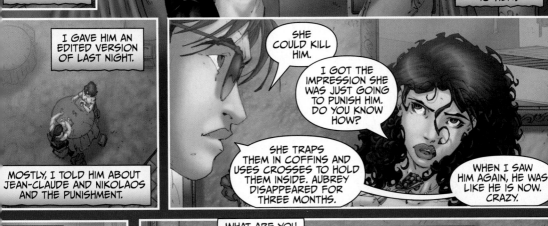

I GAVE HIM AN EDITED VERSION OF LAST NIGHT.

SHE COULD KILL HIM.

I GOT THE IMPRESSION SHE WAS JUST GOING TO PUNISH HIM. DO YOU KNOW HOW?

SHE TRAPS THEM IN COFFINS AND USES CROSSES TO HOLD THEM INSIDE. AUBREY DISAPPEARED FOR THREE MONTHS.

WHEN I SAW HIM AGAIN, HE WAS LIKE HE IS NOW. CRAZY.

MOSTLY, I TOLD HIM ABOUT JEAN-CLAUDE AND NIKOLAOS AND THE PUNISHMENT.

[WOULD] [JE]AN-CLAUDE [G]O CRAZY?

BLACKBERRIES, YUCK. I GOT THE WRONG PIE. WHAT WAS THE MATTER WITH ME?

WHAT ARE YOU GOING TO DO NOW?

PHILLIP WAS THE DAYTIME EYES-AND-EARS OF THE UNDEAD. I DIDN'T WANT TO SHARE INFORMATION WITH HIM.

YET WHEN I TALKED WITH THE VICTIM'S NEAREST AND DEAREST IN THE COMPANY OF THE POLICE, SHE TOLD US ZIP.

I NEEDED INFORMATION, AND FAST.

I'M GOING TO TALK TO REBECCA MILES.

I KNOW HER. SHE WAS MAURICE'S... PROPERTY.

I MIGHT BE ABLE TO HELP.

I DON'T WANT A CIVILIAN ALONG WHILE I WORK.

HOW ARE YOU GOING TO CONVINCE REBECCA THAT YOU WORK FOR THE MASTER VAMPIRE OF THE CITY? THE EXECUTIONER WORKING FOR VAMPIRES?

I DON'T KNOW.

I'LL COME ALONG AND HELP SMOOTH THE WATERS.

IF PHILLIP COULD HELP ME, I SAW NO HARM IN IT.

AS LONG AS HE DIDN'T FLASH THAT SMILE AT THE WRONG TIME AND GET MOLESTED BY NUNS, WE WOULD BE SAFE.

ALL RIGHT. LET'S GO.

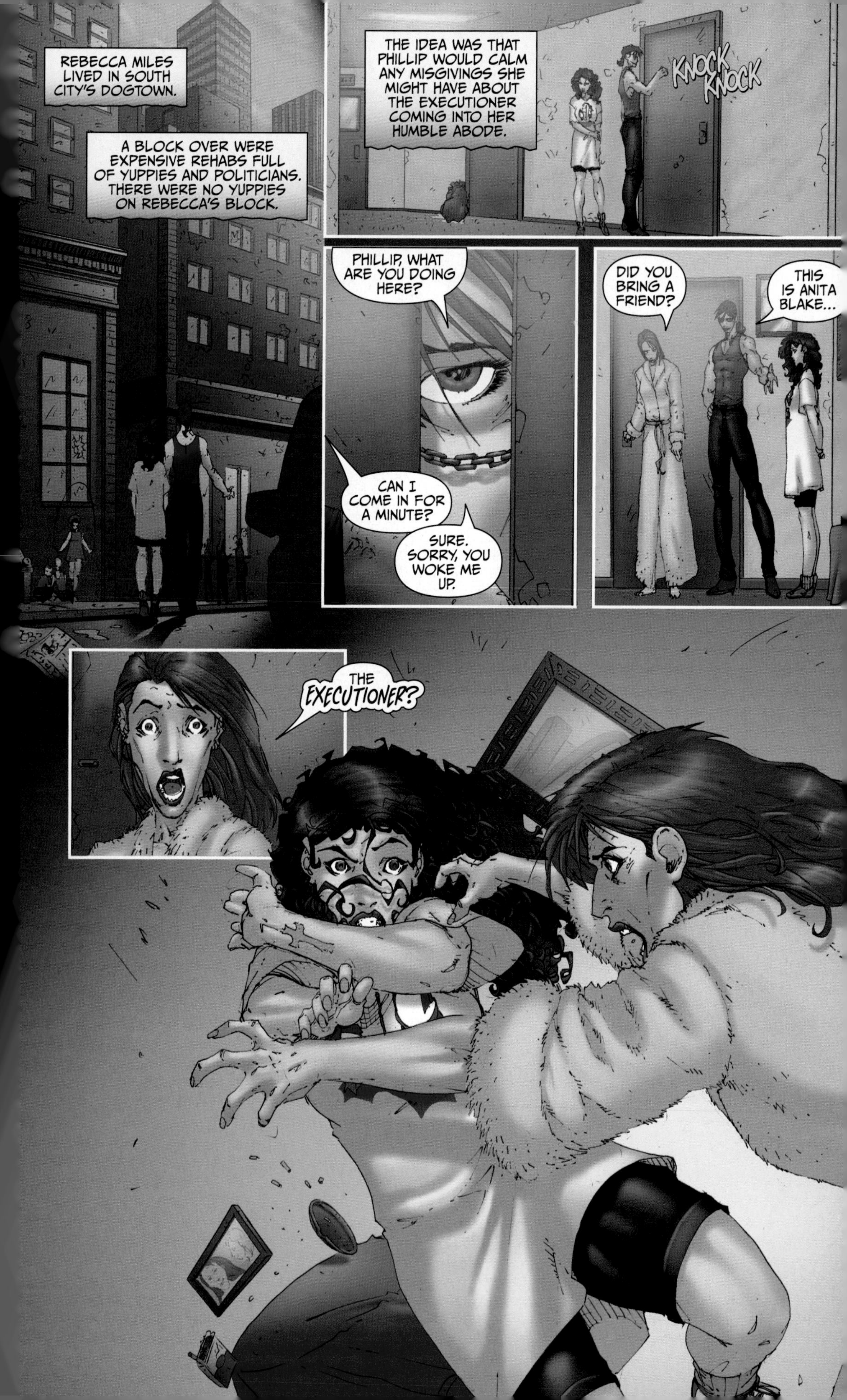

REBECCA MILES LIVED IN SOUTH CITY'S DOGTOWN.
A BLOCK OVER WERE EXPENSIVE REHABS FULL OF YUPPIES AND POLITICIANS. THERE WERE NO YUPPIES ON REBECCA'S BLOCK.
THE IDEA WAS THAT PHILLIP WOULD CALM ANY MISGIVINGS SHE MIGHT HAVE ABOUT THE EXECUTIONER COMING INTO HER HUMBLE ABODE.
KNOCK KNOCK
PHILLIP, WHAT ARE YOU DOING HERE?
CAN I COME IN FOR A MINUTE?
SURE. SORRY, YOU WOKE ME UP.
DID YOU BRING A FRIEND?
THIS IS ANITA BLAKE...
THE EXECUTIONER?

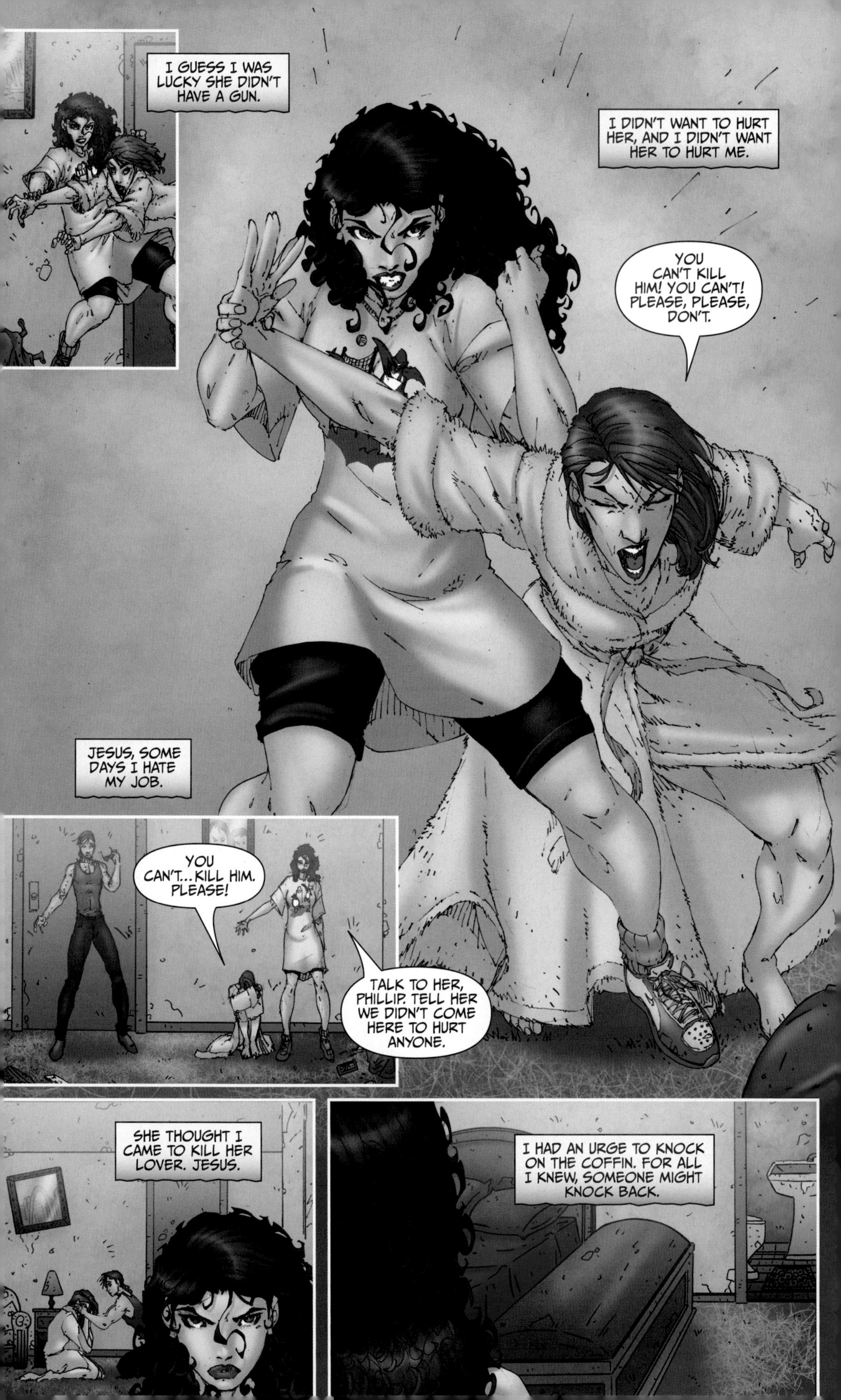

I GUESS I WAS LUCKY SHE DIDN'T HAVE A GUN.
I DIDN'T WANT TO HURT HER, AND I DIDN'T WANT HER TO HURT ME.
YOU CAN'T KILL HIM! YOU CAN'T! PLEASE, PLEASE, DON'T.
JESUS, SOME DAYS I HATE MY JOB.
YOU CAN'T...KILL HIM. PLEASE!
TALK TO HER, PHILLIP. TELL HER WE DIDN'T COME HERE TO HURT ANYONE.
SHE THOUGHT I CAME TO KILL HER LOVER. JESUS.
I HAD AN URGE TO KNOCK ON THE COFFIN. FOR ALL I KNEW, SOMEONE MIGHT KNOCK BACK.

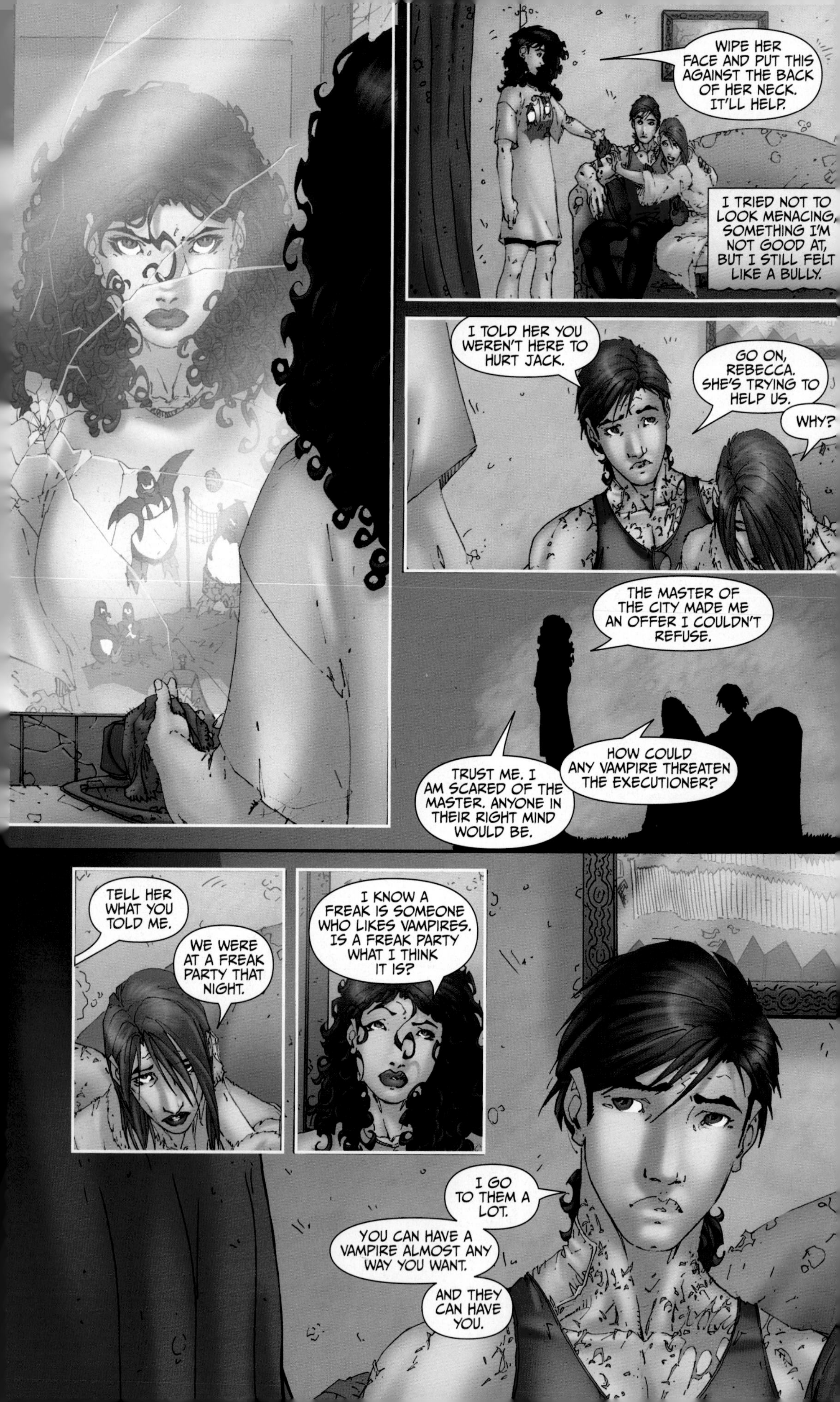
WIPE HER FACE AND PUT THIS AGAINST THE BACK OF HER NECK. IT'LL HELP.
I TRIED NOT TO LOOK MENACING, SOMETHING I'M NOT GOOD AT, BUT I STILL FELT LIKE A BULLY.
I TOLD HER YOU WEREN'T HERE TO HURT JACK.
GO ON, REBECCA. SHE'S TRYING TO HELP US.
WHY?
THE MASTER OF THE CITY MADE ME AN OFFER I COULDN'T REFUSE.
HOW COULD ANY VAMPIRE THREATEN THE EXECUTIONER?
TRUST ME. I AM SCARED OF THE MASTER. ANYONE IN THEIR RIGHT MIND WOULD BE.
TELL HER WHAT YOU TOLD ME.
WE WERE AT A FREAK PARTY THAT NIGHT.
I KNOW A FREAK IS SOMEONE WHO LIKES VAMPIRES. IS A FREAK PARTY WHAT I THINK IT IS?
I GO TO THEM A LOT.
YOU CAN HAVE A VAMPIRE ALMOST ANY WAY YOU WANT.
AND THEY CAN HAVE YOU.

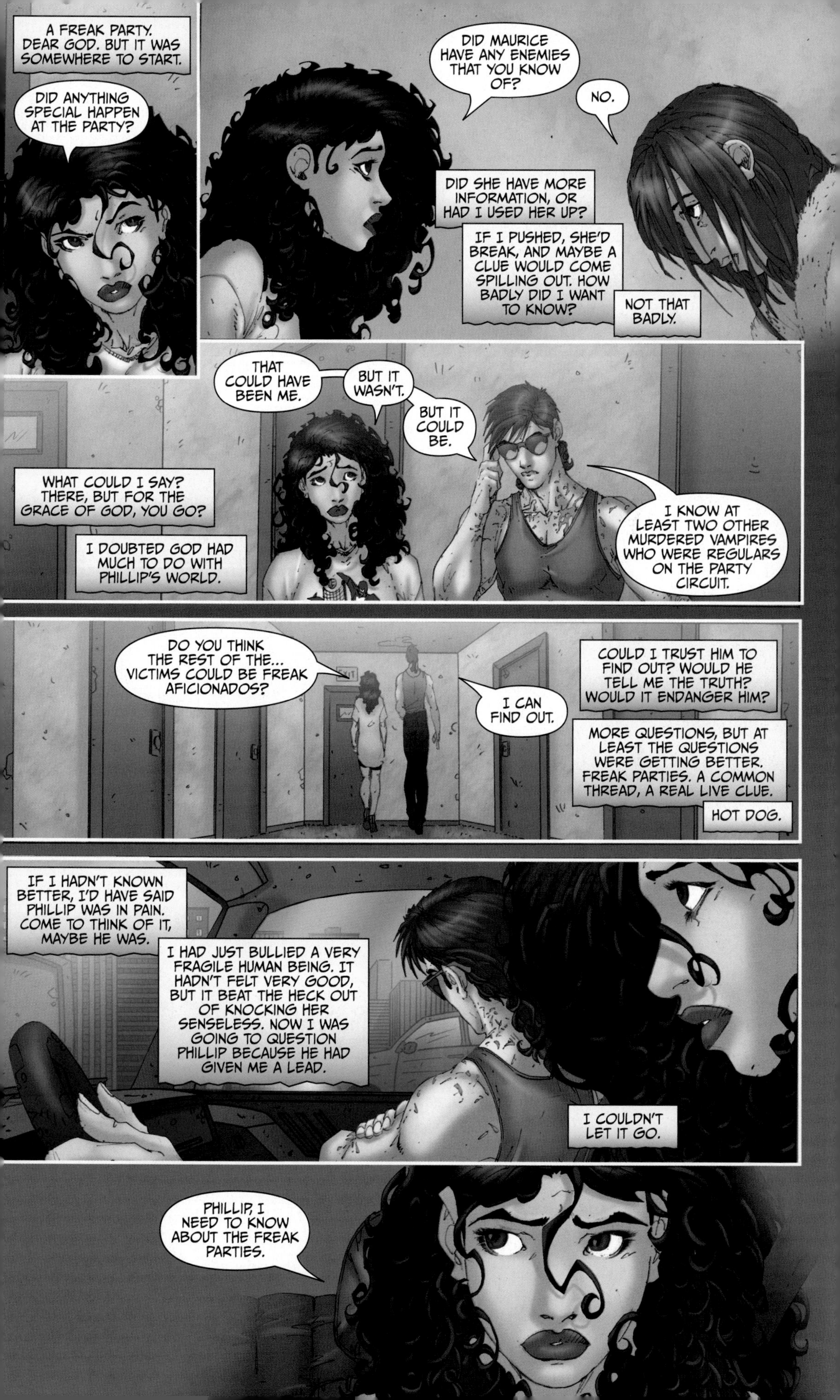
A FREAK PARTY. DEAR GOD. BUT IT WAS SOMEWHERE TO START.
DID ANYTHING SPECIAL HAPPEN AT THE PARTY?
DID MAURICE HAVE ANY ENEMIES THAT YOU KNOW OF?
NO.
DID SHE HAVE MORE INFORMATION, OR HAD I USED HER UP?
IF I PUSHED, SHE'D BREAK, AND MAYBE A CLUE WOULD COME SPILLING OUT. HOW BADLY DID I WANT TO KNOW?
NOT THAT BADLY.
THAT COULD HAVE BEEN ME.
BUT IT WASN'T.
BUT IT COULD BE.
WHAT COULD I SAY? THERE, BUT FOR THE GRACE OF GOD, YOU GO?
I DOUBTED GOD HAD MUCH TO DO WITH PHILLIP'S WORLD.
I KNOW AT LEAST TWO OTHER MURDERED VAMPIRES WHO WERE REGULARS ON THE PARTY CIRCUIT.
DO YOU THINK THE REST OF THE... VICTIMS COULD BE FREAK AFICIONADOS?
I CAN FIND OUT.
COULD I TRUST HIM TO FIND OUT? WOULD HE TELL ME THE TRUTH? WOULD IT ENDANGER HIM?
MORE QUESTIONS, BUT AT LEAST THE QUESTIONS WERE GETTING BETTER. FREAK PARTIES. A COMMON THREAD, A REAL LIVE CLUE.
HOT DOG.
IF I HADN'T KNOWN BETTER, I'D HAVE SAID PHILLIP WAS IN PAIN. COME TO THINK OF IT, MAYBE HE WAS.
I HAD JUST BULLIED A VERY FRAGILE HUMAN BEING. IT HADN'T FELT VERY GOOD, BUT IT BEAT THE HECK OUT OF KNOCKING HER SENSELESS. NOW I WAS GOING TO QUESTION PHILLIP BECAUSE HE HAD GIVEN ME A LEAD.
I COULDN'T LET IT GO.
PHILLIP, I NEED TO KNOW ABOUT THE FREAK PARTIES.

DROP ME AT *GUILTY PLEASURES.*

DON'T YOU NEED TO PICK UP YOUR CAR?

MONICA DROPPED ME OFF AT YOUR OFFICE.

DID SHE NOW?

WHY ARE YOU SO ANGRY AT HER? ALL SHE DID WAS GET YOU TO THE CLUB.

SHE'S HUMAN, AND SHE BETRAYED OTHER HUMANS TO NONHUMANS.

AND THAT'S A WORSE CRIME THAN JEAN-CLAUDE CHOOSING YOU TO BE OUR CHAMPION?

JEAN-CLAUDE IS A VAMPIRE. YOU EXPECT TREACHERY FROM VAMPIRES.

YOU DO. I DO NOT.

VAMPIRES ARE NOT HUMAN. THEIR LOYALTY MUST BE TO THEIR OWN KIND.

I UNDERSTAND THAT.

MONICA BETRAYED HER OWN KIND. SHE ALSO BETRAYED A FRIEND. THAT IS UNFORGIVABLE.

SO IF SOMEONE WAS YOUR FRIEND, YOU WOULD DO ANYTHING FOR THEM?

ANYTHING? THAT WAS A TALL ORDER.

ALMOST ANYTHING.

SO LOYALTY AND FRIENDSHIP ARE VERY IMPORTANT TO YOU?

YES.

BECAUSE YOU BELIEVE MONICA BETRAYED BOTH OF THOSE THINGS, WHAT SHE DID WAS WORSE THAN ANYTHING THE VAMPIRES DID?

I AM NOT BIG ON ANALYZING PEOPLE. I KNOW WHO I AM AND WHAT I DO, AND THAT'S ENOUGH.

NOT ALWAYS, BUT MOST OF THE TIME.

NOT ANYTHING. I DON'T BELIEVE IN MANY ABSOLUTES.

BUT IF YOU WANT TH SHORT VERSIC YES, THAT'S W I'M ANGRY A MONICA.

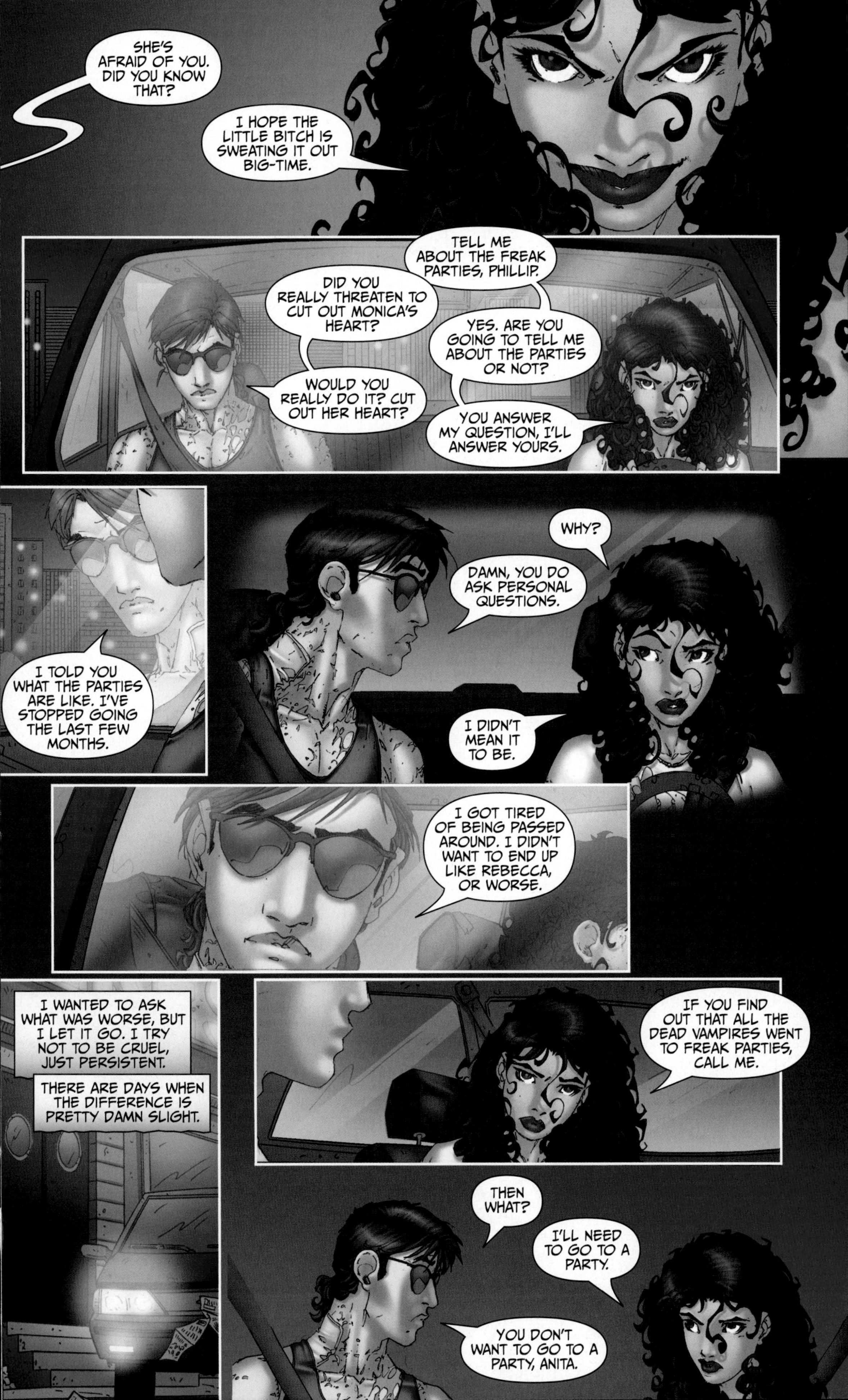
SHE'S AFRAID OF YOU. DID YOU KNOW THAT?
I HOPE THE LITTLE BITCH IS SWEATING IT OUT BIG-TIME.
TELL ME ABOUT THE FREAK PARTIES, PHILLIP.
DID YOU REALLY THREATEN TO CUT OUT MONICA'S HEART?
YES. ARE YOU GOING TO TELL ME ABOUT THE PARTIES OR NOT?
WOULD YOU REALLY DO IT? CUT OUT HER HEART?
YOU ANSWER MY QUESTION, I'LL ANSWER YOURS.
I TOLD YOU WHAT THE PARTIES ARE LIKE. I'VE STOPPED GOING THE LAST FEW MONTHS.
WHY?
DAMN, YOU DO ASK PERSONAL QUESTIONS.
I DIDN'T MEAN IT TO BE.
I GOT TIRED OF BEING PASSED AROUND. I DIDN'T WANT TO END UP LIKE REBECCA, OR WORSE.
I WANTED TO ASK WHAT WAS WORSE, BUT I LET IT GO. I TRY NOT TO BE CRUEL, JUST PERSISTENT.
THERE ARE DAYS WHEN THE DIFFERENCE IS PRETTY DAMN SLIGHT.
IF YOU FIND OUT THAT ALL THE DEAD VAMPIRES WENT TO FREAK PARTIES, CALL ME.
THEN WHAT?
I'LL NEED TO GO TO A PARTY.
YOU DON'T WANT TO GO TO A PARTY, ANITA.

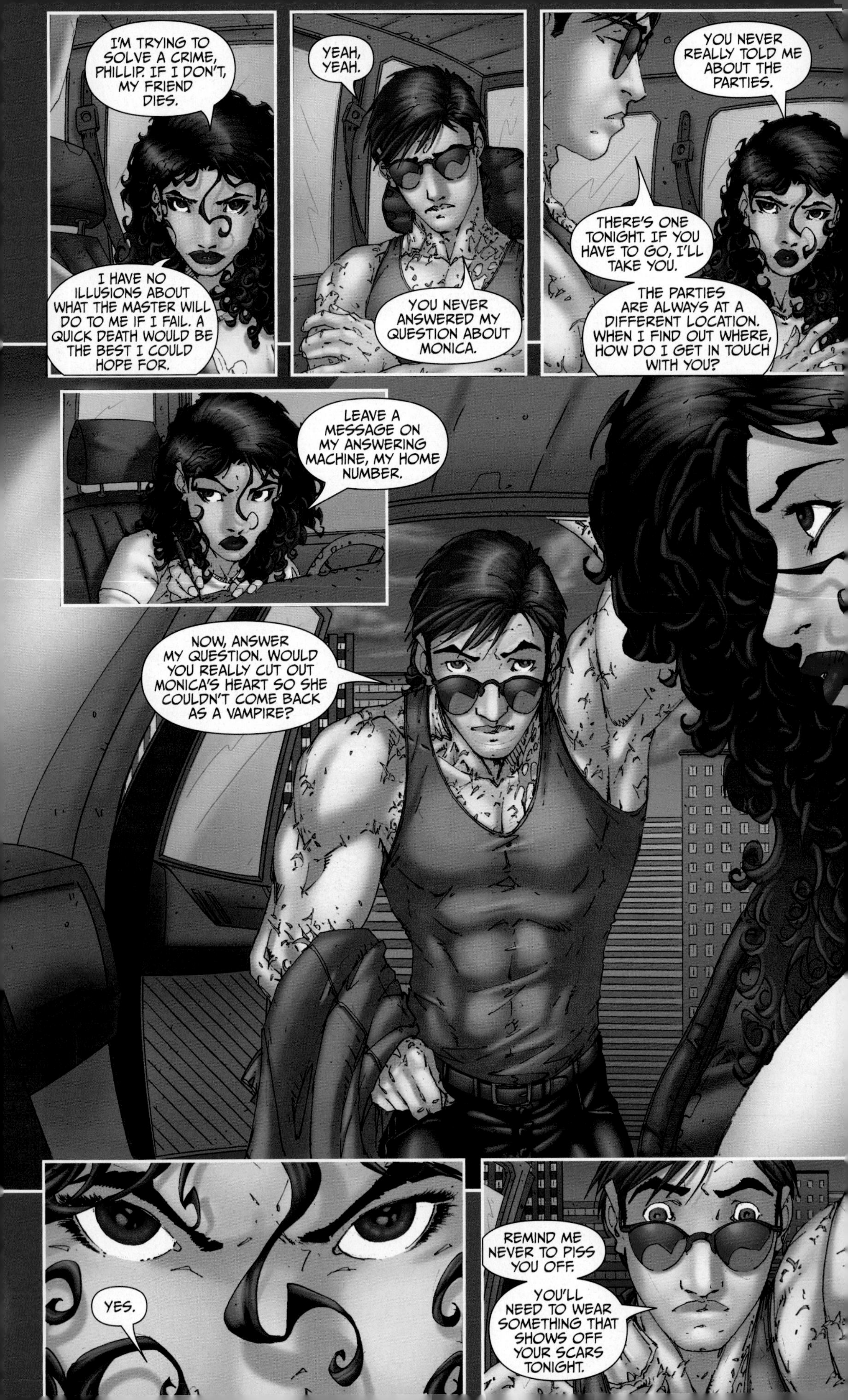
I'M TRYING TO SOLVE A CRIME, PHILLIP. IF I DON'T, MY FRIEND DIES.
I HAVE NO ILLUSIONS ABOUT WHAT THE MASTER WILL DO TO ME IF I FAIL. A QUICK DEATH WOULD BE THE BEST I COULD HOPE FOR.
YEAH, YEAH.
YOU NEVER ANSWERED MY QUESTION ABOUT MONICA.
YOU NEVER REALLY TOLD ME ABOUT THE PARTIES.
THERE'S ONE TONIGHT. IF YOU HAVE TO GO, I'LL TAKE YOU.
THE PARTIES ARE ALWAYS AT A DIFFERENT LOCATION. WHEN I FIND OUT WHERE, HOW DO I GET IN TOUCH WITH YOU?
LEAVE A MESSAGE ON MY ANSWERING MACHINE, MY HOME NUMBER.
NOW, ANSWER MY QUESTION. WOULD YOU REALLY CUT OUT MONICA'S HEART SO SHE COULDN'T COME BACK AS A VAMPIRE?
YES.
REMIND ME NEVER TO PISS YOU OFF.
YOU'LL NEED TO WEAR SOMETHING THAT SHOWS OFF YOUR SCARS TONIGHT.

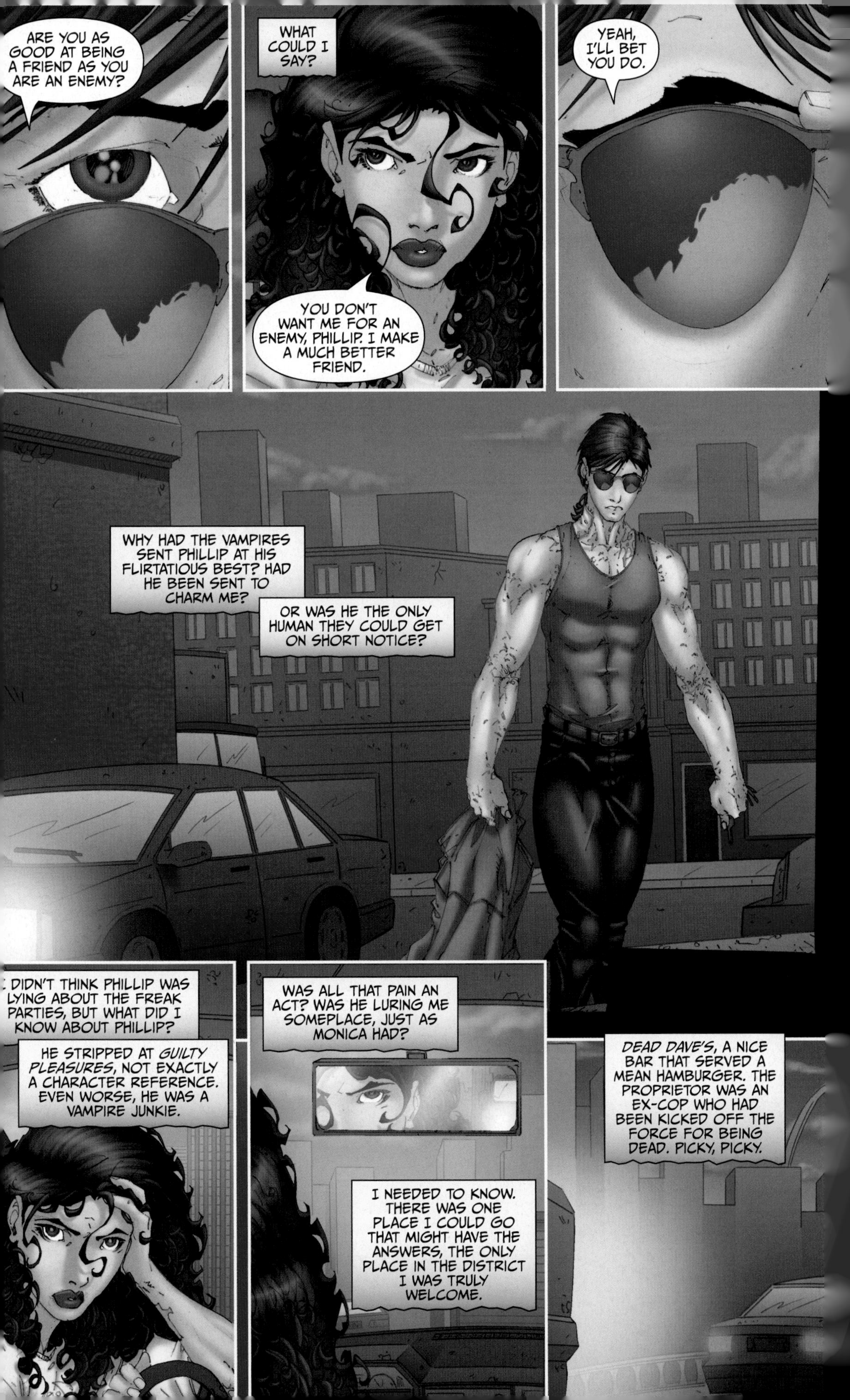
ARE YOU AS GOOD AT BEING A FRIEND AS YOU ARE AN ENEMY?
WHAT COULD I SAY?
YOU DON'T WANT ME FOR AN ENEMY, PHILLIP. I MAKE A MUCH BETTER FRIEND.
YEAH, I'LL BET YOU DO.
WHY HAD THE VAMPIRES SENT PHILLIP AT HIS FLIRTATIOUS BEST? HAD HE BEEN SENT TO CHARM ME?
OR WAS HE THE ONLY HUMAN THEY COULD GET ON SHORT NOTICE?
DIDN'T THINK PHILLIP WAS LYING ABOUT THE FREAK PARTIES, BUT WHAT DID I KNOW ABOUT PHILLIP?
HE STRIPPED AT *GUILTY PLEASURES*, NOT EXACTLY A CHARACTER REFERENCE. EVEN WORSE, HE WAS A VAMPIRE JUNKIE.
WAS ALL THAT PAIN AN ACT? WAS HE LURING ME SOMEPLACE, JUST AS MONICA HAD?
I NEEDED TO KNOW. THERE WAS ONE PLACE I COULD GO THAT MIGHT HAVE THE ANSWERS, THE ONLY PLACE IN THE DISTRICT I WAS TRULY WELCOME.
DEAD DAVE'S, A NICE BAR THAT SERVED A MEAN HAMBURGER. THE PROPRIETOR WAS AN EX-COP WHO HAD BEEN KICKED OFF THE FORCE FOR BEING DEAD. PICKY, PICKY.

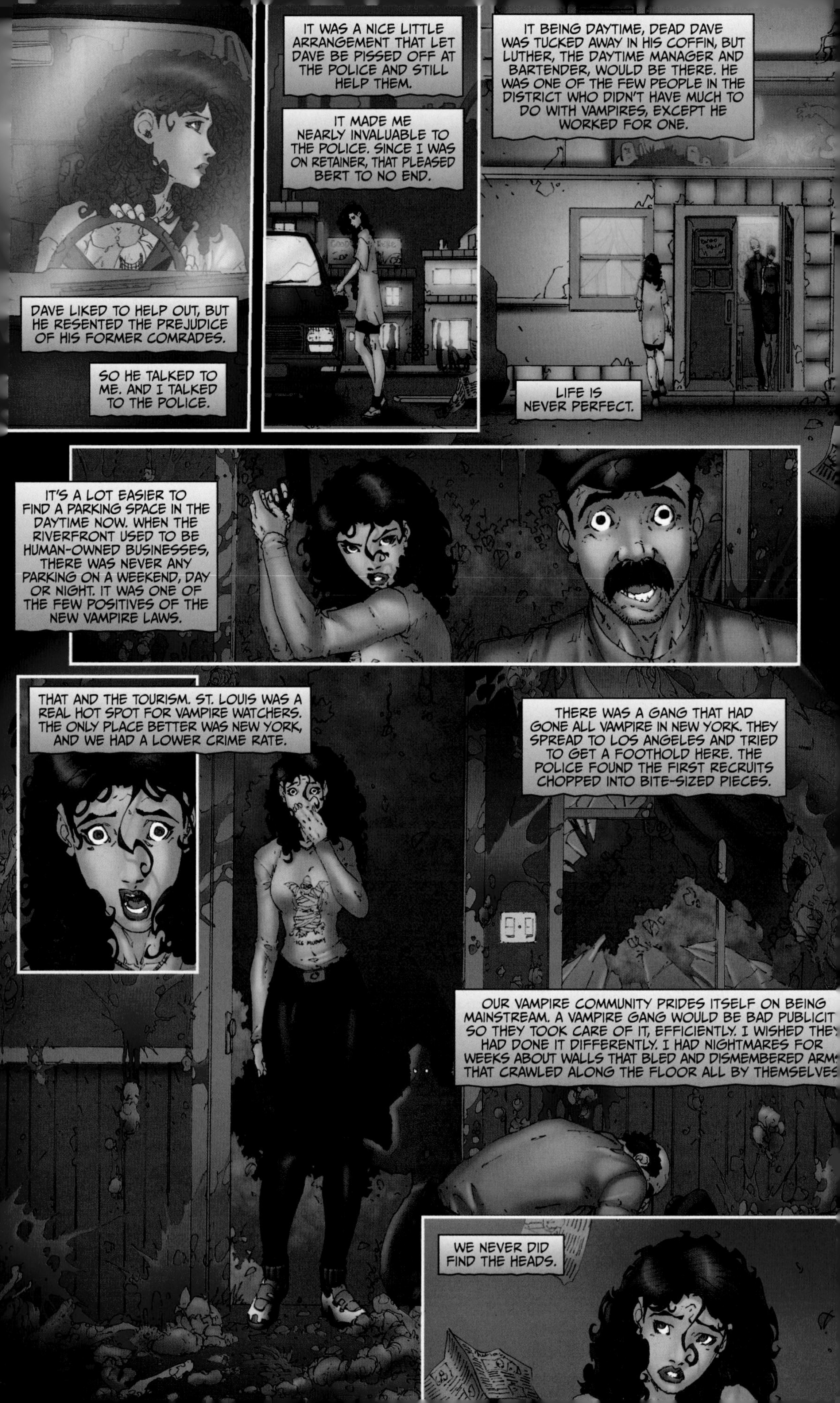

DAVE LIKED TO HELP OUT, BUT HE RESENTED THE PREJUDICE OF HIS FORMER COMRADES.
SO HE TALKED TO ME. AND I TALKED TO THE POLICE.
IT WAS A NICE LITTLE ARRANGEMENT THAT LET DAVE BE PISSED OFF AT THE POLICE AND STILL HELP THEM.
IT MADE ME NEARLY INVALUABLE TO THE POLICE. SINCE I WAS ON RETAINER, THAT PLEASED BERT TO NO END.
IT BEING DAYTIME, DEAD DAVE WAS TUCKED AWAY IN HIS COFFIN, BUT LUTHER, THE DAYTIME MANAGER AND BARTENDER, WOULD BE THERE. HE WAS ONE OF THE FEW PEOPLE IN THE DISTRICT WHO DIDN'T HAVE MUCH TO DO WITH VAMPIRES, EXCEPT HE WORKED FOR ONE.
LIFE IS NEVER PERFECT.
IT'S A LOT EASIER TO FIND A PARKING SPACE IN THE DAYTIME NOW. WHEN THE RIVERFRONT USED TO BE HUMAN-OWNED BUSINESSES, THERE WAS NEVER ANY PARKING ON A WEEKEND, DAY OR NIGHT. IT WAS ONE OF THE FEW POSITIVES OF THE NEW VAMPIRE LAWS.
THAT AND THE TOURISM. ST. LOUIS WAS A REAL HOT SPOT FOR VAMPIRE WATCHERS. THE ONLY PLACE BETTER WAS NEW YORK, AND WE HAD A LOWER CRIME RATE.
THERE WAS A GANG THAT HAD GONE ALL VAMPIRE IN NEW YORK. THEY SPREAD TO LOS ANGELES AND TRIED TO GET A FOOTHOLD HERE. THE POLICE FOUND THE FIRST RECRUITS CHOPPED INTO BITE-SIZED PIECES.
OUR VAMPIRE COMMUNITY PRIDES ITSELF ON BEING MAINSTREAM. A VAMPIRE GANG WOULD BE BAD PUBLICIT SO THEY TOOK CARE OF IT, EFFICIENTLY. I WISHED THE HAD DONE IT DIFFERENTLY. I HAD NIGHTMARES FOR WEEKS ABOUT WALLS THAT BLED AND DISMEMBERED ARM THAT CRAWLED ALONG THE FLOOR ALL BY THEMSELVES
WE NEVER DID FIND THE HEADS.

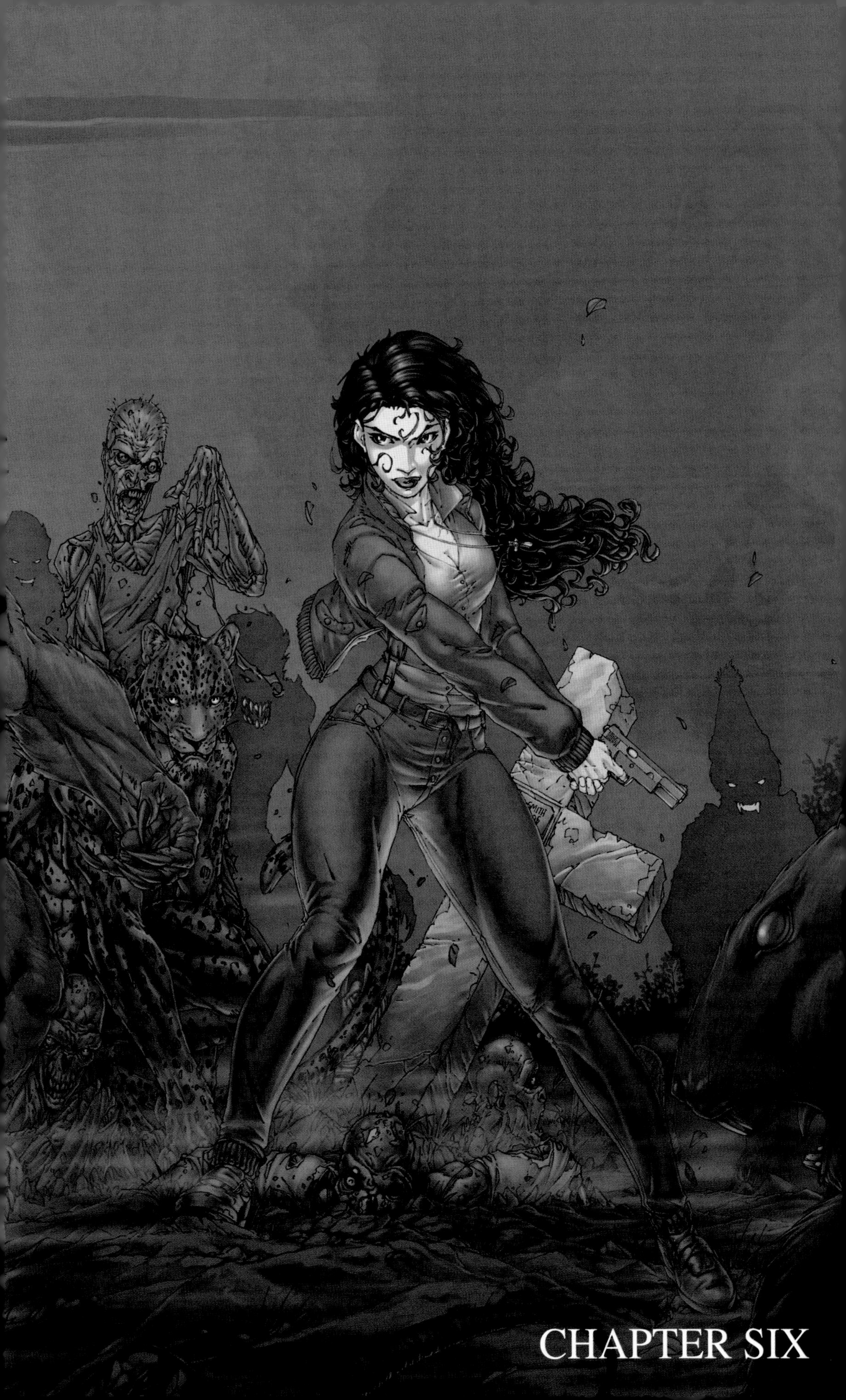

CHAPTER SIX

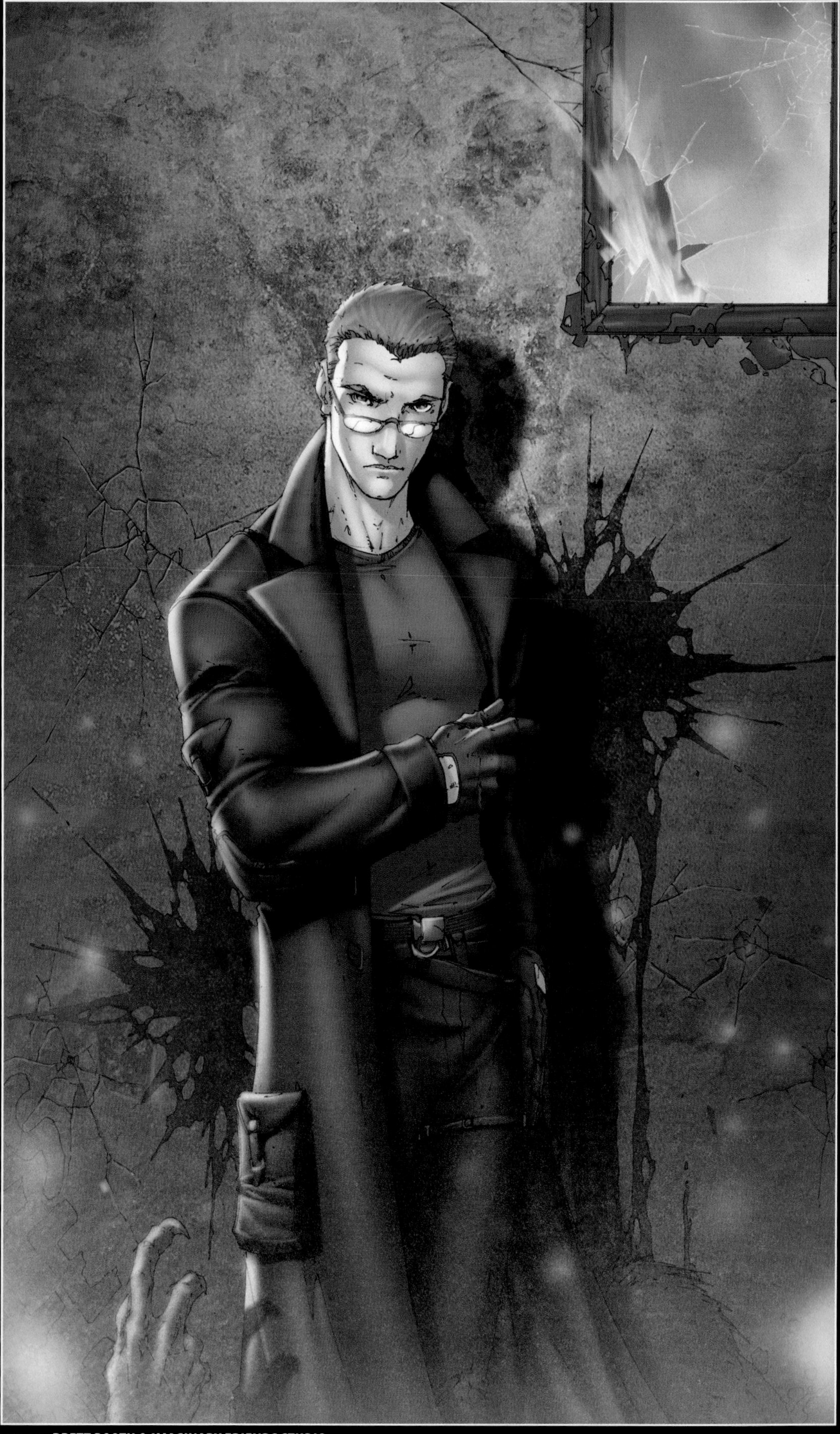

COVER BY: BRETT BOOTH & IMAGINARY FRIENDS STUDIO

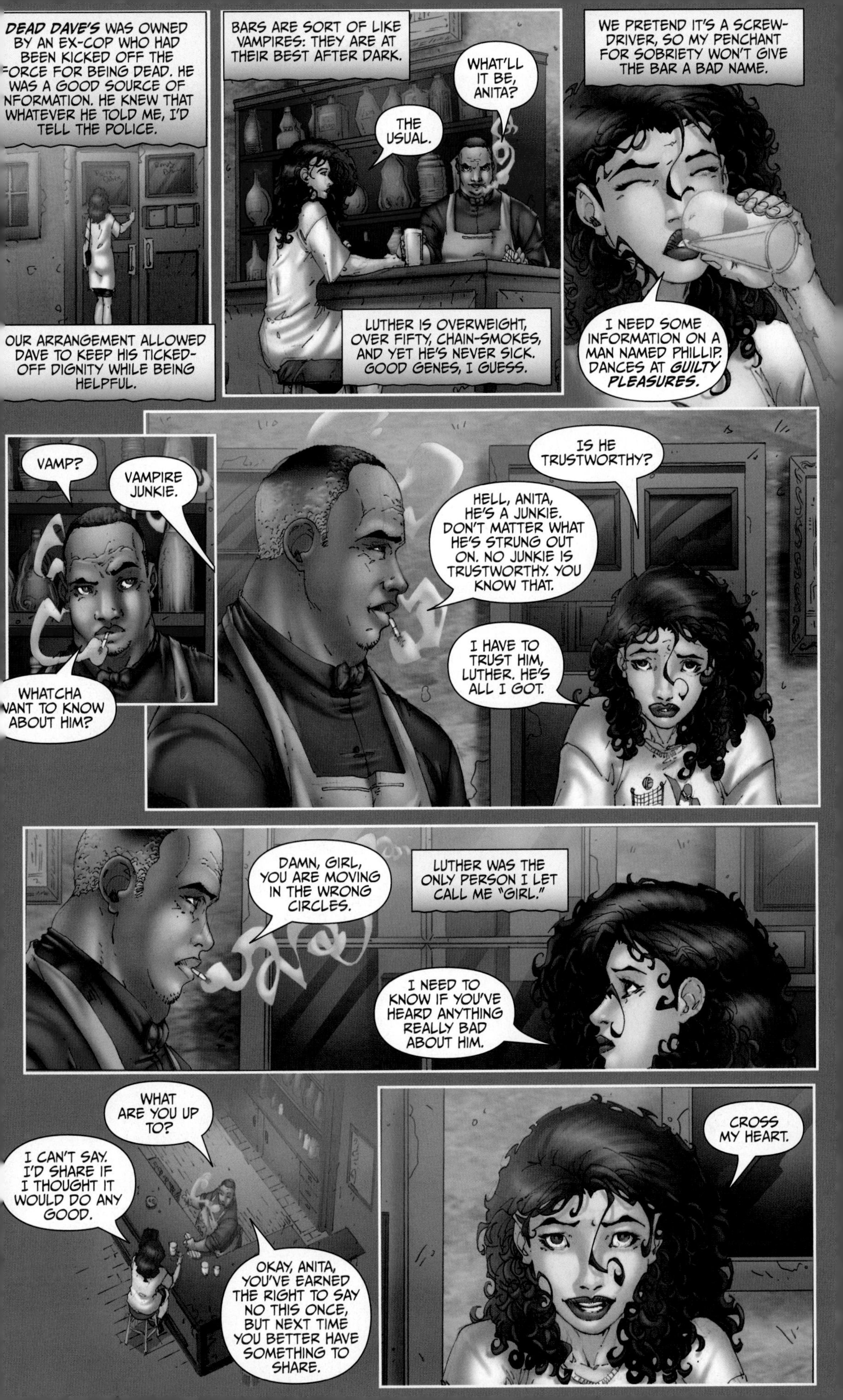
DEAD DAVE'S WAS OWNED BY AN EX-COP WHO HAD BEEN KICKED OFF THE FORCE FOR BEING DEAD. HE WAS A GOOD SOURCE OF INFORMATION. HE KNEW THAT WHATEVER HE TOLD ME, I'D TELL THE POLICE.
OUR ARRANGEMENT ALLOWED DAVE TO KEEP HIS TICKED-OFF DIGNITY WHILE BEING HELPFUL.
BARS ARE SORT OF LIKE VAMPIRES: THEY ARE AT THEIR BEST AFTER DARK.
WHAT'LL IT BE, ANITA?
THE USUAL.
LUTHER IS OVERWEIGHT, OVER FIFTY, CHAIN-SMOKES, AND YET HE'S NEVER SICK. GOOD GENES, I GUESS.
WE PRETEND IT'S A SCREW-DRIVER, SO MY PENCHANT FOR SOBRIETY WON'T GIVE THE BAR A BAD NAME.
I NEED SOME INFORMATION ON A MAN NAMED PHILLIP. DANCES AT GUILTY PLEASURES.
VAMP?
VAMPIRE JUNKIE.
WHATCHA WANT TO KNOW ABOUT HIM?
IS HE TRUSTWORTHY?
HELL, ANITA, HE'S A JUNKIE. DON'T MATTER WHAT HE'S STRUNG OUT ON. NO JUNKIE IS TRUSTWORTHY. YOU KNOW THAT.
I HAVE TO TRUST HIM, LUTHER. HE'S ALL I GOT.
DAMN, GIRL, YOU ARE MOVING IN THE WRONG CIRCLES.
LUTHER WAS THE ONLY PERSON I LET CALL ME "GIRL."
I NEED TO KNOW IF YOU'VE HEARD ANYTHING REALLY BAD ABOUT HIM.
WHAT ARE YOU UP TO?
I CAN'T SAY. I'D SHARE IF I THOUGHT IT WOULD DO ANY GOOD.
OKAY, ANITA, YOU'VE EARNED THE RIGHT TO SAY NO THIS ONCE, BUT NEXT TIME YOU BETTER HAVE SOMETHING TO SHARE.
CROSS MY HEART.

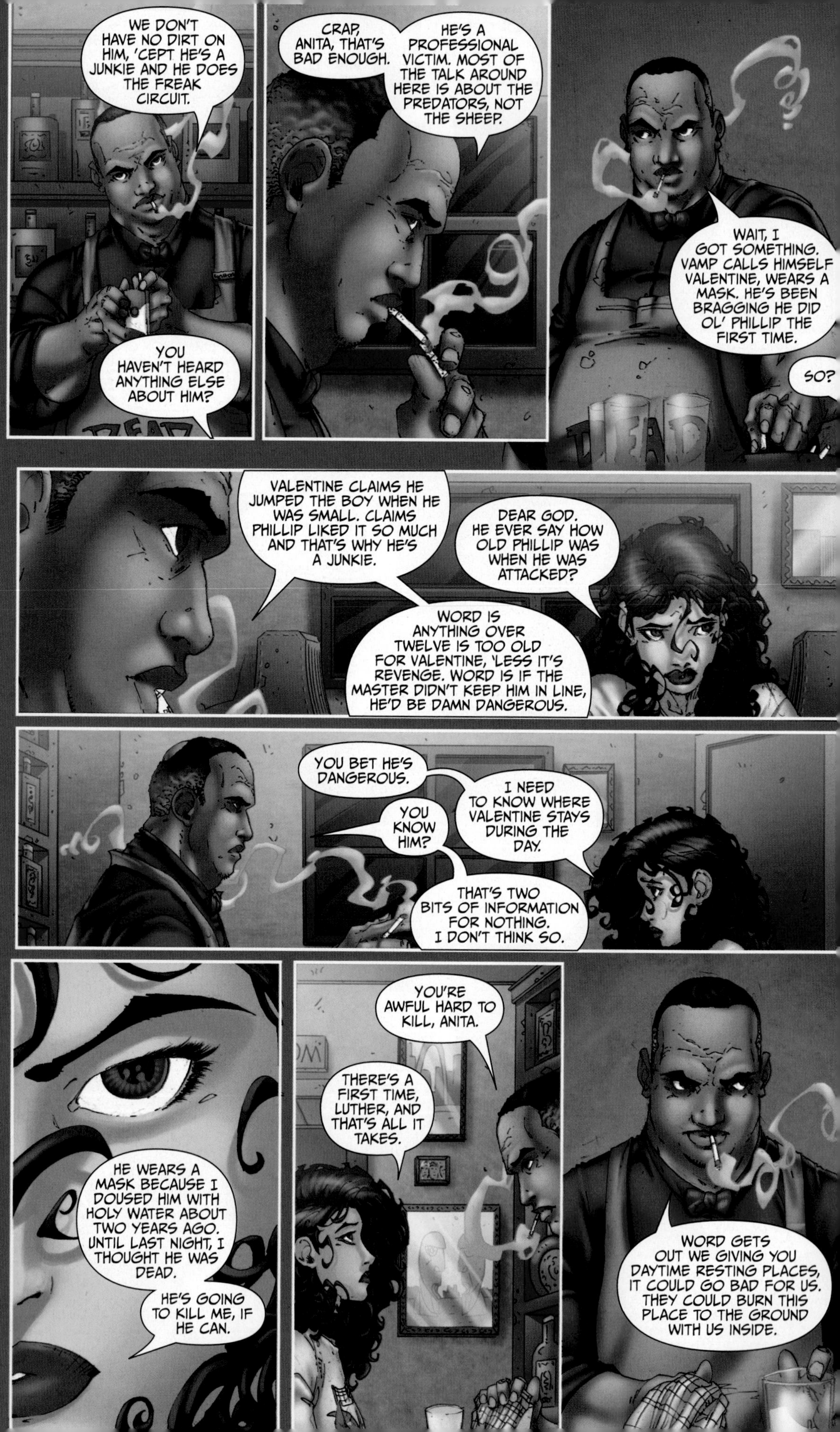
WE DON'T HAVE NO DIRT ON HIM, 'CEPT HE'S A JUNKIE AND HE DOES THE FREAK CIRCUIT.
YOU HAVEN'T HEARD ANYTHING ELSE ABOUT HIM?
CRAP, ANITA, THAT'S BAD ENOUGH.
HE'S A PROFESSIONAL VICTIM. MOST OF THE TALK AROUND HERE IS ABOUT THE PREDATORS, NOT THE SHEEP.
WAIT, I GOT SOMETHING. VAMP CALLS HIMSELF VALENTINE, WEARS A MASK. HE'S BEEN BRAGGING HE DID OL' PHILLIP THE FIRST TIME.
SO?
VALENTINE CLAIMS HE JUMPED THE BOY WHEN HE WAS SMALL. CLAIMS PHILLIP LIKED IT SO MUCH AND THAT'S WHY HE'S A JUNKIE.
DEAR GOD. HE EVER SAY HOW OLD PHILLIP WAS WHEN HE WAS ATTACKED?
WORD IS ANYTHING OVER TWELVE IS TOO OLD FOR VALENTINE, 'LESS IT'S REVENGE. WORD IS IF THE MASTER DIDN'T KEEP HIM IN LINE, HE'D BE DAMN DANGEROUS.
YOU BET HE'S DANGEROUS.
I NEED TO KNOW WHERE VALENTINE STAYS DURING THE DAY.
YOU KNOW HIM?
THAT'S TWO BITS OF INFORMATION FOR NOTHING. I DON'T THINK SO.
HE WEARS A MASK BECAUSE I DOUSED HIM WITH HOLY WATER ABOUT TWO YEARS AGO. UNTIL LAST NIGHT, I THOUGHT HE WAS DEAD.
HE'S GOING TO KILL ME, IF HE CAN.
YOU'RE AWFUL HARD TO KILL, ANITA.
THERE'S A FIRST TIME, LUTHER, AND THAT'S ALL IT TAKES.
WORD GETS OUT WE GIVING YOU DAYTIME RESTING PLACES, IT COULD GO BAD FOR US. THEY COULD BURN THIS PLACE TO THE GROUND WITH US INSIDE.

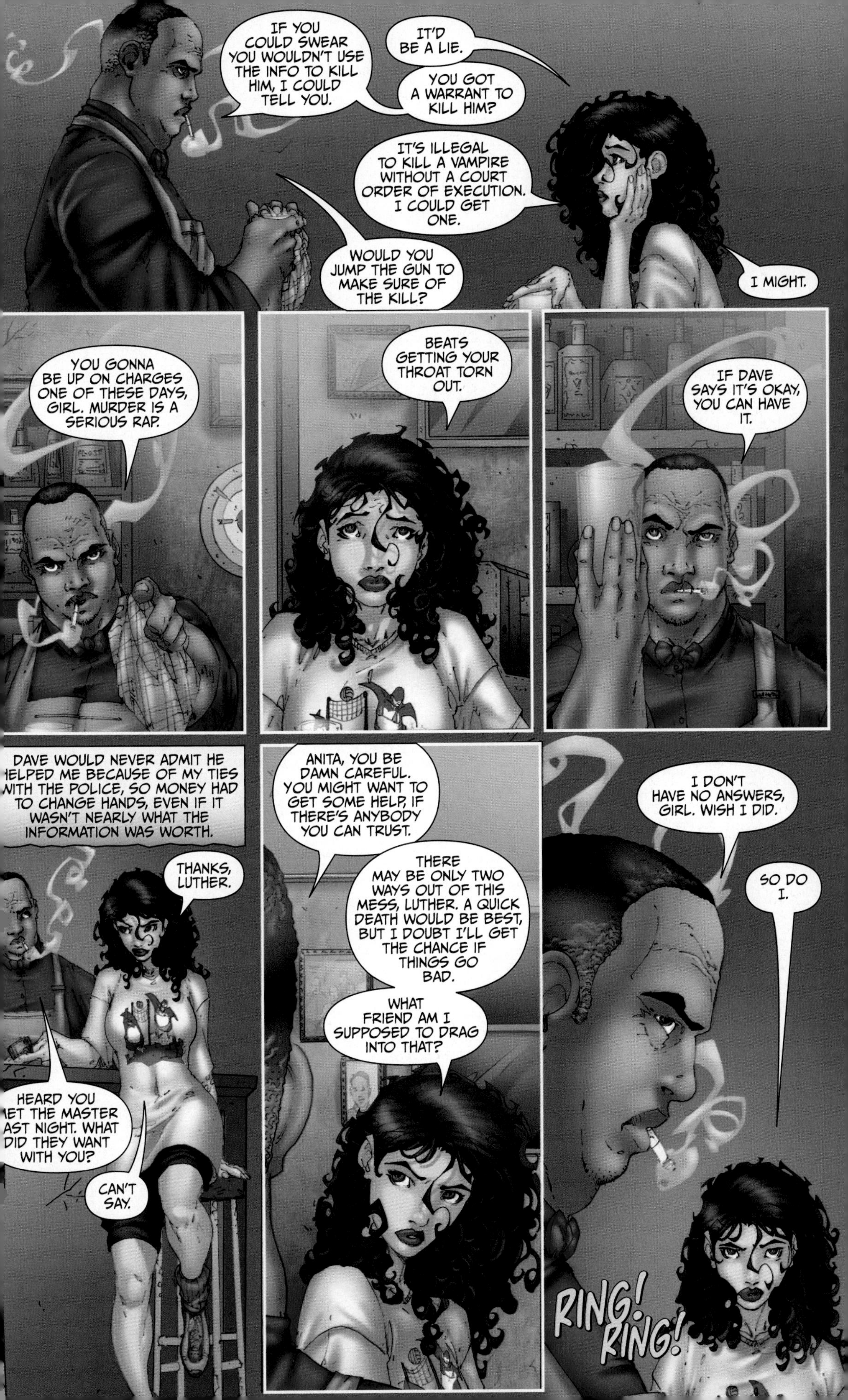
IF YOU COULD SWEAR YOU WOULDN'T USE THE INFO TO KILL HIM, I COULD TELL YOU.
IT'D BE A LIE.
YOU GOT A WARRANT TO KILL HIM?
IT'S ILLEGAL TO KILL A VAMPIRE WITHOUT A COURT ORDER OF EXECUTION. I COULD GET ONE.
WOULD YOU JUMP THE GUN TO MAKE SURE OF THE KILL?
I MIGHT.
YOU GONNA BE UP ON CHARGES ONE OF THESE DAYS, GIRL. MURDER IS A SERIOUS RAP.
BEATS GETTING YOUR THROAT TORN OUT.
IF DAVE SAYS IT'S OKAY, YOU CAN HAVE IT.
DAVE WOULD NEVER ADMIT HE IELPED ME BECAUSE OF MY TIES VITH THE POLICE, SO MONEY HAD TO CHANGE HANDS, EVEN IF IT WASN'T NEARLY WHAT THE INFORMATION WAS WORTH.
THANKS, LUTHER.
HEARD YOU IET THE MASTER AST NIGHT. WHAT DID THEY WANT WITH YOU?
CAN'T SAY.
ANITA, YOU BE DAMN CAREFUL. YOU MIGHT WANT TO GET SOME HELP, IF THERE'S ANYBODY YOU CAN TRUST.
THERE MAY BE ONLY TWO WAYS OUT OF THIS MESS, LUTHER. A QUICK DEATH WOULD BE BEST, BUT I DOUBT I'LL GET THE CHANCE IF THINGS GO BAD.
WHAT FRIEND AM I SUPPOSED TO DRAG INTO THAT?
I DON'T HAVE NO ANSWERS, GIRL. WISH I DID.
SO DO I.
RING! RING!

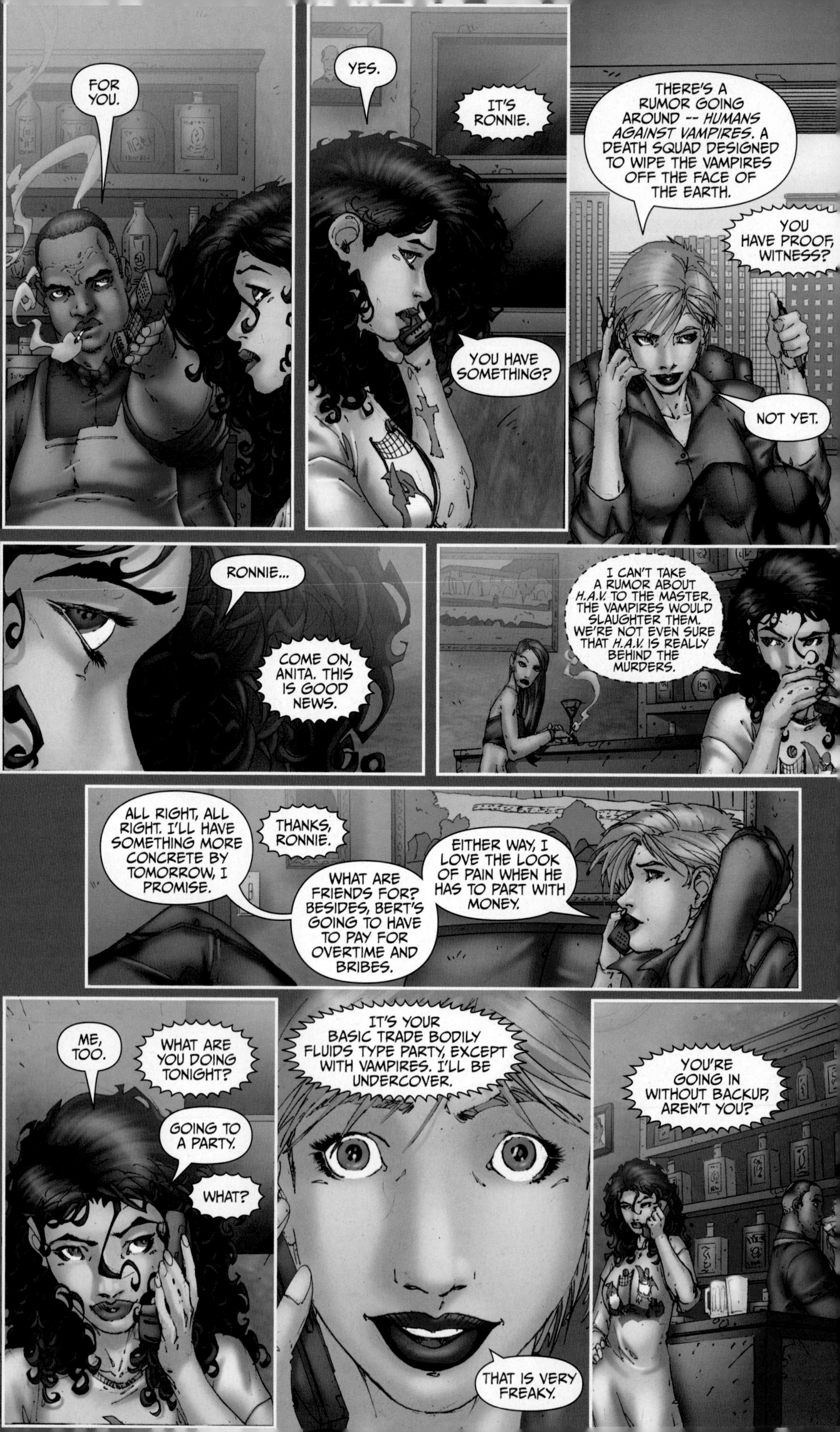
FOR YOU.
YES.
IT'S RONNIE.
YOU HAVE SOMETHING?
THERE'S A RUMOR GOING AROUND -- HUMANS AGAINST VAMPIRES. A DEATH SQUAD DESIGNED TO WIPE THE VAMPIRES OFF THE FACE OF THE EARTH.
YOU HAVE PROOF, WITNESS?
NOT YET.
RONNIE...
COME ON, ANITA. THIS IS GOOD NEWS.
I CAN'T TAKE A RUMOR ABOUT H.A.V. TO THE MASTER. THE VAMPIRES WOULD SLAUGHTER THEM. WE'RE NOT EVEN SURE THAT H.A.V. IS REALLY BEHIND THE MURDERS.
ALL RIGHT, ALL RIGHT. I'LL HAVE SOMETHING MORE CONCRETE BY TOMORROW, I PROMISE.
THANKS, RONNIE.
WHAT ARE FRIENDS FOR? BESIDES, BERT'S GOING TO HAVE TO PAY FOR OVERTIME AND BRIBES.
EITHER WAY, I LOVE THE LOOK OF PAIN WHEN HE HAS TO PART WITH MONEY.
ME, TOO.
WHAT ARE YOU DOING TONIGHT?
GOING TO A PARTY.
WHAT?
IT'S YOUR BASIC TRADE BODILY FLUIDS TYPE PARTY, EXCEPT WITH VAMPIRES. I'LL BE UNDERCOVER.
THAT IS VERY FREAKY.
YOU'RE GOING IN WITHOUT BACKUP, AREN'T YOU?

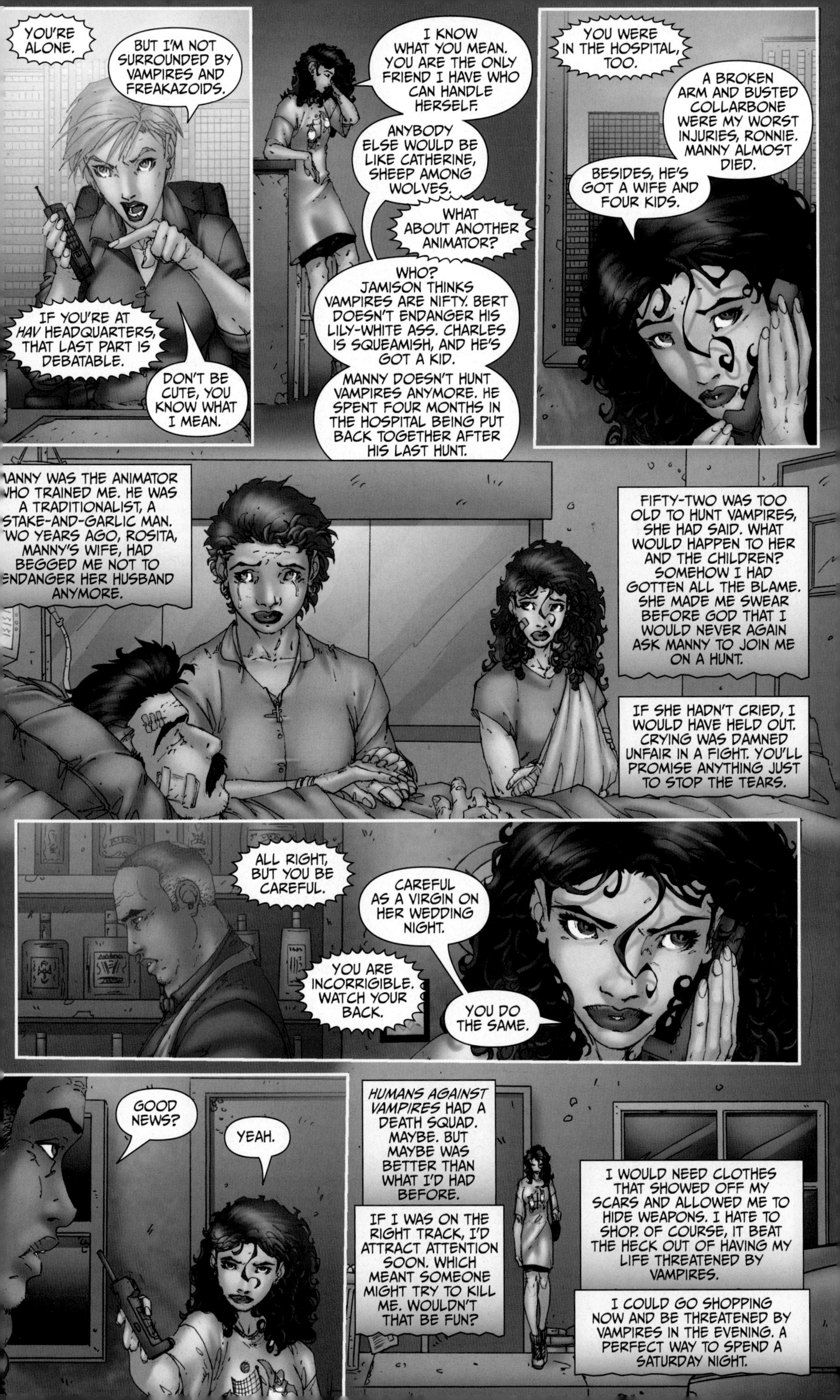

YOU'RE ALONE.
BUT I'M NOT SURROUNDED BY VAMPIRES AND FREAKAZOIDS.
IF YOU'RE AT *HAV* HEADQUARTERS, THAT LAST PART IS DEBATABLE.
DON'T BE CUTE, YOU KNOW WHAT I MEAN.
I KNOW WHAT YOU MEAN. YOU ARE THE ONLY FRIEND I HAVE WHO CAN HANDLE HERSELF.
ANYBODY ELSE WOULD BE LIKE CATHERINE, SHEEP AMONG WOLVES.
WHAT ABOUT ANOTHER ANIMATOR?
WHO? JAMISON THINKS VAMPIRES ARE NIFTY. BERT DOESN'T ENDANGER HIS LILY-WHITE ASS. CHARLES IS SQUEAMISH, AND HE'S GOT A KID.
MANNY DOESN'T HUNT VAMPIRES ANYMORE. HE SPENT FOUR MONTHS IN THE HOSPITAL BEING PUT BACK TOGETHER AFTER HIS LAST HUNT.
YOU WERE IN THE HOSPITAL, TOO.
A BROKEN ARM AND BUSTED COLLARBONE WERE MY WORST INJURIES, RONNIE. MANNY ALMOST DIED.
BESIDES, HE'S GOT A WIFE AND FOUR KIDS.
MANNY WAS THE ANIMATOR WHO TRAINED ME. HE WAS A TRADITIONALIST, A STAKE-AND-GARLIC MAN. TWO YEARS AGO, ROSITA, MANNY'S WIFE, HAD BEGGED ME NOT TO ENDANGER HER HUSBAND ANYMORE.
FIFTY-TWO WAS TOO OLD TO HUNT VAMPIRES, SHE HAD SAID. WHAT WOULD HAPPEN TO HER AND THE CHILDREN? SOMEHOW I HAD GOTTEN ALL THE BLAME. SHE MADE ME SWEAR BEFORE GOD THAT I WOULD NEVER AGAIN ASK MANNY TO JOIN ME ON A HUNT.
IF SHE HADN'T CRIED, I WOULD HAVE HELD OUT. CRYING WAS DAMNED UNFAIR IN A FIGHT. YOU'LL PROMISE ANYTHING JUST TO STOP THE TEARS.
ALL RIGHT, BUT YOU BE CAREFUL.
CAREFUL AS A VIRGIN ON HER WEDDING NIGHT.
YOU ARE INCORRIGIBLE. WATCH YOUR BACK.
YOU DO THE SAME.
GOOD NEWS?
YEAH.
HUMANS AGAINST VAMPIRES HAD A DEATH SQUAD. MAYBE. BUT MAYBE WAS BETTER THAN WHAT I'D HAD BEFORE.
IF I WAS ON THE RIGHT TRACK, I'D ATTRACT ATTENTION SOON. WHICH MEANT SOMEONE MIGHT TRY TO KILL ME. WOULDN'T THAT BE FUN?
I WOULD NEED CLOTHES THAT SHOWED OFF MY SCARS AND ALLOWED ME TO HIDE WEAPONS. I HATE TO SHOP. OF COURSE, IT BEAT THE HECK OUT OF HAVING MY LIFE THREATENED BY VAMPIRES.
I COULD GO SHOPPING NOW AND BE THREATENED BY VAMPIRES IN THE EVENING. A PERFECT WAY TO SPEND A SATURDAY NIGHT.

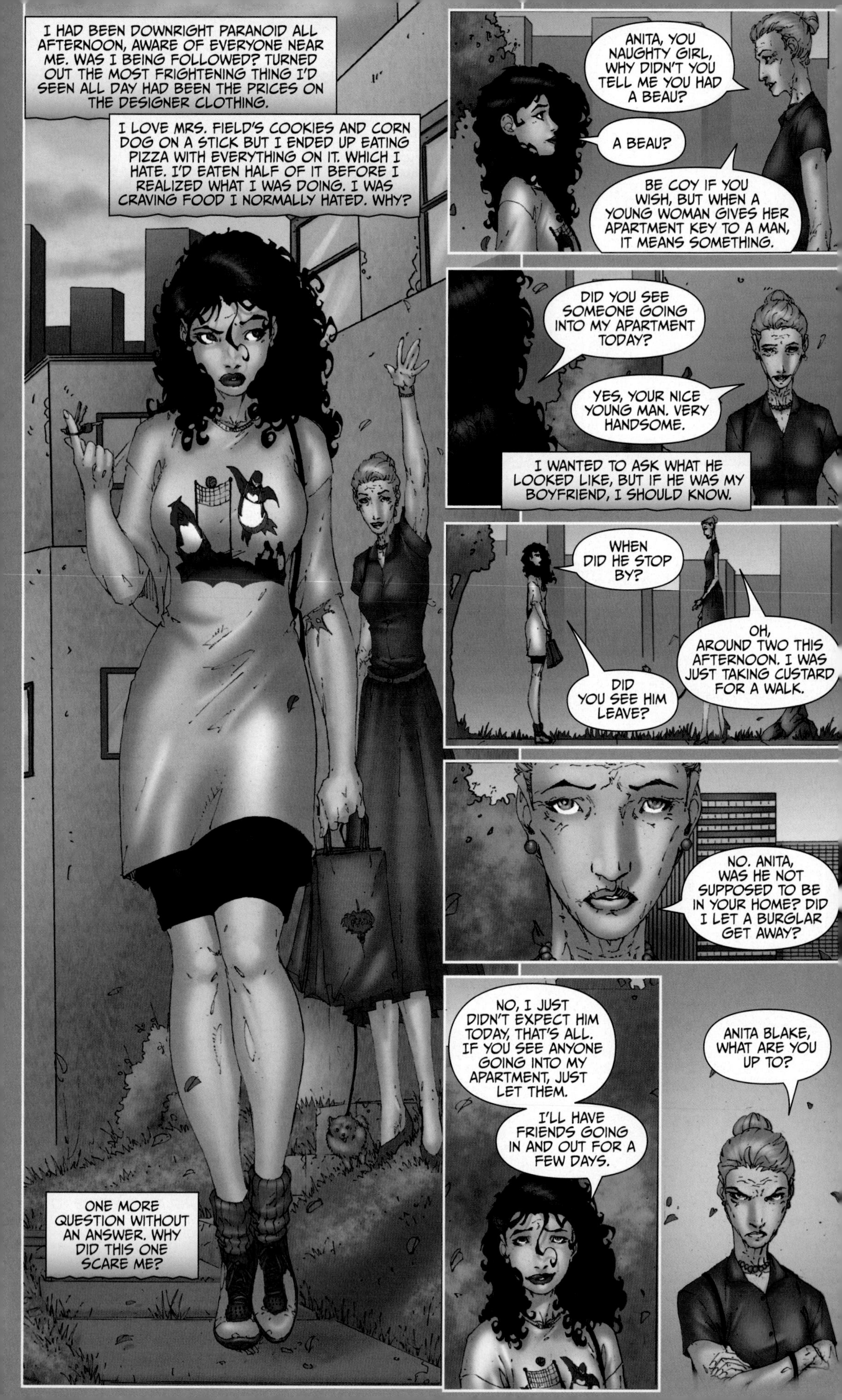
I HAD BEEN DOWNRIGHT PARANOID ALL AFTERNOON, AWARE OF EVERYONE NEAR ME. WAS I BEING FOLLOWED? TURNED OUT THE MOST FRIGHTENING THING I'D SEEN ALL DAY HAD BEEN THE PRICES ON THE DESIGNER CLOTHING.
I LOVE MRS. FIELD'S COOKIES AND CORN DOG ON A STICK BUT I ENDED UP EATING PIZZA WITH EVERYTHING ON IT. WHICH I HATE. I'D EATEN HALF OF IT BEFORE I REALIZED WHAT I WAS DOING. I WAS CRAVING FOOD I NORMALLY HATED. WHY?
ONE MORE QUESTION WITHOUT AN ANSWER. WHY DID THIS ONE SCARE ME?
ANITA, YOU NAUGHTY GIRL, WHY DIDN'T YOU TELL ME YOU HAD A BEAU?
A BEAU?
BE COY IF YOU WISH, BUT WHEN A YOUNG WOMAN GIVES HER APARTMENT KEY TO A MAN, IT MEANS SOMETHING.
DID YOU SEE SOMEONE GOING INTO MY APARTMENT TODAY?
YES, YOUR NICE YOUNG MAN. VERY HANDSOME.
I WANTED TO ASK WHAT HE LOOKED LIKE, BUT IF HE WAS MY BOYFRIEND, I SHOULD KNOW.
WHEN DID HE STOP BY?
OH, AROUND TWO THIS AFTERNOON. I WAS JUST TAKING CUSTARD FOR A WALK.
DID YOU SEE HIM LEAVE?
NO. ANITA, WAS HE NOT SUPPOSED TO BE IN YOUR HOME? DID I LET A BURGLAR GET AWAY?
NO, I JUST DIDN'T EXPECT HIM TODAY, THAT'S ALL. IF YOU SEE ANYONE GOING INTO MY APARTMENT, JUST LET THEM.
I'LL HAVE FRIENDS GOING IN AND OUT FOR A FEW DAYS.
ANITA BLAKE, WHAT ARE YOU UP TO?

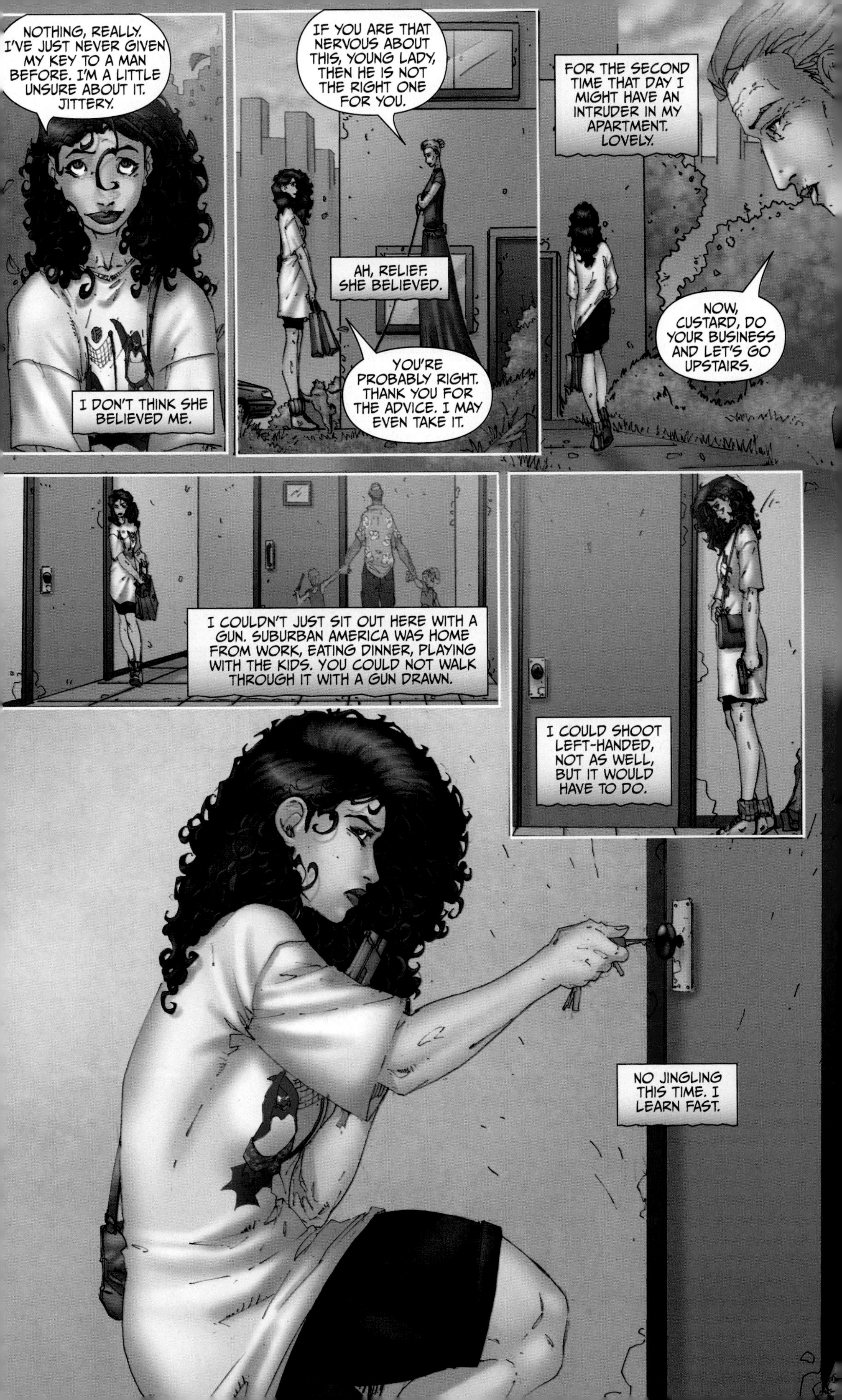

NOTHING, REALLY. I'VE JUST NEVER GIVEN MY KEY TO A MAN BEFORE. I'M A LITTLE UNSURE ABOUT IT. JITTERY.
I DON'T THINK SHE BELIEVED ME.
IF YOU ARE THAT NERVOUS ABOUT THIS, YOUNG LADY, THEN HE IS NOT THE RIGHT ONE FOR YOU.
AH, RELIEF. SHE BELIEVED.
YOU'RE PROBABLY RIGHT. THANK YOU FOR THE ADVICE. I MAY EVEN TAKE IT.
FOR THE SECOND TIME THAT DAY I MIGHT HAVE AN INTRUDER IN MY APARTMENT. LOVELY.
NOW, CUSTARD, DO YOUR BUSINESS AND LET'S GO UPSTAIRS.
I COULDN'T JUST SIT OUT HERE WITH A GUN. SUBURBAN AMERICA WAS HOME FROM WORK, EATING DINNER, PLAYING WITH THE KIDS. YOU COULD NOT WALK THROUGH IT WITH A GUN DRAWN.
I COULD SHOOT LEFT-HANDED, NOT AS WELL, BUT IT WOULD HAVE TO DO.
NO JINGLING THIS TIME. I LEARN FAST.

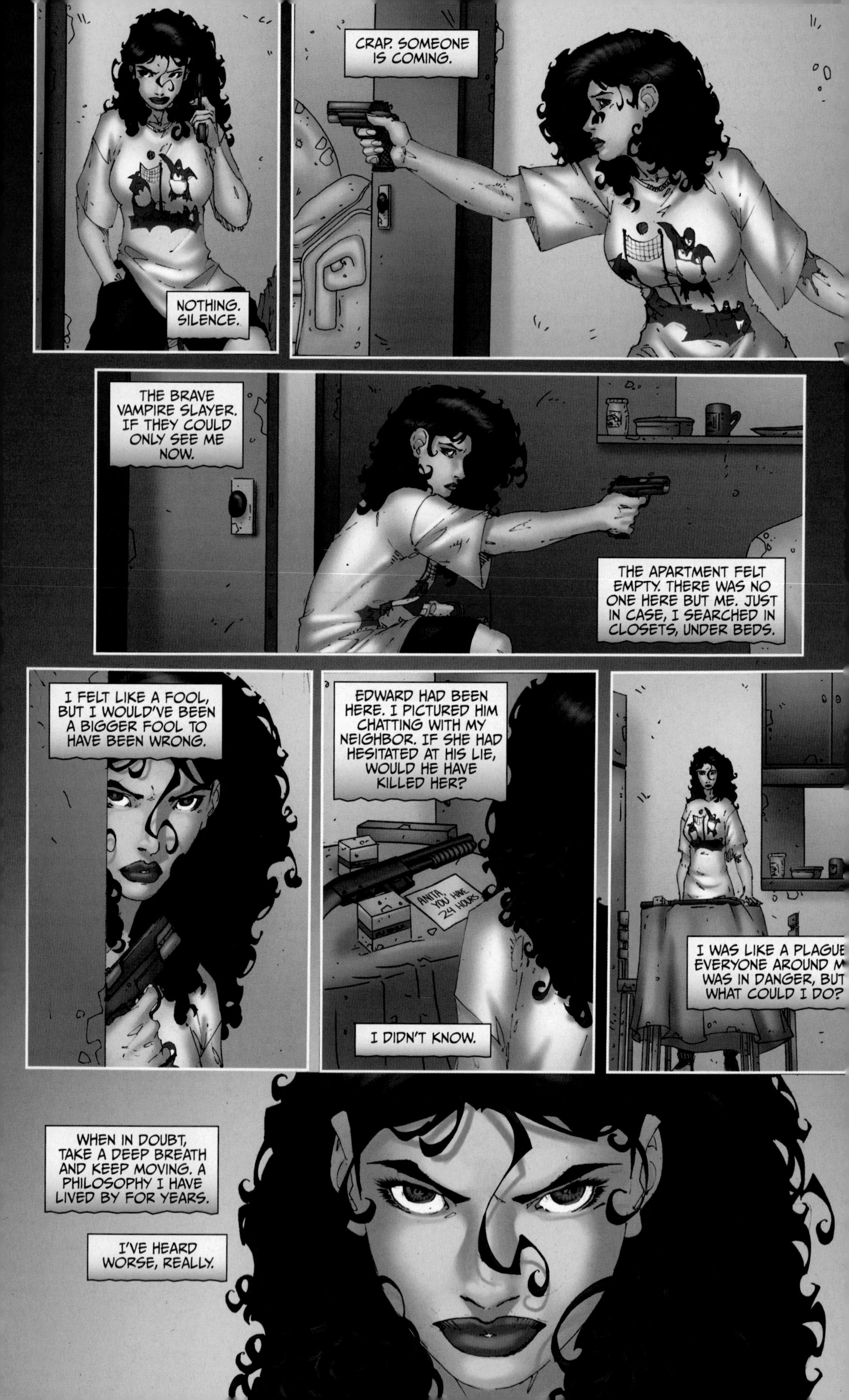
NOTHING. SILENCE.
CRAP. SOMEONE IS COMING.
THE BRAVE VAMPIRE SLAYER. IF THEY COULD ONLY SEE ME NOW.
THE APARTMENT FELT EMPTY. THERE WAS NO ONE HERE BUT ME. JUST IN CASE, I SEARCHED IN CLOSETS, UNDER BEDS.
I FELT LIKE A FOOL, BUT I WOULD'VE BEEN A BIGGER FOOL TO HAVE BEEN WRONG.
EDWARD HAD BEEN HERE. I PICTURED HIM CHATTING WITH MY NEIGHBOR. IF SHE HAD HESITATED AT HIS LIE, WOULD HE HAVE KILLED HER?
ANITA, YOU HAVE 24 HOURS
I DIDN'T KNOW.
I WAS LIKE A PLAGUE
EVERYONE AROUND M
WAS IN DANGER, BUT
WHAT COULD I DO?
WHEN IN DOUBT, TAKE A DEEP BREATH AND KEEP MOVING. A PHILOSOPHY I HAVE LIVED BY FOR YEARS.
I'VE HEARD WORSE, REALLY.

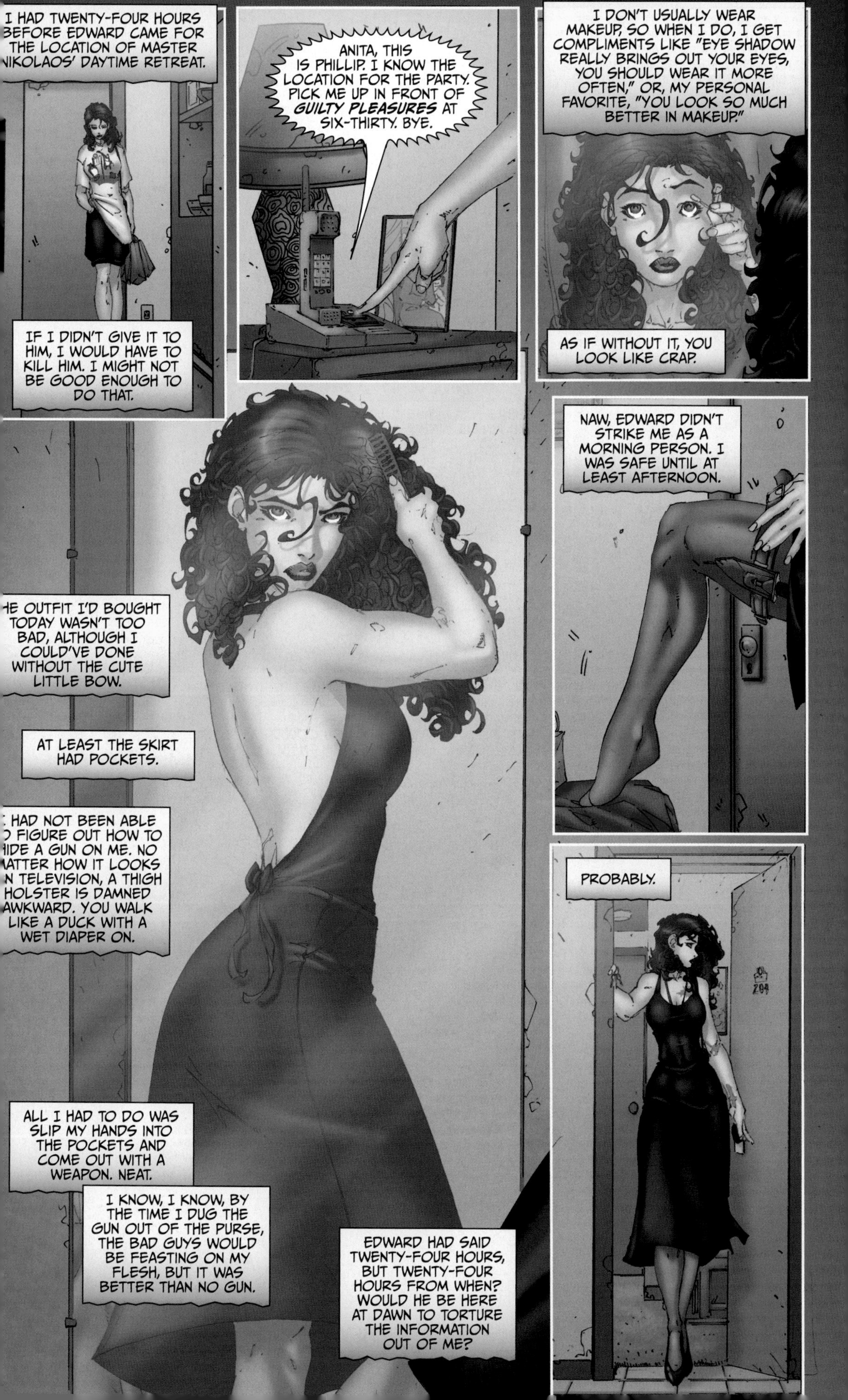
I HAD TWENTY-FOUR HOURS BEFORE EDWARD CAME FOR THE LOCATION OF MASTER NIKOLAOS' DAYTIME RETREAT.
IF I DIDN'T GIVE IT TO HIM, I WOULD HAVE TO KILL HIM. I MIGHT NOT BE GOOD ENOUGH TO DO THAT.
ANITA, THIS IS PHILLIP. I KNOW THE LOCATION FOR THE PARTY. PICK ME UP IN FRONT OF GUILTY PLEASURES AT SIX-THIRTY. BYE.
I DON'T USUALLY WEAR MAKEUP, SO WHEN I DO, I GET COMPLIMENTS LIKE "EYE SHADOW REALLY BRINGS OUT YOUR EYES, YOU SHOULD WEAR IT MORE OFTEN," OR, MY PERSONAL FAVORITE, "YOU LOOK SO MUCH BETTER IN MAKEUP."
AS IF WITHOUT IT, YOU LOOK LIKE CRAP.
HE OUTFIT I'D BOUGHT TODAY WASN'T TOO BAD, ALTHOUGH I COULD'VE DONE WITHOUT THE CUTE LITTLE BOW.
AT LEAST THE SKIRT HAD POCKETS.
HAD NOT BEEN ABLE FIGURE OUT HOW TO HIDE A GUN ON ME. NO MATTER HOW IT LOOKS N TELEVISION, A THIGH HOLSTER IS DAMNED AWKWARD. YOU WALK LIKE A DUCK WITH A WET DIAPER ON.
ALL I HAD TO DO WAS SLIP MY HANDS INTO THE POCKETS AND COME OUT WITH A WEAPON. NEAT.
I KNOW, I KNOW, BY THE TIME I DUG THE GUN OUT OF THE PURSE, THE BAD GUYS WOULD BE FEASTING ON MY FLESH, BUT IT WAS BETTER THAN NO GUN.
EDWARD HAD SAID TWENTY-FOUR HOURS, BUT TWENTY-FOUR HOURS FROM WHEN? WOULD HE BE HERE AT DAWN TO TORTURE THE INFORMATION OUT OF ME?
NAW, EDWARD DIDN'T STRIKE ME AS A MORNING PERSON. I WAS SAFE UNTIL AT LEAST AFTERNOON.
PROBABLY.
204

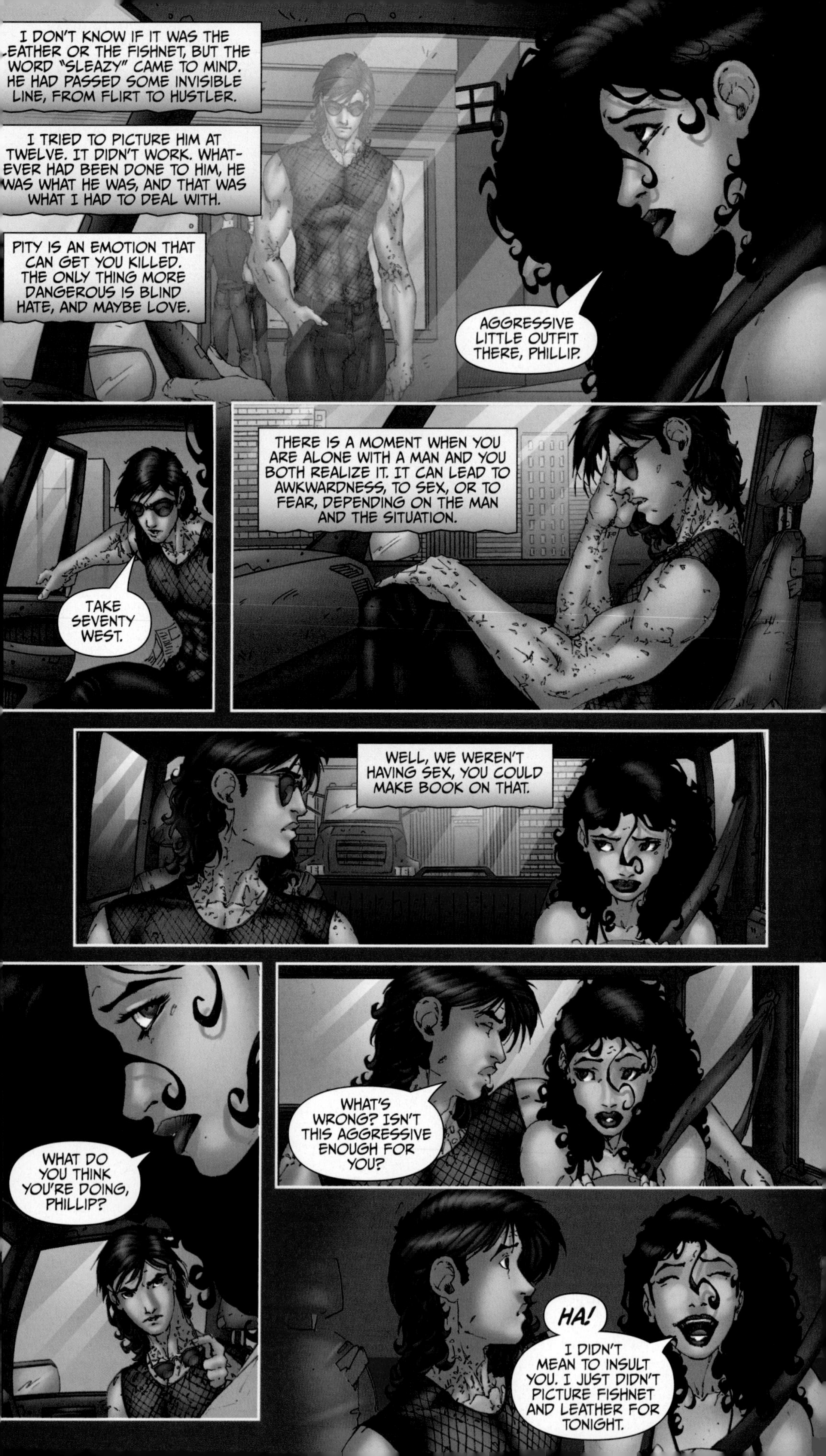

I DON'T KNOW IF IT WAS THE LEATHER OR THE FISHNET, BUT THE WORD "SLEAZY" CAME TO MIND. HE HAD PASSED SOME INVISIBLE LINE, FROM FLIRT TO HUSTLER.
I TRIED TO PICTURE HIM AT TWELVE. IT DIDN'T WORK. WHATEVER HAD BEEN DONE TO HIM, HE WAS WHAT HE WAS, AND THAT WAS WHAT I HAD TO DEAL WITH.
PITY IS AN EMOTION THAT CAN GET YOU KILLED. THE ONLY THING MORE DANGEROUS IS BLIND HATE, AND MAYBE LOVE.
AGGRESSIVE LITTLE OUTFIT THERE, PHILLIP.
TAKE SEVENTY WEST.
THERE IS A MOMENT WHEN YOU ARE ALONE WITH A MAN AND YOU BOTH REALIZE IT. IT CAN LEAD TO AWKWARDNESS, TO SEX, OR TO FEAR, DEPENDING ON THE MAN AND THE SITUATION.
WELL, WE WEREN'T HAVING SEX, YOU COULD MAKE BOOK ON THAT.
WHAT DO YOU THINK YOU'RE DOING, PHILLIP?
WHAT'S WRONG? ISN'T THIS AGGRESSIVE ENOUGH FOR YOU?
HA!
I DIDN'T MEAN TO INSULT YOU. I JUST DIDN'T PICTURE FISHNET AND LEATHER FOR TONIGHT.

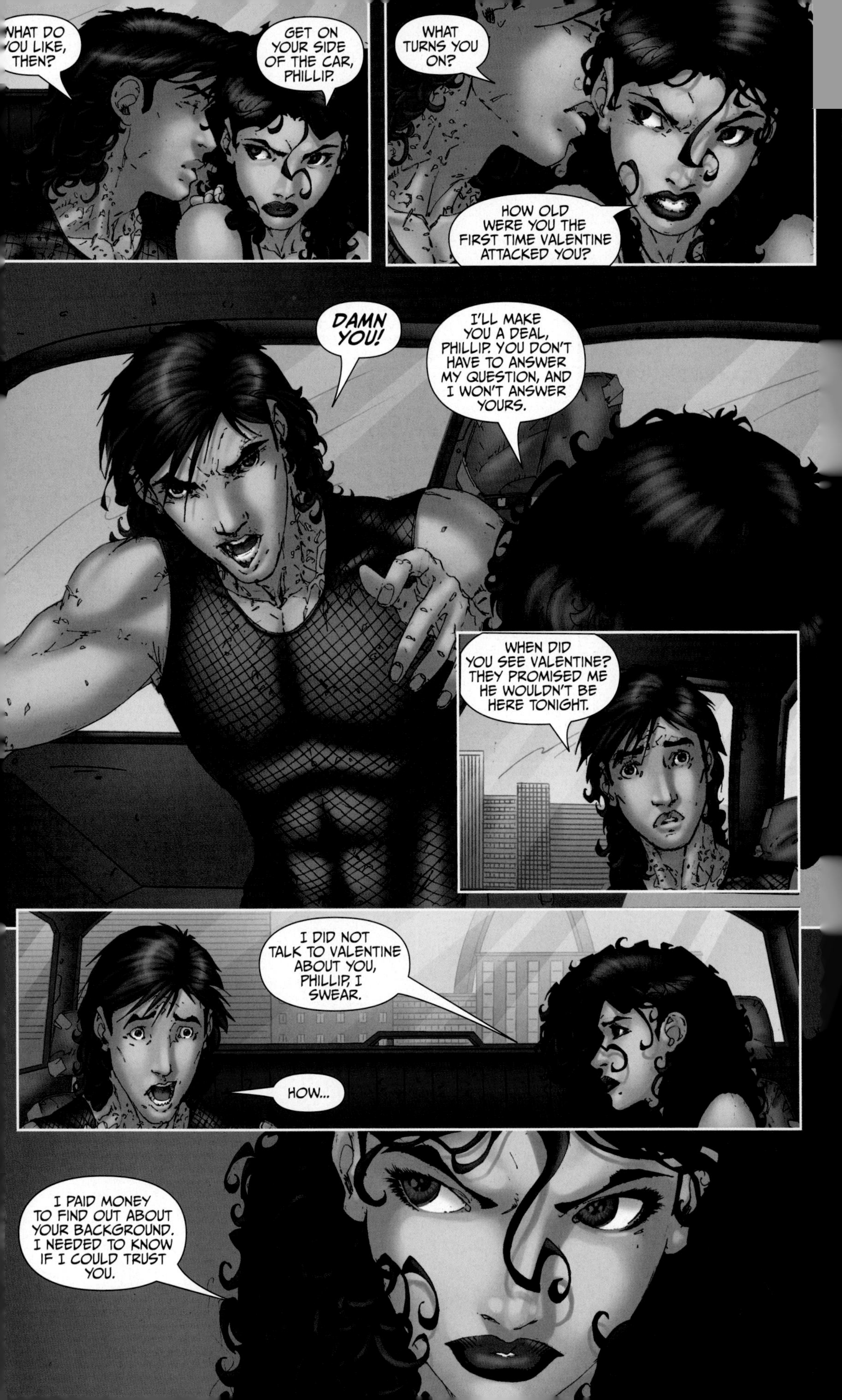
WHAT DO YOU LIKE, THEN?
GET ON YOUR SIDE OF THE CAR, PHILLIP.
WHAT TURNS YOU ON?
HOW OLD WERE YOU THE FIRST TIME VALENTINE ATTACKED YOU?
DAMN YOU!
I'LL MAKE YOU A DEAL, PHILLIP. YOU DON'T HAVE TO ANSWER MY QUESTION, AND I WON'T ANSWER YOURS.
WHEN DID YOU SEE VALENTINE? THEY PROMISED ME HE WOULDN'T BE HERE TONIGHT.
I DID NOT TALK TO VALENTINE ABOUT YOU, PHILLIP, I SWEAR.
HOW...
I PAID MONEY TO FIND OUT ABOUT YOUR BACKGROUND. I NEEDED TO KNOW IF I COULD TRUST YOU.

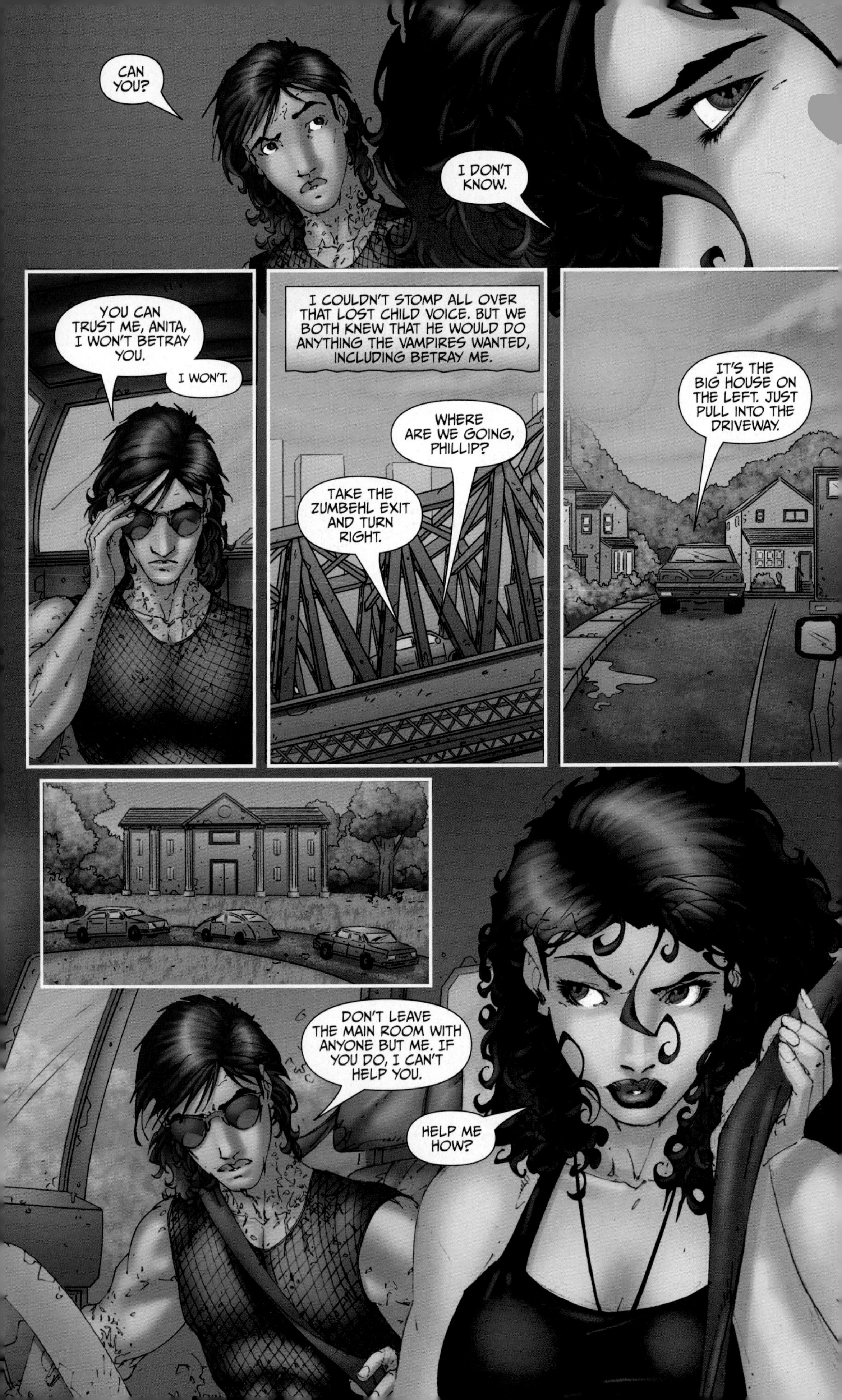
CAN YOU?
I DON'T KNOW.
YOU CAN TRUST ME, ANITA, I WON'T BETRAY YOU.
I WON'T.
I COULDN'T STOMP ALL OVER THAT LOST CHILD VOICE. BUT WE BOTH KNEW THAT HE WOULD DO ANYTHING THE VAMPIRES WANTED, INCLUDING BETRAY ME.
WHERE ARE WE GOING, PHILLIP?
TAKE THE ZUMBEHL EXIT AND TURN RIGHT.
IT'S THE BIG HOUSE ON THE LEFT. JUST PULL INTO THE DRIVEWAY.
DON'T LEAVE THE MAIN ROOM WITH ANYONE BUT ME. IF YOU DO, I CAN'T HELP YOU.
HELP ME HOW?

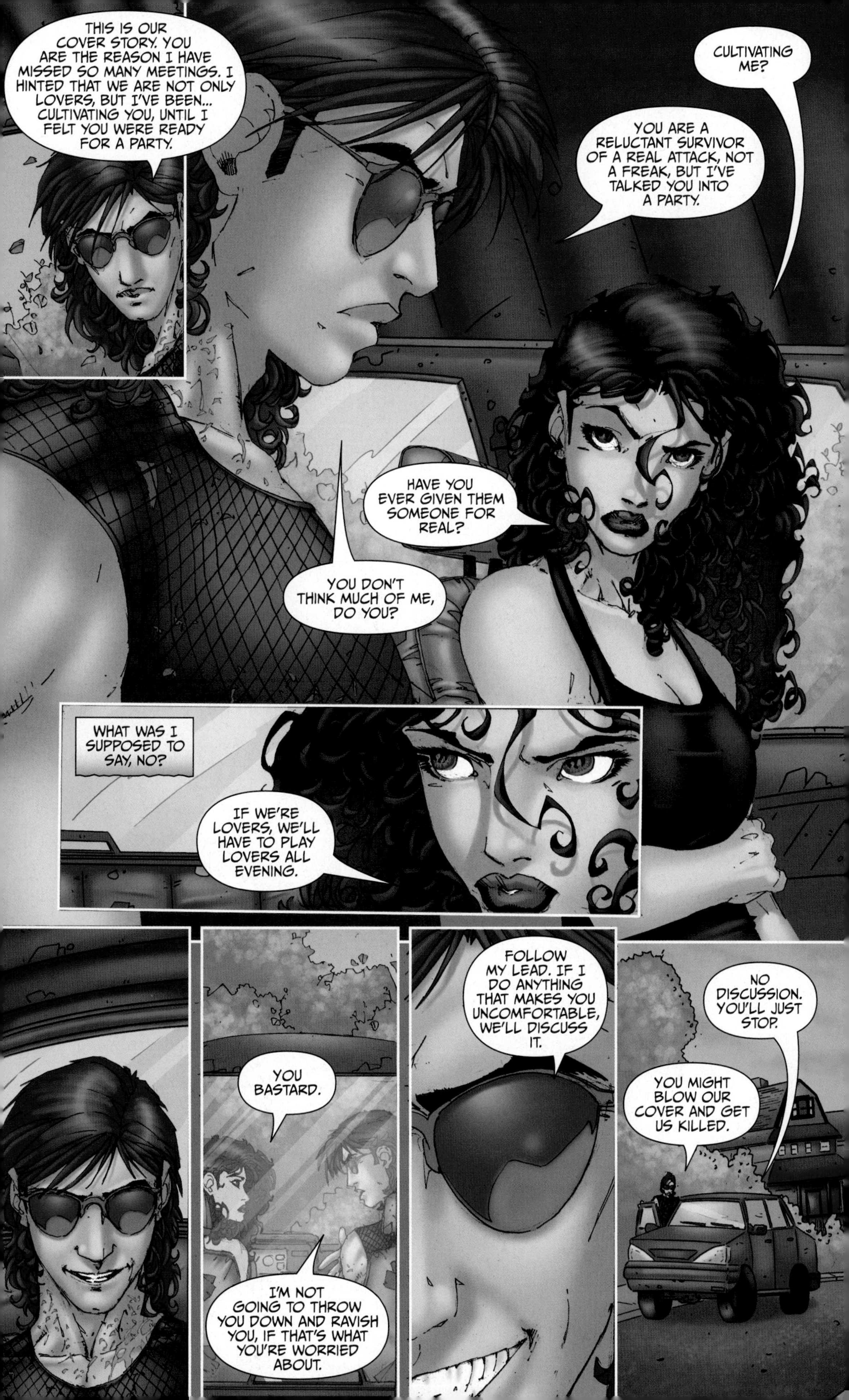
THIS IS OUR COVER STORY. YOU ARE THE REASON I HAVE MISSED SO MANY MEETINGS. I HINTED THAT WE ARE NOT ONLY LOVERS, BUT I'VE BEEN... CULTIVATING YOU, UNTIL I FELT YOU WERE READY FOR A PARTY.
CULTIVATING ME?
YOU ARE A RELUCTANT SURVIVOR OF A REAL ATTACK, NOT A FREAK, BUT I'VE TALKED YOU INTO A PARTY.
HAVE YOU EVER GIVEN THEM SOMEONE FOR REAL?
YOU DON'T THINK MUCH OF ME, DO YOU?
WHAT WAS I SUPPOSED TO SAY, NO?
IF WE'RE LOVERS, WE'LL HAVE TO PLAY LOVERS ALL EVENING.
YOU BASTARD.
I'M NOT GOING TO THROW YOU DOWN AND RAVISH YOU, IF THAT'S WHAT YOU'RE WORRIED ABOUT.
FOLLOW MY LEAD. IF I DO ANYTHING THAT MAKES YOU UNCOMFORTABLE, WE'LL DISCUSS IT.
NO DISCUSSION. YOU'LL JUST STOP.
YOU MIGHT BLOW OUR COVER AND GET US KILLED.

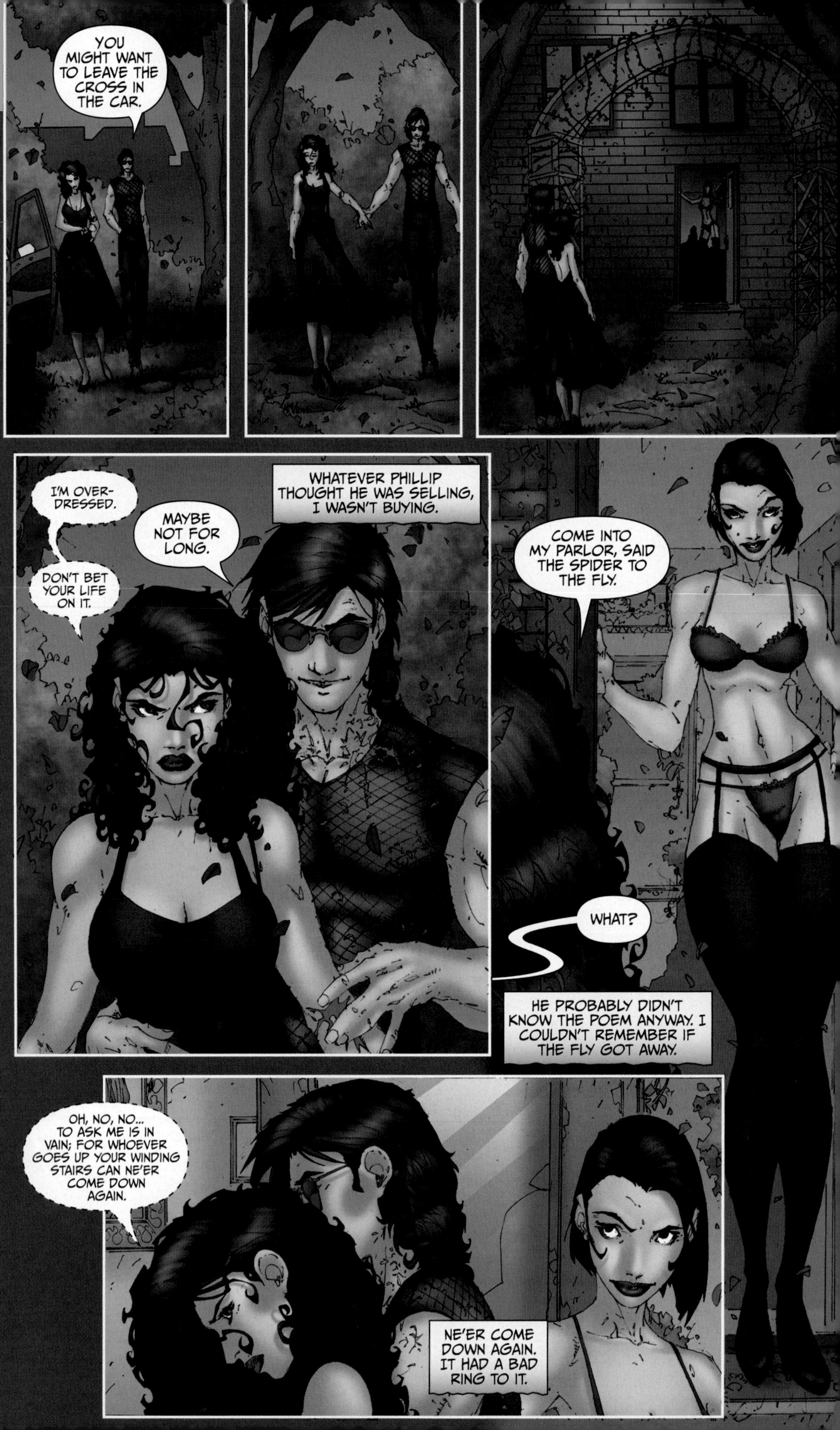
YOU MIGHT WANT TO LEAVE THE CROSS IN THE CAR.
I'M OVER-DRESSED.
MAYBE NOT FOR LONG.
DON'T BET YOUR LIFE ON IT.
WHATEVER PHILLIP THOUGHT HE WAS SELLING, I WASN'T BUYING.
COME INTO MY PARLOR, SAID THE SPIDER TO THE FLY.
WHAT?
HE PROBABLY DIDN'T KNOW THE POEM ANYWAY. I COULDN'T REMEMBER IF THE FLY GOT AWAY.
OH, NO, NO... TO ASK ME IS IN VAIN; FOR WHOEVER GOES UP YOUR WINDING STAIRS CAN NE'ER COME DOWN AGAIN.
NE'ER COME DOWN AGAIN. IT HAD A BAD RING TO IT.

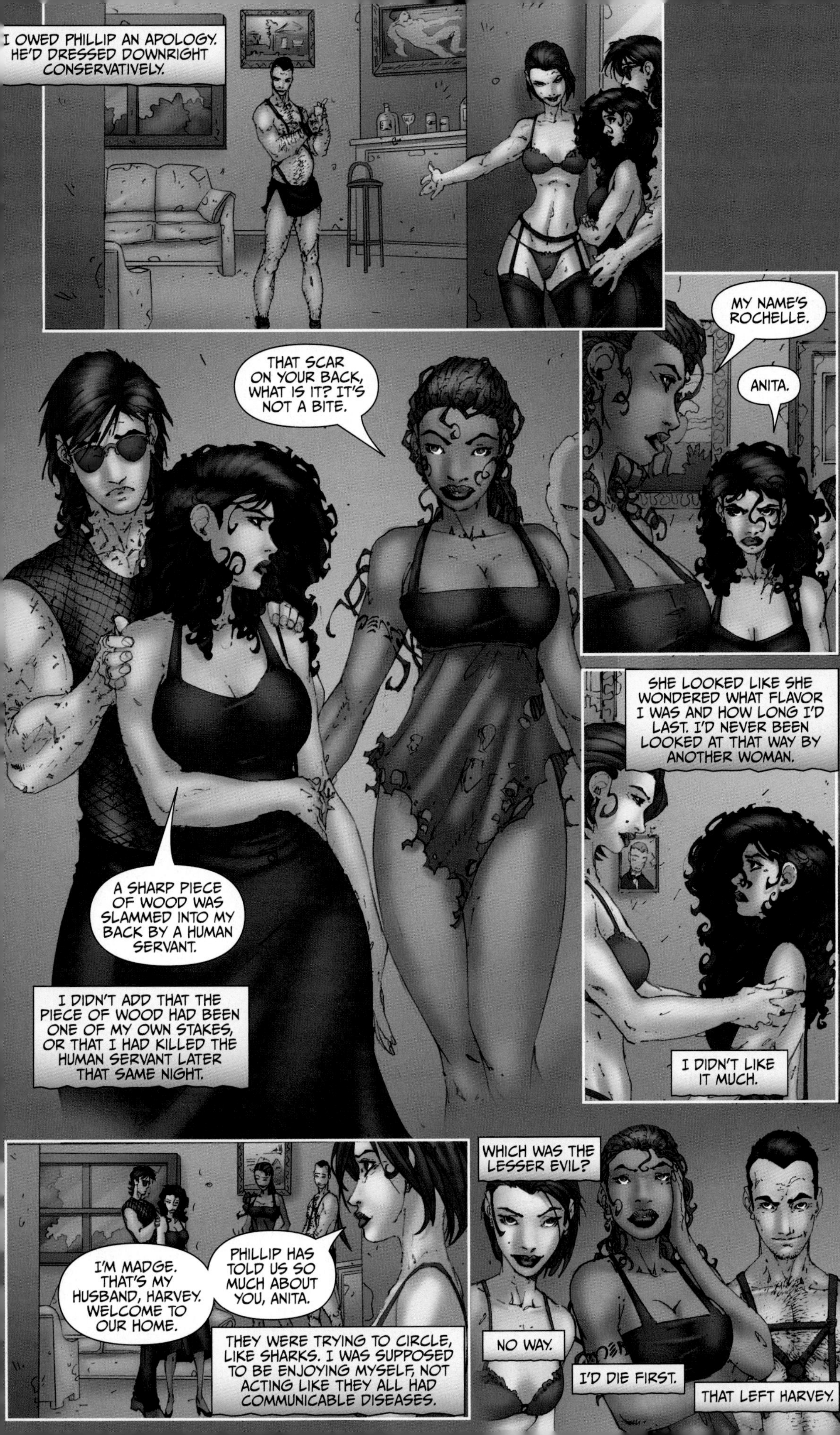
I OWED PHILLIP AN APOLOGY. HE'D DRESSED DOWNRIGHT CONSERVATIVELY.
THAT SCAR ON YOUR BACK, WHAT IS IT? IT'S NOT A BITE.
A SHARP PIECE OF WOOD WAS SLAMMED INTO MY BACK BY A HUMAN SERVANT.
I DIDN'T ADD THAT THE PIECE OF WOOD HAD BEEN ONE OF MY OWN STAKES, OR THAT I HAD KILLED THE HUMAN SERVANT LATER THAT SAME NIGHT.
MY NAME'S ROCHELLE.
ANITA.
SHE LOOKED LIKE SHE WONDERED WHAT FLAVOR I WAS AND HOW LONG I'D LAST. I'D NEVER BEEN LOOKED AT THAT WAY BY ANOTHER WOMAN.
I DIDN'T LIKE IT MUCH.
I'M MADGE. THAT'S MY HUSBAND, HARVEY. WELCOME TO OUR HOME.
PHILLIP HAS TOLD US SO MUCH ABOUT YOU, ANITA.
THEY WERE TRYING TO CIRCLE, LIKE SHARKS. I WAS SUPPOSED TO BE ENJOYING MYSELF, NOT ACTING LIKE THEY ALL HAD COMMUNICABLE DISEASES.
WHICH WAS THE LESSER EVIL?
NO WAY.
I'D DIE FIRST.
THAT LEFT HARVEY.

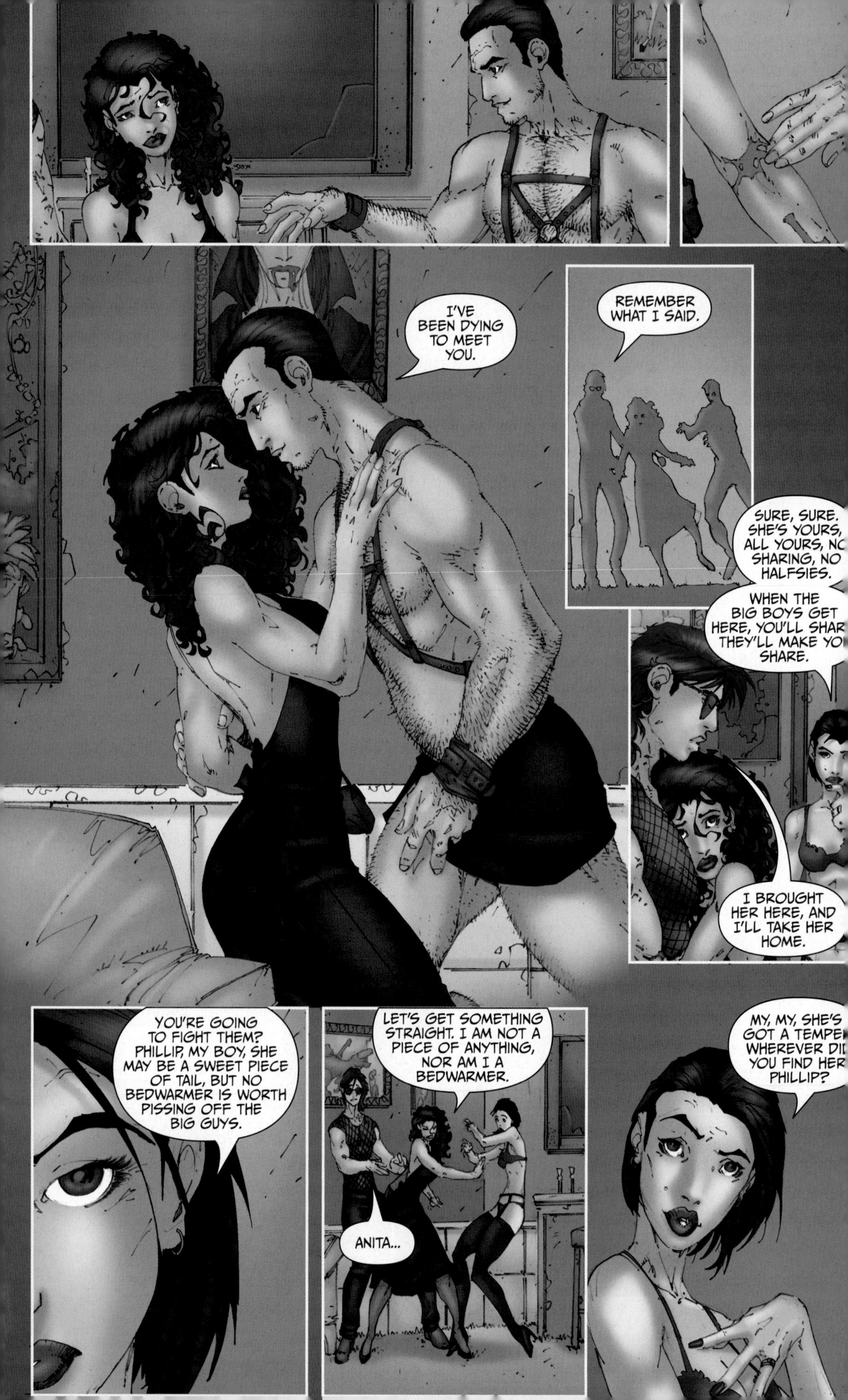
I'VE BEEN DYING TO MEET YOU.
REMEMBER WHAT I SAID.
SURE, SURE. SHE'S YOURS, ALL YOURS, NO SHARING, NO HALFSIES.
WHEN THE BIG BOYS GET HERE, YOU'LL SHARE. THEY'LL MAKE YOU SHARE.
I BROUGHT HER HERE, AND I'LL TAKE HER HOME.
YOU'RE GOING TO FIGHT THEM? PHILLIP, MY BOY, SHE MAY BE A SWEET PIECE OF TAIL, BUT NO BEDWARMER IS WORTH PISSING OFF THE BIG GUYS.
LET'S GET SOMETHING STRAIGHT. I AM NOT A PIECE OF ANYTHING, NOR AM I A BEDWARMER.
ANITA...
MY, MY, SHE'S GOT A TEMPER. WHEREVER DID YOU FIND HER, PHILLIP?

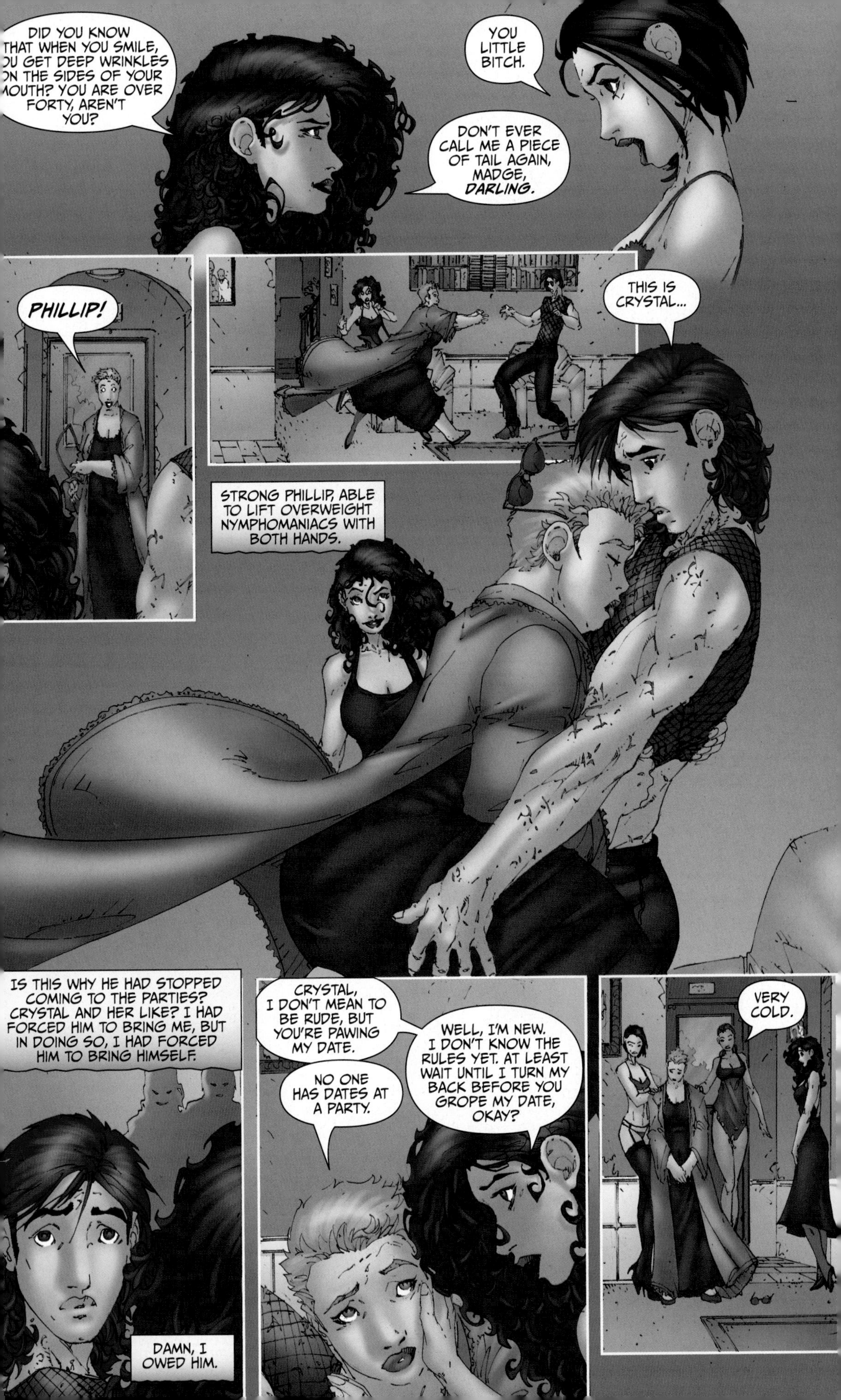
DID YOU KNOW THAT WHEN YOU SMILE, YOU GET DEEP WRINKLES ON THE SIDES OF YOUR MOUTH? YOU ARE OVER FORTY, AREN'T YOU?
YOU LITTLE BITCH.
DON'T EVER CALL ME A PIECE OF TAIL AGAIN, MADGE, DARLING.
PHILLIP!
THIS IS CRYSTAL...
STRONG PHILLIP, ABLE TO LIFT OVERWEIGHT NYMPHOMANIACS WITH BOTH HANDS.
IS THIS WHY HE HAD STOPPED COMING TO THE PARTIES? CRYSTAL AND HER LIKE? I HAD FORCED HIM TO BRING ME, BUT IN DOING SO, I HAD FORCED HIM TO BRING HIMSELF.
DAMN, I OWED HIM.
CRYSTAL, I DON'T MEAN TO BE RUDE, BUT YOU'RE PAWING MY DATE.
NO ONE HAS DATES AT A PARTY.
WELL, I'M NEW. I DON'T KNOW THE RULES YET. AT LEAST WAIT UNTIL I TURN MY BACK BEFORE YOU GROPE MY DATE, OKAY?
VERY COLD.

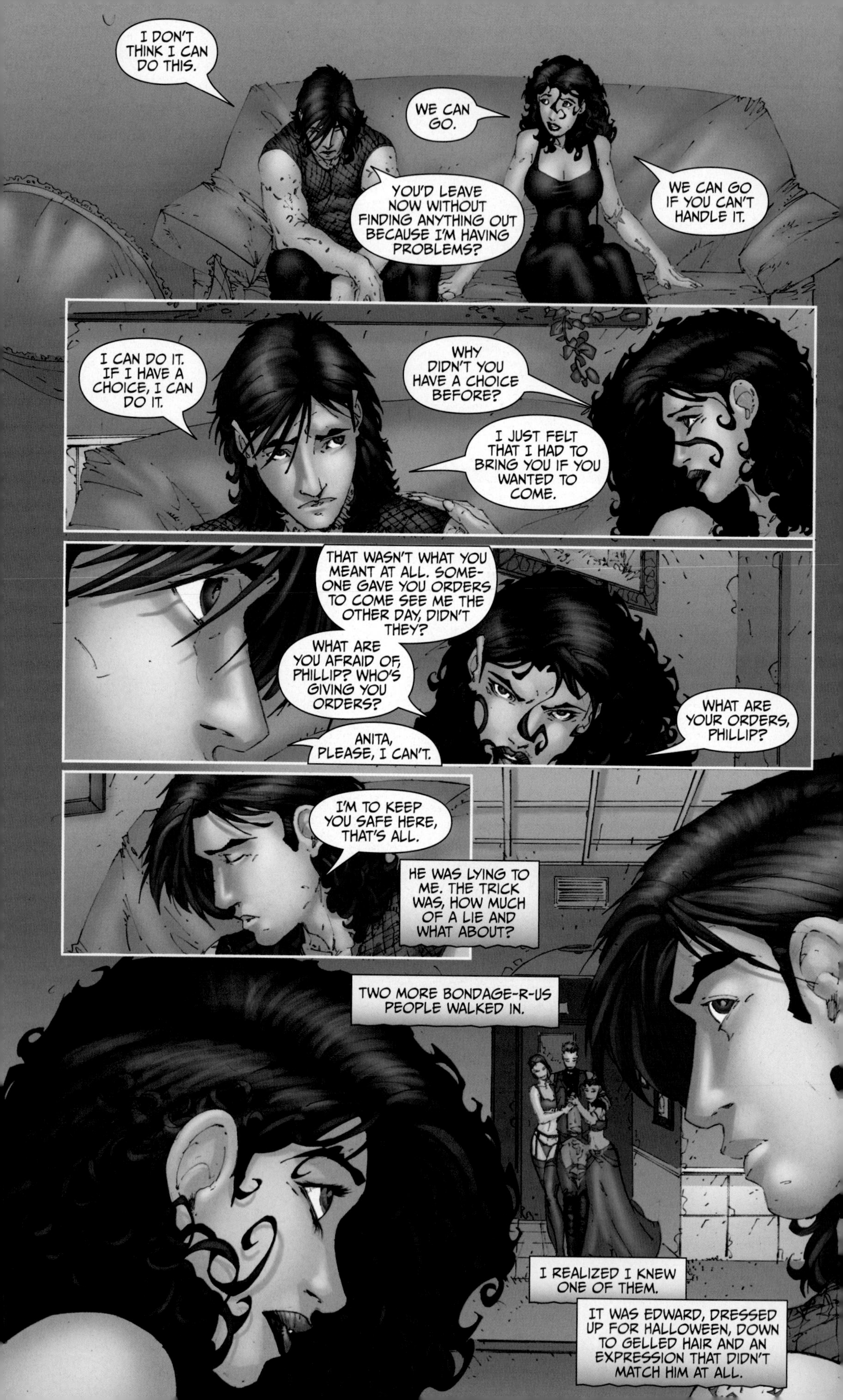
I DON'T THINK I CAN DO THIS.
WE CAN GO.
YOU'D LEAVE NOW WITHOUT FINDING ANYTHING OUT BECAUSE I'M HAVING PROBLEMS?
WE CAN GO IF YOU CAN'T HANDLE IT.
I CAN DO IT. IF I HAVE A CHOICE, I CAN DO IT.
WHY DIDN'T YOU HAVE A CHOICE BEFORE?
I JUST FELT THAT I HAD TO BRING YOU IF YOU WANTED TO COME.
THAT WASN'T WHAT YOU MEANT AT ALL. SOME-ONE GAVE YOU ORDERS TO COME SEE ME THE OTHER DAY, DIDN'T THEY?
WHAT ARE YOU AFRAID OF, PHILLIP? WHO'S GIVING YOU ORDERS?
ANITA, PLEASE, I CAN'T.
WHAT ARE YOUR ORDERS, PHILLIP?
I'M TO KEEP YOU SAFE HERE, THAT'S ALL.
HE WAS LYING TO ME. THE TRICK WAS, HOW MUCH OF A LIE AND WHAT ABOUT?
TWO MORE BONDAGE-R-US PEOPLE WALKED IN.
I REALIZED I KNEW ONE OF THEM.
IT WAS EDWARD, DRESSED UP FOR HALLOWEEN, DOWN TO GELLED HAIR AND AN EXPRESSION THAT DIDN'T MATCH HIM AT ALL.

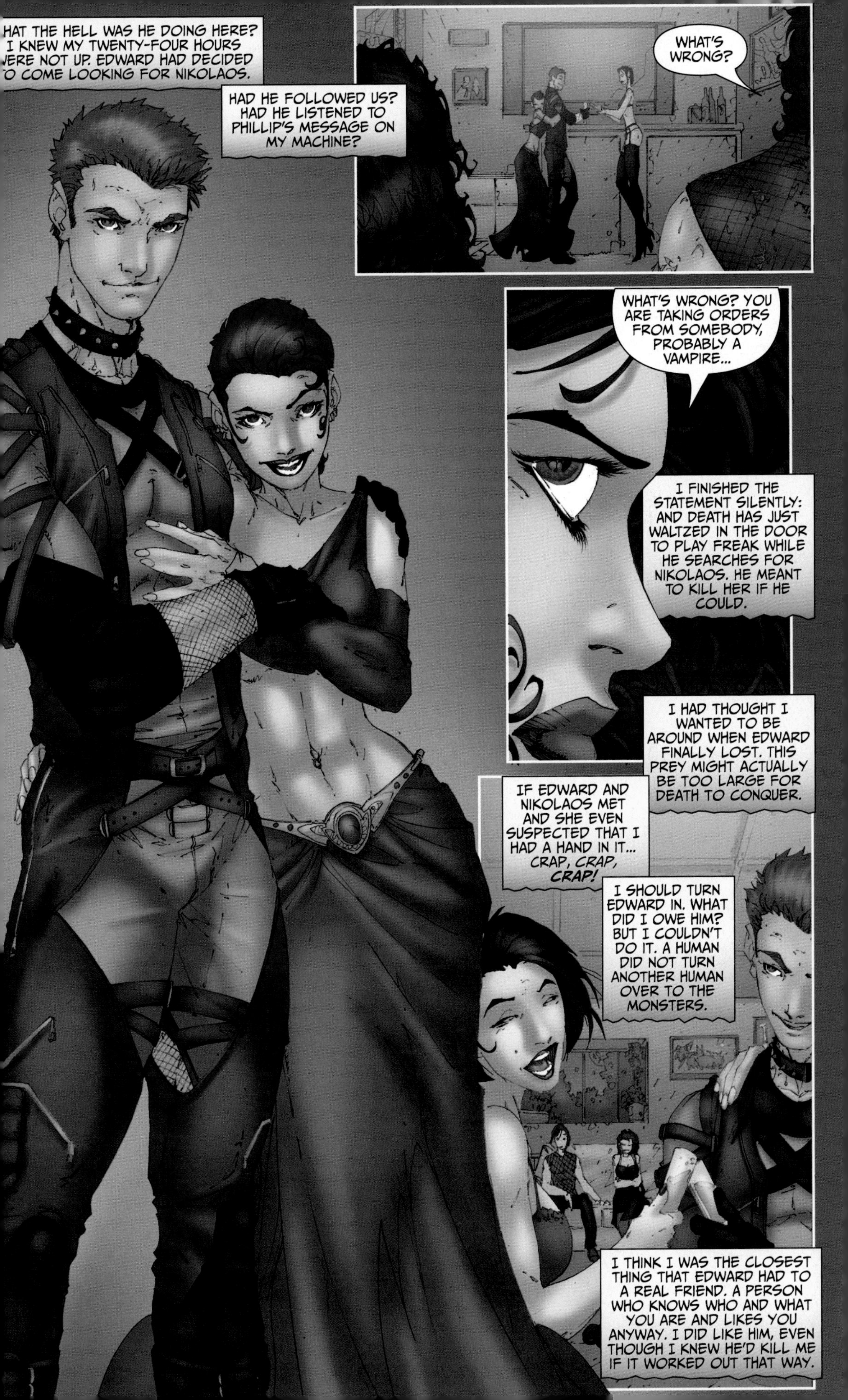
HAT THE HELL WAS HE DOING HERE? I KNEW MY TWENTY-FOUR HOURS ERE NOT UP. EDWARD HAD DECIDED O COME LOOKING FOR NIKOLAOS.
HAD HE FOLLOWED US? HAD HE LISTENED TO PHILLIP'S MESSAGE ON MY MACHINE?
WHAT'S WRONG?
WHAT'S WRONG? YOU ARE TAKING ORDERS FROM SOMEBODY, PROBABLY A VAMPIRE...
I FINISHED THE STATEMENT SILENTLY: AND DEATH HAS JUST WALTZED IN THE DOOR TO PLAY FREAK WHILE HE SEARCHES FOR NIKOLAOS. HE MEANT TO KILL HER IF HE COULD.
I HAD THOUGHT I WANTED TO BE AROUND WHEN EDWARD FINALLY LOST. THIS PREY MIGHT ACTUALLY BE TOO LARGE FOR DEATH TO CONQUER.
IF EDWARD AND NIKOLAOS MET AND SHE EVEN SUSPECTED THAT I HAD A HAND IN IT... CRAP, CRAP, CRAP!
I SHOULD TURN EDWARD IN. WHAT DID I OWE HIM? BUT I COULDN'T DO IT. A HUMAN DID NOT TURN ANOTHER HUMAN OVER TO THE MONSTERS.
I THINK I WAS THE CLOSEST THING THAT EDWARD HAD TO A REAL FRIEND. A PERSON WHO KNOWS WHO AND WHAT YOU ARE AND LIKES YOU ANYWAY. I DID LIKE HIM, EVEN THOUGH I KNEW HE'D KILL ME IF IT WORKED OUT THAT WAY.

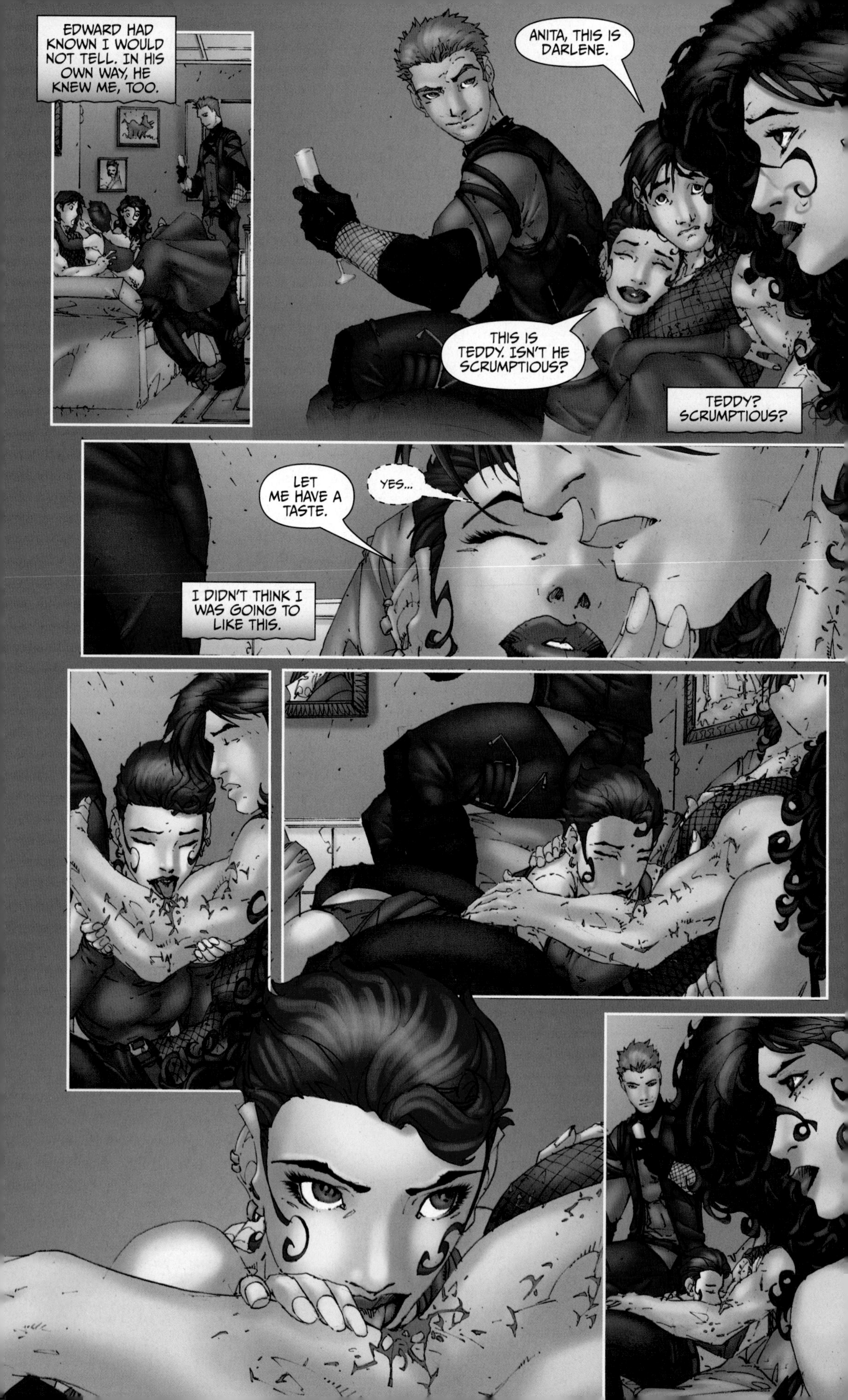
EDWARD HAD KNOWN I WOULD NOT TELL. IN HIS OWN WAY, HE KNEW ME, TOO.
ANITA, THIS IS DARLENE.
THIS IS TEDDY. ISN'T HE SCRUMPTIOUS?
TEDDY? SCRUMPTIOUS?
LET ME HAVE A TASTE.
YES...
I DIDN'T THINK I WAS GOING TO LIKE THIS.

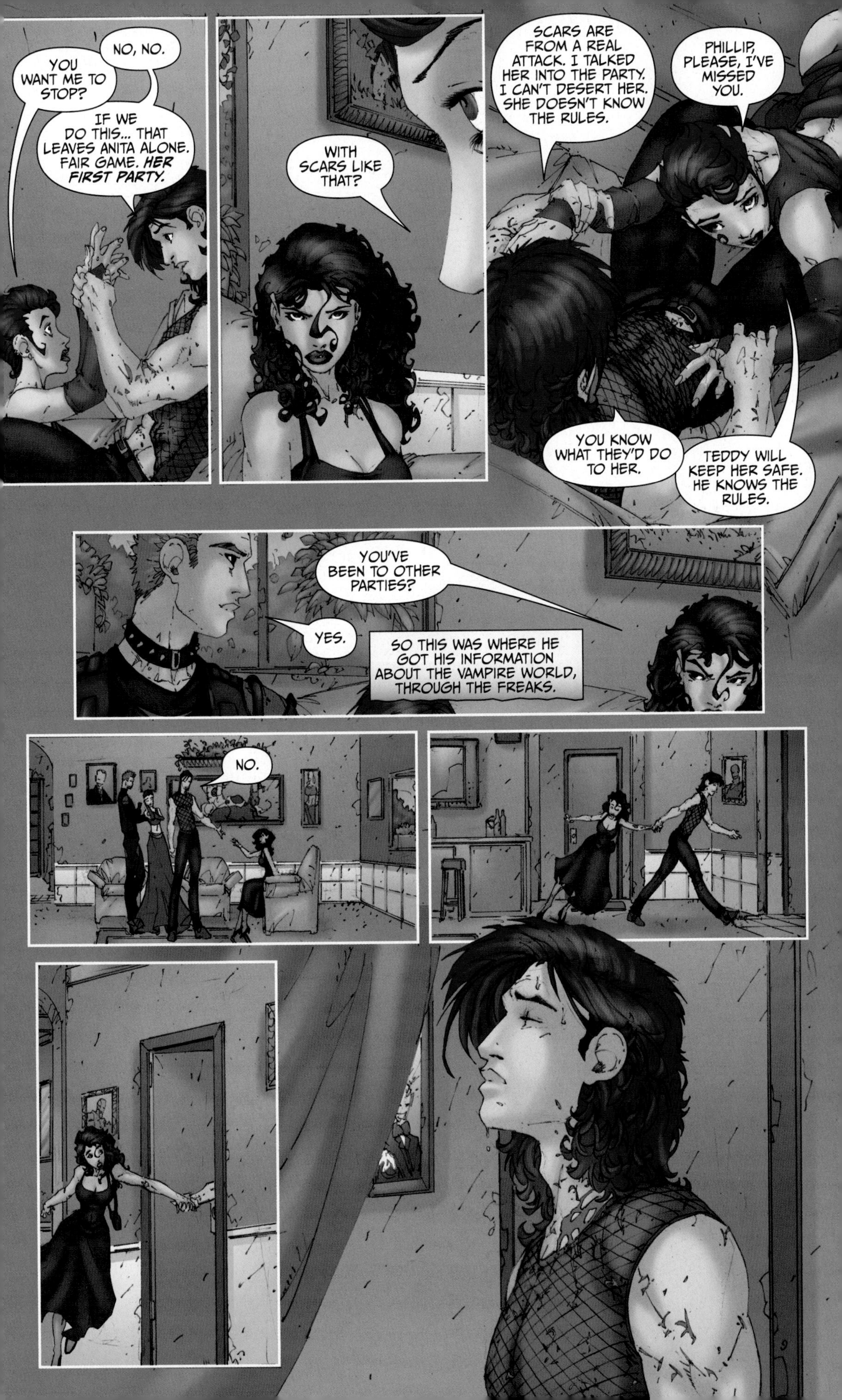
YOU WANT ME TO STOP?
NO, NO.
IF WE DO THIS... THAT LEAVES ANITA ALONE. FAIR GAME. *HER FIRST PARTY.*
WITH SCARS LIKE THAT?
SCARS ARE FROM A REAL ATTACK. I TALKED HER INTO THE PARTY. I CAN'T DESERT HER. SHE DOESN'T KNOW THE RULES.
PHILLIP, PLEASE, I'VE MISSED YOU.
YOU KNOW WHAT THEY'D DO TO HER.
TEDDY WILL KEEP HER SAFE. HE KNOWS THE RULES.
YOU'VE BEEN TO OTHER PARTIES?
YES.
SO THIS WAS WHERE HE GOT HIS INFORMATION ABOUT THE VAMPIRE WORLD, THROUGH THE FREAKS.
NO.

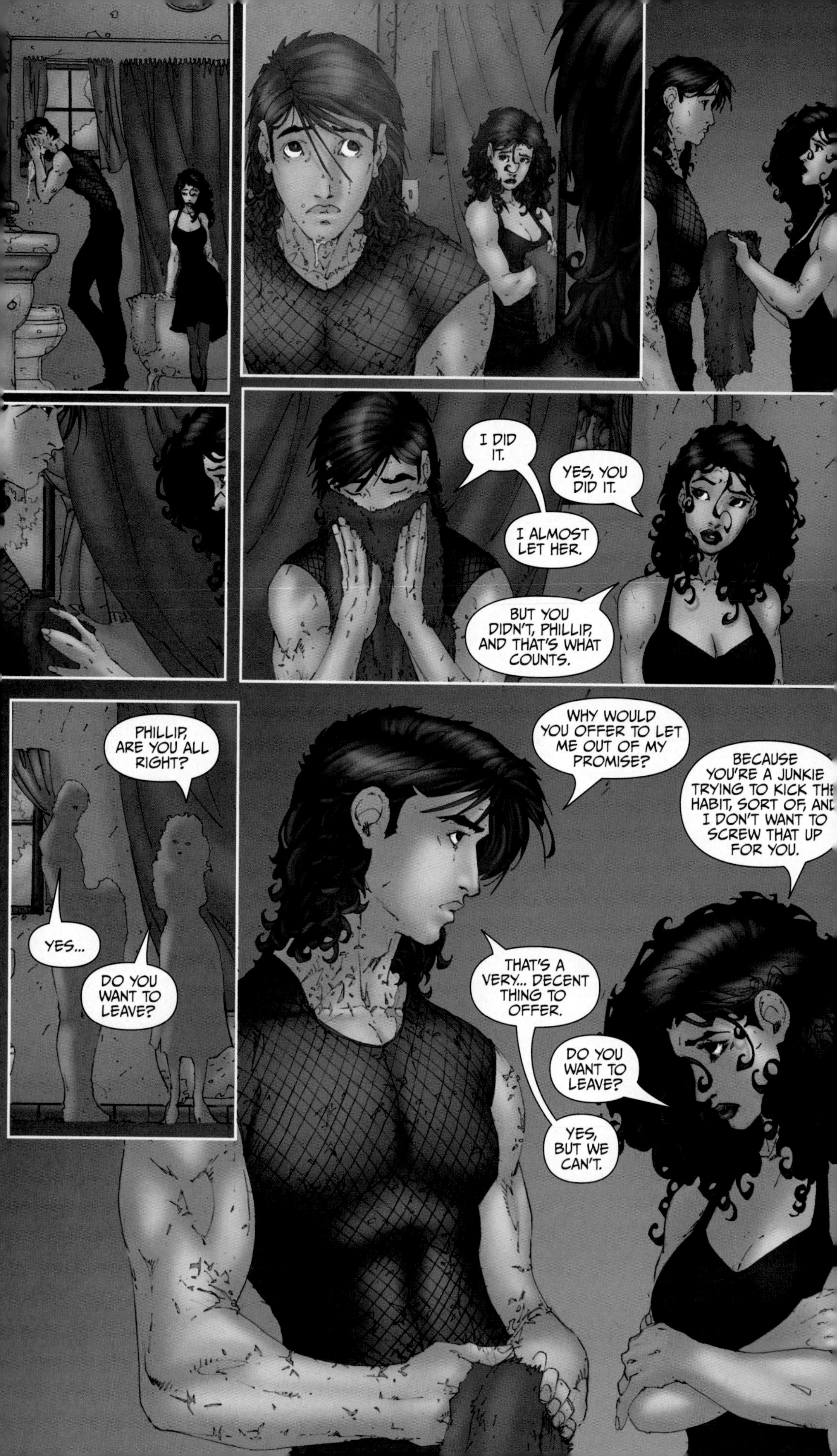
I DID IT.
YES, YOU DID IT.
I ALMOST LET HER.
BUT YOU DIDN'T, PHILLIP, AND THAT'S WHAT COUNTS.
PHILLIP, ARE YOU ALL RIGHT?
YES...
DO YOU WANT TO LEAVE?
WHY WOULD YOU OFFER TO LET ME OUT OF MY PROMISE?
BECAUSE YOU'RE A JUNKIE TRYING TO KICK THE HABIT, SORT OF, AND I DON'T WANT TO SCREW THAT UP FOR YOU.
THAT'S A VERY... DECENT THING TO OFFER.
DO YOU WANT TO LEAVE?
YES, BUT WE CAN'T.

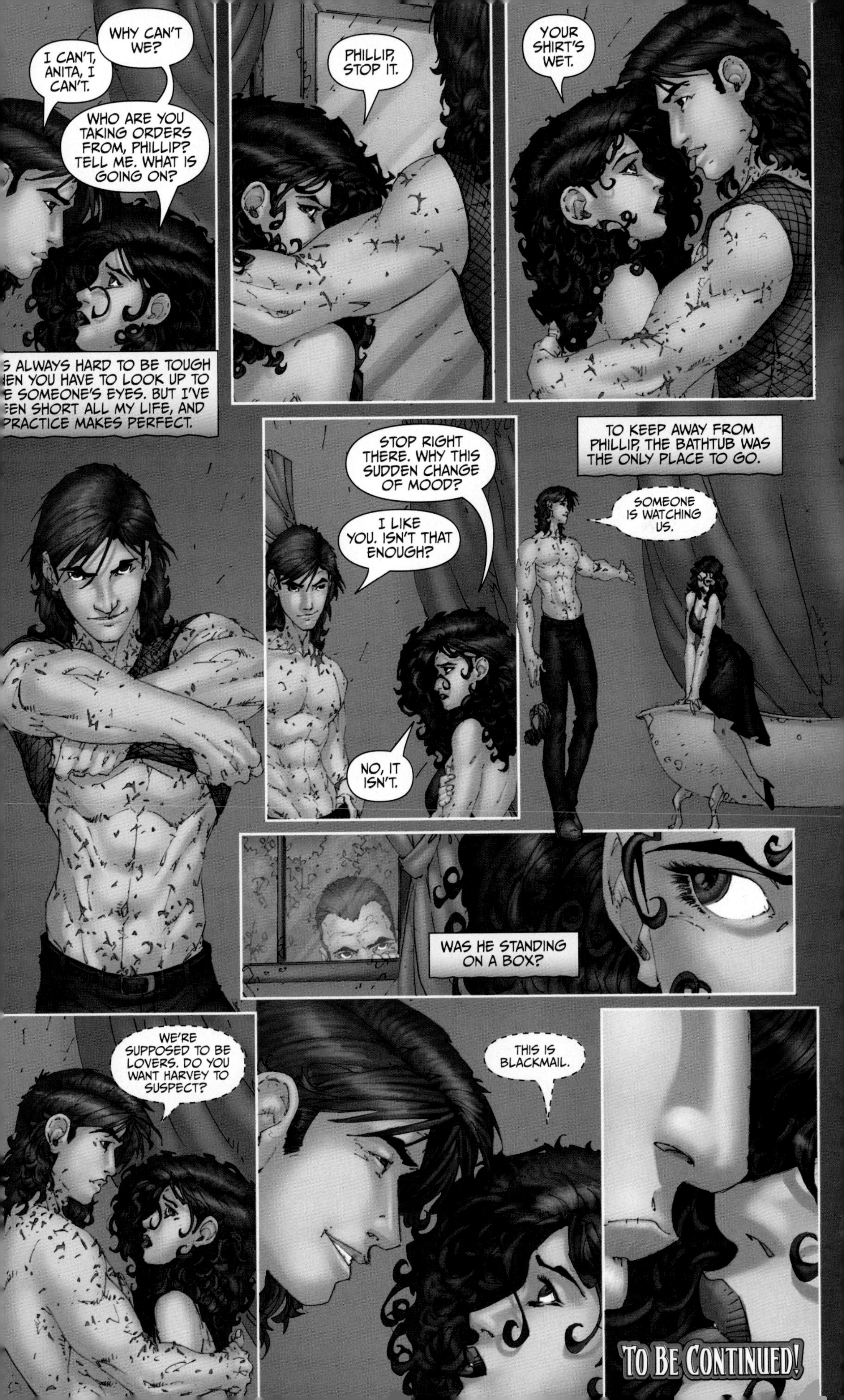
WHY CAN'T WE?
I CAN'T, ANITA, I CAN'T.
WHO ARE YOU TAKING ORDERS FROM, PHILLIP? TELL ME. WHAT IS GOING ON?
S ALWAYS HARD TO BE TOUGH HEN YOU HAVE TO LOOK UP TO E SOMEONE'S EYES. BUT I'VE EEN SHORT ALL MY LIFE, AND PRACTICE MAKES PERFECT.
PHILLIP, STOP IT.
YOUR SHIRT'S WET.
STOP RIGHT THERE. WHY THIS SUDDEN CHANGE OF MOOD?
I LIKE YOU. ISN'T THAT ENOUGH?
NO, IT ISN'T.
TO KEEP AWAY FROM PHILLIP, THE BATHTUB WAS THE ONLY PLACE TO GO.
SOMEONE IS WATCHING US.
WAS HE STANDING ON A BOX?
WE'RE SUPPOSED TO BE LOVERS. DO YOU WANT HARVEY TO SUSPECT?
THIS IS BLACKMAIL.
TO BE CONTINUED!

VAMPIRE VICTIM

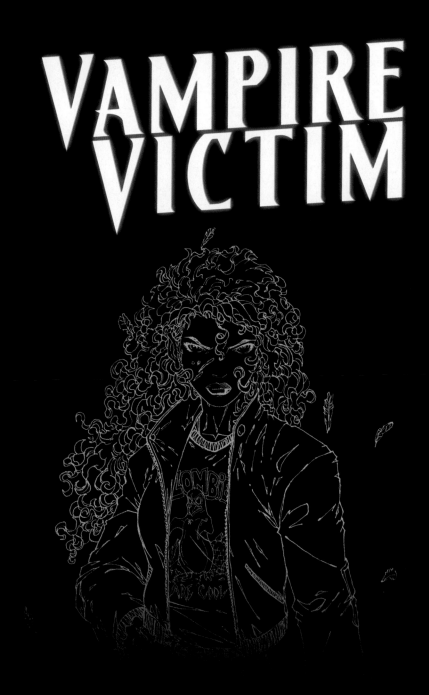

WRITER **LAURELL K. HAMILTON & JONATHON GREEN**

ARTWORK **BRETT BOOTH**

COLORS **LARRY MOLINAR** (SPECIAL THANKS TO JESS RUFFNER-BOOTH)

LETTERS **BILL TORTOLINI**

EDITOR **MIKE RAICHT**

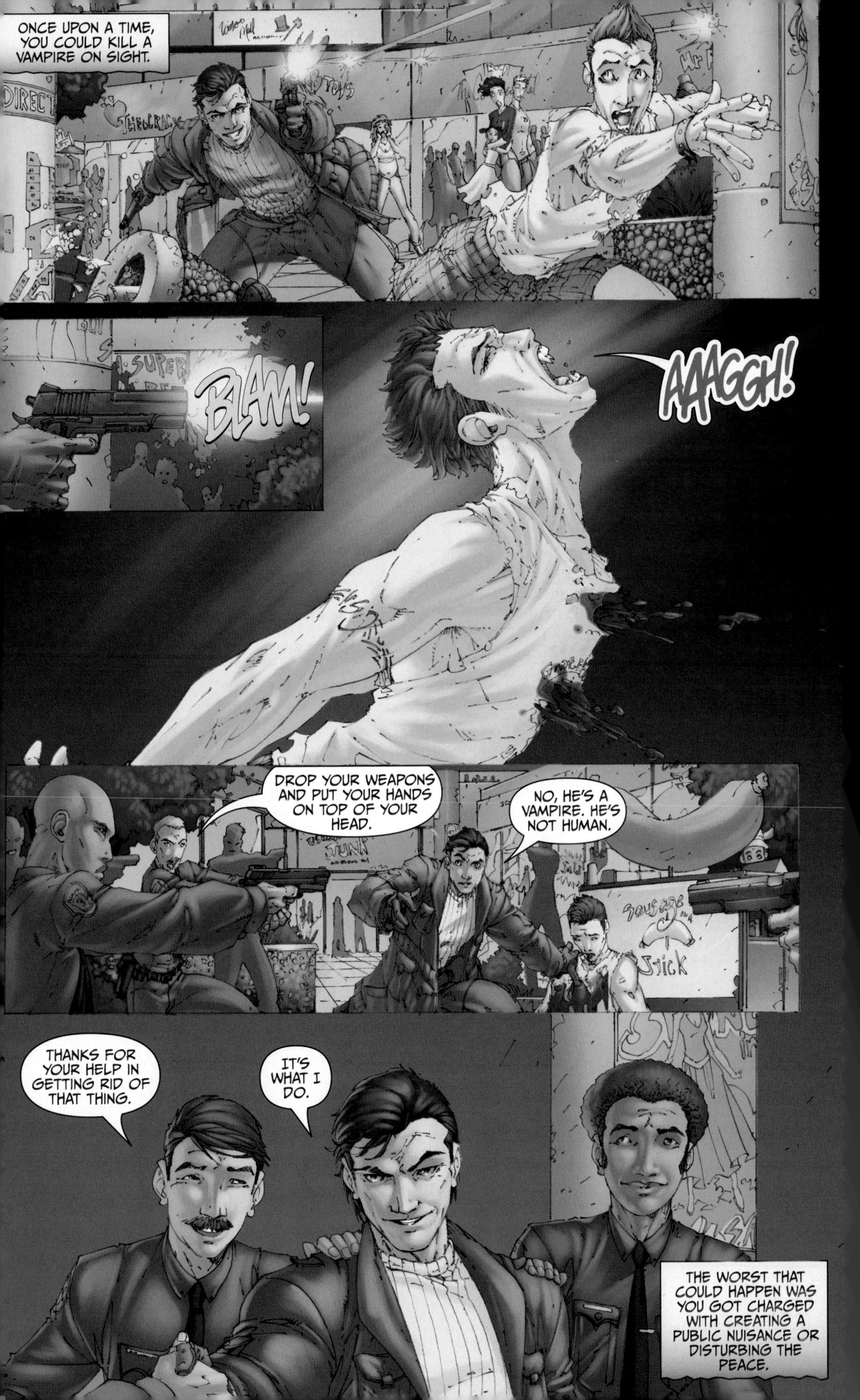
ONCE UPON A TIME, YOU COULD KILL A VAMPIRE ON SIGHT.
BLAM!
AAAGGH!
DROP YOUR WEAPONS AND PUT YOUR HANDS ON TOP OF YOUR HEAD.
NO, HE'S A VAMPIRE. HE'S NOT HUMAN.
THANKS FOR YOUR HELP IN GETTING RID OF THAT THING.
IT'S WHAT I DO.
THE WORST THAT COULD HAPPEN WAS YOU GOT CHARGED WITH CREATING A PUBLIC NUISANCE OR DISTURBING THE PEACE.

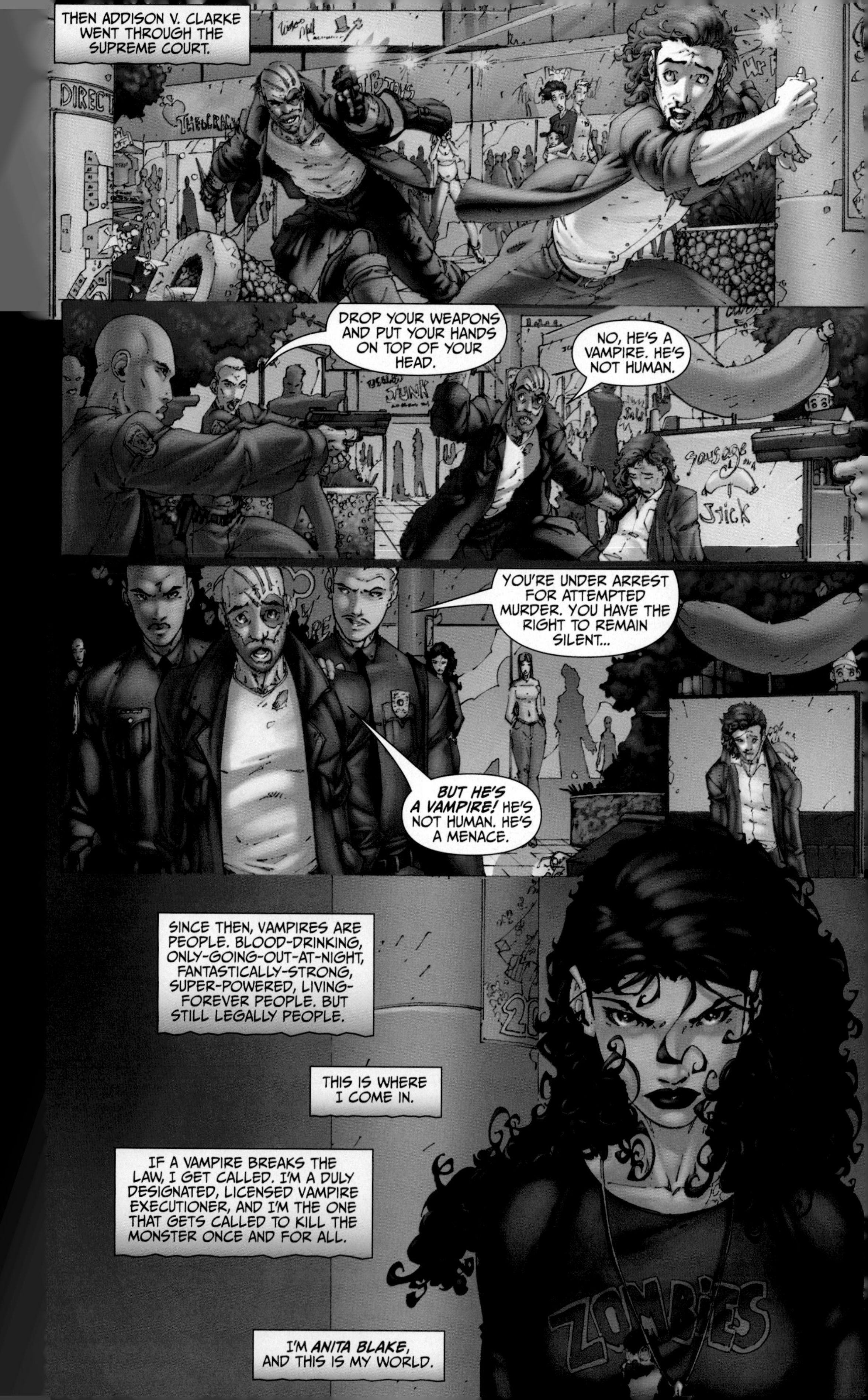
THEN ADDISON V. CLARKE WENT THROUGH THE SUPREME COURT.
DROP YOUR WEAPONS AND PUT YOUR HANDS ON TOP OF YOUR HEAD.
NO, HE'S A VAMPIRE. HE'S NOT HUMAN.
YOU'RE UNDER ARREST FOR ATTEMPTED MURDER. YOU HAVE THE RIGHT TO REMAIN SILENT...
BUT HE'S A VAMPIRE! HE'S NOT HUMAN. HE'S A MENACE.
SINCE THEN, VAMPIRES ARE PEOPLE. BLOOD-DRINKING, ONLY-GOING-OUT-AT-NIGHT, FANTASTICALLY-STRONG, SUPER-POWERED, LIVING-FOREVER PEOPLE. BUT STILL LEGALLY PEOPLE.
THIS IS WHERE I COME IN.
IF A VAMPIRE BREAKS THE LAW, I GET CALLED. I'M A DULY DESIGNATED, LICENSED VAMPIRE EXECUTIONER, AND I'M THE ONE THAT GETS CALLED TO KILL THE MONSTER ONCE AND FOR ALL.
I'M *ANITA BLAKE,* AND THIS IS MY WORLD.
ZOMBIES

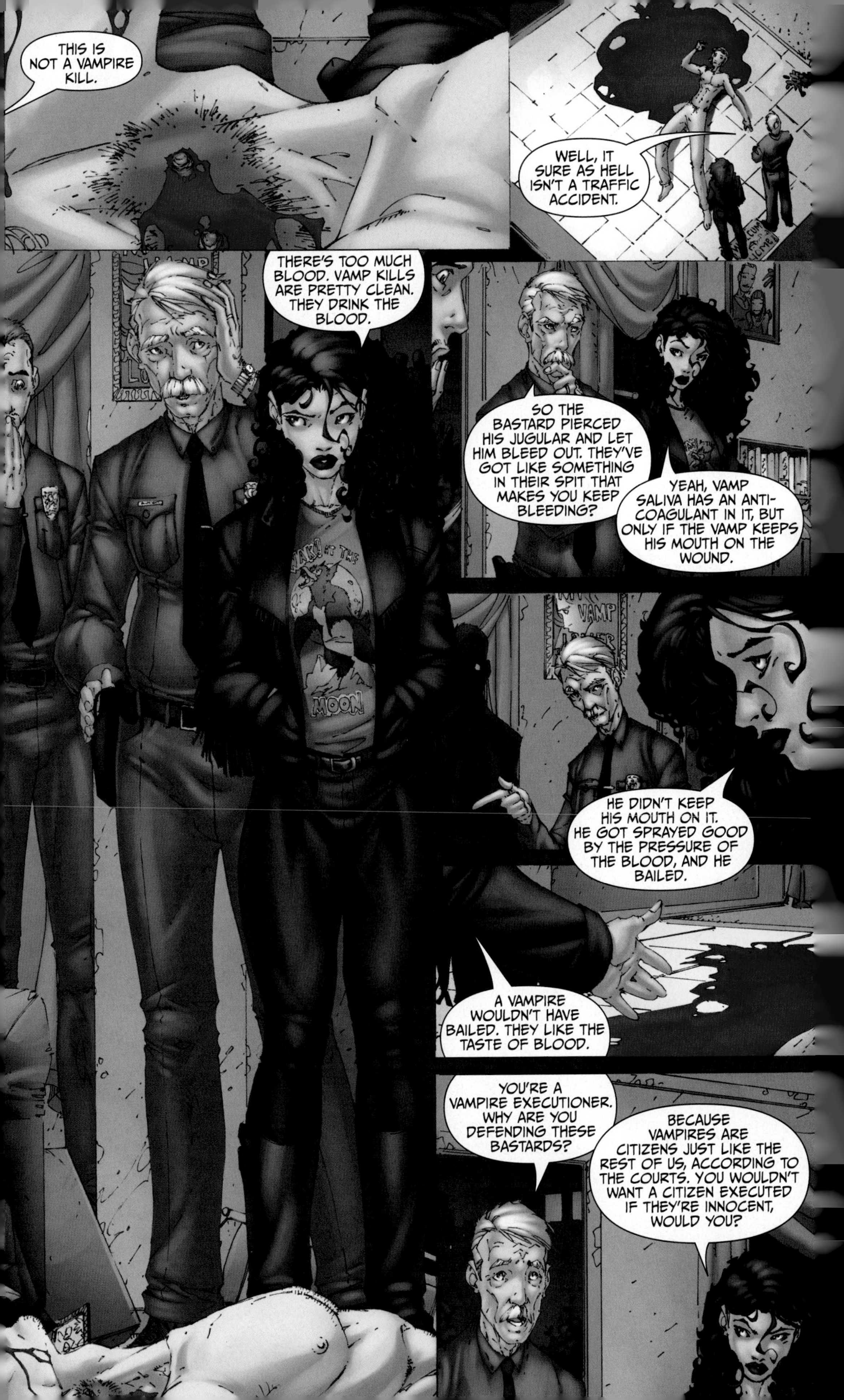
THIS IS NOT A VAMPIRE KILL.
WELL, IT SURE AS HELL ISN'T A TRAFFIC ACCIDENT.
THERE'S TOO MUCH BLOOD. VAMP KILLS ARE PRETTY CLEAN. THEY DRINK THE BLOOD.
SO THE BASTARD PIERCED HIS JUGULAR AND LET HIM BLEED OUT. THEY'VE GOT LIKE SOMETHING IN THEIR SPIT THAT MAKES YOU KEEP BLEEDING?
YEAH, VAMP SALIVA HAS AN ANTI-COAGULANT IN IT, BUT ONLY IF THE VAMP KEEPS HIS MOUTH ON THE WOUND.
HE DIDN'T KEEP HIS MOUTH ON IT. HE GOT SPRAYED GOOD BY THE PRESSURE OF THE BLOOD, AND HE BAILED.
A VAMPIRE WOULDN'T HAVE BAILED. THEY LIKE THE TASTE OF BLOOD.
YOU'RE A VAMPIRE EXECUTIONER. WHY ARE YOU DEFENDING THESE BASTARDS?
BECAUSE VAMPIRES ARE CITIZENS JUST LIKE THE REST OF US, ACCORDING TO THE COURTS. YOU WOULDN'T WANT A CITIZEN EXECUTED IF THEY'RE INNOCENT, WOULD YOU?

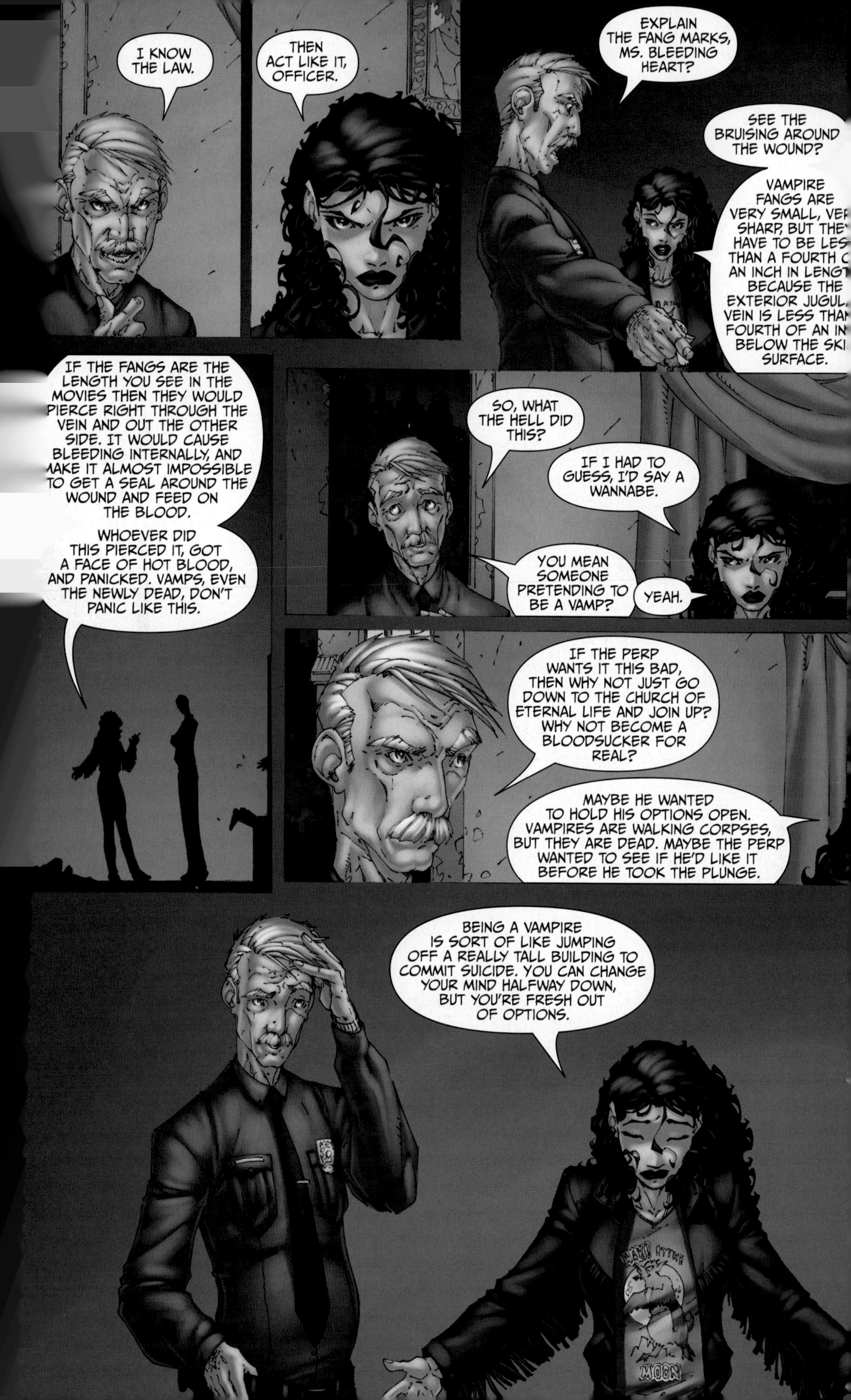

I KNOW THE LAW.
THEN ACT LIKE IT, OFFICER.
EXPLAIN THE FANG MARKS, MS. BLEEDING HEART?
SEE THE BRUISING AROUND THE WOUND?
VAMPIRE FANGS ARE VERY SMALL, VER SHARP, BUT THE HAVE TO BE LES THAN A FOURTH C AN INCH IN LENG BECAUSE THE EXTERIOR JUGUL VEIN IS LESS THA FOURTH OF AN IN BELOW THE SKI SURFACE.
IF THE FANGS ARE THE LENGTH YOU SEE IN THE MOVIES THEN THEY WOULD PIERCE RIGHT THROUGH THE VEIN AND OUT THE OTHER SIDE. IT WOULD CAUSE BLEEDING INTERNALLY, AND MAKE IT ALMOST IMPOSSIBLE TO GET A SEAL AROUND THE WOUND AND FEED ON THE BLOOD.
WHOEVER DID THIS PIERCED IT, GOT A FACE OF HOT BLOOD, AND PANICKED. VAMPS, EVEN THE NEWLY DEAD, DON'T PANIC LIKE THIS.
SO, WHAT THE HELL DID THIS?
IF I HAD TO GUESS, I'D SAY A WANNABE.
YOU MEAN SOMEONE PRETENDING TO BE A VAMP?
YEAH.
IF THE PERP WANTS IT THIS BAD, THEN WHY NOT JUST GO DOWN TO THE CHURCH OF ETERNAL LIFE AND JOIN UP? WHY NOT BECOME A BLOODSUCKER FOR REAL?
MAYBE HE WANTED TO HOLD HIS OPTIONS OPEN. VAMPIRES ARE WALKING CORPSES, BUT THEY ARE DEAD. MAYBE THE PERP WANTED TO SEE IF HE'D LIKE IT BEFORE HE TOOK THE PLUNGE.
BEING A VAMPIRE IS SORT OF LIKE JUMPING OFF A REALLY TALL BUILDING TO COMMIT SUICIDE. YOU CAN CHANGE YOUR MIND HALFWAY DOWN, BUT YOU'RE FRESH OUT OF OPTIONS.
MOON

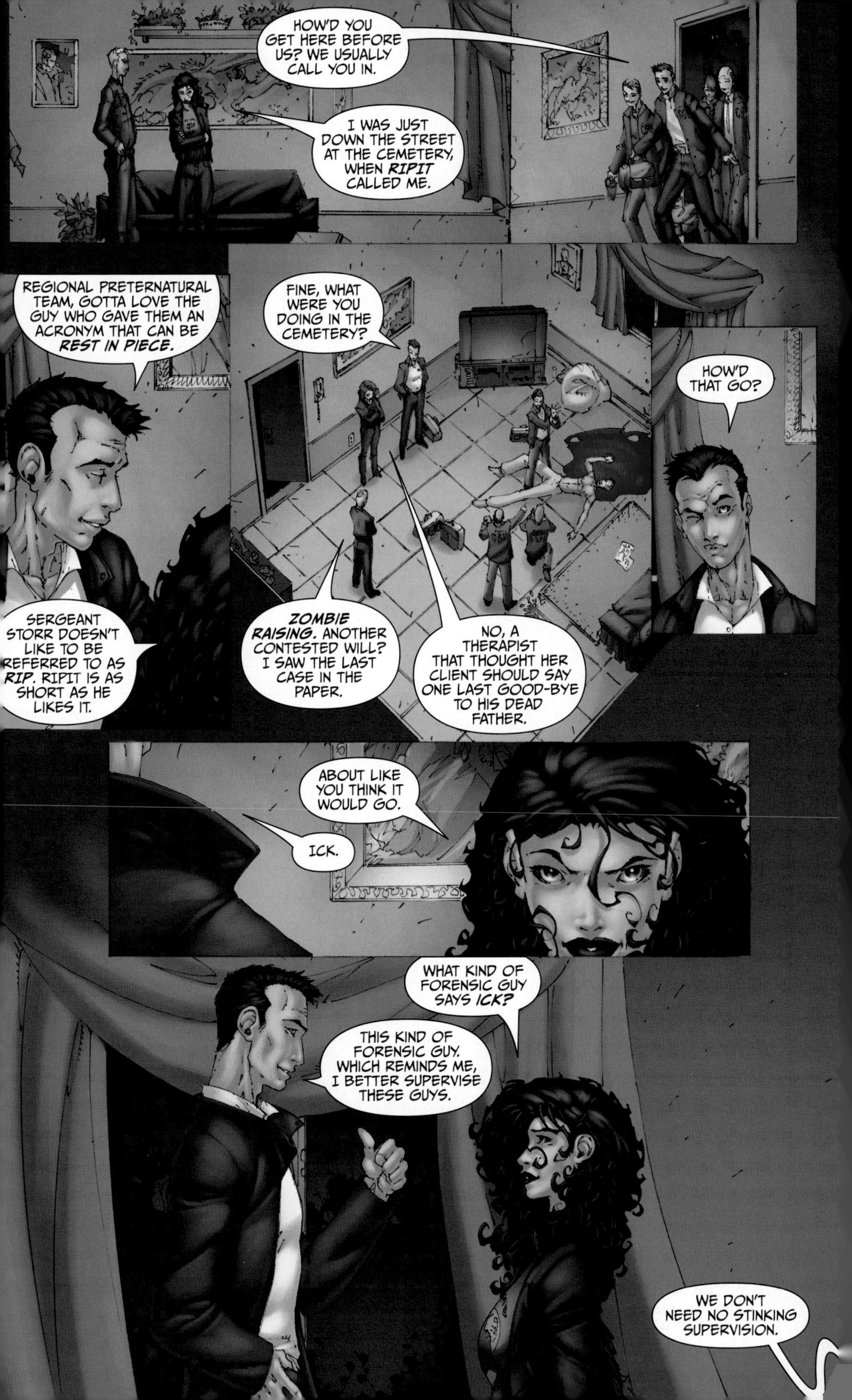
HOW'D YOU GET HERE BEFORE US? WE USUALLY CALL YOU IN.
I WAS JUST DOWN THE STREET AT THE CEMETERY, WHEN RIPIT CALLED ME.
REGIONAL PRETERNATURAL TEAM, GOTTA LOVE THE GUY WHO GAVE THEM AN ACRONYM THAT CAN BE REST IN PIECE.
SERGEANT STORR DOESN'T LIKE TO BE REFERRED TO AS RIP. RIPIT IS AS SHORT AS HE LIKES IT.
FINE, WHAT WERE YOU DOING IN THE CEMETERY?
ZOMBIE RAISING. ANOTHER CONTESTED WILL? I SAW THE LAST CASE IN THE PAPER.
NO, A THERAPIST THAT THOUGHT HER CLIENT SHOULD SAY ONE LAST GOOD-BYE TO HIS DEAD FATHER.
HOW'D THAT GO?
ABOUT LIKE YOU THINK IT WOULD GO.
ICK.
WHAT KIND OF FORENSIC GUY SAYS ICK?
THIS KIND OF FORENSIC GUY. WHICH REMINDS ME, I BETTER SUPERVISE THESE GUYS.
WE DON'T NEED NO STINKING SUPERVISION.

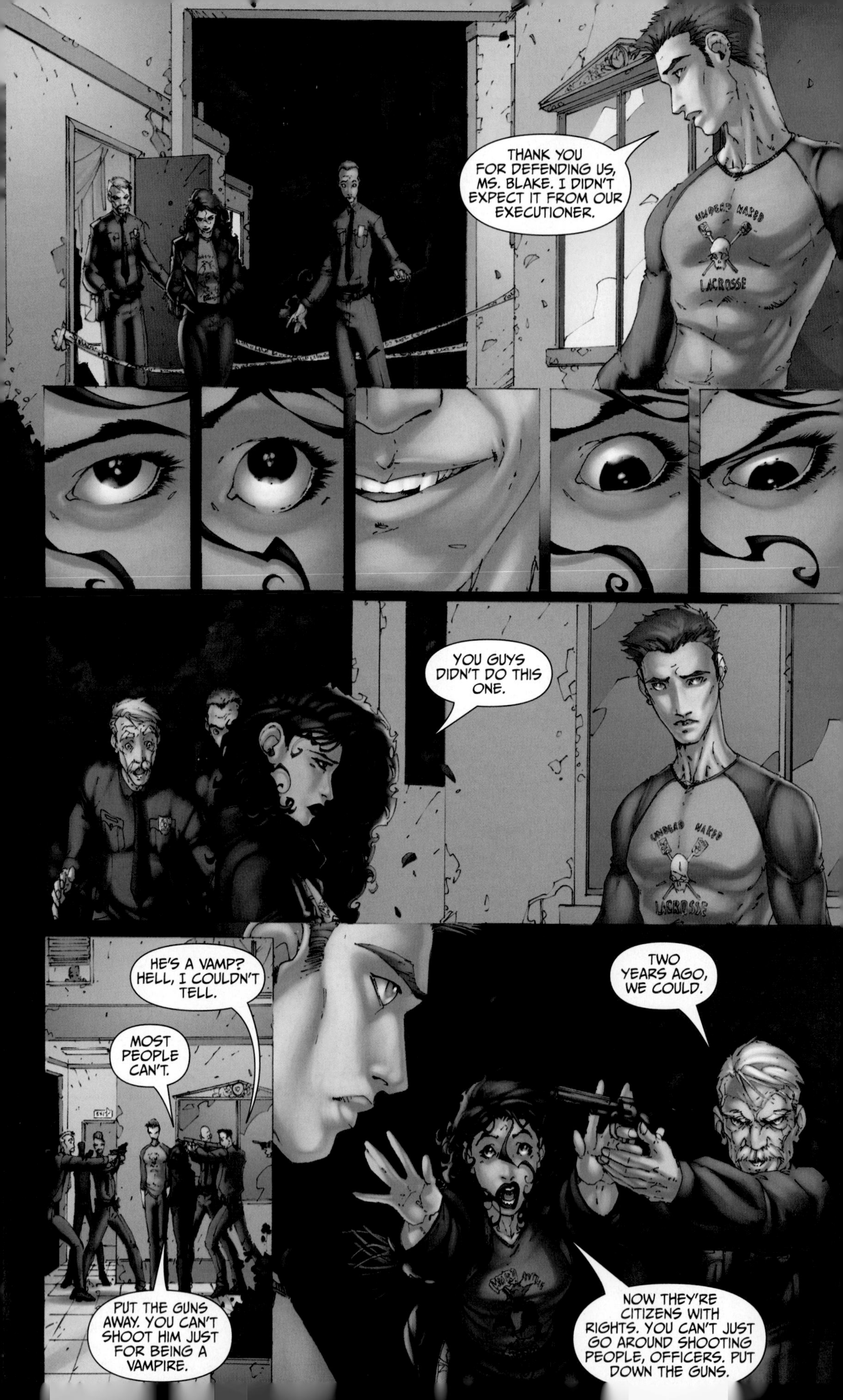
THANK YOU FOR DEFENDING US, MS. BLAKE. I DIDN'T EXPECT IT FROM OUR EXECUTIONER.
UNDEAD NAKED
LACROSSE
YOU GUYS DIDN'T DO THIS ONE.
UNDEAD NAKED
LACROSSE
HE'S A VAMP? HELL, I COULDN'T TELL.
MOST PEOPLE CAN'T.
PUT THE GUNS AWAY. YOU CAN'T SHOOT HIM JUST FOR BEING A VAMPIRE.
TWO YEARS AGO, WE COULD.
NOW THEY'RE CITIZENS WITH RIGHTS. YOU CAN'T JUST GO AROUND SHOOTING PEOPLE, OFFICERS. PUT DOWN THE GUNS.

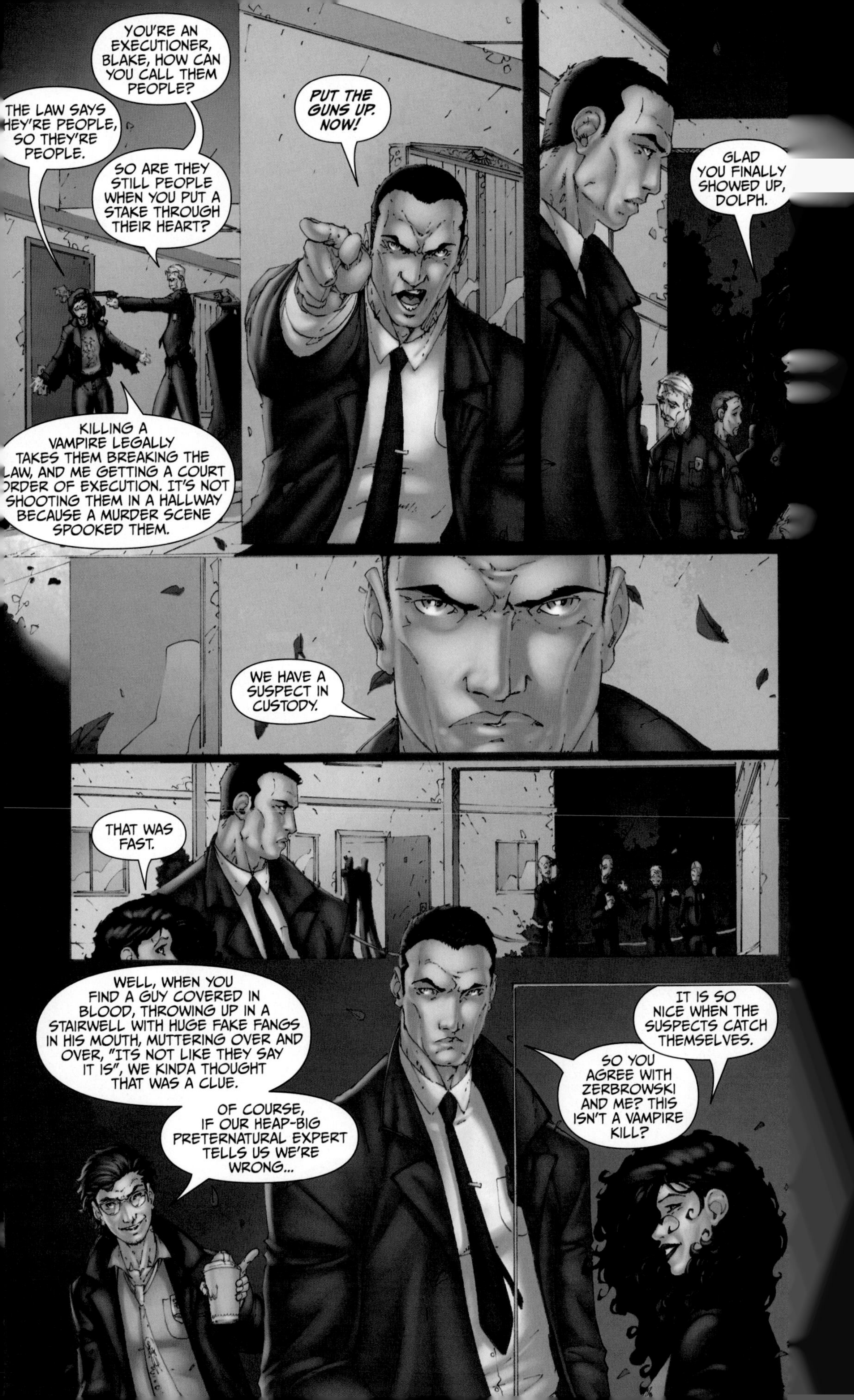
YOU'RE AN EXECUTIONER, BLAKE, HOW CAN YOU CALL THEM PEOPLE?
THE LAW SAYS THEY'RE PEOPLE, SO THEY'RE PEOPLE.
SO ARE THEY STILL PEOPLE WHEN YOU PUT A STAKE THROUGH THEIR HEART?
KILLING A VAMPIRE LEGALLY TAKES THEM BREAKING THE LAW, AND ME GETTING A COURT ORDER OF EXECUTION. IT'S NOT SHOOTING THEM IN A HALLWAY BECAUSE A MURDER SCENE SPOOKED THEM.
PUT THE GUNS UP. NOW!
GLAD YOU FINALLY SHOWED UP, DOLPH.
WE HAVE A SUSPECT IN CUSTODY.
THAT WAS FAST.
WELL, WHEN YOU FIND A GUY COVERED IN BLOOD, THROWING UP IN A STAIRWELL WITH HUGE FAKE FANGS IN HIS MOUTH, MUTTERING OVER AND OVER, "ITS NOT LIKE THEY SAY IT IS", WE KINDA THOUGHT THAT WAS A CLUE.
OF COURSE, IF OUR HEAP-BIG PRETERNATURAL EXPERT TELLS US WE'RE WRONG...
IT IS SO NICE WHEN THE SUSPECTS CATCH THEMSELVES.
SO YOU AGREE WITH ZERBROWSKI AND ME? THIS ISN'T A VAMPIRE KILL?

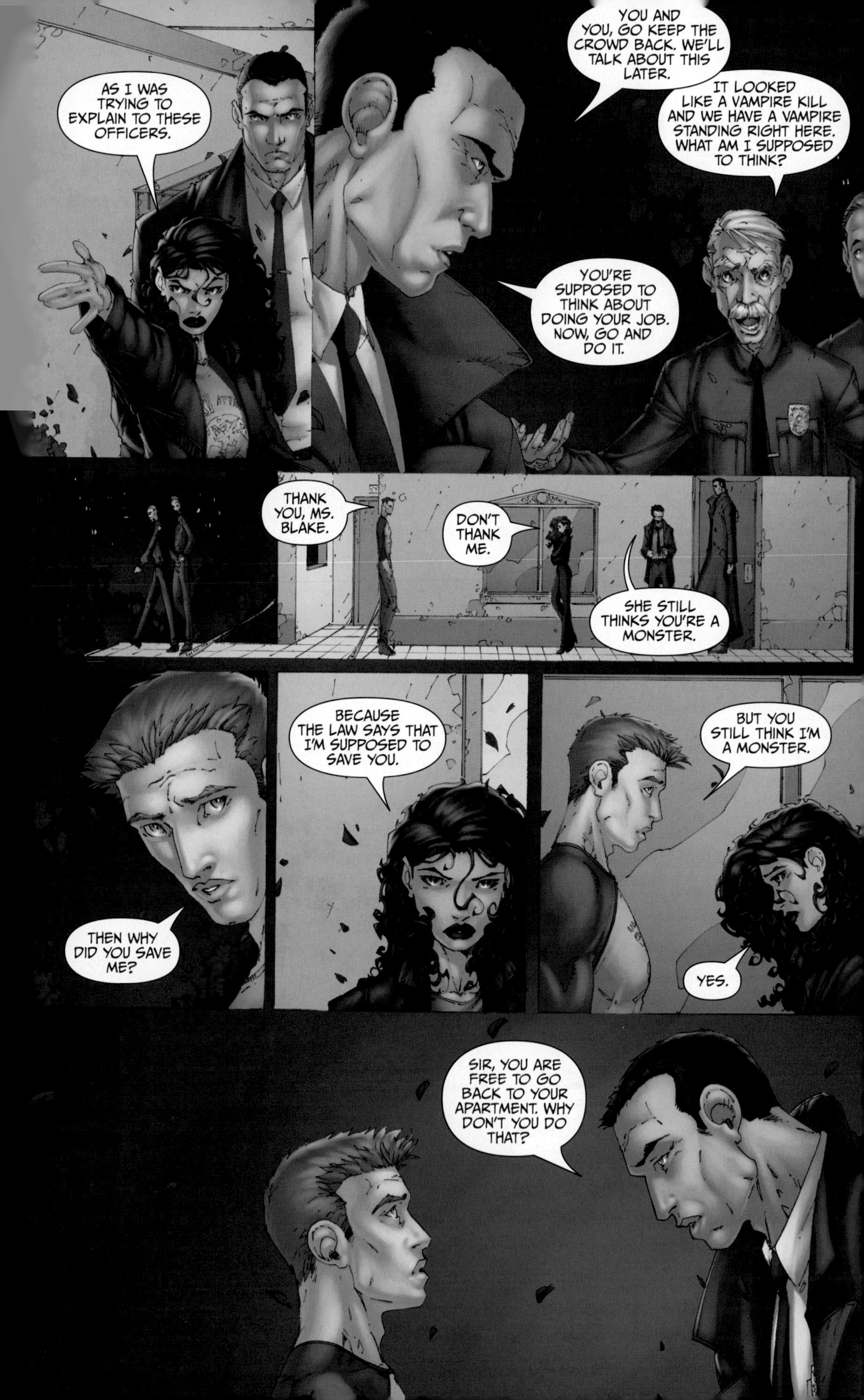
AS I WAS TRYING TO EXPLAIN TO THESE OFFICERS.
YOU AND YOU, GO KEEP THE CROWD BACK. WE'LL TALK ABOUT THIS LATER.
IT LOOKED LIKE A VAMPIRE KILL AND WE HAVE A VAMPIRE STANDING RIGHT HERE. WHAT AM I SUPPOSED TO THINK?
YOU'RE SUPPOSED TO THINK ABOUT DOING YOUR JOB. NOW, GO AND DO IT.
THANK YOU, MS. BLAKE.
DON'T THANK ME.
SHE STILL THINKS YOU'RE A MONSTER.
THEN WHY DID YOU SAVE ME?
BECAUSE THE LAW SAYS THAT I'M SUPPOSED TO SAVE YOU.
BUT YOU STILL THINK I'M A MONSTER.
YES.
SIR, YOU ARE FREE TO GO BACK TO YOUR APARTMENT. WHY DON'T YOU DO THAT?

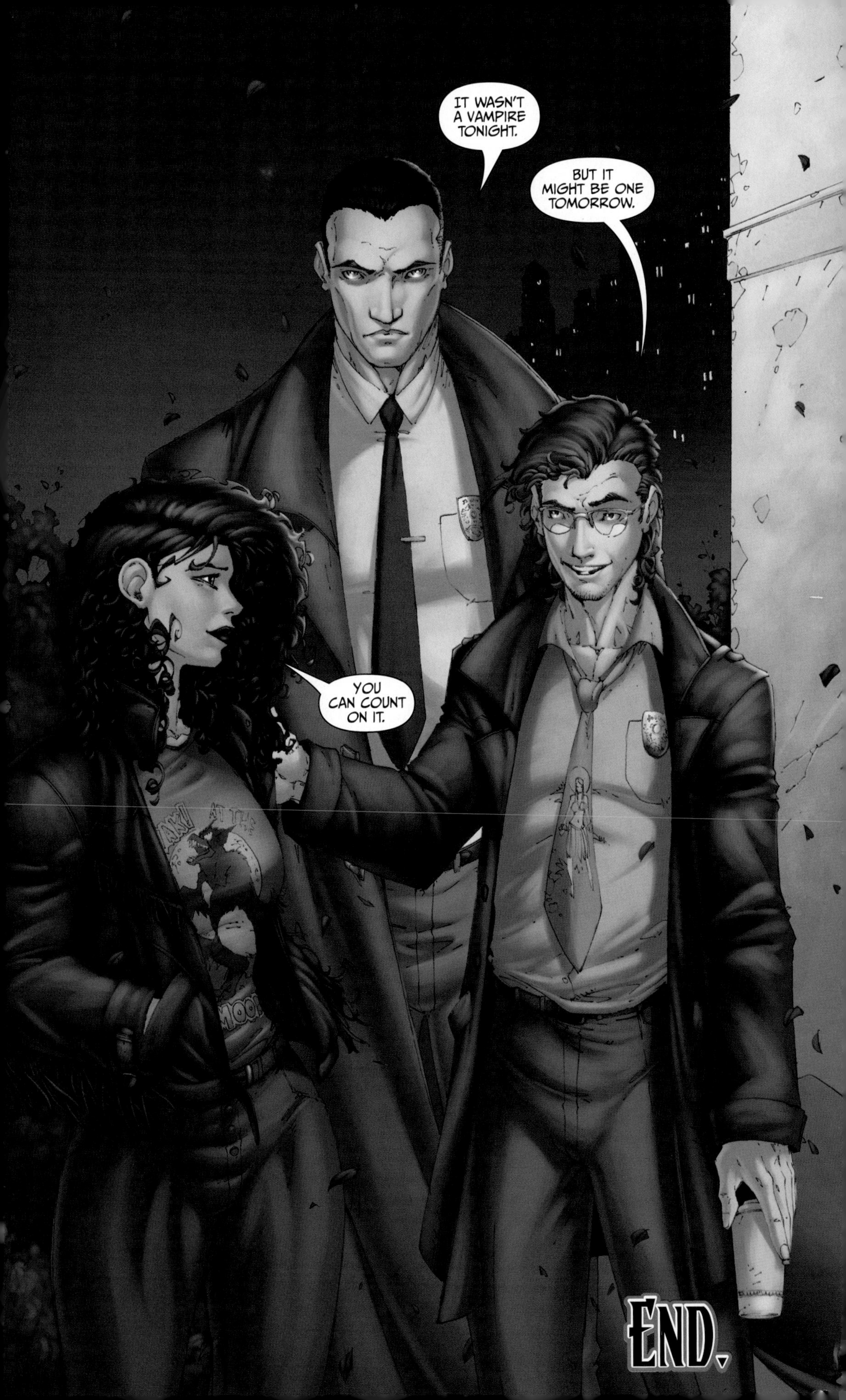
IT WASN'T A VAMPIRE TONIGHT.
BUT IT MIGHT BE ONE TOMORROW.
YOU CAN COUNT ON IT.
END.

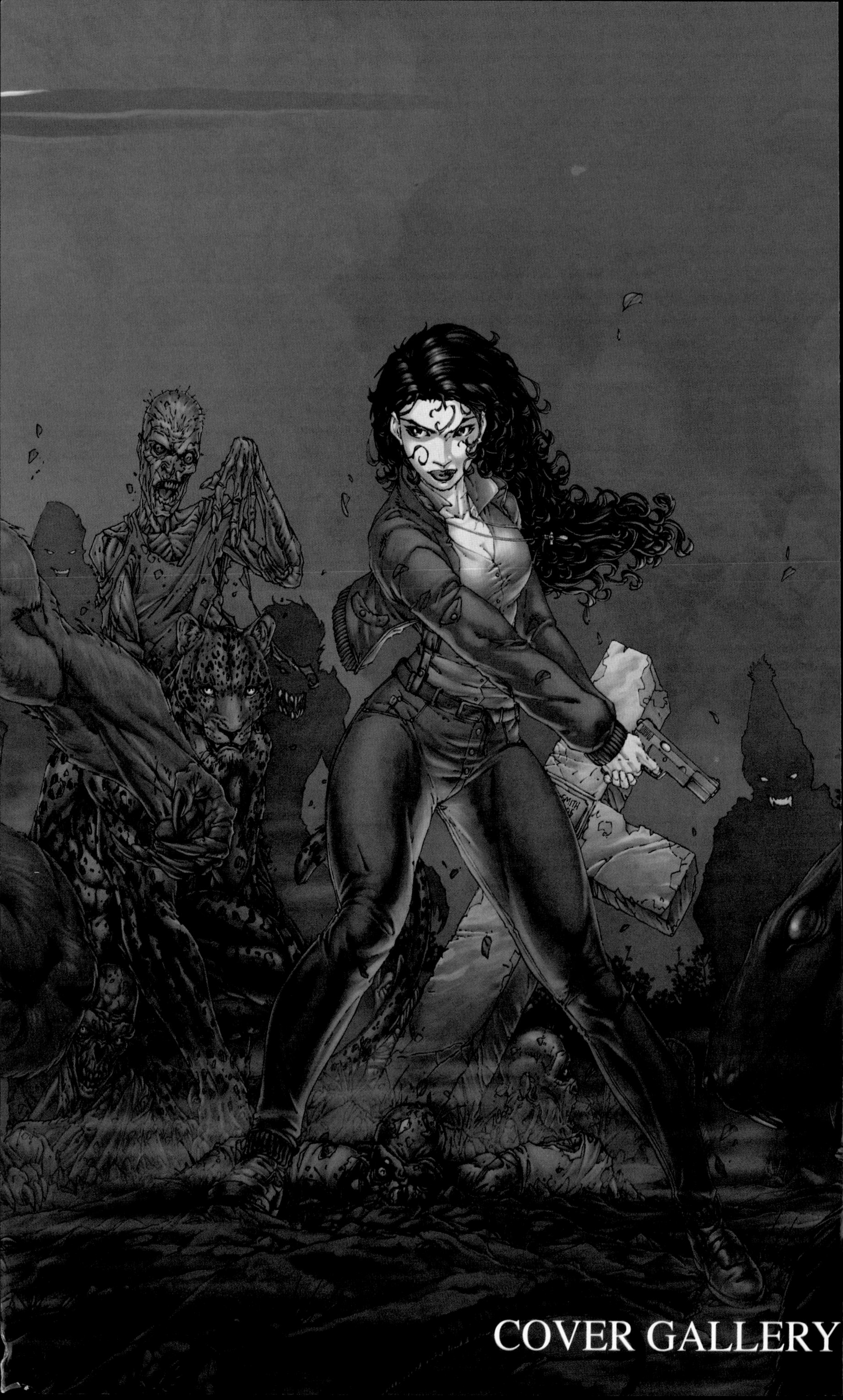

COVER GALLERY

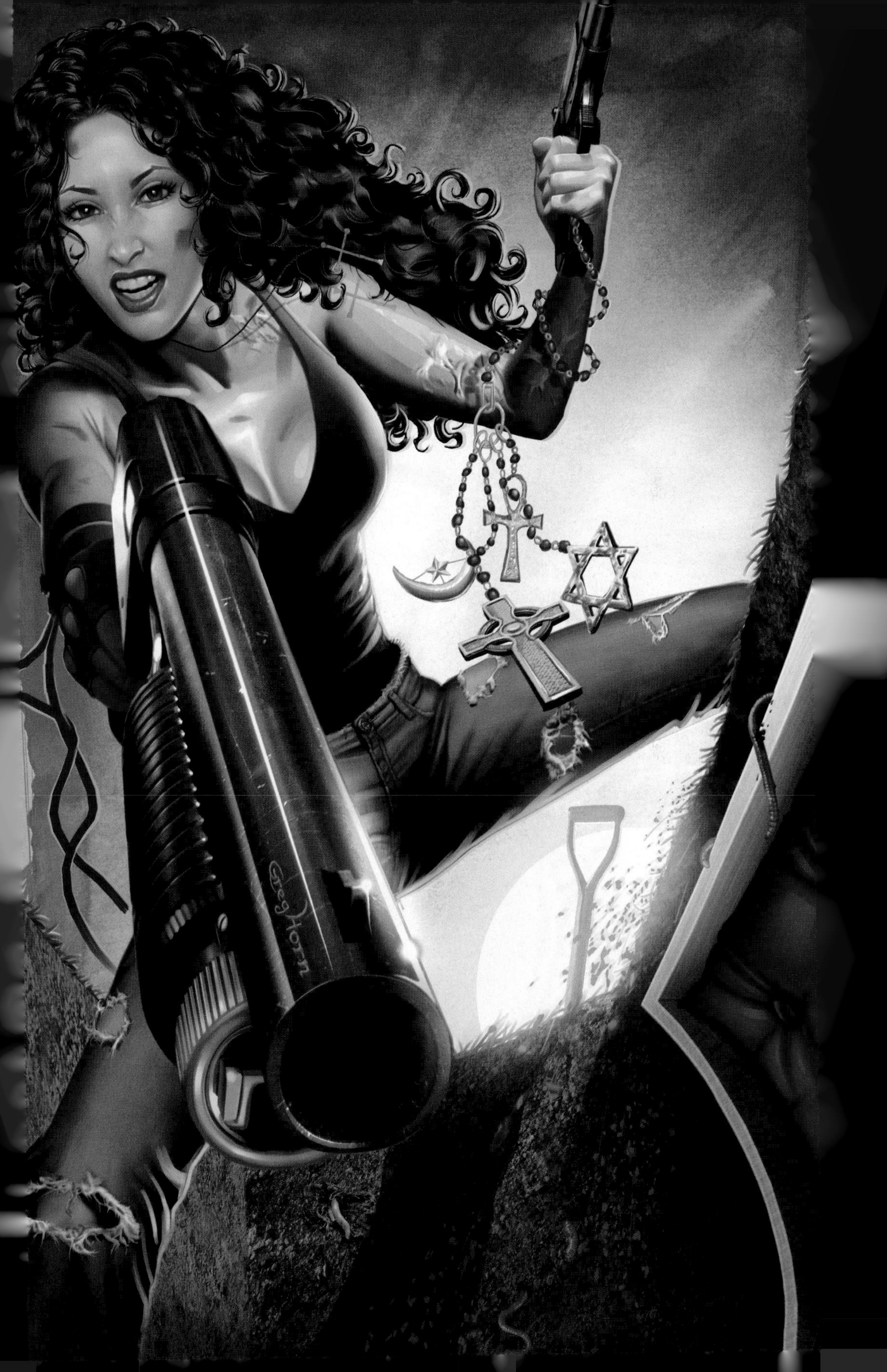
Greg Horn

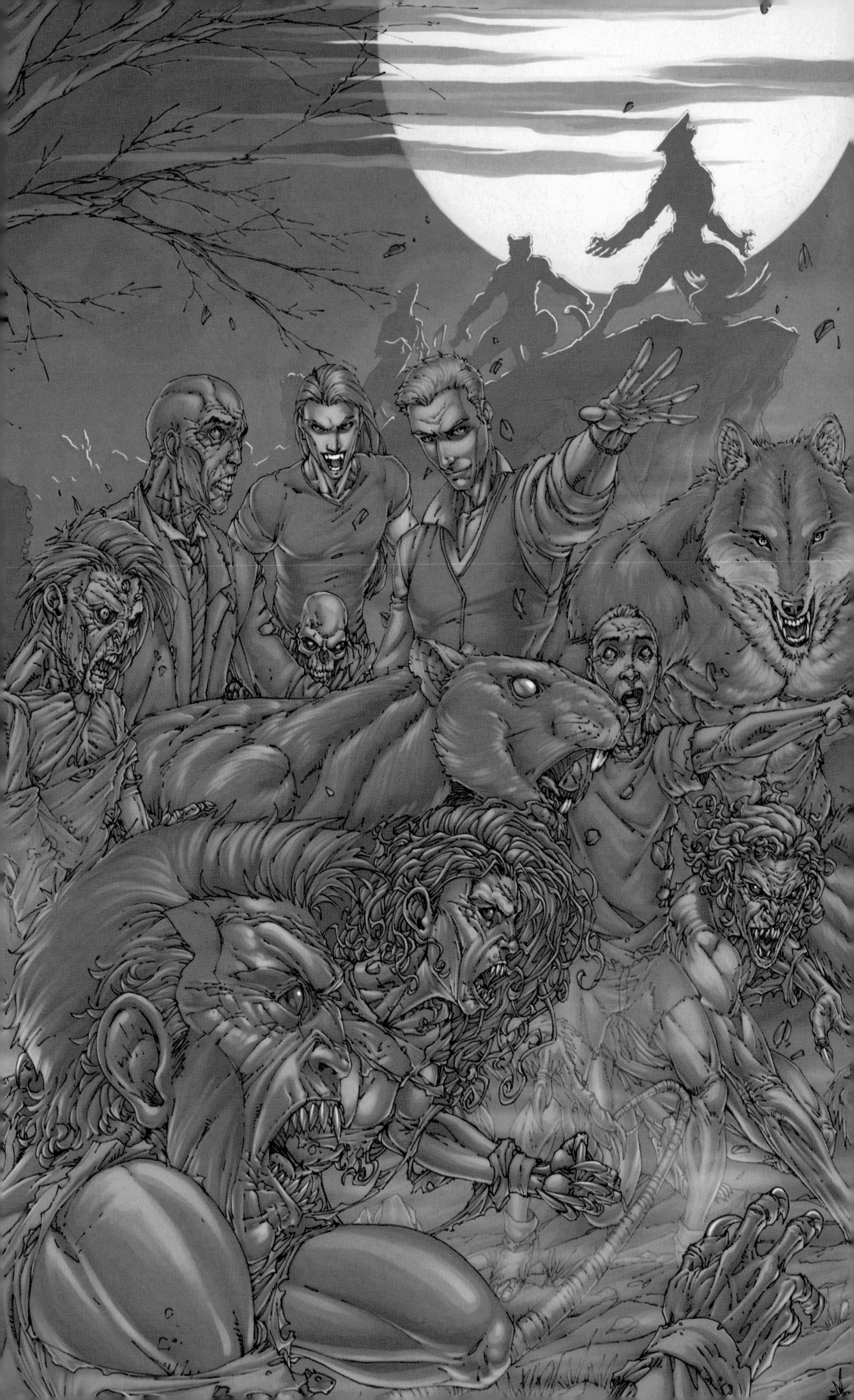

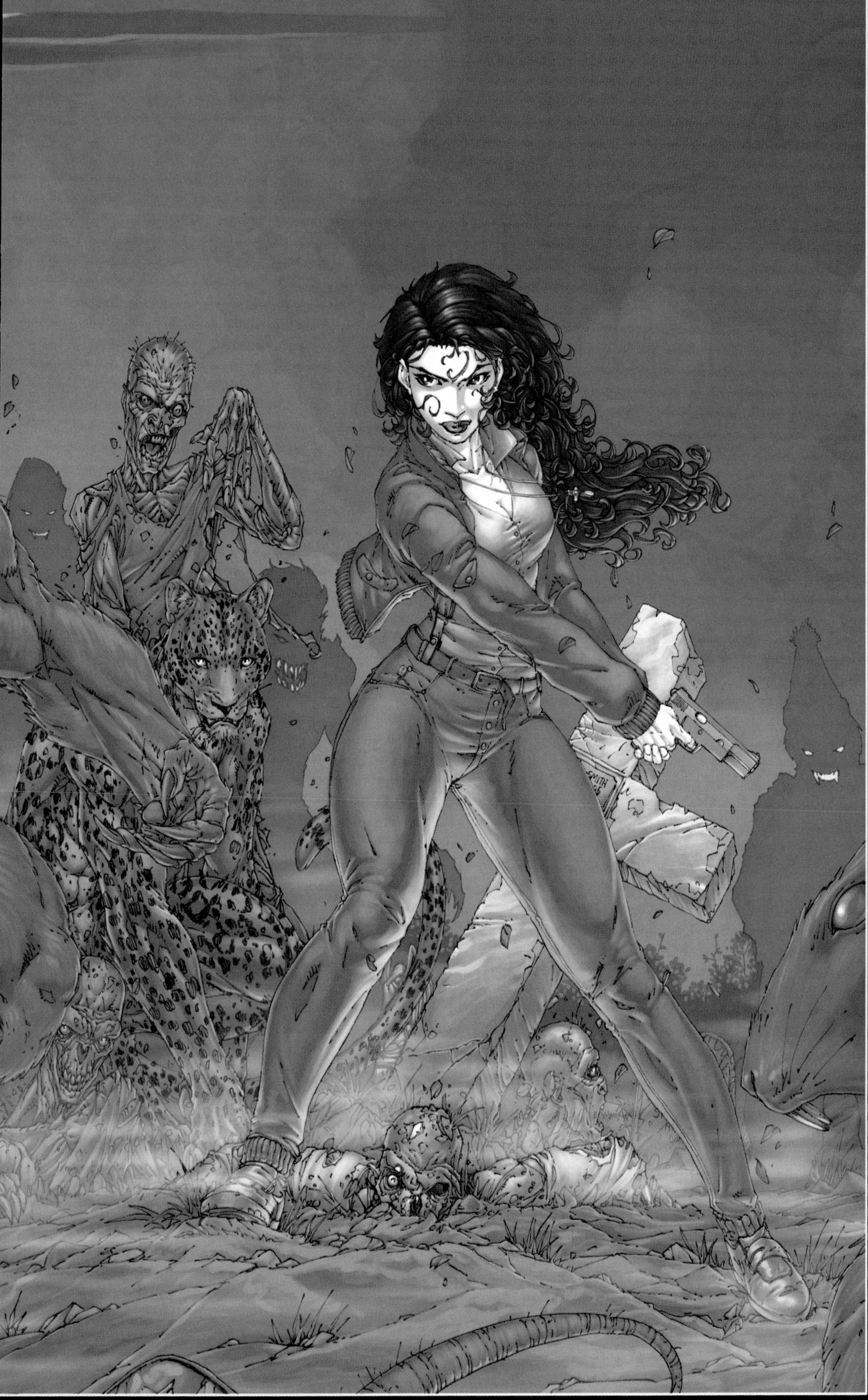

ISSUE #1 WRAPAROUND COVER BY: **BRETT BOOTH & JESS RUFFNER-BOOTH**

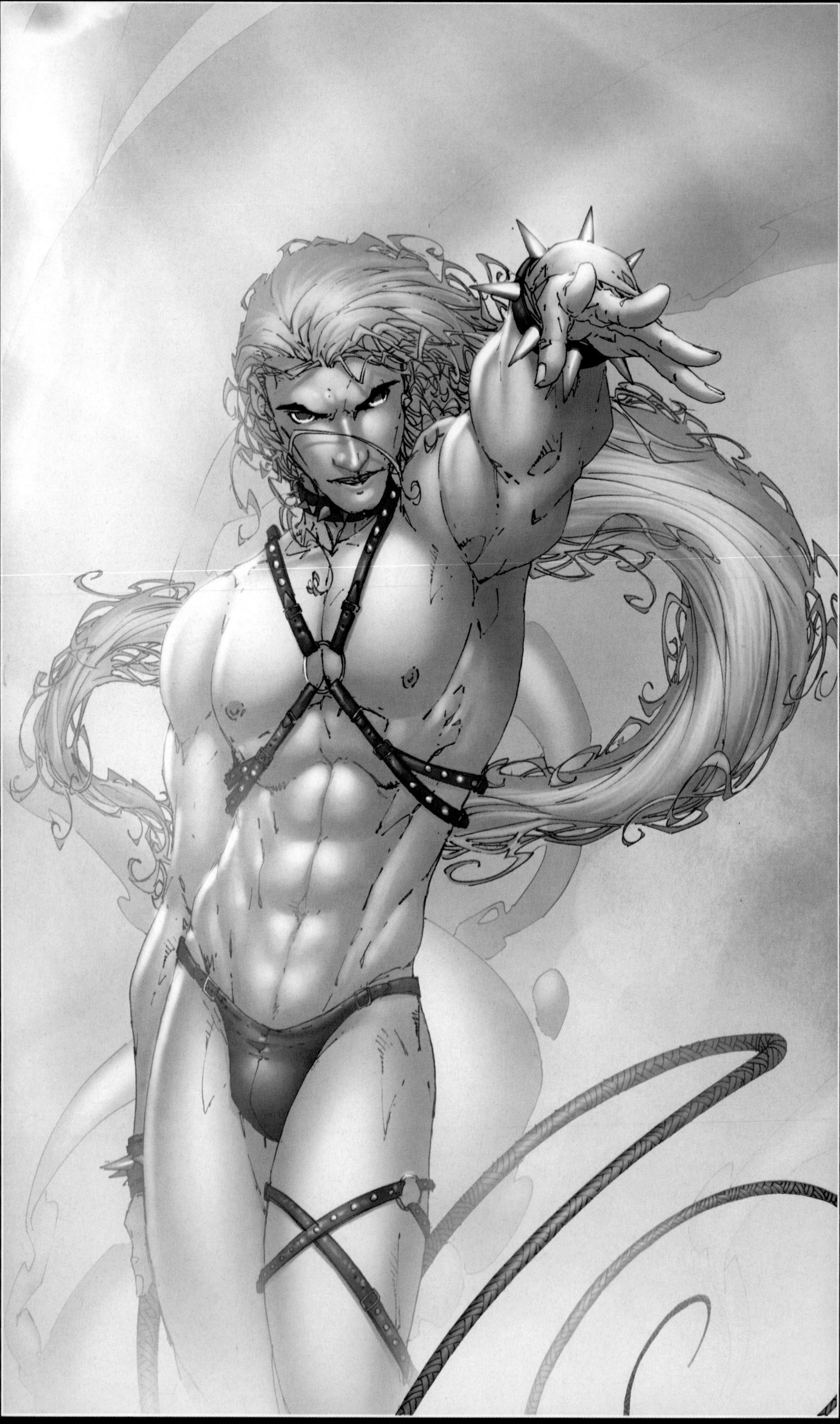

ISSUE #1 THIRD PRINTING COVER BY: **BRETT BOOTH & JESS RUFFNER-BOOTH**

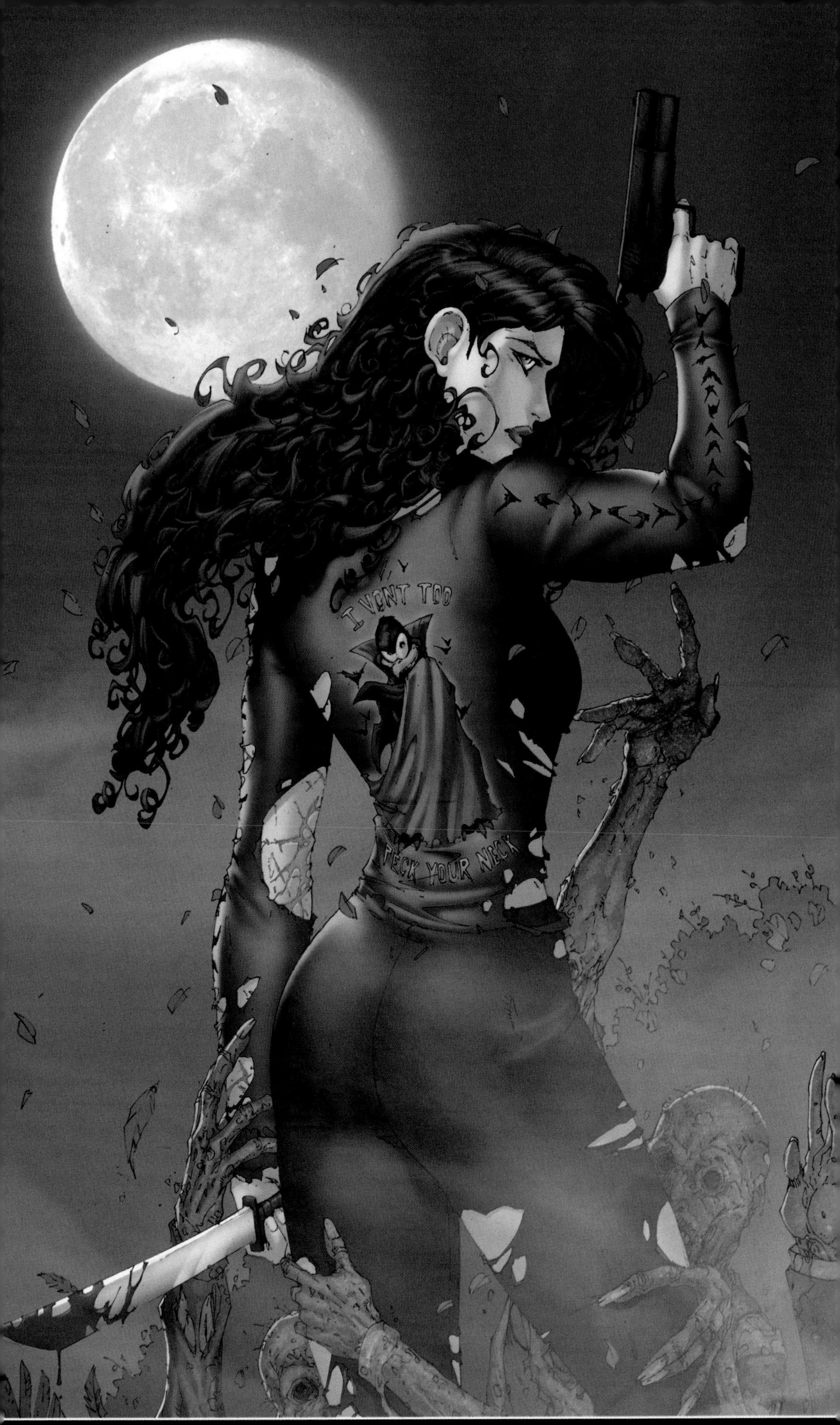
I VONT TOO
PECK YOUR NECK

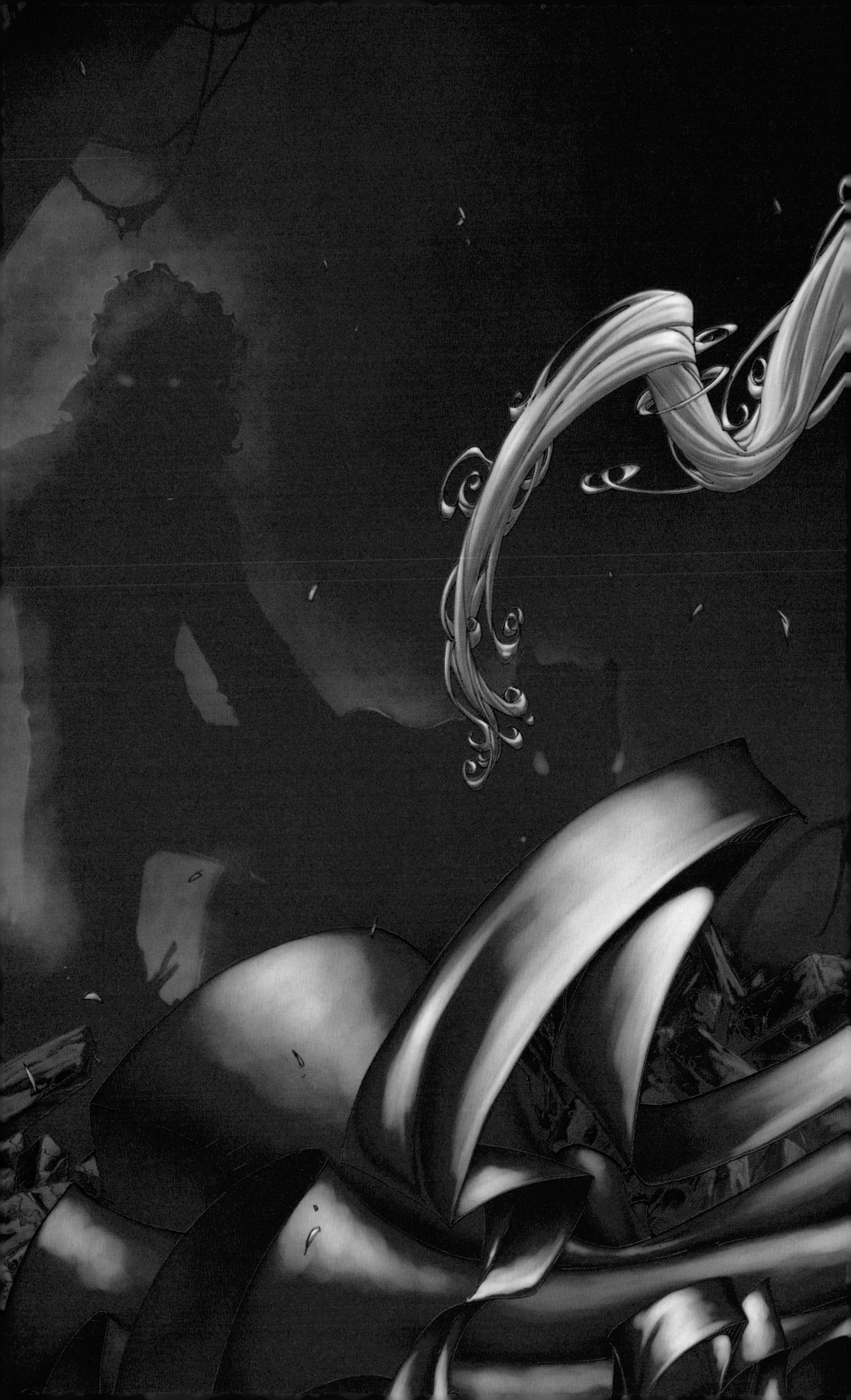

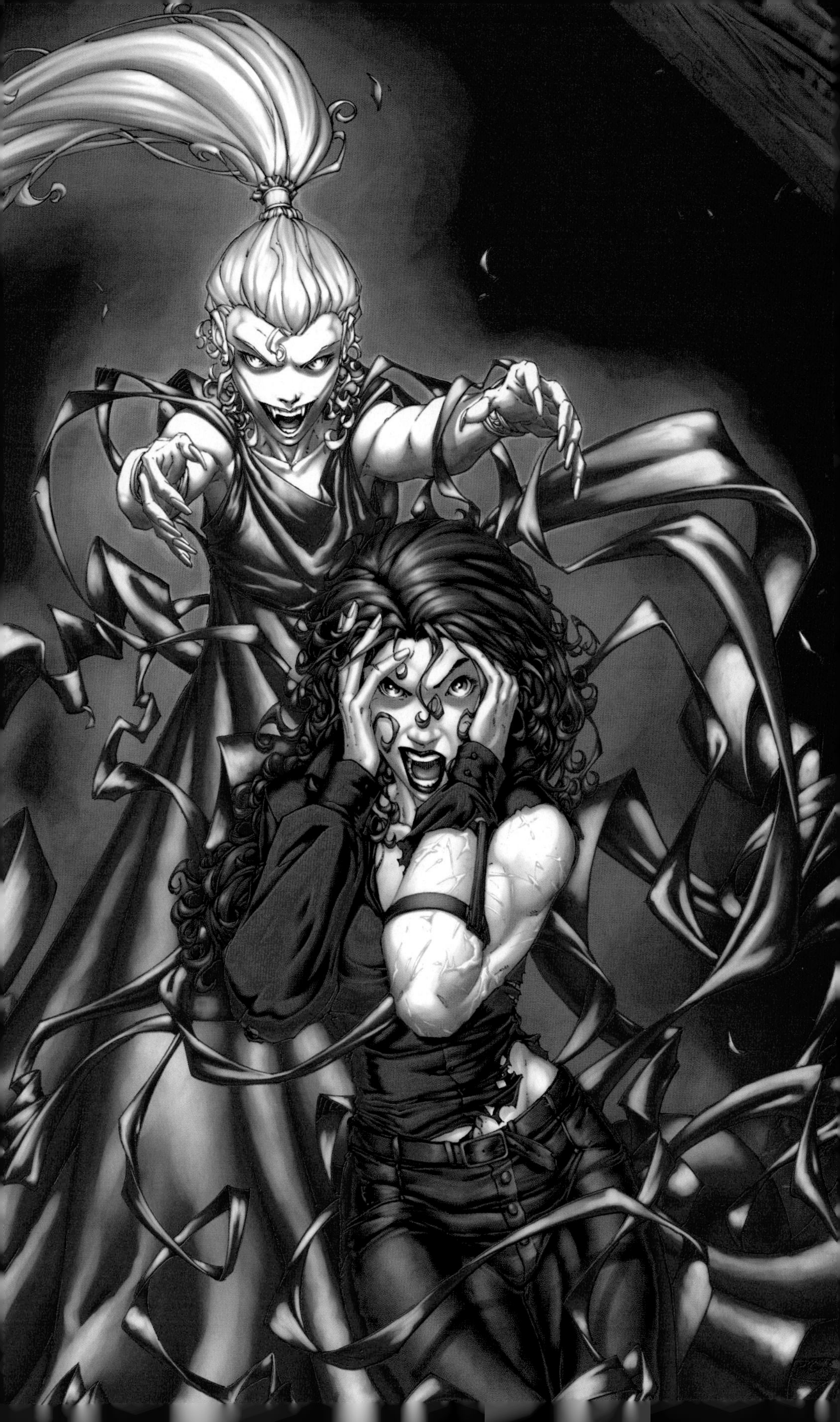

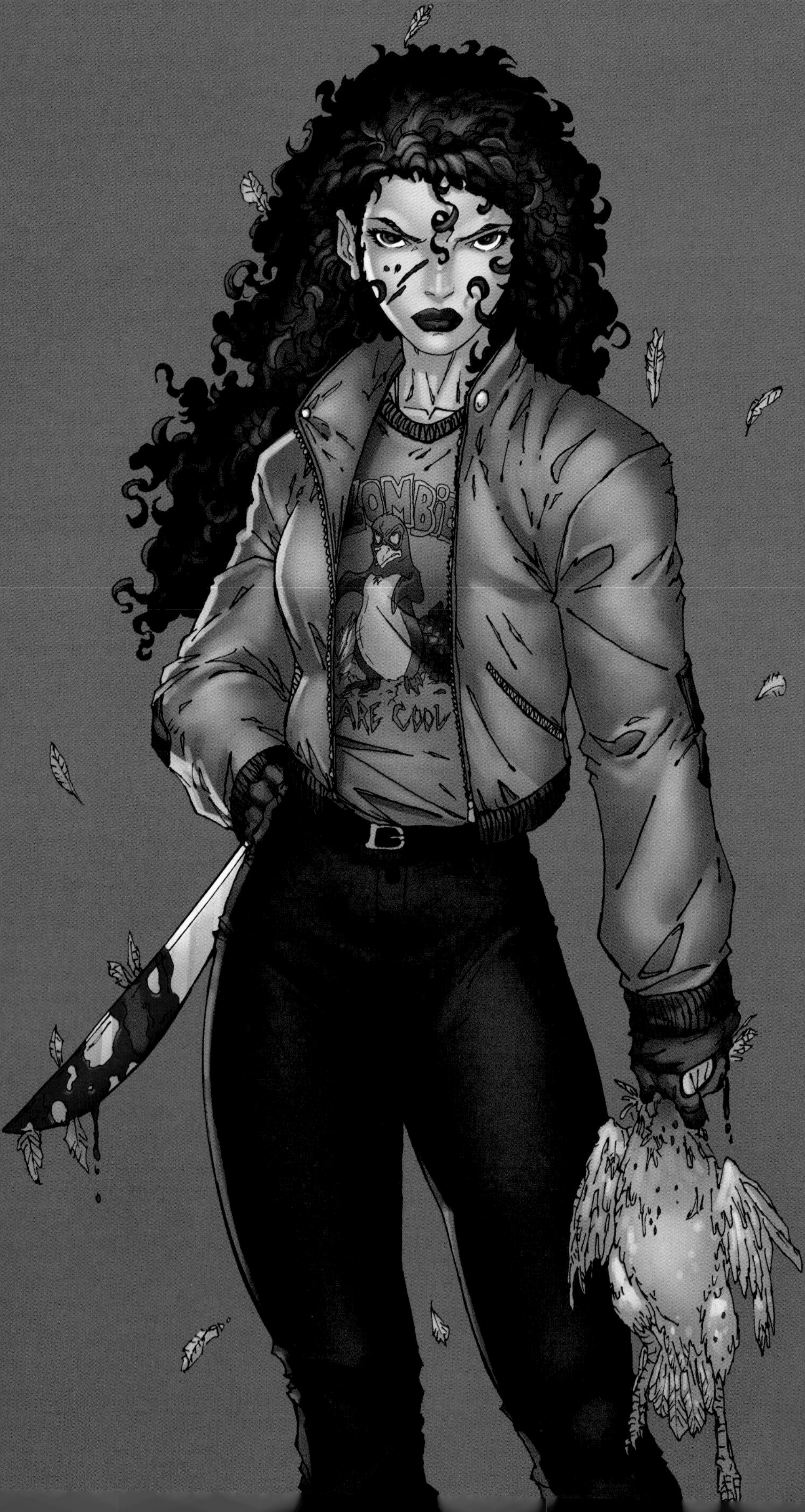
ARE COOL

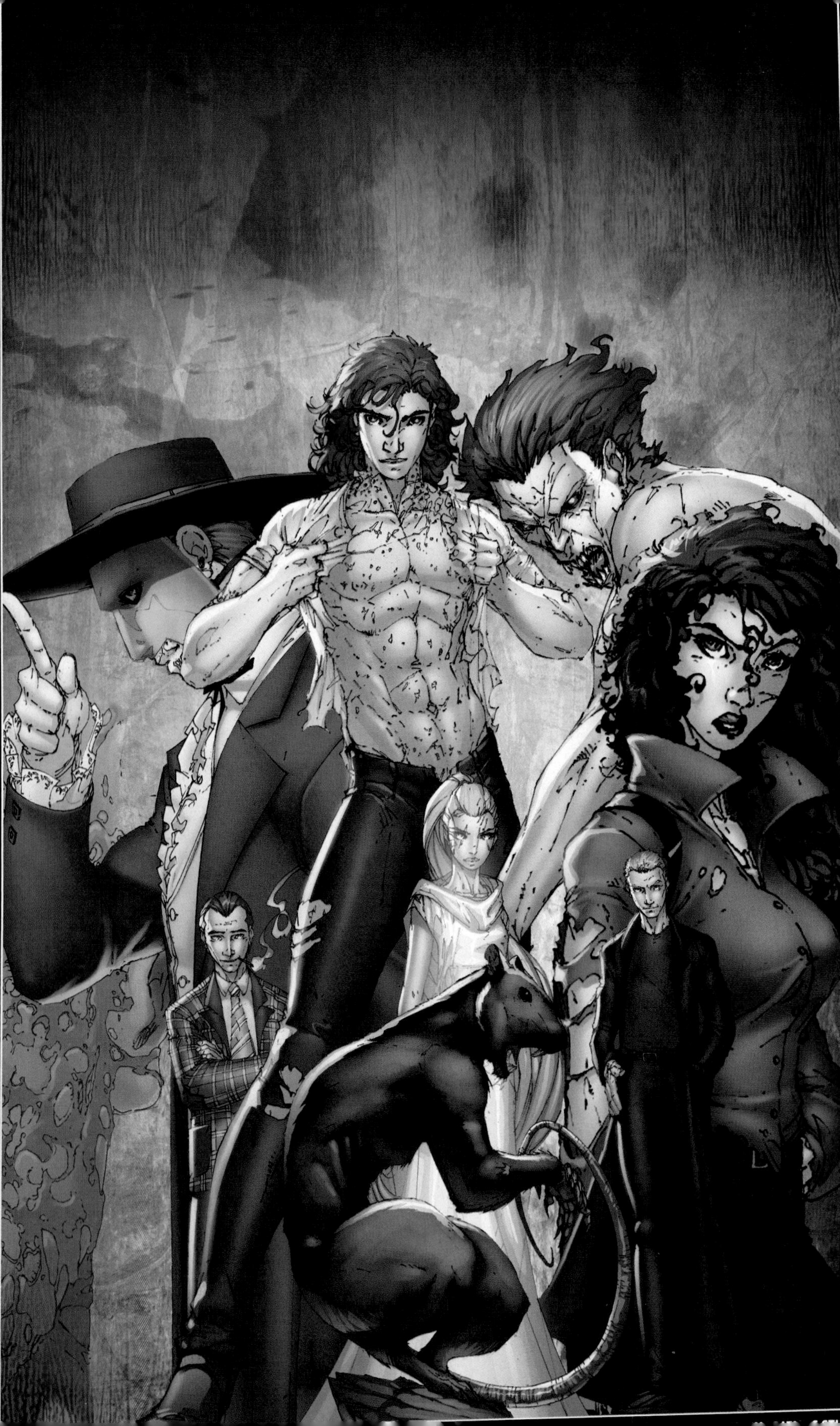

ANITA BLAKE

The Laughing Corpse

ANIMATOR

ANITA BLAKE, VAMPIRE HUNTER: THE LAUGHING CORPSE BOOK 1 — ANIMATOR. Contains material originally published in magazine form as ANITA BLAKE: THE LAUGHING CORPSE — ANIMATOR #1-5. First printing 2009. Hardcover ISBN# 978-0-7851-3632-3. Softcover ISBN# 978-0-7851-3527-2. Published by MARVEL PUBLISHING, INC., a subsidiary of MARVEL ENTERTAINMENT, INC. OFFICE OF PUBLICATION: 417 5th Avenue, New York, NY 10016. Copyright © 2008 and 2009 Laurell K. Hamilton. All rights reserved. Hardcover: $19.99 per copy in the U.S. (GST #R127032852). Softcover: $16.99 per copy in the U.S. (GST #R127032852). Canadian Agreement #40668537. Anita Blake: Vampire Hunter and all characters featured in this issue and the distinctive names and likenesses thereof, and all related indicia are trademarks of Laurell K. Hamilton. Marvel, Wolverine, Captain America, Thor, the Incredible Hulk, Spider-Man and the Fantastic Four, and their distinctive likenesses are TM and (c) 2009 Marvel Entertainment, Inc. and it's subsidiaries. All rights reserved. No similarity between any of the names, characters, persons, and/or institutions in this magazine with those of any living or dead person or institution is intended, and any such similarity which may exist is purely coincidental. **Printed in the U.S.A. ALAN** FINE, CEO Marvel Toys & Publishing Divisions and CMO Marvel Characters, Inc.; JIM SOKOLOWSKI, Chief Operating Officer; DAVID GABRIEL, SVP of Publishing Sales & Circulation; DAVID BOGART, SVP of Business Affairs & Talent Management; MICHAEL PASCIULLO, VP Merchandising & Communications; JIM O'KEEFE, VP of Operations & Logistics; DAN CARR, Executive Director of Publishing Technology; JUSTIN F. GABRIE, Director of Publishing & Editorial Operations; SUSAN CRESPI, Editorial Operations Manager; ALEX MORALES, Publishing Operations Manager; STAN LEE, Chairman Emeritus. For information regarding advertising in Marvel Comics or on Marvel.com, please contact Mitch Dane, Advertising Director, at mdane@marvel.com. For Marvel subscription inquiries, please call 800-217-9158.

10 9 8 7 6 5 4 3 2 1

ANITA BLAKE
The Laughing Corpse
ANIMATOR

WRITER	LAURELL K. HAMILTON
ADAPTATION	JESS RUFFNER-BOOTH
ART	RON LIM
COLORS	JOEL SEGUIN & JUNE CHUNG
LETTERS	BILL TORTOLINI
ASSISTANT EDITOR	JORDAN D. WHITE
EDITOR	MICHAEL HORWITZ
SENIOR EDITORS	MARK PANICCIA & RALPH MACCHIO

SPECIAL THANKS TO JONATHON GREEN, MELISSA MCALISTER & ANNE TREDWAY

COLLECTION EDITOR	CORY LEVINE
EDITORIAL ASSISTANT	ALEX STARBUCK
ASSISTANT EDITOR	JOHN DENNING
EDITORS, SPECIAL PROJECTS	JENNIFER GRÜNWALD & MARK D. BEAZLEY
SENIOR EDITOR, SPECIAL PROJECTS	JEFF YOUNGQUIST
SENIOR VICE PRESIDENT OF SALES	DAVID GABRIEL
SENIOR VICE PRESIDENT OF STRATEGIC DEVELOPMENT	RUWAN JAYATILLEKE
PRODUCTION	JERRY KALINOWSKI
BOOK DESIGN	SPRING HOTELING
EDITOR IN CHIEF	JOE QUESADA
PUBLISHER	DAN BUCKLEY

St. Louis isn't just a city of the living anymore. Vampires and werewolves prowl the back alleys and quarters of this beautiful and damned city, fearing nothing...nothing, that is, except for Anita Blake, the Executioner. A court-appointed vampire executioner, Anita reminds these monsters that the laws of man apply to the undead...

But Anita isn't only known for her deadly talents; she is also an Animator, capable of resurrecting the recently deceased as zombies. Recovering from a case involving the previous vampiric Master of the City, Anita's vacation is cut short when her manager offers her what may be the strangest assignment of her career...

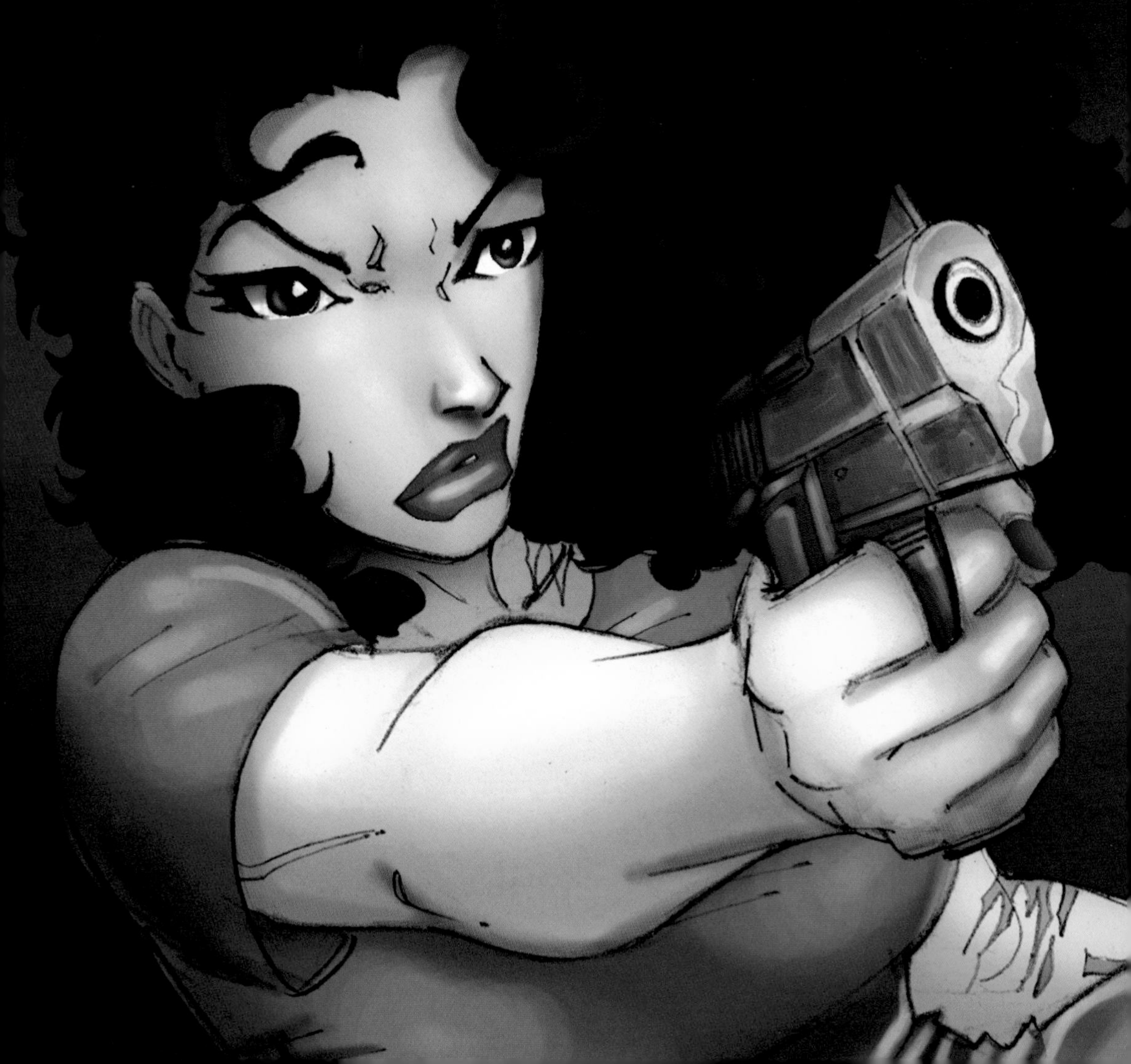

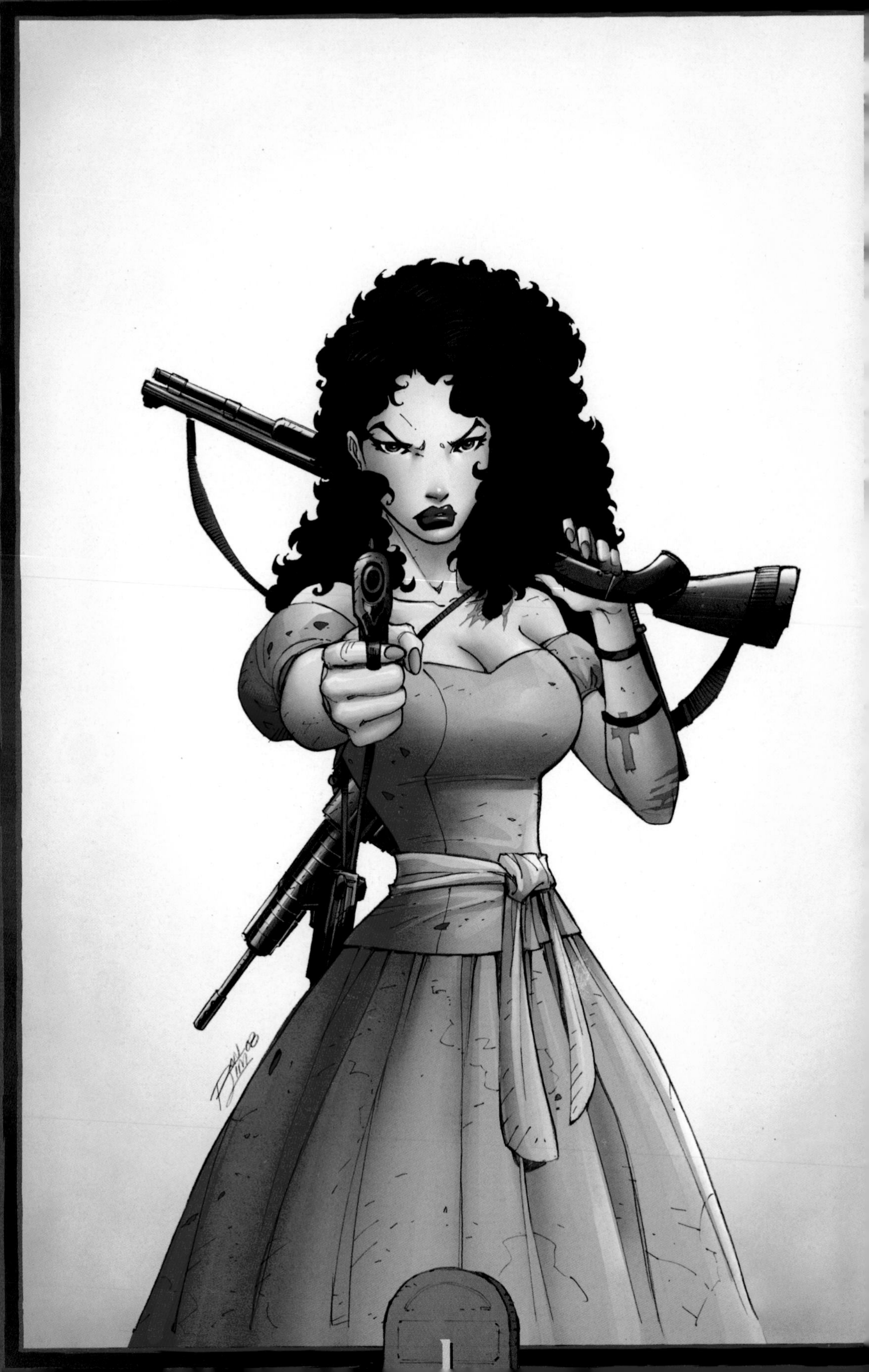

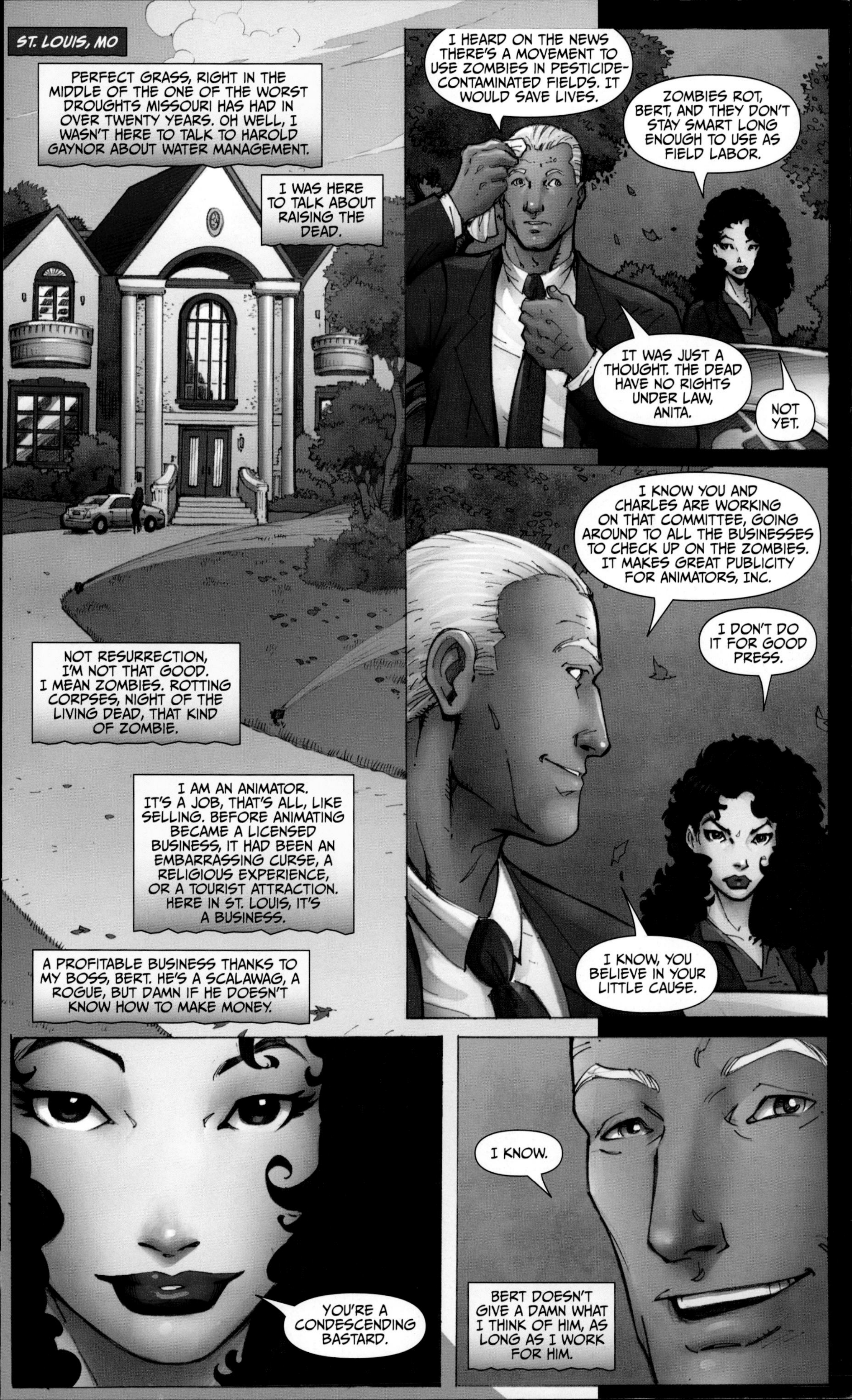
ST. LOUIS, MO
PERFECT GRASS, RIGHT IN THE MIDDLE OF THE ONE OF THE WORST DROUGHTS MISSOURI HAS HAD IN OVER TWENTY YEARS. OH WELL, I WASN'T HERE TO TALK TO HAROLD GAYNOR ABOUT WATER MANAGEMENT.
I WAS HERE TO TALK ABOUT RAISING THE DEAD.
NOT RESURRECTION, I'M NOT THAT GOOD. I MEAN ZOMBIES. ROTTING CORPSES, NIGHT OF THE LIVING DEAD, THAT KIND OF ZOMBIE.
I AM AN ANIMATOR. IT'S A JOB, THAT'S ALL, LIKE SELLING. BEFORE ANIMATING BECAME A LICENSED BUSINESS, IT HAD BEEN AN EMBARRASSING CURSE, A RELIGIOUS EXPERIENCE, OR A TOURIST ATTRACTION. HERE IN ST. LOUIS, IT'S A BUSINESS.
A PROFITABLE BUSINESS THANKS TO MY BOSS, BERT. HE'S A SCALAWAG, A ROGUE, BUT DAMN IF HE DOESN'T KNOW HOW TO MAKE MONEY.
I HEARD ON THE NEWS THERE'S A MOVEMENT TO USE ZOMBIES IN PESTICIDE-CONTAMINATED FIELDS. IT WOULD SAVE LIVES.
ZOMBIES ROT, BERT, AND THEY DON'T STAY SMART LONG ENOUGH TO USE AS FIELD LABOR.
IT WAS JUST A THOUGHT. THE DEAD HAVE NO RIGHTS UNDER LAW, ANITA.
NOT YET.
I KNOW YOU AND CHARLES ARE WORKING ON THAT COMMITTEE, GOING AROUND TO ALL THE BUSINESSES TO CHECK UP ON THE ZOMBIES. IT MAKES GREAT PUBLICITY FOR ANIMATORS, INC.
I DON'T DO IT FOR GOOD PRESS.
I KNOW, YOU BELIEVE IN YOUR LITTLE CAUSE.
YOU'RE A CONDESCENDING BASTARD.
I KNOW.
BERT DOESN'T GIVE A DAMN WHAT I THINK OF HIM, AS LONG AS I WORK FOR HIM.

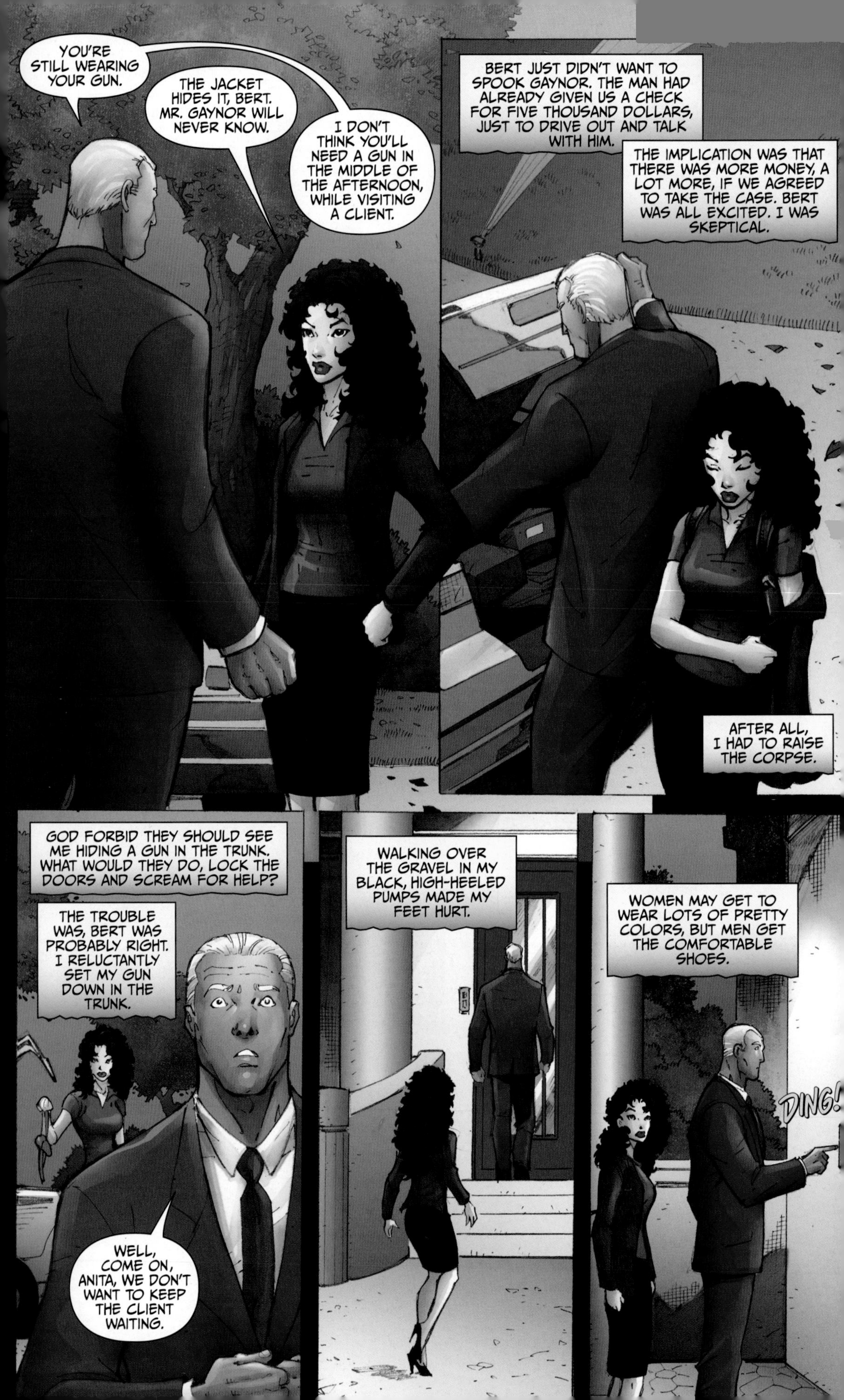
YOU'RE STILL WEARING YOUR GUN.
THE JACKET HIDES IT, BERT. MR. GAYNOR WILL NEVER KNOW.
I DON'T THINK YOU'LL NEED A GUN IN THE MIDDLE OF THE AFTERNOON, WHILE VISITING A CLIENT.
BERT JUST DIDN'T WANT TO SPOOK GAYNOR. THE MAN HAD ALREADY GIVEN US A CHECK FOR FIVE THOUSAND DOLLARS, JUST TO DRIVE OUT AND TALK WITH HIM.
THE IMPLICATION WAS THAT THERE WAS MORE MONEY, A LOT MORE, IF WE AGREED TO TAKE THE CASE. BERT WAS ALL EXCITED. I WAS SKEPTICAL.
AFTER ALL, I HAD TO RAISE THE CORPSE.
GOD FORBID THEY SHOULD SEE ME HIDING A GUN IN THE TRUNK. WHAT WOULD THEY DO, LOCK THE DOORS AND SCREAM FOR HELP?
THE TROUBLE WAS, BERT WAS PROBABLY RIGHT. I RELUCTANTLY SET MY GUN DOWN IN THE TRUNK.
WELL, COME ON, ANITA, WE DON'T WANT TO KEEP THE CLIENT WAITING.
WALKING OVER THE GRAVEL IN MY BLACK, HIGH-HEELED PUMPS MADE MY FEET HURT.
WOMEN MAY GET TO WEAR LOTS OF PRETTY COLORS, BUT MEN GET THE COMFORTABLE SHOES.
DING!

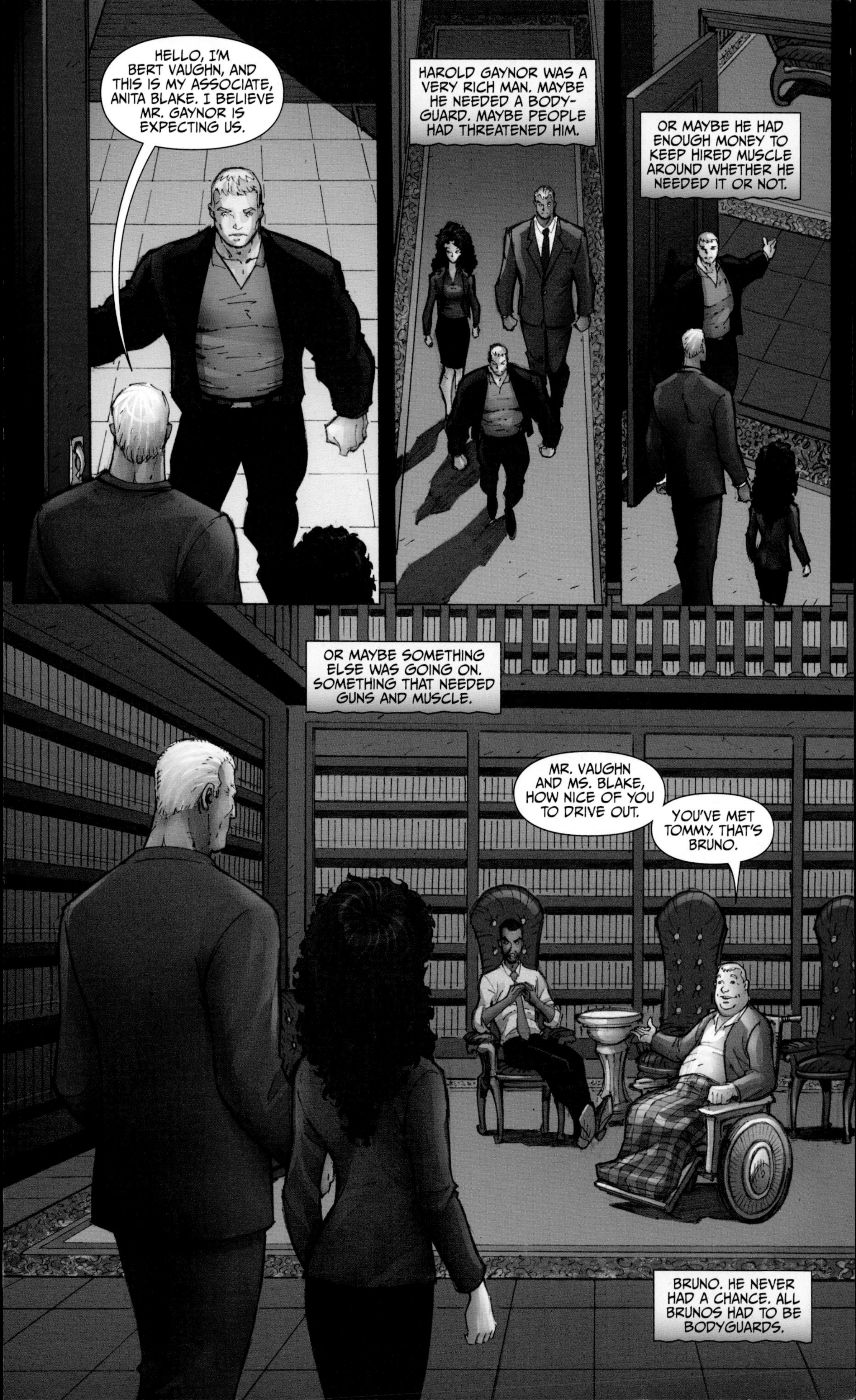
HELLO, I'M BERT VAUGHN, AND THIS IS MY ASSOCIATE, ANITA BLAKE. I BELIEVE MR. GAYNOR IS EXPECTING US.
HAROLD GAYNOR WAS A VERY RICH MAN. MAYBE HE NEEDED A BODY-GUARD. MAYBE PEOPLE HAD THREATENED HIM.
OR MAYBE HE HAD ENOUGH MONEY TO KEEP HIRED MUSCLE AROUND WHETHER HE NEEDED IT OR NOT.
OR MAYBE SOMETHING ELSE WAS GOING ON. SOMETHING THAT NEEDED GUNS AND MUSCLE.
MR. VAUGHN AND MS. BLAKE, HOW NICE OF YOU TO DRIVE OUT.
YOU'VE MET TOMMY. THAT'S BRUNO.
BRUNO. HE NEVER HAD A CHANCE. ALL BRUNOS HAD TO BE BODYGUARDS.

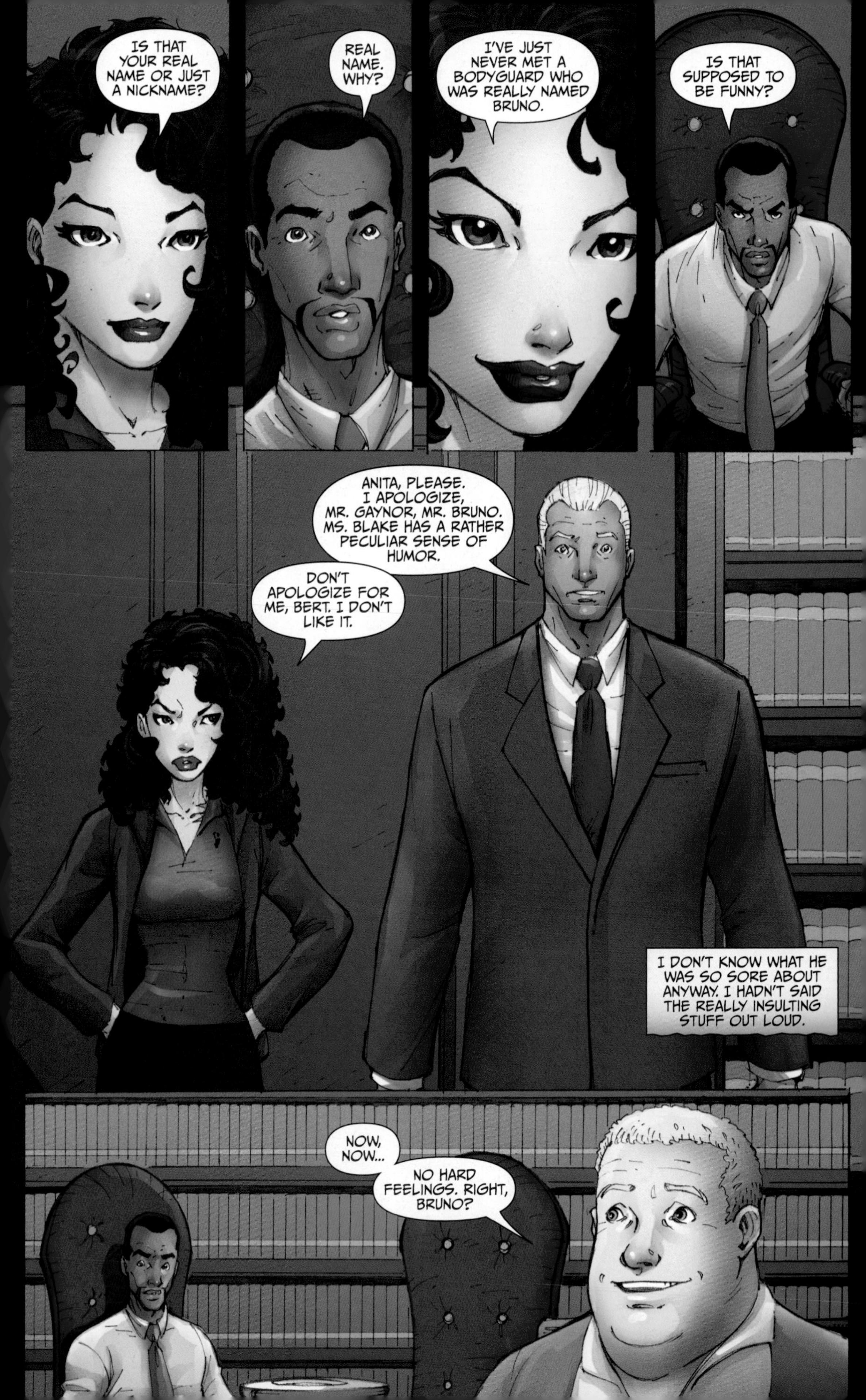
IS THAT YOUR REAL NAME OR JUST A NICKNAME?
REAL NAME. WHY?
I'VE JUST NEVER MET A BODYGUARD WHO WAS REALLY NAMED BRUNO.
IS THAT SUPPOSED TO BE FUNNY?
ANITA, PLEASE. I APOLOGIZE, MR. GAYNOR, MR. BRUNO. MS. BLAKE HAS A RATHER PECULIAR SENSE OF HUMOR.
DON'T APOLOGIZE FOR ME, BERT. I DON'T LIKE IT.
I DON'T KNOW WHAT HE WAS SO SORE ABOUT ANYWAY. I HADN'T SAID THE REALLY INSULTING STUFF OUT LOUD.
NOW, NOW...
NO HARD FEELINGS. RIGHT, BRUNO?

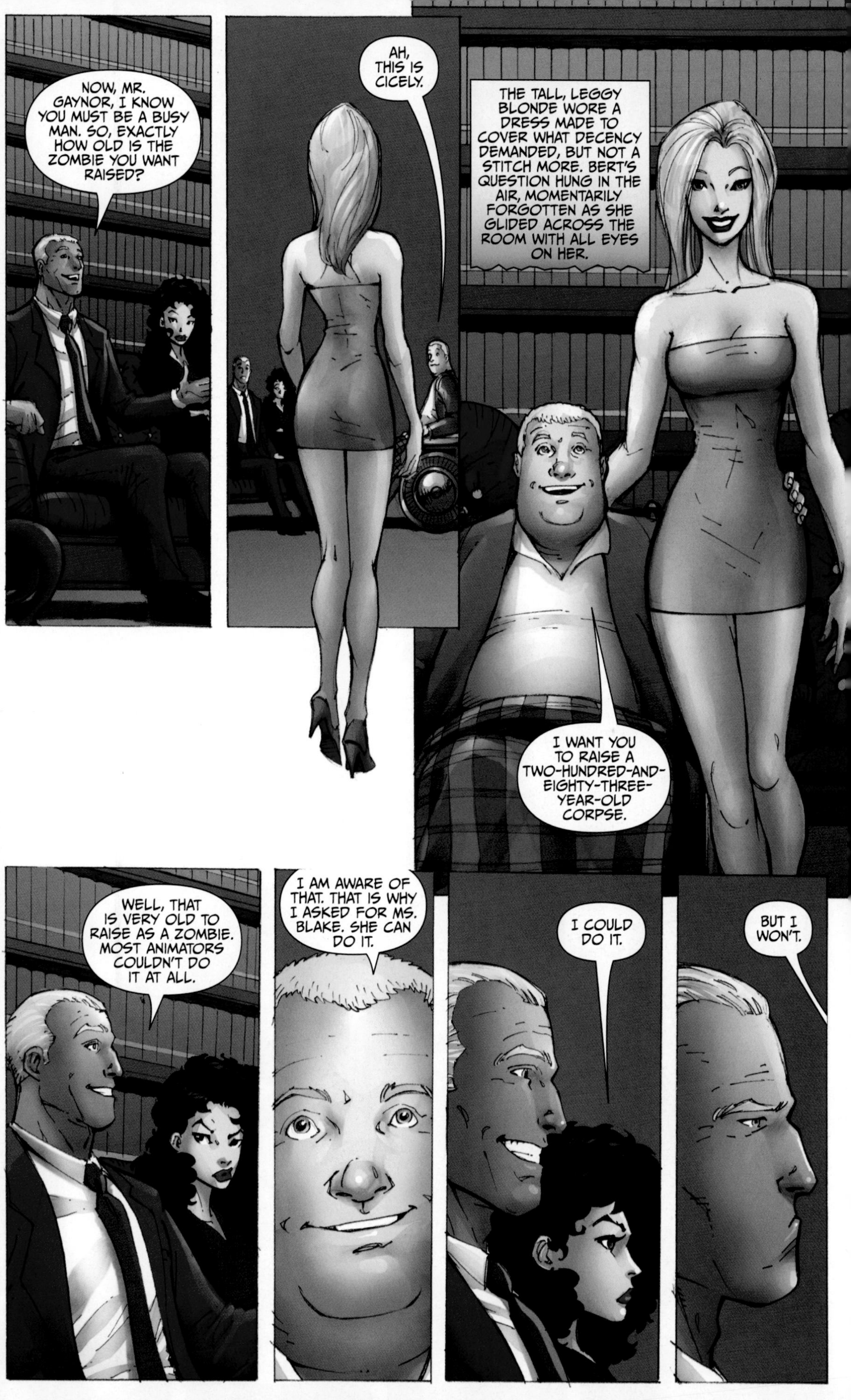
NOW, MR. GAYNOR, I KNOW YOU MUST BE A BUSY MAN. SO, EXACTLY HOW OLD IS THE ZOMBIE YOU WANT RAISED?
AH, THIS IS CICELY.
THE TALL, LEGGY BLONDE WORE A DRESS MADE TO COVER WHAT DECENCY DEMANDED, BUT NOT A STITCH MORE. BERT'S QUESTION HUNG IN THE AIR, MOMENTARILY FORGOTTEN AS SHE GLIDED ACROSS THE ROOM WITH ALL EYES ON HER.
I WANT YOU TO RAISE A TWO-HUNDRED-AND-EIGHTY-THREE-YEAR-OLD CORPSE.
WELL, THAT IS VERY OLD TO RAISE AS A ZOMBIE. MOST ANIMATORS COULDN'T DO IT AT ALL.
I AM AWARE OF THAT. THAT IS WHY I ASKED FOR MS. BLAKE. SHE CAN DO IT.
I COULD DO IT.
BUT I WON'T.

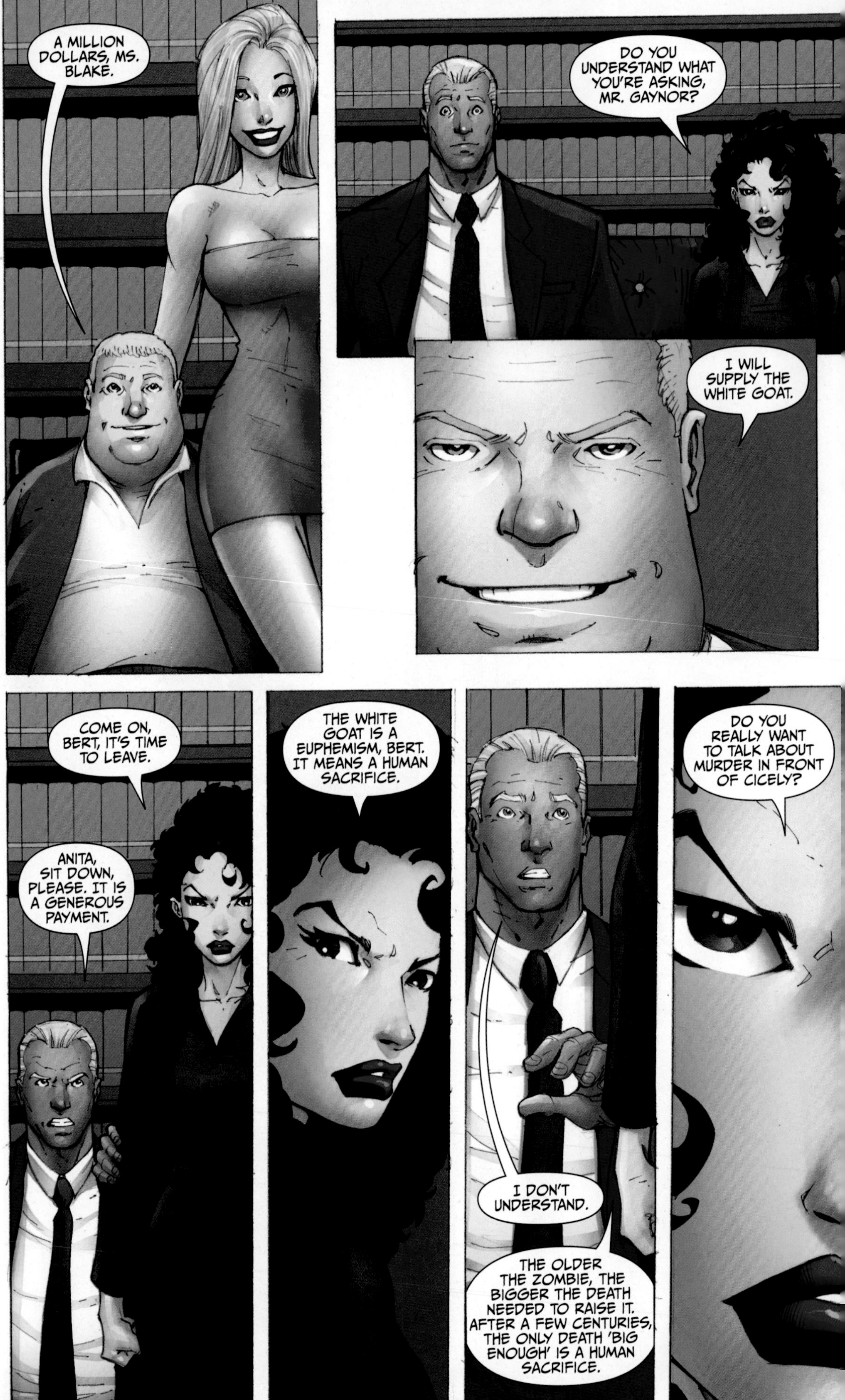
A MILLION DOLLARS, MS. BLAKE.
DO YOU UNDERSTAND WHAT YOU'RE ASKING, MR. GAYNOR?
I WILL SUPPLY THE WHITE GOAT.
COME ON, BERT, IT'S TIME TO LEAVE.
ANITA, SIT DOWN, PLEASE. IT IS A GENEROUS PAYMENT.
THE WHITE GOAT IS A EUPHEMISM, BERT. IT MEANS A HUMAN SACRIFICE.
I DON'T UNDERSTAND.
THE OLDER THE ZOMBIE, THE BIGGER THE DEATH NEEDED TO RAISE IT. AFTER A FEW CENTURIES, THE ONLY DEATH 'BIG ENOUGH' IS A HUMAN SACRIFICE.
DO YOU REALLY WANT TO TALK ABOUT MURDER IN FRONT OF CICELY?

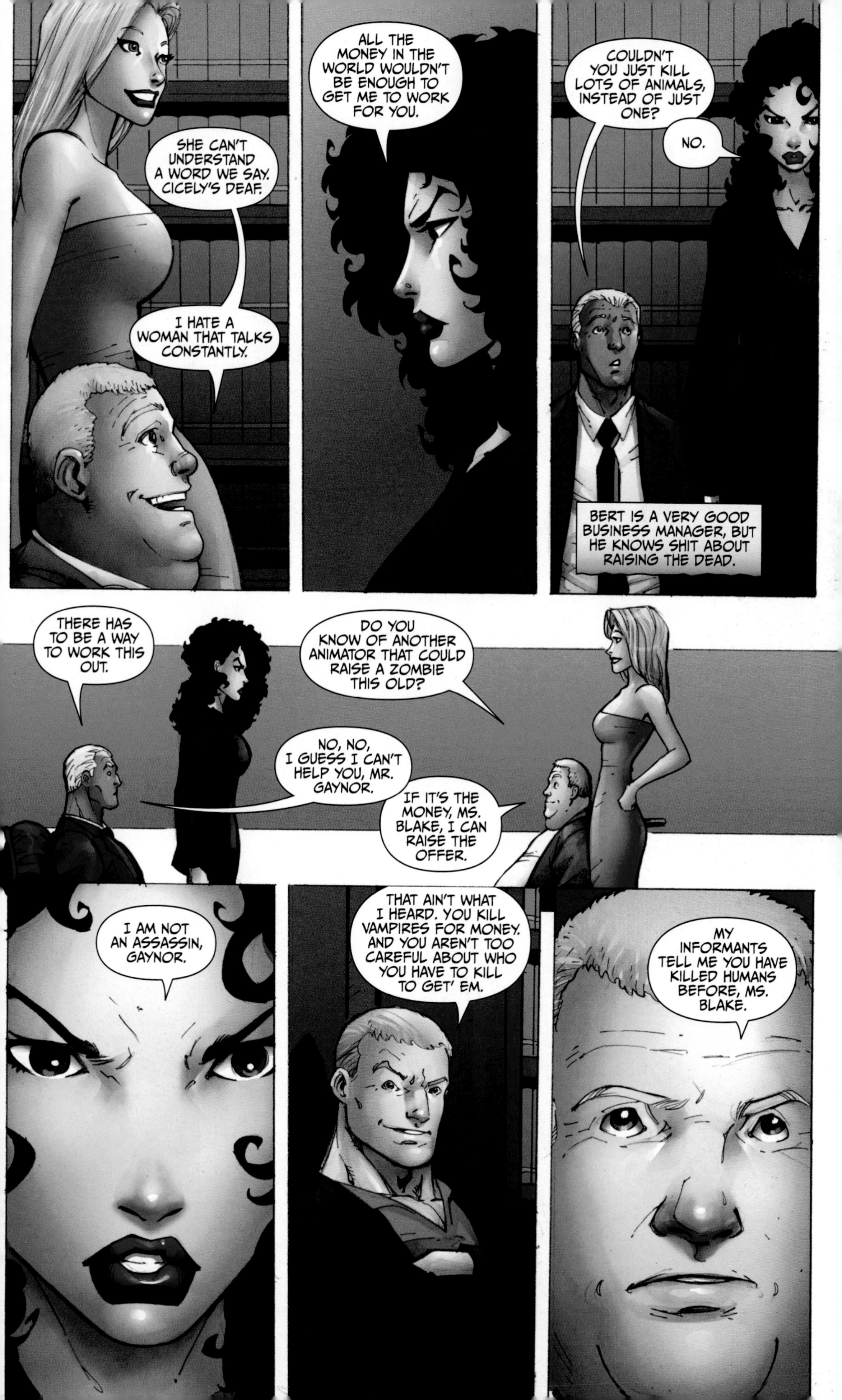
SHE CAN'T UNDERSTAND A WORD WE SAY. CICELY'S DEAF.
I HATE A WOMAN THAT TALKS CONSTANTLY.
ALL THE MONEY IN THE WORLD WOULDN'T BE ENOUGH TO GET ME TO WORK FOR YOU.
COULDN'T YOU JUST KILL LOTS OF ANIMALS, INSTEAD OF JUST ONE?
NO.
BERT IS A VERY GOOD BUSINESS MANAGER, BUT HE KNOWS SHIT ABOUT RAISING THE DEAD.
THERE HAS TO BE A WAY TO WORK THIS OUT.
DO YOU KNOW OF ANOTHER ANIMATOR THAT COULD RAISE A ZOMBIE THIS OLD?
NO, NO, I GUESS I CAN'T HELP YOU, MR. GAYNOR.
IF IT'S THE MONEY, MS. BLAKE, I CAN RAISE THE OFFER.
I AM NOT AN ASSASSIN, GAYNOR.
THAT AIN'T WHAT I HEARD. YOU KILL VAMPIRES FOR MONEY. AND YOU AREN'T TOO CAREFUL ABOUT WHO YOU HAVE TO KILL TO GET' EM.
MY INFORMANTS TELL ME YOU HAVE KILLED HUMANS BEFORE, MS. BLAKE.

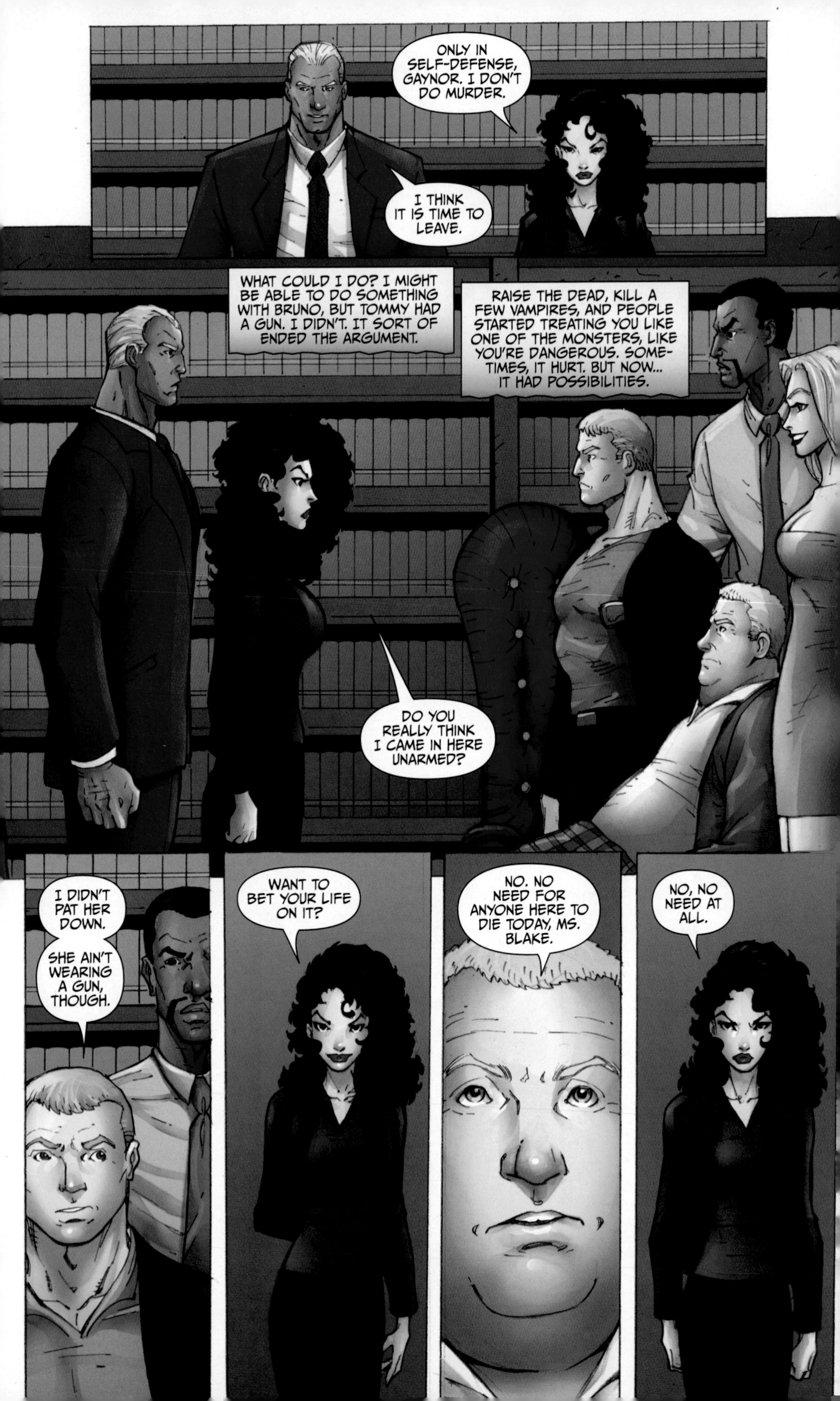
ONLY IN SELF-DEFENSE, GAYNOR. I DON'T DO MURDER.
I THINK IT IS TIME TO LEAVE.
WHAT COULD I DO? I MIGHT BE ABLE TO DO SOMETHING WITH BRUNO, BUT TOMMY HAD A GUN. I DIDN'T. IT SORT OF ENDED THE ARGUMENT.
RAISE THE DEAD, KILL A FEW VAMPIRES, AND PEOPLE STARTED TREATING YOU LIKE ONE OF THE MONSTERS, LIKE YOU'RE DANGEROUS. SOME-TIMES, IT HURT. BUT NOW... IT HAD POSSIBILITIES.
DO YOU REALLY THINK I CAME IN HERE UNARMED?
I DIDN'T PAT HER DOWN.
SHE AIN'T WEARING A GUN, THOUGH.
WANT TO BET YOUR LIFE ON IT?
NO. NO NEED FOR ANYONE HERE TO DIE TODAY, MS. BLAKE.
NO, NO NEED AT ALL.

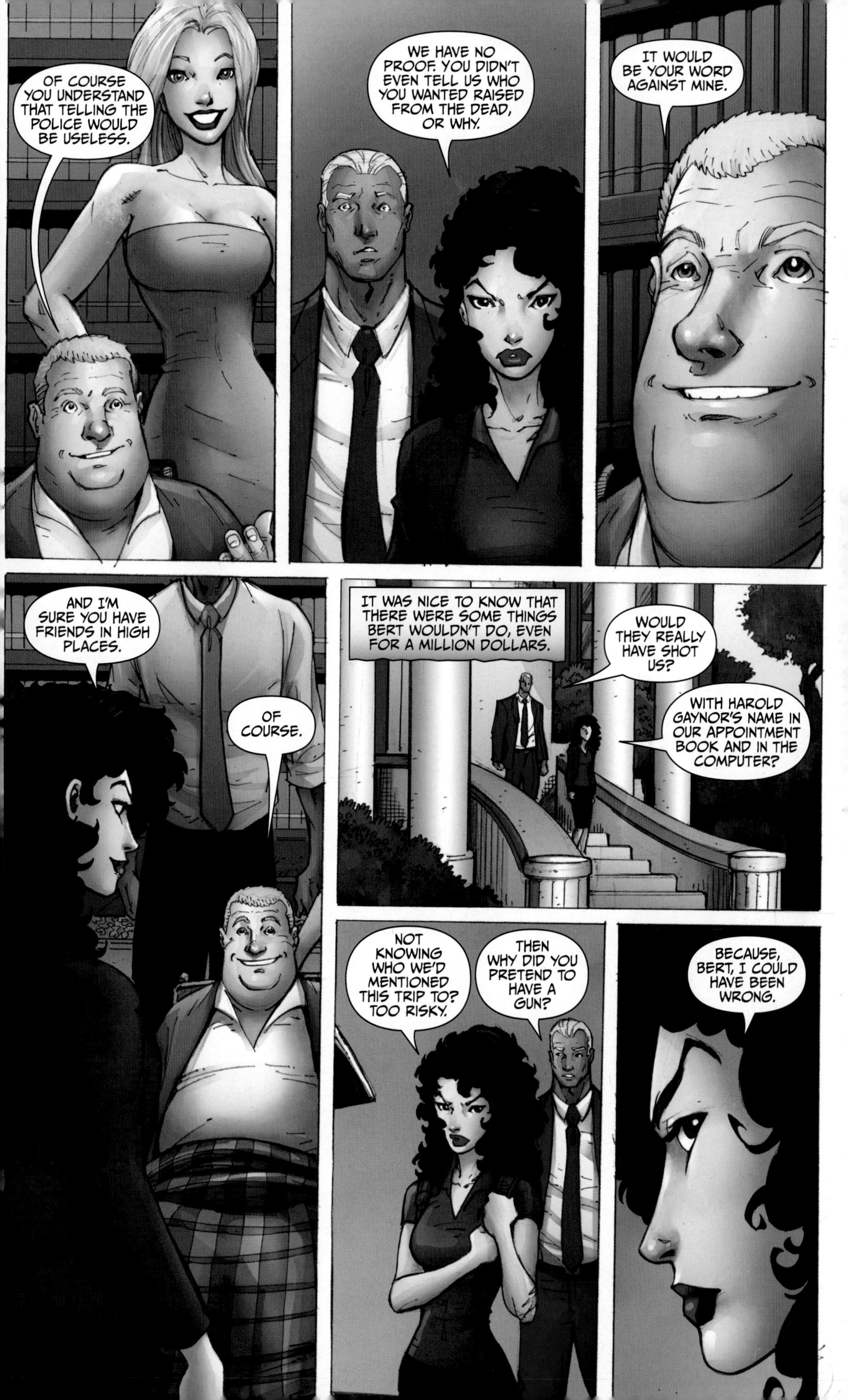
OF COURSE YOU UNDERSTAND THAT TELLING THE POLICE WOULD BE USELESS.
WE HAVE NO PROOF. YOU DIDN'T EVEN TELL US WHO YOU WANTED RAISED FROM THE DEAD, OR WHY.
IT WOULD BE YOUR WORD AGAINST MINE.
AND I'M SURE YOU HAVE FRIENDS IN HIGH PLACES.
OF COURSE.
IT WAS NICE TO KNOW THAT THERE WERE SOME THINGS BERT WOULDN'T DO, EVEN FOR A MILLION DOLLARS.
WOULD THEY REALLY HAVE SHOT US?
WITH HAROLD GAYNOR'S NAME IN OUR APPOINTMENT BOOK AND IN THE COMPUTER?
NOT KNOWING WHO WE'D MENTIONED THIS TRIP TO? TOO RISKY.
THEN WHY DID YOU PRETEND TO HAVE A GUN?
BECAUSE, BERT, I COULD HAVE BEEN WRONG.

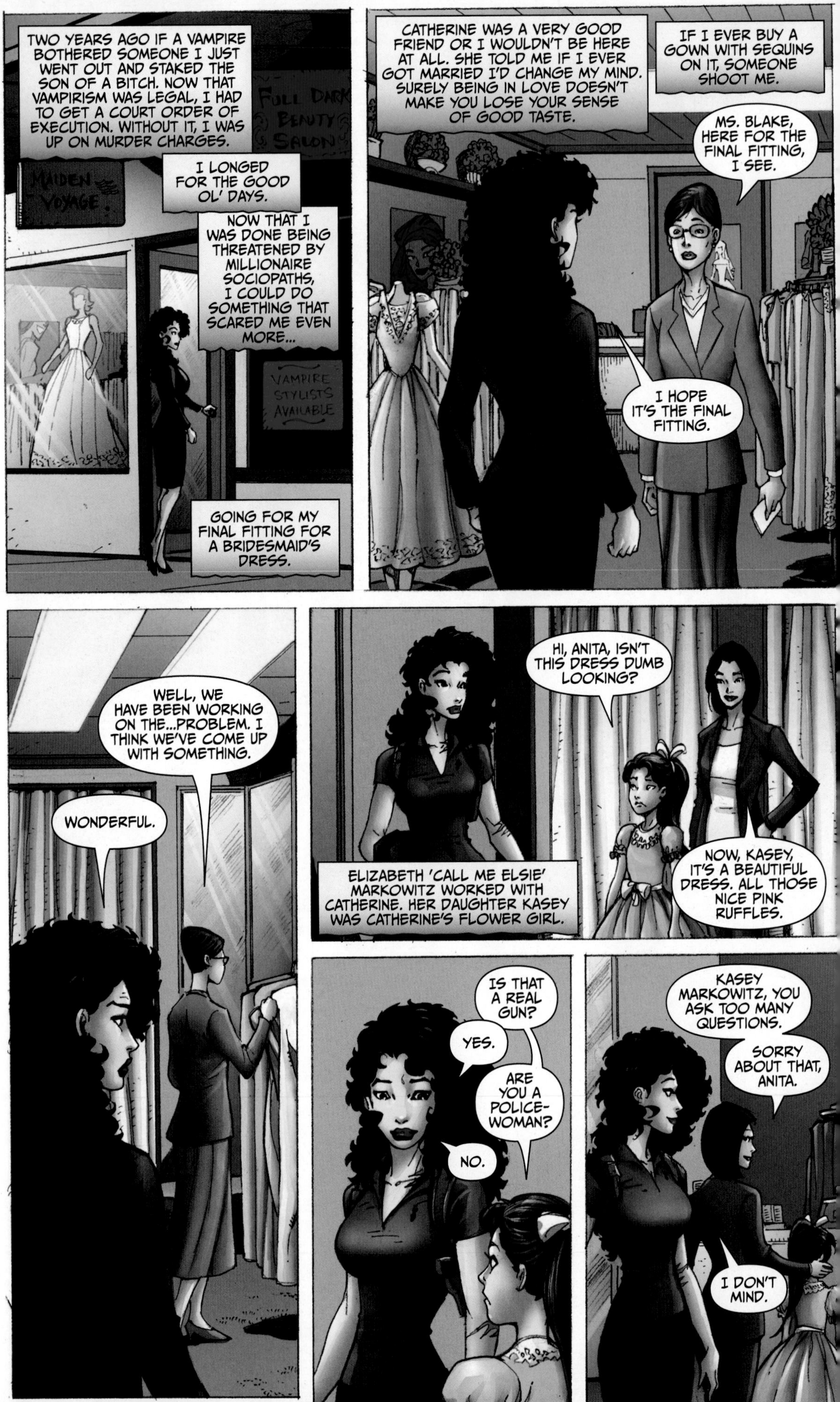
TWO YEARS AGO IF A VAMPIRE BOTHERED SOMEONE I JUST WENT OUT AND STAKED THE SON OF A BITCH. NOW THAT VAMPIRISM WAS LEGAL, I HAD TO GET A COURT ORDER OF EXECUTION. WITHOUT IT, I WAS UP ON MURDER CHARGES.
FULL DARK BEAUTY SALON
MAIDEN VOYAGE
I LONGED FOR THE GOOD OL' DAYS.
NOW THAT I WAS DONE BEING THREATENED BY MILLIONAIRE SOCIOPATHS, I COULD DO SOMETHING THAT SCARED ME EVEN MORE...
VAMPIRE STYLISTS AVAILABLE
GOING FOR MY FINAL FITTING FOR A BRIDESMAID'S DRESS.
CATHERINE WAS A VERY GOOD FRIEND OR I WOULDN'T BE HERE AT ALL. SHE TOLD ME IF I EVER GOT MARRIED I'D CHANGE MY MIND. SURELY BEING IN LOVE DOESN'T MAKE YOU LOSE YOUR SENSE OF GOOD TASTE.
IF I EVER BUY A GOWN WITH SEQUINS ON IT, SOMEONE SHOOT ME.
MS. BLAKE, HERE FOR THE FINAL FITTING, I SEE.
I HOPE IT'S THE FINAL FITTING.
WELL, WE HAVE BEEN WORKING ON THE...PROBLEM. I THINK WE'VE COME UP WITH SOMETHING.
WONDERFUL.
HI, ANITA, ISN'T THIS DRESS DUMB LOOKING?
ELIZABETH 'CALL ME ELSIE' MARKOWITZ WORKED WITH CATHERINE. HER DAUGHTER KASEY WAS CATHERINE'S FLOWER GIRL.
NOW, KASEY, IT'S A BEAUTIFUL DRESS. ALL THOSE NICE PINK RUFFLES.
IS THAT A REAL GUN?
YES.
ARE YOU A POLICE-WOMAN?
NO.
KASEY MARKOWITZ, YOU ASK TOO MANY QUESTIONS.
SORRY ABOUT THAT, ANITA.
I DON'T MIND.

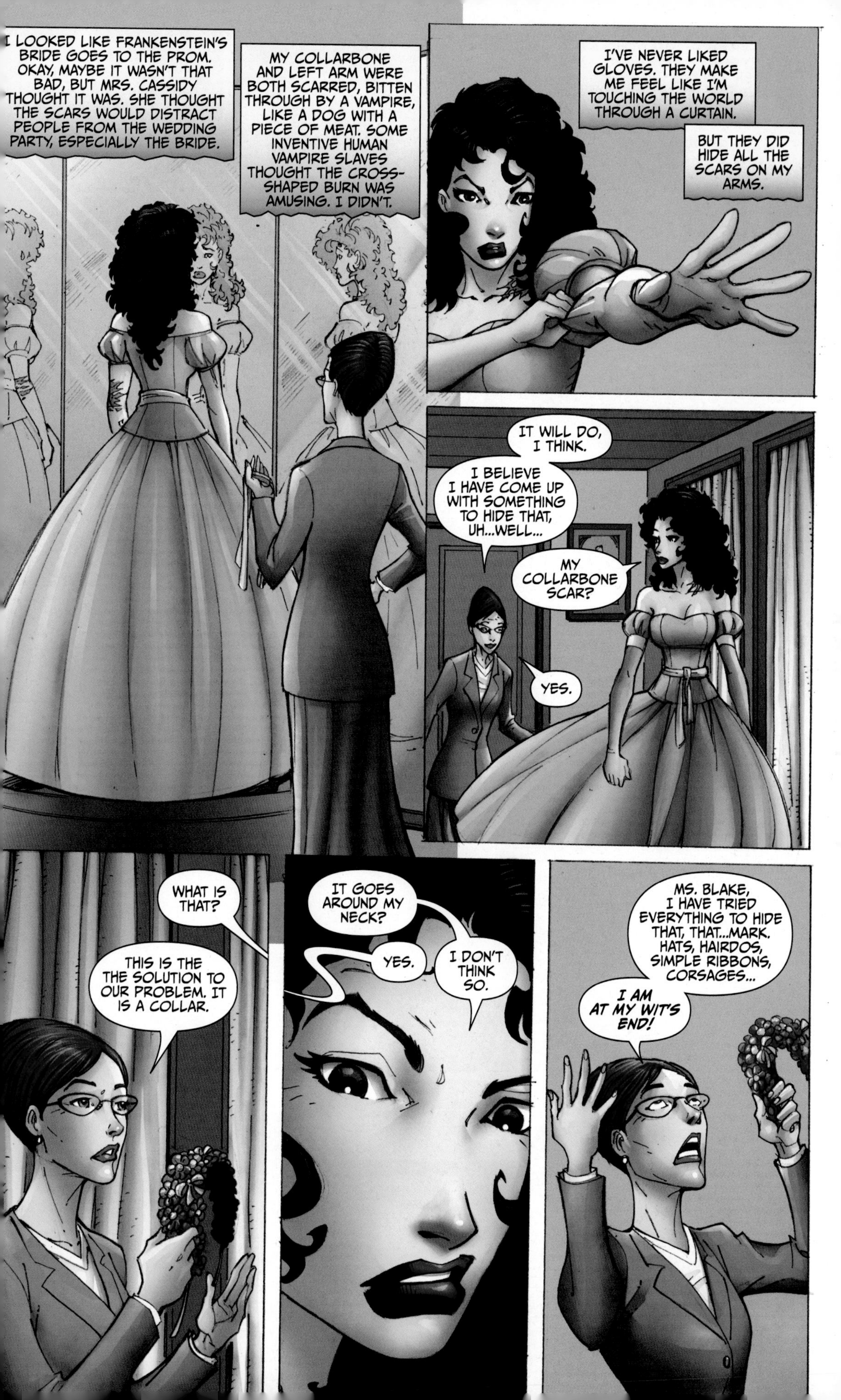

I LOOKED LIKE FRANKENSTEIN'S BRIDE GOES TO THE PROM. OKAY, MAYBE IT WASN'T THAT BAD, BUT MRS. CASSIDY THOUGHT IT WAS. SHE THOUGHT THE SCARS WOULD DISTRACT PEOPLE FROM THE WEDDING PARTY, ESPECIALLY THE BRIDE.
MY COLLARBONE AND LEFT ARM WERE BOTH SCARRED, BITTEN THROUGH BY A VAMPIRE, LIKE A DOG WITH A PIECE OF MEAT. SOME INVENTIVE HUMAN VAMPIRE SLAVES THOUGHT THE CROSS-SHAPED BURN WAS AMUSING. I DIDN'T.
I'VE NEVER LIKED GLOVES. THEY MAKE ME FEEL LIKE I'M TOUCHING THE WORLD THROUGH A CURTAIN.
BUT THEY DID HIDE ALL THE SCARS ON MY ARMS.
IT WILL DO, I THINK.
I BELIEVE I HAVE COME UP WITH SOMETHING TO HIDE THAT, UH...WELL...
MY COLLARBONE SCAR?
YES.
WHAT IS THAT?
THIS IS THE THE SOLUTION TO OUR PROBLEM. IT IS A COLLAR.
IT GOES AROUND MY NECK?
YES.
I DON'T THINK SO.
MS. BLAKE, I HAVE TRIED EVERYTHING TO HIDE THAT, THAT...MARK. HATS, HAIRDOS, SIMPLE RIBBONS, CORSAGES...
I AM AT MY WIT'S END!

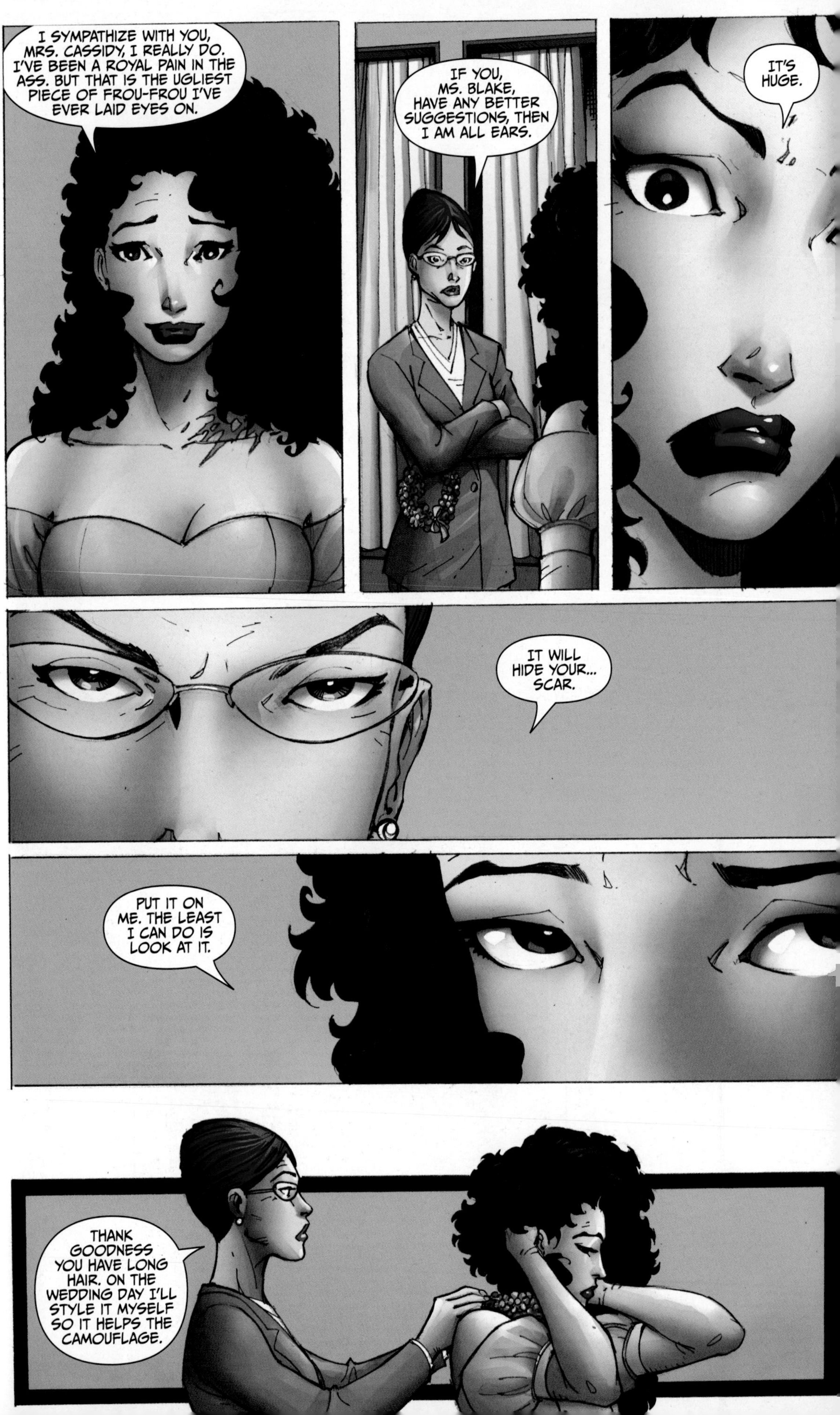
I SYMPATHIZE WITH YOU, MRS. CASSIDY, I REALLY DO. I'VE BEEN A ROYAL PAIN IN THE ASS. BUT THAT IS THE UGLIEST PIECE OF FROU-FROU I'VE EVER LAID EYES ON.
IF YOU, MS. BLAKE, HAVE ANY BETTER SUGGESTIONS, THEN I AM ALL EARS.
IT'S HUGE.
IT WILL HIDE YOUR... SCAR.
PUT IT ON ME. THE LEAST I CAN DO IS LOOK AT IT.
THANK GOODNESS YOU HAVE LONG HAIR. ON THE WEDDING DAY I'LL STYLE IT MYSELF SO IT HELPS THE CAMOUFLAGE.

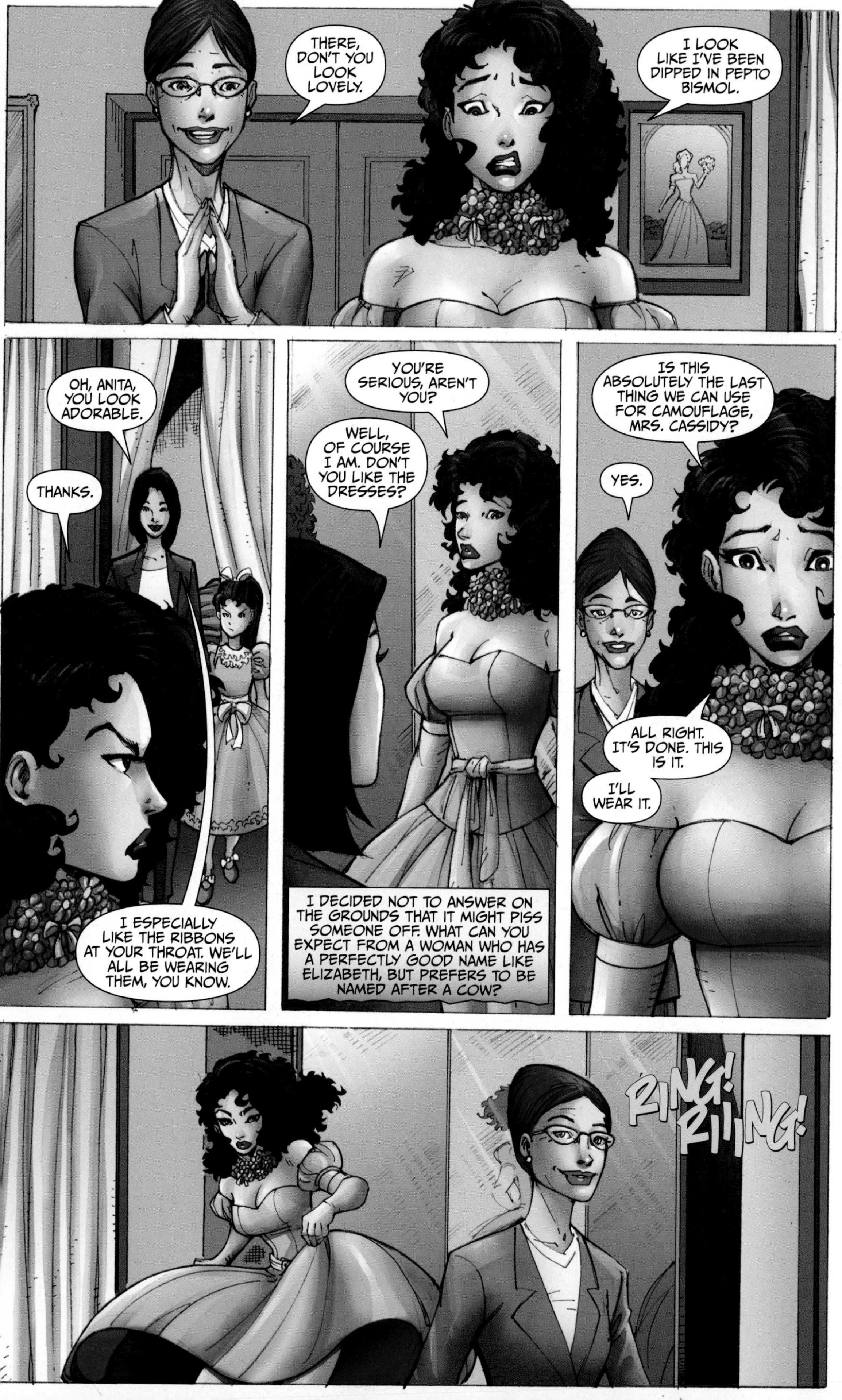
THERE, DON'T YOU LOOK LOVELY.
I LOOK LIKE I'VE BEEN DIPPED IN PEPTO BISMOL.
OH, ANITA, YOU LOOK ADORABLE.
THANKS.
I ESPECIALLY LIKE THE RIBBONS AT YOUR THROAT. WE'LL ALL BE WEARING THEM, YOU KNOW.
YOU'RE SERIOUS, AREN'T YOU?
WELL, OF COURSE I AM. DON'T YOU LIKE THE DRESSES?
I DECIDED NOT TO ANSWER ON THE GROUNDS THAT IT MIGHT PISS SOMEONE OFF. WHAT CAN YOU EXPECT FROM A WOMAN WHO HAS A PERFECTLY GOOD NAME LIKE ELIZABETH, BUT PREFERS TO BE NAMED AFTER A COW?
IS THIS ABSOLUTELY THE LAST THING WE CAN USE FOR CAMOUFLAGE, MRS. CASSIDY?
YES.
ALL RIGHT. IT'S DONE. THIS IS IT.
I'LL WEAR IT.
RING! RIIING!

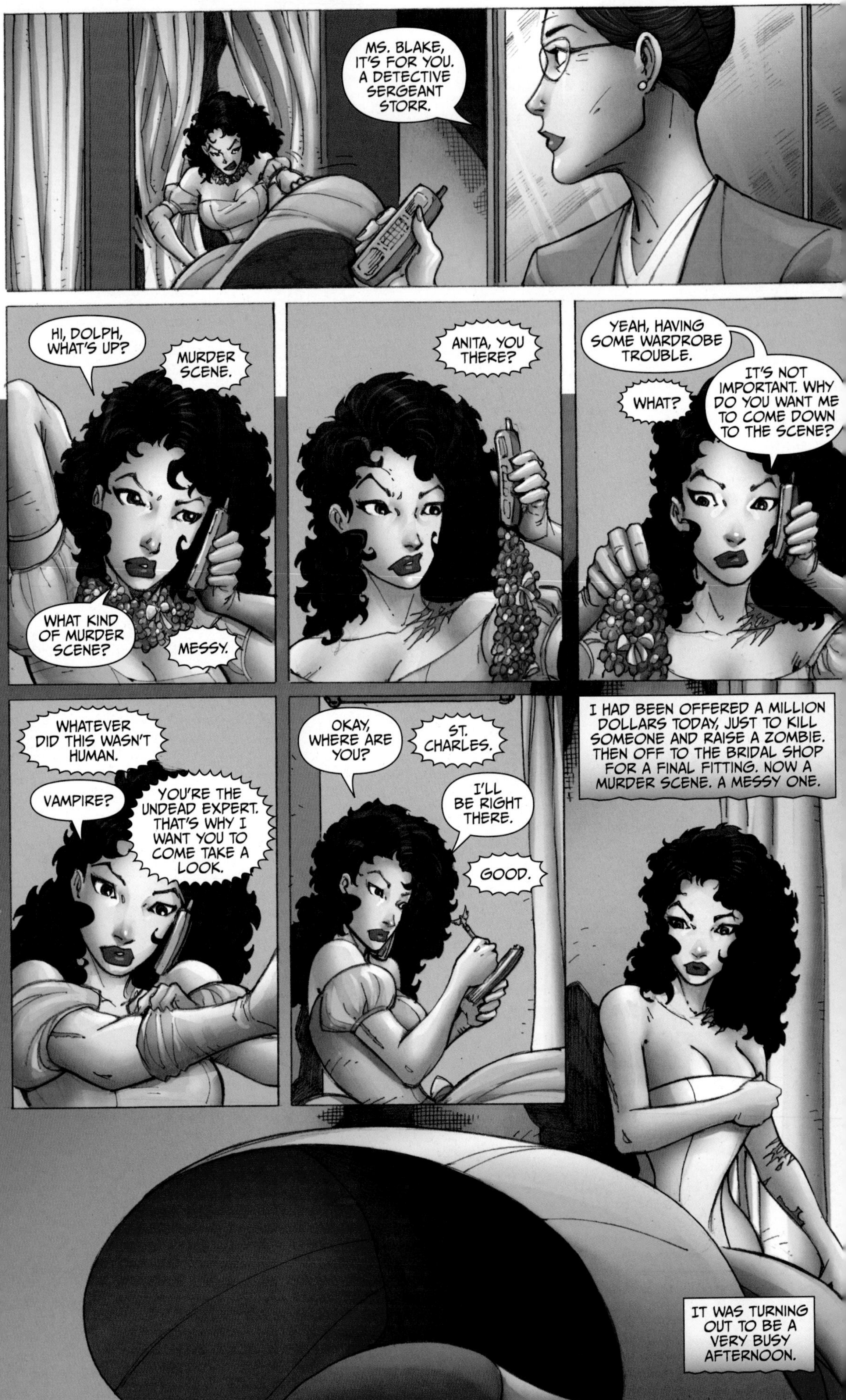
MS. BLAKE, IT'S FOR YOU. A DETECTIVE SERGEANT STORR.
HI, DOLPH, WHAT'S UP?
MURDER SCENE.
WHAT KIND OF MURDER SCENE?
MESSY.
ANITA, YOU THERE?
YEAH, HAVING SOME WARDROBE TROUBLE.
WHAT?
IT'S NOT IMPORTANT. WHY DO YOU WANT ME TO COME DOWN TO THE SCENE?
WHATEVER DID THIS WASN'T HUMAN.
VAMPIRE?
YOU'RE THE UNDEAD EXPERT. THAT'S WHY I WANT YOU TO COME TAKE A LOOK.
OKAY, WHERE ARE YOU?
ST. CHARLES.
I'LL BE RIGHT THERE.
GOOD.
I HAD BEEN OFFERED A MILLION DOLLARS TODAY, JUST TO KILL SOMEONE AND RAISE A ZOMBIE. THEN OFF TO THE BRIDAL SHOP FOR A FINAL FITTING. NOW A MURDER SCENE. A MESSY ONE.
IT WAS TURNING OUT TO BE A VERY BUSY AFTERNOON.

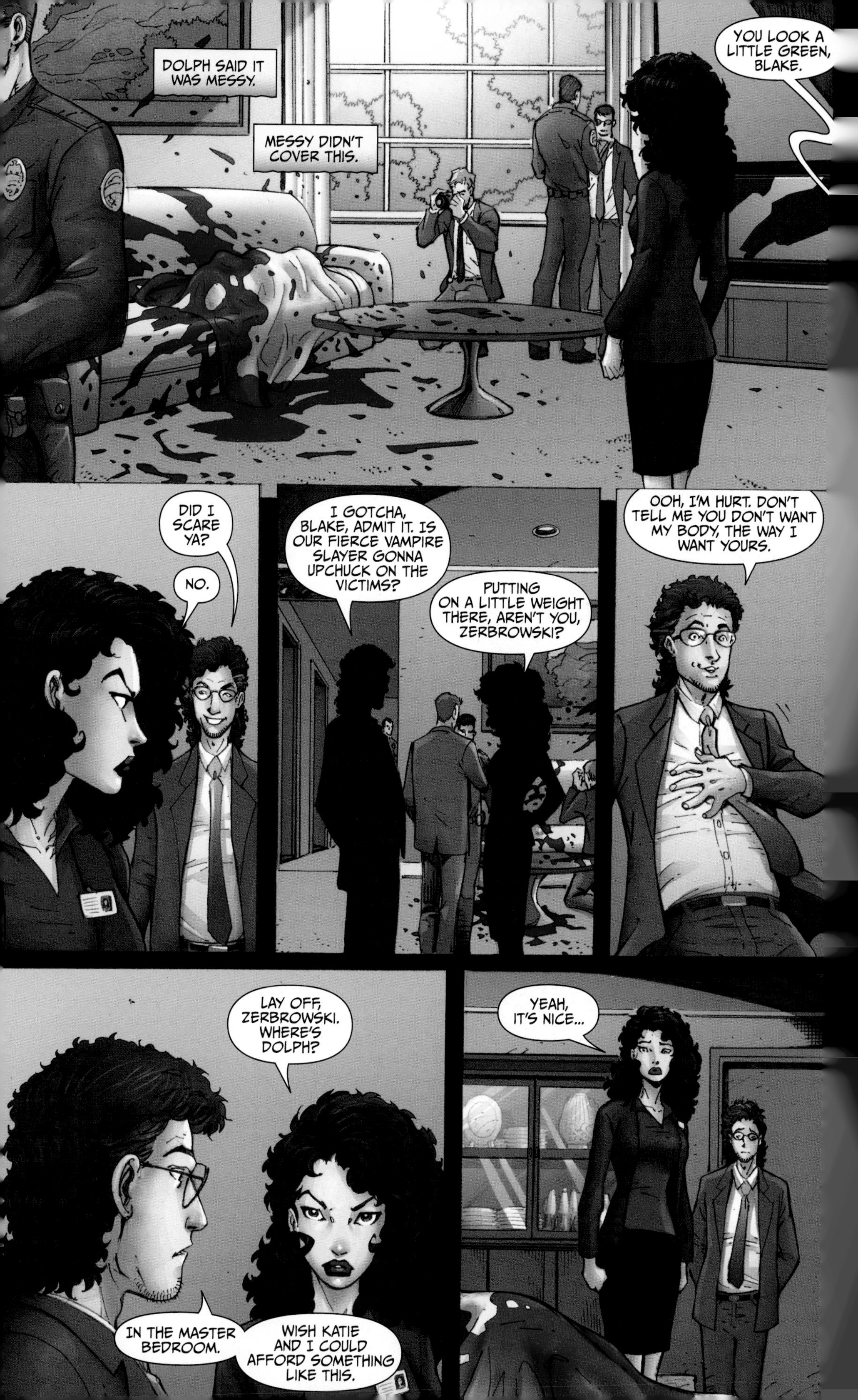
DOLPH SAID IT WAS MESSY.
MESSY DIDN'T COVER THIS.
YOU LOOK A LITTLE GREEN, BLAKE.
DID I SCARE YA?
NO.
I GOTCHA, BLAKE, ADMIT IT. IS OUR FIERCE VAMPIRE SLAYER GONNA UPCHUCK ON THE VICTIMS?
PUTTING ON A LITTLE WEIGHT THERE, AREN'T YOU, ZERBROWSKI?
OOH, I'M HURT. DON'T TELL ME YOU DON'T WANT MY BODY, THE WAY I WANT YOURS.
LAY OFF, ZERBROWSKI. WHERE'S DOLPH?
IN THE MASTER BEDROOM.
WISH KATIE AND I COULD AFFORD SOMETHING LIKE THIS.
YEAH, IT'S NICE...

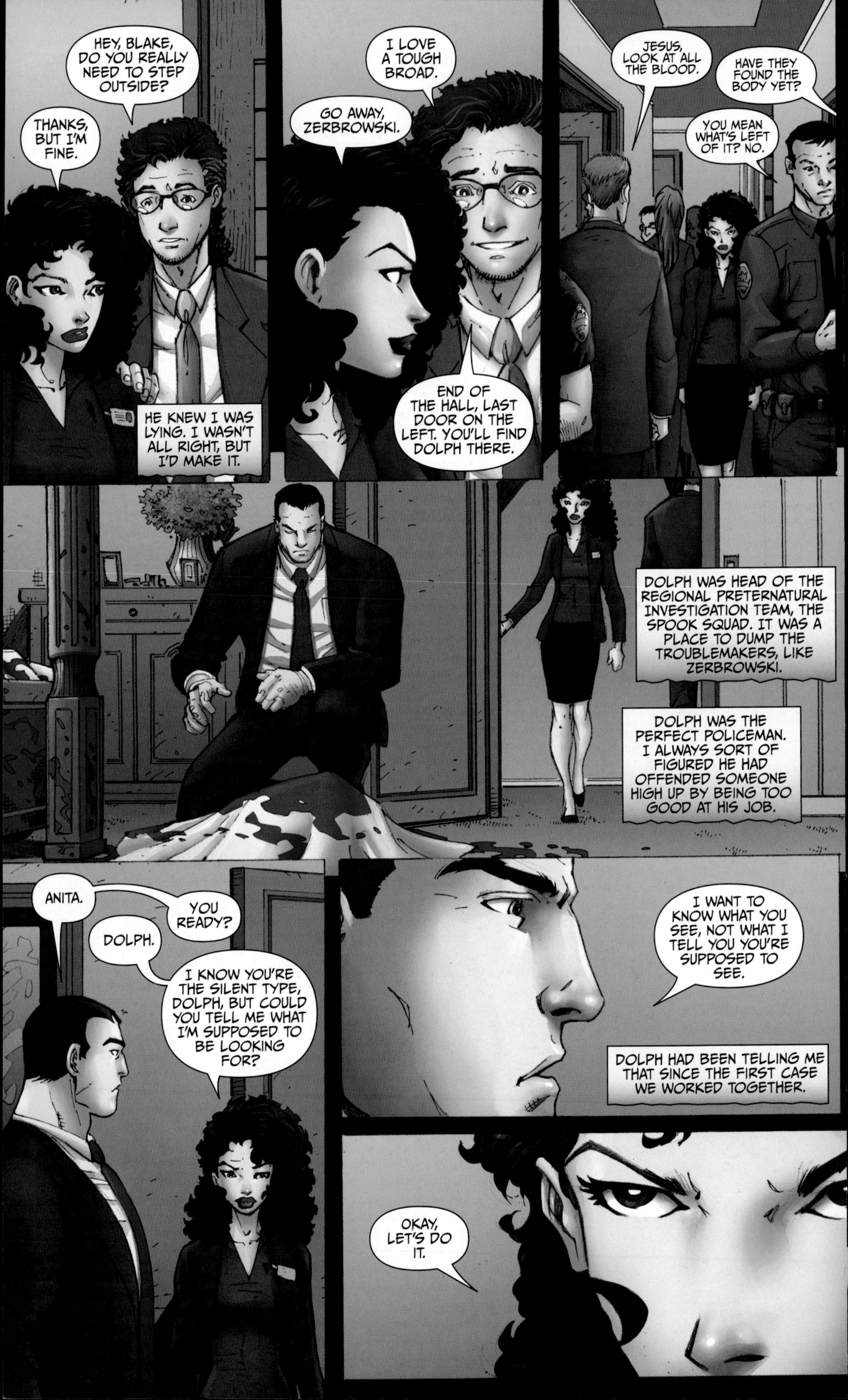
HEY, BLAKE, DO YOU REALLY NEED TO STEP OUTSIDE?
THANKS, BUT I'M FINE.
HE KNEW I WAS LYING. I WASN'T ALL RIGHT, BUT I'D MAKE IT.
I LOVE A TOUGH BROAD.
GO AWAY, ZERBROWSKI.
END OF THE HALL, LAST DOOR ON THE LEFT. YOU'LL FIND DOLPH THERE.
JESUS, LOOK AT ALL THE BLOOD.
HAVE THEY FOUND THE BODY YET?
YOU MEAN WHAT'S LEFT OF IT? NO.
DOLPH WAS HEAD OF THE REGIONAL PRETERNATURAL INVESTIGATION TEAM, THE SPOOK SQUAD. IT WAS A PLACE TO DUMP THE TROUBLEMAKERS, LIKE ZERBROWSKI.
DOLPH WAS THE PERFECT POLICEMAN. I ALWAYS SORT OF FIGURED HE HAD OFFENDED SOMEONE HIGH UP BY BEING TOO GOOD AT HIS JOB.
ANITA.
YOU READY?
DOLPH.
I KNOW YOU'RE THE SILENT TYPE, DOLPH, BUT COULD YOU TELL ME WHAT I'M SUPPOSED TO BE LOOKING FOR?
I WANT TO KNOW WHAT YOU SEE, NOT WHAT I TELL YOU YOU'RE SUPPOSED TO SEE.
DOLPH HAD BEEN TELLING ME THAT SINCE THE FIRST CASE WE WORKED TOGETHER.
OKAY, LET'S DO IT.

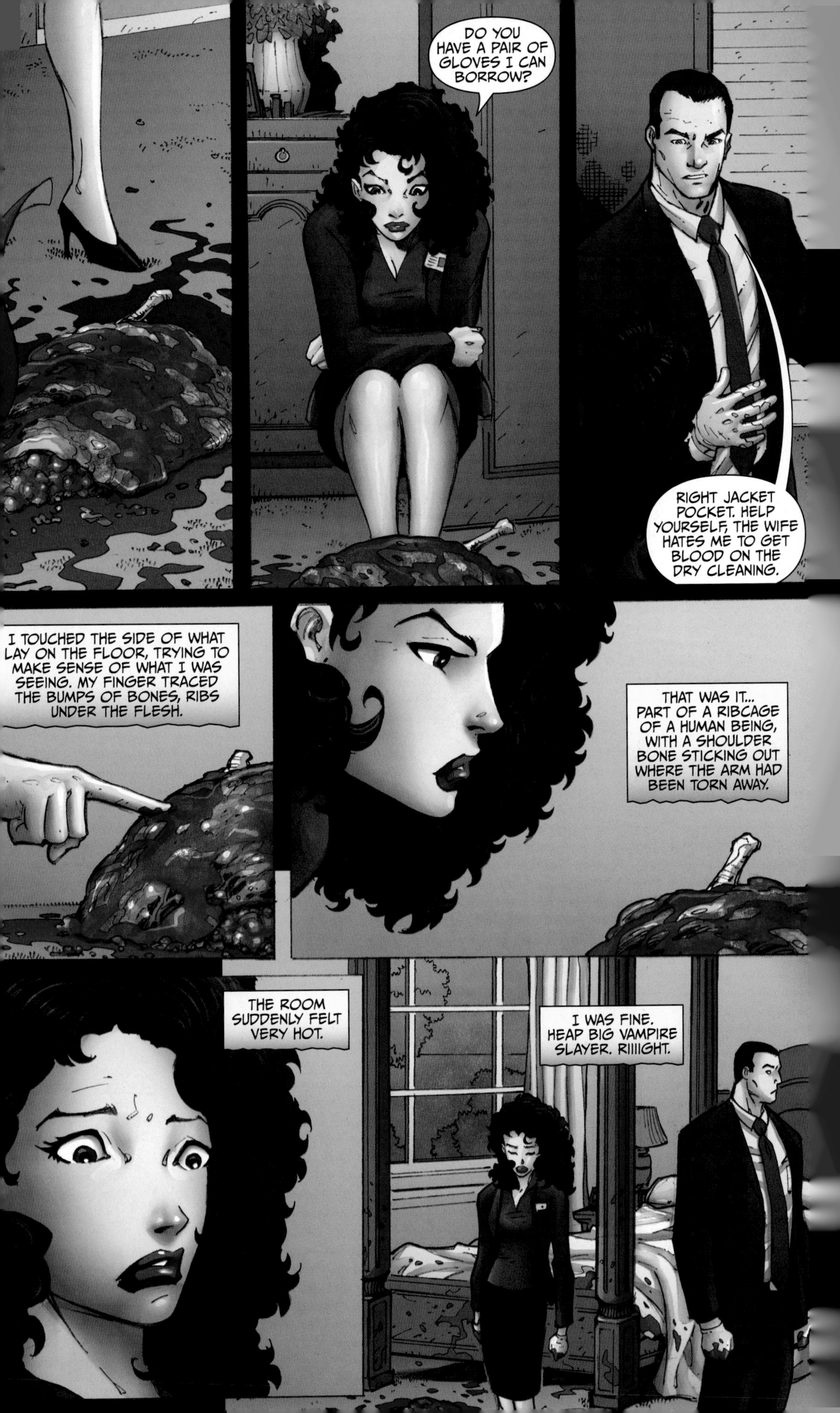
DO YOU HAVE A PAIR OF GLOVES I CAN BORROW?
RIGHT JACKET POCKET. HELP YOURSELF, THE WIFE HATES ME TO GET BLOOD ON THE DRY CLEANING.
I TOUCHED THE SIDE OF WHAT LAY ON THE FLOOR, TRYING TO MAKE SENSE OF WHAT I WAS SEEING. MY FINGER TRACED THE BUMPS OF BONES, RIBS UNDER THE FLESH.
THAT WAS IT... PART OF A RIBCAGE OF A HUMAN BEING, WITH A SHOULDER BONE STICKING OUT WHERE THE ARM HAD BEEN TORN AWAY.
THE ROOM SUDDENLY FELT VERY HOT.
I WAS FINE. HEAP BIG VAMPIRE SLAYER. RIIIIGHT.

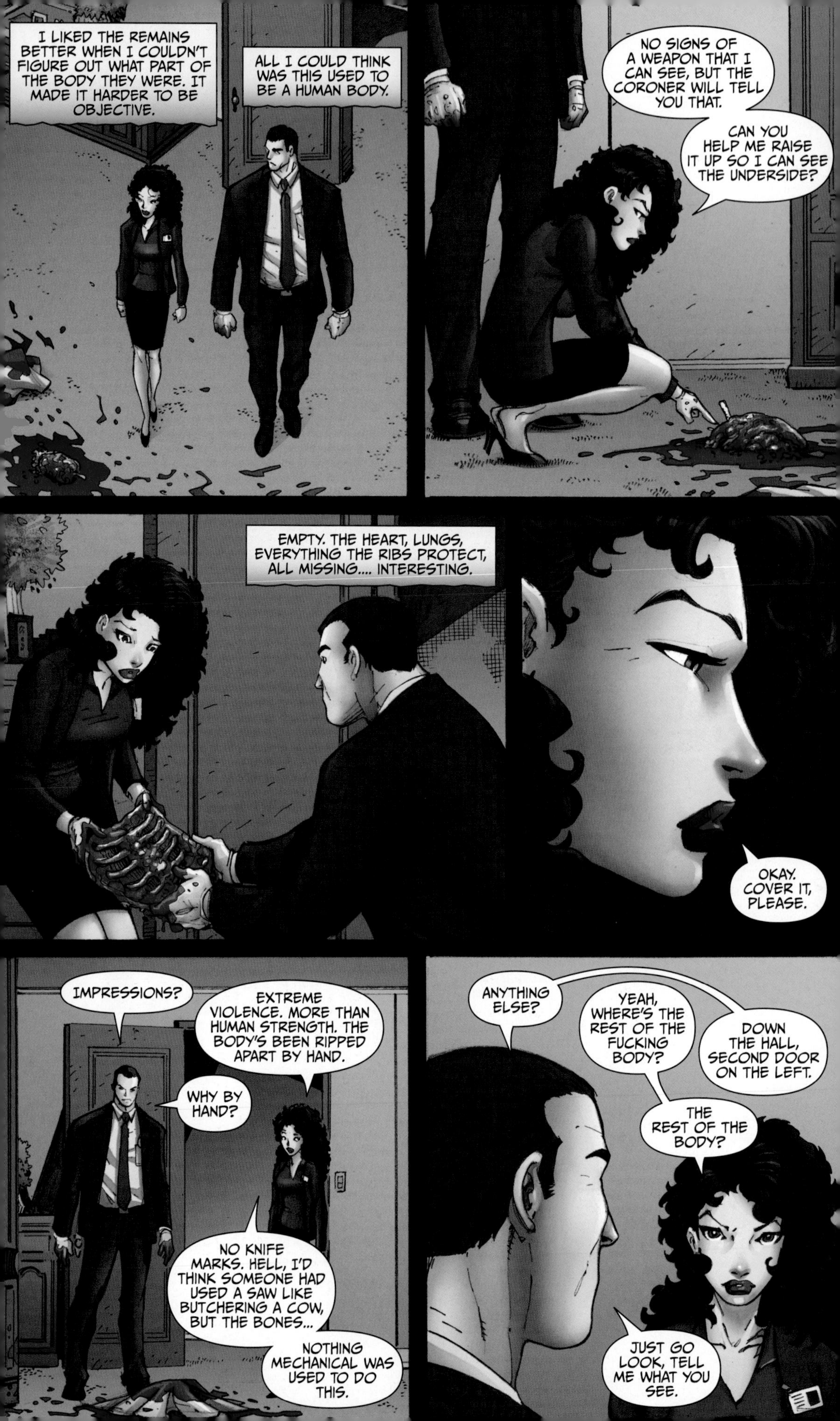
I LIKED THE REMAINS BETTER WHEN I COULDN'T FIGURE OUT WHAT PART OF THE BODY THEY WERE. IT MADE IT HARDER TO BE OBJECTIVE.
ALL I COULD THINK WAS THIS USED TO BE A HUMAN BODY.
NO SIGNS OF A WEAPON THAT I CAN SEE, BUT THE CORONER WILL TELL YOU THAT.
CAN YOU HELP ME RAISE IT UP SO I CAN SEE THE UNDERSIDE?
EMPTY. THE HEART, LUNGS, EVERYTHING THE RIBS PROTECT, ALL MISSING.... INTERESTING.
OKAY. COVER IT, PLEASE.
IMPRESSIONS?
EXTREME VIOLENCE. MORE THAN HUMAN STRENGTH. THE BODY'S BEEN RIPPED APART BY HAND.
WHY BY HAND?
NO KNIFE MARKS. HELL, I'D THINK SOMEONE HAD USED A SAW LIKE BUTCHERING A COW, BUT THE BONES...
NOTHING MECHANICAL WAS USED TO DO THIS.
ANYTHING ELSE?
YEAH, WHERE'S THE REST OF THE FUCKING BODY?
DOWN THE HALL, SECOND DOOR ON THE LEFT.
THE REST OF THE BODY?
JUST GO LOOK, TELL ME WHAT YOU SEE.

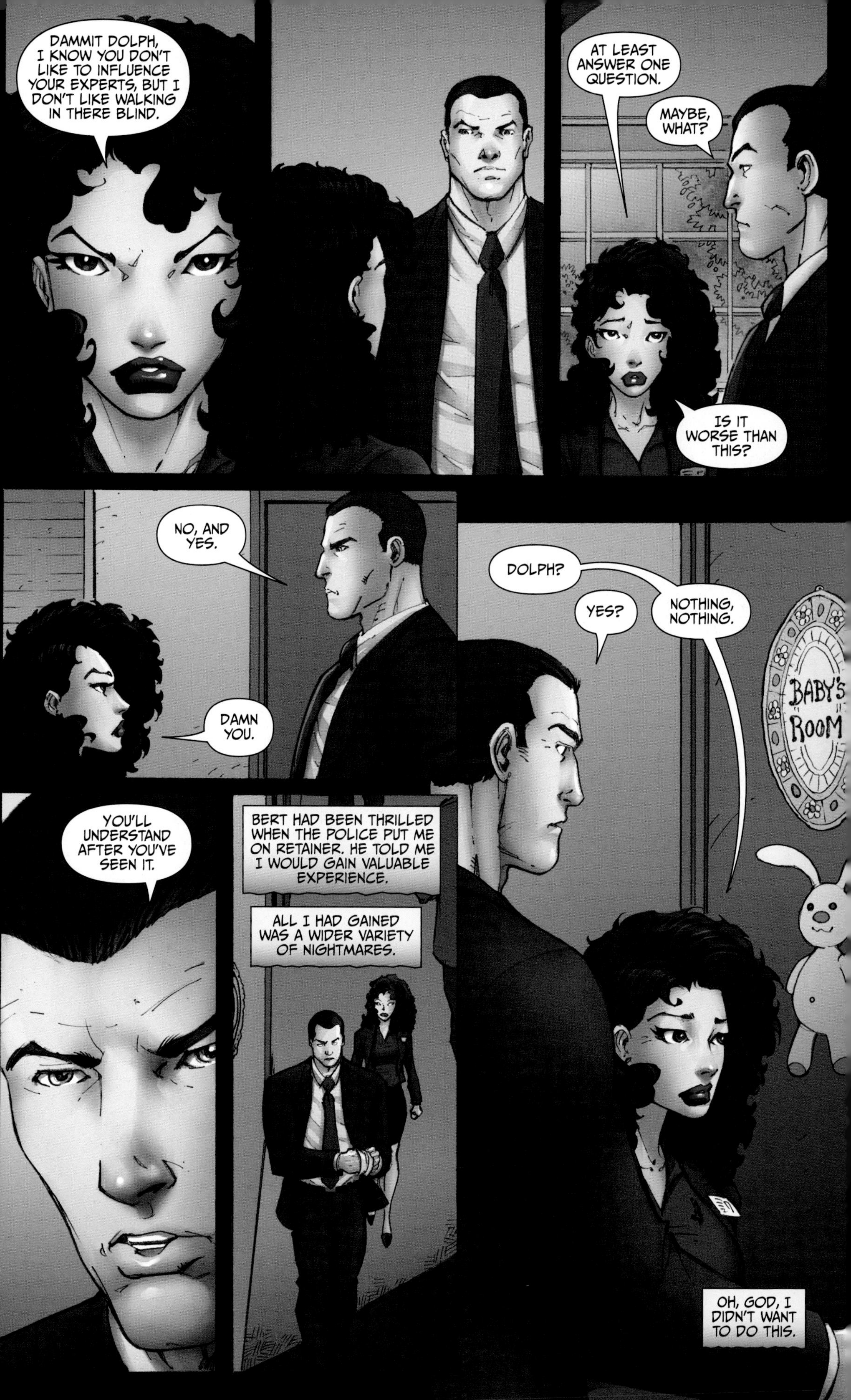

DAMMIT DOLPH, I KNOW YOU DON'T LIKE TO INFLUENCE YOUR EXPERTS, BUT I DON'T LIKE WALKING IN THERE BLIND.
AT LEAST ANSWER ONE QUESTION.
MAYBE, WHAT?
IS IT WORSE THAN THIS?
NO, AND YES.
DAMN YOU.
DOLPH?
YES?
NOTHING, NOTHING.
BABY'S ROOM
YOU'LL UNDERSTAND AFTER YOU'VE SEEN IT.
BERT HAD BEEN THRILLED WHEN THE POLICE PUT ME ON RETAINER. HE TOLD ME I WOULD GAIN VALUABLE EXPERIENCE.
ALL I HAD GAINED WAS A WIDER VARIETY OF NIGHTMARES.
OH, GOD, I DIDN'T WANT TO DO THIS.

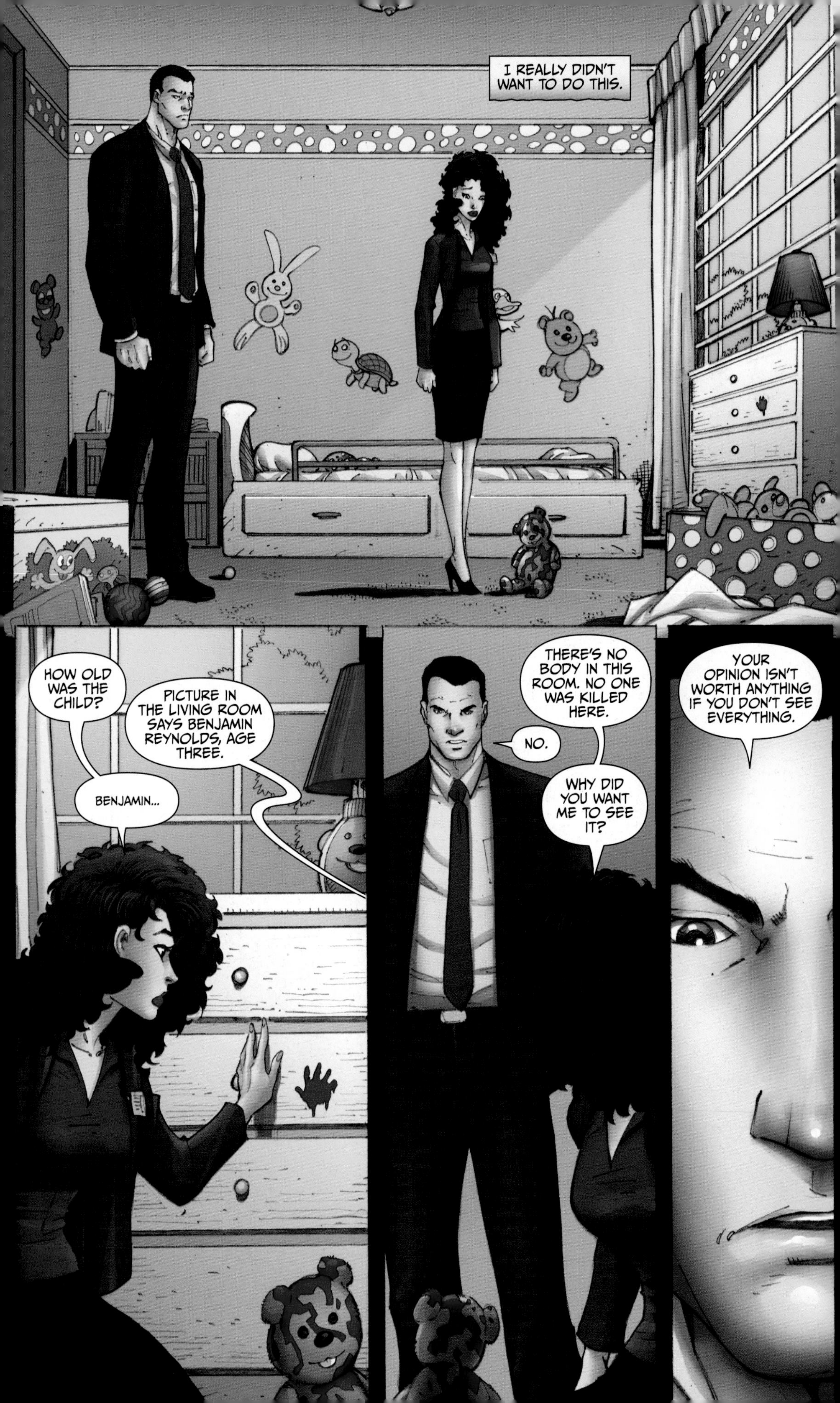
I REALLY DIDN'T WANT TO DO THIS.
HOW OLD WAS THE CHILD?
PICTURE IN THE LIVING ROOM SAYS BENJAMIN REYNOLDS, AGE THREE.
BENJAMIN...
THERE'S NO BODY IN THIS ROOM. NO ONE WAS KILLED HERE.
NO.
WHY DID YOU WANT ME TO SEE IT?
YOUR OPINION ISN'T WORTH ANYTHING IF YOU DON'T SEE EVERYTHING.

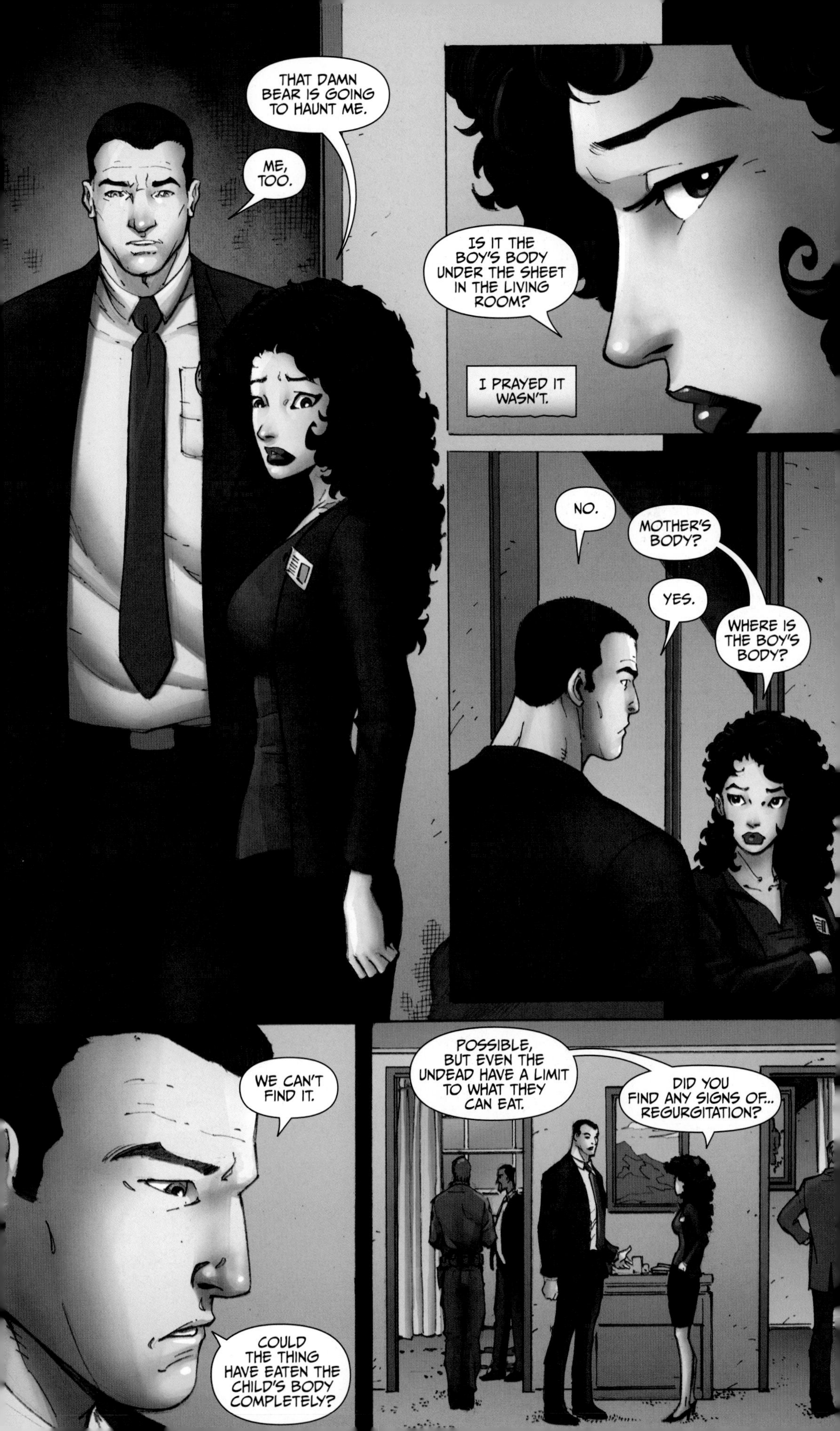
THAT DAMN BEAR IS GOING TO HAUNT ME.
ME, TOO.
IS IT THE BOY'S BODY UNDER THE SHEET IN THE LIVING ROOM?
I PRAYED IT WASN'T.
NO.
MOTHER'S BODY?
YES.
WHERE IS THE BOY'S BODY?
WE CAN'T FIND IT.
COULD THE THING HAVE EATEN THE CHILD'S BODY COMPLETELY?
POSSIBLE, BUT EVEN THE UNDEAD HAVE A LIMIT TO WHAT THEY CAN EAT.
DID YOU FIND ANY SIGNS OF.. REGURGITATION?

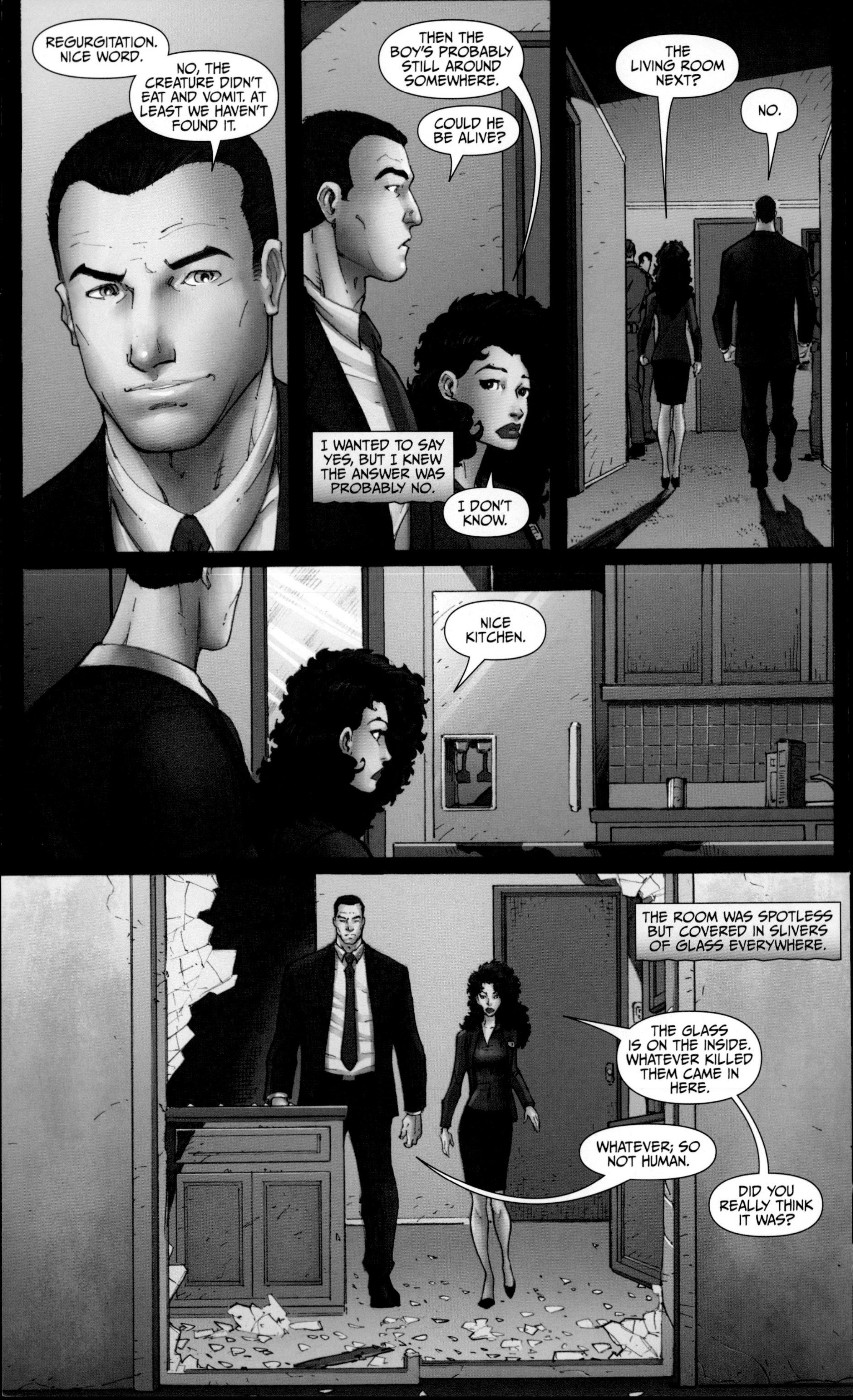
REGURGITATION. NICE WORD.
NO, THE CREATURE DIDN'T EAT AND VOMIT. AT LEAST WE HAVEN'T FOUND IT.
THEN THE BOY'S PROBABLY STILL AROUND SOMEWHERE.
COULD HE BE ALIVE?
I WANTED TO SAY YES, BUT I KNEW THE ANSWER WAS PROBABLY NO.
I DON'T KNOW.
THE LIVING ROOM NEXT?
NO.
NICE KITCHEN.
THE ROOM WAS SPOTLESS BUT COVERED IN SLIVERS OF GLASS EVERYWHERE.
THE GLASS IS ON THE INSIDE. WHATEVER KILLED THEM CAME IN HERE.
WHATEVER; SO NOT HUMAN.
DID YOU REALLY THINK IT WAS?

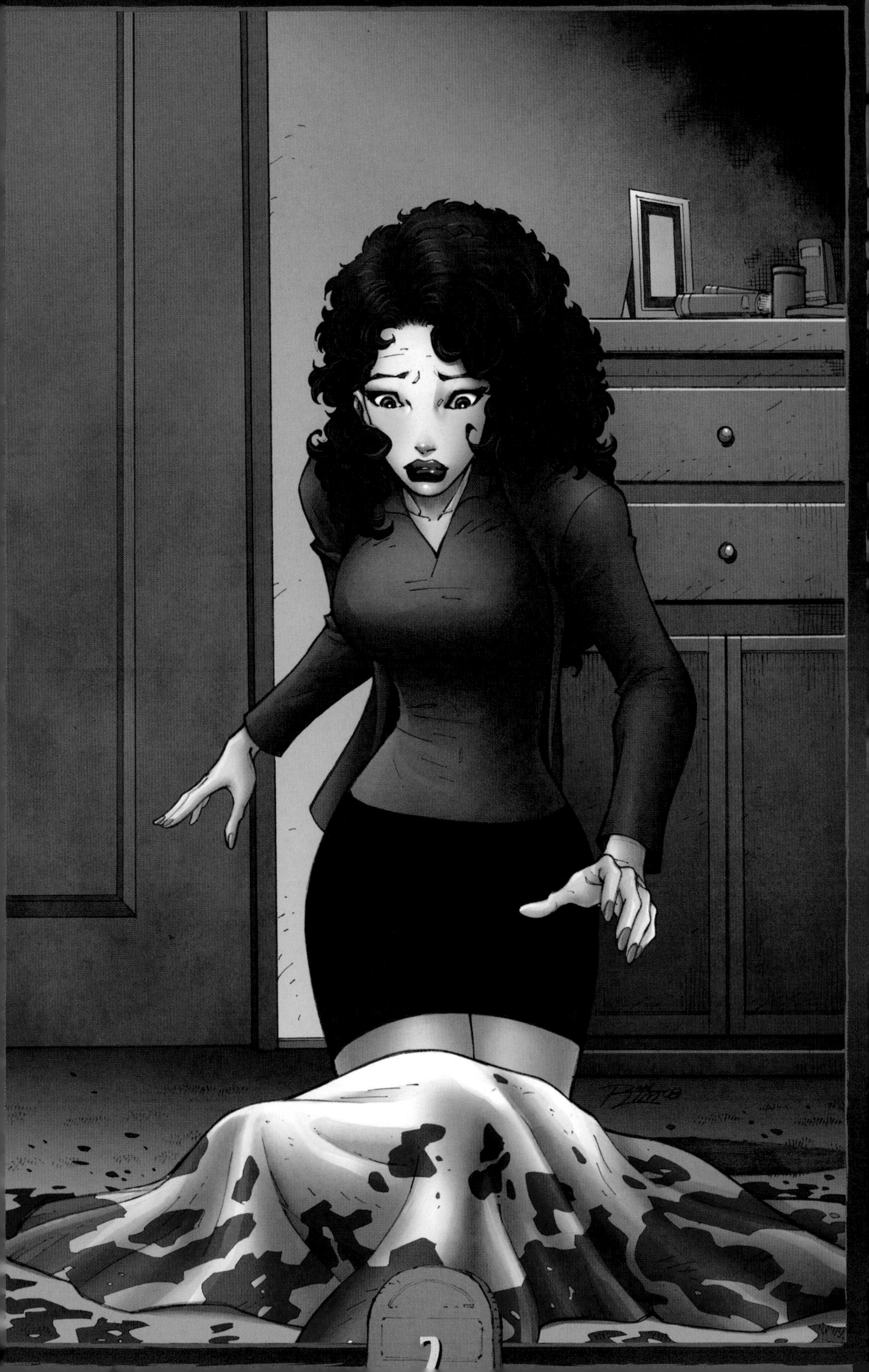

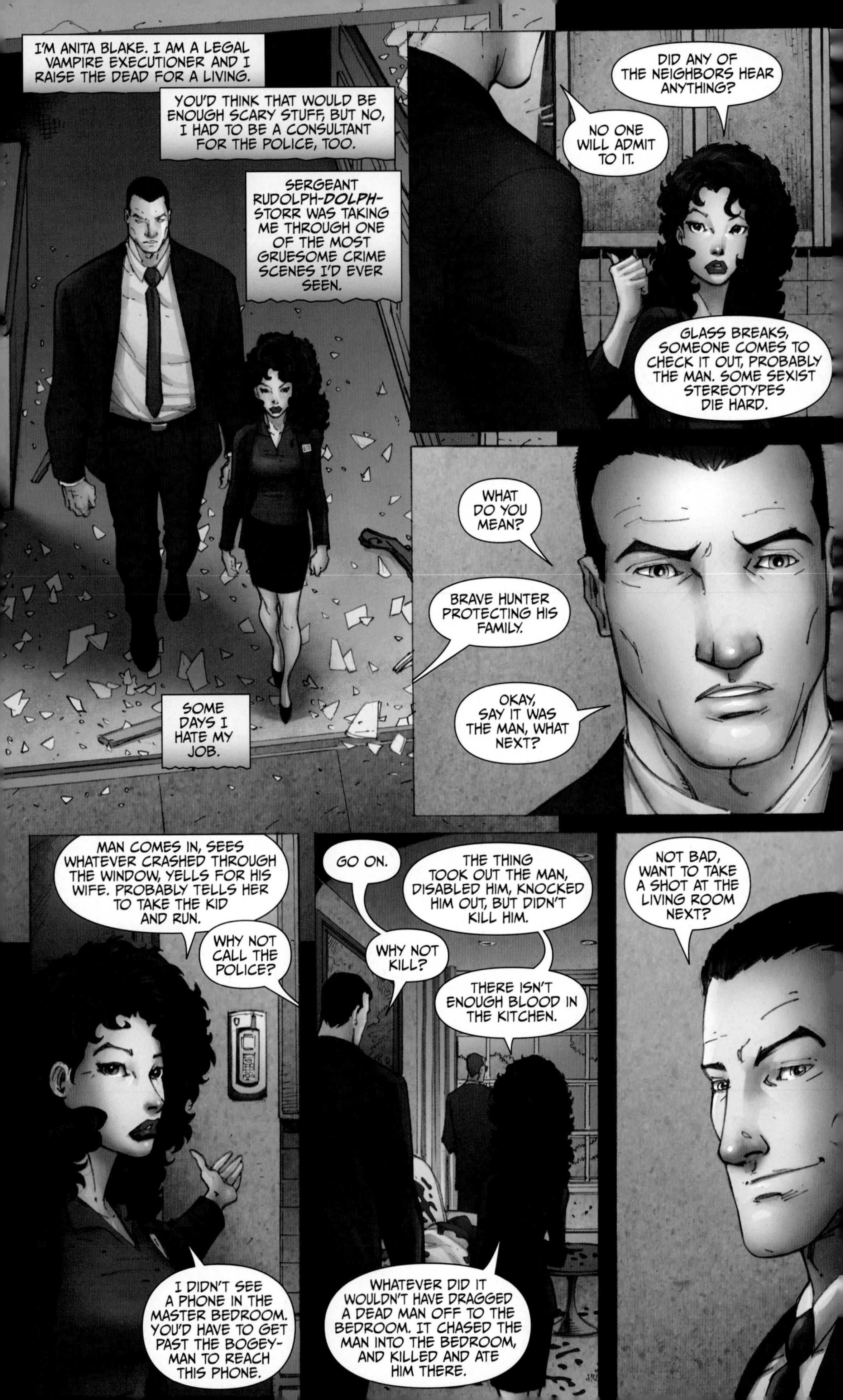
I'M ANITA BLAKE. I AM A LEGAL VAMPIRE EXECUTIONER AND I RAISE THE DEAD FOR A LIVING.
YOU'D THINK THAT WOULD BE ENOUGH SCARY STUFF, BUT NO, I HAD TO BE A CONSULTANT FOR THE POLICE, TOO.
SERGEANT RUDOLPH-**DOLPH**-STORR WAS TAKING ME THROUGH ONE OF THE MOST GRUESOME CRIME SCENES I'D EVER SEEN.
SOME DAYS I HATE MY JOB.
DID ANY OF THE NEIGHBORS HEAR ANYTHING?
NO ONE WILL ADMIT TO IT.
GLASS BREAKS, SOMEONE COMES TO CHECK IT OUT, PROBABLY THE MAN. SOME SEXIST STEREOTYPES DIE HARD.
WHAT DO YOU MEAN?
BRAVE HUNTER PROTECTING HIS FAMILY.
OKAY, SAY IT WAS THE MAN, WHAT NEXT?
MAN COMES IN, SEES WHATEVER CRASHED THROUGH THE WINDOW, YELLS FOR HIS WIFE. PROBABLY TELLS HER TO TAKE THE KID AND RUN.
WHY NOT CALL THE POLICE?
I DIDN'T SEE A PHONE IN THE MASTER BEDROOM. YOU'D HAVE TO GET PAST THE BOGEY-MAN TO REACH THIS PHONE.
GO ON.
THE THING TOOK OUT THE MAN, DISABLED HIM, KNOCKED HIM OUT, BUT DIDN'T KILL HIM.
WHY NOT KILL?
THERE ISN'T ENOUGH BLOOD IN THE KITCHEN.
WHATEVER DID IT WOULDN'T HAVE DRAGGED A DEAD MAN OFF TO THE BEDROOM. IT CHASED THE MAN INTO THE BEDROOM, AND KILLED AND ATE HIM THERE.
NOT BAD, WANT TO TAKE A SHOT AT THE LIVING ROOM NEXT?

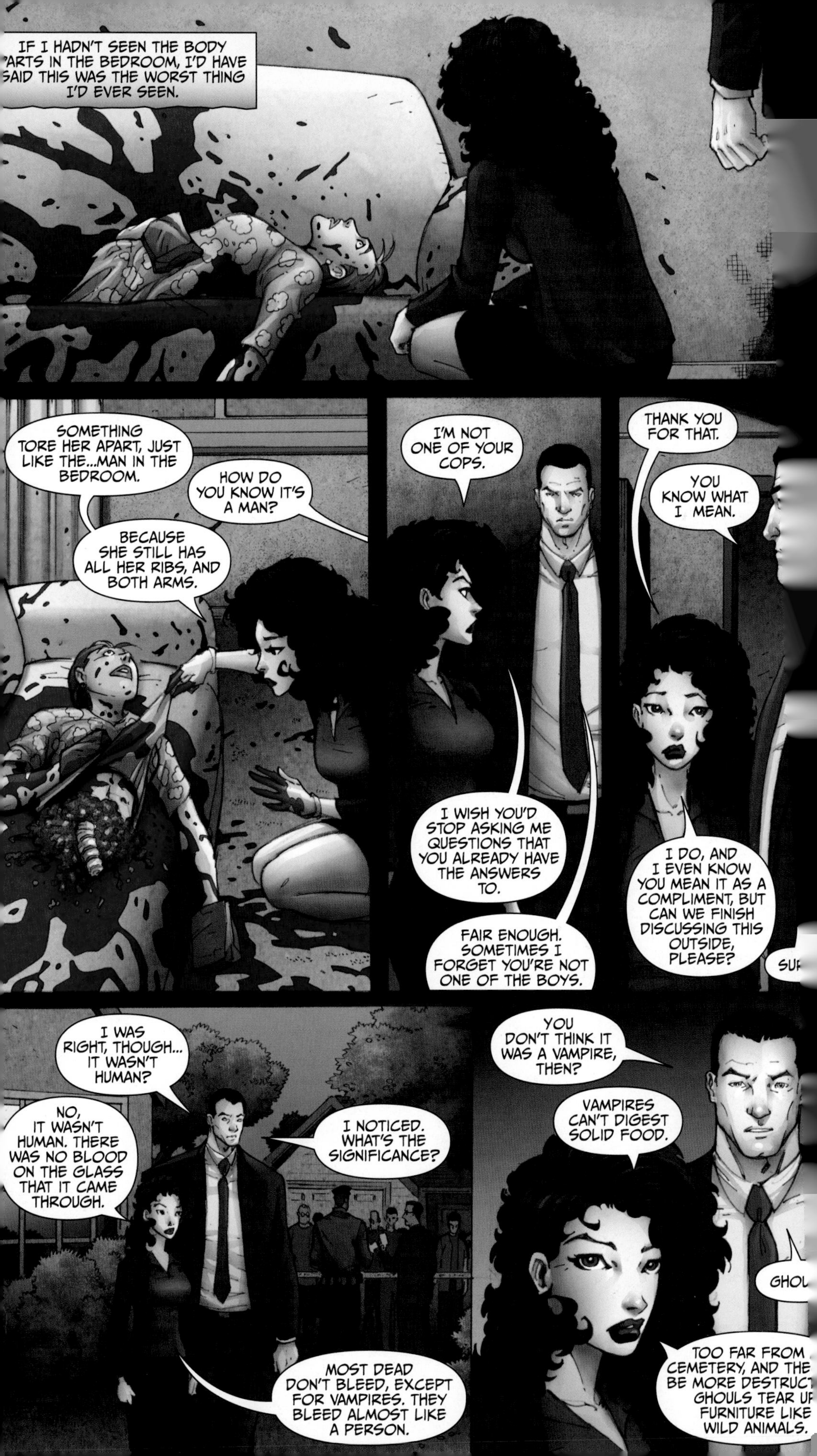
IF I HADN'T SEEN THE BODY PARTS IN THE BEDROOM, I'D HAVE SAID THIS WAS THE WORST THING I'D EVER SEEN.
SOMETHING TORE HER APART, JUST LIKE THE...MAN IN THE BEDROOM.
HOW DO YOU KNOW IT'S A MAN?
BECAUSE SHE STILL HAS ALL HER RIBS, AND BOTH ARMS.
I'M NOT ONE OF YOUR COPS.
I WISH YOU'D STOP ASKING ME QUESTIONS THAT YOU ALREADY HAVE THE ANSWERS TO.
FAIR ENOUGH. SOMETIMES I FORGET YOU'RE NOT ONE OF THE BOYS.
THANK YOU FOR THAT.
YOU KNOW WHAT I MEAN.
I DO, AND I EVEN KNOW YOU MEAN IT AS A COMPLIMENT, BUT CAN WE FINISH DISCUSSING THIS OUTSIDE, PLEASE?
SU
I WAS RIGHT, THOUGH... IT WASN'T HUMAN?
NO, IT WASN'T HUMAN. THERE WAS NO BLOOD ON THE GLASS THAT IT CAME THROUGH.
I NOTICED. WHAT'S THE SIGNIFICANCE?
MOST DEAD DON'T BLEED, EXCEPT FOR VAMPIRES. THEY BLEED ALMOST LIKE A PERSON.
YOU DON'T THINK IT WAS A VAMPIRE, THEN?
VAMPIRES CAN'T DIGEST SOLID FOOD.
GHOU
TOO FAR FROM CEMETERY, AND THE BE MORE DESTRUCT GHOULS TEAR UP FURNITURE LIKE WILD ANIMALS.

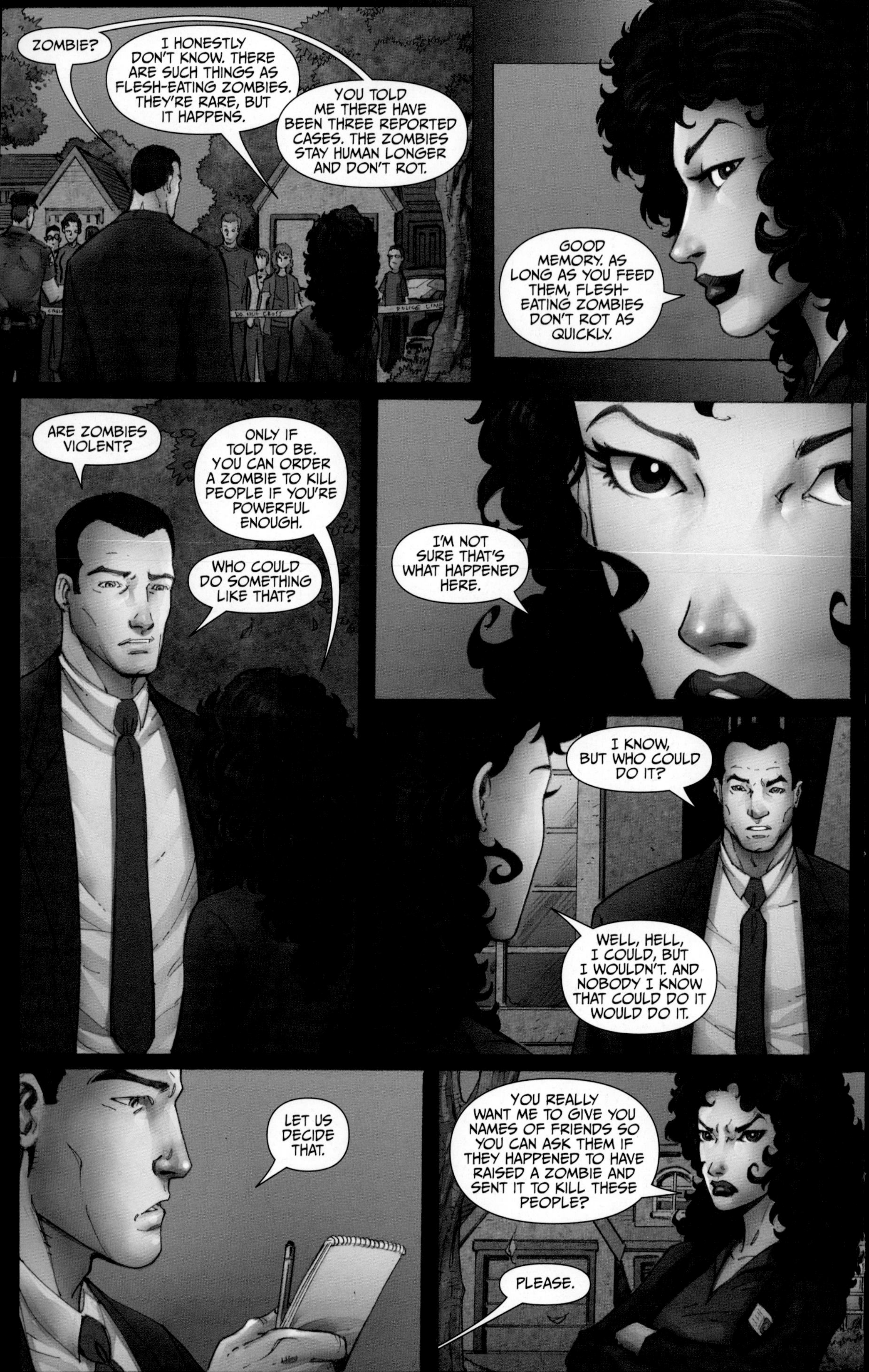

ZOMBIE?
I HONESTLY DON'T KNOW. THERE ARE SUCH THINGS AS FLESH-EATING ZOMBIES. THEY'RE RARE, BUT IT HAPPENS.
YOU TOLD ME THERE HAVE BEEN THREE REPORTED CASES. THE ZOMBIES STAY HUMAN LONGER AND DON'T ROT.
GOOD MEMORY. AS LONG AS YOU FEED THEM, FLESH-EATING ZOMBIES DON'T ROT AS QUICKLY.
ARE ZOMBIES VIOLENT?
ONLY IF TOLD TO BE. YOU CAN ORDER A ZOMBIE TO KILL PEOPLE IF YOU'RE POWERFUL ENOUGH.
WHO COULD DO SOMETHING LIKE THAT?
I'M NOT SURE THAT'S WHAT HAPPENED HERE.
I KNOW, BUT WHO COULD DO IT?
WELL, HELL, I COULD, BUT I WOULDN'T. AND NOBODY I KNOW THAT COULD DO IT WOULD DO IT.
LET US DECIDE THAT.
YOU REALLY WANT ME TO GIVE YOU NAMES OF FRIENDS SO YOU CAN ASK THEM IF THEY HAPPENED TO HAVE RAISED A ZOMBIE AND SENT IT TO KILL THESE PEOPLE?
PLEASE.

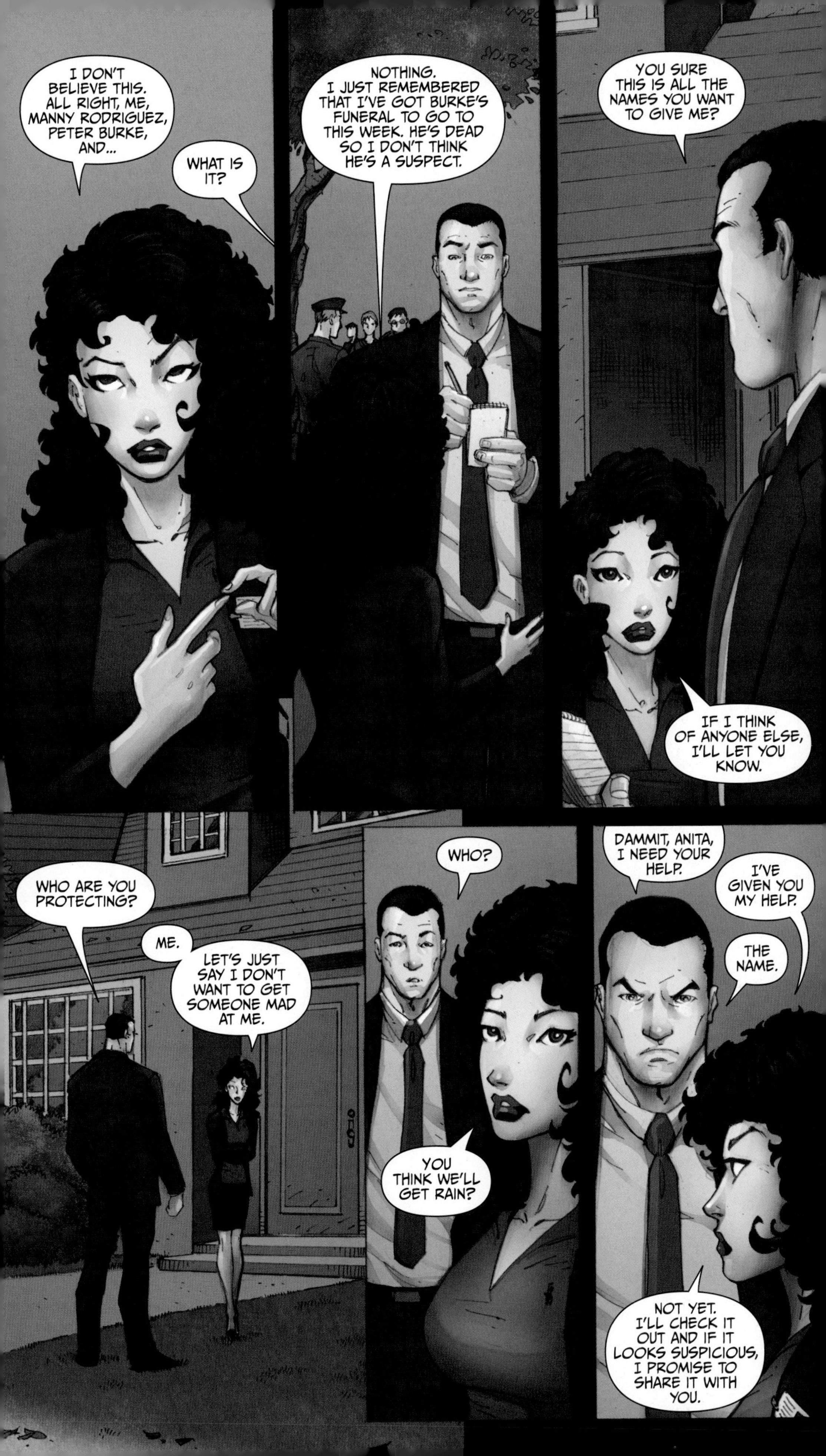
I DON'T BELIEVE THIS. ALL RIGHT, ME, MANNY RODRIGUEZ, PETER BURKE, AND...
WHAT IS IT?
NOTHING. I JUST REMEMBERED THAT I'VE GOT BURKE'S FUNERAL TO GO TO THIS WEEK. HE'S DEAD SO I DON'T THINK HE'S A SUSPECT.
YOU SURE THIS IS ALL THE NAMES YOU WANT TO GIVE ME?
IF I THINK OF ANYONE ELSE, I'LL LET YOU KNOW.
WHO ARE YOU PROTECTING?
ME.
LET'S JUST SAY I DON'T WANT TO GET SOMEONE MAD AT ME.
WHO?
YOU THINK WE'LL GET RAIN?
DAMMIT, ANITA, I NEED YOUR HELP.
I'VE GIVEN YOU MY HELP.
THE NAME.
NOT YET. I'LL CHECK IT OUT AND IF IT LOOKS SUSPICIOUS, I PROMISE TO SHARE IT WITH YOU.

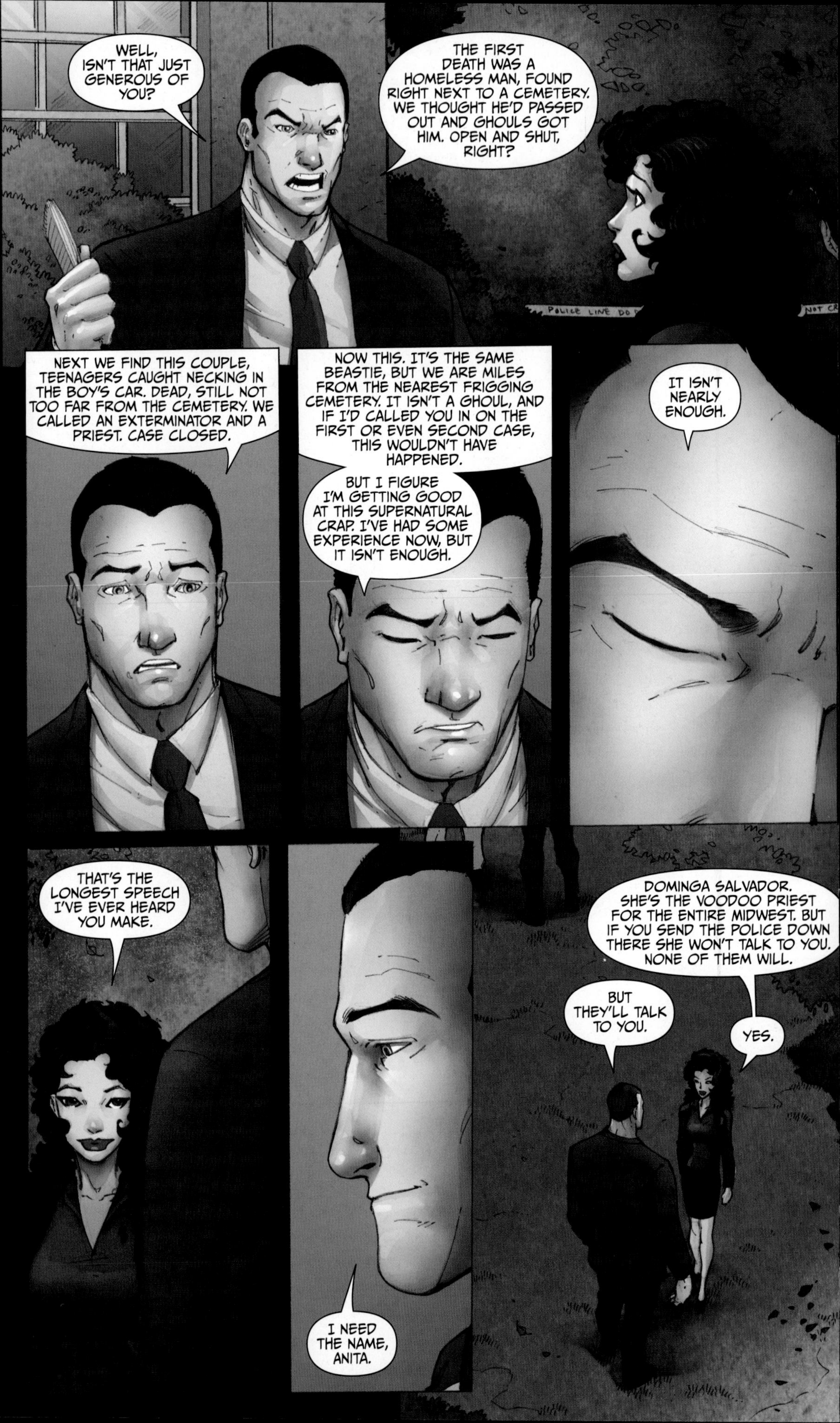

WELL, ISN'T THAT JUST GENEROUS OF YOU?
THE FIRST DEATH WAS A HOMELESS MAN, FOUND RIGHT NEXT TO A CEMETERY. WE THOUGHT HE'D PASSED OUT AND GHOULS GOT HIM. OPEN AND SHUT, RIGHT?
NEXT WE FIND THIS COUPLE, TEENAGERS CAUGHT NECKING IN THE BOY'S CAR. DEAD, STILL NOT TOO FAR FROM THE CEMETERY. WE CALLED AN EXTERMINATOR AND A PRIEST. CASE CLOSED.
NOW THIS. IT'S THE SAME BEASTIE, BUT WE ARE MILES FROM THE NEAREST FRIGGING CEMETERY. IT ISN'T A GHOUL, AND IF I'D CALLED YOU IN ON THE FIRST OR EVEN SECOND CASE, THIS WOULDN'T HAVE HAPPENED.
BUT I FIGURE I'M GETTING GOOD AT THIS SUPERNATURAL CRAP. I'VE HAD SOME EXPERIENCE NOW, BUT IT ISN'T ENOUGH.
IT ISN'T NEARLY ENOUGH.
THAT'S THE LONGEST SPEECH I'VE EVER HEARD YOU MAKE.
I NEED THE NAME, ANITA.
DOMINGA SALVADOR. SHE'S THE VOODOO PRIEST FOR THE ENTIRE MIDWEST. BUT IF YOU SEND THE POLICE DOWN THERE SHE WON'T TALK TO YOU. NONE OF THEM WILL.
BUT THEY'LL TALK TO YOU.
YES.

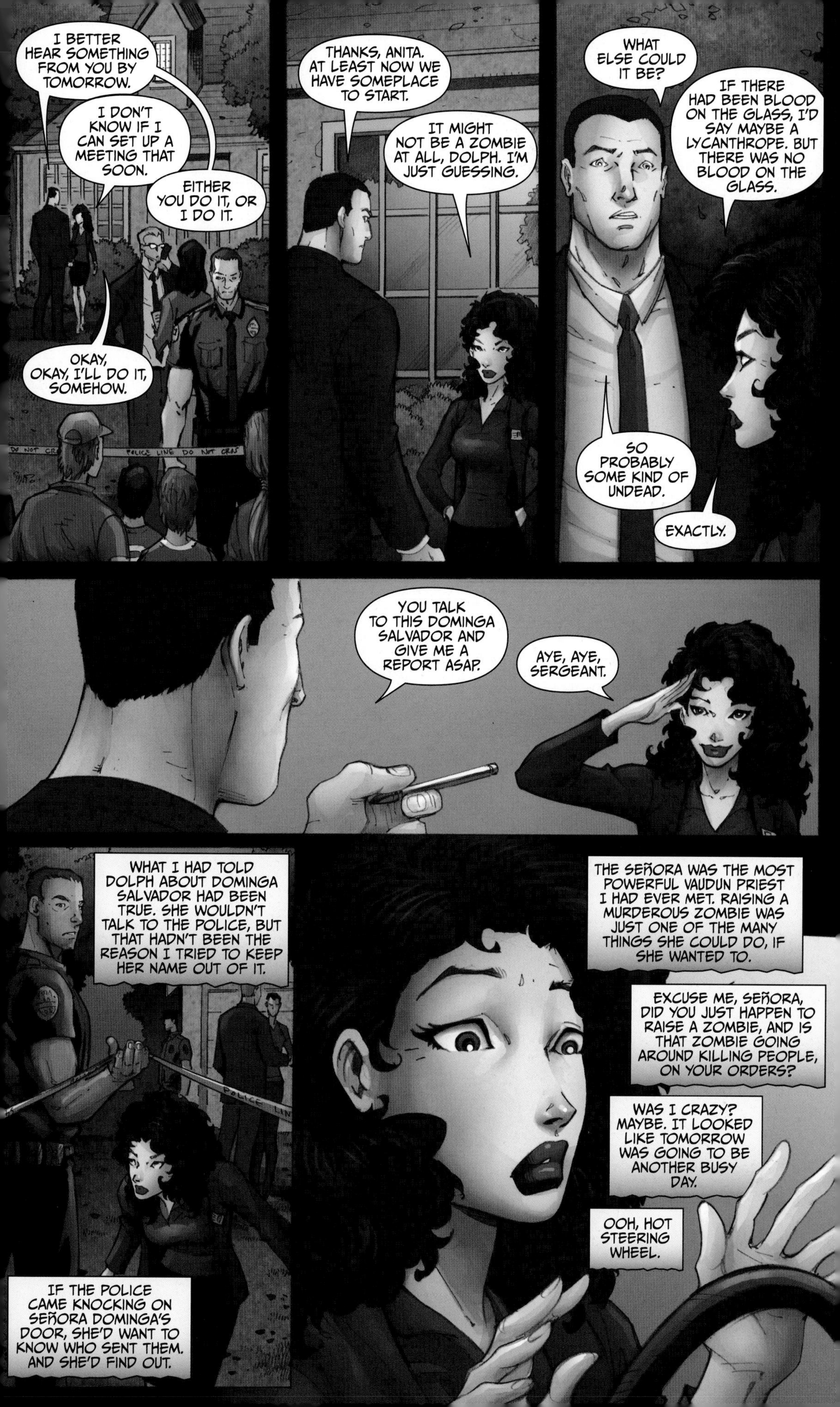

I BETTER HEAR SOMETHING FROM YOU BY TOMORROW.
I DON'T KNOW IF I CAN SET UP A MEETING THAT SOON.
EITHER YOU DO IT, OR I DO IT.
OKAY, OKAY, I'LL DO IT, SOMEHOW.
POLICE LINE DO NOT CROS
THANKS, ANITA. AT LEAST NOW WE HAVE SOMEPLACE TO START.
IT MIGHT NOT BE A ZOMBIE AT ALL, DOLPH. I'M JUST GUESSING.
WHAT ELSE COULD IT BE?
IF THERE HAD BEEN BLOOD ON THE GLASS, I'D SAY MAYBE A LYCANTHROPE. BUT THERE WAS NO BLOOD ON THE GLASS.
SO PROBABLY SOME KIND OF UNDEAD.
EXACTLY.
YOU TALK TO THIS DOMINGA SALVADOR AND GIVE ME A REPORT ASAP.
AYE, AYE, SERGEANT.
WHAT I HAD TOLD DOLPH ABOUT DOMINGA SALVADOR HAD BEEN TRUE. SHE WOULDN'T TALK TO THE POLICE, BUT THAT HADN'T BEEN THE REASON I TRIED TO KEEP HER NAME OUT OF IT.
IF THE POLICE CAME KNOCKING ON SEñORA DOMINGA'S DOOR, SHE'D WANT TO KNOW WHO SENT THEM. AND SHE'D FIND OUT.
THE SEñORA WAS THE MOST POWERFUL VAUDUN PRIEST I HAD EVER MET. RAISING A MURDEROUS ZOMBIE WAS JUST ONE OF THE MANY THINGS SHE COULD DO, IF SHE WANTED TO.
EXCUSE ME, SEñORA, DID YOU JUST HAPPEN TO RAISE A ZOMBIE, AND IS THAT ZOMBIE GOING AROUND KILLING PEOPLE, ON YOUR ORDERS?
WAS I CRAZY? MAYBE. IT LOOKED LIKE TOMORROW WAS GOING TO BE ANOTHER BUSY DAY.
OOH, HOT STEERING WHEEL.

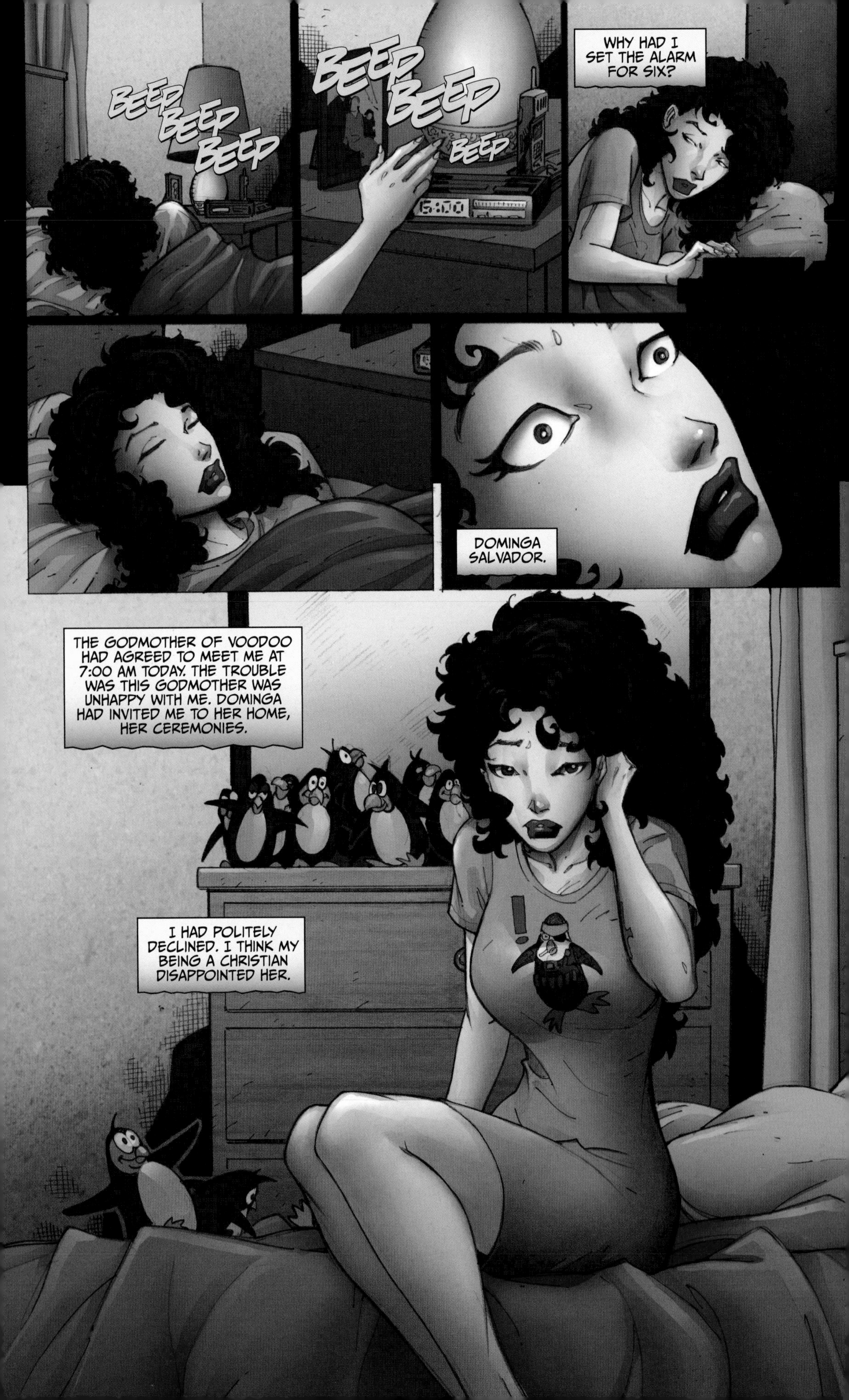
BEEP BEEP BEEP
BEEP BEEP BEEP
WHY HAD I SET THE ALARM FOR SIX?
DOMINGA SALVADOR.
THE GODMOTHER OF VOODOO HAD AGREED TO MEET ME AT 7:00 AM TODAY. THE TROUBLE WAS THIS GODMOTHER WAS UNHAPPY WITH ME. DOMINGA HAD INVITED ME TO HER HOME, HER CEREMONIES.
I HAD POLITELY DECLINED. I THINK MY BEING A CHRISTIAN DISAPPOINTED HER.

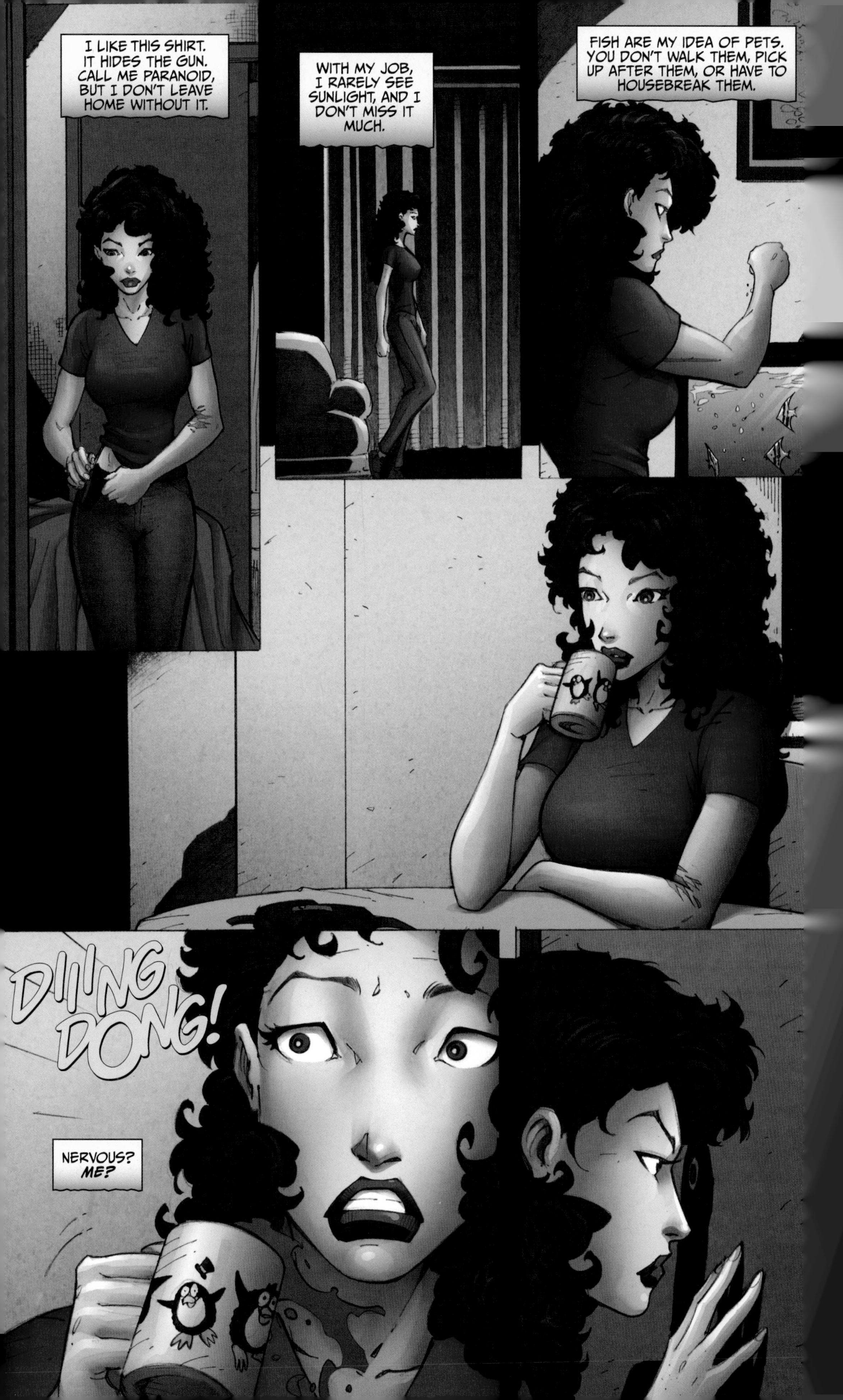

I LIKE THIS SHIRT. IT HIDES THE GUN. CALL ME PARANOID, BUT I DON'T LEAVE HOME WITHOUT IT.
WITH MY JOB, I RARELY SEE SUNLIGHT, AND I DON'T MISS IT MUCH.
FISH ARE MY IDEA OF PETS. YOU DON'T WALK THEM, PICK UP AFTER THEM, OR HAVE TO HOUSEBREAK THEM.
DIIING DONG!
NERVOUS? *ME?*

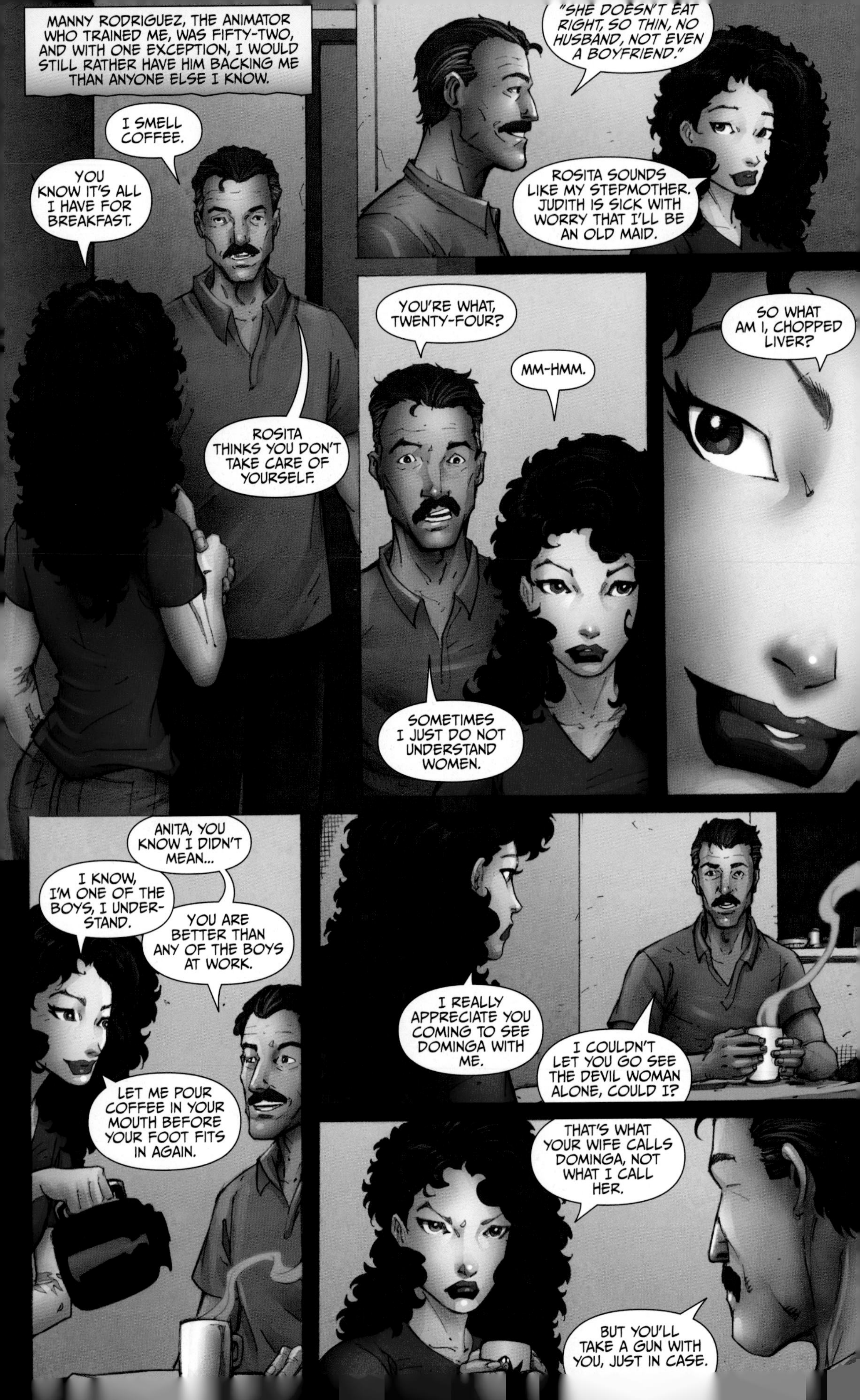
MANNY RODRIGUEZ, THE ANIMATOR WHO TRAINED ME, WAS FIFTY-TWO, AND WITH ONE EXCEPTION, I WOULD STILL RATHER HAVE HIM BACKING ME THAN ANYONE ELSE I KNOW.
I SMELL COFFEE.
YOU KNOW IT'S ALL I HAVE FOR BREAKFAST.
ROSITA THINKS YOU DON'T TAKE CARE OF YOURSELF.
"SHE DOESN'T EAT RIGHT, SO THIN, NO HUSBAND, NOT EVEN A BOYFRIEND."
ROSITA SOUNDS LIKE MY STEPMOTHER. JUDITH IS SICK WITH WORRY THAT I'LL BE AN OLD MAID.
YOU'RE WHAT, TWENTY-FOUR?
MM-HMM.
SOMETIMES I JUST DO NOT UNDERSTAND WOMEN.
SO WHAT AM I, CHOPPED LIVER?
ANITA, YOU KNOW I DIDN'T MEAN...
I KNOW, I'M ONE OF THE BOYS, I UNDER-STAND.
YOU ARE BETTER THAN ANY OF THE BOYS AT WORK.
LET ME POUR COFFEE IN YOUR MOUTH BEFORE YOUR FOOT FITS IN AGAIN.
I REALLY APPRECIATE YOU COMING TO SEE DOMINGA WITH ME.
I COULDN'T LET YOU GO SEE THE DEVIL WOMAN ALONE, COULD I?
THAT'S WHAT YOUR WIFE CALLS DOMINGA, NOT WHAT I CALL HER.
BUT YOU'LL TAKE A GUN WITH YOU, JUST IN CASE.

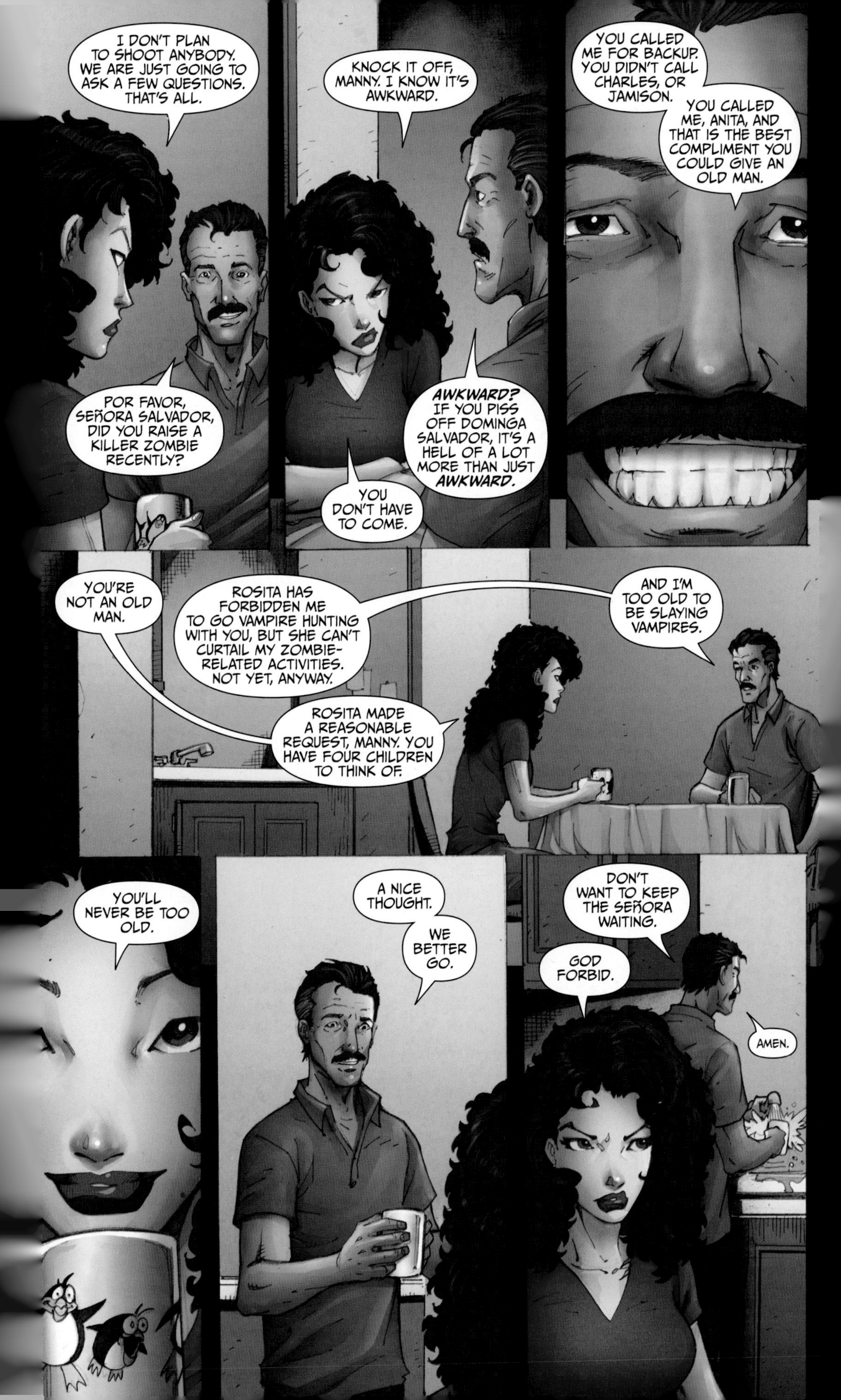
I DON'T PLAN TO SHOOT ANYBODY. WE ARE JUST GOING TO ASK A FEW QUESTIONS. THAT'S ALL.
POR FAVOR, SEÑORA SALVADOR, DID YOU RAISE A KILLER ZOMBIE RECENTLY?
KNOCK IT OFF, MANNY. I KNOW IT'S AWKWARD.
AWKWARD? IF YOU PISS OFF DOMINGA SALVADOR, IT'S A HELL OF A LOT MORE THAN JUST AWKWARD.
YOU DON'T HAVE TO COME.
YOU CALLED ME FOR BACKUP. YOU DIDN'T CALL CHARLES, OR JAMISON.
YOU CALLED ME, ANITA, AND THAT IS THE BEST COMPLIMENT YOU COULD GIVE AN OLD MAN.
YOU'RE NOT AN OLD MAN.
ROSITA HAS FORBIDDEN ME TO GO VAMPIRE HUNTING WITH YOU, BUT SHE CAN'T CURTAIL MY ZOMBIE-RELATED ACTIVITIES. NOT YET, ANYWAY.
AND I'M TOO OLD TO BE SLAYING VAMPIRES.
ROSITA MADE A REASONABLE REQUEST, MANNY. YOU HAVE FOUR CHILDREN TO THINK OF.
YOU'LL NEVER BE TOO OLD.
A NICE THOUGHT.
WE BETTER GO.
DON'T WANT TO KEEP THE SEÑORA WAITING.
GOD FORBID.
AMEN.

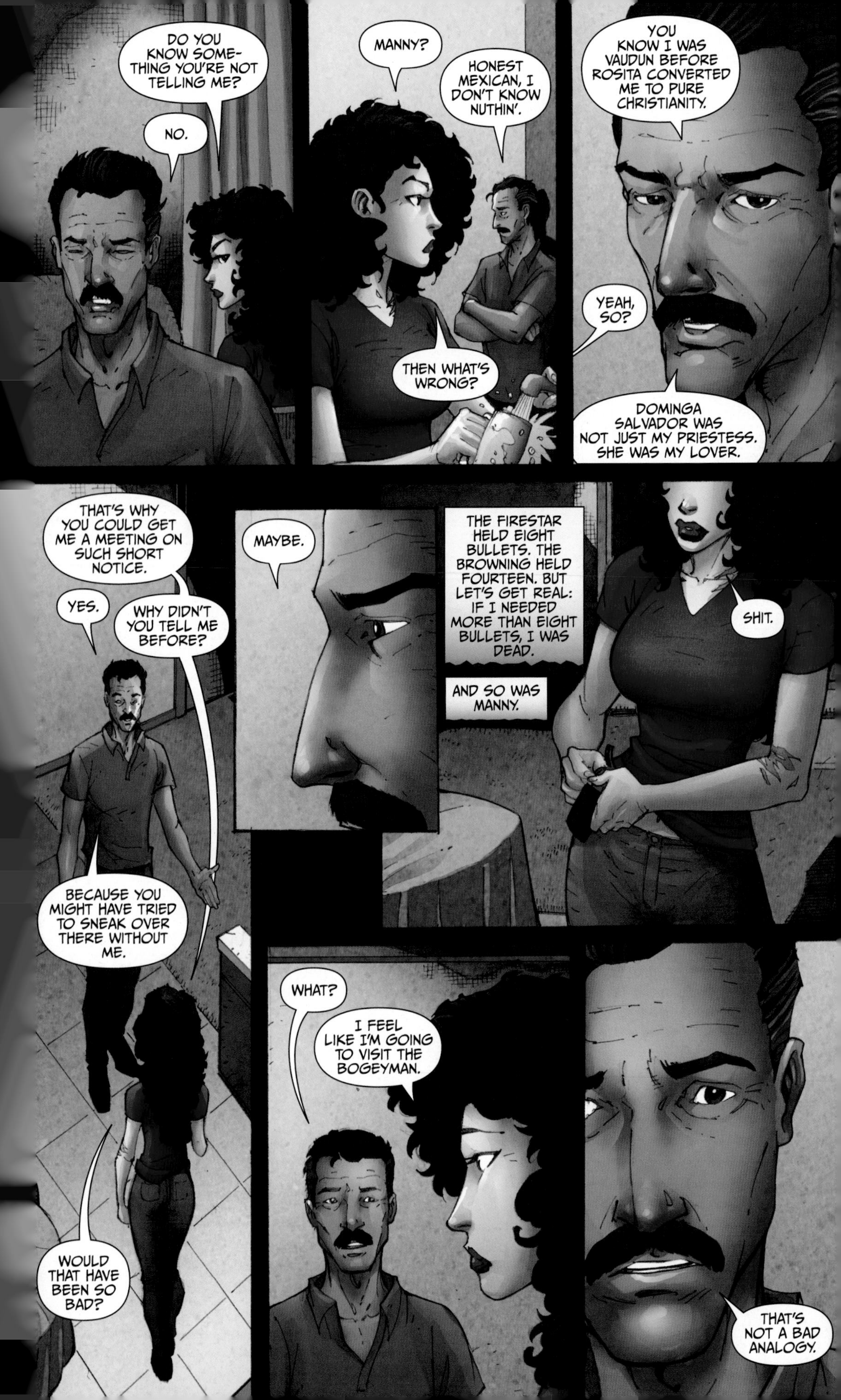

DO YOU KNOW SOME-THING YOU'RE NOT TELLING ME?
NO.
MANNY?
HONEST MEXICAN, I DON'T KNOW NUTHIN'.
THEN WHAT'S WRONG?
YOU KNOW I WAS VAUDUN BEFORE ROSITA CONVERTED ME TO PURE CHRISTIANITY.
YEAH, SO?
DOMINGA SALVADOR WAS NOT JUST MY PRIESTESS. SHE WAS MY LOVER.
THAT'S WHY YOU COULD GET ME A MEETING ON SUCH SHORT NOTICE.
YES.
WHY DIDN'T YOU TELL ME BEFORE?
BECAUSE YOU MIGHT HAVE TRIED TO SNEAK OVER THERE WITHOUT ME.
WOULD THAT HAVE BEEN SO BAD?
MAYBE.
THE FIRESTAR HELD EIGHT BULLETS. THE BROWNING HELD FOURTEEN. BUT LET'S GET REAL: IF I NEEDED MORE THAN EIGHT BULLETS, I WAS DEAD.
AND SO WAS MANNY.
SHIT.
WHAT?
I FEEL LIKE I'M GOING TO VISIT THE BOGEYMAN.
THAT'S NOT A BAD ANALOGY.

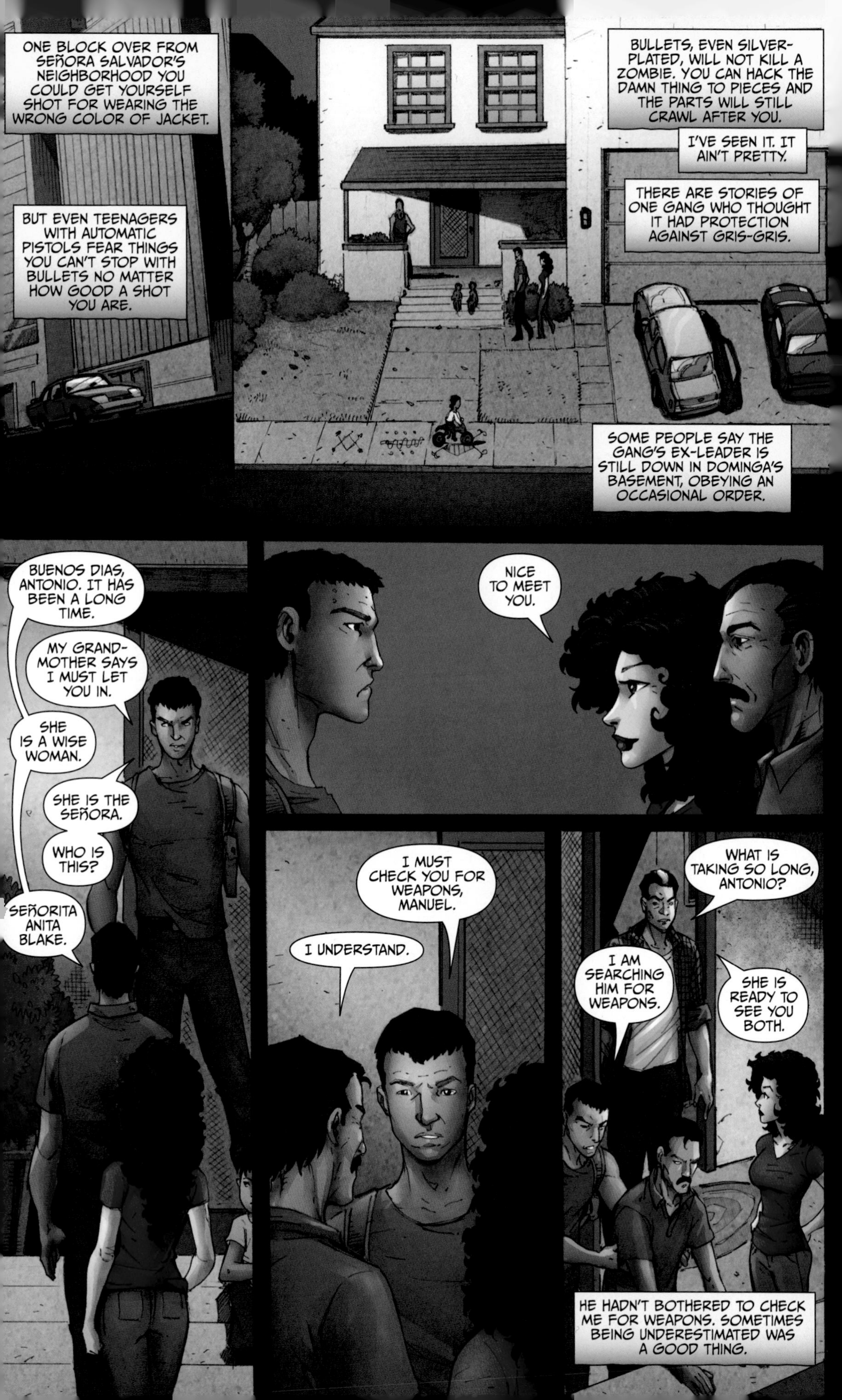

ONE BLOCK OVER FROM SEÑORA SALVADOR'S NEIGHBORHOOD YOU COULD GET YOURSELF SHOT FOR WEARING THE WRONG COLOR OF JACKET.
BUT EVEN TEENAGERS WITH AUTOMATIC PISTOLS FEAR THINGS YOU CAN'T STOP WITH BULLETS NO MATTER HOW GOOD A SHOT YOU ARE.
BULLETS, EVEN SILVER-PLATED, WILL NOT KILL A ZOMBIE. YOU CAN HACK THE DAMN THING TO PIECES AND THE PARTS WILL STILL CRAWL AFTER YOU.
I'VE SEEN IT. IT AIN'T PRETTY.
THERE ARE STORIES OF ONE GANG WHO THOUGHT IT HAD PROTECTION AGAINST GRIS-GRIS.
SOME PEOPLE SAY THE GANG'S EX-LEADER IS STILL DOWN IN DOMINGA'S BASEMENT, OBEYING AN OCCASIONAL ORDER.
BUENOS DIAS, ANTONIO. IT HAS BEEN A LONG TIME.
MY GRAND-MOTHER SAYS I MUST LET YOU IN.
SHE IS A WISE WOMAN.
SHE IS THE SEÑORA.
WHO IS THIS?
SEÑORITA ANITA BLAKE.
NICE TO MEET YOU.
I MUST CHECK YOU FOR WEAPONS, MANUEL.
I UNDERSTAND.
WHAT IS TAKING SO LONG, ANTONIO?
I AM SEARCHING HIM FOR WEAPONS.
SHE IS READY TO SEE YOU BOTH.
HE HADN'T BOTHERED TO CHECK ME FOR WEAPONS. SOMETIMES BEING UNDERESTIMATED WAS A GOOD THING.

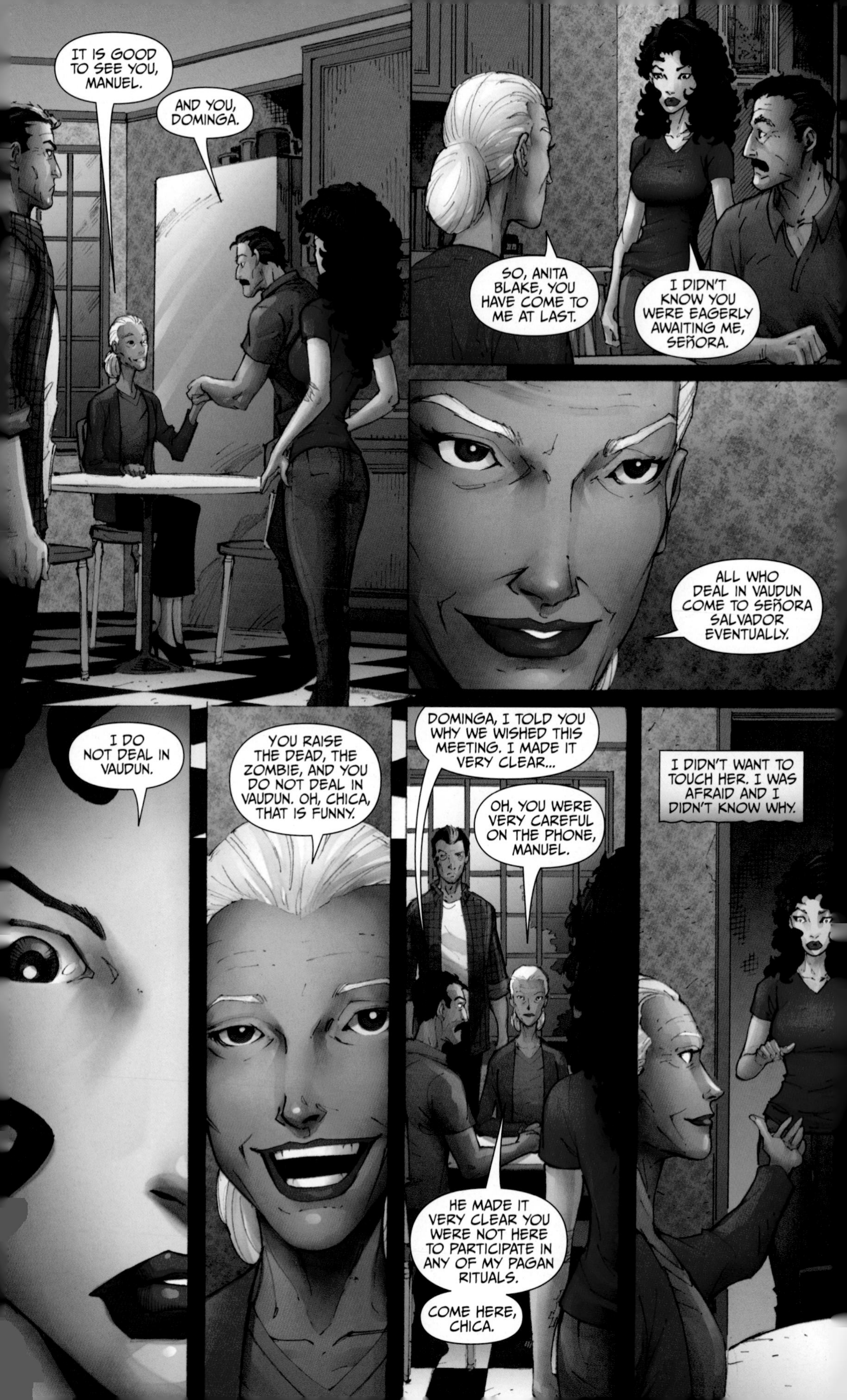
IT IS GOOD TO SEE YOU, MANUEL.
AND YOU, DOMINGA.
SO, ANITA BLAKE, YOU HAVE COME TO ME AT LAST.
I DIDN'T KNOW YOU WERE EAGERLY AWAITING ME, SEÑORA.
ALL WHO DEAL IN VAUDUN COME TO SEÑORA SALVADOR EVENTUALLY.
I DO NOT DEAL IN VAUDUN.
YOU RAISE THE DEAD, THE ZOMBIE, AND YOU DO NOT DEAL IN VAUDUN. OH, CHICA, THAT IS FUNNY.
DOMINGA, I TOLD YOU WHY WE WISHED THIS MEETING. I MADE IT VERY CLEAR...
OH, YOU WERE VERY CAREFUL ON THE PHONE, MANUEL.
HE MADE IT VERY CLEAR YOU WERE NOT HERE TO PARTICIPATE IN ANY OF MY PAGAN RITUALS.
COME HERE, CHICA.
I DIDN'T WANT TO TOUCH HER. I WAS AFRAID AND I DIDN'T KNOW WHY.

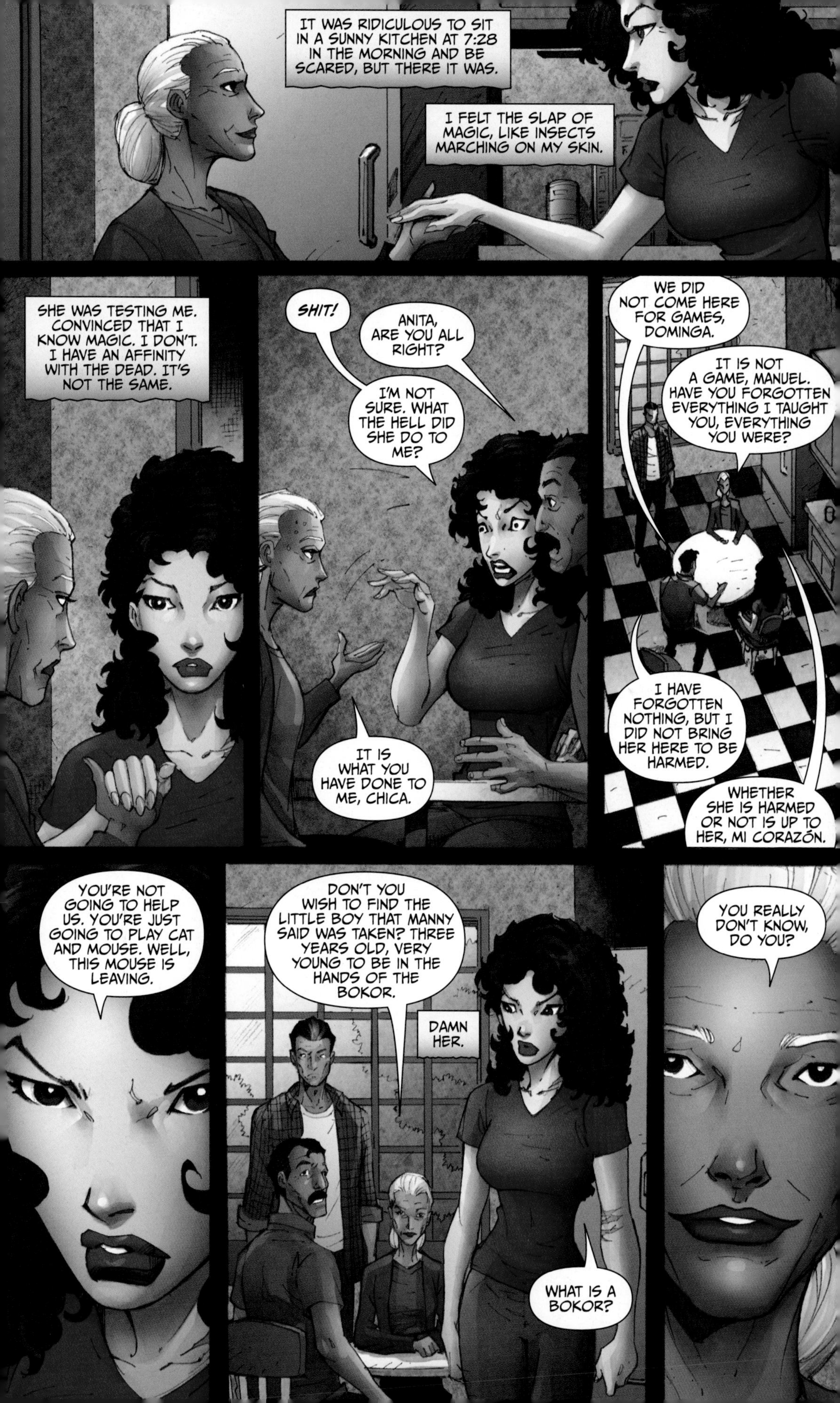
IT WAS RIDICULOUS TO SIT IN A SUNNY KITCHEN AT 7:28 IN THE MORNING AND BE SCARED, BUT THERE IT WAS.
I FELT THE SLAP OF MAGIC, LIKE INSECTS MARCHING ON MY SKIN.
SHE WAS TESTING ME. CONVINCED THAT I KNOW MAGIC. I DON'T. I HAVE AN AFFINITY WITH THE DEAD. IT'S NOT THE SAME.
SHIT!
ANITA, ARE YOU ALL RIGHT?
I'M NOT SURE. WHAT THE HELL DID SHE DO TO ME?
IT IS WHAT YOU HAVE DONE TO ME, CHICA.
WE DID NOT COME HERE FOR GAMES, DOMINGA.
IT IS NOT A GAME, MANUEL. HAVE YOU FORGOTTEN EVERYTHING I TAUGHT YOU, EVERYTHING YOU WERE?
I HAVE FORGOTTEN NOTHING, BUT I DID NOT BRING HER HERE TO BE HARMED.
WHETHER SHE IS HARMED OR NOT IS UP TO HER, MI CORAZÓN.
YOU'RE NOT GOING TO HELP US. YOU'RE JUST GOING TO PLAY CAT AND MOUSE. WELL, THIS MOUSE IS LEAVING.
DON'T YOU WISH TO FIND THE LITTLE BOY THAT MANNY SAID WAS TAKEN? THREE YEARS OLD, VERY YOUNG TO BE IN THE HANDS OF THE BOKOR.
DAMN HER.
WHAT IS A BOKOR?
YOU REALLY DON'T KNOW, DO YOU?

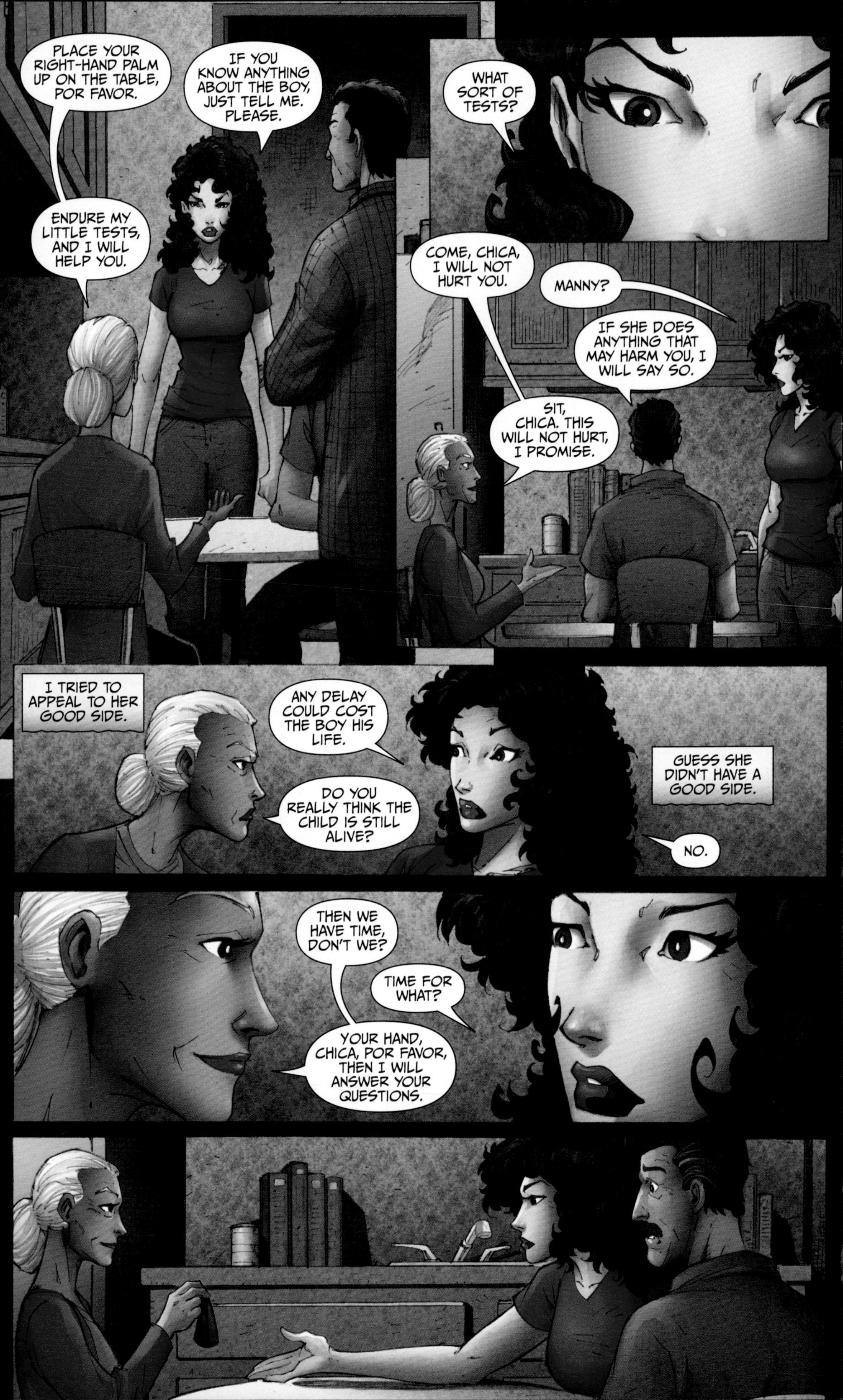
PLACE YOUR RIGHT-HAND PALM UP ON THE TABLE, POR FAVOR.
IF YOU KNOW ANYTHING ABOUT THE BOY, JUST TELL ME. PLEASE.
ENDURE MY LITTLE TESTS, AND I WILL HELP YOU.
WHAT SORT OF TESTS?
COME, CHICA, I WILL NOT HURT YOU.
MANNY?
IF SHE DOES ANYTHING THAT MAY HARM YOU, I WILL SAY SO.
SIT, CHICA. THIS WILL NOT HURT, I PROMISE.
I TRIED TO APPEAL TO HER GOOD SIDE.
ANY DELAY COULD COST THE BOY HIS LIFE.
DO YOU REALLY THINK THE CHILD IS STILL ALIVE?
GUESS SHE DIDN'T HAVE A GOOD SIDE.
NO.
THEN WE HAVE TIME, DON'T WE?
TIME FOR WHAT?
YOUR HAND, CHICA, POR FAVOR, THEN I WILL ANSWER YOUR QUESTIONS.

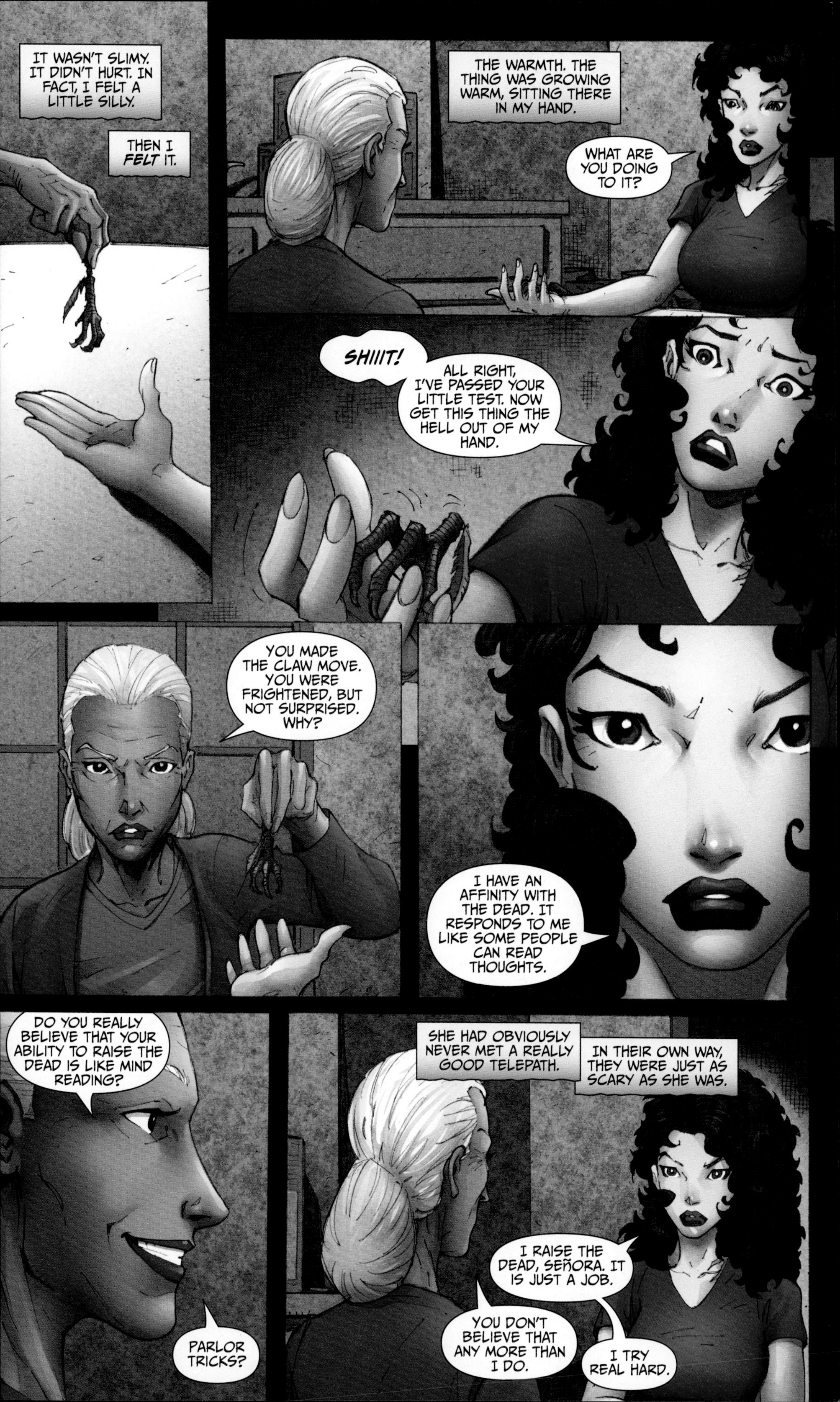

IT WASN'T SLIMY. IT DIDN'T HURT. IN FACT, I FELT A LITTLE SILLY.
THEN I *FELT* IT.
THE WARMTH. THE THING WAS GROWING WARM, SITTING THERE IN MY HAND.
WHAT ARE YOU DOING TO IT?
SHIIIT!
ALL RIGHT, I'VE PASSED YOUR LITTLE TEST. NOW GET THIS THING THE HELL OUT OF MY HAND.
YOU MADE THE CLAW MOVE. YOU WERE FRIGHTENED, BUT NOT SURPRISED. WHY?
I HAVE AN AFFINITY WITH THE DEAD. IT RESPONDS TO ME LIKE SOME PEOPLE CAN READ THOUGHTS.
DO YOU REALLY BELIEVE THAT YOUR ABILITY TO RAISE THE DEAD IS LIKE MIND READING?
PARLOR TRICKS?
SHE HAD OBVIOUSLY NEVER MET A REALLY GOOD TELEPATH.
IN THEIR OWN WAY, THEY WERE JUST AS SCARY AS SHE WAS.
I RAISE THE DEAD, SEÑORA. IT IS JUST A JOB.
YOU DON'T BELIEVE THAT ANY MORE THAN I DO.
I TRY REAL HARD.

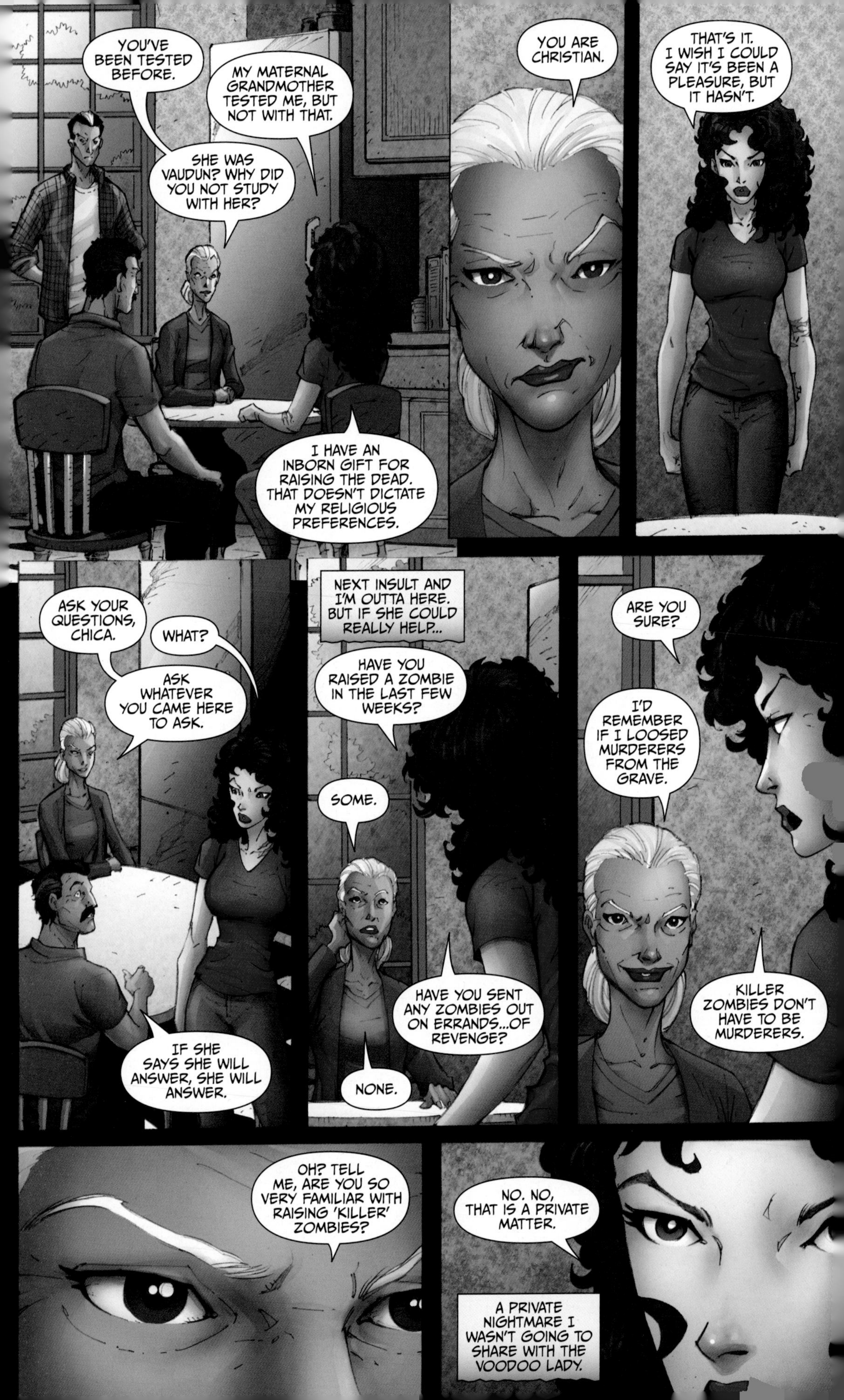
YOU'VE BEEN TESTED BEFORE.
MY MATERNAL GRANDMOTHER TESTED ME, BUT NOT WITH THAT.
SHE WAS VAUDUN? WHY DID YOU NOT STUDY WITH HER?
I HAVE AN INBORN GIFT FOR RAISING THE DEAD. THAT DOESN'T DICTATE MY RELIGIOUS PREFERENCES.
YOU ARE CHRISTIAN.
THAT'S IT. I WISH I COULD SAY IT'S BEEN A PLEASURE, BUT IT HASN'T.
ASK YOUR QUESTIONS, CHICA.
WHAT?
ASK WHATEVER YOU CAME HERE TO ASK.
IF SHE SAYS SHE WILL ANSWER, SHE WILL ANSWER.
NEXT INSULT AND I'M OUTTA HERE. BUT IF SHE COULD REALLY HELP...
HAVE YOU RAISED A ZOMBIE IN THE LAST FEW WEEKS?
SOME.
HAVE YOU SENT ANY ZOMBIES OUT ON ERRANDS...OF REVENGE?
NONE.
ARE YOU SURE?
I'D REMEMBER IF I LOOSED MURDERERS FROM THE GRAVE.
KILLER ZOMBIES DON'T HAVE TO BE MURDERERS.
OH? TELL ME, ARE YOU SO VERY FAMILIAR WITH RAISING 'KILLER' ZOMBIES?
NO. NO, THAT IS A PRIVATE MATTER.
A PRIVATE NIGHTMARE I WASN'T GOING TO SHARE WITH THE VOODOO LADY.

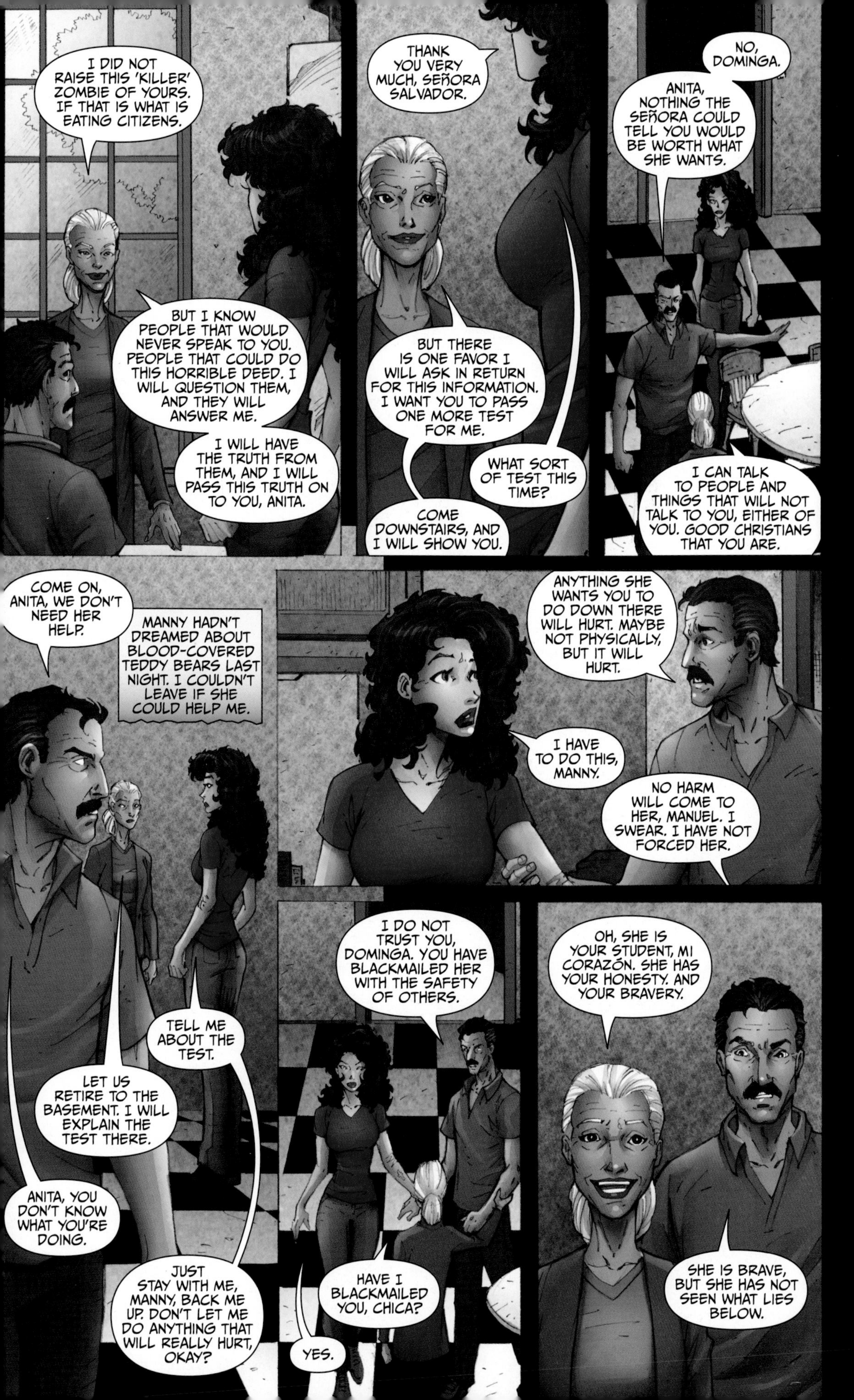

I DID NOT RAISE THIS 'KILLER' ZOMBIE OF YOURS. IF THAT IS WHAT IS EATING CITIZENS.
BUT I KNOW PEOPLE THAT WOULD NEVER SPEAK TO YOU. PEOPLE THAT COULD DO THIS HORRIBLE DEED. I WILL QUESTION THEM, AND THEY WILL ANSWER ME.
I WILL HAVE THE TRUTH FROM THEM, AND I WILL PASS THIS TRUTH ON TO YOU, ANITA.
THANK YOU VERY MUCH, SEÑORA SALVADOR.
BUT THERE IS ONE FAVOR I WILL ASK IN RETURN FOR THIS INFORMATION. I WANT YOU TO PASS ONE MORE TEST FOR ME.
WHAT SORT OF TEST THIS TIME?
COME DOWNSTAIRS, AND I WILL SHOW YOU.
NO, DOMINGA.
ANITA, NOTHING THE SEÑORA COULD TELL YOU WOULD BE WORTH WHAT SHE WANTS.
I CAN TALK TO PEOPLE AND THINGS THAT WILL NOT TALK TO YOU, EITHER OF YOU. GOOD CHRISTIANS THAT YOU ARE.
COME ON, ANITA, WE DON'T NEED HER HELP.
MANNY HADN'T DREAMED ABOUT BLOOD-COVERED TEDDY BEARS LAST NIGHT. I COULDN'T LEAVE IF SHE COULD HELP ME.
TELL ME ABOUT THE TEST.
LET US RETIRE TO THE BASEMENT. I WILL EXPLAIN THE TEST THERE.
ANITA, YOU DON'T KNOW WHAT YOU'RE DOING.
JUST STAY WITH ME, MANNY, BACK ME UP. DON'T LET ME DO ANYTHING THAT WILL REALLY HURT, OKAY?
ANYTHING SHE WANTS YOU TO DO DOWN THERE WILL HURT. MAYBE NOT PHYSICALLY, BUT IT WILL HURT.
I HAVE TO DO THIS, MANNY.
NO HARM WILL COME TO HER, MANUEL. I SWEAR. I HAVE NOT FORCED HER.
I DO NOT TRUST YOU, DOMINGA. YOU HAVE BLACKMAILED HER WITH THE SAFETY OF OTHERS.
HAVE I BLACKMAILED YOU, CHICA?
YES.
OH, SHE IS YOUR STUDENT, MI CORAZÓN. SHE HAS YOUR HONESTY. AND YOUR BRAVERY.
SHE IS BRAVE, BUT SHE HAS NOT SEEN WHAT LIES BELOW.

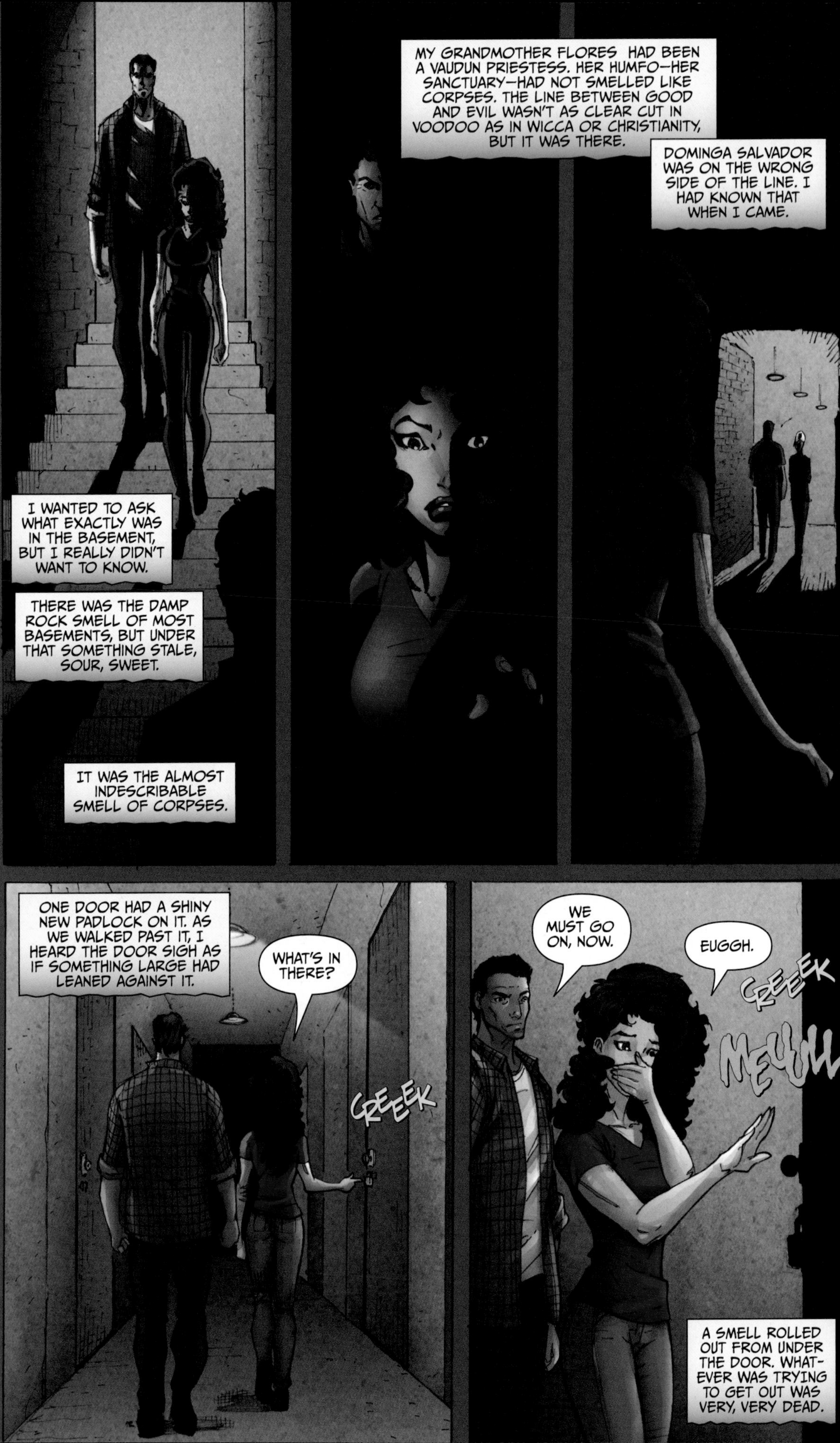
I WANTED TO ASK WHAT EXACTLY WAS IN THE BASEMENT, BUT I REALLY DIDN'T WANT TO KNOW.
THERE WAS THE DAMP ROCK SMELL OF MOST BASEMENTS, BUT UNDER THAT SOMETHING STALE, SOUR, SWEET.
IT WAS THE ALMOST INDESCRIBABLE SMELL OF CORPSES.
MY GRANDMOTHER FLORES HAD BEEN A VAUDUN PRIESTESS. HER HUMFO—HER SANCTUARY—HAD NOT SMELLED LIKE CORPSES. THE LINE BETWEEN GOOD AND EVIL WASN'T AS CLEAR CUT IN VOODOO AS IN WICCA OR CHRISTIANITY, BUT IT WAS THERE.
DOMINGA SALVADOR WAS ON THE WRONG SIDE OF THE LINE. I HAD KNOWN THAT WHEN I CAME.
ONE DOOR HAD A SHINY NEW PADLOCK ON IT. AS WE WALKED PAST IT, I HEARD THE DOOR SIGH AS IF SOMETHING LARGE HAD LEANED AGAINST IT.
WHAT'S IN THERE?
CREEEK
WE MUST GO ON, NOW.
EUGGH.
CREEEK
MEUUU
A SMELL ROLLED OUT FROM UNDER THE DOOR. WHATEVER WAS TRYING TO GET OUT WAS VERY, VERY DEAD.

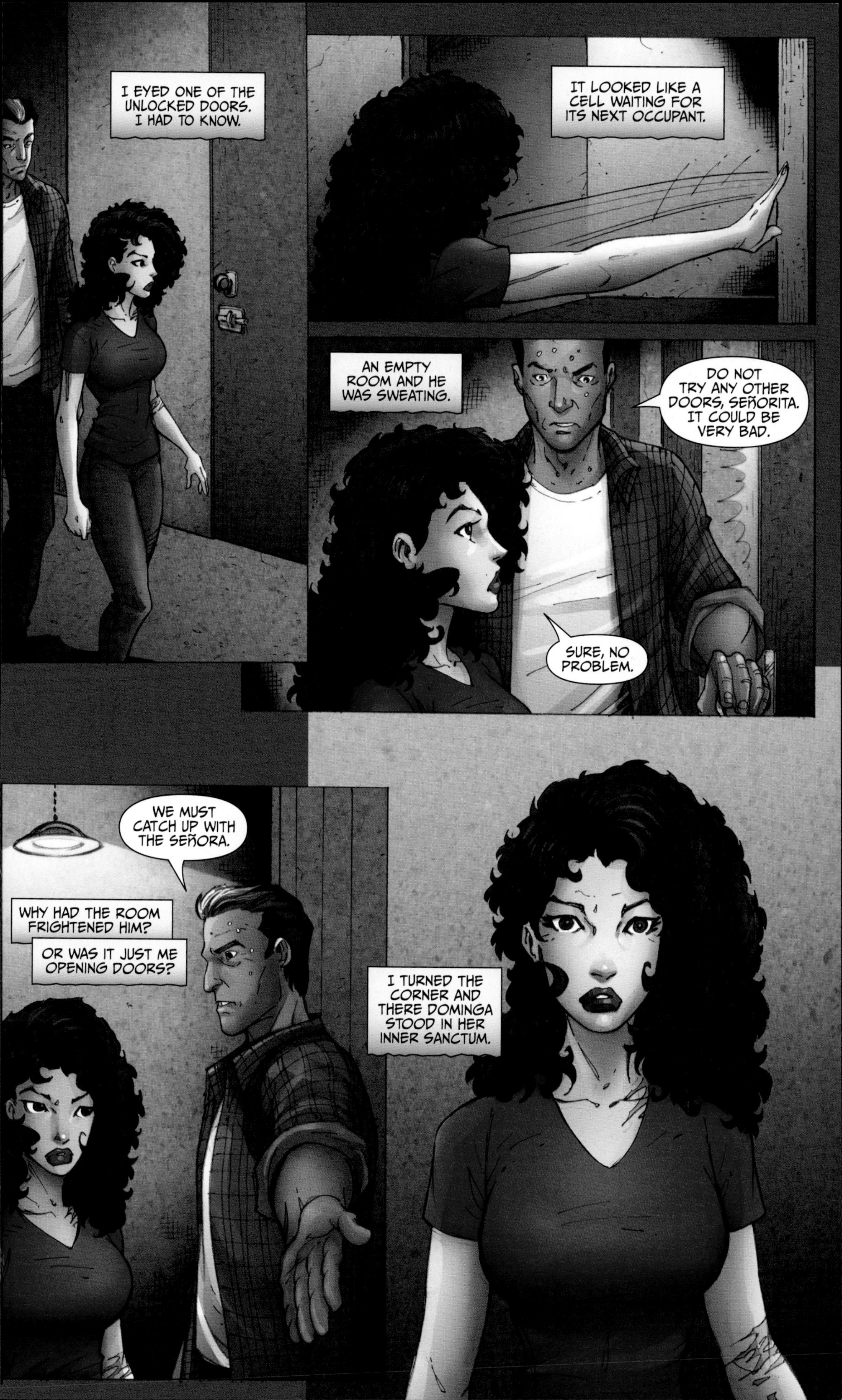
I EYED ONE OF THE UNLOCKED DOORS. I HAD TO KNOW.
IT LOOKED LIKE A CELL WAITING FOR ITS NEXT OCCUPANT.
AN EMPTY ROOM AND HE WAS SWEATING.
DO NOT TRY ANY OTHER DOORS, SEÑORITA. IT COULD BE VERY BAD.
SURE, NO PROBLEM.
WE MUST CATCH UP WITH THE SEÑORA.
WHY HAD THE ROOM FRIGHTENED HIM?
OR WAS IT JUST ME OPENING DOORS?
I TURNED THE CORNER AND THERE DOMINGA STOOD IN HER INNER SANCTUM.

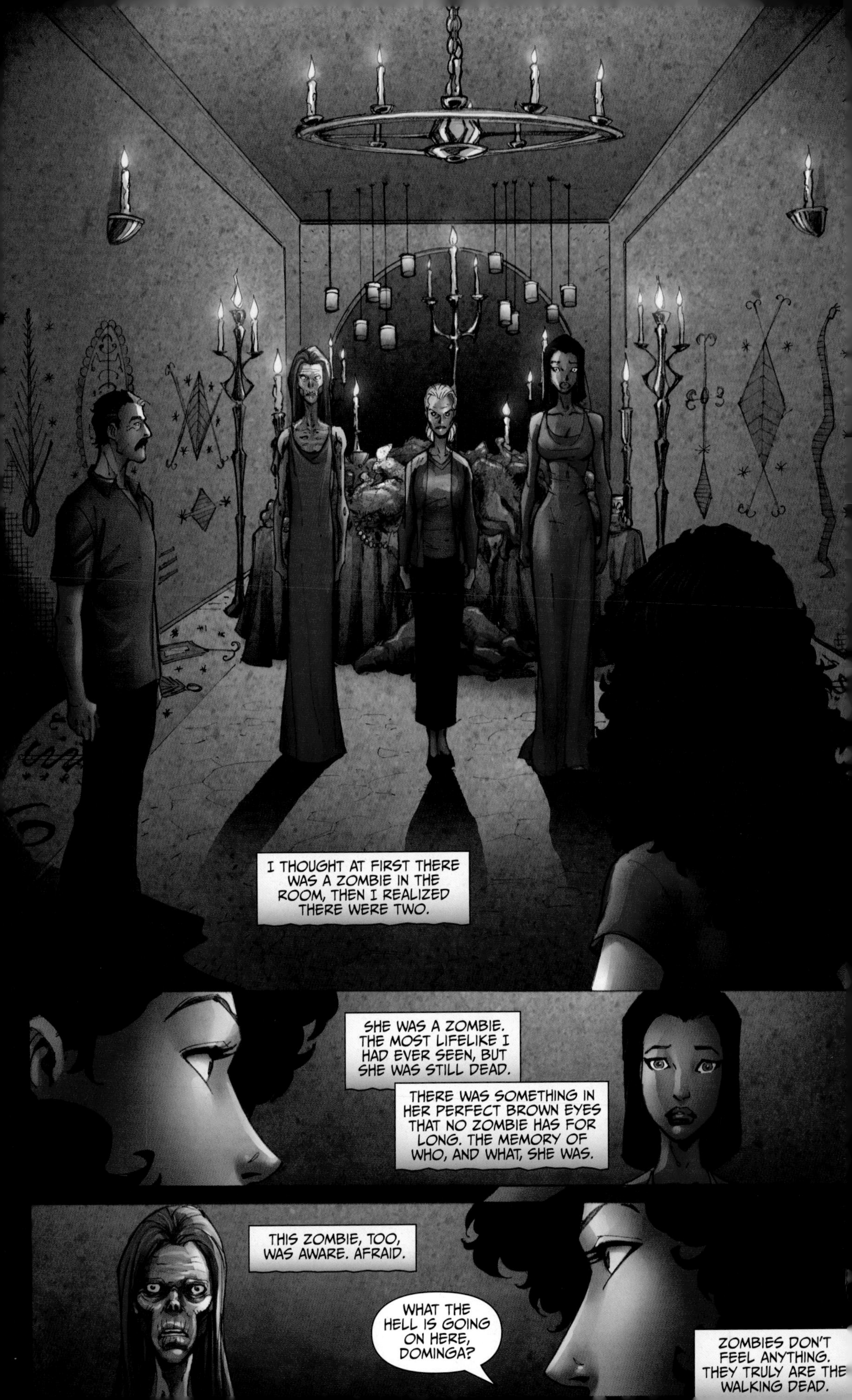
I THOUGHT AT FIRST THERE WAS A ZOMBIE IN THE ROOM, THEN I REALIZED THERE WERE TWO.
SHE WAS A ZOMBIE. THE MOST LIFELIKE I HAD EVER SEEN, BUT SHE WAS STILL DEAD.
THERE WAS SOMETHING IN HER PERFECT BROWN EYES THAT NO ZOMBIE HAS FOR LONG. THE MEMORY OF WHO, AND WHAT, SHE WAS.
THIS ZOMBIE, TOO, WAS AWARE. AFRAID.
WHAT THE HELL IS GOING ON HERE, DOMINGA?
ZOMBIES DON'T FEEL ANYTHING. THEY TRULY ARE THE WALKING DEAD.

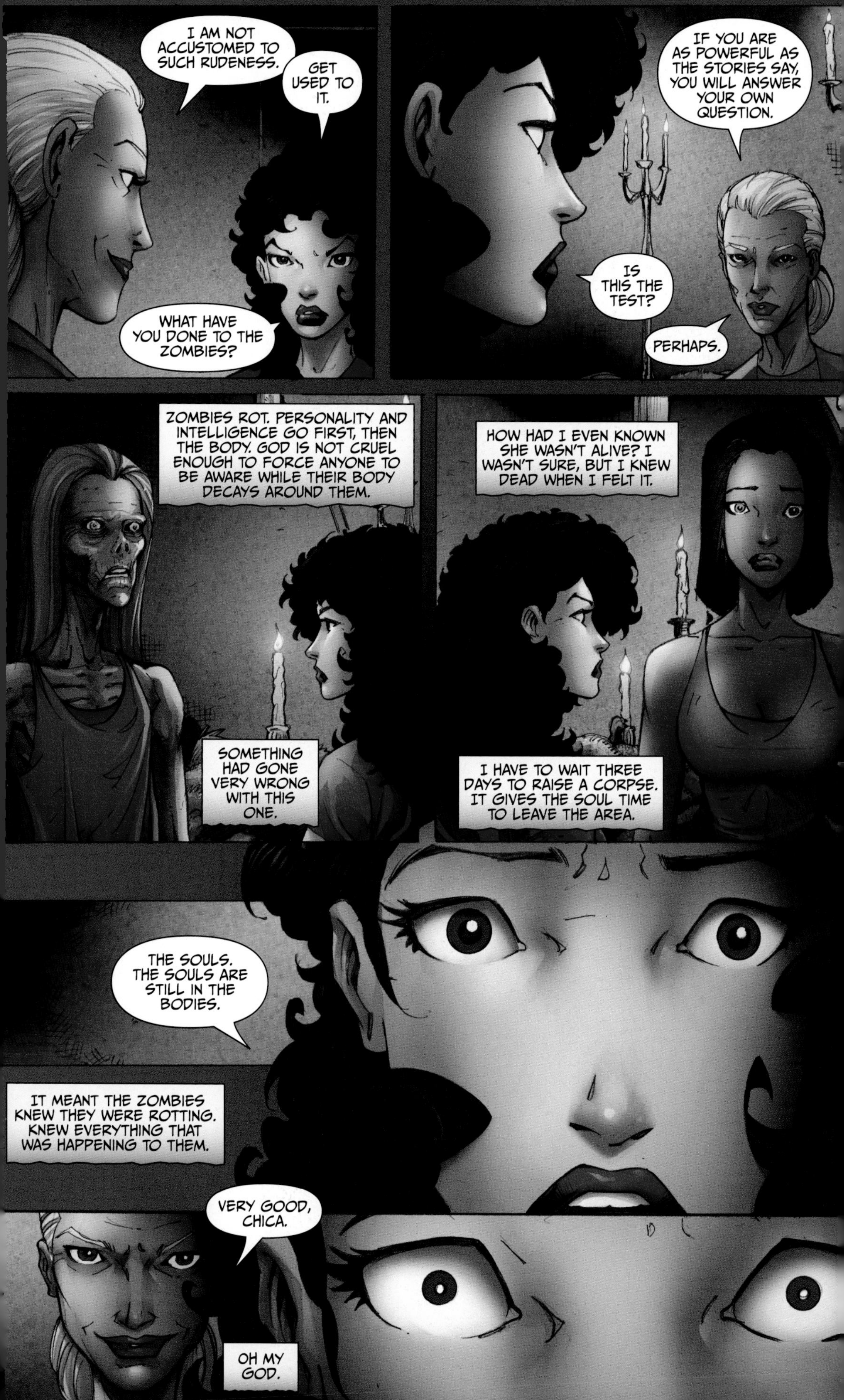
I AM NOT ACCUSTOMED TO SUCH RUDENESS.
GET USED TO IT.
WHAT HAVE YOU DONE TO THE ZOMBIES?
IF YOU ARE AS POWERFUL AS THE STORIES SAY, YOU WILL ANSWER YOUR OWN QUESTION.
IS THIS THE TEST?
PERHAPS.
ZOMBIES ROT. PERSONALITY AND INTELLIGENCE GO FIRST, THEN THE BODY. GOD IS NOT CRUEL ENOUGH TO FORCE ANYONE TO BE AWARE WHILE THEIR BODY DECAYS AROUND THEM.
SOMETHING HAD GONE VERY WRONG WITH THIS ONE.
HOW HAD I EVEN KNOWN SHE WASN'T ALIVE? I WASN'T SURE, BUT I KNEW DEAD WHEN I FELT IT.
I HAVE TO WAIT THREE DAYS TO RAISE A CORPSE. IT GIVES THE SOUL TIME TO LEAVE THE AREA.
THE SOULS. THE SOULS ARE STILL IN THE BODIES.
IT MEANT THE ZOMBIES KNEW THEY WERE ROTTING. KNEW EVERYTHING THAT WAS HAPPENING TO THEM.
VERY GOOD, CHICA.
OH MY GOD.

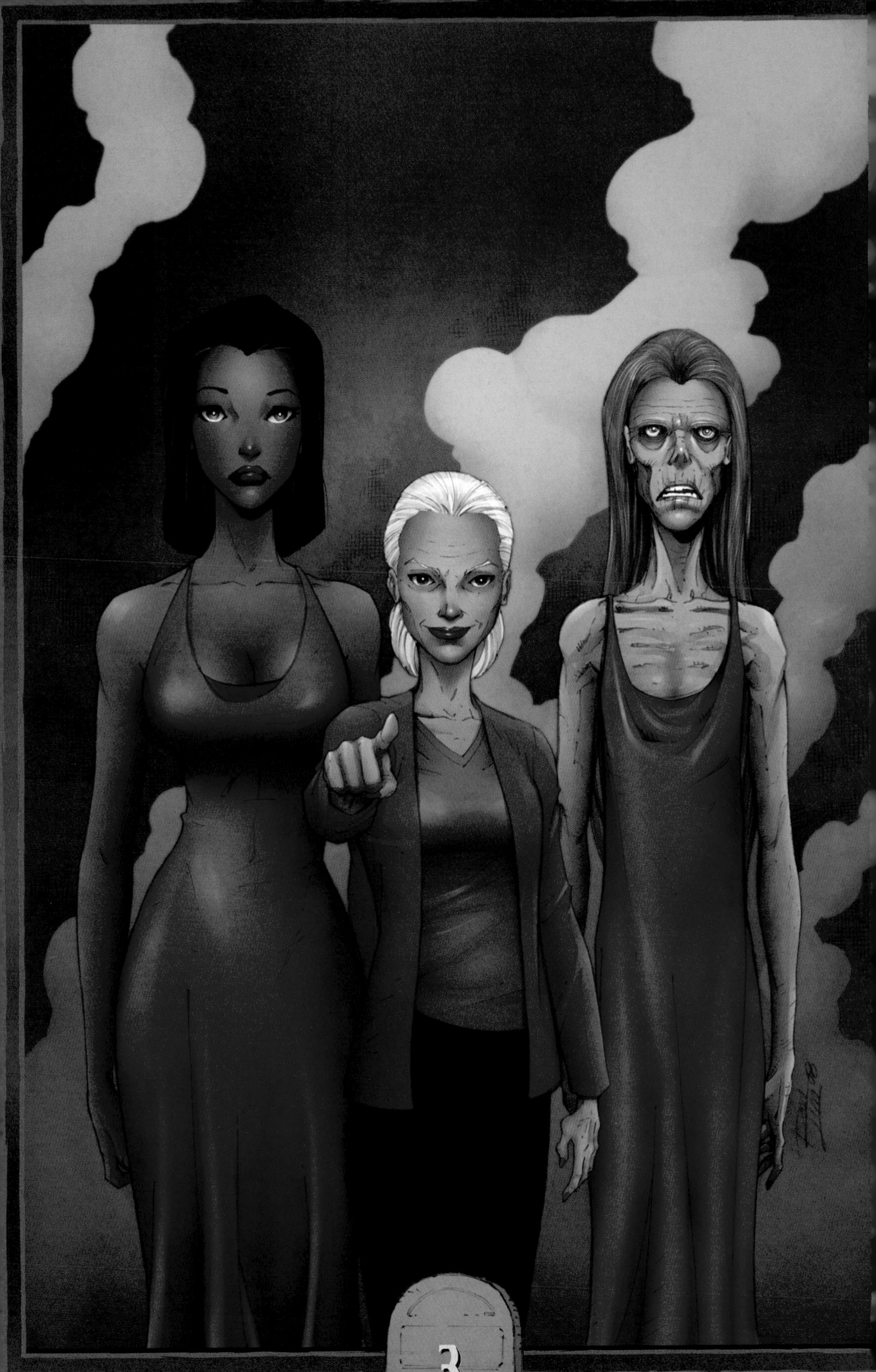
3

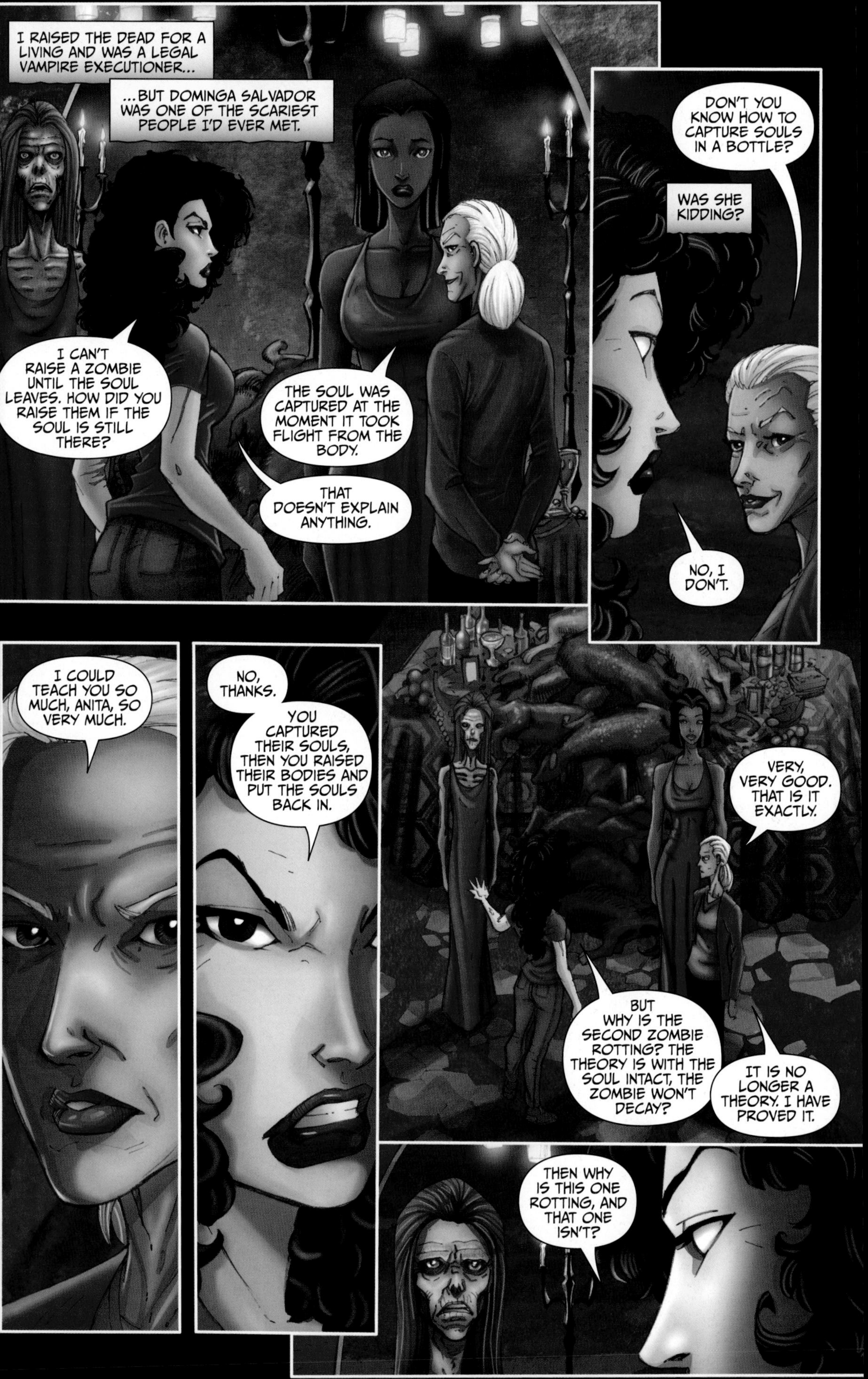
I RAISED THE DEAD FOR A LIVING AND WAS A LEGAL VAMPIRE EXECUTIONER...
...BUT DOMINGA SALVADOR WAS ONE OF THE SCARIEST PEOPLE I'D EVER MET.
I CAN'T RAISE A ZOMBIE UNTIL THE SOUL LEAVES. HOW DID YOU RAISE THEM IF THE SOUL IS STILL THERE?
THE SOUL WAS CAPTURED AT THE MOMENT IT TOOK FLIGHT FROM THE BODY.
THAT DOESN'T EXPLAIN ANYTHING.
DON'T YOU KNOW HOW TO CAPTURE SOULS IN A BOTTLE?
WAS SHE KIDDING?
NO, I DON'T.
I COULD TEACH YOU SO MUCH, ANITA, SO VERY MUCH.
NO, THANKS.
YOU CAPTURED THEIR SOULS, THEN YOU RAISED THEIR BODIES AND PUT THE SOULS BACK IN.
VERY, VERY GOOD. THAT IS IT EXACTLY.
BUT WHY IS THE SECOND ZOMBIE ROTTING? THE THEORY IS WITH THE SOUL INTACT, THE ZOMBIE WON'T DECAY?
IT IS NO LONGER A THEORY. I HAVE PROVED IT.
THEN WHY IS THIS ONE ROTTING, AND THAT ONE ISN'T?

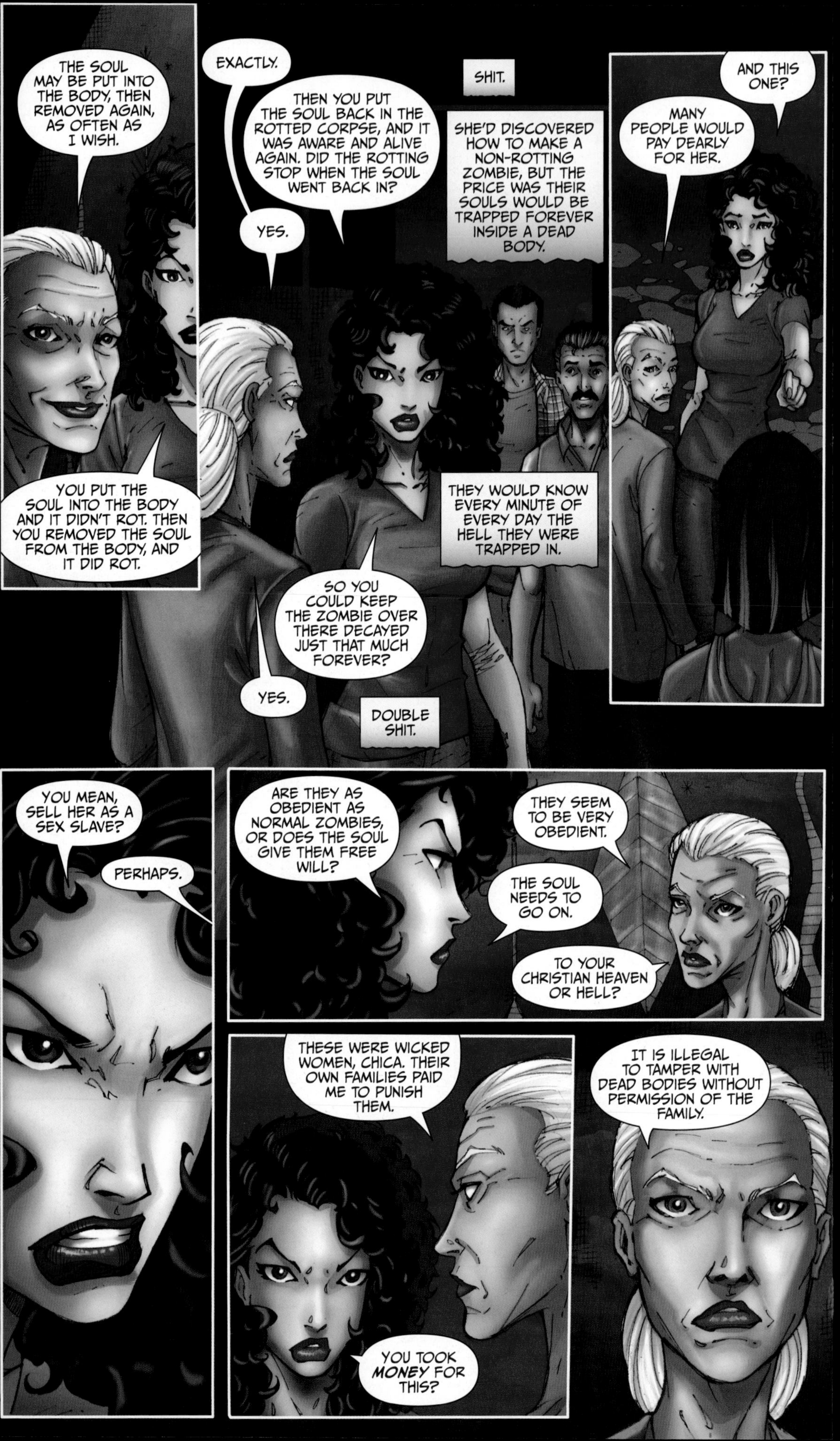

THE SOUL MAY BE PUT INTO THE BODY, THEN REMOVED AGAIN, AS OFTEN AS I WISH.
YOU PUT THE SOUL INTO THE BODY AND IT DIDN'T ROT. THEN YOU REMOVED THE SOUL FROM THE BODY, AND IT DID ROT.
EXACTLY.
THEN YOU PUT THE SOUL BACK IN THE ROTTED CORPSE, AND IT WAS AWARE AND ALIVE AGAIN. DID THE ROTTING STOP WHEN THE SOUL WENT BACK IN?
YES.
SHIT.
SHE'D DISCOVERED HOW TO MAKE A NON-ROTTING ZOMBIE, BUT THE PRICE WAS THEIR SOULS WOULD BE TRAPPED FOREVER INSIDE A DEAD BODY.
THEY WOULD KNOW EVERY MINUTE OF EVERY DAY THE HELL THEY WERE TRAPPED IN.
SO YOU COULD KEEP THE ZOMBIE OVER THERE DECAYED JUST THAT MUCH FOREVER?
YES.
DOUBLE SHIT.
AND THIS ONE?
MANY PEOPLE WOULD PAY DEARLY FOR HER.
YOU MEAN, SELL HER AS A SEX SLAVE?
PERHAPS.
ARE THEY AS OBEDIENT AS NORMAL ZOMBIES, OR DOES THE SOUL GIVE THEM FREE WILL?
THEY SEEM TO BE VERY OBEDIENT.
THE SOUL NEEDS TO GO ON.
TO YOUR CHRISTIAN HEAVEN OR HELL?
THESE WERE WICKED WOMEN, CHICA. THEIR OWN FAMILIES PAID ME TO PUNISH THEM.
YOU TOOK MONEY FOR THIS?
IT IS ILLEGAL TO TAMPER WITH DEAD BODIES WITHOUT PERMISSION OF THE FAMILY.

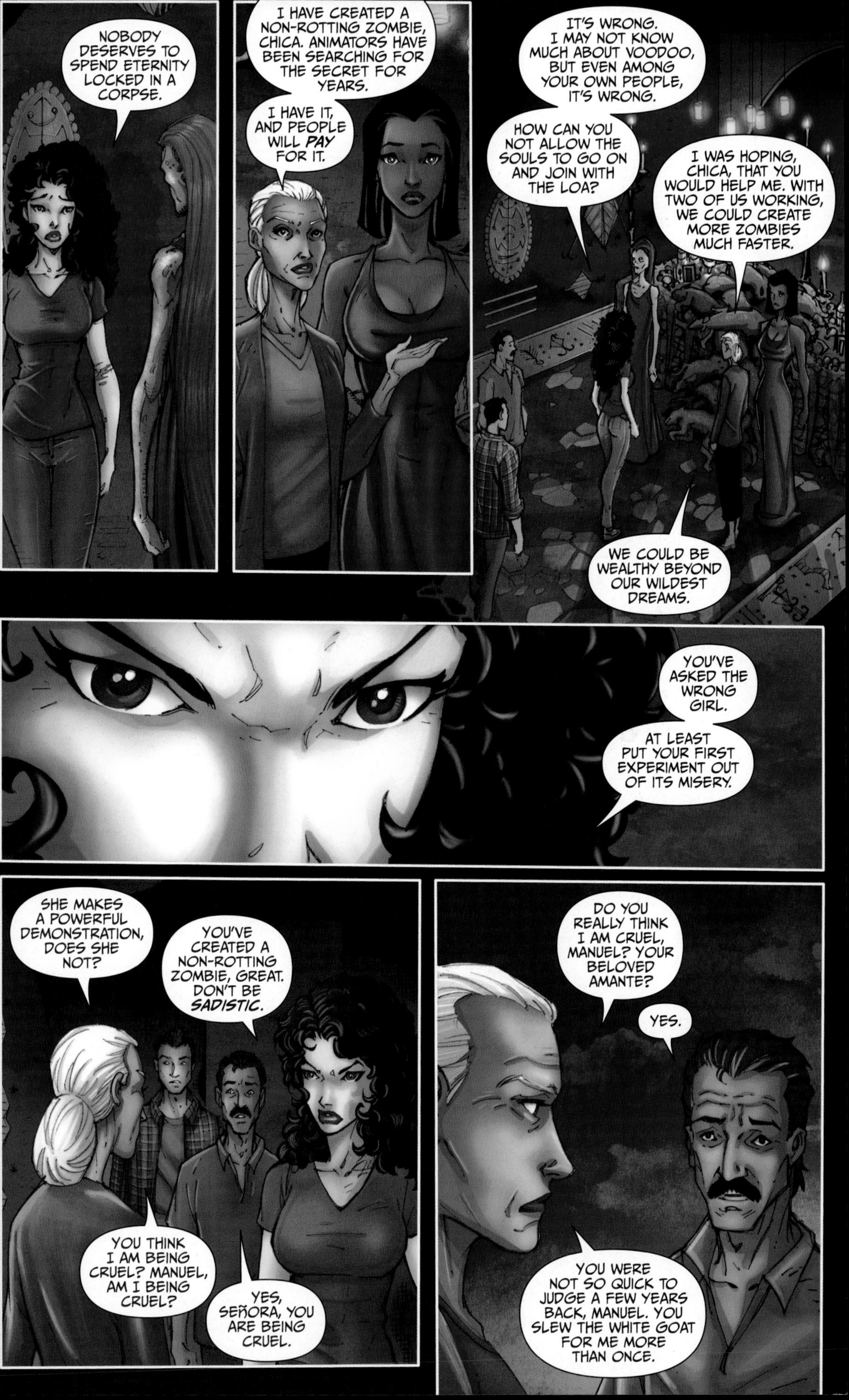
NOBODY DESERVES TO SPEND ETERNITY LOCKED IN A CORPSE.
I HAVE CREATED A NON-ROTTING ZOMBIE, CHICA. ANIMATORS HAVE BEEN SEARCHING FOR THE SECRET FOR YEARS.
I HAVE IT, AND PEOPLE WILL *PAY* FOR IT.
IT'S WRONG. I MAY NOT KNOW MUCH ABOUT VOODOO, BUT EVEN AMONG YOUR OWN PEOPLE, IT'S WRONG.
HOW CAN YOU NOT ALLOW THE SOULS TO GO ON AND JOIN WITH THE LOA?
I WAS HOPING, CHICA, THAT YOU WOULD HELP ME. WITH TWO OF US WORKING, WE COULD CREATE MORE ZOMBIES MUCH FASTER.
WE COULD BE WEALTHY BEYOND OUR WILDEST DREAMS.
YOU'VE ASKED THE WRONG GIRL.
AT LEAST PUT YOUR FIRST EXPERIMENT OUT OF ITS MISERY.
SHE MAKES A POWERFUL DEMONSTRATION, DOES SHE NOT?
YOU'VE CREATED A NON-ROTTING ZOMBIE, GREAT. DON'T BE *SADISTIC*.
YOU THINK I AM BEING CRUEL? MANUEL, AM I BEING CRUEL?
YES, SEÑORA, YOU ARE BEING CRUEL.
DO YOU REALLY THINK I AM CRUEL, MANUEL? YOUR BELOVED AMANTE?
YES.
YOU WERE NOT SO QUICK TO JUDGE A FEW YEARS BACK, MANUEL. YOU SLEW THE WHITE GOAT FOR ME MORE THAN ONCE.

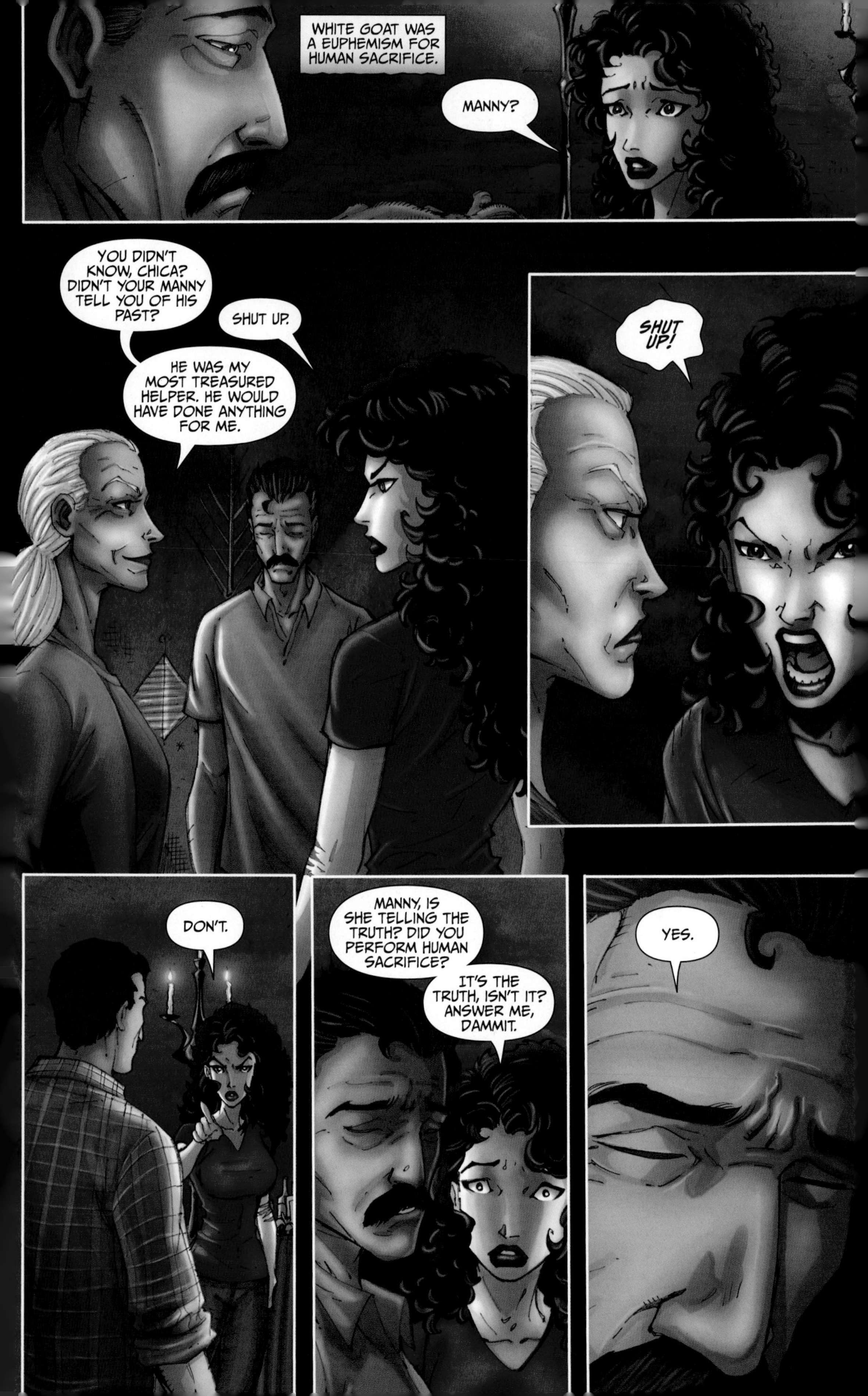
WHITE GOAT WAS A EUPHEMISM FOR HUMAN SACRIFICE.
MANNY?
YOU DIDN'T KNOW, CHICA? DIDN'T YOUR MANNY TELL YOU OF HIS PAST?
SHUT UP.
HE WAS MY MOST TREASURED HELPER. HE WOULD HAVE DONE ANYTHING FOR ME.
SHUT UP!
DON'T.
MANNY, IS SHE TELLING THE TRUTH? DID YOU PERFORM HUMAN SACRIFICE?
IT'S THE TRUTH, ISN'T IT? ANSWER ME, DAMMIT.
YES.

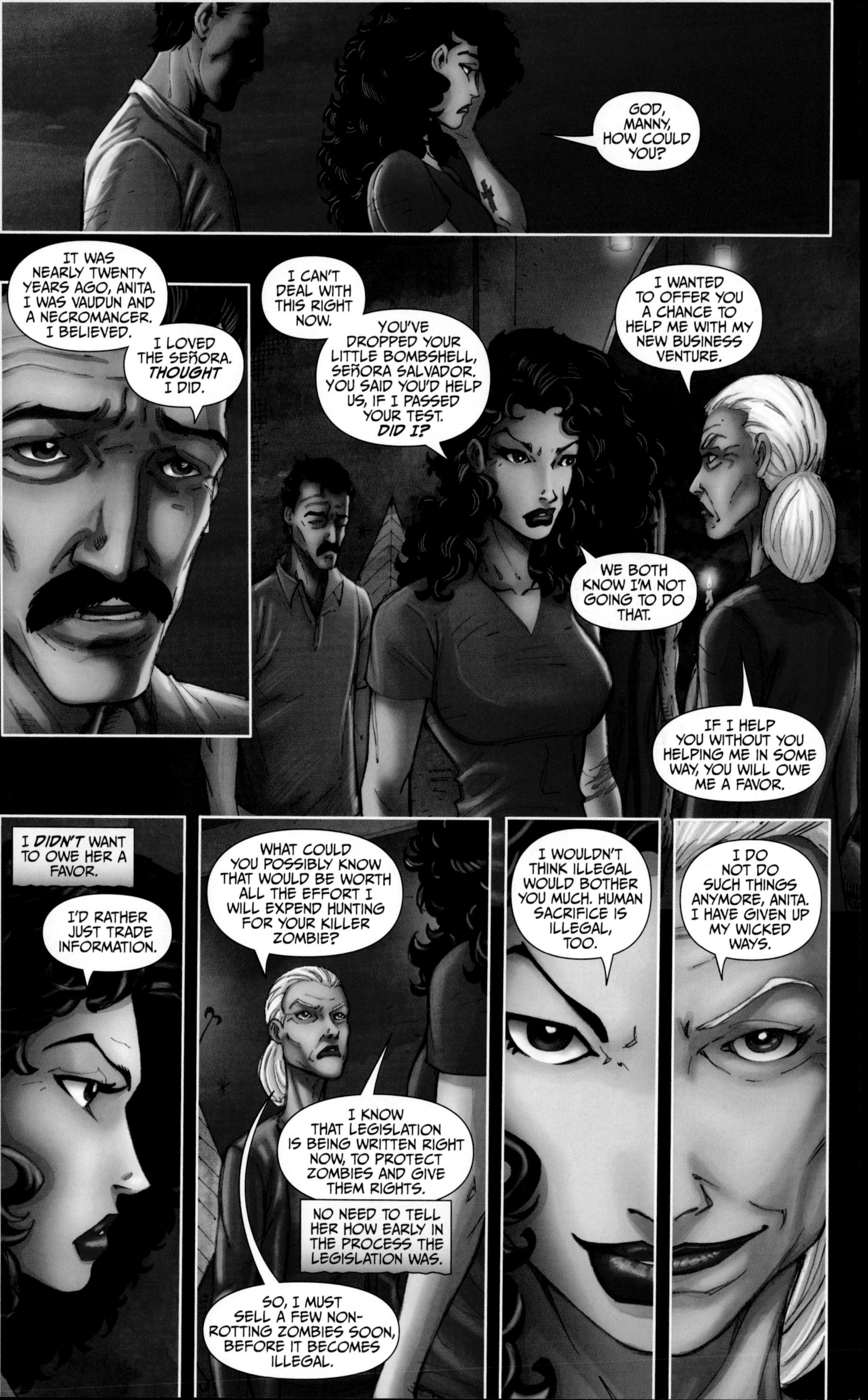
GOD, MANNY, HOW COULD YOU?
IT WAS NEARLY TWENTY YEARS AGO, ANITA. I WAS VAUDUN AND A NECROMANCER. I BELIEVED.
I LOVED THE SEÑORA. *THOUGHT* I DID.
I CAN'T DEAL WITH THIS RIGHT NOW.
YOU'VE DROPPED YOUR LITTLE BOMBSHELL, SEÑORA SALVADOR. YOU SAID YOU'D HELP US, IF I PASSED YOUR TEST. *DID I?*
I WANTED TO OFFER YOU A CHANCE TO HELP ME WITH MY NEW BUSINESS VENTURE.
WE BOTH KNOW I'M NOT GOING TO DO THAT.
IF I HELP YOU WITHOUT YOU HELPING ME IN SOME WAY, YOU WILL OWE ME A FAVOR.
I *DIDN'T* WANT TO OWE HER A FAVOR.
I'D RATHER JUST TRADE INFORMATION.
WHAT COULD YOU POSSIBLY KNOW THAT WOULD BE WORTH ALL THE EFFORT I WILL EXPEND HUNTING FOR YOUR KILLER ZOMBIE?
I KNOW THAT LEGISLATION IS BEING WRITTEN RIGHT NOW, TO PROTECT ZOMBIES AND GIVE THEM RIGHTS.
NO NEED TO TELL HER HOW EARLY IN THE PROCESS THE LEGISLATION WAS.
SO, I MUST SELL A FEW NON-ROTTING ZOMBIES SOON, BEFORE IT BECOMES ILLEGAL.
I WOULDN'T THINK ILLEGAL WOULD BOTHER YOU MUCH. HUMAN SACRIFICE IS ILLEGAL, TOO.
I DO NOT DO SUCH THINGS ANYMORE, ANITA. I HAVE GIVEN UP MY WICKED WAYS.

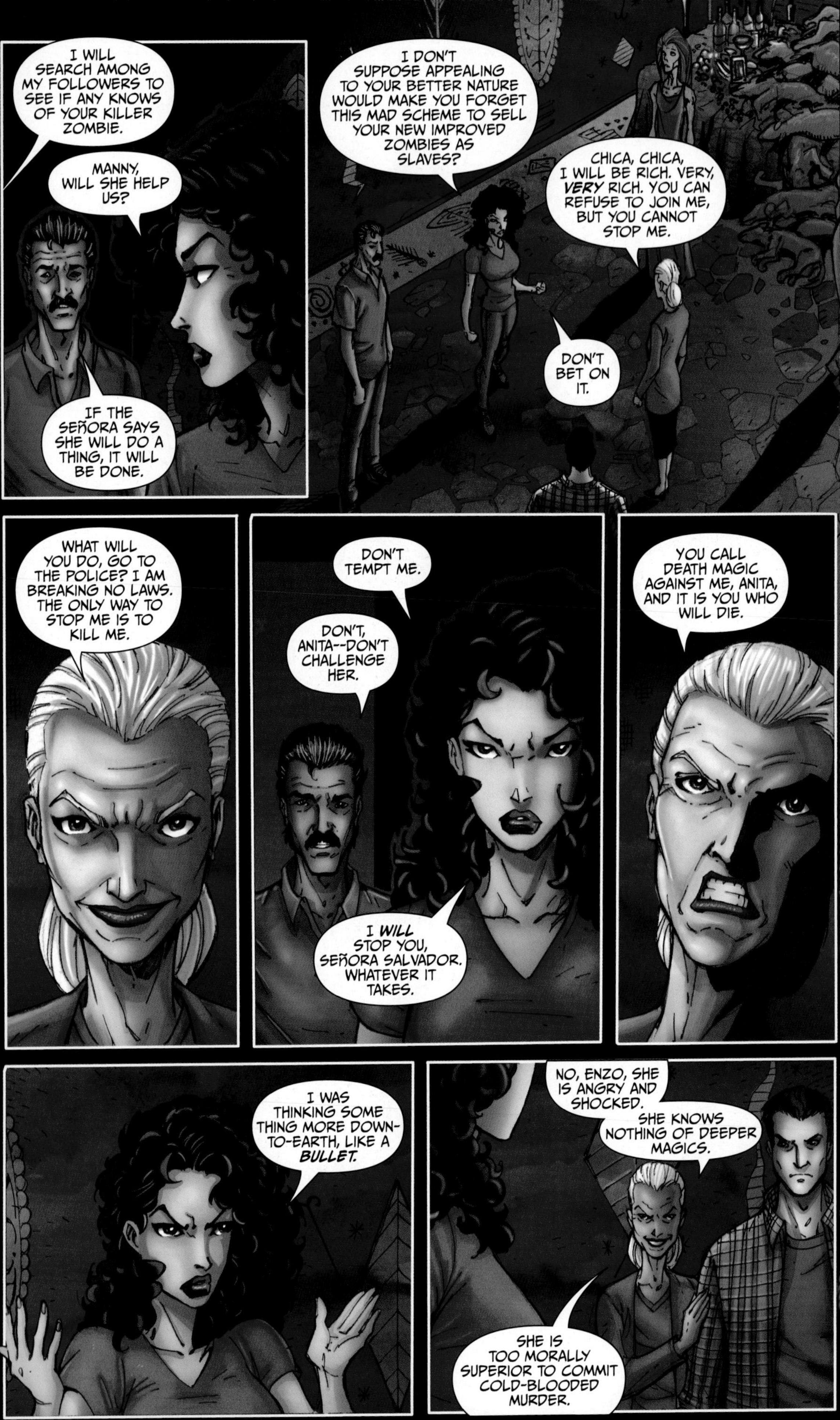
I WILL SEARCH AMONG MY FOLLOWERS TO SEE IF ANY KNOWS OF YOUR KILLER ZOMBIE.
MANNY, WILL SHE HELP US?
IF THE SEÑORA SAYS SHE WILL DO A THING, IT WILL BE DONE.
I DON'T SUPPOSE APPEALING TO YOUR BETTER NATURE WOULD MAKE YOU FORGET THIS MAD SCHEME TO SELL YOUR NEW IMPROVED ZOMBIES AS SLAVES?
CHICA, CHICA, I WILL BE RICH. VERY, ***VERY*** RICH. YOU CAN REFUSE TO JOIN ME, BUT YOU CANNOT STOP ME.
DON'T BET ON IT.
WHAT WILL YOU DO, GO TO THE POLICE? I AM BREAKING NO LAWS. THE ONLY WAY TO STOP ME IS TO KILL ME.
DON'T TEMPT ME.
DON'T, ANITA--DON'T CHALLENGE HER.
I ***WILL*** STOP YOU, SEÑORA SALVADOR. WHATEVER IT TAKES.
YOU CALL DEATH MAGIC AGAINST ME, ANITA, AND IT IS YOU WHO WILL DIE.
I WAS THINKING SOME THING MORE DOWN-TO-EARTH, LIKE A ***BULLET.***
NO, ENZO, SHE IS ANGRY AND SHOCKED.
SHE KNOWS NOTHING OF DEEPER MAGICS.
SHE IS TOO MORALLY SUPERIOR TO COMMIT COLD-BLOODED MURDER.

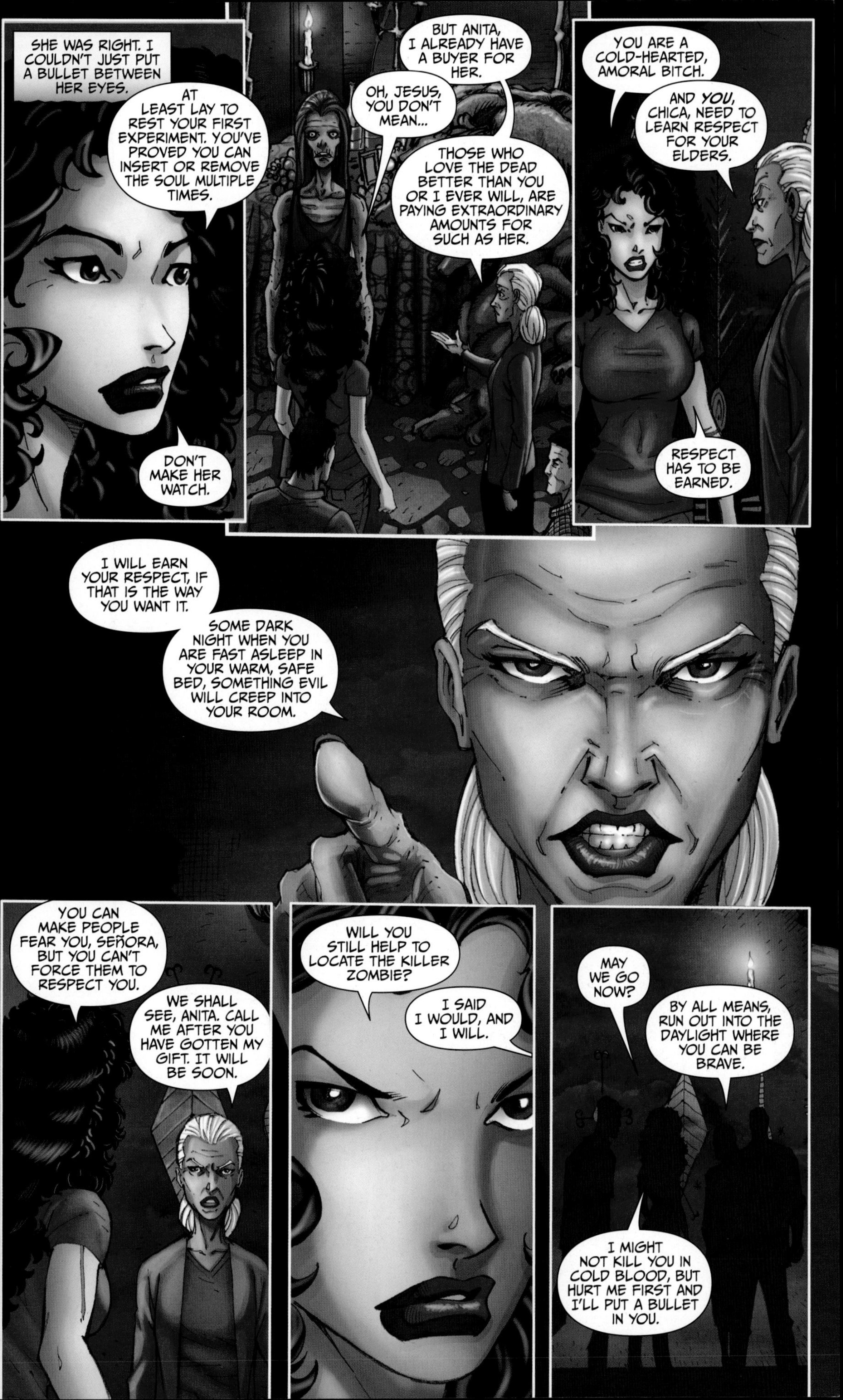

SHE WAS RIGHT. I COULDN'T JUST PUT A BULLET BETWEEN HER EYES.
AT LEAST LAY TO REST YOUR FIRST EXPERIMENT. YOU'VE PROVED YOU CAN INSERT OR REMOVE THE SOUL MULTIPLE TIMES.
DON'T MAKE HER WATCH.
BUT ANITA, I ALREADY HAVE A BUYER FOR HER.
OH, JESUS, YOU DON'T MEAN...
THOSE WHO LOVE THE DEAD BETTER THAN YOU OR I EVER WILL, ARE PAYING EXTRAORDINARY AMOUNTS FOR SUCH AS HER.
YOU ARE A COLD-HEARTED, AMORAL BITCH.
AND *YOU*, CHICA, NEED TO LEARN RESPECT FOR YOUR ELDERS.
RESPECT HAS TO BE EARNED.
I WILL EARN YOUR RESPECT, IF THAT IS THE WAY YOU WANT IT.
SOME DARK NIGHT WHEN YOU ARE FAST ASLEEP IN YOUR WARM, SAFE BED, SOMETHING EVIL WILL CREEP INTO YOUR ROOM.
YOU CAN MAKE PEOPLE FEAR YOU, SEÑORA, BUT YOU CAN'T FORCE THEM TO RESPECT YOU.
WE SHALL SEE, ANITA. CALL ME AFTER YOU HAVE GOTTEN MY GIFT. IT WILL BE SOON.
WILL YOU STILL HELP TO LOCATE THE KILLER ZOMBIE?
I SAID I WOULD, AND I WILL.
MAY WE GO NOW?
BY ALL MEANS, RUN OUT INTO THE DAYLIGHT WHERE YOU CAN BE BRAVE.
I MIGHT NOT KILL YOU IN COLD BLOOD, BUT HURT ME FIRST AND I'LL PUT A BULLET IN YOU.

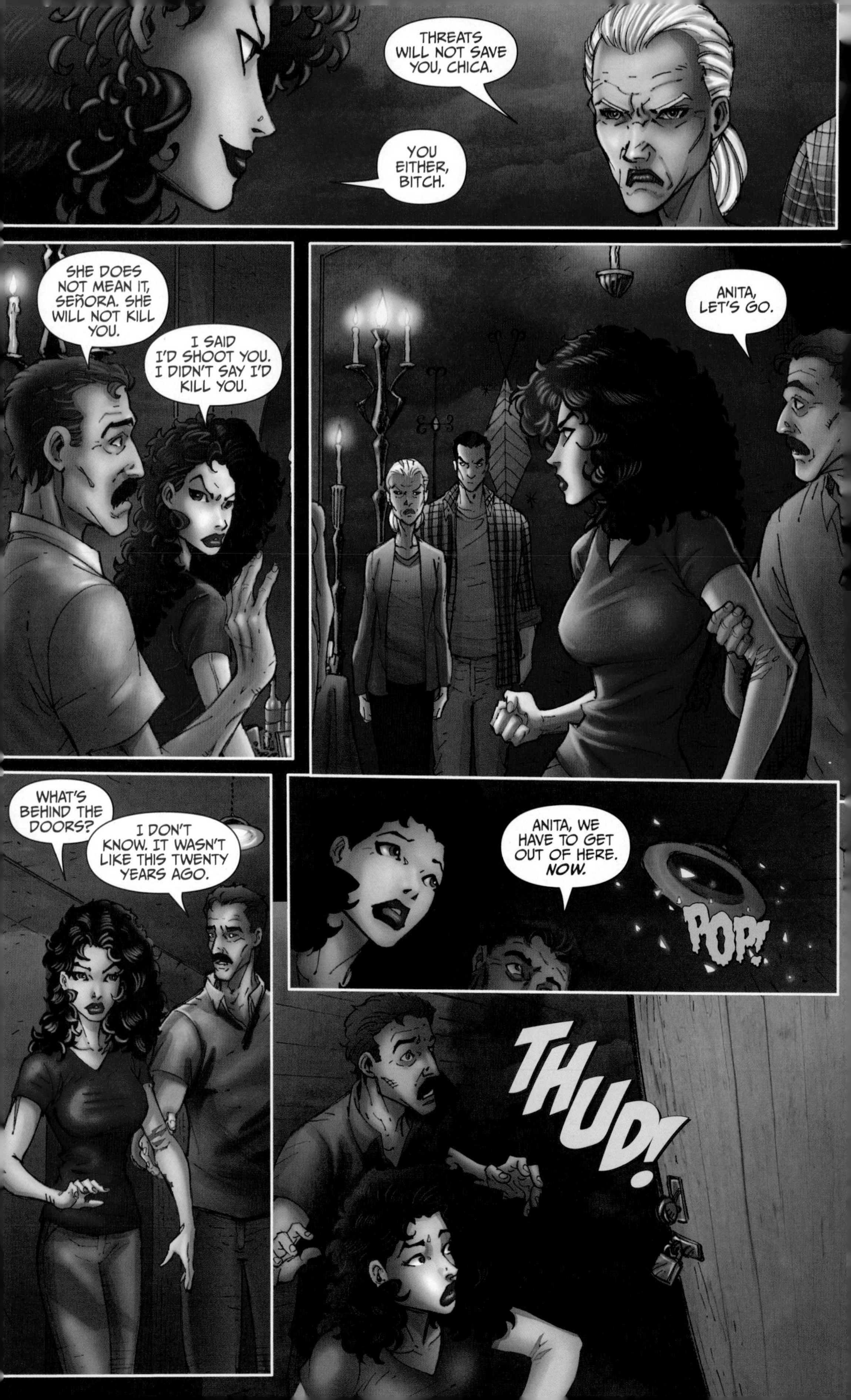

THREATS WILL NOT SAVE YOU, CHICA.
YOU EITHER, BITCH.
SHE DOES NOT MEAN IT, SEñORA. SHE WILL NOT KILL YOU.
I SAID I'D SHOOT YOU. I DIDN'T SAY I'D KILL YOU.
ANITA, LET'S GO.
WHAT'S BEHIND THE DOORS?
I DON'T KNOW. IT WASN'T LIKE THIS TWENTY YEARS AGO.
ANITA, WE HAVE TO GET OUT OF HERE. *NOW.*
POP!
THUD!

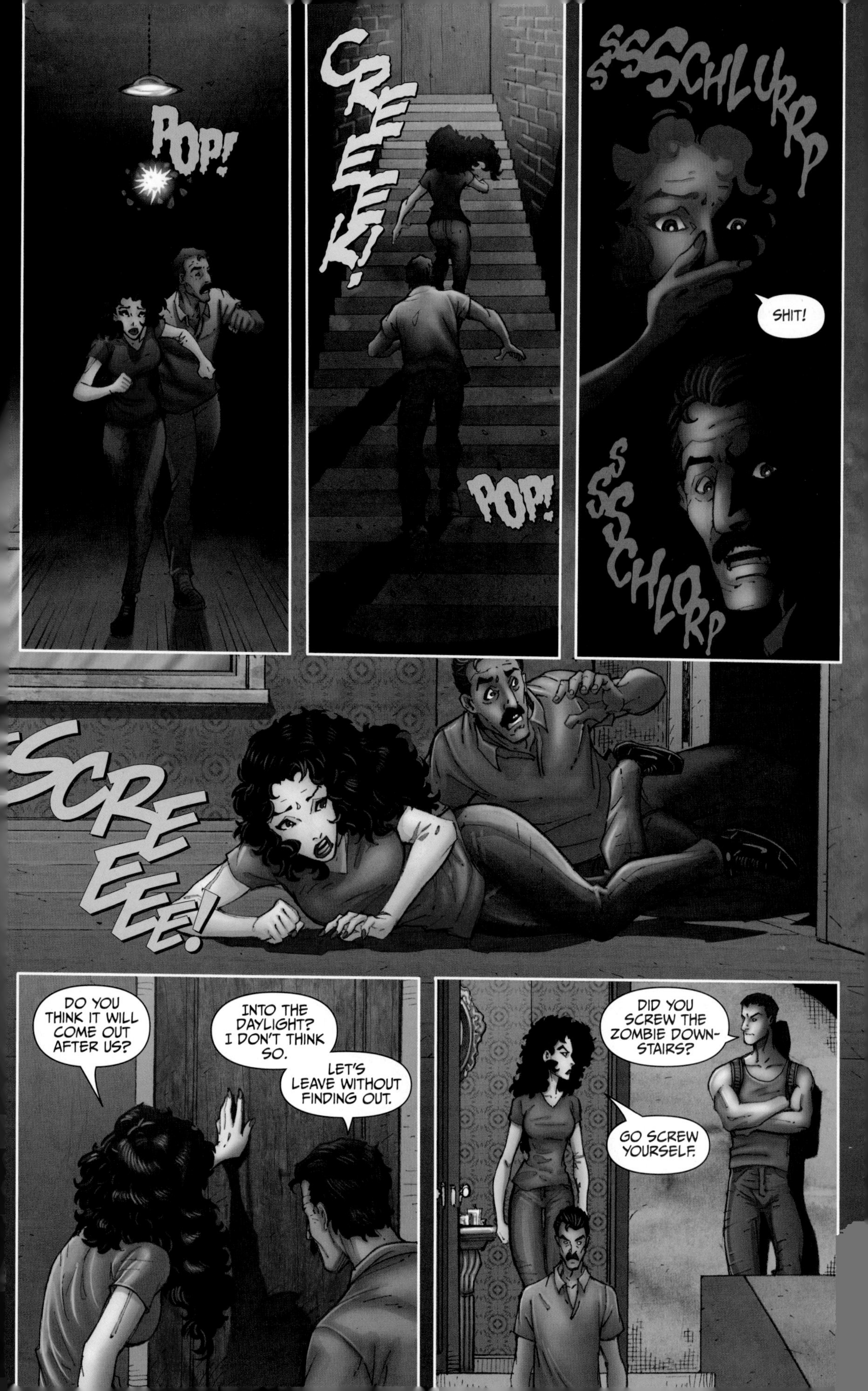
POP!
CREEEK!
POP!
SSSSCHLURRP
SHIT!
SSSSCHLORP
SCREEEE!
DO YOU THINK IT WILL COME OUT AFTER US?
INTO THE DAYLIGHT? I DON'T THINK SO.
LET'S LEAVE WITHOUT FINDING OUT.
DID YOU SCREW THE ZOMBIE DOWN-STAIRS?
GO SCREW YOURSELF.

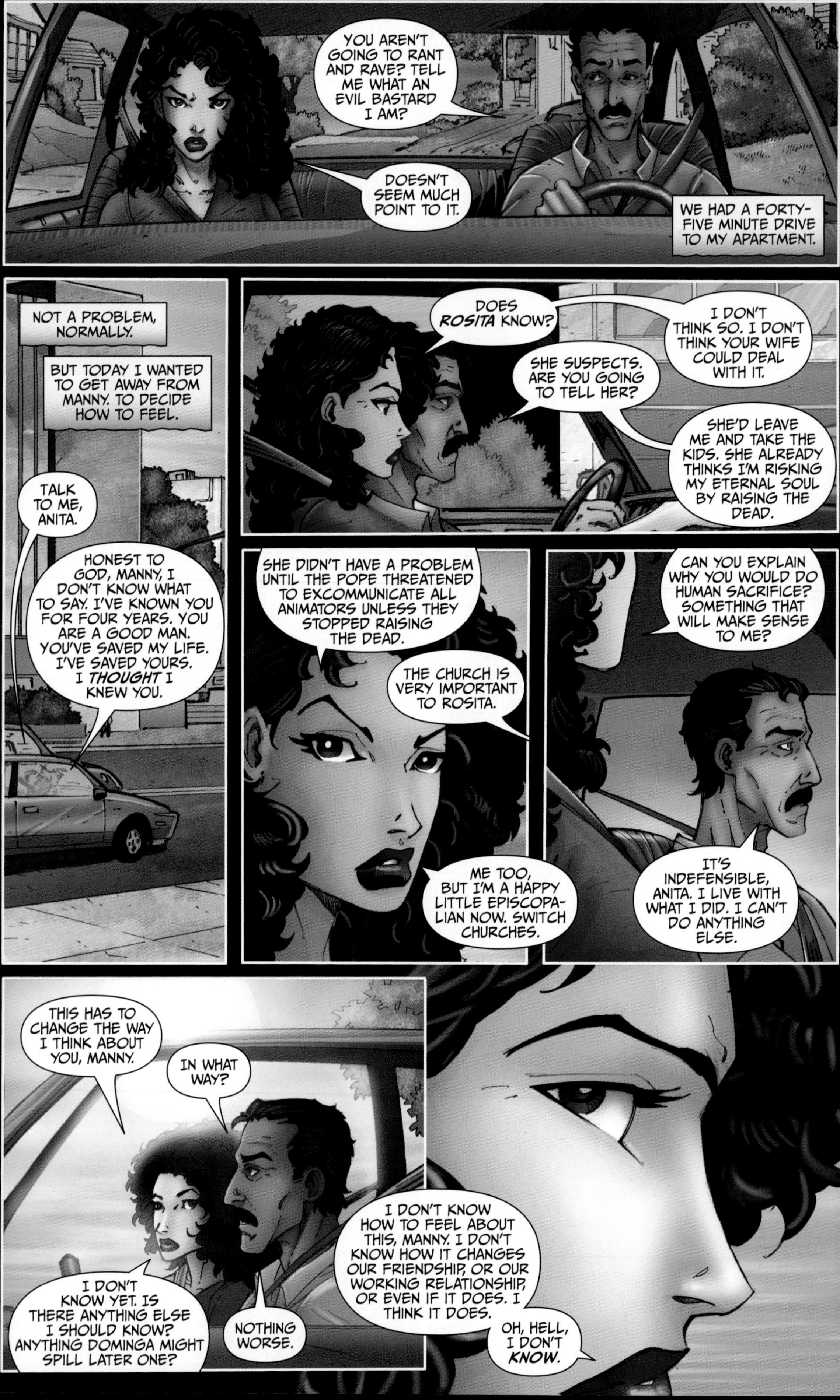
YOU AREN'T GOING TO RANT AND RAVE? TELL ME WHAT AN EVIL BASTARD I AM?
DOESN'T SEEM MUCH POINT TO IT.
WE HAD A FORTY-FIVE MINUTE DRIVE TO MY APARTMENT.
NOT A PROBLEM, NORMALLY.
BUT TODAY I WANTED TO GET AWAY FROM MANNY. TO DECIDE HOW TO FEEL.
TALK TO ME, ANITA.
HONEST TO GOD, MANNY, I DON'T KNOW WHAT TO SAY. I'VE KNOWN YOU FOR FOUR YEARS. YOU ARE A GOOD MAN. YOU'VE SAVED MY LIFE. I'VE SAVED YOURS. I *THOUGHT* I KNEW YOU.
DOES *ROSITA* KNOW?
I DON'T THINK SO. I DON'T THINK YOUR WIFE COULD DEAL WITH IT.
SHE SUSPECTS. ARE YOU GOING TO TELL HER?
SHE'D LEAVE ME AND TAKE THE KIDS. SHE ALREADY THINKS I'M RISKING MY ETERNAL SOUL BY RAISING THE DEAD.
SHE DIDN'T HAVE A PROBLEM UNTIL THE POPE THREATENED TO EXCOMMUNICATE ALL ANIMATORS UNLESS THEY STOPPED RAISING THE DEAD.
THE CHURCH IS VERY IMPORTANT TO ROSITA.
ME TOO, BUT I'M A HAPPY LITTLE EPISCOPA-LIAN NOW. SWITCH CHURCHES.
CAN YOU EXPLAIN WHY YOU WOULD DO HUMAN SACRIFICE? SOMETHING THAT WILL MAKE SENSE TO ME?
IT'S INDEFENSIBLE, ANITA. I LIVE WITH WHAT I DID. I CAN'T DO ANYTHING ELSE.
THIS HAS TO CHANGE THE WAY I THINK ABOUT YOU, MANNY.
IN WHAT WAY?
I DON'T KNOW YET. IS THERE ANYTHING ELSE I SHOULD KNOW? ANYTHING DOMINGA MIGHT SPILL LATER ONE?
NOTHING WORSE.
I DON'T KNOW HOW TO FEEL ABOUT THIS, MANNY. I DON'T KNOW HOW IT CHANGES OUR FRIENDSHIP, OR OUR WORKING RELATIONSHIP, OR EVEN IF IT DOES. I THINK IT DOES.
OH, HELL, I DON'T *KNOW*.

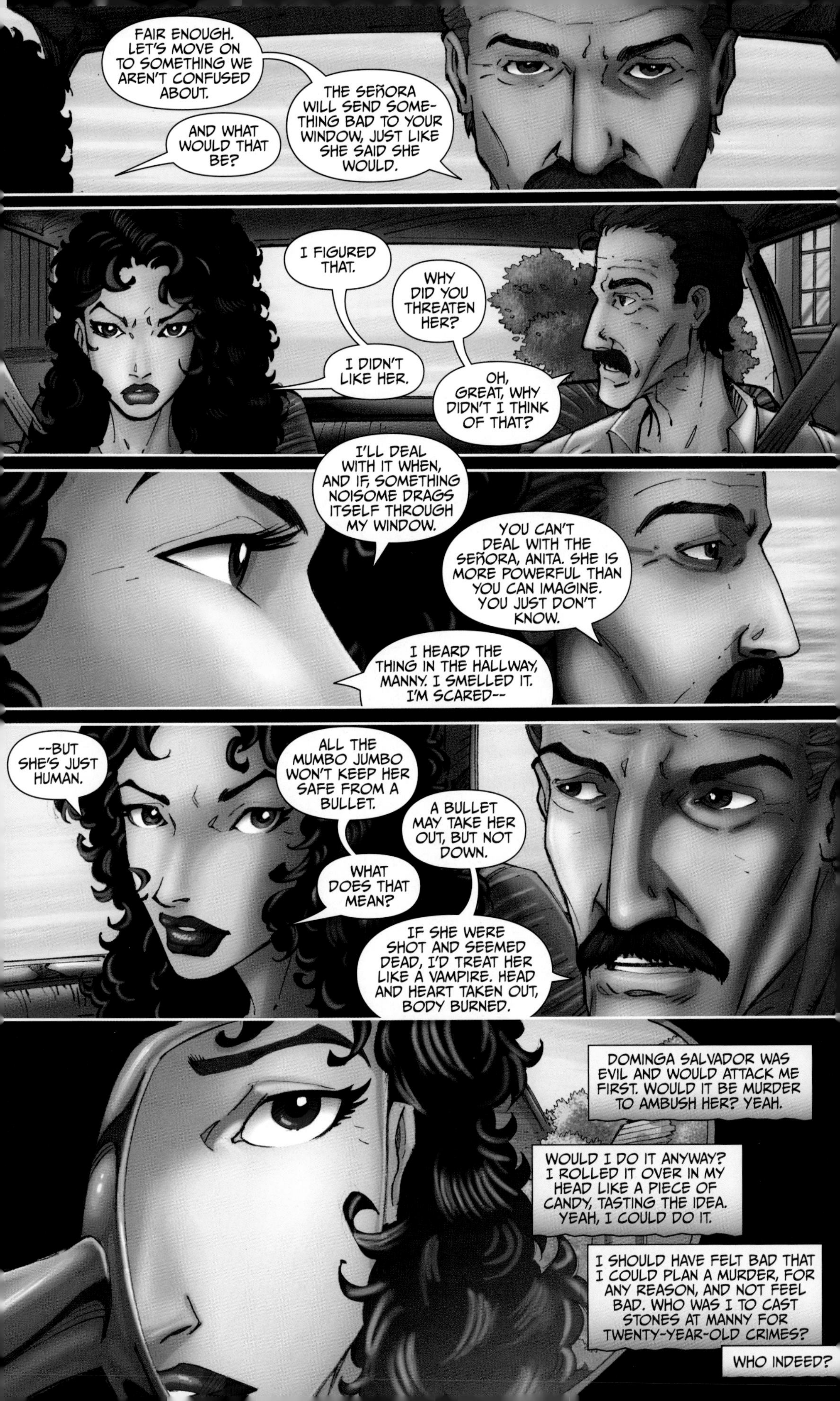
FAIR ENOUGH. LET'S MOVE ON TO SOMETHING WE AREN'T CONFUSED ABOUT.
AND WHAT WOULD THAT BE?
THE SEÑORA WILL SEND SOME-THING BAD TO YOUR WINDOW, JUST LIKE SHE SAID SHE WOULD.
I FIGURED THAT.
WHY DID YOU THREATEN HER?
I DIDN'T LIKE HER.
OH, GREAT, WHY DIDN'T I THINK OF THAT?
I'LL DEAL WITH IT WHEN, AND IF, SOMETHING NOISOME DRAGS ITSELF THROUGH MY WINDOW.
YOU CAN'T DEAL WITH THE SEÑORA, ANITA. SHE IS MORE POWERFUL THAN YOU CAN IMAGINE. YOU JUST DON'T KNOW.
I HEARD THE THING IN THE HALLWAY, MANNY. I SMELLED IT. I'M SCARED--
--BUT SHE'S JUST HUMAN.
ALL THE MUMBO JUMBO WON'T KEEP HER SAFE FROM A BULLET.
A BULLET MAY TAKE HER OUT, BUT NOT DOWN.
WHAT DOES THAT MEAN?
IF SHE WERE SHOT AND SEEMED DEAD, I'D TREAT HER LIKE A VAMPIRE. HEAD AND HEART TAKEN OUT, BODY BURNED.
DOMINGA SALVADOR WAS EVIL AND WOULD ATTACK ME FIRST. WOULD IT BE MURDER TO AMBUSH HER? YEAH.
WOULD I DO IT ANYWAY? I ROLLED IT OVER IN MY HEAD LIKE A PIECE OF CANDY, TASTING THE IDEA. YEAH, I COULD DO IT.
I SHOULD HAVE FELT BAD THAT I COULD PLAN A MURDER, FOR ANY REASON, AND NOT FEEL BAD. WHO WAS I TO CAST STONES AT MANNY FOR TWENTY-YEAR-OLD CRIMES?
WHO INDEED?

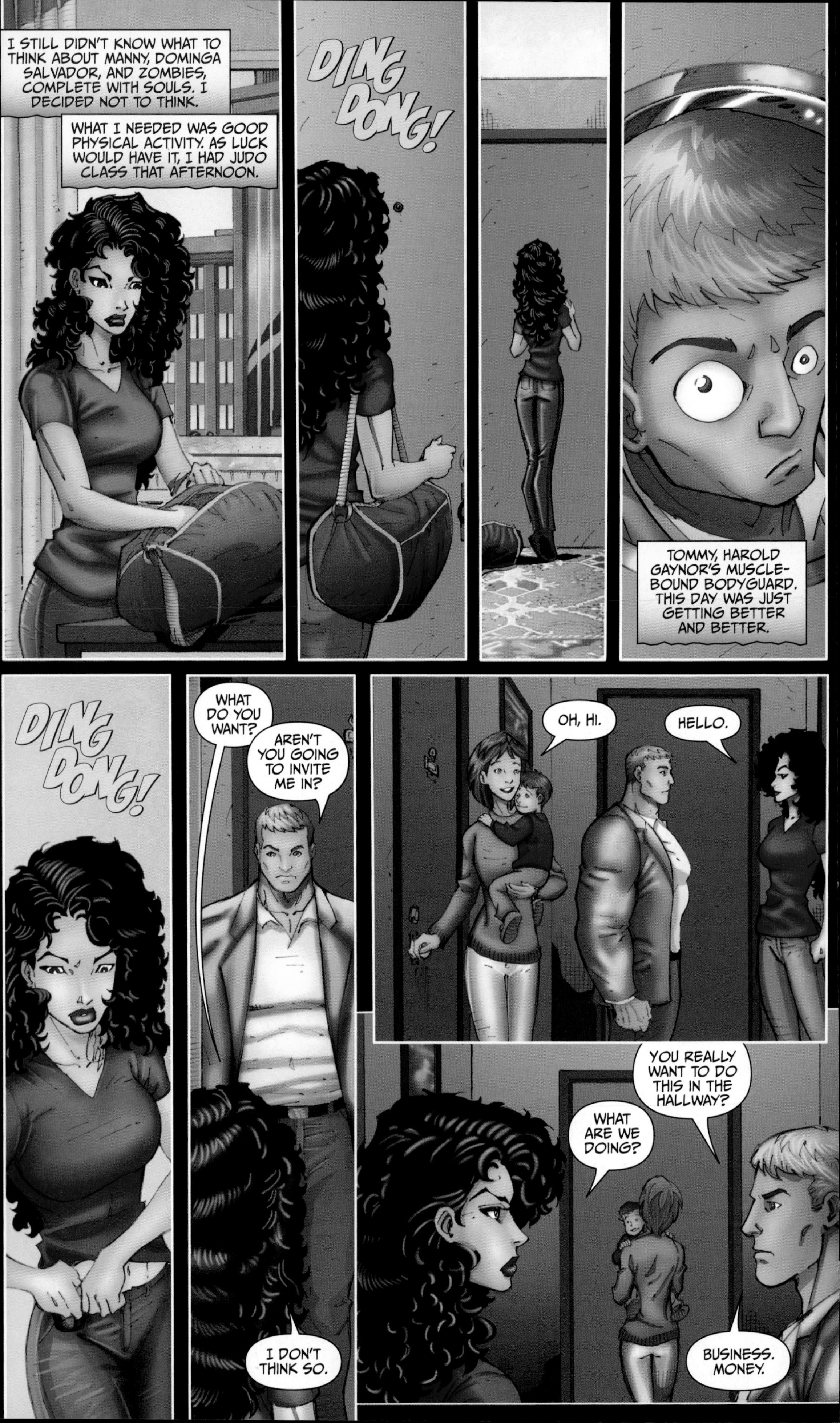
I STILL DIDN'T KNOW WHAT TO THINK ABOUT MANNY, DOMINGA SALVADOR, AND ZOMBIES, COMPLETE WITH SOULS. I DECIDED NOT TO THINK.
WHAT I NEEDED WAS GOOD PHYSICAL ACTIVITY. AS LUCK WOULD HAVE IT, I HAD JUDO CLASS THAT AFTERNOON.
DING DONG!
TOMMY, HAROLD GAYNOR'S MUSCLE-BOUND BODYGUARD. THIS DAY WAS JUST GETTING BETTER AND BETTER.
DING DONG!
WHAT DO YOU WANT?
AREN'T YOU GOING TO INVITE ME IN?
I DON'T THINK SO.
OH, HI.
HELLO.
YOU REALLY WANT TO DO THIS IN THE HALLWAY?
WHAT ARE WE DOING?
BUSINESS. MONEY.

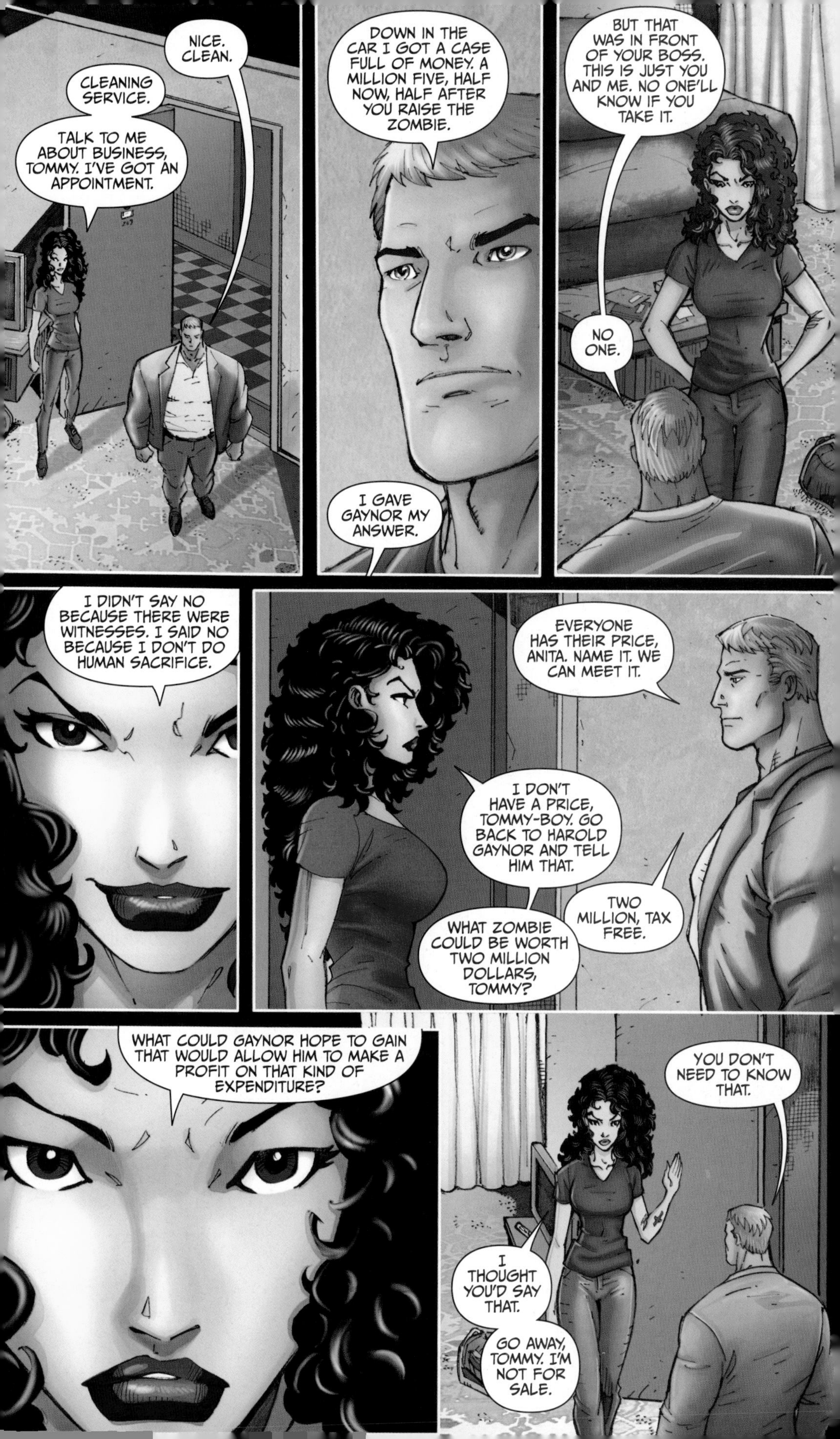
NICE. CLEAN.
CLEANING SERVICE.
TALK TO ME ABOUT BUSINESS, TOMMY. I'VE GOT AN APPOINTMENT.
DOWN IN THE CAR I GOT A CASE FULL OF MONEY. A MILLION FIVE, HALF NOW, HALF AFTER YOU RAISE THE ZOMBIE.
I GAVE GAYNOR MY ANSWER.
BUT THAT WAS IN FRONT OF YOUR BOSS. THIS IS JUST YOU AND ME. NO ONE'LL KNOW IF YOU TAKE IT.
NO ONE.
I DIDN'T SAY NO BECAUSE THERE WERE WITNESSES. I SAID NO BECAUSE I DON'T DO HUMAN SACRIFICE.
EVERYONE HAS THEIR PRICE, ANITA. NAME IT. WE CAN MEET IT.
I DON'T HAVE A PRICE, TOMMY-BOY. GO BACK TO HAROLD GAYNOR AND TELL HIM THAT.
TWO MILLION, TAX FREE.
WHAT ZOMBIE COULD BE WORTH TWO MILLION DOLLARS, TOMMY?
WHAT COULD GAYNOR HOPE TO GAIN THAT WOULD ALLOW HIM TO MAKE A PROFIT ON THAT KIND OF EXPENDITURE?
YOU DON'T NEED TO KNOW THAT.
I THOUGHT YOU'D SAY THAT.
GO AWAY, TOMMY. I'M NOT FOR SALE.

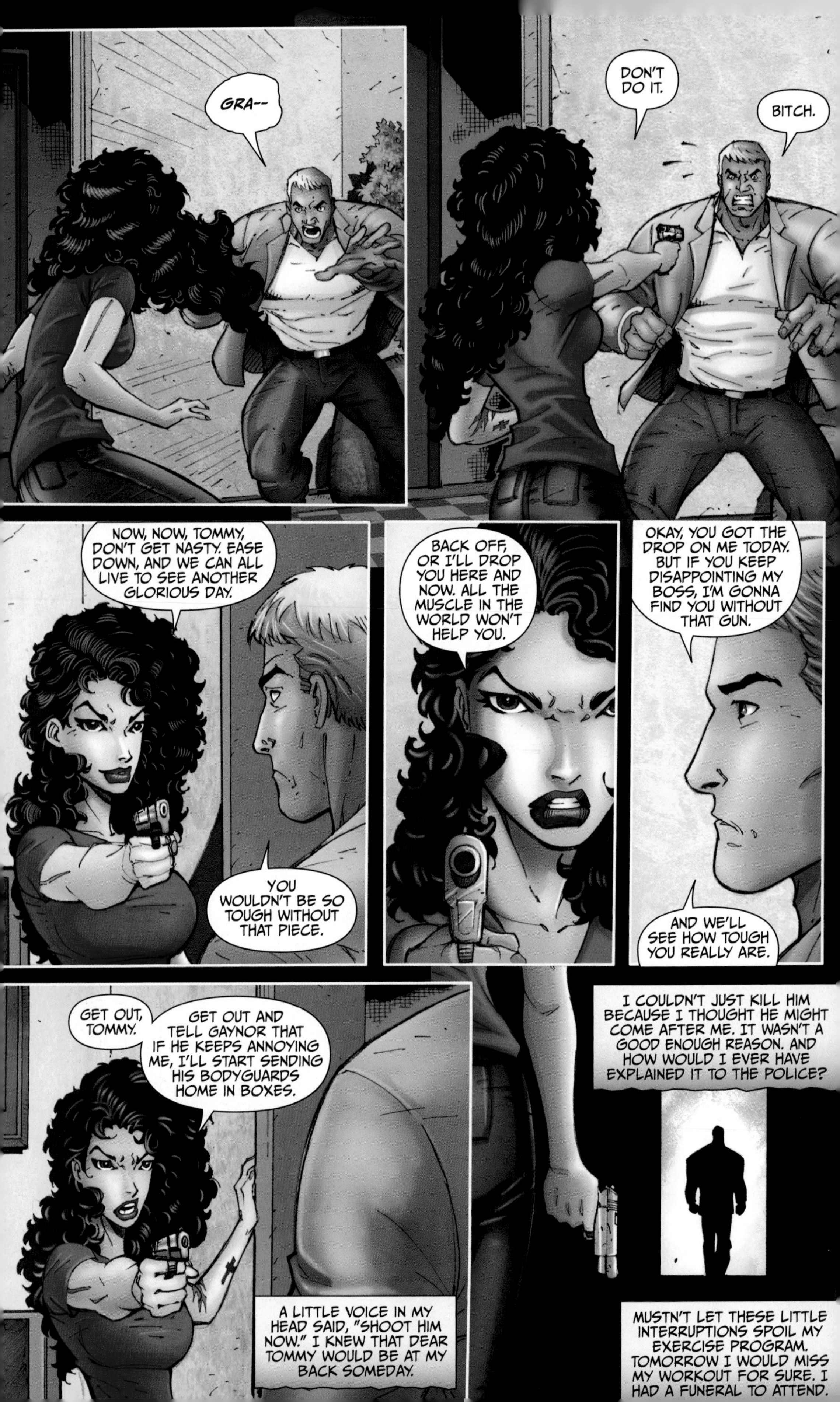

GRA--
DON'T DO IT.
BITCH.
NOW, NOW, TOMMY, DON'T GET NASTY. EASE DOWN, AND WE CAN ALL LIVE TO SEE ANOTHER GLORIOUS DAY.
YOU WOULDN'T BE SO TOUGH WITHOUT THAT PIECE.
BACK OFF, OR I'LL DROP YOU HERE AND NOW. ALL THE MUSCLE IN THE WORLD WON'T HELP YOU.
OKAY, YOU GOT THE DROP ON ME TODAY. BUT IF YOU KEEP DISAPPOINTING MY BOSS, I'M GONNA FIND YOU WITHOUT THAT GUN.
AND WE'LL SEE HOW TOUGH YOU REALLY ARE.
GET OUT, TOMMY.
GET OUT AND TELL GAYNOR THAT IF HE KEEPS ANNOYING ME, I'LL START SENDING HIS BODYGUARDS HOME IN BOXES.
A LITTLE VOICE IN MY HEAD SAID, "SHOOT HIM NOW." I KNEW THAT DEAR TOMMY WOULD BE AT MY BACK SOMEDAY.
I COULDN'T JUST KILL HIM BECAUSE I THOUGHT HE MIGHT COME AFTER ME. IT WASN'T A GOOD ENOUGH REASON. AND HOW WOULD I EVER HAVE EXPLAINED IT TO THE POLICE?
MUSTN'T LET THESE LITTLE INTERRUPTIONS SPOIL MY EXERCISE PROGRAM. TOMORROW I WOULD MISS MY WORKOUT FOR SURE. I HAD A FUNERAL TO ATTEND.

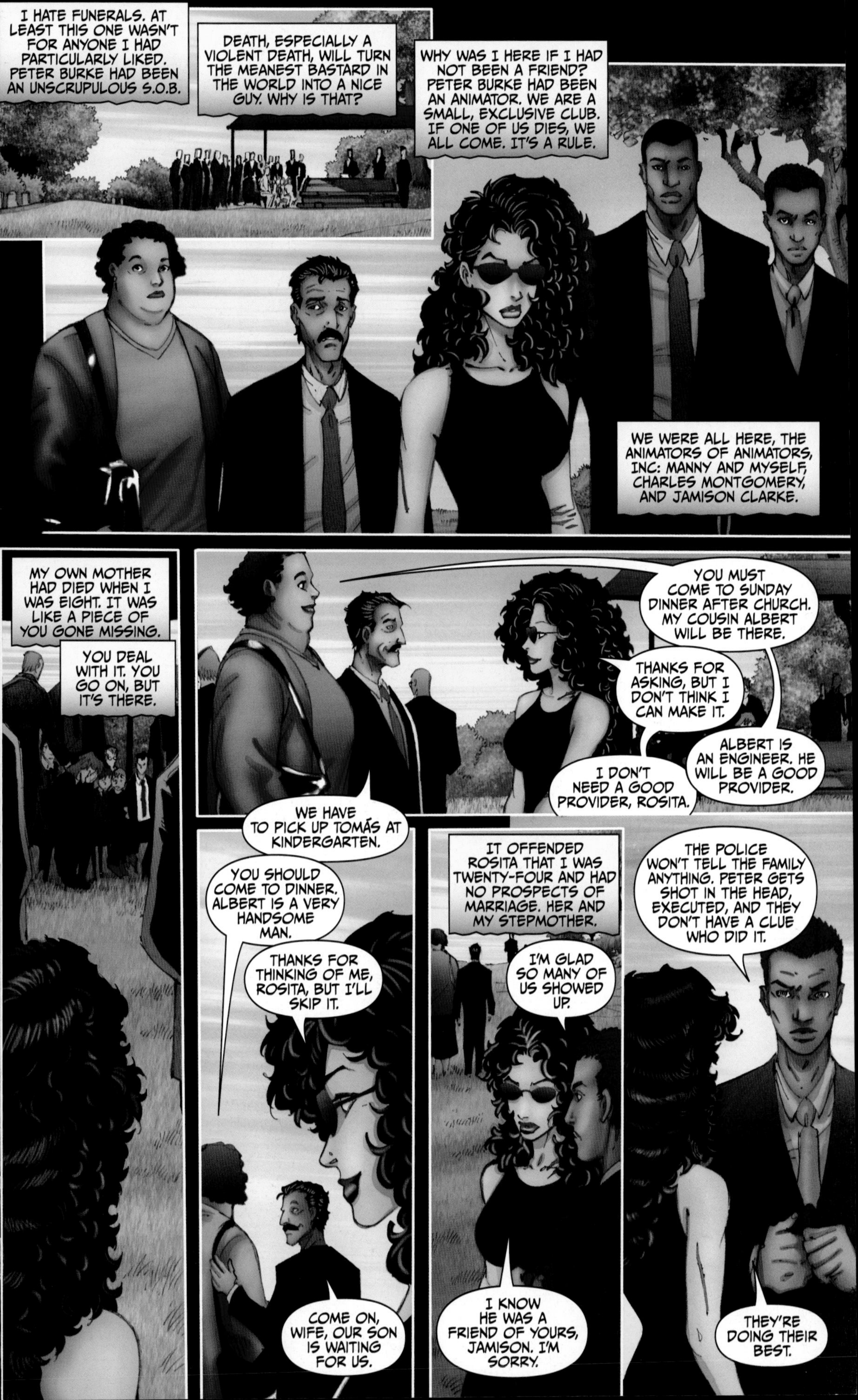

I HATE FUNERALS. AT LEAST THIS ONE WASN'T FOR ANYONE I HAD PARTICULARLY LIKED. PETER BURKE HAD BEEN AN UNSCRUPULOUS S.O.B.
DEATH, ESPECIALLY A VIOLENT DEATH, WILL TURN THE MEANEST BASTARD IN THE WORLD INTO A NICE GUY. WHY IS THAT?
WHY WAS I HERE IF I HAD NOT BEEN A FRIEND? PETER BURKE HAD BEEN AN ANIMATOR. WE ARE A SMALL, EXCLUSIVE CLUB. IF ONE OF US DIES, WE ALL COME. IT'S A RULE.
WE WERE ALL HERE, THE ANIMATORS OF ANIMATORS, INC: MANNY AND MYSELF, CHARLES MONTGOMERY, AND JAMISON CLARKE.
MY OWN MOTHER HAD DIED WHEN I WAS EIGHT. IT WAS LIKE A PIECE OF YOU GONE MISSING.
YOU DEAL WITH IT. YOU GO ON, BUT IT'S THERE.
YOU MUST COME TO SUNDAY DINNER AFTER CHURCH. MY COUSIN ALBERT WILL BE THERE.
THANKS FOR ASKING, BUT I DON'T THINK I CAN MAKE IT.
ALBERT IS AN ENGINEER. HE WILL BE A GOOD PROVIDER.
I DON'T NEED A GOOD PROVIDER, ROSITA.
WE HAVE TO PICK UP TOMÁS AT KINDERGARTEN.
YOU SHOULD COME TO DINNER. ALBERT IS A VERY HANDSOME MAN.
THANKS FOR THINKING OF ME, ROSITA, BUT I'LL SKIP IT.
COME ON, WIFE, OUR SON IS WAITING FOR US.
IT OFFENDED ROSITA THAT I WAS TWENTY-FOUR AND HAD NO PROSPECTS OF MARRIAGE. HER AND MY STEPMOTHER.
I'M GLAD SO MANY OF US SHOWED UP.
I KNOW HE WAS A FRIEND OF YOURS, JAMISON. I'M SORRY.
THE POLICE WON'T TELL THE FAMILY ANYTHING. PETER GETS SHOT IN THE HEAD, EXECUTED, AND THEY DON'T HAVE A CLUE WHO DID IT.
THEY'RE DOING THEIR BEST.

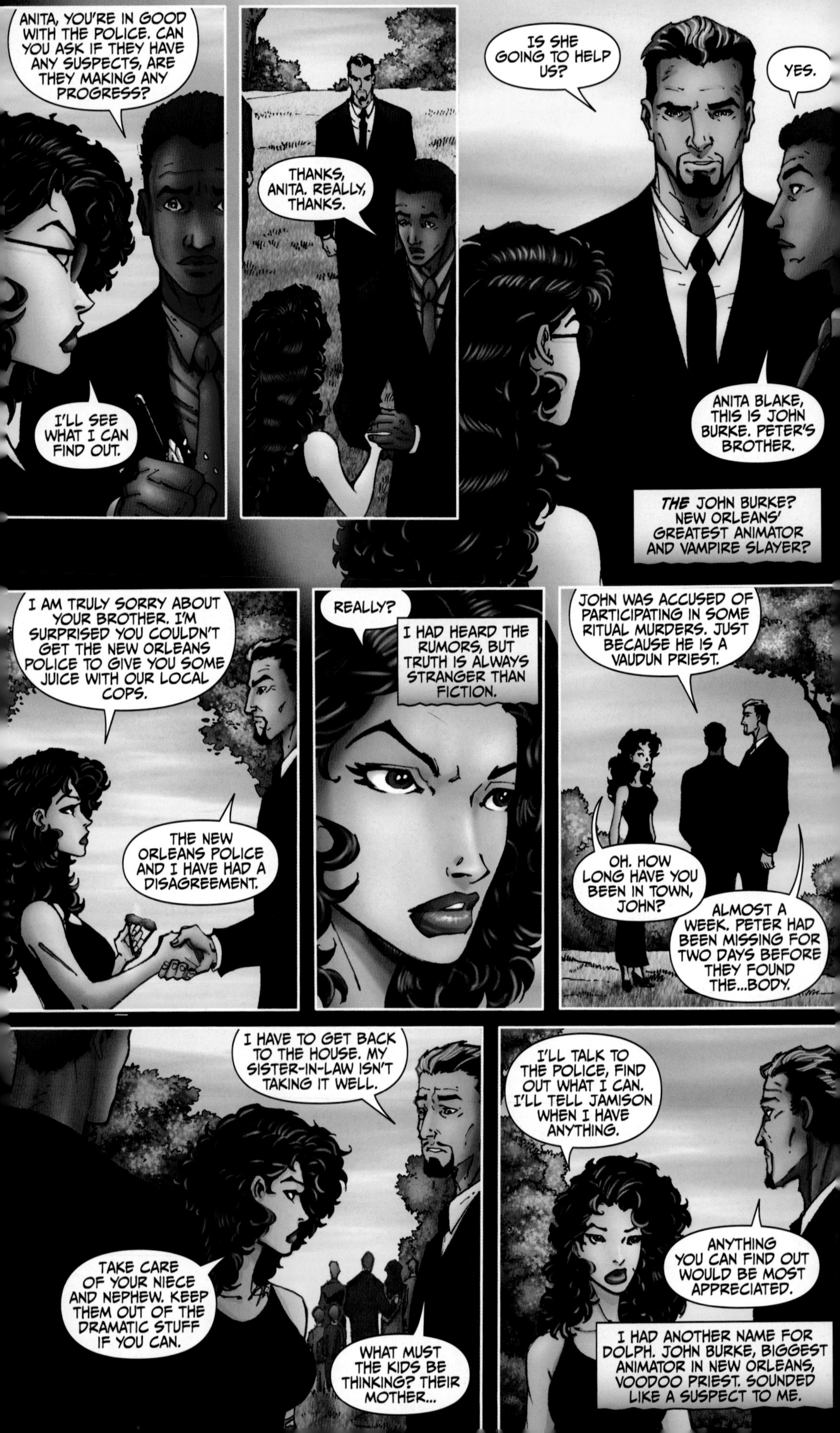

ANITA, YOU'RE IN GOOD WITH THE POLICE. CAN YOU ASK IF THEY HAVE ANY SUSPECTS, ARE THEY MAKING ANY PROGRESS?
I'LL SEE WHAT I CAN FIND OUT.
THANKS, ANITA. REALLY, THANKS.
IS SHE GOING TO HELP US?
YES.
ANITA BLAKE, THIS IS JOHN BURKE. PETER'S BROTHER.
THE JOHN BURKE? NEW ORLEANS' GREATEST ANIMATOR AND VAMPIRE SLAYER?
I AM TRULY SORRY ABOUT YOUR BROTHER. I'M SURPRISED YOU COULDN'T GET THE NEW ORLEANS POLICE TO GIVE YOU SOME JUICE WITH OUR LOCAL COPS.
THE NEW ORLEANS POLICE AND I HAVE HAD A DISAGREEMENT.
REALLY?
I HAD HEARD THE RUMORS, BUT TRUTH IS ALWAYS STRANGER THAN FICTION.
JOHN WAS ACCUSED OF PARTICIPATING IN SOME RITUAL MURDERS. JUST BECAUSE HE IS A VAUDUN PRIEST.
OH. HOW LONG HAVE YOU BEEN IN TOWN, JOHN?
ALMOST A WEEK. PETER HAD BEEN MISSING FOR TWO DAYS BEFORE THEY FOUND THE...BODY.
I HAVE TO GET BACK TO THE HOUSE. MY SISTER-IN-LAW ISN'T TAKING IT WELL.
TAKE CARE OF YOUR NIECE AND NEPHEW. KEEP THEM OUT OF THE DRAMATIC STUFF IF YOU CAN.
WHAT MUST THE KIDS BE THINKING? THEIR MOTHER...
I'LL TALK TO THE POLICE, FIND OUT WHAT I CAN. I'LL TELL JAMISON WHEN I HAVE ANYTHING.
ANYTHING YOU CAN FIND OUT WOULD BE MOST APPRECIATED.
I HAD ANOTHER NAME FOR DOLPH. JOHN BURKE, BIGGEST ANIMATOR IN NEW ORLEANS, VOODOO PRIEST. SOUNDED LIKE A SUSPECT TO ME.

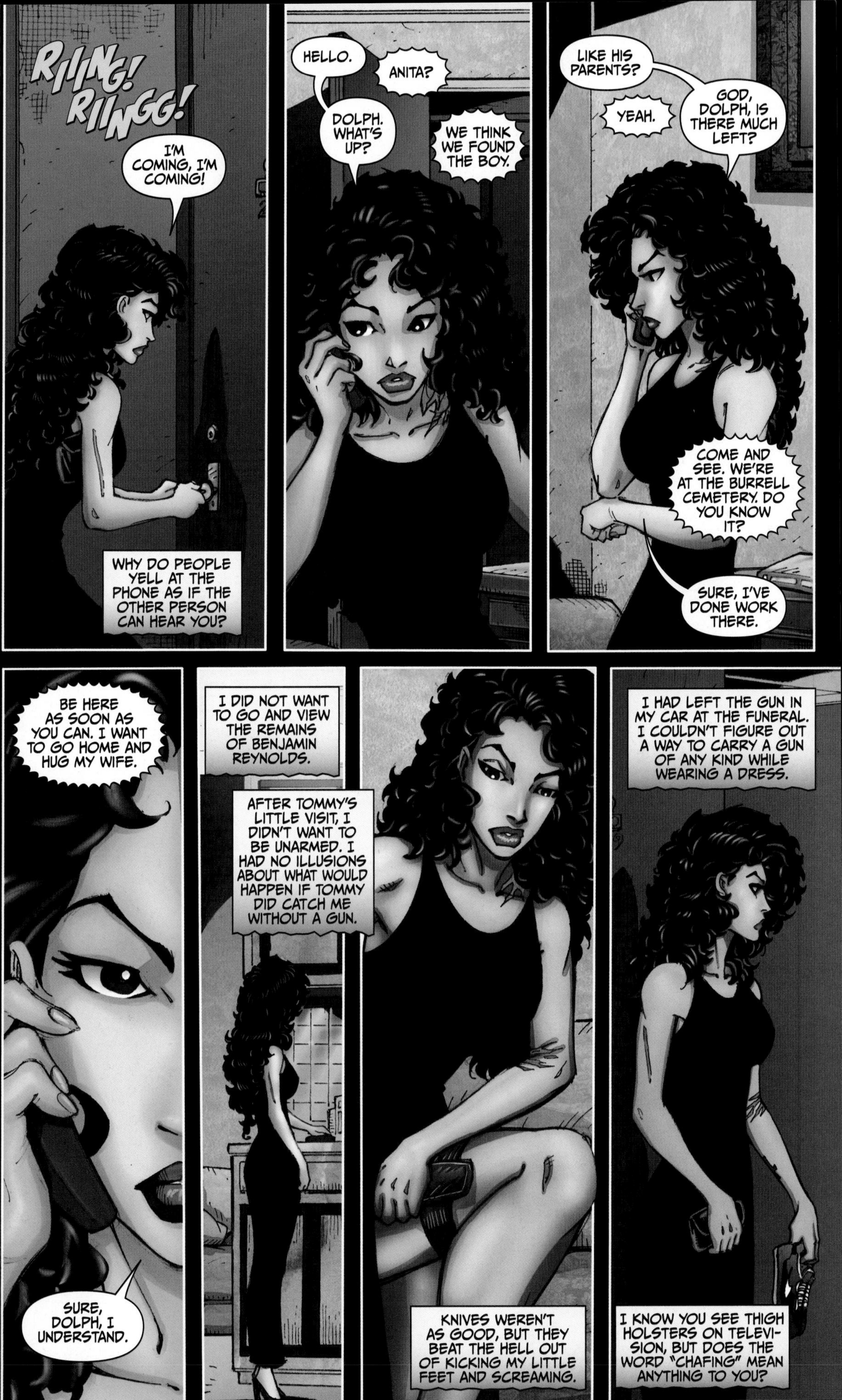
RIIING! RIINGG!
I'M COMING, I'M COMING!
WHY DO PEOPLE YELL AT THE PHONE AS IF THE OTHER PERSON CAN HEAR YOU?
HELLO.
ANITA?
DOLPH. WHAT'S UP?
WE THINK WE FOUND THE BOY.
LIKE HIS PARENTS?
YEAH.
GOD, DOLPH, IS THERE MUCH LEFT?
COME AND SEE. WE'RE AT THE BURRELL CEMETERY. DO YOU KNOW IT?
SURE, I'VE DONE WORK THERE.
BE HERE AS SOON AS YOU CAN. I WANT TO GO HOME AND HUG MY WIFE.
SURE, DOLPH, I UNDERSTAND.
I DID NOT WANT TO GO AND VIEW THE REMAINS OF BENJAMIN REYNOLDS.
AFTER TOMMY'S LITTLE VISIT, I DIDN'T WANT TO BE UNARMED. I HAD NO ILLUSIONS ABOUT WHAT WOULD HAPPEN IF TOMMY DID CATCH ME WITHOUT A GUN.
KNIVES WEREN'T AS GOOD, BUT THEY BEAT THE HELL OUT OF KICKING MY LITTLE FEET AND SCREAMING.
I HAD LEFT THE GUN IN MY CAR AT THE FUNERAL. I COULDN'T FIGURE OUT A WAY TO CARRY A GUN OF ANY KIND WHILE WEARING A DRESS.
I KNOW YOU SEE THIGH HOLSTERS ON TELEVISION, BUT DOES THE WORD "CHAFING" MEAN ANYTHING TO YOU?

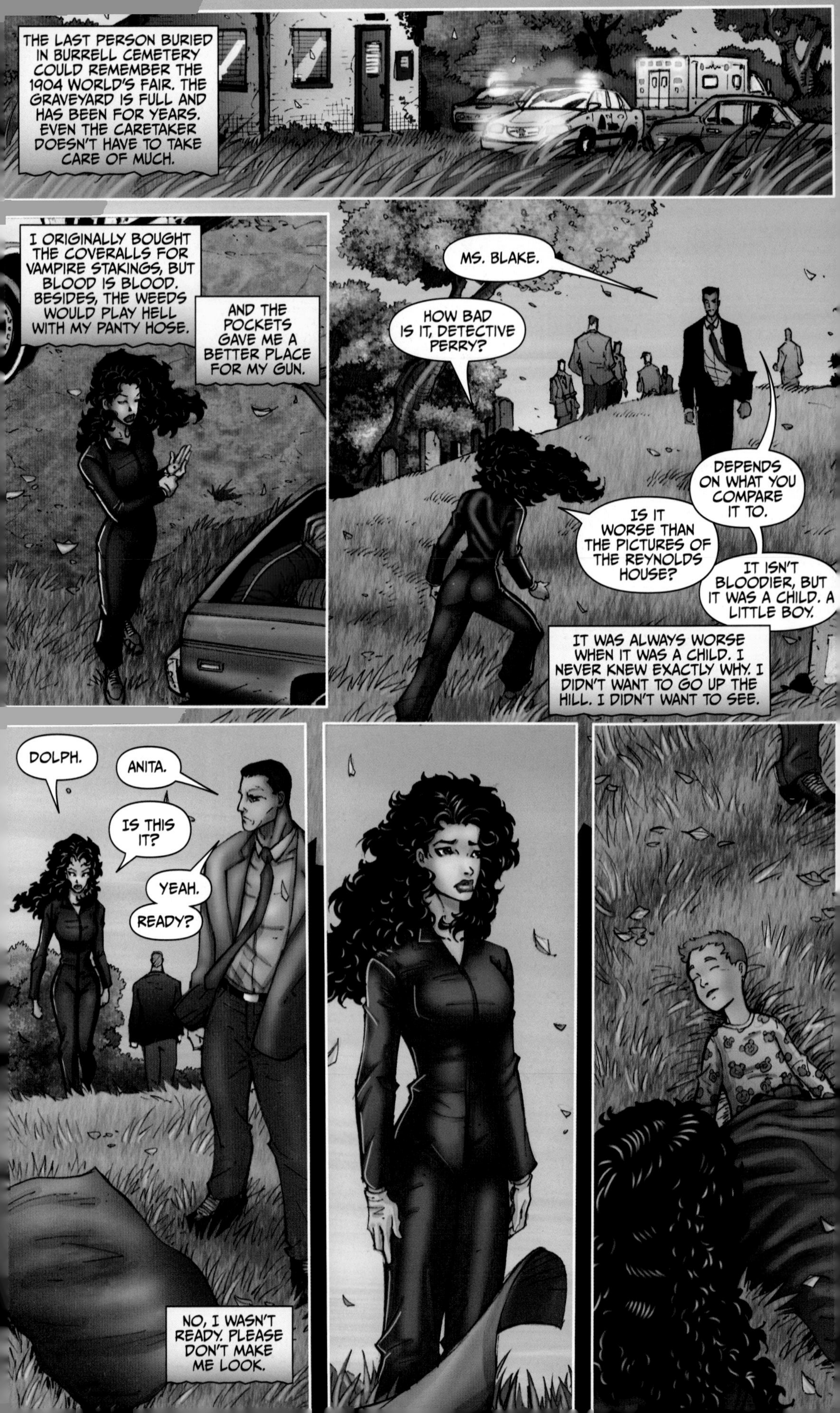
THE LAST PERSON BURIED IN BURRELL CEMETERY COULD REMEMBER THE 1904 WORLD'S FAIR. THE GRAVEYARD IS FULL AND HAS BEEN FOR YEARS. EVEN THE CARETAKER DOESN'T HAVE TO TAKE CARE OF MUCH.
I ORIGINALLY BOUGHT THE COVERALLS FOR VAMPIRE STAKINGS, BUT BLOOD IS BLOOD. BESIDES, THE WEEDS WOULD PLAY HELL WITH MY PANTY HOSE.
AND THE POCKETS GAVE ME A BETTER PLACE FOR MY GUN.
MS. BLAKE.
HOW BAD IS IT, DETECTIVE PERRY?
DEPENDS ON WHAT YOU COMPARE IT TO.
IS IT WORSE THAN THE PICTURES OF THE REYNOLDS HOUSE?
IT ISN'T BLOODIER, BUT IT WAS A CHILD. A LITTLE BOY.
IT WAS ALWAYS WORSE WHEN IT WAS A CHILD. I NEVER KNEW EXACTLY WHY. I DIDN'T WANT TO GO UP THE HILL. I DIDN'T WANT TO SEE.
DOLPH.
ANITA.
IS THIS IT?
YEAH.
READY?
NO, I WASN'T READY. PLEASE DON'T MAKE ME LOOK.

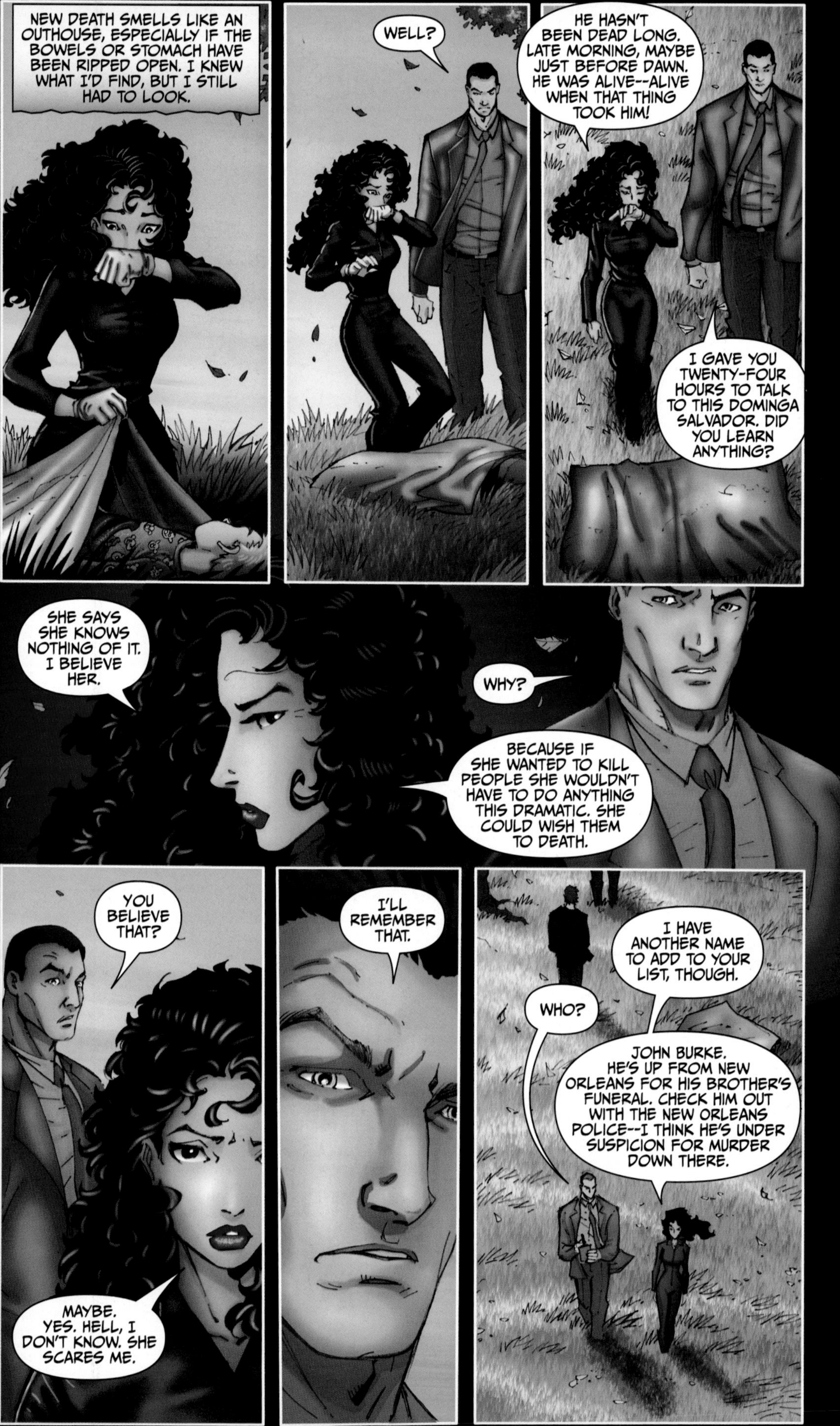
NEW DEATH SMELLS LIKE AN OUTHOUSE, ESPECIALLY IF THE BOWELS OR STOMACH HAVE BEEN RIPPED OPEN. I KNEW WHAT I'D FIND, BUT I STILL HAD TO LOOK.
WELL?
HE HASN'T BEEN DEAD LONG. LATE MORNING, MAYBE JUST BEFORE DAWN. HE WAS ALIVE--ALIVE WHEN THAT THING TOOK HIM!
I GAVE YOU TWENTY-FOUR HOURS TO TALK TO THIS DOMINGA SALVADOR. DID YOU LEARN ANYTHING?
SHE SAYS SHE KNOWS NOTHING OF IT. I BELIEVE HER.
WHY?
BECAUSE IF SHE WANTED TO KILL PEOPLE SHE WOULDN'T HAVE TO DO ANYTHING THIS DRAMATIC. SHE COULD WISH THEM TO DEATH.
YOU BELIEVE THAT?
MAYBE. YES. HELL, I DON'T KNOW. SHE SCARES ME.
I'LL REMEMBER THAT.
I HAVE ANOTHER NAME TO ADD TO YOUR LIST, THOUGH.
WHO?
JOHN BURKE. HE'S UP FROM NEW ORLEANS FOR HIS BROTHER'S FUNERAL. CHECK HIM OUT WITH THE NEW ORLEANS POLICE--I THINK HE'S UNDER SUSPICION FOR MURDER DOWN THERE.

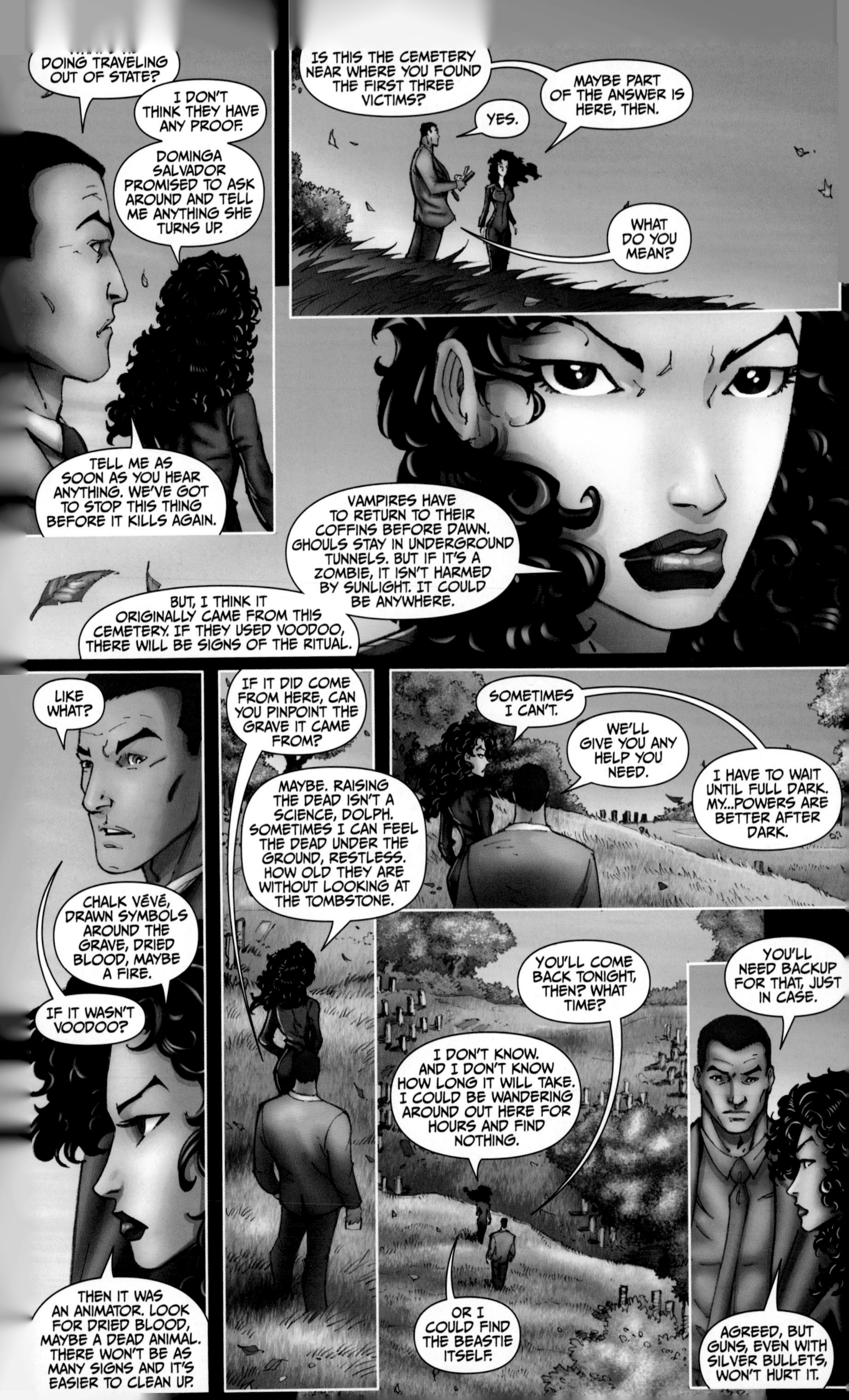
DOING TRAVELING OUT OF STATE?
I DON'T THINK THEY HAVE ANY PROOF.
DOMINGA SALVADOR PROMISED TO ASK AROUND AND TELL ME ANYTHING SHE TURNS UP.
TELL ME AS SOON AS YOU HEAR ANYTHING. WE'VE GOT TO STOP THIS THING BEFORE IT KILLS AGAIN.
IS THIS THE CEMETERY NEAR WHERE YOU FOUND THE FIRST THREE VICTIMS?
YES.
MAYBE PART OF THE ANSWER IS HERE, THEN.
WHAT DO YOU MEAN?
VAMPIRES HAVE TO RETURN TO THEIR COFFINS BEFORE DAWN. GHOULS STAY IN UNDERGROUND TUNNELS. BUT IF IT'S A ZOMBIE, IT ISN'T HARMED BY SUNLIGHT. IT COULD BE ANYWHERE.
BUT, I THINK IT ORIGINALLY CAME FROM THIS CEMETERY. IF THEY USED VOODOO, THERE WILL BE SIGNS OF THE RITUAL.
LIKE WHAT?
CHALK VÉVÉ, DRAWN SYMBOLS AROUND THE GRAVE, DRIED BLOOD, MAYBE A FIRE.
IF IT WASN'T VOODOO?
THEN IT WAS AN ANIMATOR. LOOK FOR DRIED BLOOD, MAYBE A DEAD ANIMAL. THERE WON'T BE AS MANY SIGNS AND IT'S EASIER TO CLEAN UP.
IF IT DID COME FROM HERE, CAN YOU PINPOINT THE GRAVE IT CAME FROM?
MAYBE. RAISING THE DEAD ISN'T A SCIENCE, DOLPH. SOMETIMES I CAN FEEL THE DEAD UNDER THE GROUND, RESTLESS. HOW OLD THEY ARE WITHOUT LOOKING AT THE TOMBSTONE.
SOMETIMES I CAN'T.
WE'LL GIVE YOU ANY HELP YOU NEED.
I HAVE TO WAIT UNTIL FULL DARK. MY...POWERS ARE BETTER AFTER DARK.
YOU'LL COME BACK TONIGHT, THEN? WHAT TIME?
I DON'T KNOW. AND I DON'T KNOW HOW LONG IT WILL TAKE. I COULD BE WANDERING AROUND OUT HERE FOR HOURS AND FIND NOTHING.
OR I COULD FIND THE BEASTIE ITSELF.
YOU'LL NEED BACKUP FOR THAT, JUST IN CASE.
AGREED, BUT GUNS, EVEN WITH SILVER BULLETS, WON'T HURT IT.

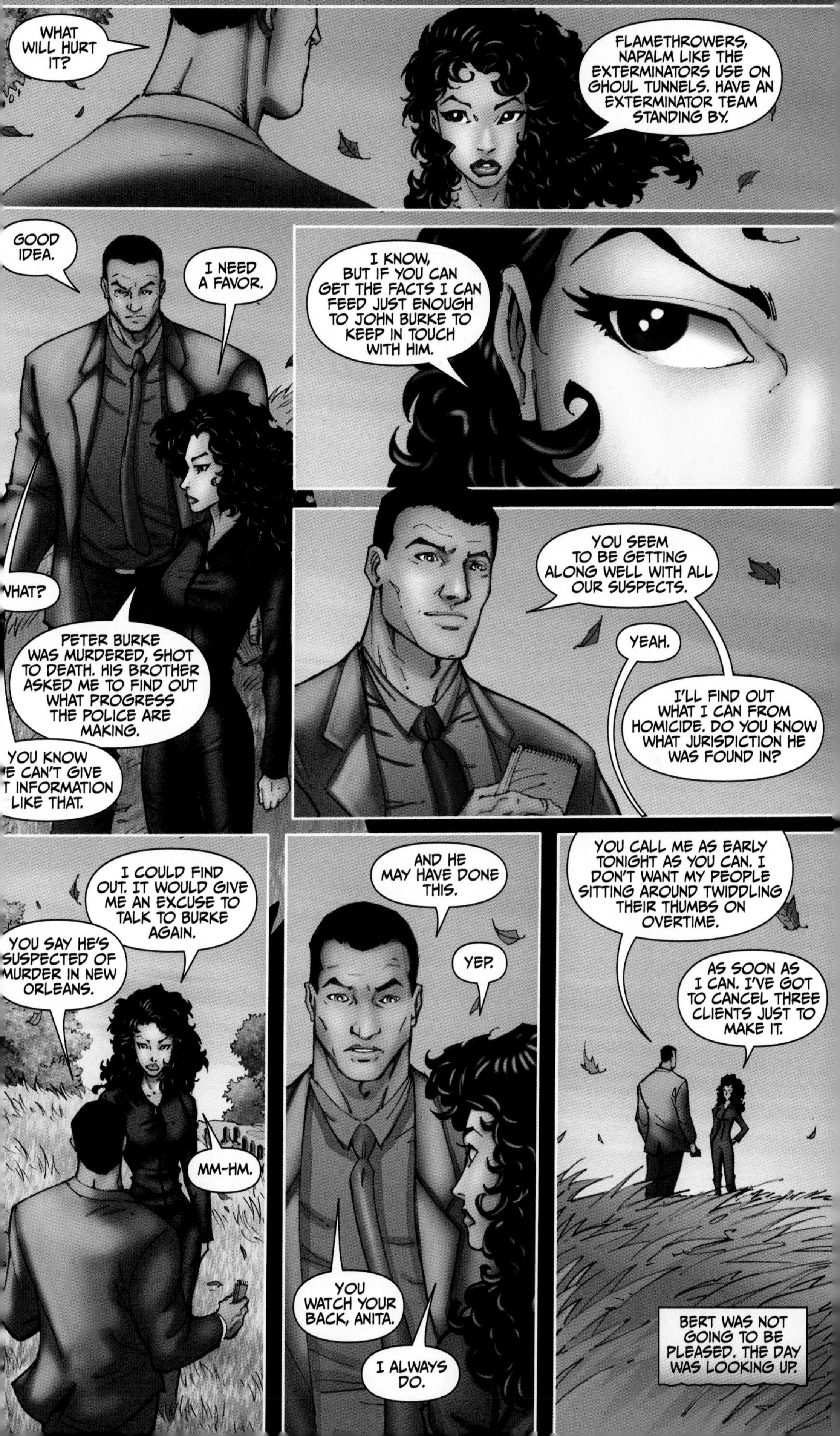
WHAT WILL HURT IT?
FLAMETHROWERS, NAPALM LIKE THE EXTERMINATORS USE ON GHOUL TUNNELS. HAVE AN EXTERMINATOR TEAM STANDING BY.
GOOD IDEA.
I NEED A FAVOR.
WHAT?
PETER BURKE WAS MURDERED, SHOT TO DEATH. HIS BROTHER ASKED ME TO FIND OUT WHAT PROGRESS THE POLICE ARE MAKING.
YOU KNOW WE CAN'T GIVE OUT INFORMATION LIKE THAT.
I KNOW, BUT IF YOU CAN GET THE FACTS I CAN FEED JUST ENOUGH TO JOHN BURKE TO KEEP IN TOUCH WITH HIM.
YOU SEEM TO BE GETTING ALONG WELL WITH ALL OUR SUSPECTS.
YEAH.
I'LL FIND OUT WHAT I CAN FROM HOMICIDE. DO YOU KNOW WHAT JURISDICTION HE WAS FOUND IN?
I COULD FIND OUT. IT WOULD GIVE ME AN EXCUSE TO TALK TO BURKE AGAIN.
YOU SAY HE'S SUSPECTED OF MURDER IN NEW ORLEANS.
MM-HM.
AND HE MAY HAVE DONE THIS.
YEP.
YOU WATCH YOUR BACK, ANITA.
I ALWAYS DO.
YOU CALL ME AS EARLY TONIGHT AS YOU CAN. I DON'T WANT MY PEOPLE SITTING AROUND TWIDDLING THEIR THUMBS ON OVERTIME.
AS SOON AS I CAN. I'VE GOT TO CANCEL THREE CLIENTS JUST TO MAKE IT.
BERT WAS NOT GOING TO BE PLEASED. THE DAY WAS LOOKING UP.

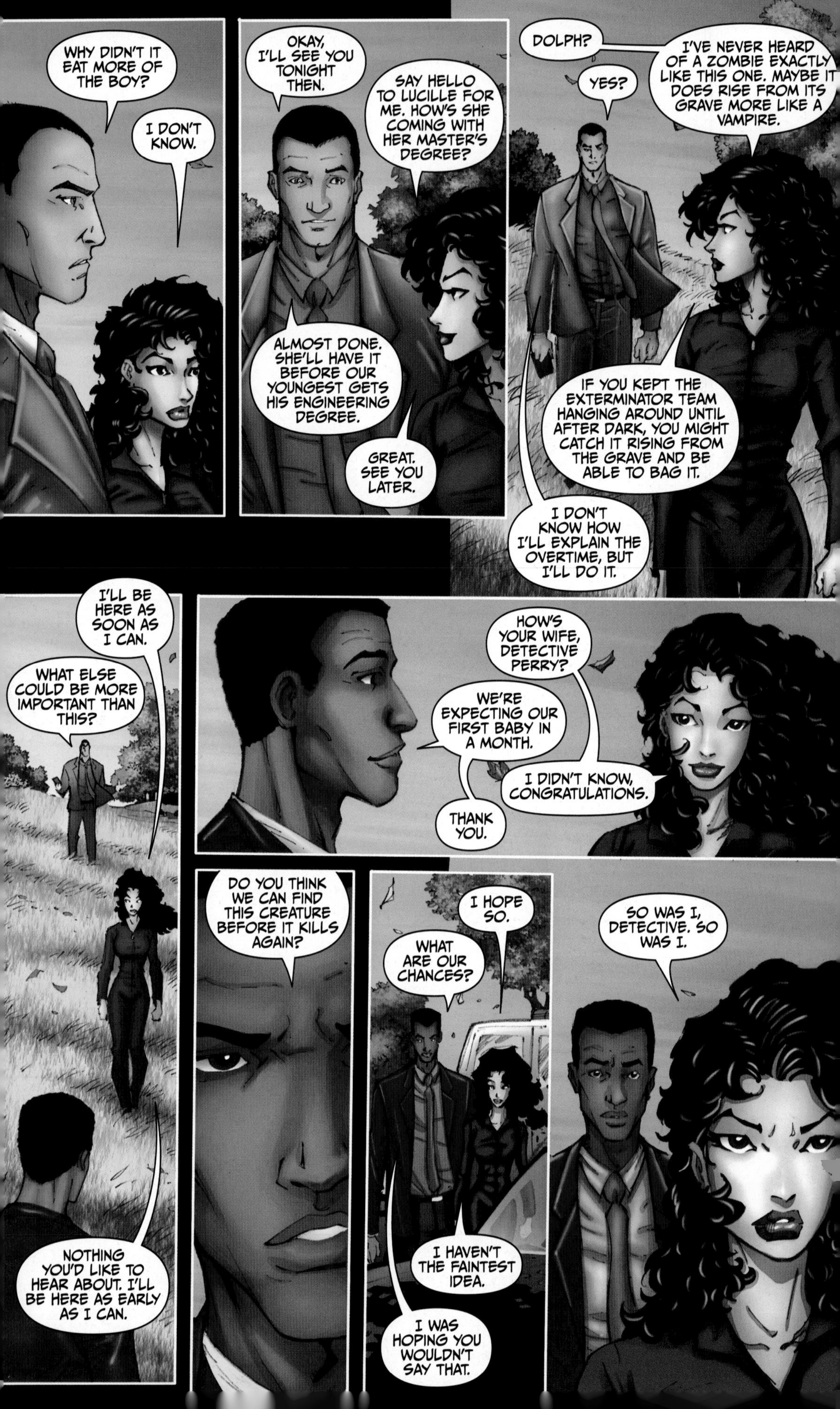
WHY DIDN'T IT EAT MORE OF THE BOY?
I DON'T KNOW.
OKAY, I'LL SEE YOU TONIGHT THEN.
SAY HELLO TO LUCILLE FOR ME. HOW'S SHE COMING WITH HER MASTER'S DEGREE?
ALMOST DONE. SHE'LL HAVE IT BEFORE OUR YOUNGEST GETS HIS ENGINEERING DEGREE.
GREAT. SEE YOU LATER.
DOLPH?
YES?
I'VE NEVER HEARD OF A ZOMBIE EXACTLY LIKE THIS ONE. MAYBE IT DOES RISE FROM ITS GRAVE MORE LIKE A VAMPIRE.
IF YOU KEPT THE EXTERMINATOR TEAM HANGING AROUND UNTIL AFTER DARK, YOU MIGHT CATCH IT RISING FROM THE GRAVE AND BE ABLE TO BAG IT.
I DON'T KNOW HOW I'LL EXPLAIN THE OVERTIME, BUT I'LL DO IT.
I'LL BE HERE AS SOON AS I CAN.
WHAT ELSE COULD BE MORE IMPORTANT THAN THIS?
NOTHING YOU'D LIKE TO HEAR ABOUT. I'LL BE HERE AS EARLY AS I CAN.
HOW'S YOUR WIFE, DETECTIVE PERRY?
WE'RE EXPECTING OUR FIRST BABY IN A MONTH.
I DIDN'T KNOW, CONGRATULATIONS.
THANK YOU.
DO YOU THINK WE CAN FIND THIS CREATURE BEFORE IT KILLS AGAIN?
I HOPE SO.
WHAT ARE OUR CHANCES?
I HAVEN'T THE FAINTEST IDEA.
I WAS HOPING YOU WOULDN'T SAY THAT.
SO WAS I, DETECTIVE. SO WAS I.

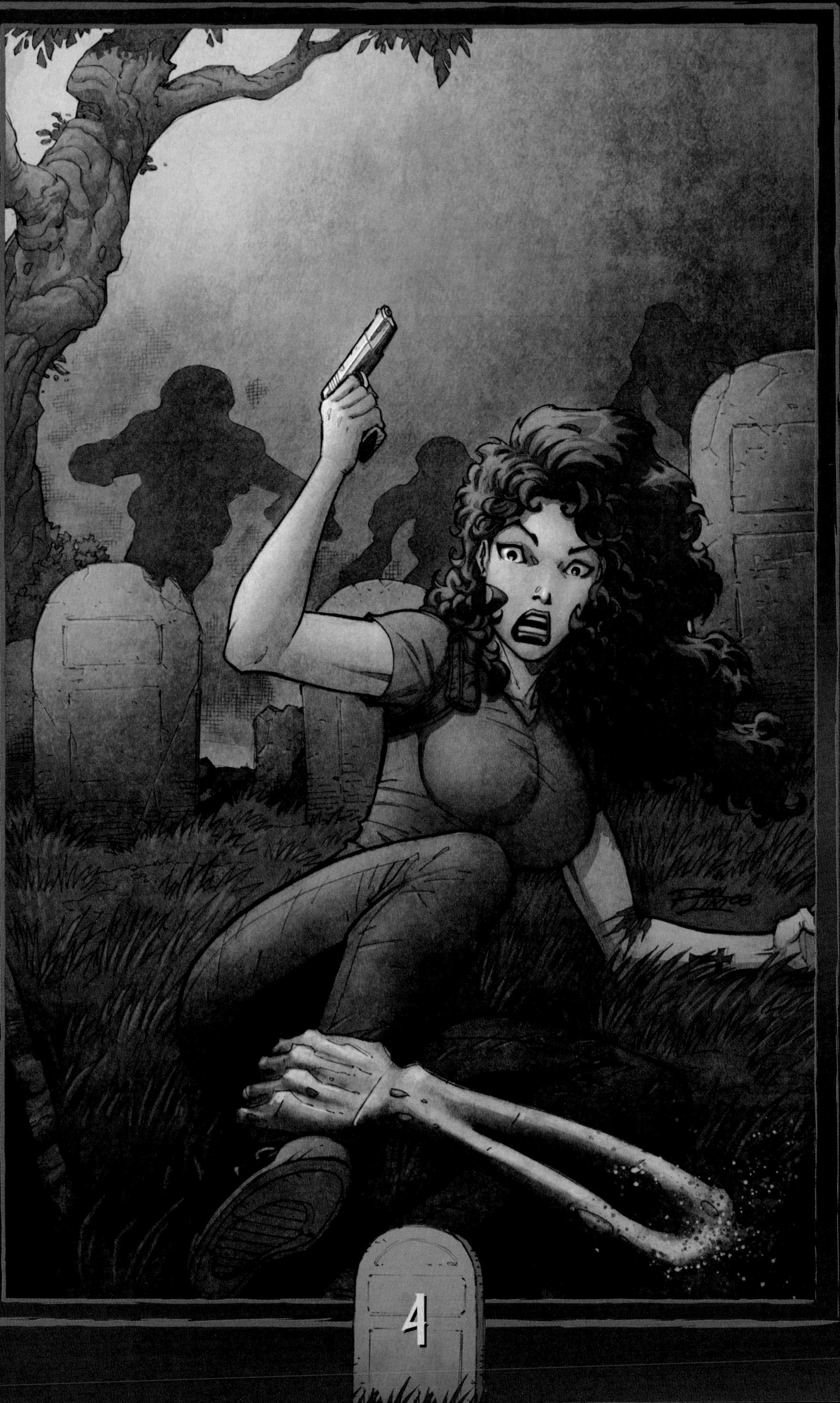

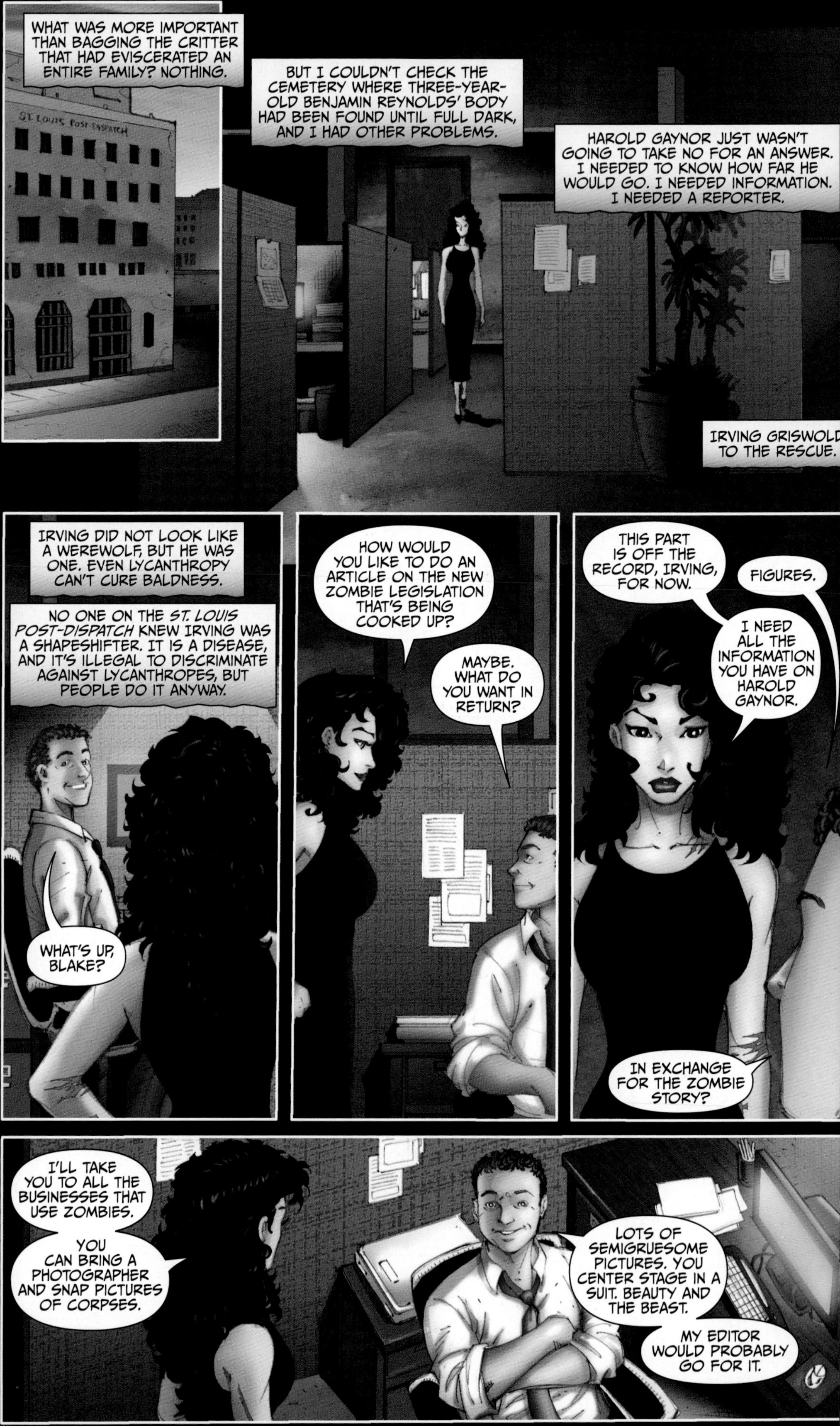

WHAT WAS MORE IMPORTANT THAN BAGGING THE CRITTER THAT HAD EVISCERATED AN ENTIRE FAMILY? NOTHING.
ST. LOUIS POST-DISPATCH
BUT I COULDN'T CHECK THE CEMETERY WHERE THREE-YEAR-OLD BENJAMIN REYNOLDS' BODY HAD BEEN FOUND UNTIL FULL DARK, AND I HAD OTHER PROBLEMS.
HAROLD GAYNOR JUST WASN'T GOING TO TAKE NO FOR AN ANSWER. I NEEDED TO KNOW HOW FAR HE WOULD GO. I NEEDED INFORMATION. I NEEDED A REPORTER.
IRVING GRISWOLD TO THE RESCUE.
IRVING DID NOT LOOK LIKE A WEREWOLF, BUT HE WAS ONE. EVEN LYCANTHROPY CAN'T CURE BALDNESS.
NO ONE ON THE *ST. LOUIS POST-DISPATCH* KNEW IRVING WAS A SHAPESHIFTER. IT IS A DISEASE, AND IT'S ILLEGAL TO DISCRIMINATE AGAINST LYCANTHROPES, BUT PEOPLE DO IT ANYWAY.
WHAT'S UP, BLAKE?
HOW WOULD YOU LIKE TO DO AN ARTICLE ON THE NEW ZOMBIE LEGISLATION THAT'S BEING COOKED UP?
MAYBE. WHAT DO YOU WANT IN RETURN?
THIS PART IS OFF THE RECORD, IRVING, FOR NOW.
FIGURES.
I NEED ALL THE INFORMATION YOU HAVE ON HAROLD GAYNOR.
IN EXCHANGE FOR THE ZOMBIE STORY?
I'LL TAKE YOU TO ALL THE BUSINESSES THAT USE ZOMBIES.
YOU CAN BRING A PHOTOGRAPHER AND SNAP PICTURES OF CORPSES.
LOTS OF SEMIGRUESOME PICTURES. YOU CENTER STAGE IN A SUIT. BEAUTY AND THE BEAST.
MY EDITOR WOULD PROBABLY GO FOR IT.

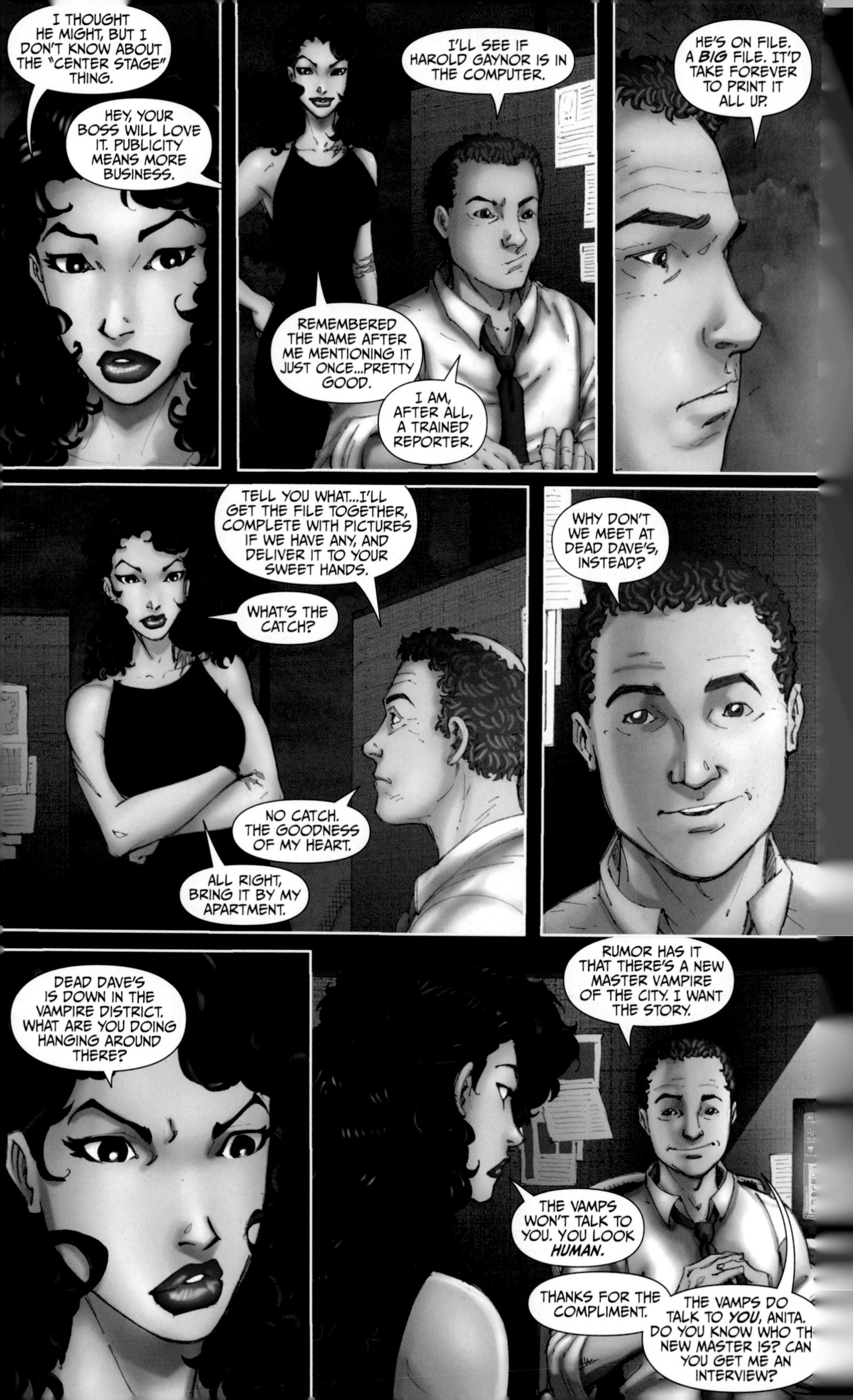
I THOUGHT HE MIGHT, BUT I DON'T KNOW ABOUT THE "CENTER STAGE" THING.
HEY, YOUR BOSS WILL LOVE IT. PUBLICITY MEANS MORE BUSINESS.
I'LL SEE IF HAROLD GAYNOR IS IN THE COMPUTER.
REMEMBERED THE NAME AFTER ME MENTIONING IT JUST ONCE...PRETTY GOOD.
I AM, AFTER ALL, A TRAINED REPORTER.
HE'S ON FILE. A BIG FILE. IT'D TAKE FOREVER TO PRINT IT ALL UP.
TELL YOU WHAT...I'LL GET THE FILE TOGETHER, COMPLETE WITH PICTURES IF WE HAVE ANY, AND DELIVER IT TO YOUR SWEET HANDS.
WHAT'S THE CATCH?
NO CATCH. THE GOODNESS OF MY HEART.
ALL RIGHT, BRING IT BY MY APARTMENT.
WHY DON'T WE MEET AT DEAD DAVE'S, INSTEAD?
DEAD DAVE'S IS DOWN IN THE VAMPIRE DISTRICT. WHAT ARE YOU DOING HANGING AROUND THERE?
RUMOR HAS IT THAT THERE'S A NEW MASTER VAMPIRE OF THE CITY. I WANT THE STORY.
THE VAMPS WON'T TALK TO YOU. YOU LOOK HUMAN.
THANKS FOR THE COMPLIMENT.
THE VAMPS DO TALK TO YOU, ANITA. DO YOU KNOW WHO TH NEW MASTER IS? CAN YOU GET ME AN INTERVIEW?

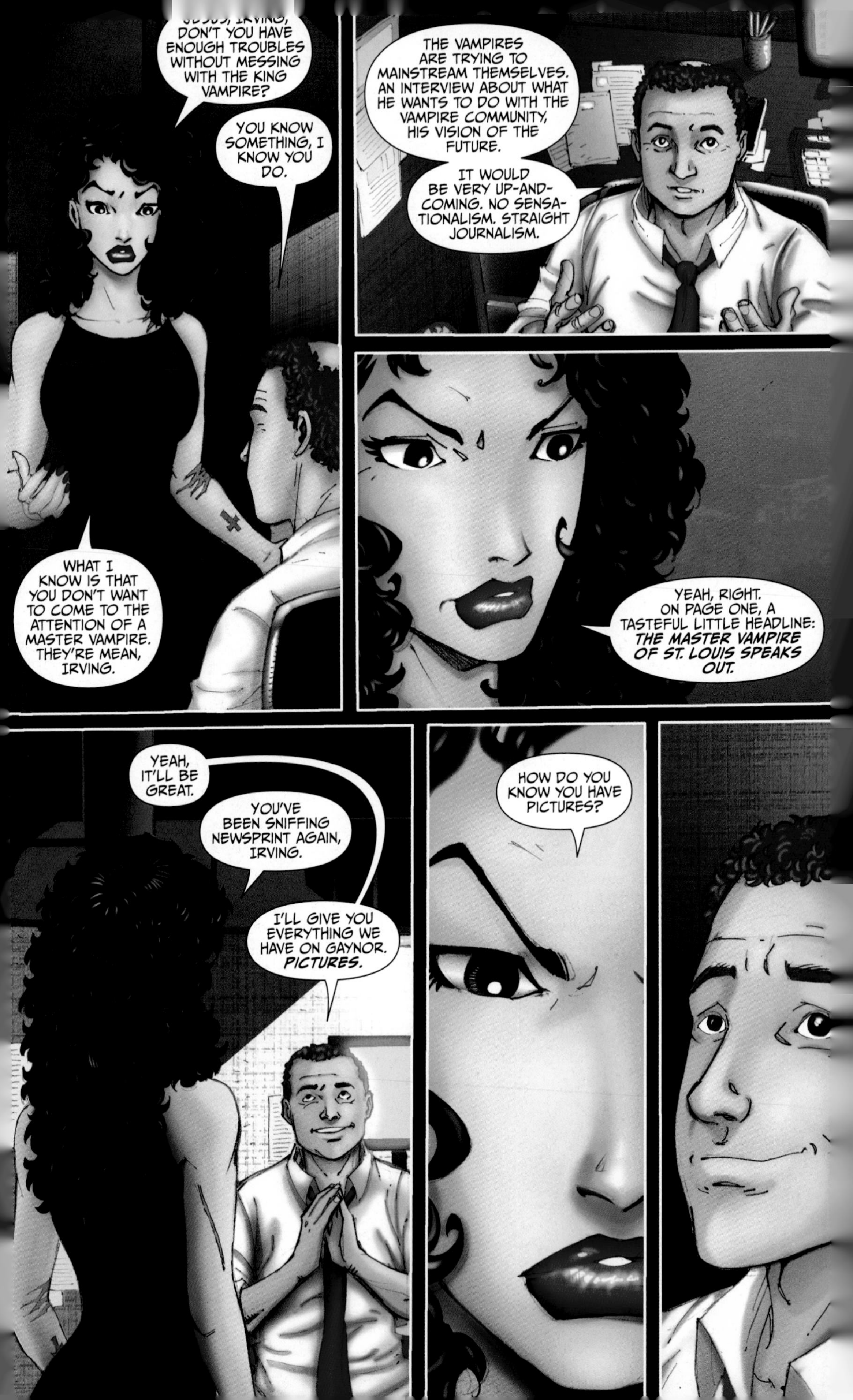

DON'T YOU HAVE ENOUGH TROUBLES WITHOUT MESSING WITH THE KING VAMPIRE?
YOU KNOW SOMETHING, I KNOW YOU DO.
WHAT I KNOW IS THAT YOU DON'T WANT TO COME TO THE ATTENTION OF A MASTER VAMPIRE. THEY'RE MEAN, IRVING.
THE VAMPIRES ARE TRYING TO MAINSTREAM THEMSELVES. AN INTERVIEW ABOUT WHAT HE WANTS TO DO WITH THE VAMPIRE COMMUNITY, HIS VISION OF THE FUTURE.
IT WOULD BE VERY UP-AND-COMING. NO SENSA-TIONALISM. STRAIGHT JOURNALISM.
YEAH, RIGHT. ON PAGE ONE, A TASTEFUL LITTLE HEADLINE: *THE MASTER VAMPIRE OF ST. LOUIS SPEAKS OUT.*
YEAH, IT'LL BE GREAT.
YOU'VE BEEN SNIFFING NEWSPRINT AGAIN, IRVING.
I'LL GIVE YOU EVERYTHING WE HAVE ON GAYNOR. *PICTURES.*
HOW DO YOU KNOW YOU HAVE PICTURES?

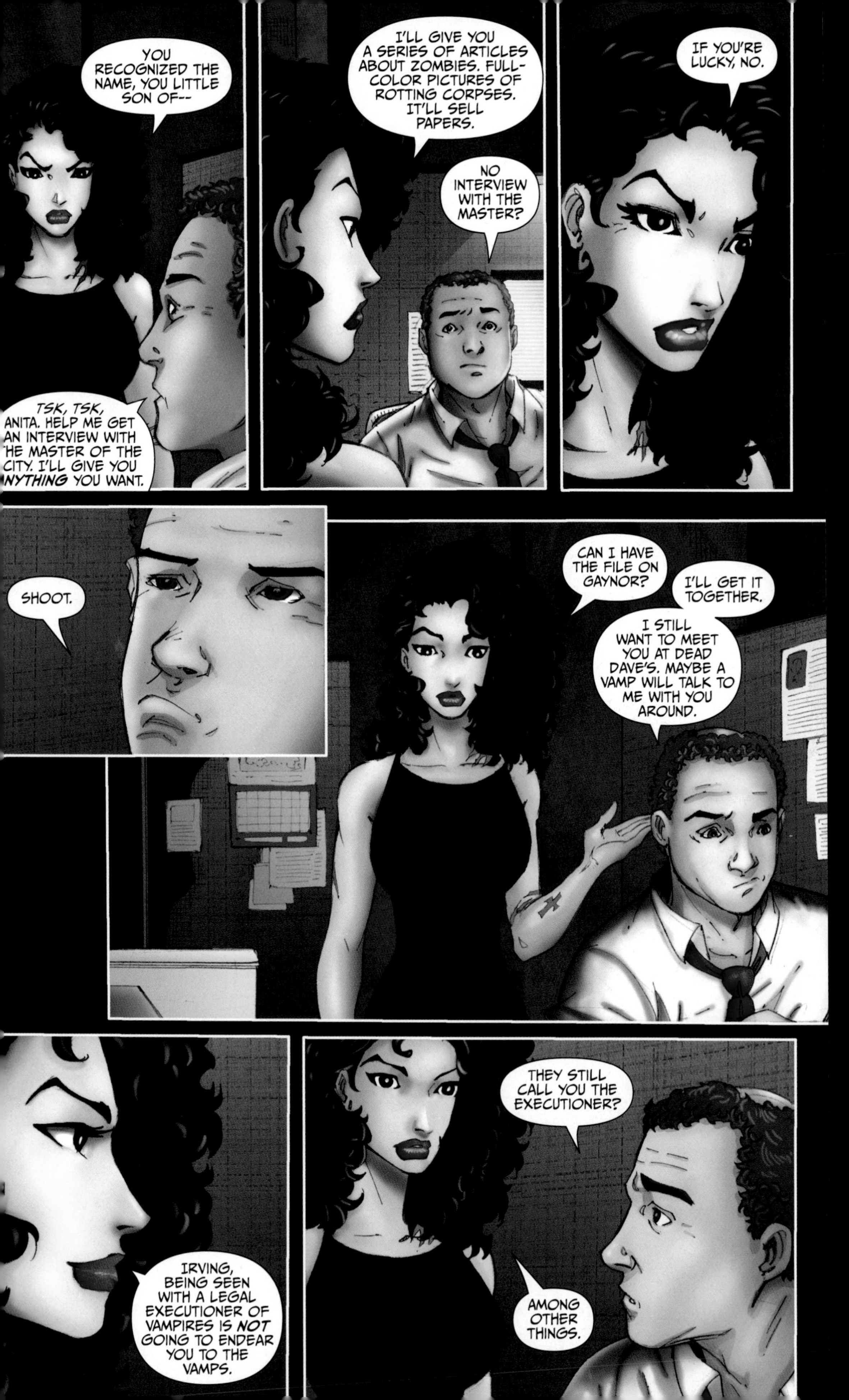
YOU RECOGNIZED THE NAME, YOU LITTLE SON OF--
TSK, TSK, ANITA. HELP ME GET AN INTERVIEW WITH HE MASTER OF THE CITY. I'LL GIVE YOU NYTHING YOU WANT.
I'LL GIVE YOU A SERIES OF ARTICLES ABOUT ZOMBIES. FULL-COLOR PICTURES OF ROTTING CORPSES. IT'LL SELL PAPERS.
NO INTERVIEW WITH THE MASTER?
IF YOU'RE LUCKY, NO.
SHOOT.
CAN I HAVE THE FILE ON GAYNOR?
I'LL GET IT TOGETHER.
I STILL WANT TO MEET YOU AT DEAD DAVE'S. MAYBE A VAMP WILL TALK TO ME WITH YOU AROUND.
IRVING, BEING SEEN WITH A LEGAL EXECUTIONER OF VAMPIRES IS NOT GOING TO ENDEAR YOU TO THE VAMPS.
THEY STILL CALL YOU THE EXECUTIONER?
AMONG OTHER THINGS.

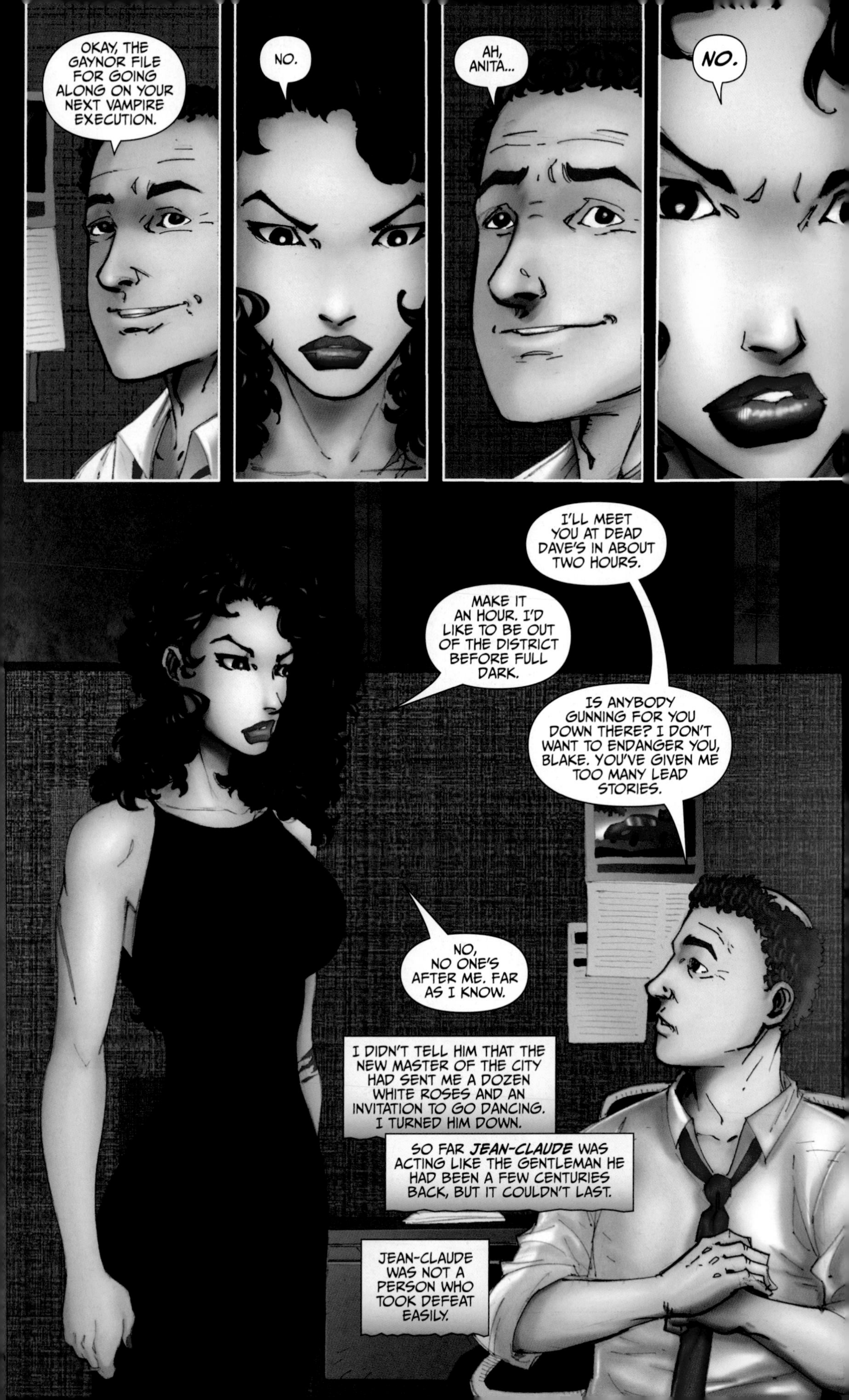

OKAY, THE GAYNOR FILE FOR GOING ALONG ON YOUR NEXT VAMPIRE EXECUTION.
NO.
AH, ANITA...
NO.
I'LL MEET YOU AT DEAD DAVE'S IN ABOUT TWO HOURS.
MAKE IT AN HOUR. I'D LIKE TO BE OUT OF THE DISTRICT BEFORE FULL DARK.
IS ANYBODY GUNNING FOR YOU DOWN THERE? I DON'T WANT TO ENDANGER YOU, BLAKE. YOU'VE GIVEN ME TOO MANY LEAD STORIES.
NO, NO ONE'S AFTER ME. FAR AS I KNOW.
I DIDN'T TELL HIM THAT THE NEW MASTER OF THE CITY HAD SENT ME A DOZEN WHITE ROSES AND AN INVITATION TO GO DANCING. I TURNED HIM DOWN.
SO FAR JEAN-CLAUDE WAS ACTING LIKE THE GENTLEMAN HE HAD BEEN A FEW CENTURIES BACK, BUT IT COULDN'T LAST.
JEAN-CLAUDE WAS NOT A PERSON WHO TOOK DEFEAT EASILY.

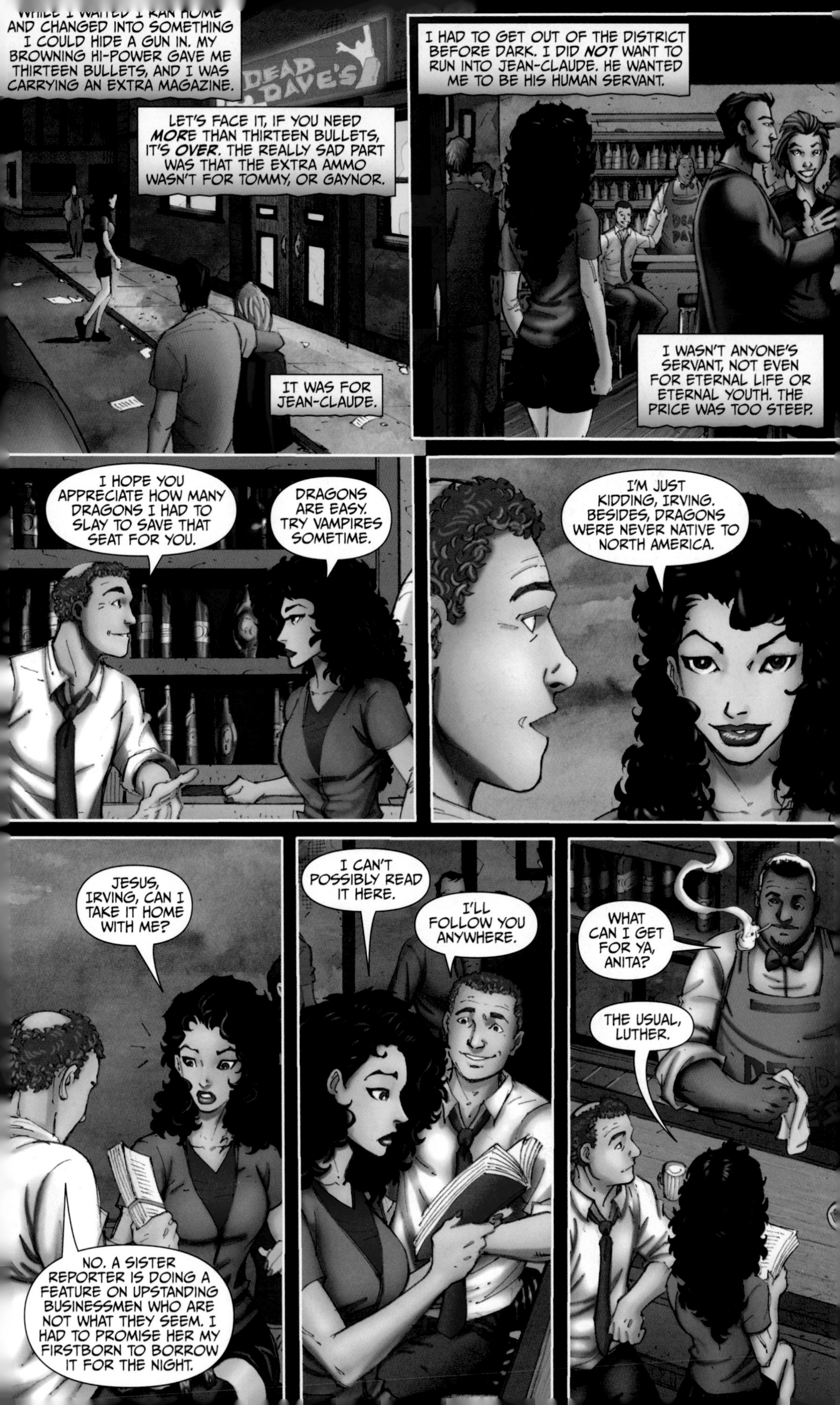

AND CHANGED INTO SOMETHING I COULD HIDE A GUN IN. MY BROWNING HI-POWER GAVE ME THIRTEEN BULLETS, AND I WAS CARRYING AN EXTRA MAGAZINE.
DEAD DAVE'S
LET'S FACE IT, IF YOU NEED MORE THAN THIRTEEN BULLETS, IT'S OVER. THE REALLY SAD PART WAS THAT THE EXTRA AMMO WASN'T FOR TOMMY, OR GAYNOR.
IT WAS FOR JEAN-CLAUDE.
I HAD TO GET OUT OF THE DISTRICT BEFORE DARK. I DID NOT WANT TO RUN INTO JEAN-CLAUDE. HE WANTED ME TO BE HIS HUMAN SERVANT.
I WASN'T ANYONE'S SERVANT, NOT EVEN FOR ETERNAL LIFE OR ETERNAL YOUTH. THE PRICE WAS TOO STEEP.
I HOPE YOU APPRECIATE HOW MANY DRAGONS I HAD TO SLAY TO SAVE THAT SEAT FOR YOU.
DRAGONS ARE EASY. TRY VAMPIRES SOMETIME.
I'M JUST KIDDING, IRVING. BESIDES, DRAGONS WERE NEVER NATIVE TO NORTH AMERICA.
JESUS, IRVING, CAN I TAKE IT HOME WITH ME?
NO. A SISTER REPORTER IS DOING A FEATURE ON UPSTANDING BUSINESSMEN WHO ARE NOT WHAT THEY SEEM. I HAD TO PROMISE HER MY FIRSTBORN TO BORROW IT FOR THE NIGHT.
I CAN'T POSSIBLY READ IT HERE.
I'LL FOLLOW YOU ANYWHERE.
WHAT CAN I GET FOR YA, ANITA?
THE USUAL, LUTHER.

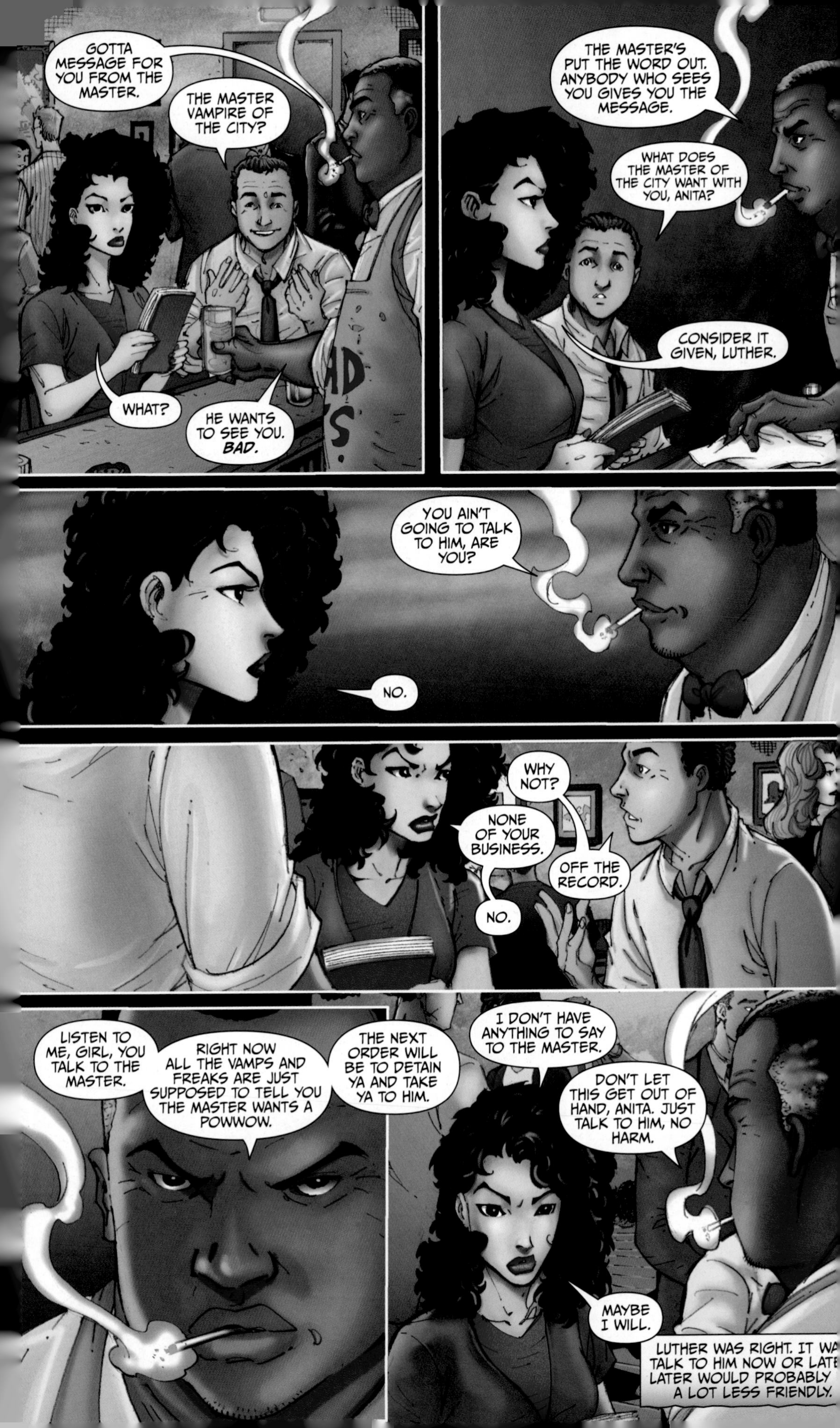

GOTTA MESSAGE FOR YOU FROM THE MASTER.
THE MASTER VAMPIRE OF THE CITY?
WHAT?
HE WANTS TO SEE YOU. BAD.
THE MASTER'S PUT THE WORD OUT. ANYBODY WHO SEES YOU GIVES YOU THE MESSAGE.
WHAT DOES THE MASTER OF THE CITY WANT WITH YOU, ANITA?
CONSIDER IT GIVEN, LUTHER.
YOU AIN'T GOING TO TALK TO HIM, ARE YOU?
NO.
WHY NOT?
NONE OF YOUR BUSINESS.
OFF THE RECORD.
NO.
LISTEN TO ME, GIRL, YOU TALK TO THE MASTER.
RIGHT NOW ALL THE VAMPS AND FREAKS ARE JUST SUPPOSED TO TELL YOU THE MASTER WANTS A POWWOW.
THE NEXT ORDER WILL BE TO DETAIN YA AND TAKE YA TO HIM.
I DON'T HAVE ANYTHING TO SAY TO THE MASTER.
DON'T LET THIS GET OUT OF HAND, ANITA. JUST TALK TO HIM, NO HARM.
MAYBE I WILL.

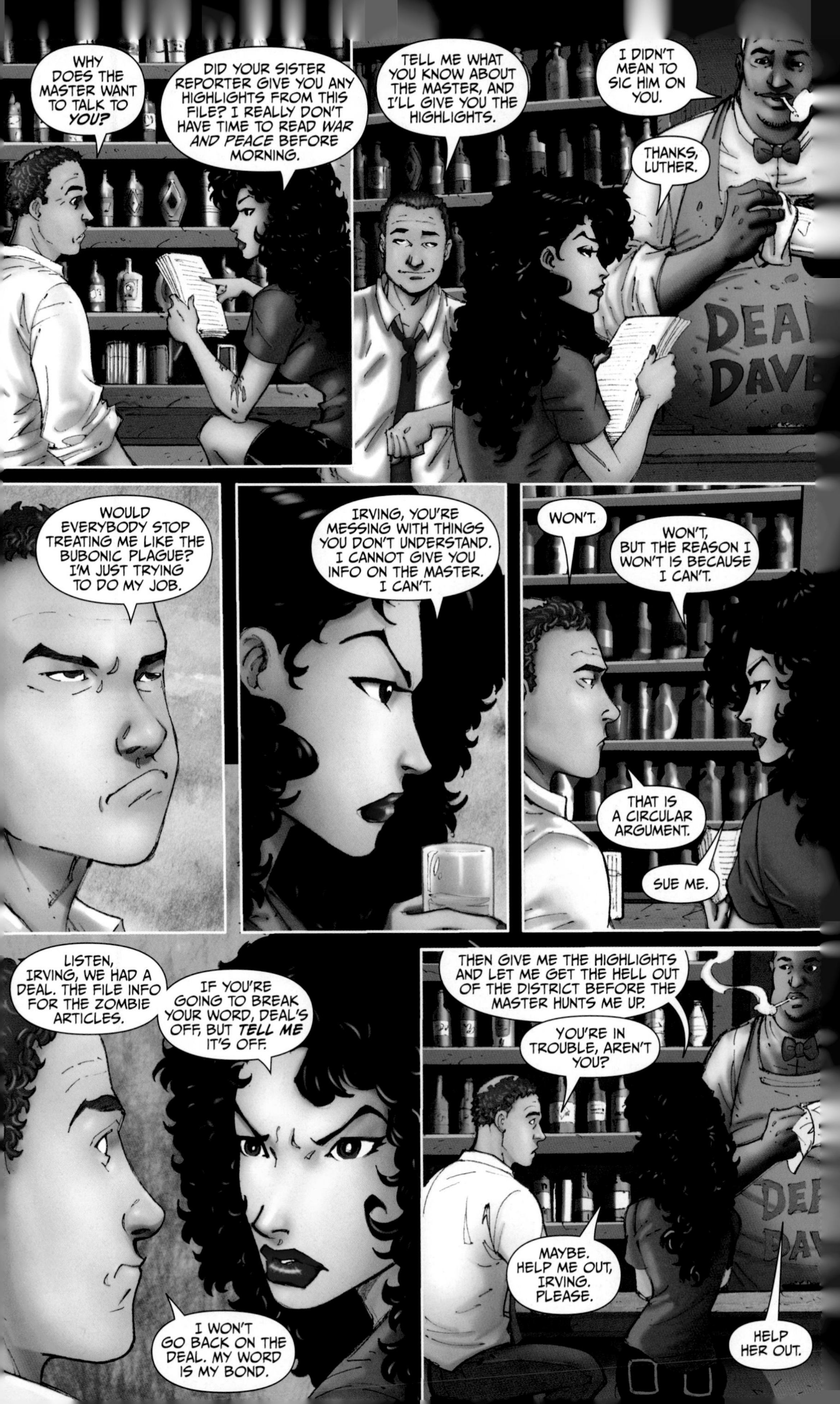
WHY DOES THE MASTER WANT TO TALK TO YOU?
DID YOUR SISTER REPORTER GIVE YOU ANY HIGHLIGHTS FROM THIS FILE? I REALLY DON'T HAVE TIME TO READ WAR AND PEACE BEFORE MORNING.
TELL ME WHAT YOU KNOW ABOUT THE MASTER, AND I'LL GIVE YOU THE HIGHLIGHTS.
I DIDN'T MEAN TO SIC HIM ON YOU.
THANKS, LUTHER.
DEAD DAVE
WOULD EVERYBODY STOP TREATING ME LIKE THE BUBONIC PLAGUE? I'M JUST TRYING TO DO MY JOB.
IRVING, YOU'RE MESSING WITH THINGS YOU DON'T UNDERSTAND. I CANNOT GIVE YOU INFO ON THE MASTER. I CAN'T.
WON'T.
WON'T, BUT THE REASON I WON'T IS BECAUSE I CAN'T.
THAT IS A CIRCULAR ARGUMENT.
SUE ME.
LISTEN, IRVING, WE HAD A DEAL. THE FILE INFO FOR THE ZOMBIE ARTICLES.
IF YOU'RE GOING TO BREAK YOUR WORD, DEAL'S OFF, BUT TELL ME IT'S OFF.
I WON'T GO BACK ON THE DEAL. MY WORD IS MY BOND.
THEN GIVE ME THE HIGHLIGHTS AND LET ME GET THE HELL OUT OF THE DISTRICT BEFORE THE MASTER HUNTS ME UP.
YOU'RE IN TROUBLE, AREN'T YOU?
MAYBE. HELP ME OUT, IRVING. PLEASE.
HELP HER OUT.

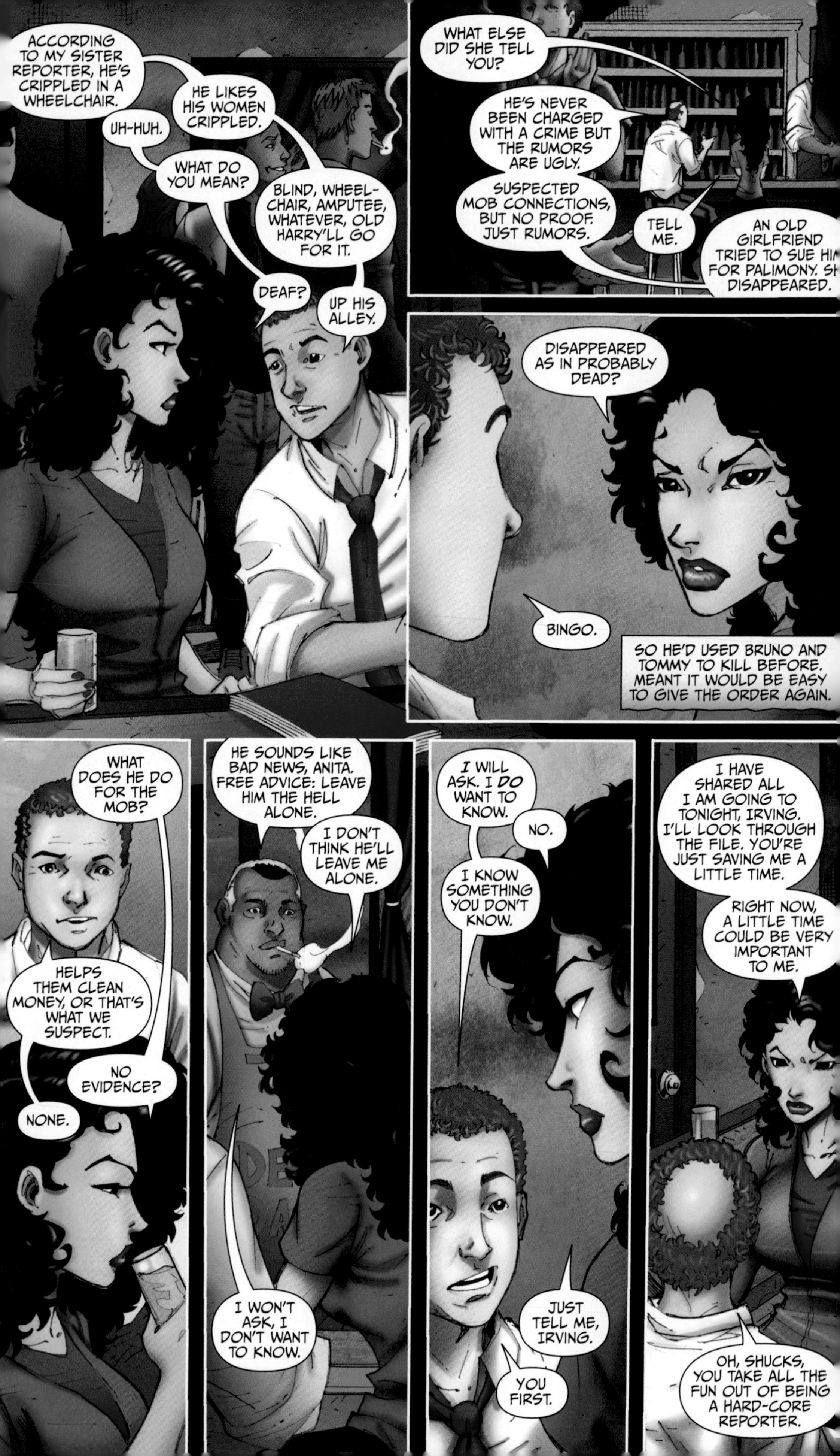
ACCORDING TO MY SISTER REPORTER, HE'S CRIPPLED IN A WHEELCHAIR.
UH-HUH.
HE LIKES HIS WOMEN CRIPPLED.
WHAT DO YOU MEAN?
BLIND, WHEEL-CHAIR, AMPUTEE, WHATEVER, OLD HARRY'LL GO FOR IT.
DEAF?
UP HIS ALLEY.
WHAT ELSE DID SHE TELL YOU?
HE'S NEVER BEEN CHARGED WITH A CRIME BUT THE RUMORS ARE UGLY.
SUSPECTED MOB CONNECTIONS, BUT NO PROOF. JUST RUMORS.
TELL ME.
AN OLD GIRLFRIEND TRIED TO SUE HI FOR PALIMONY. SH DISAPPEARED.
DISAPPEARED AS IN PROBABLY DEAD?
BINGO.
SO HE'D USED BRUNO AND TOMMY TO KILL BEFORE. MEANT IT WOULD BE EASY TO GIVE THE ORDER AGAIN.
WHAT DOES HE DO FOR THE MOB?
HELPS THEM CLEAN MONEY, OR THAT'S WHAT WE SUSPECT.
NO EVIDENCE?
NONE.
HE SOUNDS LIKE BAD NEWS, ANITA. FREE ADVICE: LEAVE HIM THE HELL ALONE.
I DON'T THINK HE'LL LEAVE ME ALONE.
I WON'T ASK, I DON'T WANT TO KNOW.
I WILL ASK. I DO WANT TO KNOW.
NO.
I KNOW SOMETHING YOU DON'T KNOW.
JUST TELL ME, IRVING.
YOU FIRST.
I HAVE SHARED ALL I AM GOING TO TONIGHT, IRVING. I'LL LOOK THROUGH THE FILE. YOU'RE JUST SAVING ME A LITTLE TIME.
RIGHT NOW, A LITTLE TIME COULD BE VERY IMPORTANT TO ME.
OH, SHUCKS, YOU TAKE ALL THE FUN OUT OF BEING A HARD-CORE REPORTER.

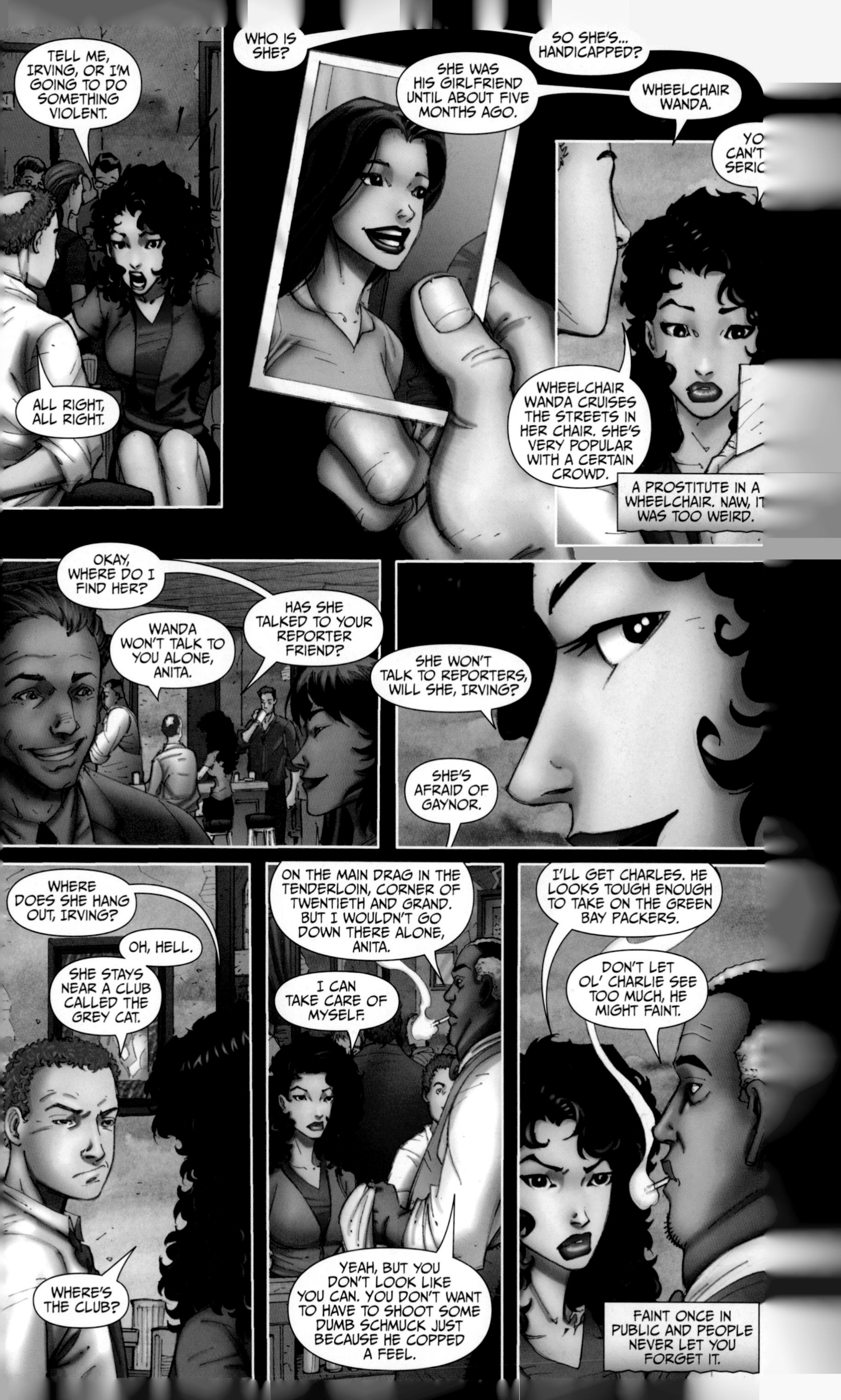
TELL ME, IRVING, OR I'M GOING TO DO SOMETHING VIOLENT.
ALL RIGHT, ALL RIGHT.
WHO IS SHE?
SHE WAS HIS GIRLFRIEND UNTIL ABOUT FIVE MONTHS AGO.
SO SHE'S... HANDICAPPED?
WHEELCHAIR WANDA.
WHEELCHAIR WANDA CRUISES THE STREETS IN HER CHAIR. SHE'S VERY POPULAR WITH A CERTAIN CROWD.
A PROSTITUTE IN A WHEELCHAIR. NAW, IT WAS TOO WEIRD.
OKAY, WHERE DO I FIND HER?
WANDA WON'T TALK TO YOU ALONE, ANITA.
HAS SHE TALKED TO YOUR REPORTER FRIEND?
SHE WON'T TALK TO REPORTERS, WILL SHE, IRVING?
SHE'S AFRAID OF GAYNOR.
WHERE DOES SHE HANG OUT, IRVING?
OH, HELL.
SHE STAYS NEAR A CLUB CALLED THE GREY CAT.
WHERE'S THE CLUB?
ON THE MAIN DRAG IN THE TENDERLOIN, CORNER OF TWENTIETH AND GRAND. BUT I WOULDN'T GO DOWN THERE ALONE, ANITA.
I CAN TAKE CARE OF MYSELF.
YEAH, BUT YOU DON'T LOOK LIKE YOU CAN. YOU DON'T WANT TO HAVE TO SHOOT SOME DUMB SCHMUCK JUST BECAUSE HE COPPED A FEEL.
I'LL GET CHARLES. HE LOOKS TOUGH ENOUGH TO TAKE ON THE GREEN BAY PACKERS.
DON'T LET OL' CHARLIE SEE TOO MUCH, HE MIGHT FAINT.
FAINT ONCE IN PUBLIC AND PEOPLE NEVER LET YOU FORGET IT.

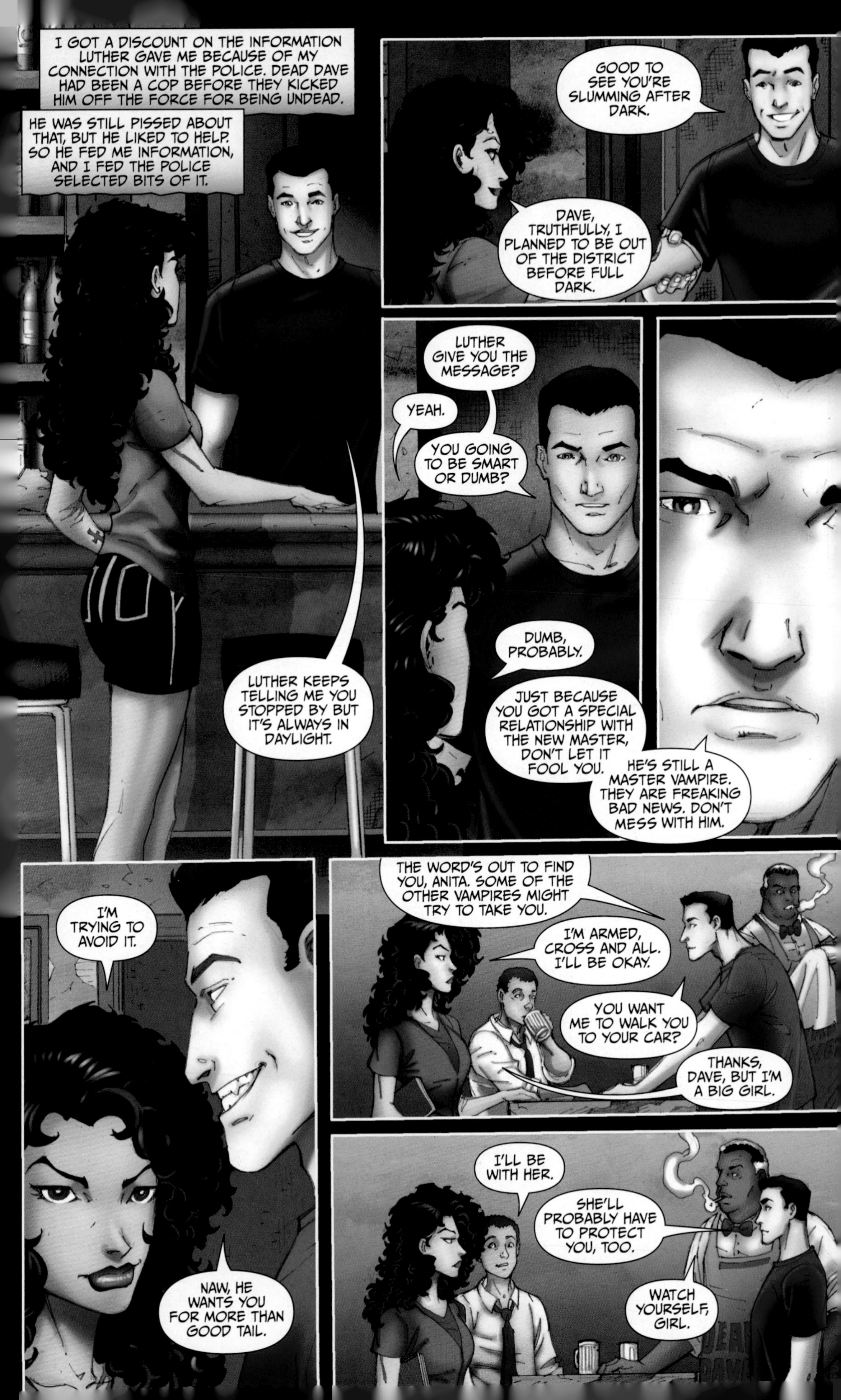
I GOT A DISCOUNT ON THE INFORMATION LUTHER GAVE ME BECAUSE OF MY CONNECTION WITH THE POLICE. DEAD DAVE HAD BEEN A COP BEFORE THEY KICKED HIM OFF THE FORCE FOR BEING UNDEAD.
HE WAS STILL PISSED ABOUT THAT, BUT HE LIKED TO HELP. SO HE FED ME INFORMATION, AND I FED THE POLICE SELECTED BITS OF IT.
LUTHER KEEPS TELLING ME YOU STOPPED BY BUT IT'S ALWAYS IN DAYLIGHT.
GOOD TO SEE YOU'RE SLUMMING AFTER DARK.
DAVE, TRUTHFULLY, I PLANNED TO BE OUT OF THE DISTRICT BEFORE FULL DARK.
LUTHER GIVE YOU THE MESSAGE?
YEAH.
YOU GOING TO BE SMART OR DUMB?
DUMB, PROBABLY.
JUST BECAUSE YOU GOT A SPECIAL RELATIONSHIP WITH THE NEW MASTER, DON'T LET IT FOOL YOU.
HE'S STILL A MASTER VAMPIRE. THEY ARE FREAKING BAD NEWS. DON'T MESS WITH HIM.
I'M TRYING TO AVOID IT.
NAW, HE WANTS YOU FOR MORE THAN GOOD TAIL.
THE WORD'S OUT TO FIND YOU, ANITA. SOME OF THE OTHER VAMPIRES MIGHT TRY TO TAKE YOU.
I'M ARMED, CROSS AND ALL. I'LL BE OKAY.
YOU WANT ME TO WALK YOU TO YOUR CAR?
THANKS, DAVE, BUT I'M A BIG GIRL.
I'LL BE WITH HER.
SHE'LL PROBABLY HAVE TO PROTECT YOU, TOO.
WATCH YOURSELF, GIRL.

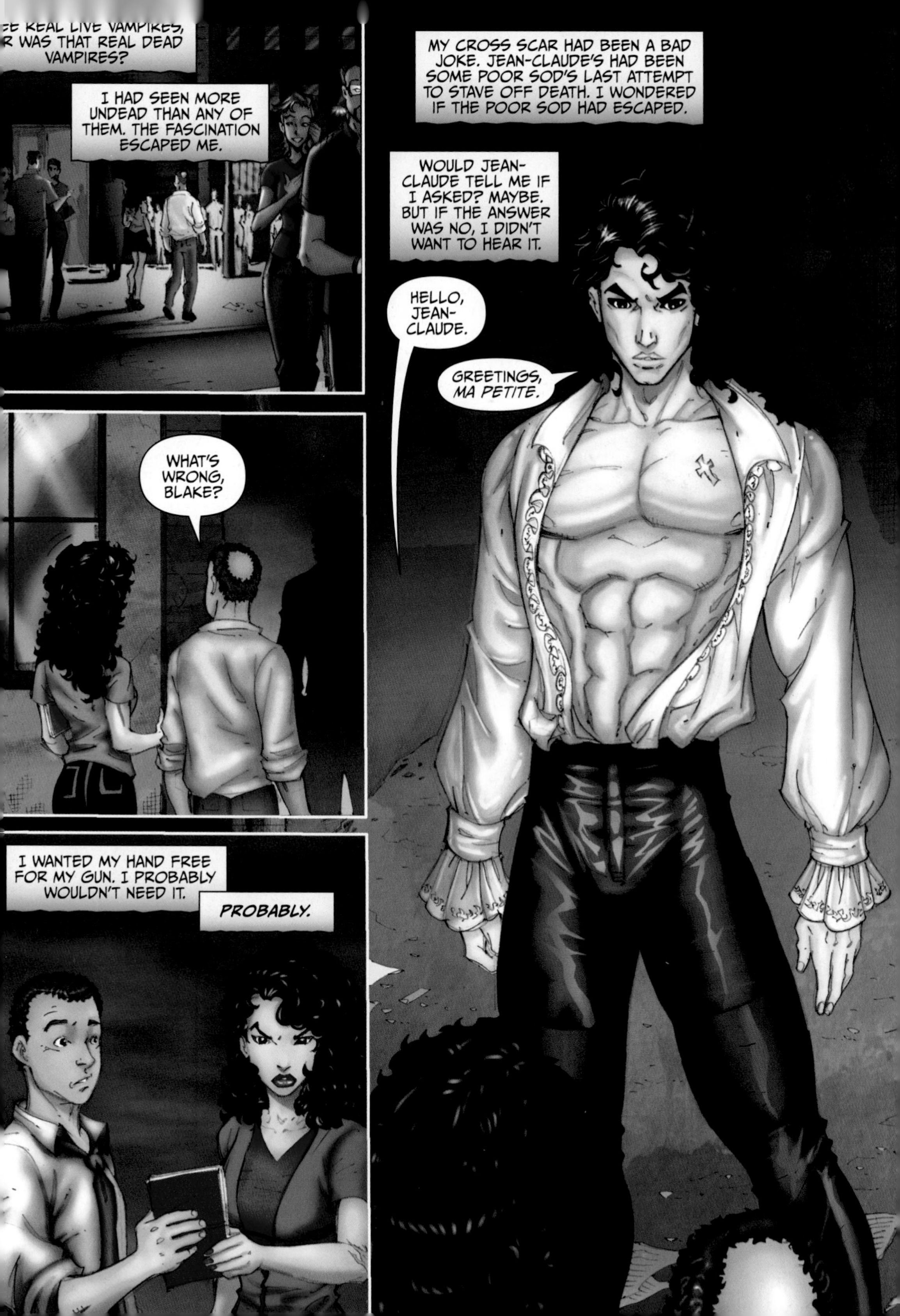
REAL LIVE VAMPIRES, WAS THAT REAL DEAD VAMPIRES?
I HAD SEEN MORE UNDEAD THAN ANY OF THEM. THE FASCINATION ESCAPED ME.
WHAT'S WRONG, BLAKE?
I WANTED MY HAND FREE FOR MY GUN. I PROBABLY WOULDN'T NEED IT.
PROBABLY.
MY CROSS SCAR HAD BEEN A BAD JOKE. JEAN-CLAUDE'S HAD BEEN SOME POOR SOD'S LAST ATTEMPT TO STAVE OFF DEATH. I WONDERED IF THE POOR SOD HAD ESCAPED.
WOULD JEAN-CLAUDE TELL ME IF I ASKED? MAYBE. BUT IF THE ANSWER WAS NO, I DIDN'T WANT TO HEAR IT.
HELLO, JEAN-CLAUDE.
GREETINGS, MA PETITE.

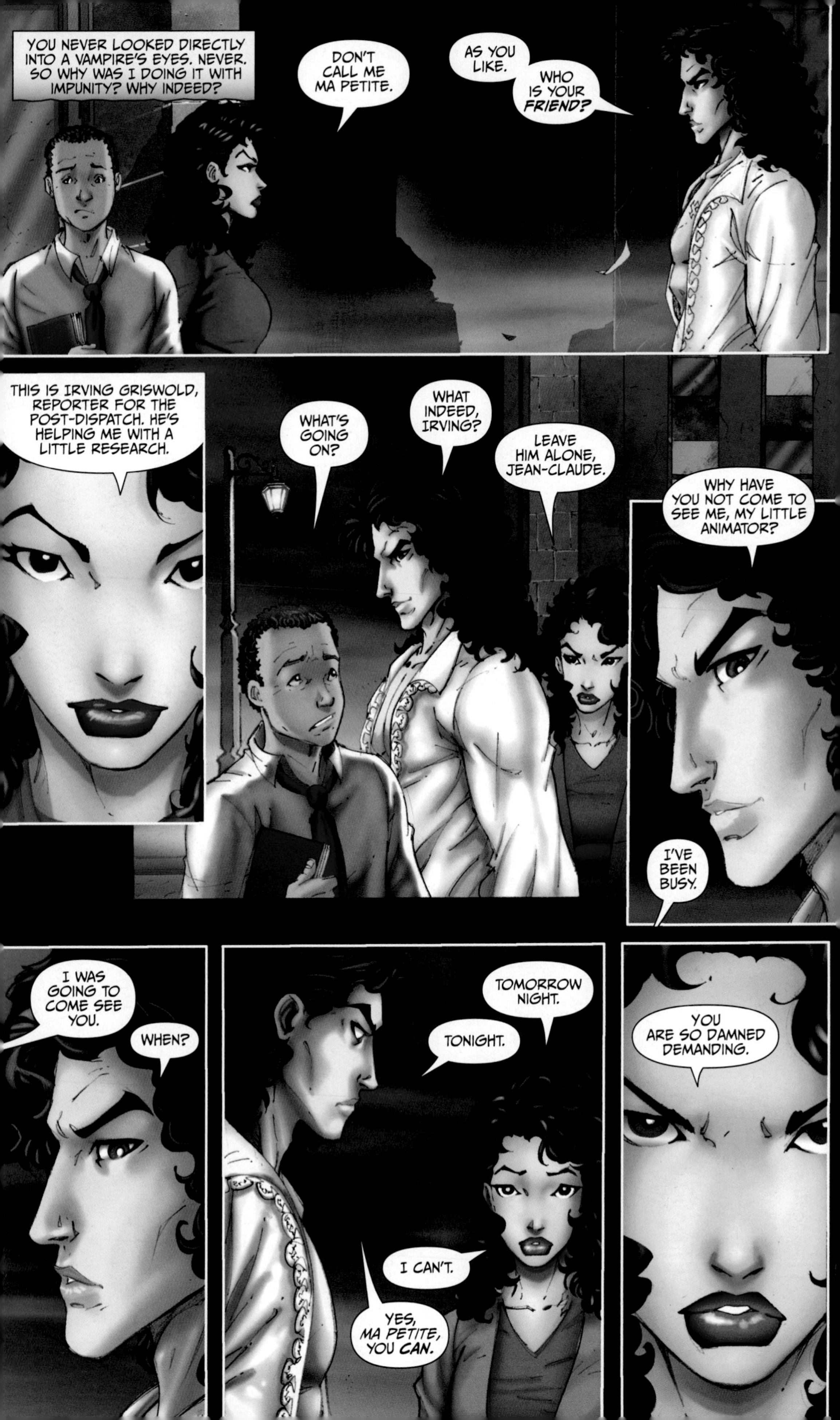
YOU NEVER LOOKED DIRECTLY INTO A VAMPIRE'S EYES. NEVER. SO WHY WAS I DOING IT WITH IMPUNITY? WHY INDEED?
DON'T CALL ME MA PETITE.
AS YOU LIKE.
WHO IS YOUR *FRIEND?*
THIS IS IRVING GRISWOLD, REPORTER FOR THE POST-DISPATCH. HE'S HELPING ME WITH A LITTLE RESEARCH.
WHAT'S GOING ON?
WHAT INDEED, IRVING?
LEAVE HIM ALONE, JEAN-CLAUDE.
WHY HAVE YOU NOT COME TO SEE ME, MY LITTLE ANIMATOR?
I'VE BEEN BUSY.
I WAS GOING TO COME SEE YOU.
WHEN?
TOMORROW NIGHT.
TONIGHT.
I CAN'T.
YES, *MA PETITE,* YOU ***CAN.***
YOU ARE SO DAMNED DEMANDING.

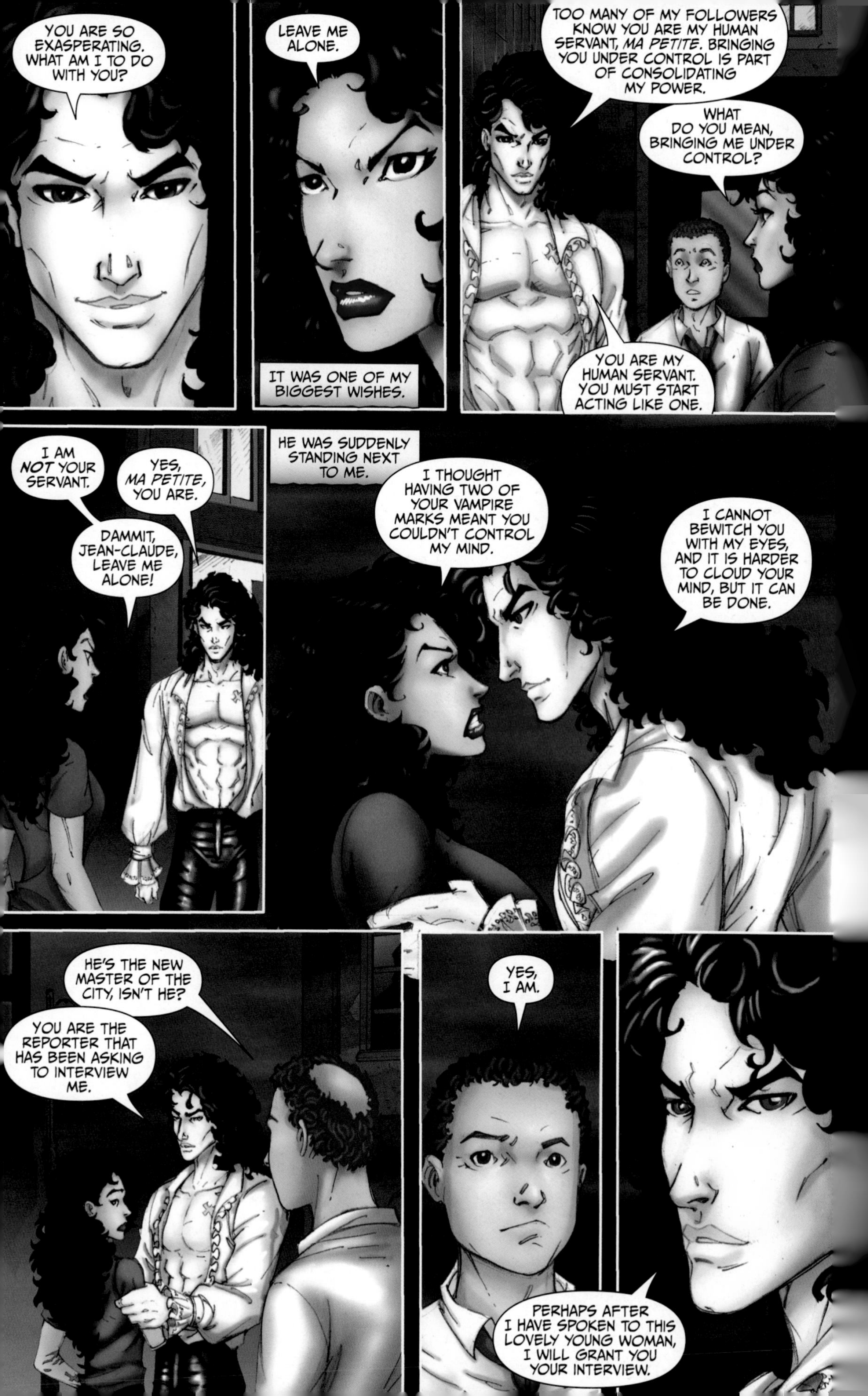

YOU ARE SO EXASPERATING. WHAT AM I TO DO WITH YOU?
LEAVE ME ALONE.
IT WAS ONE OF MY BIGGEST WISHES.
TOO MANY OF MY FOLLOWERS KNOW YOU ARE MY HUMAN SERVANT, *MA PETITE*. BRINGING YOU UNDER CONTROL IS PART OF CONSOLIDATING MY POWER.
WHAT DO YOU MEAN, BRINGING ME UNDER CONTROL?
YOU ARE MY HUMAN SERVANT. YOU MUST START ACTING LIKE ONE.
I AM *NOT* YOUR SERVANT.
YES, *MA PETITE*, YOU ARE.
DAMMIT, JEAN-CLAUDE, LEAVE ME ALONE!
HE WAS SUDDENLY STANDING NEXT TO ME.
I THOUGHT HAVING TWO OF YOUR VAMPIRE MARKS MEANT YOU COULDN'T CONTROL MY MIND.
I CANNOT BEWITCH YOU WITH MY EYES, AND IT IS HARDER TO CLOUD YOUR MIND, BUT IT CAN BE DONE.
HE'S THE NEW MASTER OF THE CITY, ISN'T HE?
YOU ARE THE REPORTER THAT HAS BEEN ASKING TO INTERVIEW ME.
YES, I AM.
PERHAPS AFTER I HAVE SPOKEN TO THIS LOVELY YOUNG WOMAN, I WILL GRANT YOU YOUR INTERVIEW.

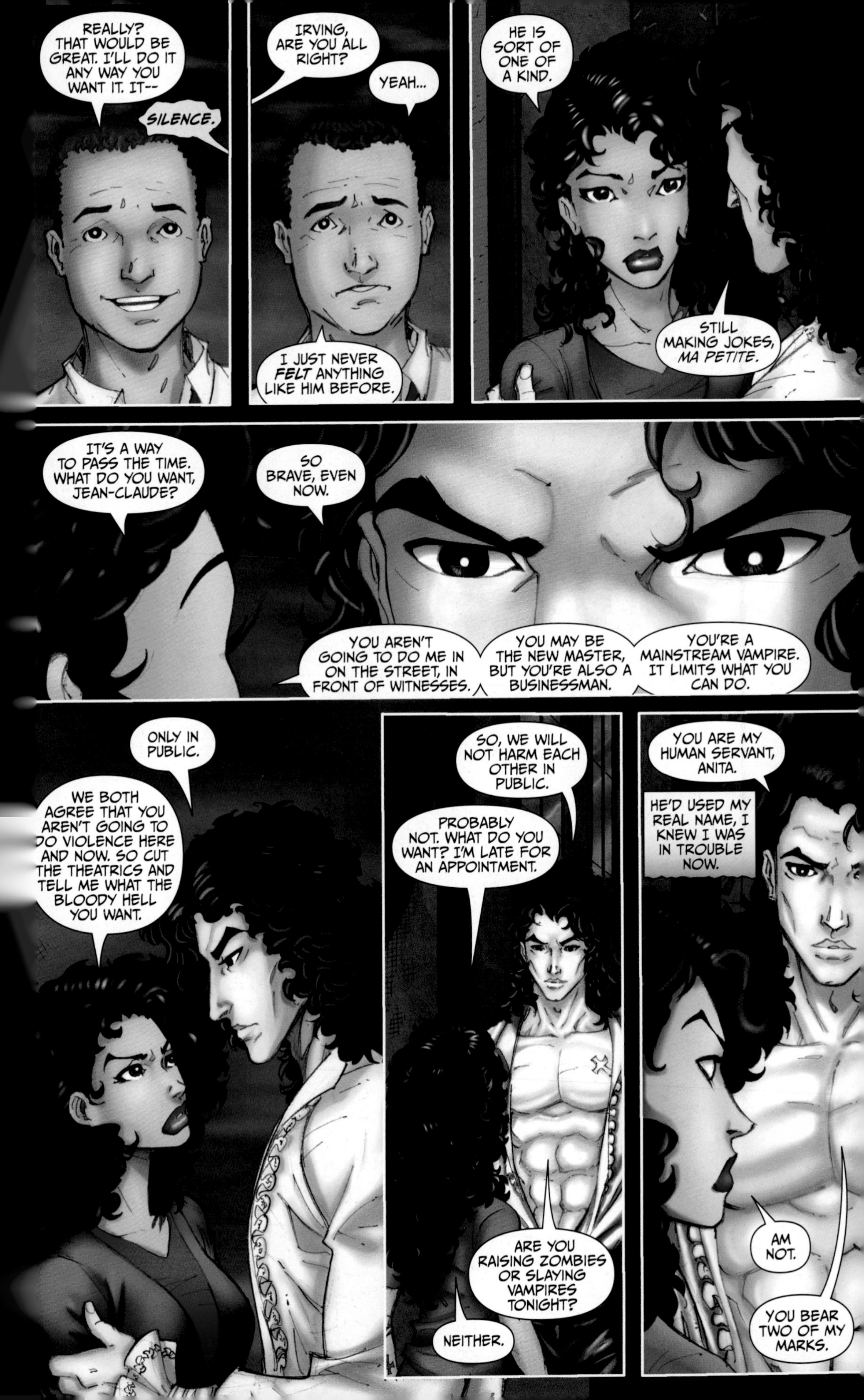
REALLY? THAT WOULD BE GREAT. I'LL DO IT ANY WAY YOU WANT IT. IT--
SILENCE.
IRVING, ARE YOU ALL RIGHT?
YEAH...
I JUST NEVER FELT ANYTHING LIKE HIM BEFORE.
HE IS SORT OF ONE OF A KIND.
STILL MAKING JOKES, MA PETITE.
IT'S A WAY TO PASS THE TIME. WHAT DO YOU WANT, JEAN-CLAUDE?
SO BRAVE, EVEN NOW.
YOU AREN'T GOING TO DO ME IN ON THE STREET, IN FRONT OF WITNESSES.
YOU MAY BE THE NEW MASTER, BUT YOU'RE ALSO A BUSINESSMAN.
YOU'RE A MAINSTREAM VAMPIRE. IT LIMITS WHAT YOU CAN DO.
ONLY IN PUBLIC.
WE BOTH AGREE THAT YOU AREN'T GOING TO DO VIOLENCE HERE AND NOW. SO CUT THE THEATRICS AND TELL ME WHAT THE BLOODY HELL YOU WANT.
SO, WE WILL NOT HARM EACH OTHER IN PUBLIC.
PROBABLY NOT. WHAT DO YOU WANT? I'M LATE FOR AN APPOINTMENT.
ARE YOU RAISING ZOMBIES OR SLAYING VAMPIRES TONIGHT?
NEITHER.
YOU ARE MY HUMAN SERVANT, ANITA.
HE'D USED MY REAL NAME, I KNEW I WAS IN TROUBLE NOW.
AM NOT.
YOU BEAR TWO OF MY MARKS.

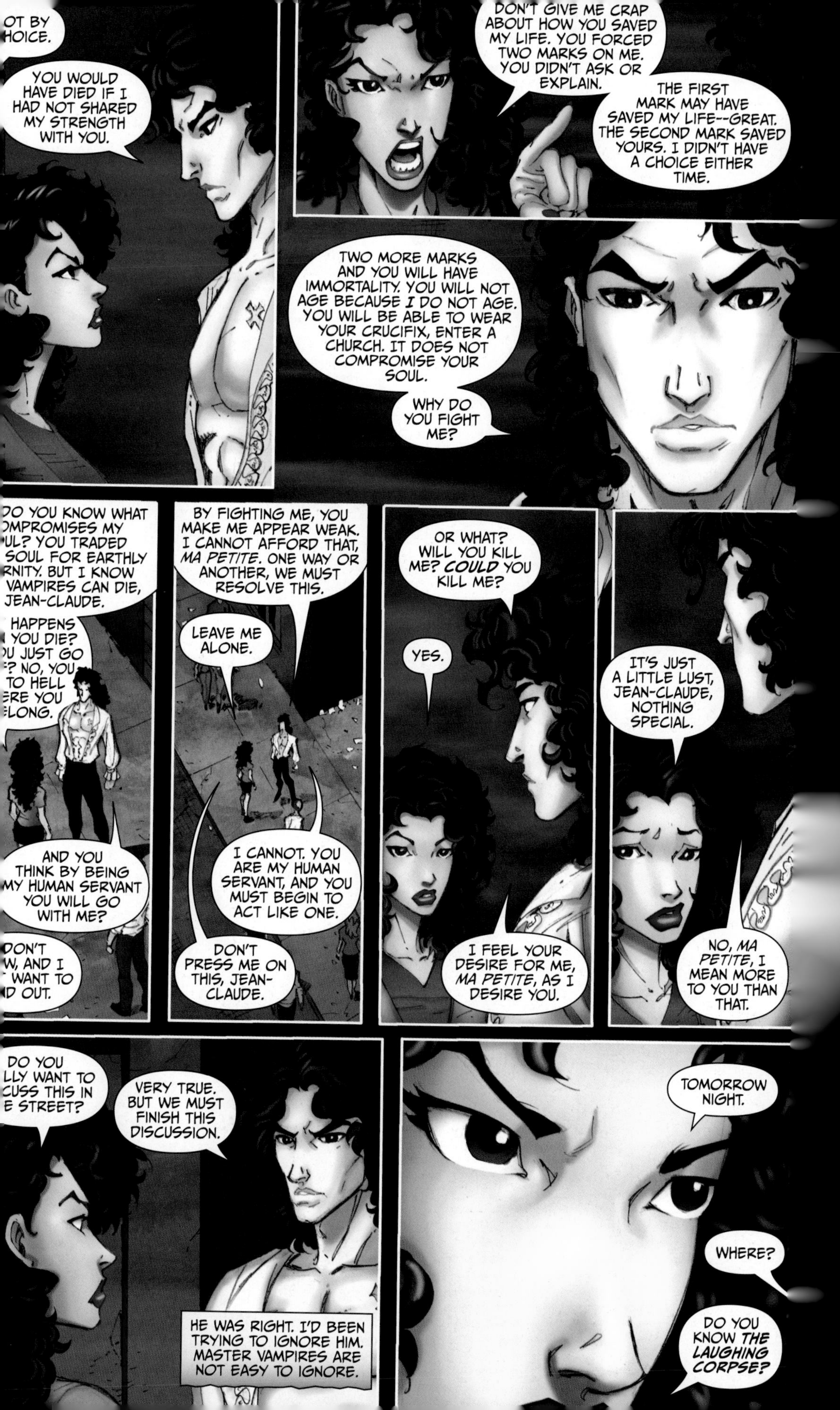

OT BY
HOICE.
YOU WOULD HAVE DIED IF I HAD NOT SHARED MY STRENGTH WITH YOU.
DON'T GIVE ME CRAP ABOUT HOW YOU SAVED MY LIFE. YOU FORCED TWO MARKS ON ME. YOU DIDN'T ASK OR EXPLAIN.
THE FIRST MARK MAY HAVE SAVED MY LIFE--GREAT. THE SECOND MARK SAVED YOURS. I DIDN'T HAVE A CHOICE EITHER TIME.
TWO MORE MARKS AND YOU WILL HAVE IMMORTALITY. YOU WILL NOT AGE BECAUSE *I* DO NOT AGE. YOU WILL BE ABLE TO WEAR YOUR CRUCIFIX, ENTER A CHURCH. IT DOES NOT COMPROMISE YOUR SOUL.
WHY DO YOU FIGHT ME?
DO YOU KNOW WHAT OMPROMISES MY UL? YOU TRADED SOUL FOR EARTHLY RNITY. BUT I KNOW VAMPIRES CAN DIE, JEAN-CLAUDE.
HAPPENS YOU DIE? U JUST GO ? NO, YOU TO HELL ERE YOU ELONG.
AND YOU THINK BY BEING MY HUMAN SERVANT YOU WILL GO WITH ME?
DON'T W, AND I WANT TO D OUT.
BY FIGHTING ME, YOU MAKE ME APPEAR WEAK. I CANNOT AFFORD THAT, *MA PETITE*. ONE WAY OR ANOTHER, WE MUST RESOLVE THIS.
LEAVE ME ALONE.
I CANNOT. YOU ARE MY HUMAN SERVANT, AND YOU MUST BEGIN TO ACT LIKE ONE.
DON'T PRESS ME ON THIS, JEAN-CLAUDE.
OR WHAT? WILL YOU KILL ME? ***COULD*** YOU KILL ME?
YES.
I FEEL YOUR DESIRE FOR ME, *MA PETITE*, AS I DESIRE YOU.
IT'S JUST A LITTLE LUST, JEAN-CLAUDE, NOTHING SPECIAL.
NO, *MA PETITE*, I MEAN MORE TO YOU THAN THAT.
DO YOU LLY WANT TO CUSS THIS IN E STREET?
VERY TRUE. BUT WE MUST FINISH THIS DISCUSSION.
HE WAS RIGHT. I'D BEEN TRYING TO IGNORE HIM. MASTER VAMPIRES ARE NOT EASY TO IGNORE.
TOMORROW NIGHT.
WHERE?
DO YOU KNOW ***THE LAUGHING CORPSE?***

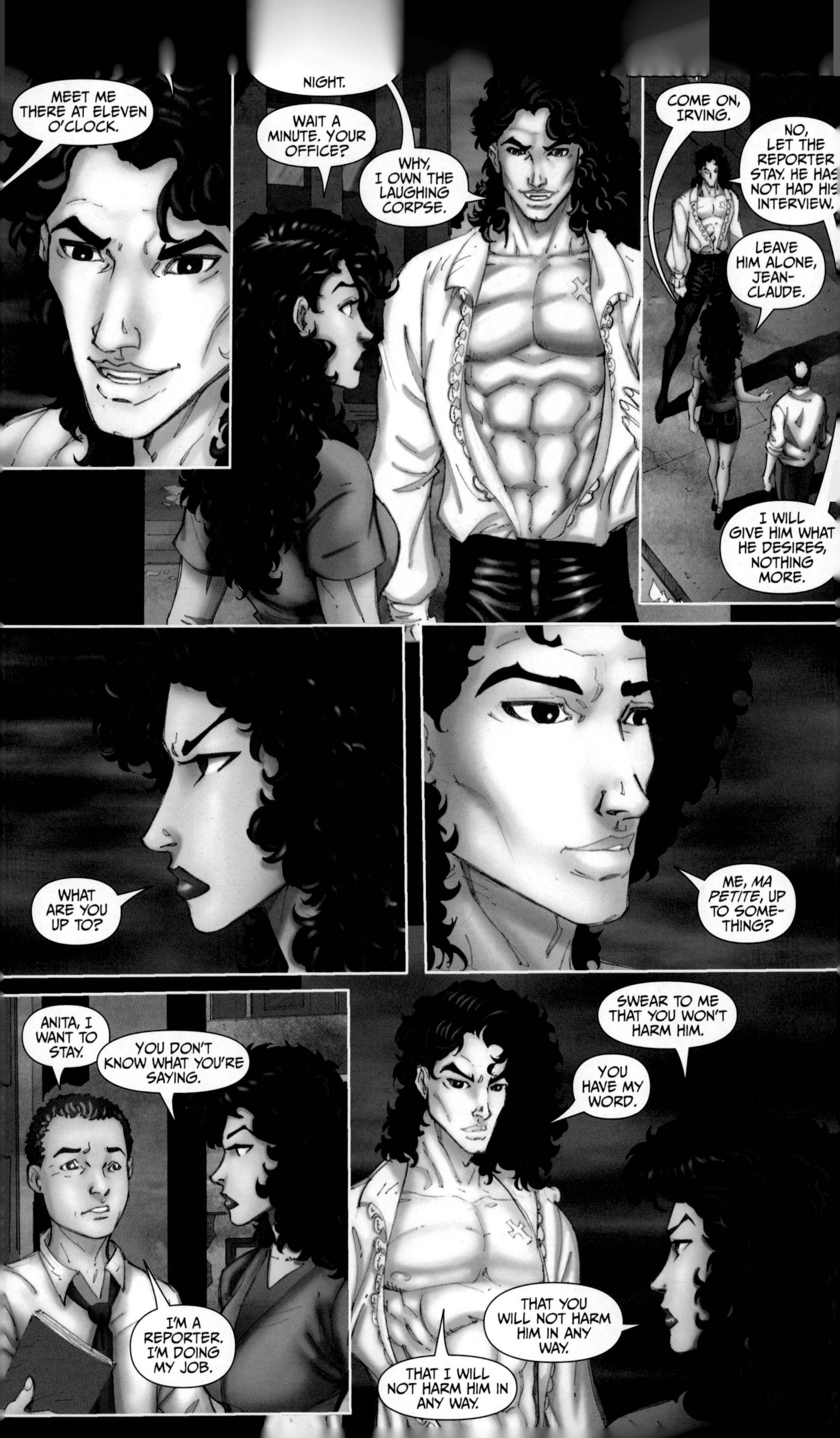
MEET ME THERE AT ELEVEN O'CLOCK.
NIGHT.
WAIT A MINUTE. YOUR OFFICE?
WHY, I OWN THE LAUGHING CORPSE.
COME ON, IRVING.
NO, LET THE REPORTER STAY. HE HAS NOT HAD HIS INTERVIEW.
LEAVE HIM ALONE, JEAN-CLAUDE.
I WILL GIVE HIM WHAT HE DESIRES, NOTHING MORE.
WHAT ARE YOU UP TO?
ME, *MA PETITE*, UP TO SOME-THING?
ANITA, I WANT TO STAY.
YOU DON'T KNOW WHAT YOU'RE SAYING.
I'M A REPORTER. I'M DOING MY JOB.
SWEAR TO ME THAT YOU WON'T HARM HIM.
YOU HAVE MY WORD.
THAT YOU WILL NOT HARM HIM IN ANY WAY.
THAT I WILL NOT HARM HIM IN ANY WAY.

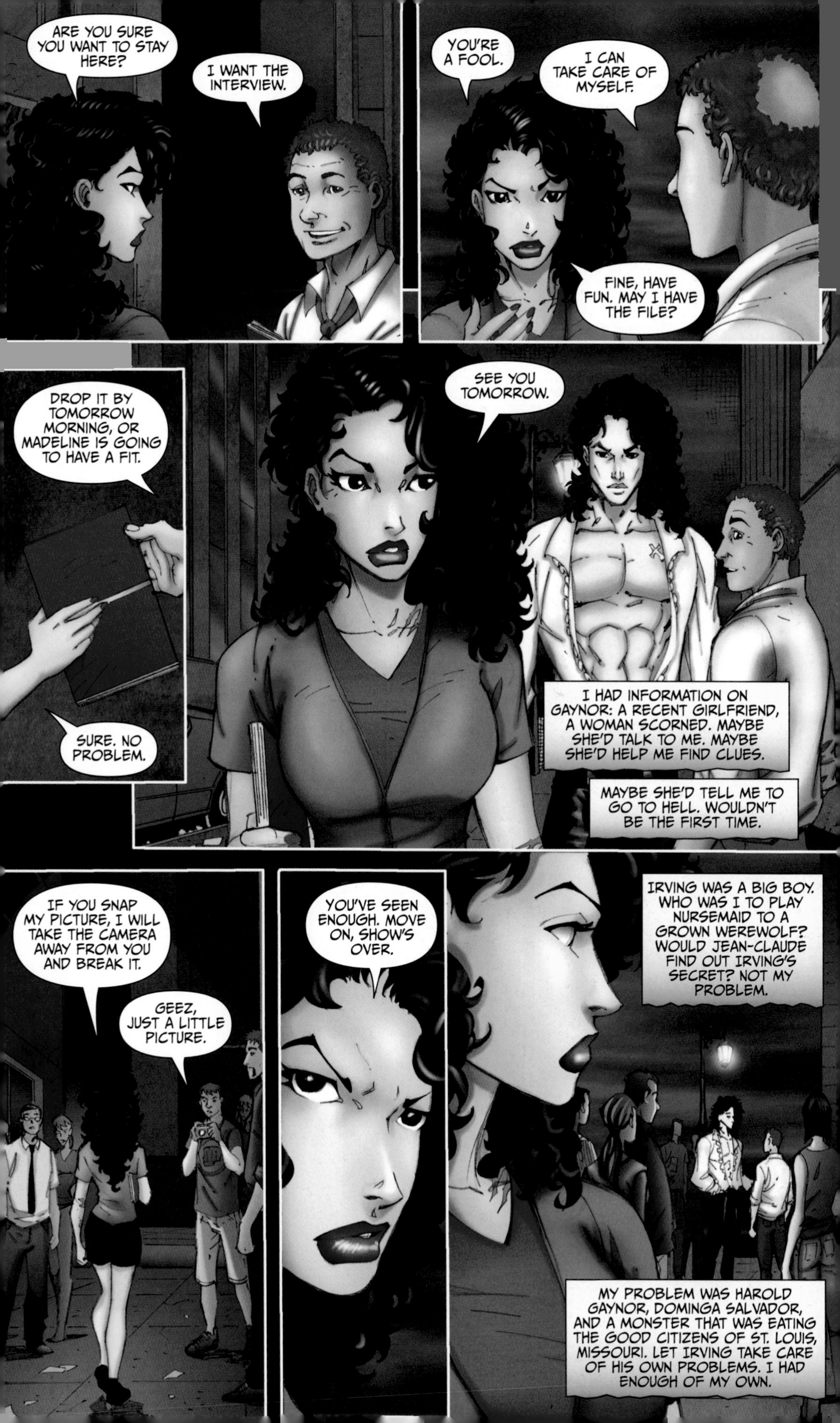
ARE YOU SURE YOU WANT TO STAY HERE?
I WANT THE INTERVIEW.
YOU'RE A FOOL.
I CAN TAKE CARE OF MYSELF.
FINE, HAVE FUN. MAY I HAVE THE FILE?
DROP IT BY TOMORROW MORNING, OR MADELINE IS GOING TO HAVE A FIT.
SURE. NO PROBLEM.
SEE YOU TOMORROW.
I HAD INFORMATION ON GAYNOR: A RECENT GIRLFRIEND, A WOMAN SCORNED. MAYBE SHE'D TALK TO ME. MAYBE SHE'D HELP ME FIND CLUES.
MAYBE SHE'D TELL ME TO GO TO HELL. WOULDN'T BE THE FIRST TIME.
IF YOU SNAP MY PICTURE, I WILL TAKE THE CAMERA AWAY FROM YOU AND BREAK IT.
GEEZ, JUST A LITTLE PICTURE.
YOU'VE SEEN ENOUGH. MOVE ON, SHOW'S OVER.
IRVING WAS A BIG BOY. WHO WAS I TO PLAY NURSEMAID TO A GROWN WEREWOLF? WOULD JEAN-CLAUDE FIND OUT IRVING'S SECRET? NOT MY PROBLEM.
MY PROBLEM WAS HAROLD GAYNOR, DOMINGA SALVADOR, AND A MONSTER THAT WAS EATING THE GOOD CITIZENS OF ST. LOUIS, MISSOURI. LET IRVING TAKE CARE OF HIS OWN PROBLEMS. I HAD ENOUGH OF MY OWN.

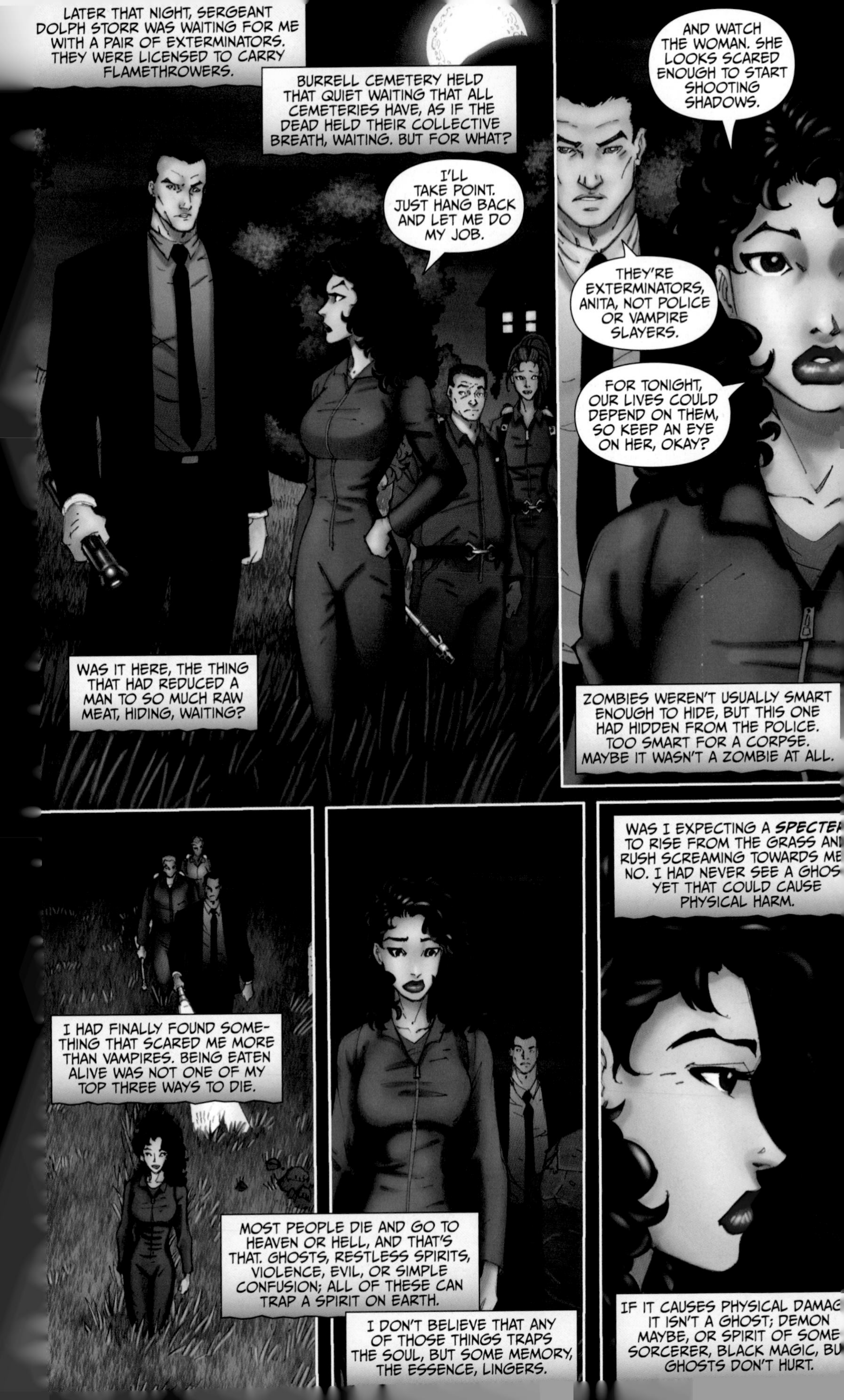
LATER THAT NIGHT, SERGEANT DOLPH STORR WAS WAITING FOR ME WITH A PAIR OF EXTERMINATORS. THEY WERE LICENSED TO CARRY FLAMETHROWERS.
BURRELL CEMETERY HELD THAT QUIET WAITING THAT ALL CEMETERIES HAVE, AS IF THE DEAD HELD THEIR COLLECTIVE BREATH, WAITING. BUT FOR WHAT?
I'LL TAKE POINT. JUST HANG BACK AND LET ME DO MY JOB.
WAS IT HERE, THE THING THAT HAD REDUCED A MAN TO SO MUCH RAW MEAT, HIDING, WAITING?
AND WATCH THE WOMAN. SHE LOOKS SCARED ENOUGH TO START SHOOTING SHADOWS.
THEY'RE EXTERMINATORS, ANITA, NOT POLICE OR VAMPIRE SLAYERS.
FOR TONIGHT, OUR LIVES COULD DEPEND ON THEM, SO KEEP AN EYE ON HER, OKAY?
ZOMBIES WEREN'T USUALLY SMART ENOUGH TO HIDE, BUT THIS ONE HAD HIDDEN FROM THE POLICE. TOO SMART FOR A CORPSE. MAYBE IT WASN'T A ZOMBIE AT ALL.
I HAD FINALLY FOUND SOMETHING THAT SCARED ME MORE THAN VAMPIRES. BEING EATEN ALIVE WAS NOT ONE OF MY TOP THREE WAYS TO DIE.
MOST PEOPLE DIE AND GO TO HEAVEN OR HELL, AND THAT'S THAT. GHOSTS, RESTLESS SPIRITS, VIOLENCE, EVIL, OR SIMPLE CONFUSION; ALL OF THESE CAN TRAP A SPIRIT ON EARTH.
I DON'T BELIEVE THAT ANY OF THOSE THINGS TRAPS THE SOUL, BUT SOME MEMORY, THE ESSENCE, LINGERS.
WAS I EXPECTING A *SPECTER* TO RISE FROM THE GRASS AND RUSH SCREAMING TOWARDS ME NO. I HAD NEVER SEE A GHOS YET THAT COULD CAUSE PHYSICAL HARM.
IF IT CAUSES PHYSICAL DAMAG IT ISN'T A GHOST; DEMON MAYBE, OR SPIRIT OF SOME SORCERER, BLACK MAGIC, BU GHOSTS DON'T HURT.

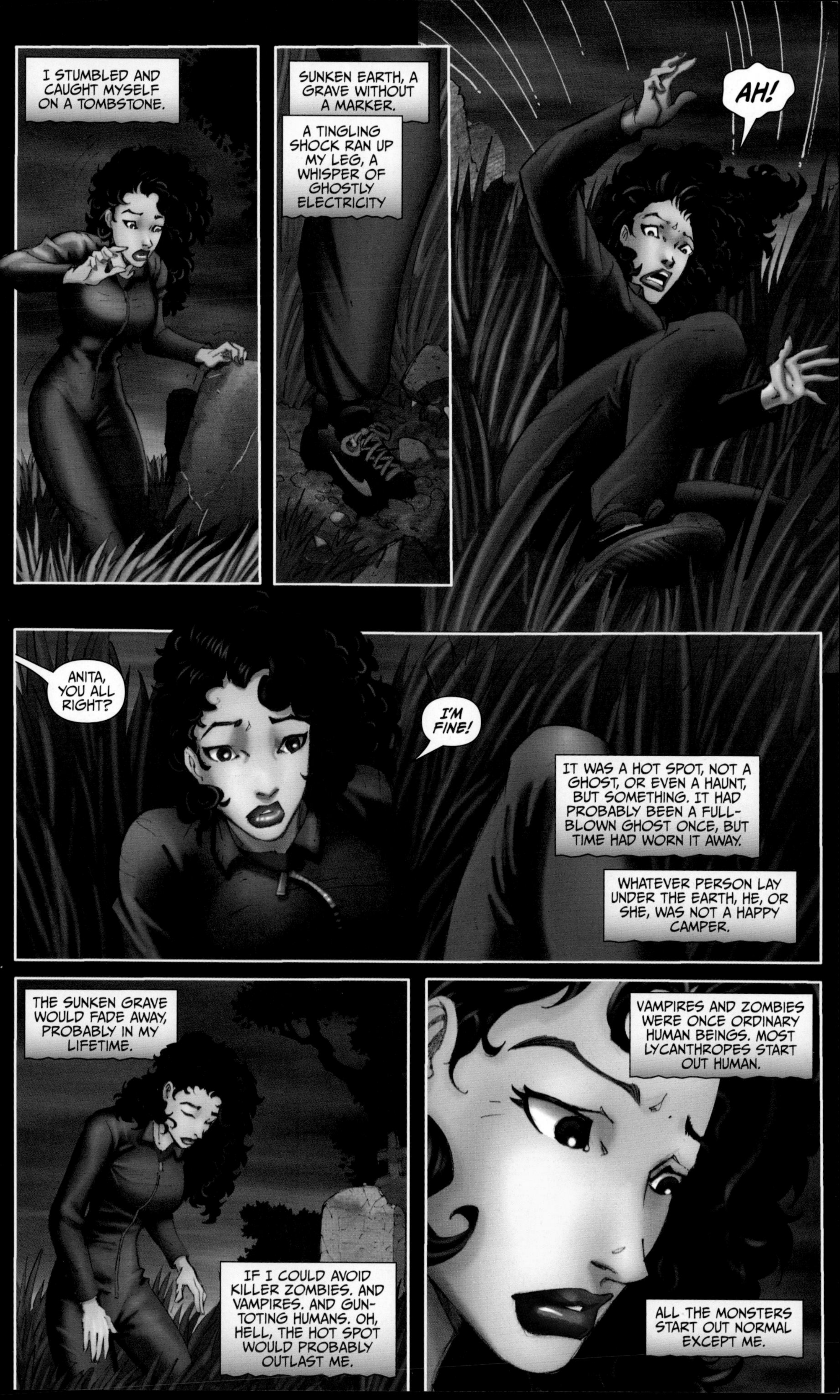
I STUMBLED AND CAUGHT MYSELF ON A TOMBSTONE.
SUNKEN EARTH, A GRAVE WITHOUT A MARKER.
A TINGLING SHOCK RAN UP MY LEG, A WHISPER OF GHOSTLY ELECTRICITY
AH!
ANITA, YOU ALL RIGHT?
I'M FINE!
IT WAS A HOT SPOT, NOT A GHOST, OR EVEN A HAUNT, BUT SOMETHING. IT HAD PROBABLY BEEN A FULL-BLOWN GHOST ONCE, BUT TIME HAD WORN IT AWAY.
WHATEVER PERSON LAY UNDER THE EARTH, HE, OR SHE, WAS NOT A HAPPY CAMPER.
THE SUNKEN GRAVE WOULD FADE AWAY, PROBABLY IN MY LIFETIME.
IF I COULD AVOID KILLER ZOMBIES. AND VAMPIRES. AND GUN-TOTING HUMANS. OH, HELL, THE HOT SPOT WOULD PROBABLY OUTLAST ME.
VAMPIRES AND ZOMBIES WERE ONCE ORDINARY HUMAN BEINGS. MOST LYCANTHROPES START OUT HUMAN.
ALL THE MONSTERS START OUT NORMAL EXCEPT ME.

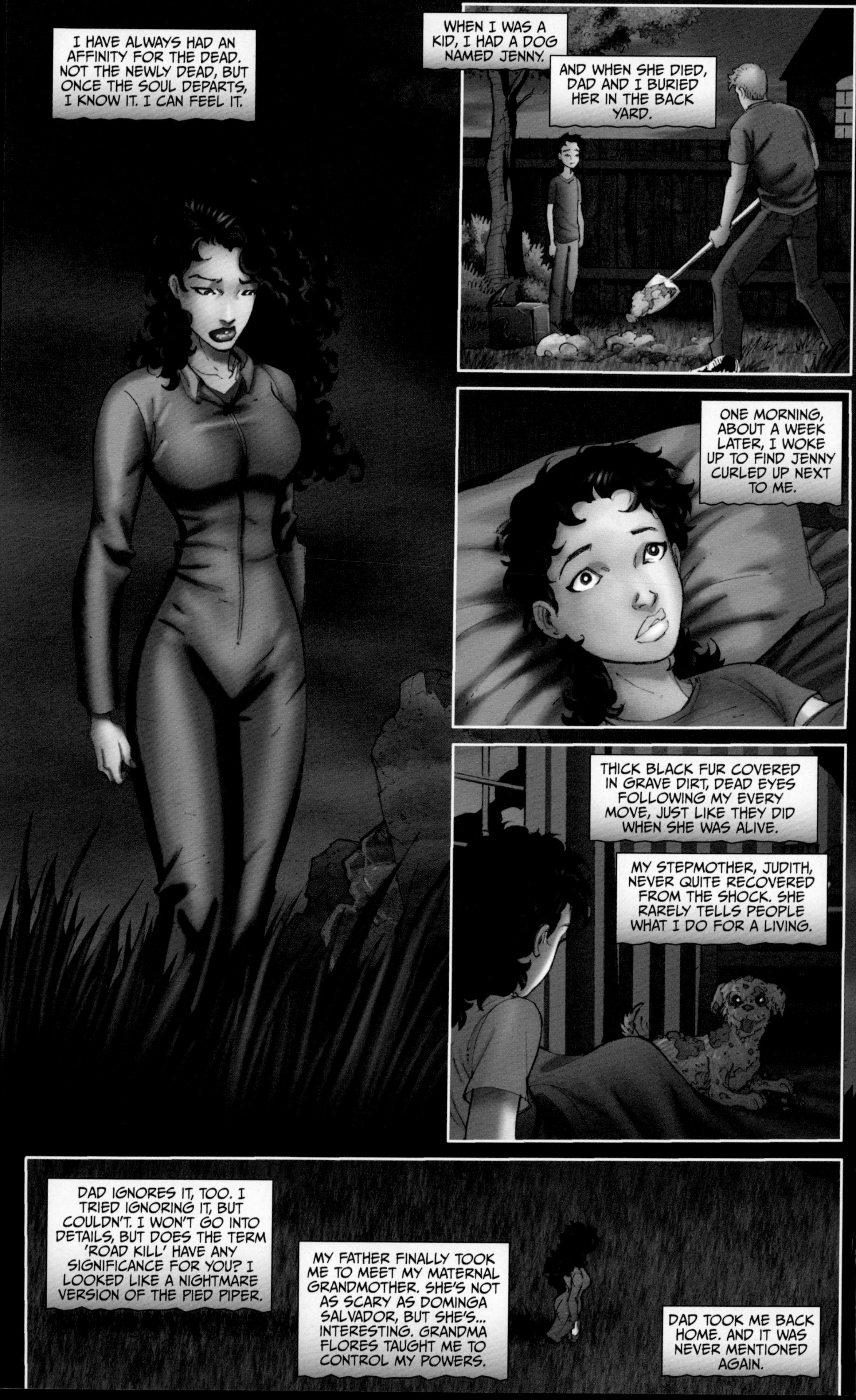

I HAVE ALWAYS HAD AN AFFINITY FOR THE DEAD. NOT THE NEWLY DEAD, BUT ONCE THE SOUL DEPARTS, I KNOW IT. I CAN FEEL IT.
WHEN I WAS A KID, I HAD A DOG NAMED JENNY.
AND WHEN SHE DIED, DAD AND I BURIED HER IN THE BACK YARD.
ONE MORNING, ABOUT A WEEK LATER, I WOKE UP TO FIND JENNY CURLED UP NEXT TO ME.
THICK BLACK FUR COVERED IN GRAVE DIRT, DEAD EYES FOLLOWING MY EVERY MOVE, JUST LIKE THEY DID WHEN SHE WAS ALIVE.
MY STEPMOTHER, JUDITH, NEVER QUITE RECOVERED FROM THE SHOCK. SHE RARELY TELLS PEOPLE WHAT I DO FOR A LIVING.
DAD IGNORES IT, TOO. I TRIED IGNORING IT, BUT COULDN'T. I WON'T GO INTO DETAILS, BUT DOES THE TERM 'ROAD KILL' HAVE ANY SIGNIFICANCE FOR YOU? I LOOKED LIKE A NIGHTMARE VERSION OF THE PIED PIPER.
MY FATHER FINALLY TOOK ME TO MEET MY MATERNAL GRANDMOTHER. SHE'S NOT AS SCARY AS DOMINGA SALVADOR, BUT SHE'S... INTERESTING. GRANDMA FLORES TAUGHT ME TO CONTROL MY POWERS.
DAD TOOK ME BACK HOME. AND IT WAS NEVER MENTIONED AGAIN.

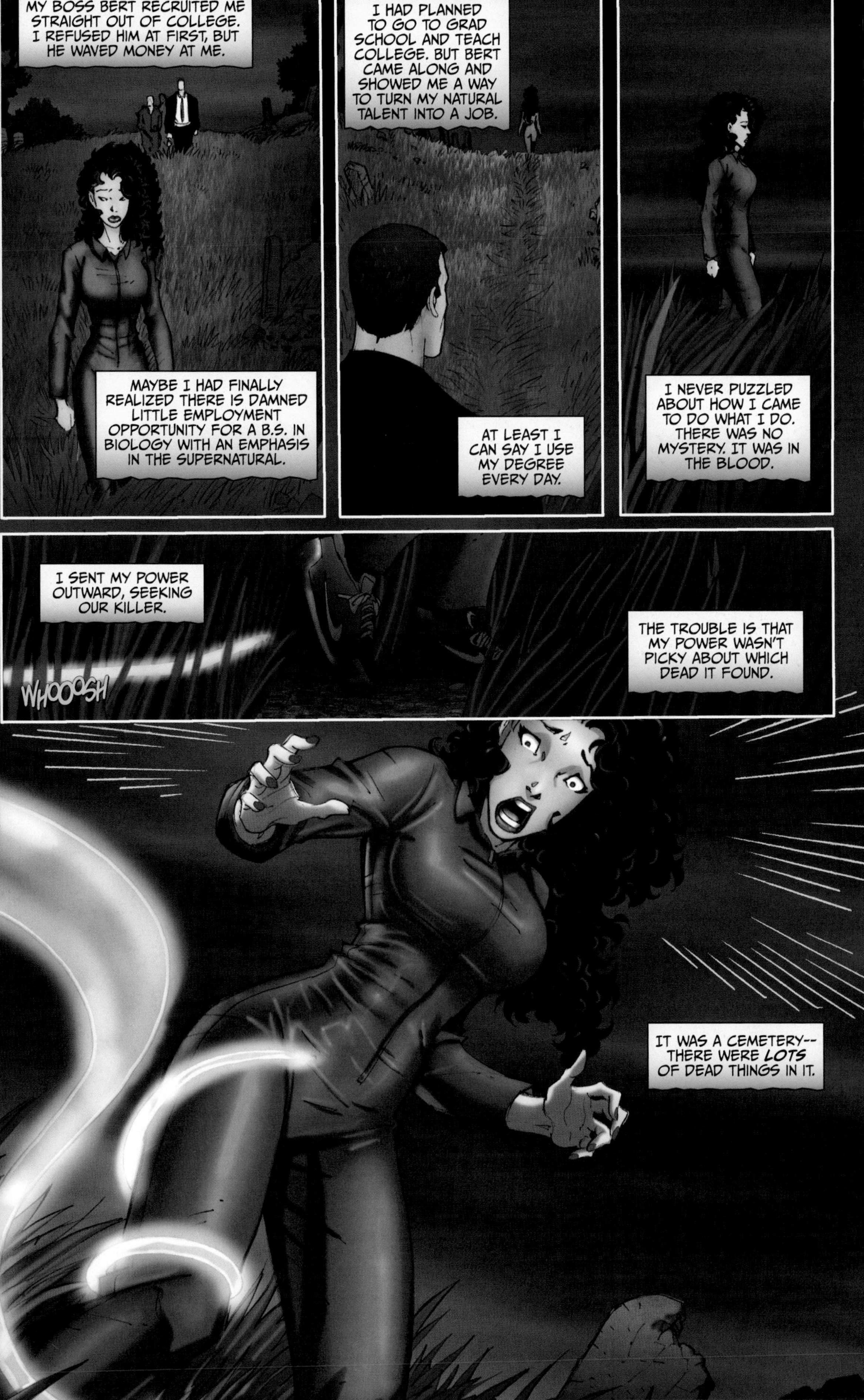
MY BOSS BERT RECRUITED ME STRAIGHT OUT OF COLLEGE. I REFUSED HIM AT FIRST, BUT HE WAVED MONEY AT ME.
MAYBE I HAD FINALLY REALIZED THERE IS DAMNED LITTLE EMPLOYMENT OPPORTUNITY FOR A B.S. IN BIOLOGY WITH AN EMPHASIS IN THE SUPERNATURAL.
I HAD PLANNED TO GO TO GRAD SCHOOL AND TEACH COLLEGE. BUT BERT CAME ALONG AND SHOWED ME A WAY TO TURN MY NATURAL TALENT INTO A JOB.
AT LEAST I CAN SAY I USE MY DEGREE EVERY DAY.
I NEVER PUZZLED ABOUT HOW I CAME TO DO WHAT I DO. THERE WAS NO MYSTERY. IT WAS IN THE BLOOD.
I SENT MY POWER OUTWARD, SEEKING OUR KILLER.
WHOOOSH
THE TROUBLE IS THAT MY POWER WASN'T PICKY ABOUT WHICH DEAD IT FOUND.
IT WAS A CEMETERY-- THERE WERE *LOTS* OF DEAD THINGS IN IT.

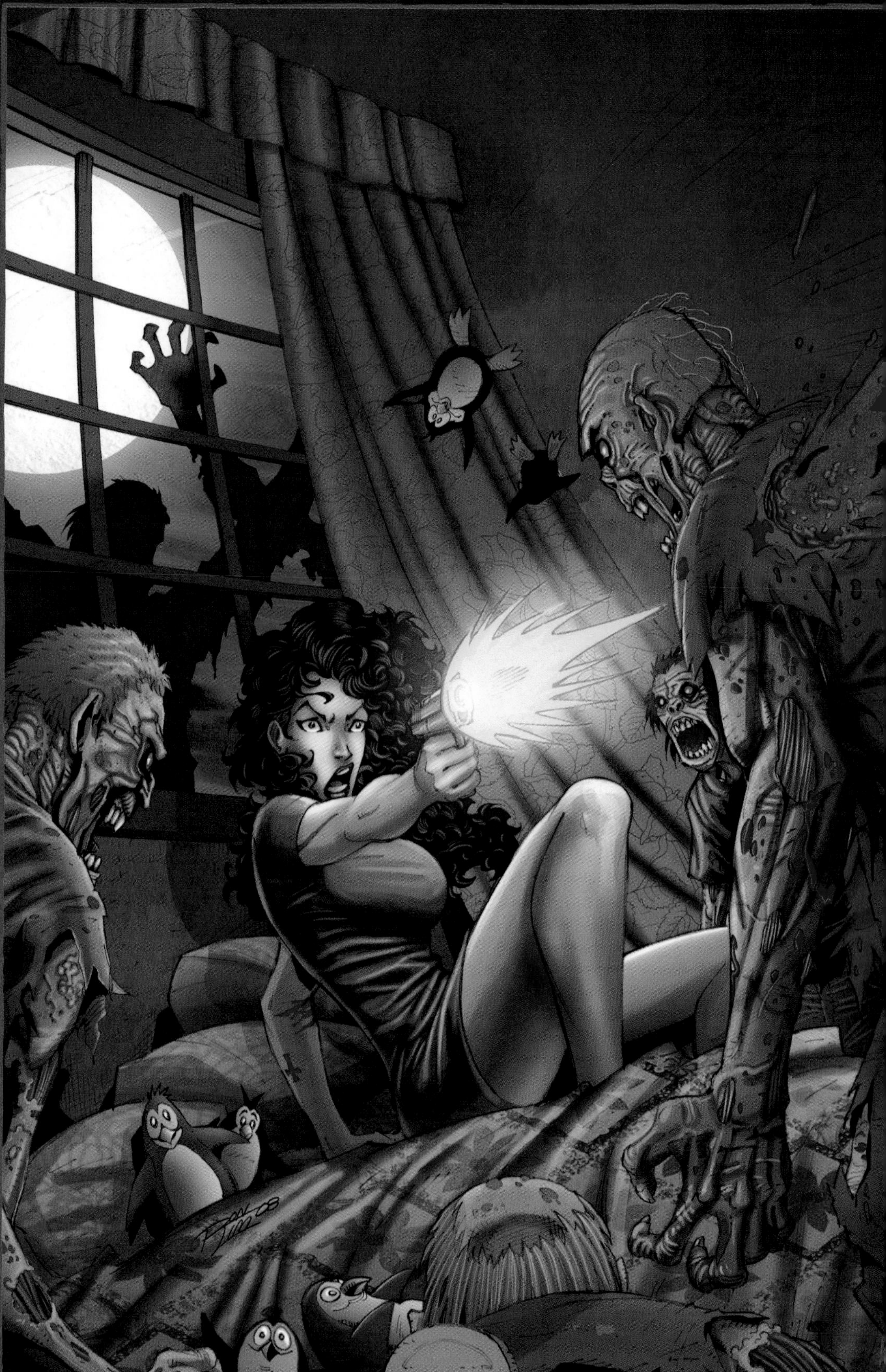

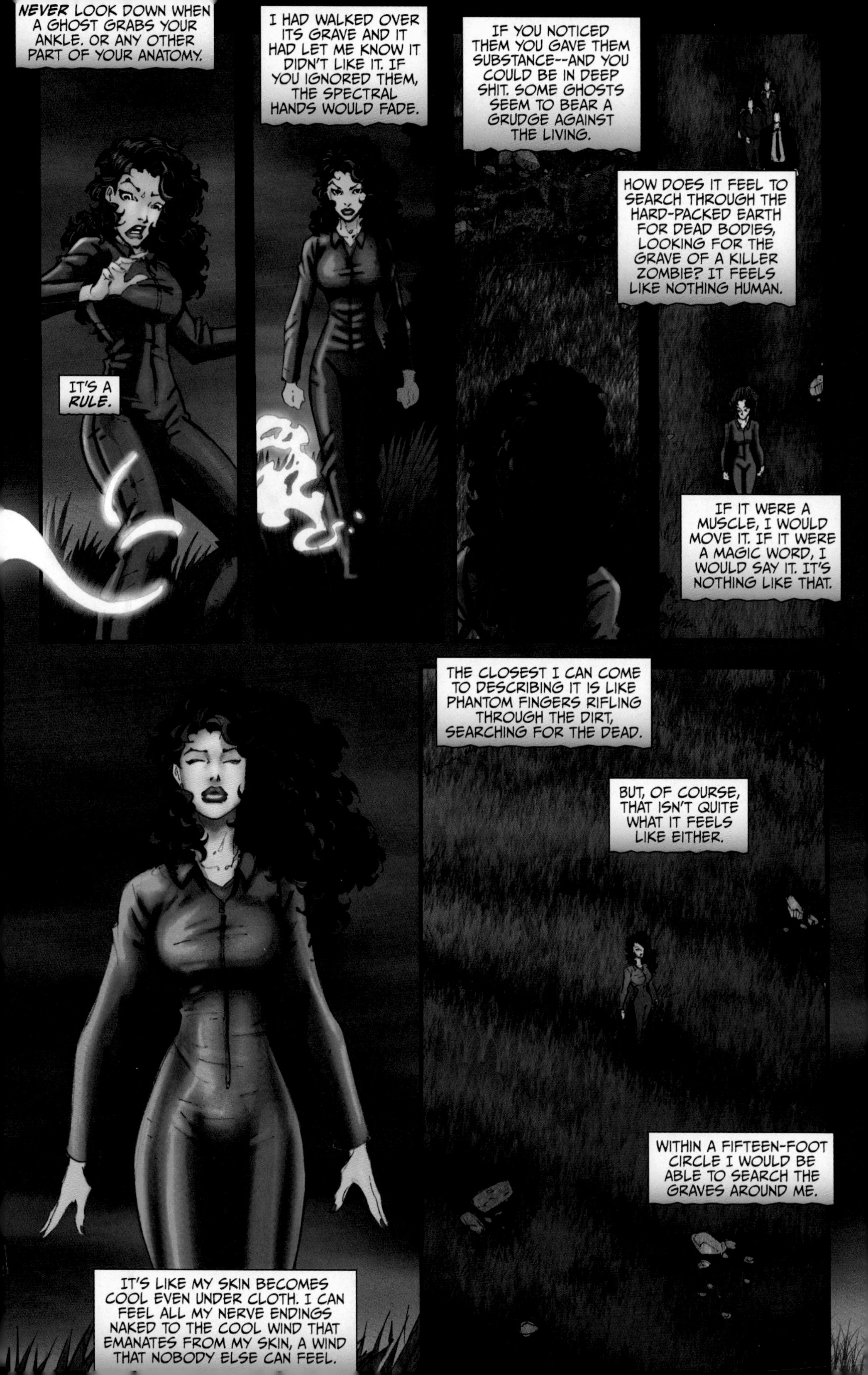
NEVER LOOK DOWN WHEN A GHOST GRABS YOUR ANKLE. OR ANY OTHER PART OF YOUR ANATOMY.
IT'S A RULE.
I HAD WALKED OVER ITS GRAVE AND IT HAD LET ME KNOW IT DIDN'T LIKE IT. IF YOU IGNORED THEM, THE SPECTRAL HANDS WOULD FADE.
IF YOU NOTICED THEM YOU GAVE THEM SUBSTANCE--AND YOU COULD BE IN DEEP SHIT. SOME GHOSTS SEEM TO BEAR A GRUDGE AGAINST THE LIVING.
HOW DOES IT FEEL TO SEARCH THROUGH THE HARD-PACKED EARTH FOR DEAD BODIES, LOOKING FOR THE GRAVE OF A KILLER ZOMBIE? IT FEELS LIKE NOTHING HUMAN.
IF IT WERE A MUSCLE, I WOULD MOVE IT. IF IT WERE A MAGIC WORD, I WOULD SAY IT. IT'S NOTHING LIKE THAT.
IT'S LIKE MY SKIN BECOMES COOL EVEN UNDER CLOTH. I CAN FEEL ALL MY NERVE ENDINGS NAKED TO THE COOL WIND THAT EMANATES FROM MY SKIN, A WIND THAT NOBODY ELSE CAN FEEL.
THE CLOSEST I CAN COME TO DESCRIBING IT IS LIKE PHANTOM FINGERS RIFLING THROUGH THE DIRT, SEARCHING FOR THE DEAD.
BUT, OF COURSE, THAT ISN'T QUITE WHAT IT FEELS LIKE EITHER.
WITHIN A FIFTEEN-FOOT CIRCLE I WOULD BE ABLE TO SEARCH THE GRAVES AROUND ME.

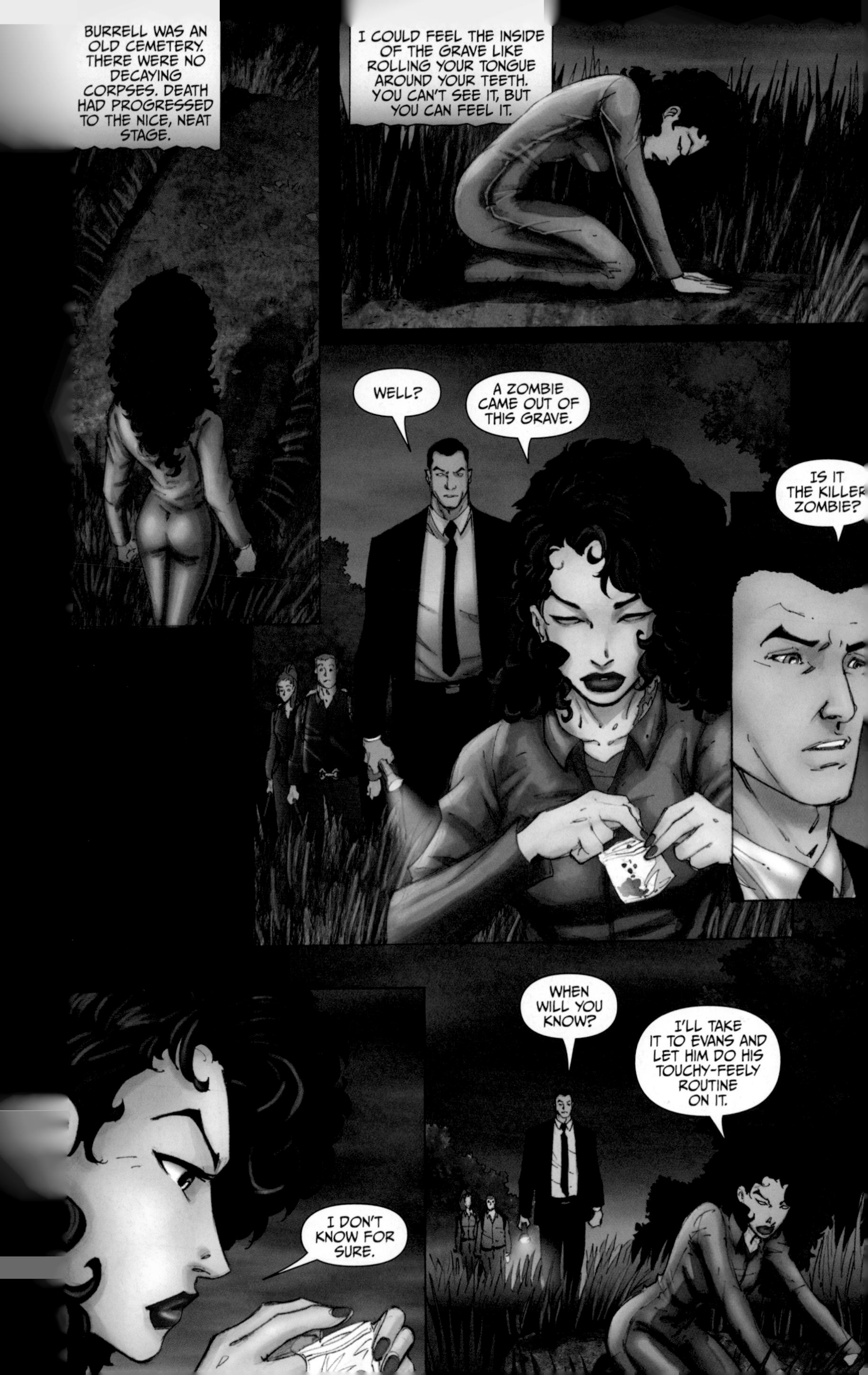
BURRELL WAS AN OLD CEMETERY. THERE WERE NO DECAYING CORPSES. DEATH HAD PROGRESSED TO THE NICE, NEAT STAGE.
I COULD FEEL THE INSIDE OF THE GRAVE LIKE ROLLING YOUR TONGUE AROUND YOUR TEETH. YOU CAN'T SEE IT, BUT YOU CAN FEEL IT.
WELL?
A ZOMBIE CAME OUT OF THIS GRAVE.
IS IT THE KILLER ZOMBIE?
I DON'T KNOW FOR SURE.
WHEN WILL YOU KNOW?
I'LL TAKE IT TO EVANS AND LET HIM DO HIS TOUCHY-FEELY ROUTINE ON IT.

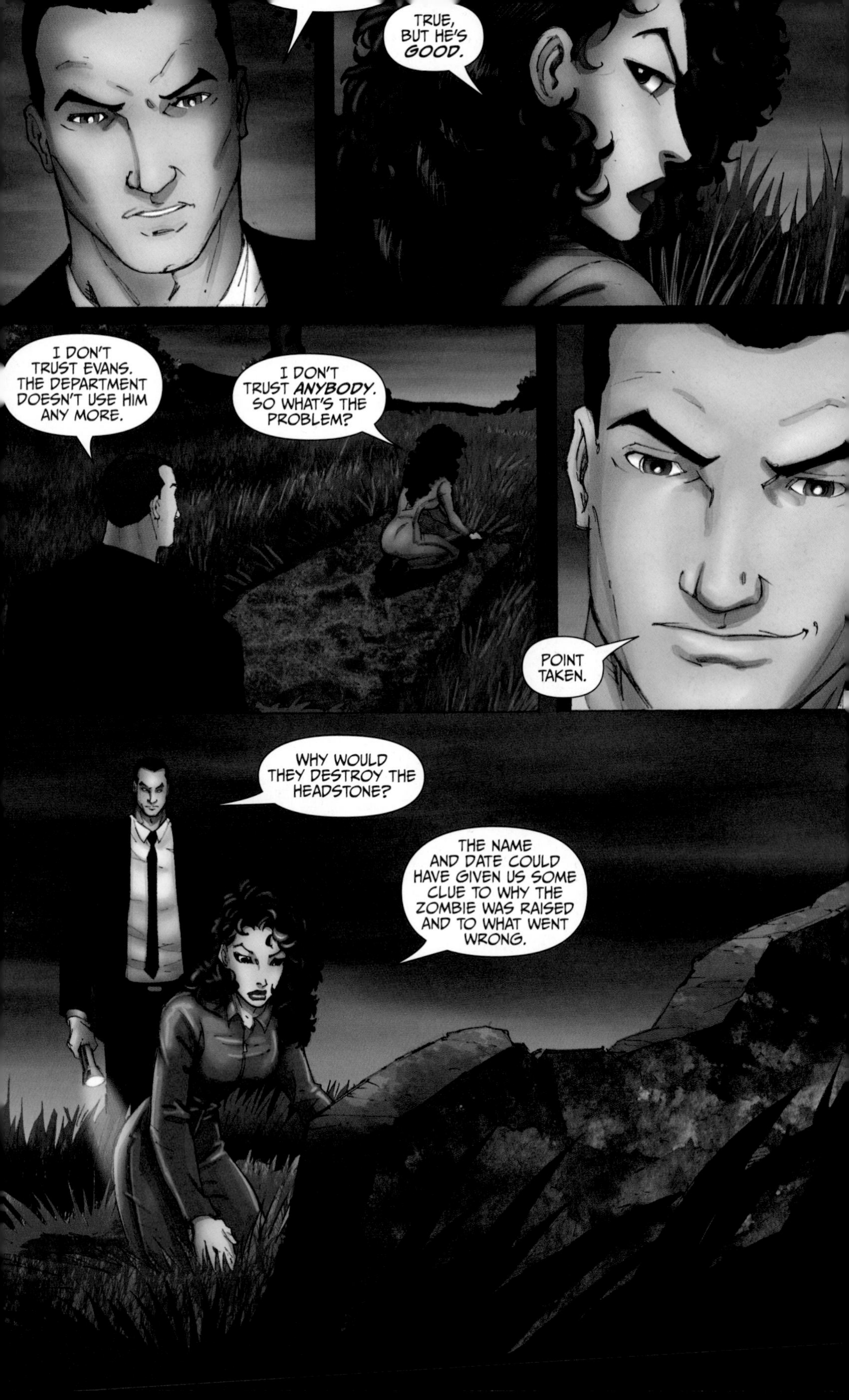
TRUE, BUT HE'S *GOOD*.
I DON'T TRUST EVANS. THE DEPARTMENT DOESN'T USE HIM ANY MORE.
I DON'T TRUST *ANYBODY*. SO WHAT'S THE PROBLEM?
POINT TAKEN.
WHY WOULD THEY DESTROY THE HEADSTONE?
THE NAME AND DATE COULD HAVE GIVEN US SOME CLUE TO WHY THE ZOMBIE WAS RAISED AND TO WHAT WENT WRONG.

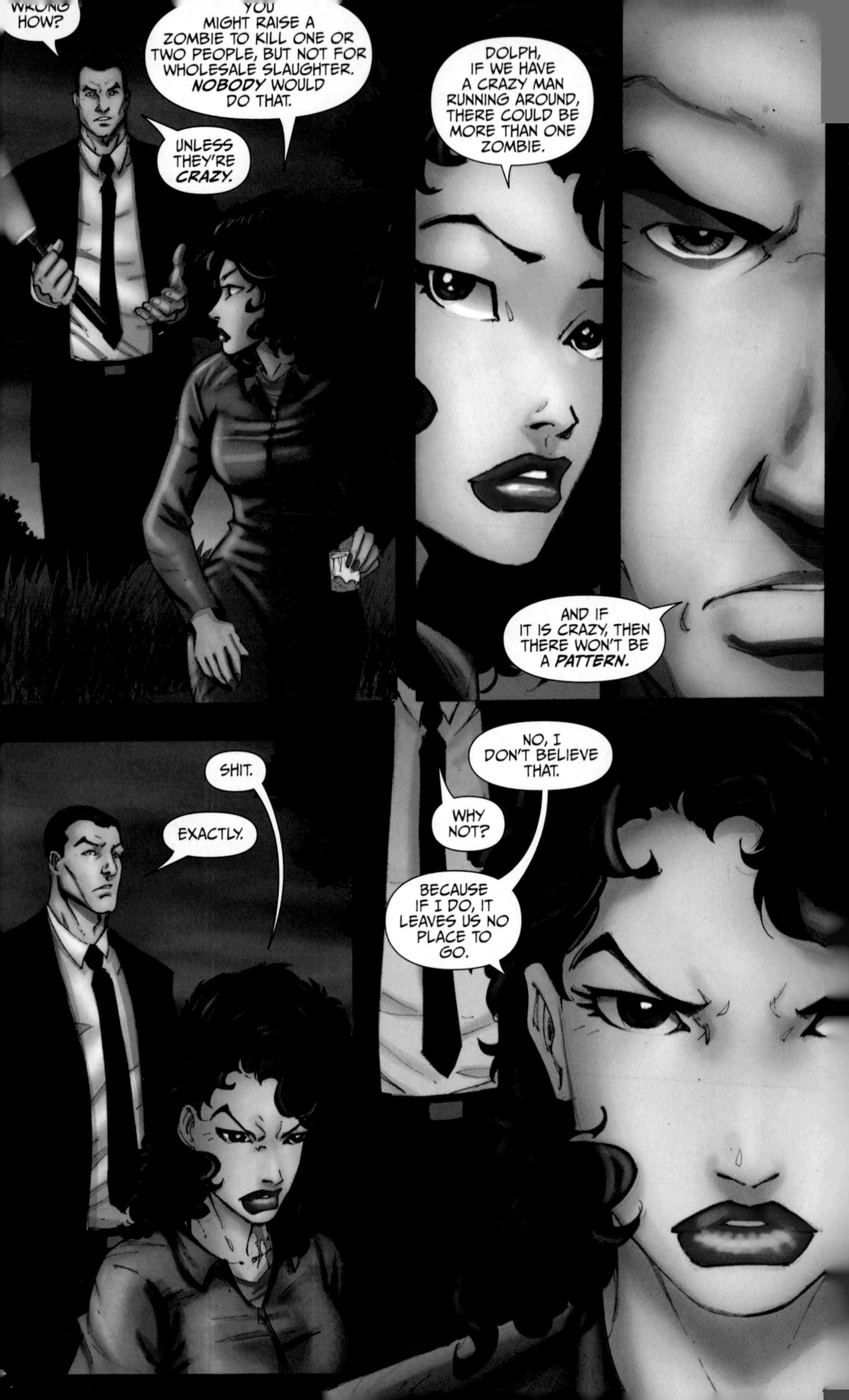
WRONG HOW?
YOU MIGHT RAISE A ZOMBIE TO KILL ONE OR TWO PEOPLE, BUT NOT FOR WHOLESALE SLAUGHTER. NOBODY WOULD DO THAT.
UNLESS THEY'RE CRAZY.
DOLPH, IF WE HAVE A CRAZY MAN RUNNING AROUND, THERE COULD BE MORE THAN ONE ZOMBIE.
AND IF IT IS CRAZY, THEN THERE WON'T BE A PATTERN.
SHIT.
EXACTLY.
NO, I DON'T BELIEVE THAT.
WHY NOT?
BECAUSE IF I DO, IT LEAVES US NO PLACE TO GO.

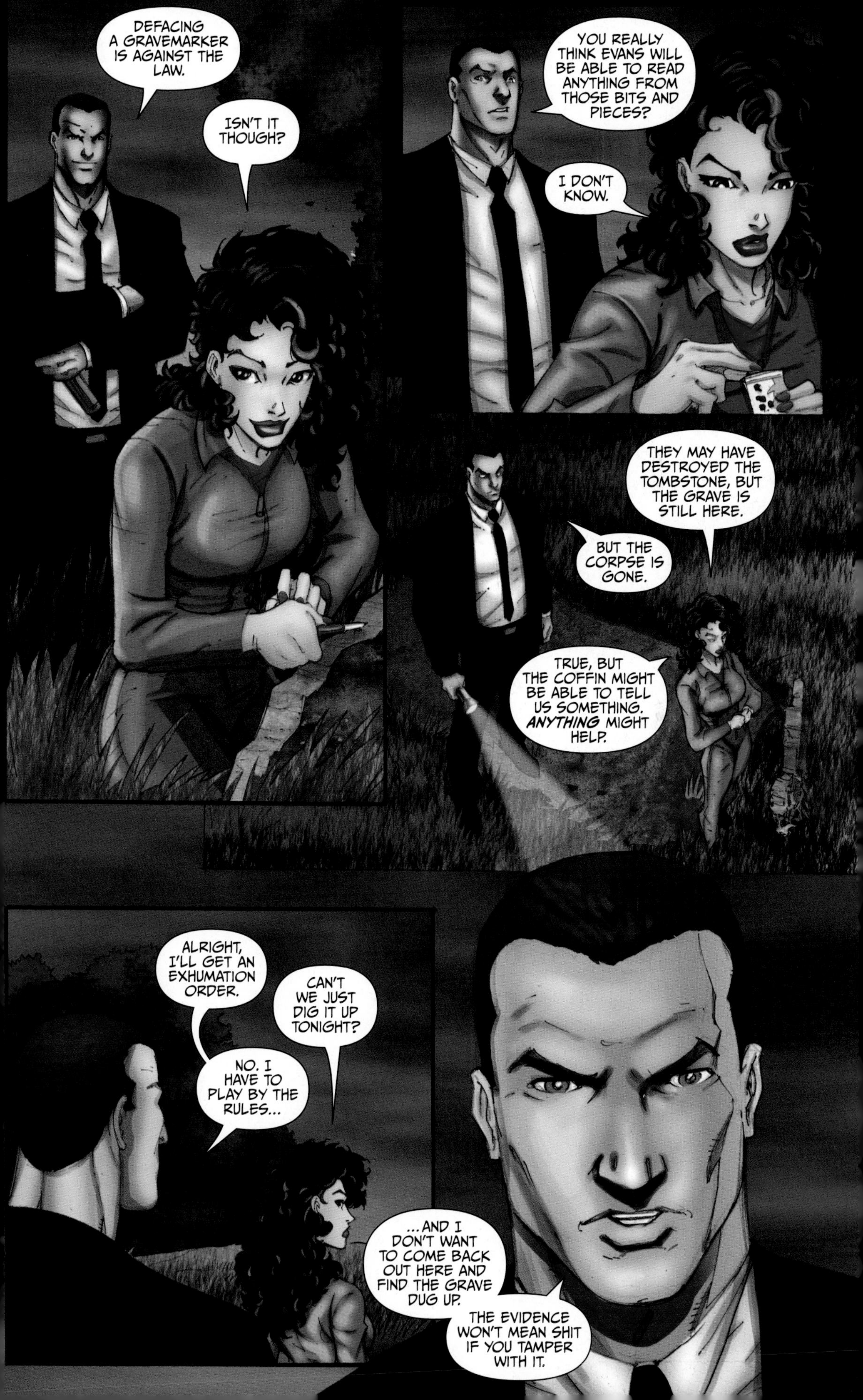
DEFACING A GRAVEMARKER IS AGAINST THE LAW.
ISN'T IT THOUGH?
YOU REALLY THINK EVANS WILL BE ABLE TO READ ANYTHING FROM THOSE BITS AND PIECES?
I DON'T KNOW.
THEY MAY HAVE DESTROYED THE TOMBSTONE, BUT THE GRAVE IS STILL HERE.
BUT THE CORPSE IS GONE.
TRUE, BUT THE COFFIN MIGHT BE ABLE TO TELL US SOMETHING. ANYTHING MIGHT HELP.
ALRIGHT, I'LL GET AN EXHUMATION ORDER.
CAN'T WE JUST DIG IT UP TONIGHT?
NO. I HAVE TO PLAY BY THE RULES...
...AND I DON'T WANT TO COME BACK OUT HERE AND FIND THE GRAVE DUG UP.
THE EVIDENCE WON'T MEAN SHIT IF YOU TAMPER WITH IT.

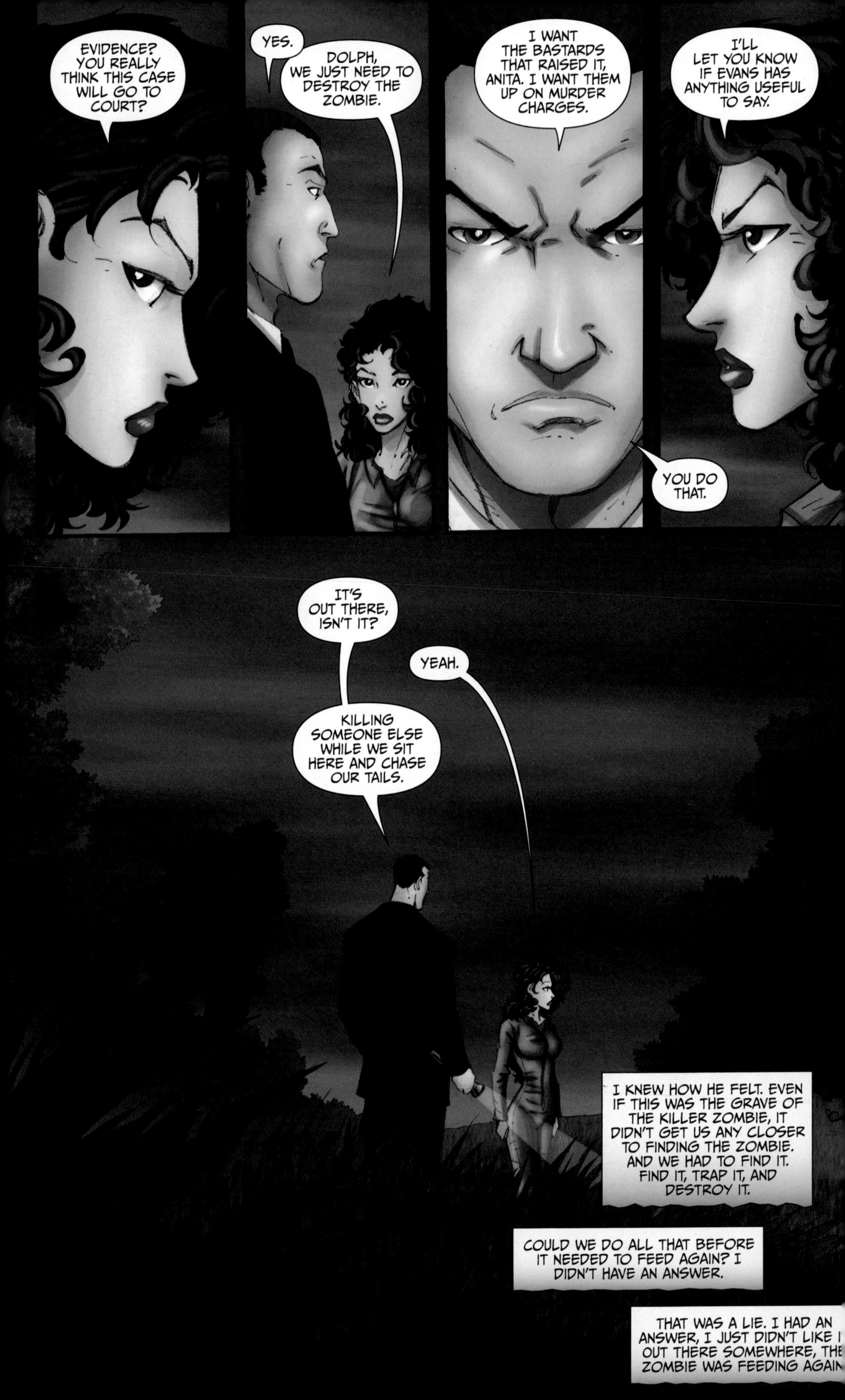
EVIDENCE? YOU REALLY THINK THIS CASE WILL GO TO COURT?
YES.
DOLPH, WE JUST NEED TO DESTROY THE ZOMBIE.
I WANT THE BASTARDS THAT RAISED IT, ANITA. I WANT THEM UP ON MURDER CHARGES.
I'LL LET YOU KNOW IF EVANS HAS ANYTHING USEFUL TO SAY.
YOU DO THAT.
IT'S OUT THERE, ISN'T IT?
YEAH.
KILLING SOMEONE ELSE WHILE WE SIT HERE AND CHASE OUR TAILS.
I KNEW HOW HE FELT. EVEN IF THIS WAS THE GRAVE OF THE KILLER ZOMBIE, IT DIDN'T GET US ANY CLOSER TO FINDING THE ZOMBIE. AND WE HAD TO FIND IT. FIND IT, TRAP IT, AND DESTROY IT.
COULD WE DO ALL THAT BEFORE IT NEEDED TO FEED AGAIN? I DIDN'T HAVE AN ANSWER.
THAT WAS A LIE. I HAD AN ANSWER, I JUST DIDN'T LIKE I OUT THERE SOMEWHERE, THE ZOMBIE WAS FEEDING AGAIN

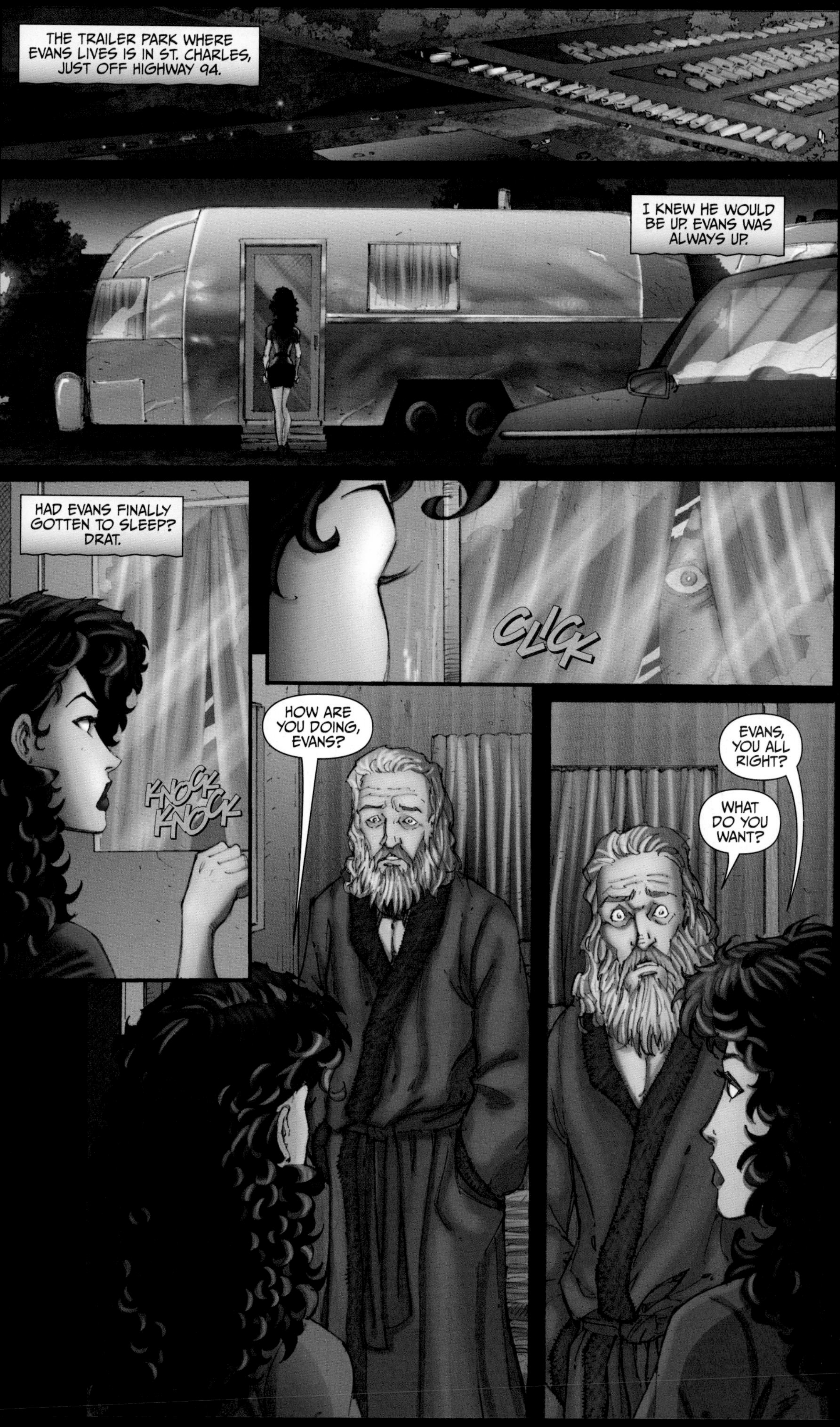
THE TRAILER PARK WHERE EVANS LIVES IS IN ST. CHARLES, JUST OFF HIGHWAY 94.
I KNEW HE WOULD BE UP. EVANS WAS ALWAYS UP.
HAD EVANS FINALLY GOTTEN TO SLEEP? DRAT.
KNOCK KNOCK
CLICK
HOW ARE YOU DOING, EVANS?
EVANS, YOU ALL RIGHT?
WHAT DO YOU WANT?

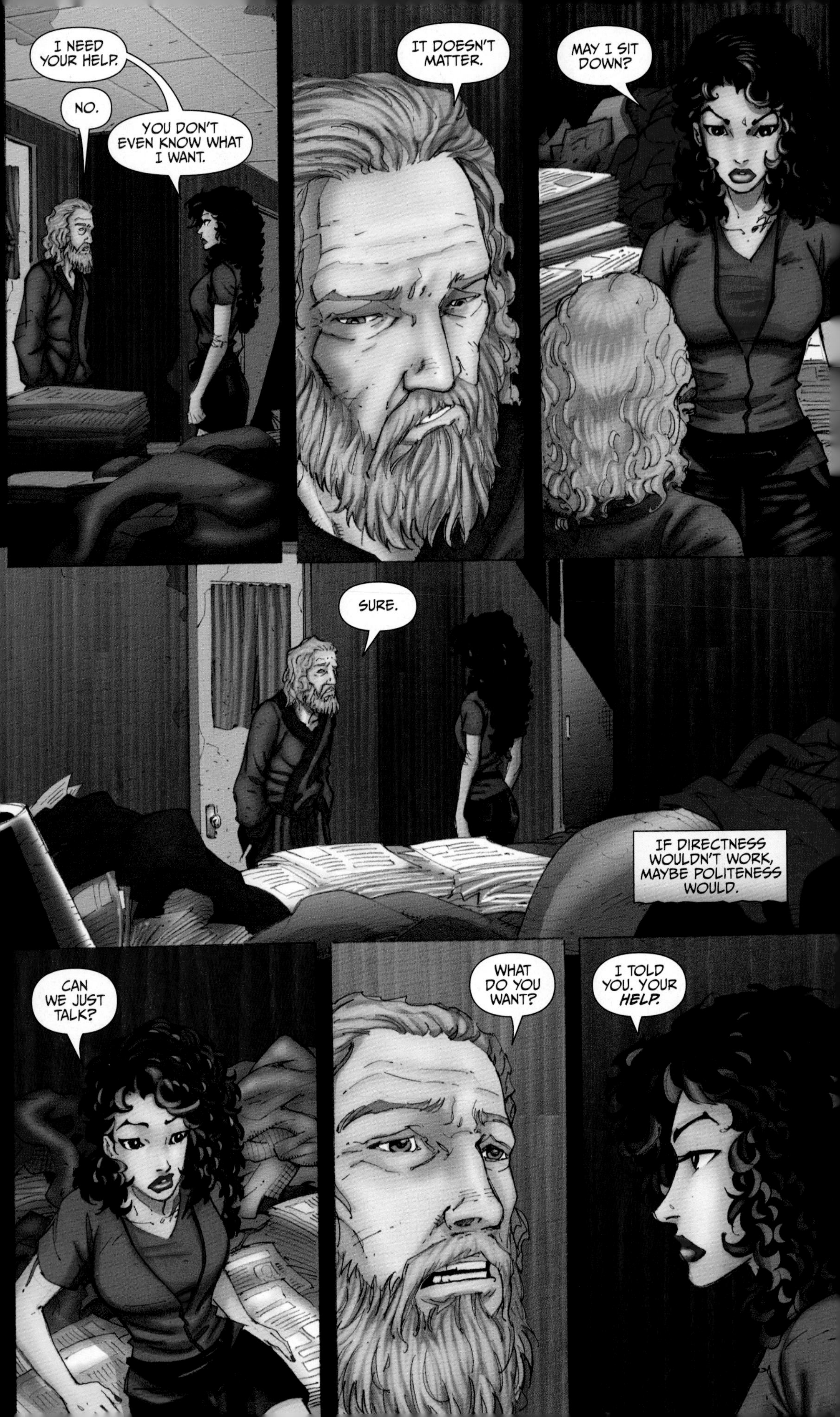

I NEED YOUR HELP.
NO.
YOU DON'T EVEN KNOW WHAT I WANT.
IT DOESN'T MATTER.
MAY I SIT DOWN?
SURE.
IF DIRECTNESS WOULDN'T WORK, MAYBE POLITENESS WOULD.
CAN WE JUST TALK?
WHAT DO YOU WANT?
I TOLD YOU. YOUR HELP.

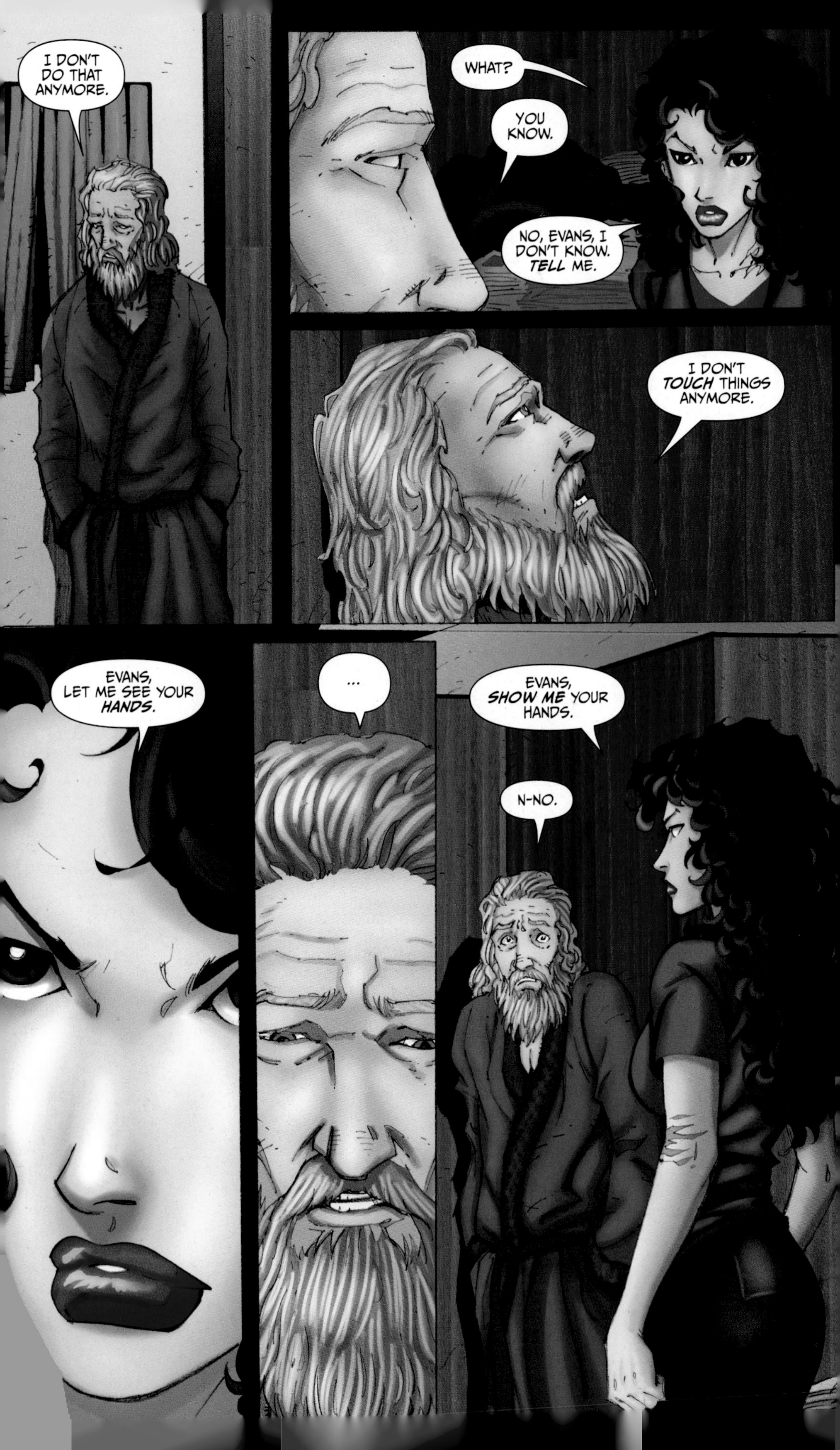
I DON'T DO THAT ANYMORE.
WHAT?
YOU KNOW.
NO, EVANS, I DON'T KNOW. *TELL* ME.
I DON'T *TOUCH* THINGS ANYMORE.
EVANS, LET ME SEE YOUR *HANDS.*
...
EVANS, *SHOW ME* YOUR HANDS.
N-NO.

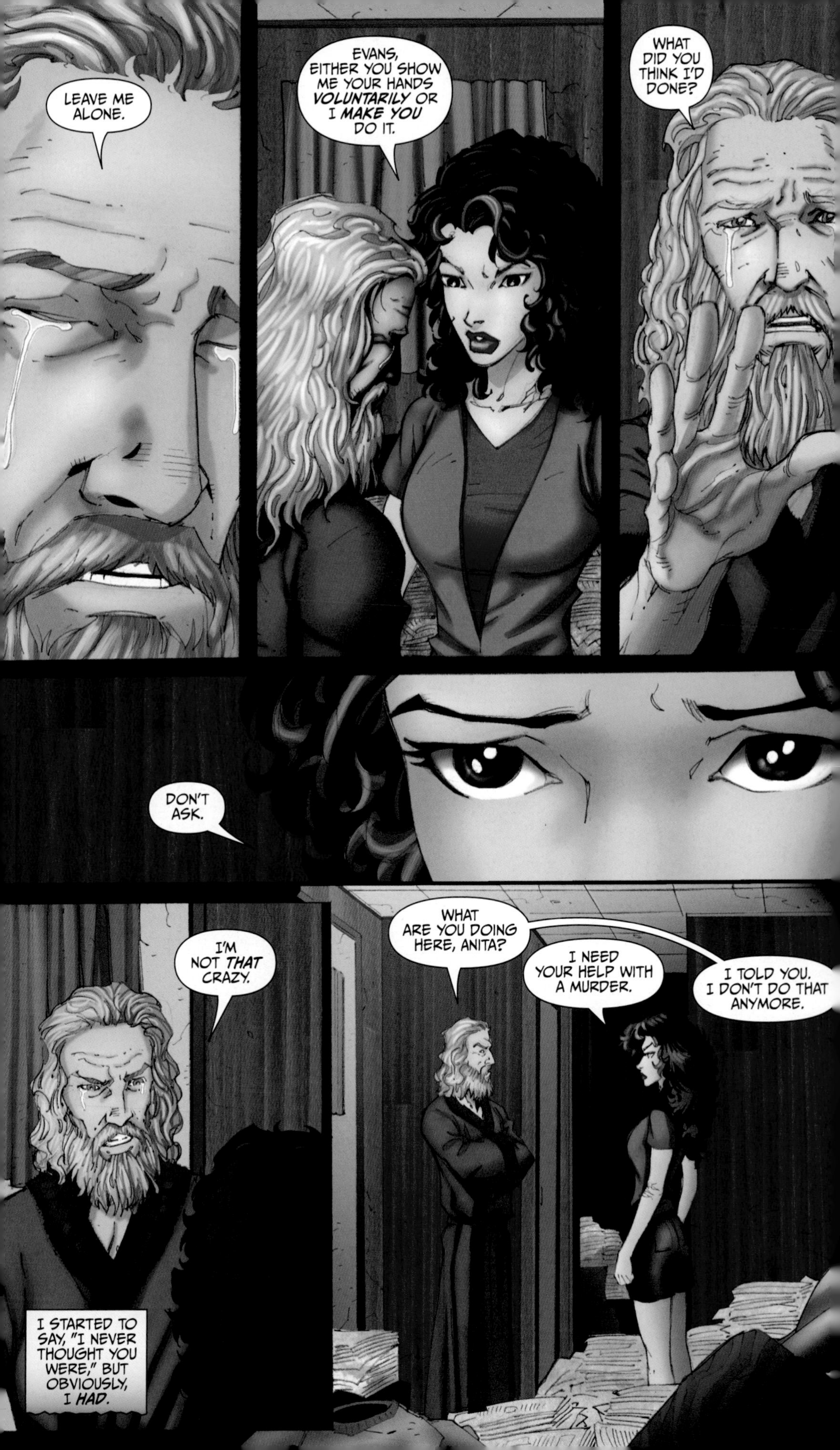
LEAVE ME ALONE.
EVANS, EITHER YOU SHOW ME YOUR HANDS VOLUNTARILY OR I MAKE YOU DO IT.
WHAT DID YOU THINK I'D DONE?
DON'T ASK.
I'M NOT THAT CRAZY.
I STARTED TO SAY, "I NEVER THOUGHT YOU WERE," BUT OBVIOUSLY, I HAD.
WHAT ARE YOU DOING HERE, ANITA?
I NEED YOUR HELP WITH A MURDER.
I TOLD YOU. I DON'T DO THAT ANYMORE.

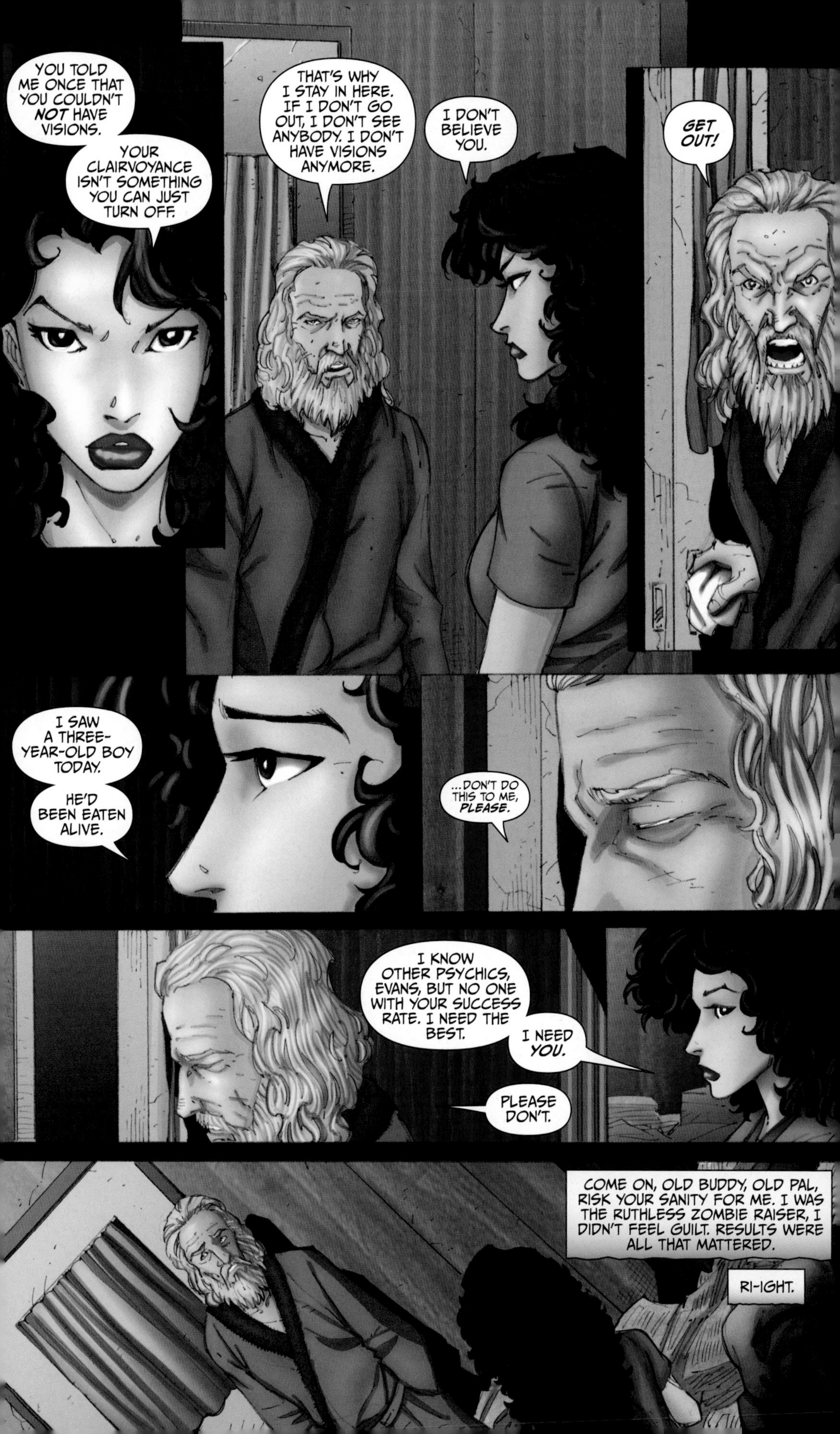

YOU TOLD ME ONCE THAT YOU COULDN'T *NOT* HAVE VISIONS.
YOUR CLAIRVOYANCE ISN'T SOMETHING YOU CAN JUST TURN OFF.
THAT'S WHY I STAY IN HERE. IF I DON'T GO OUT, I DON'T SEE ANYBODY. I DON'T HAVE VISIONS ANYMORE.
I DON'T BELIEVE YOU.
GET OUT!
I SAW A THREE-YEAR-OLD BOY TODAY.
HE'D BEEN EATEN ALIVE.
...DON'T DO THIS TO ME, *PLEASE.*
I KNOW OTHER PSYCHICS, EVANS, BUT NO ONE WITH YOUR SUCCESS RATE. I NEED THE BEST.
I NEED *YOU.*
PLEASE DON'T.
COME ON, OLD BUDDY, OLD PAL, RISK YOUR SANITY FOR ME. I WAS THE RUTHLESS ZOMBIE RAISER, I DIDN'T FEEL GUILT. RESULTS WERE ALL THAT MATTERED.
RI-IGHT.

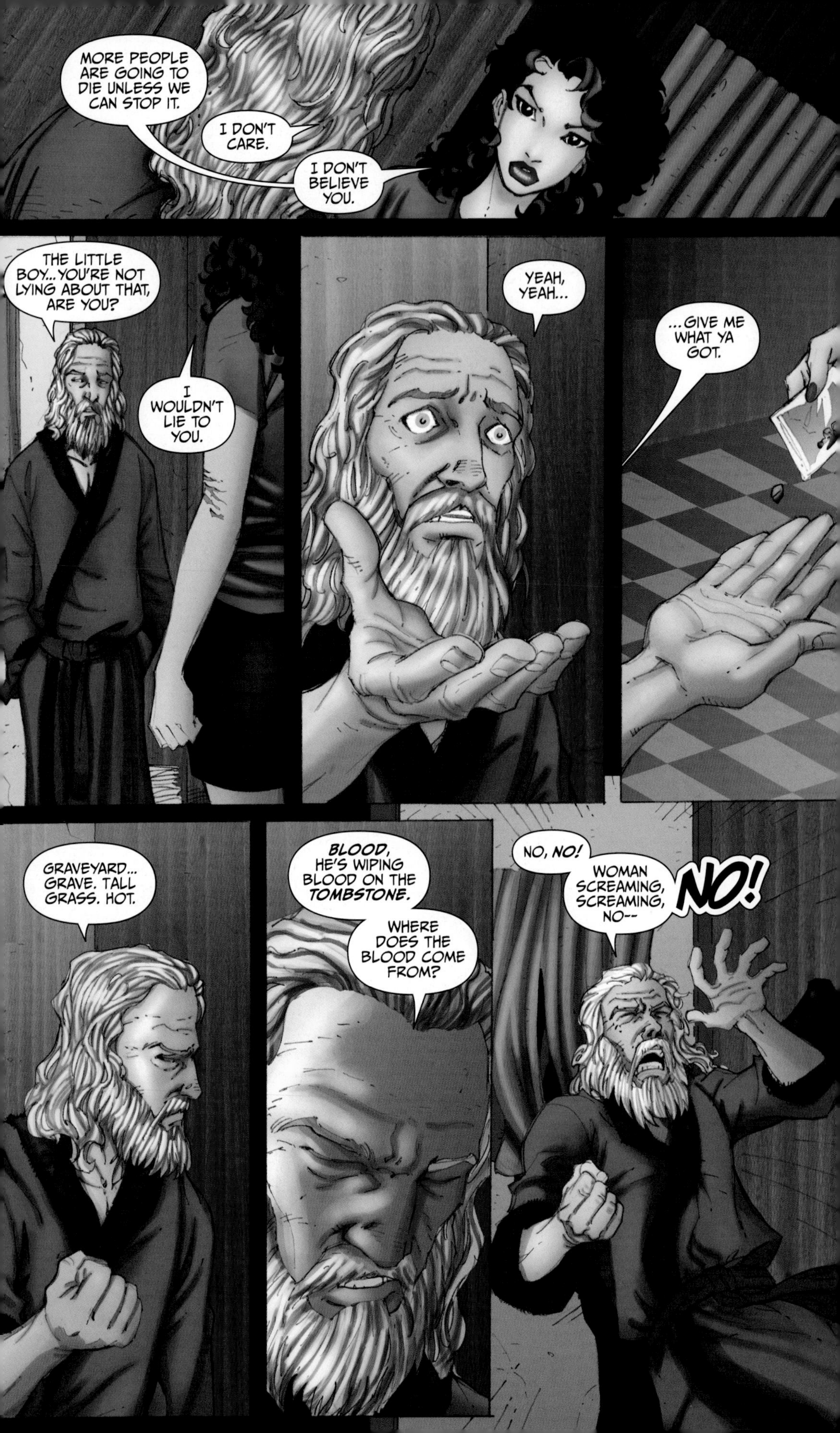
MORE PEOPLE ARE GOING TO DIE UNLESS WE CAN STOP IT.
I DON'T CARE.
I DON'T BELIEVE YOU.
THE LITTLE BOY...YOU'RE NOT LYING ABOUT THAT, ARE YOU?
I WOULDN'T LIE TO YOU.
YEAH, YEAH...
...GIVE ME WHAT YA GOT.
GRAVEYARD... GRAVE. TALL GRASS. HOT.
BLOOD, HE'S WIPING BLOOD ON THE TOMBSTONE.
WHERE DOES THE BLOOD COME FROM?
NO, NO!
WOMAN SCREAMING, SCREAMING, NO--
NO!

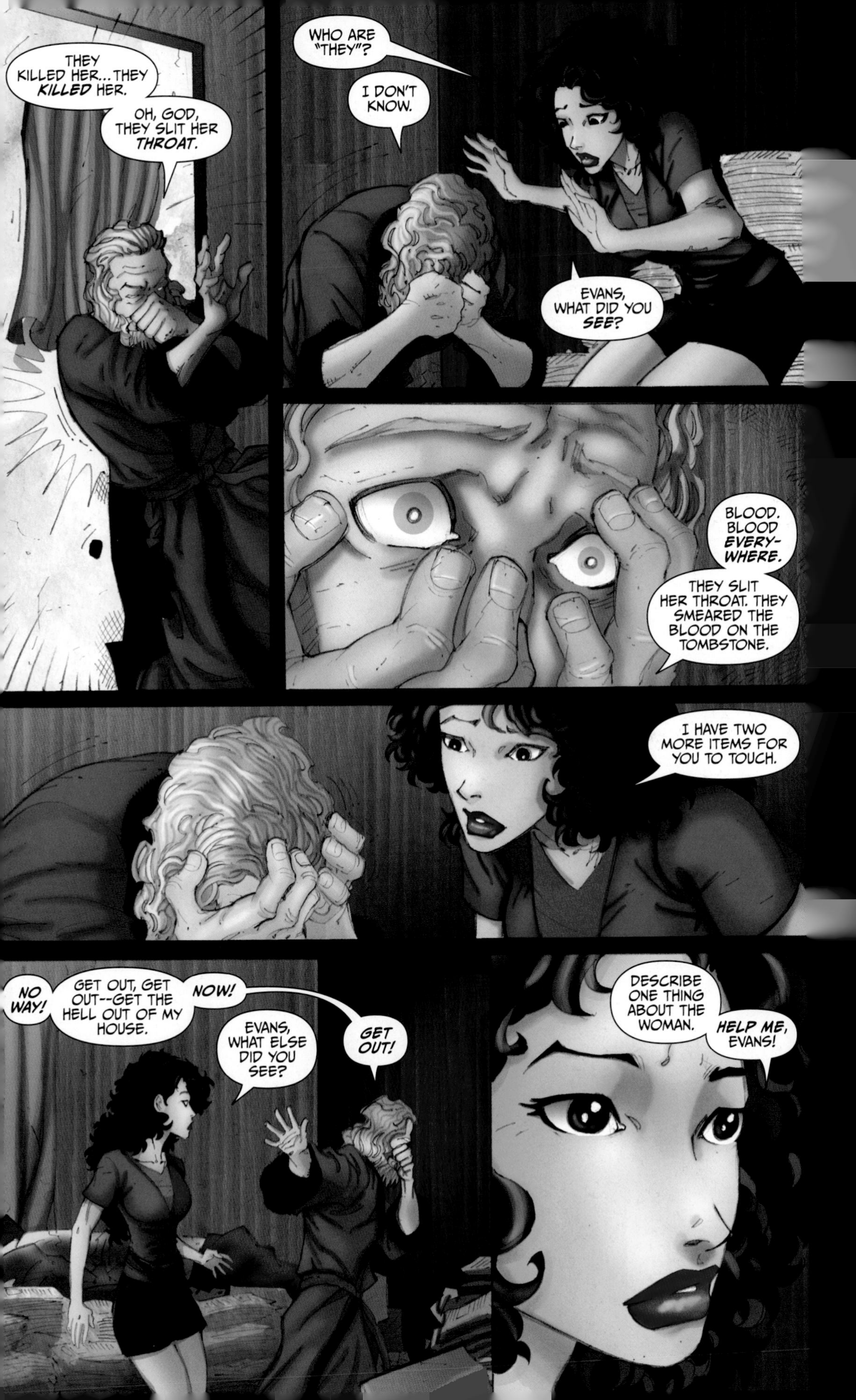

THEY KILLED HER... THEY KILLED HER.
OH, GOD, THEY SLIT HER THROAT.
WHO ARE "THEY"?
I DON'T KNOW.
EVANS, WHAT DID YOU SEE?
BLOOD. BLOOD EVERY-WHERE.
THEY SLIT HER THROAT. THEY SMEARED THE BLOOD ON THE TOMBSTONE.
I HAVE TWO MORE ITEMS FOR YOU TO TOUCH.
GET OUT, GET OUT--GET THE HELL OUT OF MY HOUSE.
NO WAY!
NOW!
EVANS, WHAT ELSE DID YOU SEE?
GET OUT!
DESCRIBE ONE THING ABOUT THE WOMAN.
HELP ME, EVANS!

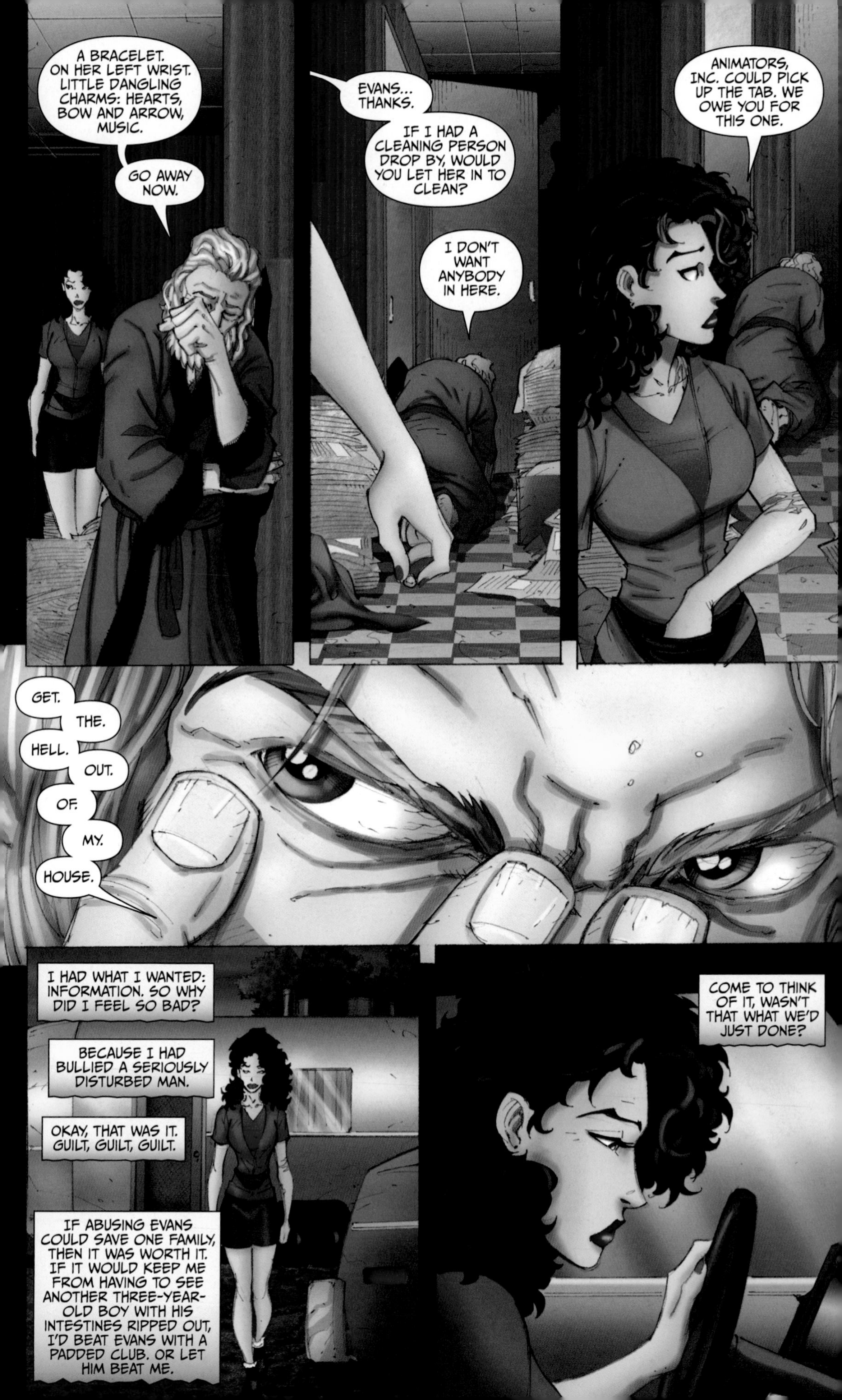
A BRACELET. ON HER LEFT WRIST. LITTLE DANGLING CHARMS: HEARTS, BOW AND ARROW, MUSIC.
GO AWAY NOW.
EVANS... THANKS.
IF I HAD A CLEANING PERSON DROP BY, WOULD YOU LET HER IN TO CLEAN?
I DON'T WANT ANYBODY IN HERE.
ANIMATORS, INC. COULD PICK UP THE TAB. WE OWE YOU FOR THIS ONE.
GET.
THE.
HELL.
OUT.
OF.
MY.
HOUSE.
I HAD WHAT I WANTED: INFORMATION. SO WHY DID I FEEL SO BAD?
BECAUSE I HAD BULLIED A SERIOUSLY DISTURBED MAN.
OKAY, THAT WAS IT. GUILT, GUILT, GUILT.
IF ABUSING EVANS COULD SAVE ONE FAMILY, THEN IT WAS WORTH IT. IF IT WOULD KEEP ME FROM HAVING TO SEE ANOTHER THREE-YEAR-OLD BOY WITH HIS INTESTINES RIPPED OUT, I'D BEAT EVANS WITH A PADDED CLUB. OR LET HIM BEAT ME.
COME TO THINK OF IT, WASN'T THAT WHAT WE'D JUST DONE?

I ALWAYS HATED THIS DREAM. I'VE BEEN HAVING IT SINCE I WAS EIGHT.

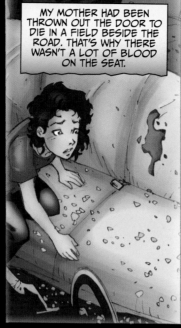

MY MOTHER HAD BEEN THROWN OUT THE DOOR TO DIE IN A FIELD BESIDE THE ROAD. THAT'S WHY THERE WASN'T A LOT OF BLOOD ON THE SEAT.

IN REAL LIFE THE BLOOD HAD BEEN DRY, JUST A STAIN. WHEN I DREAMED ABOUT IT, IT WAS ALWAYS *FRESH.*

THIS TIME THERE WAS A SMELL, OF ROTTEN FLESH. IT DIDN'T BELONG.

I WOKE FROM MY WORST NIGHTMARE TO A DIFFERENT ONE.

WHOOOSH

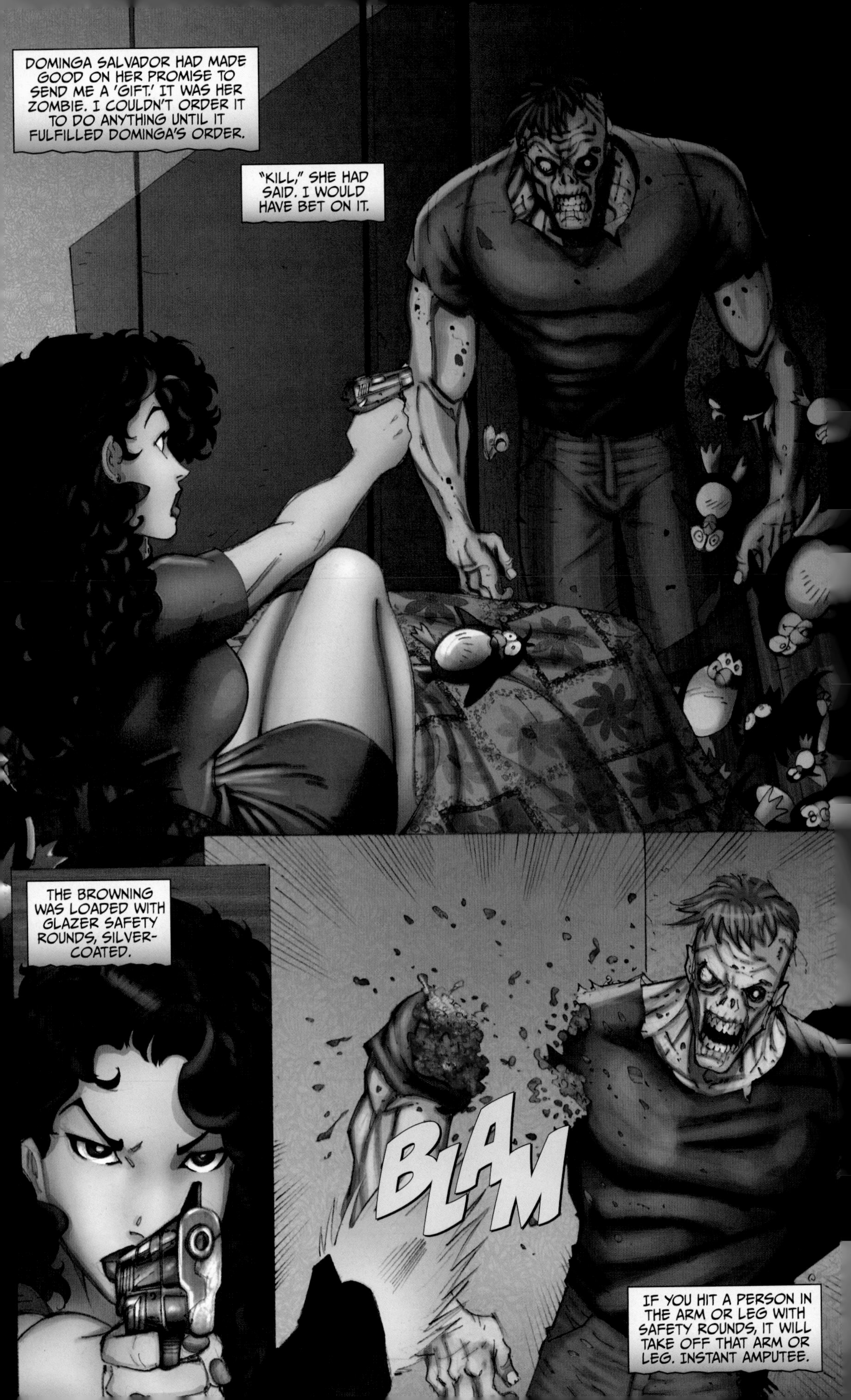
DOMINGA SALVADOR HAD MADE GOOD ON HER PROMISE TO SEND ME A 'GIFT.' IT WAS HER ZOMBIE. I COULDN'T ORDER IT TO DO ANYTHING UNTIL IT FULFILLED DOMINGA'S ORDER.
"KILL," SHE HAD SAID. I WOULD HAVE BET ON IT.
THE BROWNING WAS LOADED WITH GLAZER SAFETY ROUNDS, SILVER-COATED.
BLAM
IF YOU HIT A PERSON IN THE ARM OR LEG WITH SAFETY ROUNDS, IT WILL TAKE OFF THAT ARM OR LEG. INSTANT AMPUTEE.

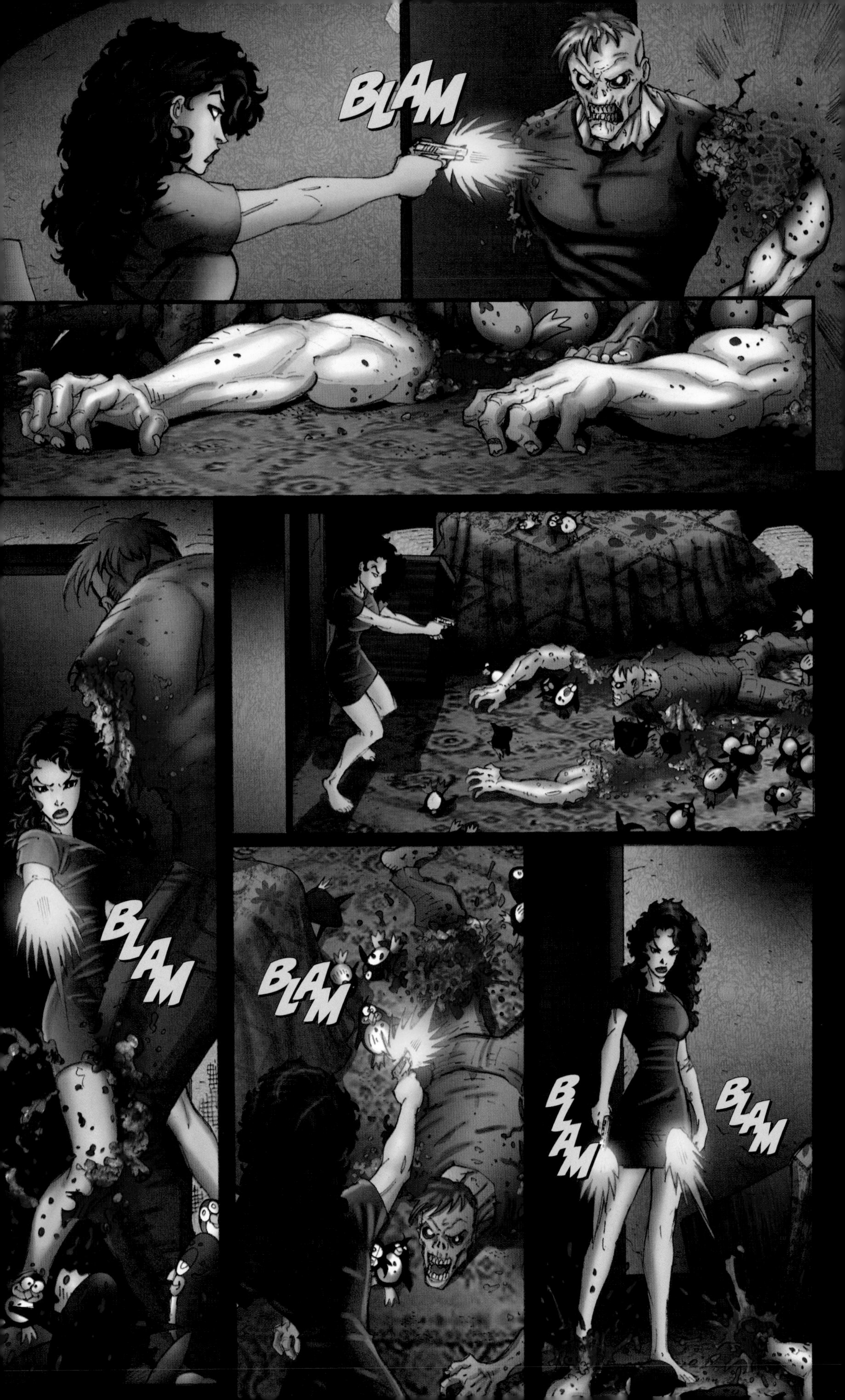
BLAM
BLAM
BLAM
BLAM
BLAM

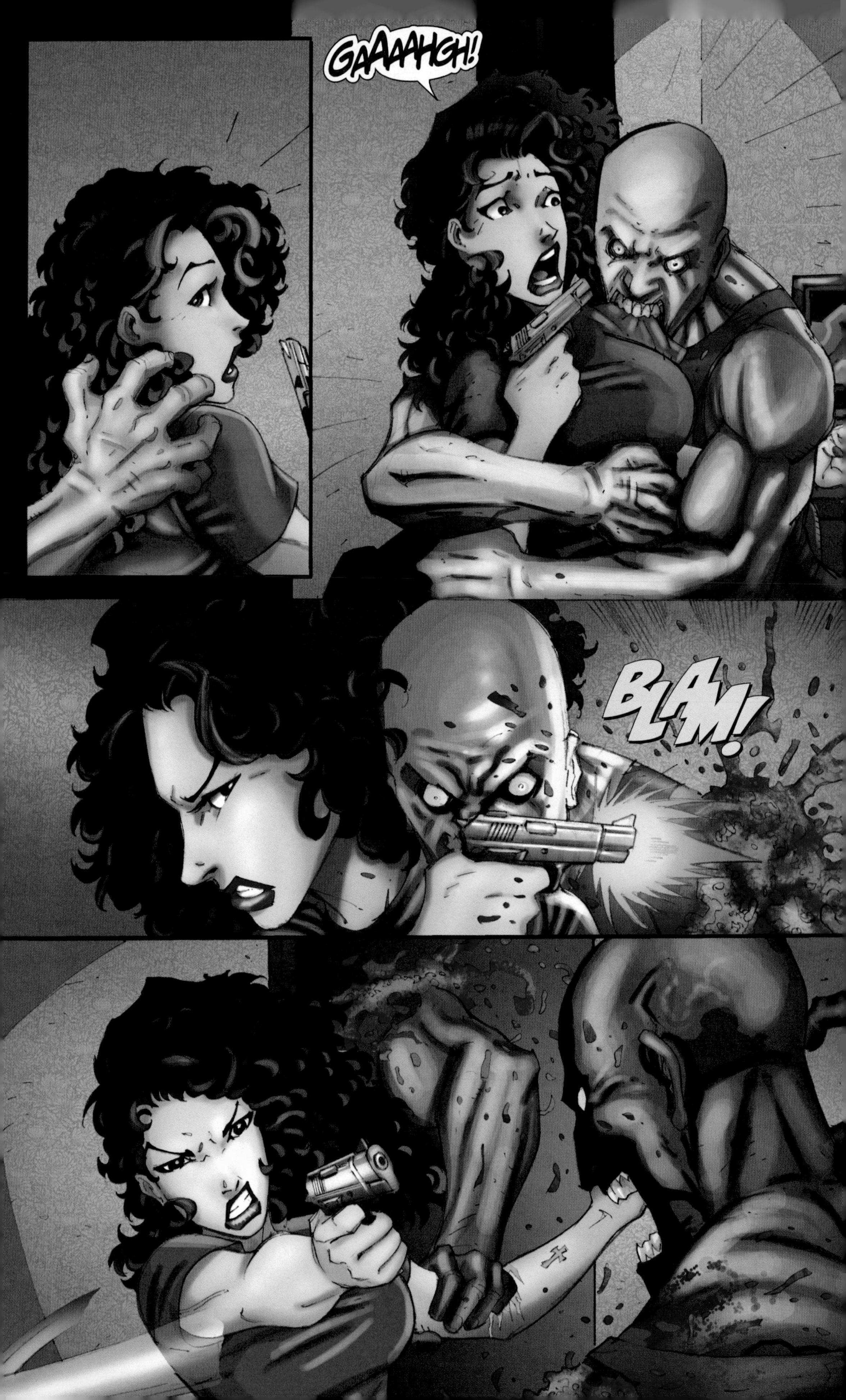

GAAAAHGH!
BLAM!

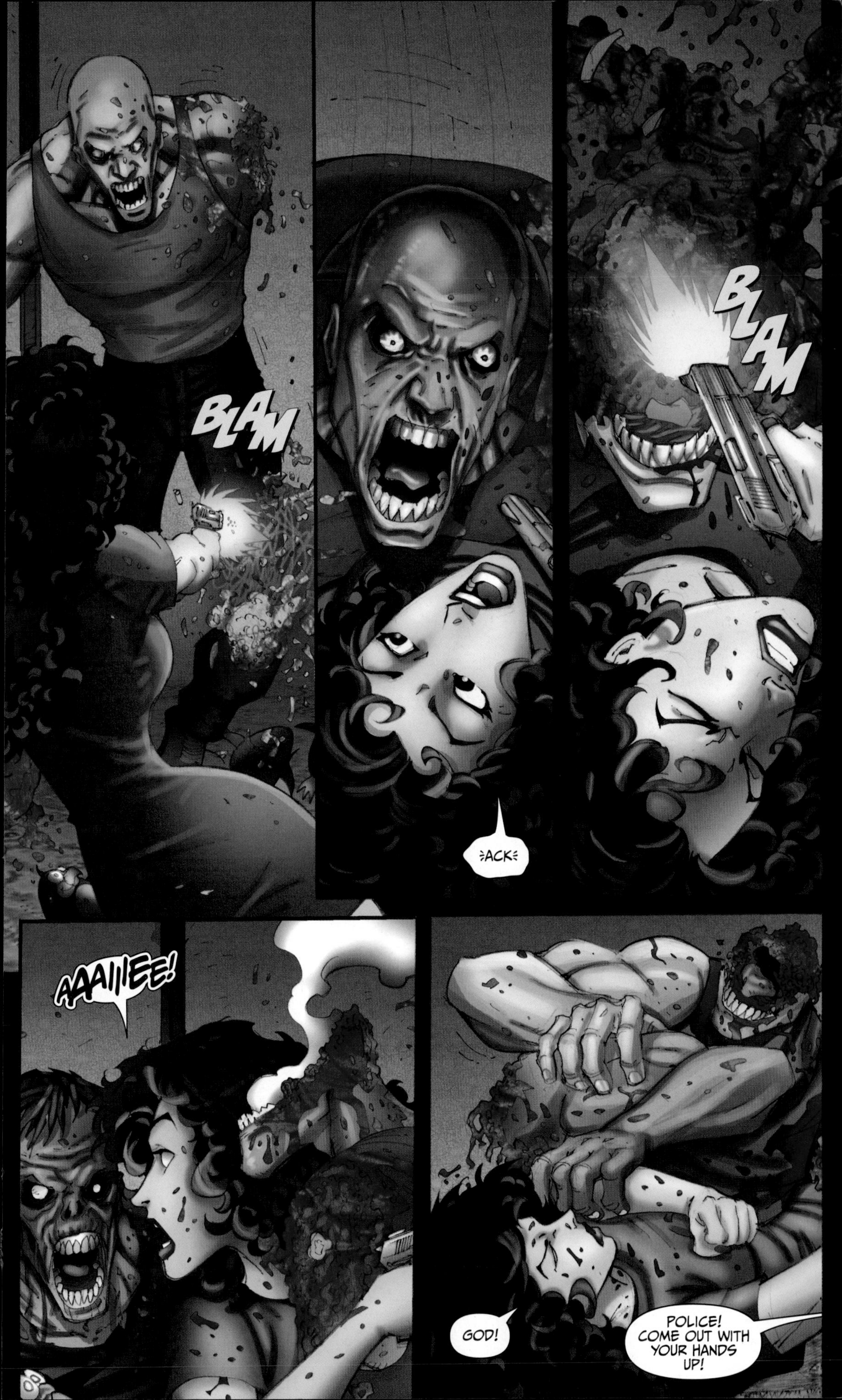
BLAM
ACK
BLAM
AAAIIIEE!
GOD!
POLICE! COME OUT WITH YOUR HANDS UP!

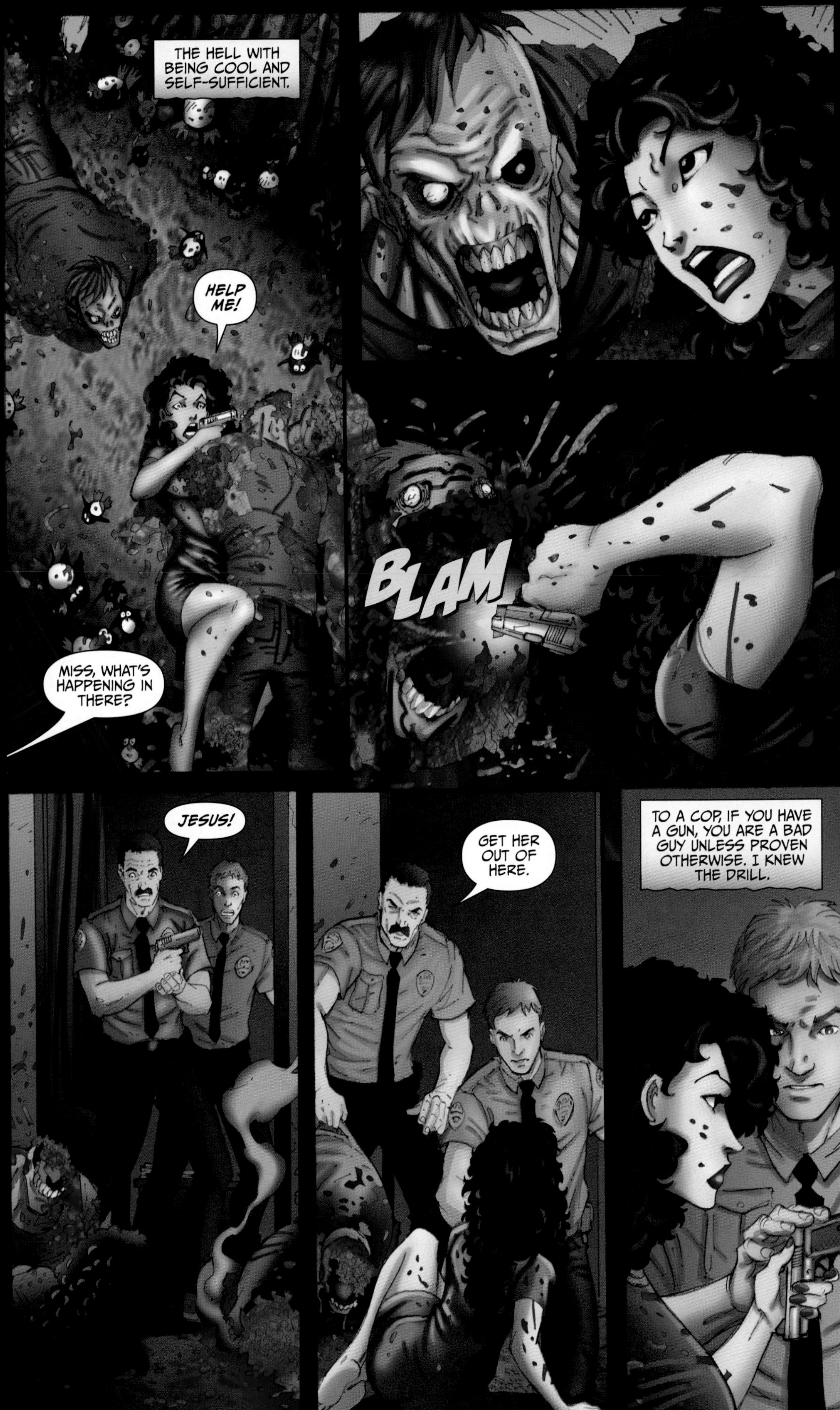
THE HELL WITH BEING COOL AND SELF-SUFFICIENT.
HELP ME!
MISS, WHAT'S HAPPENING IN THERE?
BLAM
JESUS!
GET HER OUT OF HERE.
TO A COP, IF YOU HAVE A GUN, YOU ARE A BAD GUY UNLESS PROVEN OTHERWISE. I KNEW THE DRILL.

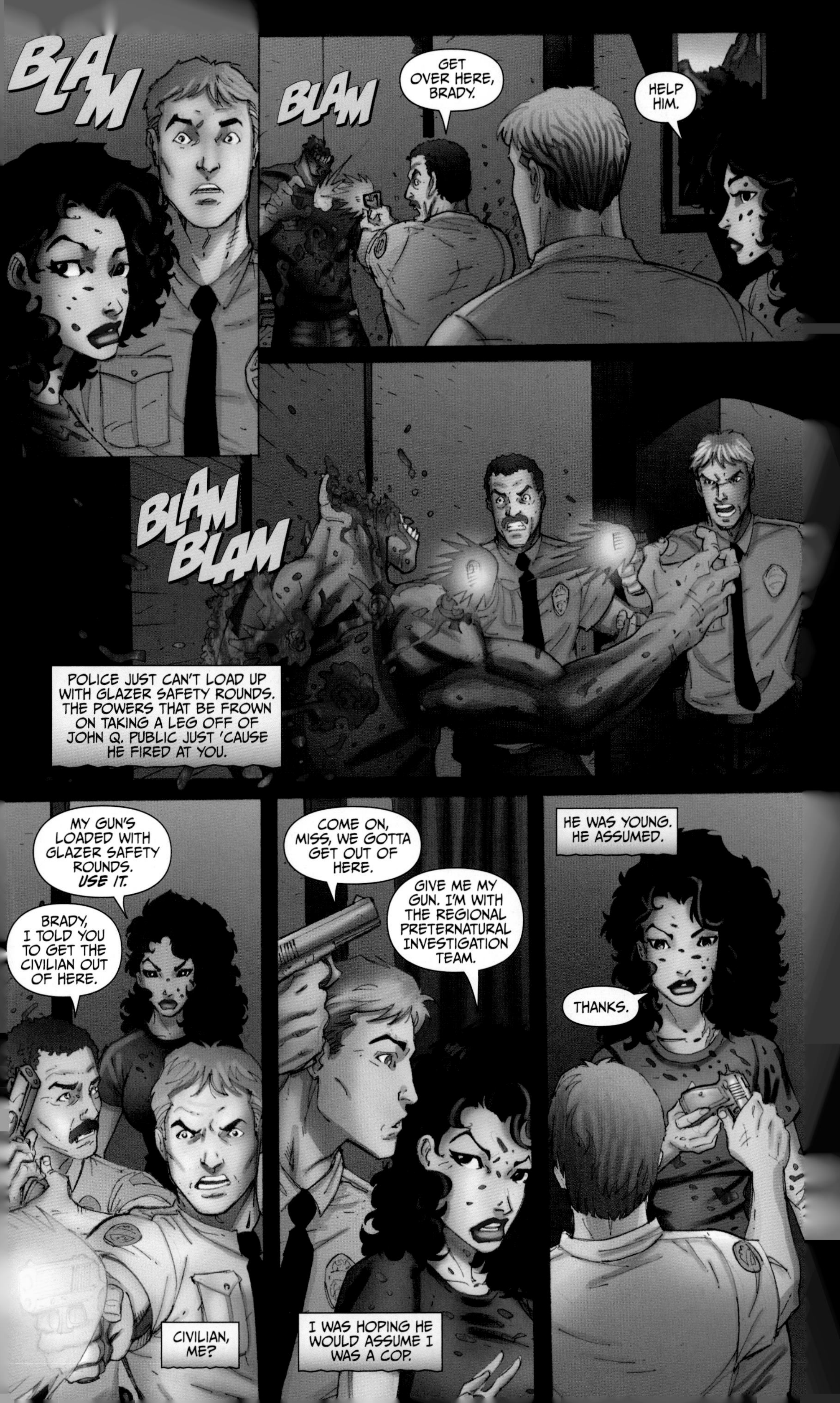
BLAM
BLAM
GET OVER HERE, BRADY.
HELP HIM.
BLAM BLAM
POLICE JUST CAN'T LOAD UP WITH GLAZER SAFETY ROUNDS. THE POWERS THAT BE FROWN ON TAKING A LEG OFF OF JOHN Q. PUBLIC JUST 'CAUSE HE FIRED AT YOU.
MY GUN'S LOADED WITH GLAZER SAFETY ROUNDS. USE IT.
BRADY, I TOLD YOU TO GET THE CIVILIAN OUT OF HERE.
CIVILIAN, ME?
COME ON, MISS, WE GOTTA GET OUT OF HERE.
GIVE ME MY GUN. I'M WITH THE REGIONAL PRETERNATURAL INVESTIGATION TEAM.
I WAS HOPING HE WOULD ASSUME I WAS A COP.
HE WAS YOUNG. HE ASSUMED.
THANKS.

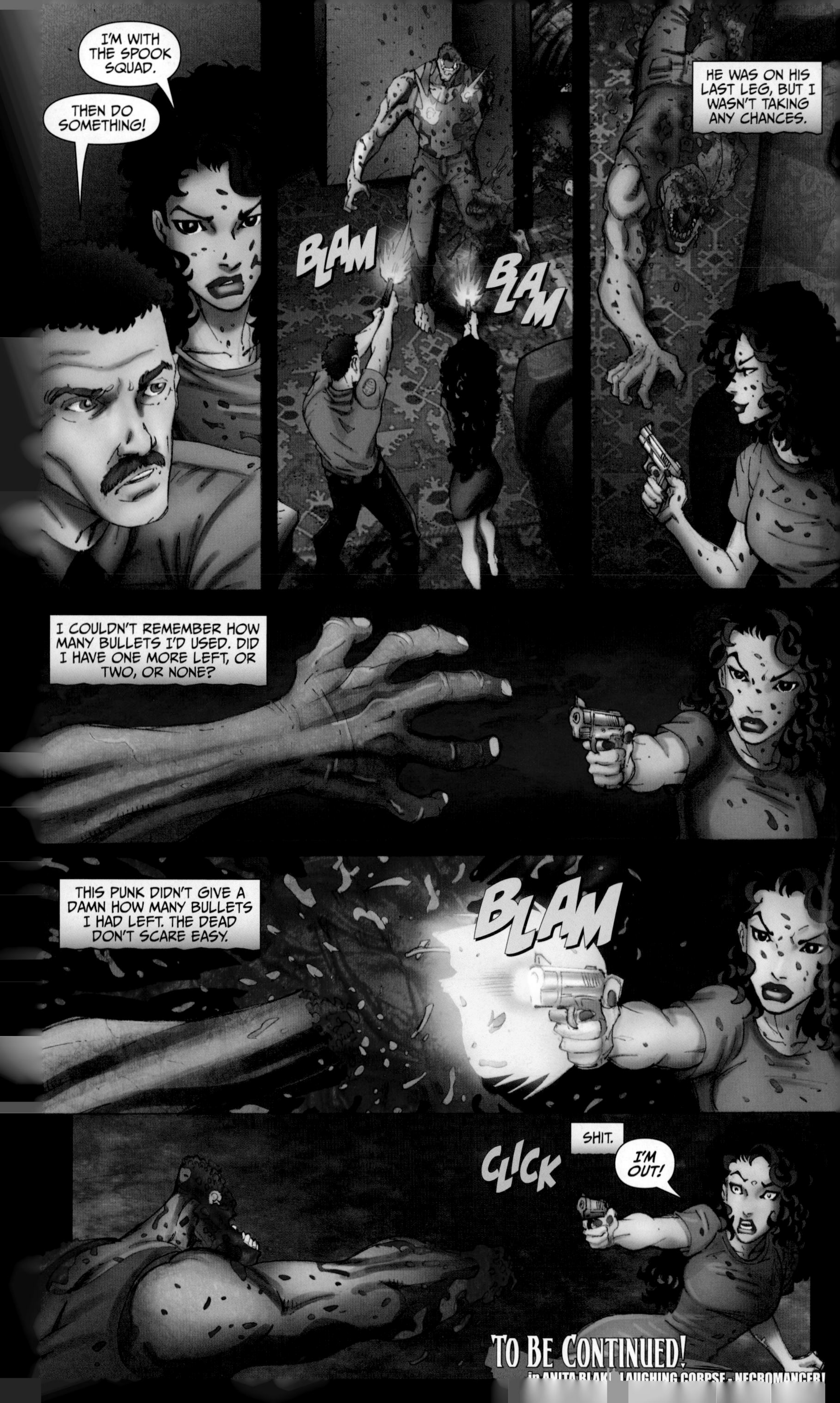

I'M WITH THE SPOOK SQUAD.
THEN DO SOMETHING!
BLAM
BLAM
HE WAS ON HIS LAST LEG, BUT I WASN'T TAKING ANY CHANCES.
I COULDN'T REMEMBER HOW MANY BULLETS I'D USED. DID I HAVE ONE MORE LEFT, OR TWO, OR NONE?
THIS PUNK DIDN'T GIVE A DAMN HOW MANY BULLETS I HAD LEFT. THE DEAD DON'T SCARE EASY.
BLAM
CLICK
SHIT.
I'M OUT!
TO BE CONTINUED!
in ANITA BLAKE: LAUGHING CORPSE - NECROMANCER!

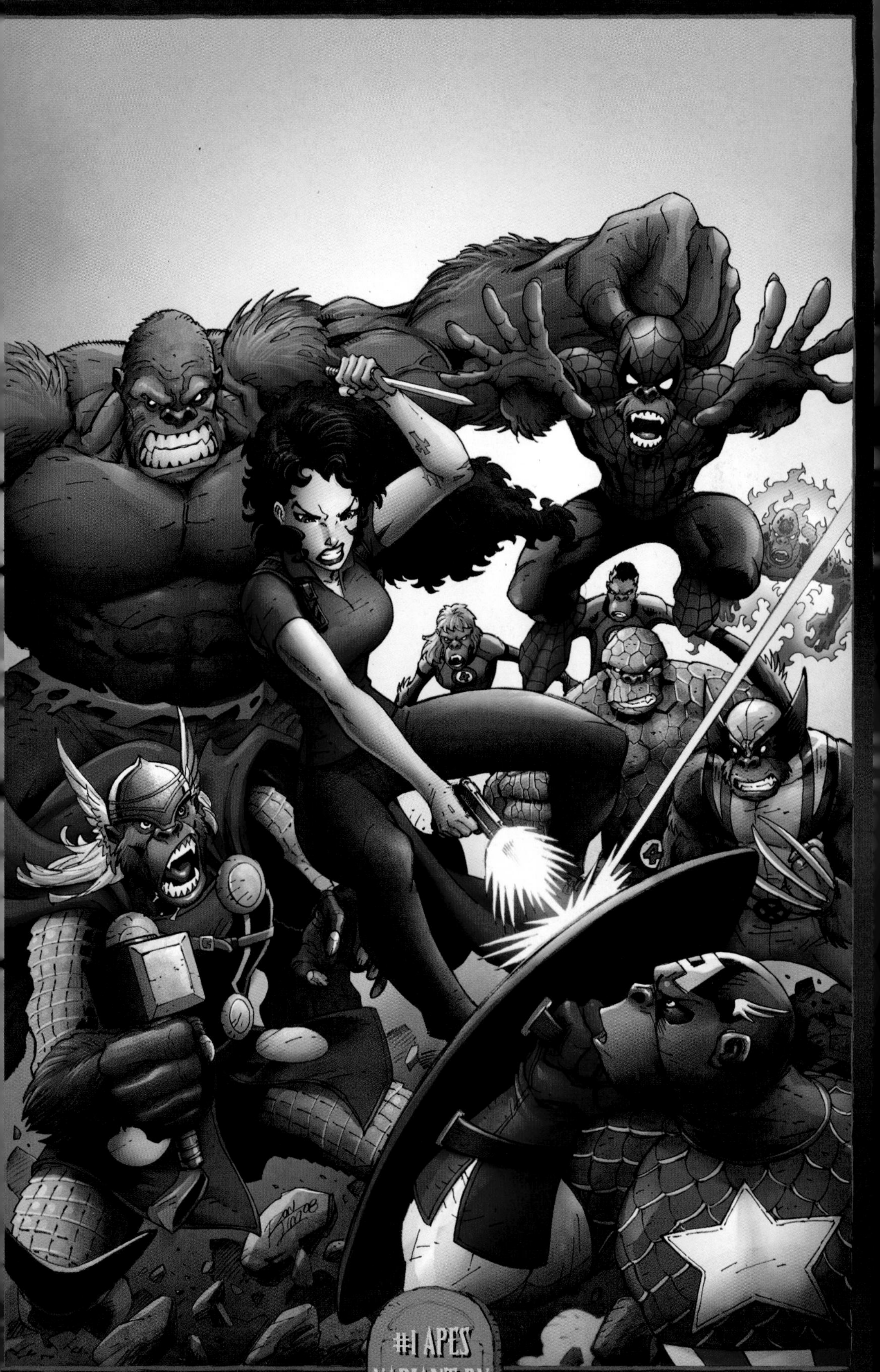
#1 APES